CAEL'S SHADOW

BOOK II OF THE SKY SEEKERS

Praise for *Cael's Shadow* and *Shorn*

"As Davila unwinds yet another series of escalating personal and political challenges affecting the survival of individuals and societies in this world, fantasy readers who look for swift action tempered by an attention to strong characterization and a solid sense of place and purpose will find *Cael's Shadow* hard to put down."

—D. Donovan, Senior Reviewer, *Midwest Book Review*

"Davila's debut novel, the first of a planned four-book series, creates a fascinating world of rival clans and sacred rituals."

—*Library Journal*

"A grand-scale fantasy . . . Fantasy fans will be impressed by Davila's deep characterization of the two main players; the focus on their internal development . . . makes them emotionally relatable and endearing . . . Scenes come alive on the page through detailed descriptions, and multiple layers of political and social intrigue . . . add remarkable depth."

—*Kirkus Reviews*

"*Shorn* is a striking debut, filled with skilled world-building, complex psychological tension, and a fine sense of nuance too seldom seen in fantasy. I was engrossed in the unfolding tale, and I look forward to the continuing journey!"

—Jacqueline Carey, *NYT* bestselling author of Kushiel's Legacy series

"Larissa N. N. Davila has created a compelling story with an original and complex hero torn between duty and desire, loyalty and freedom. She shows us a deep and fascinating culture, a believable world, struggling with issues of faith and power in ways that reflect our own fears and dreams. More please!"

—Ari Berk, author of The Undertaken trilogy

"Larissa N. N. Davila has created a fascinating world, peopled it with vivid characters, and woven an epic tale of adventure and political intrigue with thoughtful themes of duty versus desire, bigotry versus acceptance, and the truth of history that hides behind the self-serving accounts written by the victors. She has also invented one of the more convincing religions I've seen in fantasy recently—no mere window-dressing of gods and altars and a priest or two, but a fully rounded, psychologically convincing faith. An intelligent and captivating novel by a new writer of promise."

—Victoria Strauss, author of *The Burning Land*

CAEL'S SHADOW

BOOK II OF THE SKY SEEKERS

LARISSA N. N. DAVILA

Sante Fe, New Mexico

Acknowledgments

Much gratitude and affection go to the team at Stone Raven Press. In particular, I thank Ari Warner for his gorgeous frontispiece and map; Kristen McDermott for her editing skill and for being the friend willing to help me hide the body; and Geoffrey McVey for Jase's lovely "Summer Soldier" ballad. Love and hugs to Sue Bellinger at Sunset Farm, my infinitely patient riding instructor, for always helping me to escape on a horse when I needed to step back from the story and for answering funny questions about a horse's endurance. To Arturo, whose great skill and experience in the martial arts informed the combat scenes. And to my family for being proud, even when there was still much work to be done.

FOR DAD, WHO ALWAYS
ENCOURAGED ME TO FLY.

Principal Characters

Jhared Denaban, a young Shorn man
Mahla Denaban, his mother (deceased)
Madam Sarena Trianor, Elder Trianor's wife, Jhared's foster mother and Teacher
Branlen Trianor, Jhared's foster brother
Alende, Shorn waylayer, one of the caelevano
Ziabela Marcalo, Shorn scribe and musician
Vesarian, a Shorn man accused of breaking Shorn Law
Boar and Shrill, Jhared's internal Teachers

RIANA'S SERVANTS
Nemiah (Rustania) Gabriana, High Priestess of Avelos
Lady Amalia, traitorous former high priestess (deceased)
Captain Rom, Nemiah's Arionad
Commander Evorales, Rom's second-in-command
Lady Esania, High Priestess of Brenia
Enaro, Aide to Lady Esania

Leita, Bearer of Cael's Blade
Kaliska, Healer, Mistress of Guardians, Keeper of the Shadow Guards
Carian, Mistress of Novices
Bena, Mistress of Maps — RIANA'S HIGHER CIRCLE
Clemina, Mistress of Messages
Maita, Mistress of Rituals

KEY MEMBERS OF THE COUNCIL OF CLANS
Adan Rumar, High Chieftain of Avelos
Tumal the Just, heroic former high chieftain (deceased)
Elder Tierzen Trianor, Minister of the Teaching, Jhared's foster father and one of his Teachers
Elder Toren Abrigado, Minister of the Treasury, Leader of Tumal's Legacy
Elder Nadro, Clan Nadaren

FOREST GUARD
Enrian Nadel, General of the Southern Towers
Orn, General of the Northern Towers
Lieutenant Matio Sevar, Jhared's commanding officer

Commander Carn, head of Jhared's patrol
Lenaro, second to Carn
Anzo Nevia, patrolman
Grion Hariar, patrolman
Jase Relki, patrolman — JHARED'S PATROL
Esran, patrolman
Bevan Lavando, patrolman
Twitch, patrolman
Afiro, patrolman

KEY LEADERS OF THE NORTHERN FIVE CLANS
Prefect Ondal Aglar – head of Clan Aglar
Prefect Bilar Lasla – head of Clan Lasla
Commander Ciam – commanding officer of Clan Aglar's clanguard

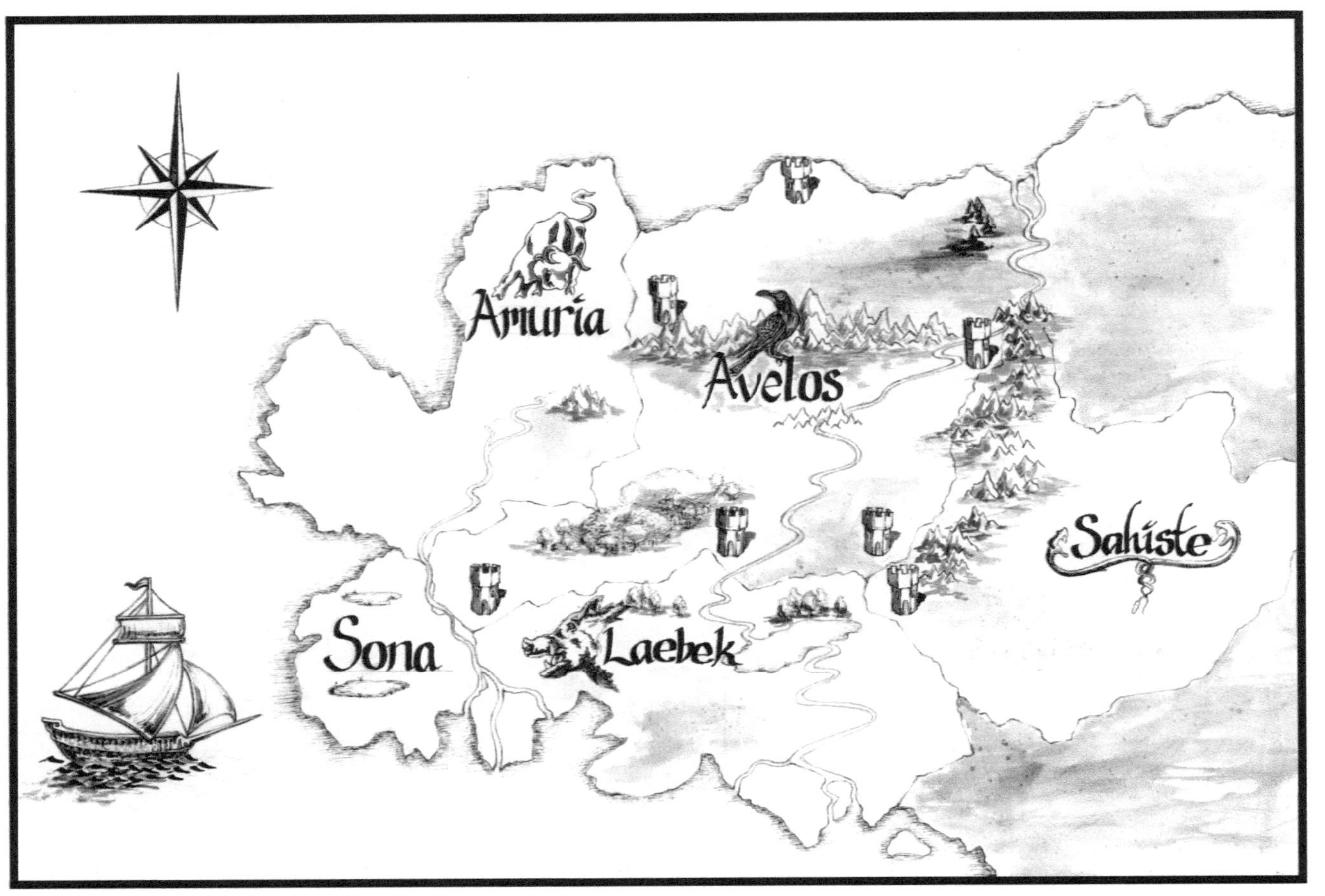

Amuria
Avelos
Sahíste
Sona
Laebek

1.
Madness

The mountain road vanished at the cliff's edge.

Or that's what it looked like from Jhared's perspective atop Seravina's broad back, halfway through the pass. His Forest Guard patrol trotted in neat formation behind him; Lieutenant Sevar and Commander Carn rode ahead, their horses' glossy hindquarters rising and falling at the trot. All Jhared could see beyond the top of the steep rise was the seductive arch of the autumn sky, sweeping toward forever in shades of blue that were sweeter than song, filling him with infinite impossibilities.

It shamed him that the mere thought of going over the edge set his heart racing and a cold sweat running between his scarred shoulders. He had faced much worse than mountain heights in the past weeks: his body still bore the marks of the Legacy's hatred and Alende's fury. It shamed him that even now, after twelve years of the Teaching and more than half that many years under the training of General Nadel, a part of him still longed to fling himself off the cliff just to experience the precious seconds of ecstasy the sky would offer before the rocks at the bottom crushed him.

Seravina trod too close to the steep incline on his left. When he twitched the reins, she tossed her head before stepping deeper onto the path toward the rock face and the priestess riding beside him. He knew the road's abrupt end must be an illusion, a veil between him and the truth: what he perceived depended on where he was standing, and just now the slope blinded him to the switchback on the other side of the ridge. He had discovered so many of his own veils recently that even though it distressed him, this new distortion didn't really surprise him. Not so long ago he wouldn't have believed he could lie to his foster father or hunger for the kiss of a traitor or shatter his oath to Avelos. But he was still Shorn, after all.

Near the rear, Anzo whistled an off-tempo version of "The Road to Velantar," torturing the old ballad into a marching tune. Jhared grimaced and pulled his gaze from the temptation of the sky to focus on what lay ahead of him. When his patrol reached the switchback, he knew he would see that the road continued on, as it had since the days of the ancients, when the council reinforced its tenuous link to the northern clans and their silver mines with stone as well as with the enticement of trade in the south. On this fall afternoon, he knew the road unrolled out of the burgundy- and copper-colored Parnas Mountains, all the way down to Aven Plains. He counted on that reality to extinguish his treacherous desires and safely ground him.

Except that it didn't.

The sheer drop ahead made Jhared's innards spin. The road no longer existed at all. It had collapsed beneath a steep slide of gravel and fallen trees. Lieutenant Sevar trotted on without apparent concern for the damage caused by the rockslide, his back straight in the saddle, his golden head turned toward Commander Carn's shaggy white one as they spoke. Jhared felt a dull thud against his breastbone.

"Soldier, is something wrong?"

He glanced at the slender, black-haired woman to whom he'd been given as a bodyguard. Her first long days of riding and nights sleeping on the ground amid a patrol of rough men hadn't doused her intensity. The Bearer of Cael's Blade watched everything around her with an all-consuming gaze. When she turned her midnight eyes on Jhared, he felt as though she knew things about him that he did not.

"Lady, look. Look ahead." He gestured toward the danger.

She frowned. Commander Carn barked a laugh at something the lieutenant said. They trotted closer to the road's end, with no sign of halting.

Jhared sucked a breath. "Lieutenant! Commander! Beware ahead!"

The patrol responded to Jhared's cry with well-drilled efficiency, wheeling their horses into a defensive line. Even in the rutted pass, they moved at speed. It would have been a perfectly executed maneuver if not for the pack animals: three hot-blooded Clan Everen coursers who never would have been used for baggage if not for the loss of Forest Guard mounts in the killing winds. They shied at the commotion, and the second of the three, a chestnut colt, tore loose his lead. Sturdy, steady Anzo kicked his mount forward and grabbed up the broken tether before the chestnut could bolt. Fast-moving, slower-thinking Twitch tried to leap his horse clear of the panicked animal and almost tumbled off the road. As Twitch scrambled away from the edge, Jhared legged Seravina close to the rock face, shielding the priestess from the frightened horses and the drop before them. The woman's gaze was on the sky.

Lieutenant Sevar's glare, however, landed squarely on Jhared. "Denaban, what in the name of—"

"Lieutenant, up there!" The priestess pointed toward the west.

Jhared turned more slowly than the others, his focus still on the rockslide. He felt the storm before he saw it, a reverberation against his chest. Seravina pinned her ears.

"Lady save us," Jase muttered, rubbing the blessing tattooed along his cheek.

"The Good Lady don't have anything t'do with that!" Esran spat.

The cloud writhed above the mountains, not five miles west of the pass. It was the color of a falcon's wing, as dark as the grey-feather curse. No man could mistake it for a natural storm. No natural storm ripped through the spirit as this one could or sliced through leather armor and tore flesh to the bone.

"Demon spawn!" Carn snarled. "You want we should run for it, Lieutenant, or try to find a hide?"

Caves honey-combed the mountains throughout the pass, but it wouldn't be an easy thing to find sufficient shelter to fit the patrol and fifteen horses. If they didn't find stone before the winds reached their killing speed, their journey would end swiftly and horribly.

Sevar faced the cloud without flinching, a terrible need twisting his wind-scarred features, a predator's need to master what hunted him. "We run. Curse the skies and the creatures in them. Once again, we run."

As the first high-pitched strains of the killing winds blew toward them, Jhared watched the cloud roiling and felt the same roiling within himself. The storm had slain so many already. In Velantar, entire families—three and four generations deep—had been wiped from the world. Men he had respected had been ripped apart. His foster brother Branlen would forever bear the scars.

He moved as though in a fever dream, every moment distant and unreal. He heard himself shout a second warning about the road. No one responded. The Bearer of Cael's Blade eyed him closely.

Jhared looked at her and his breath caught as human figures shimmered around her, silvery shadows of no substance. He couldn't turn away, though he urgently needed someone to lead him back to a place that made sense. The shadows seemed to *be her*, a host of ghostly priestesses. One smiled at him from horseback; three of them threatened him with Cael's Blade; some stared at him through the avian eyes of a demon's mask; one stared with no eyes at all. Seravina whinnied and jigged. Jhared grabbed for the pommel of his saddle, retching over her withers.

"Soldier?" one of the shadows hissed. "Are you with me?"

His stomach was turning flips like an acrobat at the summer faire. His head was being pounded into shards. He wasn't sure he would stay conscious. "I'm fine," he croaked.

"If you're fine, then you'd best sit up," she whispered. "Your lieutenant is watching you."

Jhared inhaled the reassuring scent of warm horse, struggling to find his still center amidst a force trying to suck him into darkness. Was it poison? Herbs existed that could weaken a man's mind and cause him to die raving. There were people who might be pleased to see him dead: Alende. Ziabela.

Ah, Zia. I am sorry!

"Soldier!"

Pain stabbed him back to awareness. The priestess gripped him hard across the forearm, where Alende's dagger had scored him. Her other hand was reaching under her cloak for the black hilt of her Blade.

"I'm fine," he said again, shaking free of her and straightening. "It's only a bit of fever returned. Prepare yourself, Lady. We must run."

Commander Carn bellowed commands and the patrol began to reform its neat file. After a hesitation, the lady's hand slid away from the Blade and she gathered her mare. Lieutenant Sevar called the order that sent them off at a gallop. Within a span of heartbeats, Sevar's agile border horse crossed the short stretch to the pile of gravel and rock. The beast struck the place where the road no longer existed.

And kept running.

Hooves struck the ground in a flawless cadence, first Sevar's stallion, then the commander's black. The road unrolled without interruption through the pass, as it must have done all along. Jhared stared in bewilderment. The destruction was only another illusion in this unreal moment. He glanced sidelong at the priestess. Her silvery shadows had vanished as well. Almost before he could signal Seravina, the mare leaped after the others.

The cloud of the killing winds pursued them as they fled, a dark stain spreading over the sky. Did consciousness or motive exist behind such violence or were the killing winds truly chaos, with nothing so orderly as hatred driving them? This close to the city, hundreds of people lay at risk. The small villages of Clan Manitar speckled the mountainsides, villages that supplied the city with meat, milk, and wool from their flocks of sheep and goats. Decimation of the stock would have grave consequences for already crippled Velantar. The killing winds were not only shattering lives, they were severing the country's life-veins.

The patrol fled mile after mile, but could not outrun the churning cloud. Beside Jhared, the priestess bent low in the saddle murmuring what might have been a prayer as they pounded over the steep terrain. Her foam-flecked mount ran bravely. Seravina, on the other hand, fretted and fought the bit, lengthening her stride until she was near to running over the heels of Sevar's border horse. Jhared kept her in line with effort, expecting every instant to hear the winds roar to their killing speed above him. As the land flashed past, Commander Carn's mount stumbled, then caught its balance and pushed on. Lieutenant Sevar scowled over his shoulder at the sky. After another moment, he signaled the patrol and led them off the road, down the slope and into the forested hills.

Scattered stones, gnarled tree roots, and eroded ravines forced the horses to lose speed, but they fled perpendicular to the storm's path now. Jhared didn't dare to look back, focused only on guiding Seravina away from the most dangerous terrain. She had no wish to slow. Halfway down the hill, where a small copse of pine trees cast viridian shadows over the slope, years of runoff had carved a vast gully. It was too wide to jump and too long to go around, but deep enough that the climb back out would be a scramble. The lieutenant and commander drew up their mounts and started down. The priestess slowed to follow. Jhared sat back in the saddle to ease Seravina up to the edge, but she would have none of it. With a trumpeting whinny, she charged forward, her hindquarters drawing deeper under her body. She was gathering herself for a jump.

Jhared knew he should rein her in. The gully spanned nearly twenty feet, a gulf most horses wouldn't make even on level terrain, but Seravina's ardor was contagious. He longed to see how far she could take him. He shortened the rein and balanced his weight to help her prepare. His cloak fluttered behind him. His warrior's tail tugged at his skull. Then the chasm opened, wide and abrupt. Seravina propelled them into the air with a sky-seeking leap.

The wind embraced them. Jhared closed his eyes as intense pleasure-pain rushed through him. The mare's rise and stretch formed an arc of perfect weightlessness across the chasm. It stole his breath and awoke the old need, an aching heat that radiated from his center to make his muscles hum. Like a half-forgotten dream, he knew the joy of joining with the sacred sky, of reaching lofty mountain aeries. Even as his heart soared with hope, he knew he would find no release. This was only a moment of freedom, and he desired more, a lifetime. In that instant, when he hung suspended above the ground, caught between flying and falling, he understood anew the enormity of all he had lost.

They landed with a jolt. Seravina cleared the far side with room to spare, although it seemed to Jhared they had fallen far short.

A shout from the gully made him wheel around to look behind him. Men and horses were crossing the floor of the chasm and scrabbling up the bank, dusty and sweat-soaked. Only Jase and Anzo still waited on the opposite rim for their turn to cross. Both men stared back up the mountain. Jhared followed Anzo's gaze to the sky: the cloud had not pursued them off the road. Instead, it had begun to dissipate, melting like snow in the sunshine. Tendrils of mist twisted above the mountains and disappeared. Sunlight pierced the grey as the storm shrank from the size of a fortress to the size of a house to the size of a horse. A breeze feathered over Jhared's face. Then the cloud was gone.

Silence gripped the patrol. Jhared stared in astonished relief with the others, until Jase threw back his head and roared out in victory. The other men joined him. Amidst the whooping, Jhared's gaze went to the priestess. The ride had pinked her cheeks and pulled strands of hair free of her long braid. Her dark eyes studied the now clear patch of sky as though she could read some subtle message there.

"Orders, Lieutenant?" Carn asked, once all the men had climbed onto the bank.

Sevar leaned forward and patted his stallion's shoulder. "Find a place to set camp. We've done what we must for today."

Rather than climb the long, treacherous way back to the road, the commander led them farther down the mountain. Eventually, they would cross another switchback and pick up the pass again, but Carn called a halt before they regained the road. They had pushed free of the trees, with their bronze and burgundy foliage, into a small clearing. A shepherd's cottage, abandoned for the winter, crouched on a gentle rise beside a sheepfold. At the north edge of the clearing, a creek chattered softly on its way down the hill.

The setting surrendered its peacefulness to the incursion of soldiers. Jhared dismounted with the others, feeling heavy and awkward as the earth claimed him again. He loosened Seravina's girth and led her on a circuit around the clearing to cool her. Her coat shone silver as she pranced and fidgeted, surveying her surroundings with a baleful eye.

"Well, madam, you do know how to run," he murmured.

"That's the first time I've seen you smile, soldier. It suits you. You should race the winds more often."

Jhared glanced up at the priestess, who had caught up to him on her mare. He pulled the crisp autumn air into his lungs and felt his muscles still buzzing. He must be cautious now or his body would continue to draw from its cache of Shorn energy and burn him with deadly desires. Still, he couldn't keep the pleasure from his voice. "She's a magnificent horse. I've never ridden another like her."

"I should say not. Seravina's a rare beast. Captain Mavias's blood flows in her veins."

Jhared stopped. The heat in him went suddenly chill. "She's descended from the Chosen?"

The priestess nodded cheerfully as she swung out of the saddle. "Her grandsire was one of Riana's blessed Aye, a Mavaye stallion."

"And the temple gave her to *me*? Lady, it is against Shorn Law! No man or woman Shorn shall hold sway over the Chosen, neither Aye nor Ael, and none shall command them to do the bidding of the cursed."

"Patrolman, slow down!" the priestess said, laughing. "Seravina's not Chosen. She carries only her grandsire's strength and his love for command, not his spirit. I selected her for you myself." The woman stopped laughing and her deep blue gaze grew sober. "Do you think I would lead you down the wrong Path, Jhared Denaban? Have you thought on who I am?"

She had asked him almost the same question once before, during the vigil of his Becoming, when she wore another shape: Cael's. *"Do you know who I am?"*

"You are death," Jhared had answered then. *"Chaos and death."*

"I am choice," she had responded. *"Choice and freedom."*

Another distortion, that one. Cael's unholy perspective.

"Patrolman?"

"You are the Bearer of Cael's Blade. And I am merely a Shorn soldier. Forgive me. The only paths I can speak of knowledgeably are the ones that will take us north."

"Oh, indeed?" She frowned, visibly dissatisfied with his answer, but she let him lead her back to the sheepfold, where they unsaddled and rubbed down the horses. When she had finished, she lifted a covered basket from among her packs. "As merely a Shorn soldier, do you think you might set up my tent?"

"It will be safer for you inside, Lady. In case the killing winds return." He gestured toward the cottage, ignoring her tone.

"If the winds return, I imagine I can make it the ten paces to shelter. And there are things to be learned beyond the confines of walls, Patrolman. Please do as I've asked."

"Of course, Lady." He watched her walk away, then turned to water the horses at the creek. Elongated shadows of trees striped the water. A few hardy crickets chirped unenthusiastically in the brush. He thought on what he had seen in the pass—the rockslide, the shadow priestesses—trying to make sense of them. He had told the Bearer it was illness, but his fever had broken several days ago, and the symptoms of poison wouldn't have abated so quickly.

After considering a moment, he decided not to take any chances on the last and pulled two small vials from the pouch at his belt: Madam Kaliska's restoratives. They were the only things he had ingested in the past three days that were not a part of the patrol's provisions. The high temple's healer had given them to him the night before he left Velantar. He didn't think she wished him harm, but she was a friend to Zia and had been upset by his refusal to support their treasonous plans.

He broke the seals on the vials and emptied their contents downstream of the camp. The foul-smelling liquid swirled into the water and vanished. He let his thoughts about Zia and her traitorous band go with it. Zia was far from him now, in Velantar. But his apprehension about the Bearer didn't swirl away so easily. What had he seen on the mountain? The images of the shadow priestesses still haunted him. Was he becoming disordered or did the imbalance exist within the Bearer of Cael's Blade?

I know what true chaos is. I've seen past the edges of reason and visited the places where the only reality is disorder. This woman who will travel with you, this creature of the dark, worships that chaos.

Jhared shivered at the recollection of Alende's warning, reluctant to heed the word of the unbound. Alende was anathema, a Shorn man who had failed to prove his loyalty and failed to pay the price for it. He had tried to kill the Bearer in the high temple.

Had Alende seen the priestess's spirit-shadows too?

A pattern existed here that refused to come together. The woman wasn't just a sworn servant of Riana; she was the Bearer of Cael's Blade, the priestess responsible for warning others of the dangers of Cael's ways and the second most powerful woman in the high temple. She had been there, hidden, when Jhared shattered his oath to Avelos by slaying the Legacy man who beat him. Rather than earning the high chieftain's favor by exposing the Legacy's intrigues, she had promised the faction her silence if they let Jhared live.

Now his life lay in her hands. If she revealed his crime, Lieutenant Sevar would be acting within Shorn Law and Forest Guard code to execute him.

Jhared rolled his shoulders against the impossible pain that wasn't quite in his back, but in the part of him cut away long ago. The Bearer must have some use for him. Why else had she saved his life? Why else had she insisted he be a part of this mission? Zia had sought to use him to betray Avelos. The Legacy had tried to make him a bloody message for Elder Trianor. Even his foster father had used him to inform on the garrison at Ravia.

What purpose could the Bearer of Cael's Blade possibly intend for him?

"Someone must walk the dark paths," she had told him in Velantar.

Jhared didn't want to think about what that might mean. He had already strayed so far he had lost what was dearest to him. He had lied to Elder Trianor and shielded Zia. He had killed to sate his own rage. Undisciplined. Uncontrolled. Dangerous. Jhared looked at his hands. In the dappled evening shadows, he could see blood on them again. It made him ill when he thought on that moment. The deaths he wrought in defense of Avelos were a matter of duty, and he owned no choice in them, but that night on the street, the sensation of muscle tearing beneath his steel had been deeply satisfying. For a time, it had even felt like justice.

Jhared groaned and scrubbed a hand across his face. He longed to preserve what remained of his oath and to help his patrol find an answer to the killing winds. The Bearer of Cael's Blade had seen the darkness in him. He couldn't imagine what she sought from it.

2.
STORYTELLERS

Jhared set about raising the Bearer's tent uphill from the water. The patrol was traveling light and wouldn't bother to carry tents for the men until they reached the altitudes of the Sandien Mountains, but the leather and canvas offered the priestess a bit of protection from the elements and some small privacy from eleven soldiers. He spread the tarp, inspecting the seams before pushing the iron pins and the center stakes into the ground. Once he had strung the cord through the eyes of the stakes, he hung the tarp and secured it along the bottom with the pins. He was stacking the Bearer's saddle and packs beside the tent flap, when the cottage door opened behind him. He knew Lieutenant Sevar's purposeful step and hoped it would pass him by. It didn't. Swiftly, he turned and saluted.

"Lieutenant, sir."

Sevar's gaze was withering. "I saw you on the road, Patrolman. I know it wasn't the winds that made you cry warning. You weren't even looking at the cloud. What happened? Did *a dream of flight seduce the Watcher from his post?* Or was it *the lure of the endless skies* that so distracted you?"

Jhared braced himself. When Matio Sevar began quoting the old historians, it meant trouble. "Sir, I didn't intend to—"

"Shut it! I don't want another excuse. I know you. The Shorn child raised by Tierzen Trianor can quote the eight histories in the ancient tongue, but can't control the most dire of Shorn urges."

Jhared looked at the ground. He couldn't argue: he *had* suffered that unnatural desire. He had imagined flinging himself from the cliff, mindless of anything but the need to be airborne. Desire wasn't what had disordered him, but he couldn't tell the lieutenant about shadow priestesses and vanishing rockslides. "I have no excuse, sir."

Sevar stared up at him in stony silence, his aristocratic features a mask Jhared couldn't entirely interpret. At the fortress, some called Sevar "golden boy" for his good looks and bright mane. He was well-bred and well-read, a man born to be a statesman, but instead hammered into a soldier. Many clansmen believed the lieutenant to be a soft city man who had only run to the Forest Guard to spite his father. Those clansmen surely had never seen the steel-sharp ferocity in the lieutenant that Jhared faced now.

"You're a danger," Sevar growled. "The worst kind of Shorn danger; you think yourself so far above the rest of your kind you don't see how weak you truly are. Tierzen Trianor did you no favors by making you his pet. But then, the Minister of the Teaching has always been more interested in testing his grand philosophies than in helping the Shorn to survive their flaws."

The lieutenant spat on the ground in disgust. "Very well. I'm assigning you to double watch duty. Until you've acquired the strength to restrain yourself, you'll stand from the dead-moon watch through the dawn. We've been here before, you and I. I don't expect I can make you a reliable man, but at least we're going to burn off that Shorn energy and elder-bred arrogance."

Shame formed a hard knot in Jhared's middle. "Understood, sir."

"I didn't want you on this mission," the lieutenant ground on. "The Bearer of Cael's Blade seems to think you have some value here, but I've seen the grief your kind offers to those who are too close. Take this as a warning: if you bring harm to this company, the debt you owe to Avelos will seem as nothing to what I make you pay."

Emotions more complex than anger reflected from the lieutenant's thunder-grey gaze. "Are we clear, Patrolman?"

Jhared worked to school his features, startled by his own ambivalence. He had ample reason to hate Matio Sevar, so why did he still feel the need to prove his worth to the man? "Sir, my only goal is to make reparation for the crimes of those before me."

"Before you?" Sevar gave a humorless laugh. "Worry about your own faults, Denaban. You've more than enough to answer for there."

Full dark gloved the clearing by the time the patrol had set camp and finished dinner. Jhared and his patrolmates sat around the fire, working at the odd tasks required of a unit on the march. Jase, whose hands were as neat with a needle as with the tossing of dice, mended a worn girth strap. Bevan and Grion sharpened their blades. Twitch bent his head over a bridle, rubbing at one piece for a short time with an oiled rag, dropping it aside to pick up another, then throwing that one down to return to the first. Jhared sat cross-legged with his quiver, a knife, and a handful of feathers for fletching. His patrolmates kept their distance. The feathers were a necessary evil, but no soldier would touch them who could avoid it.

The conversation ran hot and was all of the killing winds. The patrol had spent much of the summer following the trail of destruction across the southern villages. In village after village, Jhared had dug through the rubble beside his patrolmates, searching for survivors. He had lost count of the number of broken bodies he had lifted out of the wreckage. The killing winds had torn their way up from the southern border. They had devastated Velantar. Now they had reached Parnas Pass.

"Almost seems like they followed us from the city," Grion muttered, drawing his knife across a whetting stone. "Seems whoever owns that power doesn't want us t'find its source."

"Whoever?" Bevan sneered. "It's Sahiste. Who else would attack so slyly, without giving a man a chance t'face his enemy? More dishonorable even than an archer." The pale-eyed clansman shot a poisonous glare at Jhared, who was trimming feathers for the arrows beside him.

"General Nadel doesn't think it's Sahiste. That's why we're heading north." Jase flashed his quicksilver grin from across the fire. "Take a bet on it, Bevan?"

"No, he won't take a bet on who's tearing us t'pieces!" Grion roared. "Don't be a fool tempting disaster."

Jase shrugged unapologetically, but devout Esran gave the Clan Nadaren man a disapproving glance before looking up from the shirt he'd been mending. "What's the plan for us, Commander? Will we push all the way to the Sandien Mountains in one go? Try t'beat the snows?"

"Naw. We've a stop to make before." Carn offered the patrol a wolfish grin. "Orders are we pause at Brenia."

The men greeted the news with enthusiasm. Jase uttered the name of a woman with a reverence only the goddess incarnate could merit. Other of Jhared's patrolmates shared tales of the comforts the Clan Valador trade town offered to travelers. It was Twitch, married to a lovely and, rumor held, iron-tempered Clan Rehamra woman, who thought to ask something other than the cost for a night of pleasure.

"What business for us in Brenia, Commander? I thought we were headed for the northern five."

The others quieted a little. Carn pulled at his mustache, his grin turning to a scowl. "The dark priestess knows."

"I could tell you, if you'd like."

Jhared glanced up, surprised to find the priestess standing at the edge of the circle clutching a small lap loom. An awkward moment gripped the patrol as the men glanced at one another uncertainly. It was Commander Carn who bobbed his white head in what Jhared was sure was the closest the wild clansman had ever come to a bow.

" 'Course, Lady. You're always welcome to the fire and the company, such as it is."

She smiled, and the men hastily made a space for her. As she folded herself before the fire, her cloak breezed open, revealing the ebony gleam of the hilt of Cael's Blade. An uneasy murmur ran through the patrol. Esran made Riana's spiral behind his back.

"No fear, Esran of Clan Ontera. I won't vanish or shift into a raven in the face of the holy spiral." The priestess smiled as she situated herself with the small loom across her knees.

Poor Esran's fair features turned bright enough to compete with the fire. He ducked his head. "Sorry, Lady. It's just, well, I've heard stories, but I never . . ." He gestured toward her hip.

"You've never seen the Blade?"

Her hand moved toward the hilt, and Jhared checked a flinch. He *had* seen the Blade, when the demon Cael pressed it against his chest and offered him death as an escape from his duty.

The priestess flicked her gaze toward him as she patted the sheath. "Few tasks require the weapon of Cael. Do not hope for a chance to see it on this trip."

Jase leaned closer to the woman. His eyes drifted from the knife to her blue gaze with a mix of reverent awe and the hint of something less reverent. "Ya must have some good tale's t'tell," he said hopefully. "If ya can't show us the Blade, surely ya can speak'a it."

"Hush, ya rogue!" gasped Esran. "The Bearer'a Cael's Blade's not one'a your tavern maids t'tell ya stories!"

The priestess laughed, not a girl's light laughter; it was the sound of a woman who knew something of the world. "All is well, Patrolman. Riana gave men a hunger for tales so they might learn the diversity of her Paths. She blesses her Storytellers."

Jase beamed. Jhared stopped trimming the feather in his hand to peer at the woman. Storytellers? Had he heard a nuance of meaning in the way she spoke the word? Did she only refer to any tavern tale-teller who warmed a chilly night with songs and legends? Or could she mean the outlawed Storytellers who claimed to carry forbidden tales of the Avelune?

Zia had told him his mother was a Storyteller.

"I can't share tales of the Blade," the priestess said. "They are for the initiated, but I have other stories you should hear. Before I tell you why we're heading for Brenia, you should understand what we're seeking in the Sandien Mountains. Who among you knows the story of Lady Sabela?"

Quiet descended over the group. The men shook their heads or shrugged. It was Anzo who stirred from where he leaned against a log, cradling the bowl of his pipe in one hand. "I've never heard of your Lady Sabela, but if she has something to say about what we're looking for, I'm ready to listen."

"I'd hear any story ya have t'tell," Jase added with a pretty smile.

The others hadn't warmed to the priestess, but she didn't look troubled. She adjusted her little loom and took up a strand of grey wool. "Good, then. We'll speak of what Sabela gave us. You should know the goal of our journey. You're the ones who must accomplish it, after all." Her long slender fingers hovered above her weaving, like a spider over its web, and she drew a breath.

"Long before the Exile," she began in a smoky tone. "Before Velantar stood with her gleaming towers, and the fifteen first-clans spread across the lands of Avelos, our people lived amid the wonders of Altan Mar. That glorious city perched in the highest crags of a mountain range we can no longer find and stood sentinel over the sparkling waters of an ocean we can no longer name. It was the first golden age, after the Great Wars of Riana and Cael, when our people still understood how to keep the world's true balance.

"Near the end of that age, Alende Isan led the council, and Lady Sabela, Riana's high priestess, was his guide. Lady Sabela was a Pathwalker of great skill, and navigated her way safely through many sacred journeys to advise Alende. There came a time when Sabela traveled the Paths into a future and saw a terrible war that would break upon the walls of Altan Mar. The conflict between Riana and Cael would flare once more, Sabela saw. She went to Alende with the warning and urged him to prepare the people to flee. But Alende, who had followed his guide in good faith for many years, loved the spires and balconies of their mountain home too well. He was unwilling to abandon it, and so he disregarded Sabela's warning."

"Wait," Grion interjected. "Alende was the hero'a Altan Mar."

"The hero'a the migration," Afiro added, rubbing the scar across his bald head.

The priestess's dark blue eyes absorbed the firelight as she looked at each of the soldiers. Jhared followed her gaze, wondering if his expression matched the discomfort he saw on his comrades' faces.

"Hero is the name others give a man when they have a need to mask his flaws," she answered softly. "Indeed, many people named Alende hero, even then. For they needed to see him as infallible. Three times Sabela warned that the conflict between Riana and Cael would destroy Altan Mar, and three times Alende rejected her advice to flee. The people jeered at Sabela as a coward. They did not prepare to abandon the city, but instead dug in for a siege, reinforcing the battlements and bringing stock within the walls, strengthening the barricades and sealing the beautiful open arches that overlooked the sea.

"A season passed, and in the depths of a calm summer night, Altan Mar caught up to the Path Sabela had seen. The conflict between Riana and Cael erupted into the realm of man as it hadn't since the days before the Aye and Ael. Fury arose from the very bowels of the world, and the mountain exploded in fire.

The palaces on the highest cliffs of Altan Mar were broken to rubble and spewed down the mountainside. Ash and poisoned smoke threatened to choke what fire did not char.

"Alende Isan rose to defend his people, but they were trapped within the fortress they had barricaded so well. He beat his sword against stone helplessly, foiled by the searing fire. His own children perished, and his lady wife. He cried out in despair, begging the Goddess of Order for mercy.

"It was Sabela who told him to cling to hope. Drawing upon the gift Riana gave her—a power to tame the sacred skies—she gathered the winds to her call and blew the raging flames and poisonous smoke back from Altan Mar, giving Alende and his people time to flee.

"The migration that followed that night was long and arduous. With all they loved destroyed, Alende and the others wandered for five years in search of a land to name home. They passed through myriad hardships, always with Sabela as their guide.

"Only fifteen of the great families remained when Sabela led them to the northern shores of Avelos. Gratefully, our ancestors climbed into the Sandien Mountains, searching for reflections of what they had lost. For herself, Sabela chose a sacrifice, for she had failed to stir Alende to action, and her failure cost many lives. She built a temple to beg Riana's forgiveness, a structure of beauty to echo the arches of Altan Mar. When Alende traveled deeper into Avelos, Sabela parted from him and never traveled farther. She never laid eyes on the Parnas Valley, nor did she see the gleaming city Alende raised and named in the ancient tongue *Tard en' Velan*, Hold of the Heart. Velantar.

"Sabela's sacrifice is our hope. We seek her temple that we might find the key to her strength and knowledge. She owned the power to command the sacred skies. If we find her secrets, they will help us to understand the source of the killing winds and how to combat them."

The priestess's voice faded to silence; her fingers stilled over her loom. Arrows and feathers lay neglected at Jhared's side. The songs and stories with which he had grown up taught that Alende's losses were the result of Cael's destructive rage. If the Bearer's story were true, the hero of Avelos could have saved his family. In the end, the deaths at Altan Mar were on Alende's head.

"Nope." Grion spat into the fire. "Alende Isan didn't need a woman to bring our people out'a harm's way. Sabela was bad fortune for him."

Esran glared at Grion, but some of the others nodded.

"More likely she distracted Alende. Misled him," Afiro said.

"The temple has a history'a that, right enough. Look at the Exile War." Bevan, less superstitious than Grion, could also be more cruelly clever. He narrowed his eyes. "Perhaps the killing winds did belong to Sabela. Now the temple is trying t'grab hold'a the power they lost."

"Are ya totally disordered?" Esran's tone rang with devout passion. "Don't you speak against Riana or her servants!"

A distance formed on either side of the Bearer as the soldiers took sides. Disbelief and fear caused them to push her to the edge of the circle. She looked dismayed by the vehemence her tale had unleashed. Jhared didn't like the ugly glances some of the men gave her.

"Lady, you said you could share how Brenia will lead us to Sabela's secrets," he said quickly.

"Indeed." She surprised him with a grateful smile. "Some of the oldest ruins south of the Sandien exist on Clan Valador's lands. It is said a sky tower still stands somewhere outside of Brenia."

"Sky tower?" Jase asked.

The priestess nodded. "Towers the ancients used to study Riana's spirals among the stars. Surely you've heard of them, a son of the devout Clan Nadaren."

"You heard'a them," Grion muttered to Jase. "She's talking 'bout traitors' towers."

"Oh." Recognition flashed across Jase's face, followed by apprehension. "I didn't know Tumal the Just left any standing."

"Few enough," the priestess said. "He was quite thorough in destroying those treasures." She shook her head, a bitter expression tightening her features. "The towers were places of learning long before they became fortifications for the fleeing Avelune during the war. You should hope we find the Valador tower intact, for the walls will be covered with the ancients' stories and maps."

"And you expect those maps will include Sabela's temple," Jhared said, watching as Grion gave a belligerent shrug and leaned over to mutter something to Bevan. Had the woman truly just denounced Tumal the Just? Did she even realize how foreign and dangerous her words sounded?

"Or something close," she answered. "The Lady of Brenia is a student of the ancients. She'll help us to find the sky tower, and may be able to interpret whatever clues to Sabela remain there."

"Hard to see how any good can come from a traitors' tower," Grion grumbled.

"Hard t'see why we soldiers are chasing after stories," Bevan added.

"Because your high chieftain says this is our best chance to stop the killing winds," a cold voice said from the darkness, "and you swore to obey him."

Lieutenant Sevar stepped into the circle, his grim presence silencing the men instantly. Firelight illuminated the fine scars that slashed his features, a reminder that even the killing winds had not defeated him. "If any of you care to argue the matter, you can do so before a deserters' tribunal." Sevar gestured at Grion and Bevan. "Hariar. Lavando. You're on first-moon watch. Move out. Now."

The two soldiers climbed to their feet and saluted the lieutenant before taking up their weapons and marching into the woods. Jhared grimaced. They shouldn't have been sent off together where they would only nurture one another's gripes. For their disrespect to the Bearer they should have faced punishment, not empty threats. Sevar's gentle treatment of Legacy supporters like Bevan and Grion only bolstered what Jhared had learned about the lieutenant's Legacy sympathies. He searched the faces of his comrades to see if they shared his frustration and found nothing but their own varying levels of repentance.

"Believe what you will about temple stories," Sevar said impassively. "It matters not to me or to our mission. You are scouts of the Forest Guard Fourth. You will find the key to controlling the killing winds because Avelos requires it of you."

"How do you answer your lieutenant?" Commander Carn bellowed.

"Sir! Yes, sir!" the patrol roared.

Sevar nodded once, then turned away from the circle to his maps. Jhared determined to observe the lieutenant more closely. The patrol would be traveling through clans whose council elders vacillated in their support of the high chieftain. If Sevar wished to stir sentiment against Rumar, he would find rich opportunities for it. Jhared didn't think it absurd to imagine the lieutenant capable of such maneuvering; he had already betrayed his general.

As he turned back to the fire, Jhared saw the priestess staring after Sevar with a bemused and disappointed expression.

"Well, I'm old enough to regret the things I'll never learn," Anzo said, "but not so foolish as to fear the things I don't know. Whatever the ancients left us to stop these killing winds can't be anything but a gift, whether it's hiding in a tower or a temple. If it means we don't feel those knives again or find another broken child, I'll be glad for it."

"Where I grew up near the seat'a Clan Ontera was an ancient grotto by a river," Lenaro offered. "So ruined, hard t'tell what form it first took. Might've been a tower. It had wall carvings and a few paintings'a the stars. It didn't seem an evil place. Mothers would beat us if they caught us there, but we loved it. We played at being Alende Isan and his companions."

"I suppose most'a us have stories'a the old ruins or some talisman from Alende," Esran said.

"My cousin had a sliver'a Alende's staff'a warding itself!" Jase declared brightly. "Wore it on a cord 'round his neck. Said it'd keep a man hard as . . ." The Clan Nadaren soldier trailed off and offered the priestess his best chagrined smile. "Sorry, Lady."

"No shame," the priestess answered. "Fertility is Riana's gift."

"Don't encourage him," Twitch warned. "Relki is quite the gift-giver."

A few of the men chuckled. The mood lightened somewhat, although the cohesion around the fire had fractured. Esran excused himself to sleep. Afiro strode out of the circle looking sour. Jhared decided it was time to head for his own blankets.

The priestess cornered him while he was checking on Seravina.

"Does the story trouble you?" she asked.

A horse whickered softly. The others' voices droned in the background; someone laughed. "Does it trouble me that a man as great as Alende Isan needed help to save his people? No. I've never heard of a battle won by one person on his own. I only grieve Alende's obstinance."

"I meant, does it trouble you that despite her role in our history, none among you had ever heard Lady Sabela's story?"

"Oh." Jhared played with a buckle on Seravina's halter, uncertain whether he believed the priestess's version of the migration—or wanted to. "Where did you learn such a story, Lady?"

"From a source not accessible to everyone," she said. "And more's the pity for it. You haven't answered my question."

He gave a little shrug. "It seems to me the enduring truths find their ways to us."

"And who decides what truths will be *enduring*? Might not valuable stories ever be lost? Might not a tale be shunned and forgotten if it holds a truth too painful to face?"

Jhared grimaced. Why did every conversation with this woman seem like a trap waiting to close? She already owned enough to condemn him. "I'm sorry, Lady. I'm no scholar. There's no answer a simple soldier like me could possibly—"

"Stop!" she hissed, her eyes sparking with fury. "Be done with this game! Do not, *do not* hide behind the mask of soldiery and believe I will accept as little from you as from yonder clansmen. I know what home raised you."

Jhared stepped backward, hearing the threat in her words. "Lady, I'd no intention of offending. I only . . ." *Only wonder when I'll learn what use you have for an oath-broken Shorn man raised by the high chieftain's closest ally.*

The priestess's gaze blasted over him. Despite the darkness, he felt terribly exposed. He recalled the searing pain the high priestess had inflicted upon him at his Becoming with her direct gaze and a single suggestion, and forced himself to withstand the Bearer's scrutiny. Then, as quickly as the storm struck, it passed. Her eyes darkened. With a sigh, she shrank into her cloak.

"Very well," she murmured. "Nothing about this night is what I intended, either. I only thought to hear the impressions of one who has read the histories. It seems we will have to leave that discussion for a time when you trust me a little better. Come. We'll start with something easier."

She picked her way through the half-light toward her tent. Beside the tent flap, she bent to search among her saddle packs, while Jhared waited uneasily.

"Ah, here!" she said, drawing forth a narrow, cloth-wrapped bundle and laying it in his hands. "This is meant for you."

Carefully, he unrolled the little package to reveal a beautifully worked hunter's knife with a blade of twilight-colored steel. The last time he had spied the knife it was on a deadly arc toward the Bearer. He had seen to it the blade found his body instead.

"Lady, you owe me nothing! All I do goes toward reparation."

"Of course, soldier." She smiled, more gently. "However, you are my guard now, and I would have you well-armed. It seems a weapon of unusually fine workmanship."

"Very fine," he agreed. "It's from none of our forges."

Her expression shifted with interest. "Foreign made? From where?"

He turned the knife in his hands. The blade was narrow and straight, edged on both sides. An elegant guard curved toward the tip in the shape of a long-tailed fish. The grip was decorated with an interlocking pattern of palm fronds. An exquisite and deadly piece of work. The poorly balanced, sometimes brittle weapons with which the Forest Guard outfitted its soldiers were far inferior. "The design is unfamiliar, but steel as exceptional as this is likely of Amurian origin."

"I see. A rarity then." All her dark fury had fled; she seemed small and vulnerable. Jhared realized how difficult it must have been for her to leave the temple and the familiarity of the city to travel through the wilds with a company of soldiers.

"Thank you," he said. "It is a generous gift."

She reached out and ran a finger along the knife's grip. Her lips parted, a question reflecting in her eyes, but she closed her mouth again without speaking.

Jhared was relieved not to confront any more questions about the blade or the man who had wielded it. *That* Alende had likely been pushed off the top of the city wall by now, a traitor's death.

"Mahla Denaban saved my life," Alende had claimed.

Jhared shuddered.

"Ah, now I've kept you too long from rest, and you still healing," said the priestess. "You must get some sleep."

"If there's nothing more you need," he said, grateful to be dismissed.

"Go, and rest easy until you walk the Paths again."

He turned, his thoughts churning. She had given him a gift beyond expectation—the knife was more than fine steel; it was an acknowledgment of what he had done for her. Did she mean to say their debts were balanced? Or did she mean to remind him of all the ways he was bound to her?

"Oh, soldier. There is one more thing."

He halted abruptly. "Yes, Lady?"

"If your *fever* returns and you feel again as you did on the hill this afternoon, you must tell me. I have remedies for such ailments."

She knew he had lied. He saw it in her sardonic gaze. He smiled as best he could. "As you say, Lady."

"Very good." She nodded and slipped into her tent. He heard her cooing softly to herself as he strode away.

3.

HUNTERS AND PREY

The moon sank beneath the horizon, allowing the stars to gleam as sharp and bright as sword points across the purple sky. Jhared stirred at his post at the edge of camp, stretching his awareness to assess the forest around him. He started, as General Nadel had taught him, by attending to the state of his own thoughts. He drew deep breaths and set aside distractions before gradually shifting outside of himself. The myriad sensations of the world could overwhelm and confuse a scout, but he organized them into concentric rings, using himself as the center and moving ring by ring through the forest and across the hills: the scent of earth under his feet, the scuttle of insects in the leaves beside him; the howl of a predator deep among the trees; the smell of rain high in the clouds. It was glorious to open himself to the nuances of the night. His own shame-filled life shrank to splendid insignificance. To lose himself in his awareness of the world was almost as complete an escape as an exhausting run. If Lieutenant Sevar understood what a comfort it was to guard the others through the heart of the night, no doubt he would have devised some other form of discipline.

Jhared set his attention on the camp perimeter and began walking his patrol. They had spied no further sign of the killing winds, but the company remained on edge from the previous day's close escape. Silently, he glided among the trees. A breeze rose from the north. On the other side of the hill, a mountain cat yowled. Reflexively, he reached for the small carved stone in the pouch at his belt: Branlen's well-wishes talisman. Thinking of his foster brother cheered Jhared and reminded him of his goal.

Ahead, something rustled the brush. He halted, scanning the twisted tree branches, but the forest held tightly to its secret. The sound came again, purposeful. No animal sound—a footstep. Jhared moved toward the source. As he changed his line of sight, starlight fell through the leaves. The outline of a man snapped into his perception.

"Who is it? Identify yourself!"

Laughter drifted from among the branches: beautiful, lonely laughter.

21

Jhared had the dizzying sensation of living two moments at the same time. The land pitched beneath him. "In the name of High Chieftain Adan Rumar, step forward and announce yourself!"

No response. Jhared shifted to find his balance. His sword swung heavily against his hip.

"Sulosan, surma sen," the voice said softly. The foreign words were ugly, half-formed and wet sounding.

Steel shone in the starlight. A knife flew from the arched entrance of the temple garden. A man rushed at him, full of frustration and hatred. No. That attack wasn't a part of this moment; it had been weeks ago. Alende had tried to kill the Bearer in the high temple. Jhared heard the beautiful laughter again, behind him this time. How many men were out there? Memories were getting in his way, like the tree branches, making it difficult to see. On the horse lines, Seravina gave a high-pitched squeal. Jhared staggered a step. A gleam of blue flickered at the edges of his vision. Beyond the trees, men drew their blades.

"Forest Guard, attackers! Awake! To arms!"

The camp erupted as his patrolmates flung themselves out of their blankets. Bleary-eyed men scrambled for their weapons, muttering curses and eyeing the trees. Commander Carn kicked out the dying fire and barked orders for a defensive formation.

"Watchman, report!" Sevar hissed.

"Men closing from the north and west," Jhared answered, shoving through the circle of his comrades to reach the Bearer's tent. "Foreigners. Drawing steel."

The priestess was already hurrying out, her feet bare, her hair unbound. She grabbed Jhared's arm. "Thank the Pathmaker," she whispered. "You're still here with me."

"Of course, Lady! Come. You'll be safe behind our swords."

"But I thought . . ." She darted a wide-eyed glance at the men. "Wait!" she cried, running back into her tent.

"Patrolman, how many?" the lieutenant demanded.

How many? Jhared tried to sort out his memories from the truth. Was it five? Twelve? Or had there only ever been the one? "I heard them north and west. I saw blades."

"Numbers, Patrolman!"

"I don't know, sir. I don't know how many."

The lieutenant cursed. "Relki, go learn who's out there."

Jase vanished into the trees without a sound. Jhared ducked into the tent after the priestess. He almost collided with her as she emerged carrying her square basket.

"Hurry, Lady!" He shepherded her toward the circle. The soldiers opened their formation for her, and Jhared nearly threw her behind them. He took his place shoulder to shoulder with Twitch and Grion.

Then came the moment of pause, that instant before an attack when imminent danger burned away the veils between fear and truth. Jhared loosened his grip on his sword, feeling the muscles of his hands stretch and contract. He heard his comrades' breathing and smelled his own sweat. His enemy's laughter was silent now. In the next breath or the next they would come.

The silence lengthened, increasing the tension like a bowstring drawing to its limit. Next to Jhared, Twitch fidgeted. Grion coughed.

The attack didn't come.

The stars continued their spiral across the sky. Jase slipped back into camp.

"Well?" Sevar demanded.

"The perimeter's clear, sir. I couldn't find anyone."

"No one?" Sevar growled. "Did they all just fly away?"

Jase glanced apologetically at Jhared. "I didn't see signs'a anyone. There might'a been a set'a tracks near the pool, but the bank's too muddled and it's too dark t'tell for sure."

"Maybe our watchman had a bad dream and let his shadow scare him," Bevan snickered.

"I saw a man," Jhared insisted. "I heard him speak in a foreign tongue."

"Sahistens," Esran offered. "They can move as silent as witches without leaving tracks."

"No. What I heard wasn't Sahine."

"And we're too far from the border," Twitch added.

The Bearer stepped out of the circle and looked up at Jhared. "Can you repeat it?"

"Maybe." Jhared bowed his head, trying to recall the slippery words. "It was something like '*Sulosa sur . . . masen.*'"

"That almost sounds Amurian," the priestess mused. "Or something close."

"Might be it's the same group who sent the winds after us," Commander Carn offered to Sevar. "They want t'keep us from reaching Brenia. Keep us from finding the sky tower."

"If they mean to stop us," Sevar said flatly, "they're doing a piss-poor job of it, aren't they? I doubt those words are Amurian or Sahine. More likely than anything they're the whispers of the forest interpreted by a Shorn man who can't control his imagination." The lieutenant glowered at Jhared.

He should have stayed quiet. Sevar hated him, and might very well have been one of the men who arranged to have him beaten in Velantar. But Jhared had sworn to protect his patrol and to do something meaningful to stop the killing winds. That started by doing *something*. "It wasn't my imagination," he replied. "Sir, I heard someone speaking and saw blades. I know where I heard them. Please. You must let me go out to look."

"I *must?*" Sevar's tone went cold. "After all you've already done? After the warnings you've been given? You dare to use those words?" The men were silent. Somewhere in the forest, an owl questioned the night. Sevar lifted his head and met Jhared's gaze. "Five lashes for insubordination."

"Lieutenant!" the Bearer cried, round-eyed. "Not five lashes, surely! Your Forest Guard was only trying to—"

Anzo hissed a warning. "Lady!"

Too late. Sevar swung around on the Bearer. "You think not, Lady? Perhaps you are correct. It takes more than pain to teach this Shorn man anything. Not five lashes. Commander Carn, make it ten."

The Bearer uttered a sound of shock. "Lieutenant Sevar, he is my guard. Do I not have some say in how he is disciplined?"

"Lady, he is a Shorn soldier under my command. You have *no* say." Sevar turned his back on her. "Get on with it, Commander."

Jhared moved toward the closest of the trees before Carn could order one of his comrades to compel him. Someone retrieved the whip from the packs. Jhared didn't look to see who it was. He stripped off his shirt. His torso was still covered with evidence of Ilvio's fists and Bren's knife, but his patrolmates would only be staring at his scars, the ugly knobs of flesh and severed bone that defined him. The reason he could not discipline his thoughts or senses. Once he had been Avelun.

"Position, Denaban," Carn growled.

Jhared's mistakes reflected badly on the commander. He would not be feeling forgiving. Jhared took a wide stance and braced his arms against the tree trunk.

The first lash took him high across his shoulders. He exhaled hard through his teeth and pressed his palms into the rough tree bark. The second lash ripped a path around his ribcage, tearing across a still-healing gash. By the third stroke, he was clenching his jaw to prevent himself from crying out.

Carn made the rest swift and professional, but as Jhared straightened, his back screaming, the expressions of revulsion and pity from his patrolmates landed nearly as hard as the whip.

Lieutenant Sevar turned away. "All right, men. We'll call this dawn. Break camp and get to your horses. I want to reach Mirela before breakfast."

The others jumped to their tasks. As Jhared reached for his shirt, he caught the Bearer's gaze on him, pale in the predawn light. Another rush of humiliation filled his chest. He looked aside, stumbling a little as Grion shoved past him.

"Well done, Denaban," the man muttered.

Instantly, Sevar's gaze dropped onto Grion. "If any of you are unhappy riding out at this hour. I'll reassign your mount to the baggage team and you can walk to Brenia. Is that clear?"

No one else spoke.

"Commander Carn, get your boys moving. We've wasted enough time here." Sevar stalked off toward his own mount. Jhared watched him go. Were strangers still observing them from the trees, had they fled, or was the lieutenant correct that the image of a blade and the memory of foreign words had been only an illusion?

"Denaban, you looking to get left behind?" Carn barked. " 'Bout now I'd be happy to make that happen."

Jhared snapped to attention. "No, Commander."

"Then get to work!"

Dawn was still just a hope when the patrol started traveling again along Parnas Pass. Sevar kept the pace steady on the rutted road, but didn't press the horses. Beside Jhared, the priestess was a silent figure darker than the forest. He could feel her gaze on him and did his best to ignore it. He felt sick and unsettled in a way that had little to do with the fresh wounds across his back. A perverse part of him wished for an attack to spring from the forest. He needed to prove to himself, even more than to the others, that what he had seen and heard had been real.

By midday, they left the pass well behind and the terrain grew easier. The foothills rolled off the northern shoulders of the Parnas Mountains into wooded vales graced with clear-running streams and small lakes. Villages nestled between the hills and sprawled along the shores. Colorful fall markets, tiny replicas of the city's autumn gathering, spilled outside the village walls and across the farmers' fields.

As they trotted down to the low lands, the self-destructive urges that plagued Jhared in the heights released their grip. Seravina covered ground with an effortless gait. If it hadn't been for the Bearer's taut presence beside him and the pain in his back reminding him of his errors, it might have been a pleasant ride.

They made good time that day. Lieutenant halted the patrol before the sun met the western hills, and Jhared slid out of the saddle with the others. He rubbed down Seravina and rationed out her grain. She nipped his arm for his efforts.

When he finished, he approached the priestess, who was removing her bags from her mare. Jhared reached out to take the reed basket from her hands. "Lady, may I help you?"

She turned to evade his reach. "Not now, Patrolman."

With an inward sigh, he watched her march away.

"Leave it, boy. You've got trouble enough." Anzo stepped beside Jhared, a leather bag tucked under one arm.

"I wish I could leave it. I don't know what she wants of me."

"How 'bout we set ourselves to a task more fitting a Forest Guard scout, eh? Lenaro wants meat for the pot tonight."

Jhared scrubbed a hand over his face. It would be a relief to lose himself in the hunt for a time, but he hadn't yet figured out his new role. "I'm not certain I should leave her. I'm charged to be her bodyguard. If she needs—"

"Lieutenant says you're the one for this. After you and I take care of that other thing."

Jhared turned and gave Anzo a puzzled look.

"Those stripes you're wearing need cleaning," the old vet replied.

"Oh."

"Go on. Fetch your bow. We'll walk downstream for a bit of quiet, eh?"

They left the camp and made their way along the course of the nearby stream. Damp earth and dead leaves sweetened the air. Jhared rejoiced in the untamed grace around him and in the supple bow in his hands. He read the patterns of the wilds as easily as he read ancient Velos—the tales of a vixen hunting mice, the stream shifting in its bed, a stag searching for a mate—and felt himself joining those patterns, becoming the one who saw and understood them. He grew light with it, until Anzo stopped and pointed out a tumble of rocks beside the water.

"Here's good enough. Take a seat and let's see the damage."

Jhared remained standing, his arms wrapped around his chest. "You needn't do this, Anzo. No one would be the wiser."

"You getting in the habit of defying Lieutenant's orders? Sit. I'll manage."

Reluctantly, Jhared did as he was directed. As he drew up his shirt, ripping it free of the fresh scabs, Anzo hissed in dismay. Jhared hunched into himself, waiting for the condemnation to follow and knowing he deserved it. Insubordination was not a small crime. Anzo said nothing, but unpacked the healer's bag he'd been carrying and set to work.

"You'd better watch yourself, boy. You're not winning any favor these days."

"I know," Jhared muttered. "I suppose the lieutenant would like nothing better than for me to walk off a cliff."

Anzo's hands moved firmly but not cruelly across Jhared's back as he cleaned the wounds. "I don't think it's so bad as that. Could be though, if you have another night like last."

"I know," Jhared said again.

"I'm sorry you and Lieutenant started off on opposite sides of the blade so early on. I don't know what makes you hate him, but it's not a smart way to go."

That startled Jhared. He had imagined his anger well concealed. "Anzo, Lieutenant Sevar supported Tumal's Legacy against General Nadel. How can you . . . any loyal man bear him?"

"Whoa now." Anzo came around to face Jhared, a bloodied cloth in one hand. "Have a care, boy. You're talking about rumor. Rumor put about by the Legacy itself. No one believed it. Sevar's as loyal to the general as he is to the high chieftain."

Jhared looked away. What could he say to that? That he had spied on the lieutenant at Ravia? That he had heard Sevar speak the condemning words himself? Not without displaying his own capacity for guile. "Whatever the truth about

Sevar's faction alliance, Anzo, it's clear enough what he thinks about the high chieftain's closest ally. My foster father."

"Well, that's a fact." The other patrolman blew out a breath. "Lieutenant has no love for the Minister of the Teaching. I'm sorry to see that enmity bleed onto you. Although maybe you're not seeing everything clearly yourself, eh?"

"How is that?"

"Lieutenant knows what it is to have to prove himself. He would'a been an elder if his father hadn't stepped down from the council. No one thought he'd make it when he ran to the Forest Guard. I saw it myself. The officers made him suffer. But he ran the Tests of Rona alone and unsanctioned rather than let them drive him out."

Jhared had heard the story from Anzo before. It didn't warm him now any more than it had the first time. "He suffered so much that High Chieftain Rumar offered to promote him to General of the Northern Towers?"

"Don't be clever," Anzo said. "He means to make you earn your place. That's all I'm saying. He's hard, but he isn't one to turn on his own men. If he sees you're serious about reparation, he'll ease off."

"Is that something you'd lay money on, Anzo?"

The older man sucked his teeth. "Just think on what I'm telling you. It'll help to keep you in one piece, eh?"

"It might . . . I'll try. Now, haven't we been ordered to bring back something for dinner?" Jhared stood and swept up his bow, needing to end the awkwardness.

They followed a game trail until they came upon a herd of cabrin foraging for acorns. The herd was small—Jhared counted nine of the little wild goats—but fat and healthy, prepared for the approaching winter. The billy, a glossy, black beast with spiraled amber horns, watched over the others. Their hooves thumped the ground quietly and their muzzles rustled the deadfall as they searched out fodder among the trees. Without a sound, Jhared lifted his bow and stepped around a tree for a clear shot. His target was a young, spotted male. He nocked the arrow and drew the bow as easily as drawing a breath, pain only a distant thing. His heart beat steadily against his ribs as he waited for the breeze to still. The moment came. His fingers loosed the string. The arrow carved the air like yearning.

The cabrin dropped without a cry, sending the others into a panicked retreat. The billy bugled and ran after his charges. When the last had disappeared, Anzo strode over to retrieve the kill.

"Cleanly done," he said, withdrawing the arrow.

"Think the lieutenant will make it so clean for me?" Jhared asked.

Anzo glanced up with a look of shock, but laughed when his eyes met Jhared's. "I think you shouldn't test it."

When they returned to the patrol, Jhared handed his kill to Lenaro. There was a stir of appreciation among the others, most of them willing to forgive the predawn chaos in exchange for fresh meat. Jhared looked over the camp. Carn and Sevar were in conversation over a map. Grion was splitting logs for the fire. The others were occupied with various tasks.

"Where's the Bearer?" he asked.

"She walked off toward the water a bit ago," Lenaro answered. "She had a basket with her. Looked like she was hoping for a bath."

Jase looked up, his blue eyes sparkling with mischief. "Ya think I should go after her? All kinds'a dangers out there for a woman alone."

"With you the biggest," Esran said. "Give her some peace."

"Give Denaban some peace," Twitch added. "No offense, boy, but she keeps ya leashed like a temple hound. Not right for a man'a the Fourth. And after what she did this morning . . ."

"True enough," Anzo muttered.

As Jase tilted his head toward Jhared, his tattoos caught the light. "Can't deny she keeps you tightly tethered."

Jhared lifted his hands, taken aback by the others' sentiments. "Guard is what I've been named, and I'm honored to serve so. Just leave her some privacy, as Esran says. She'll return soon."

Twilight slid closer. A widow's bird hooted its sad message east of camp. The roasting cabrin gave off a rich aroma. The Bearer didn't reappear.

Jhared paced outside the ring of firelight. He remembered that her basket had something to do with women's business, and wanted no part of that, but Jase was right about the dangers that existed in these hills: ravines and gullies difficult to see in the dusk; fast-flowing rivers with slippery banks; the occasional hungry wild cat; and sometimes even the Ael—the wolfish Verael or serpent Semael—on the hunt.

As the first stars winked in a lavender sky, Jhared could wait no longer.

"You want company?" Anzo asked.

"No. This may have to do with me. She was angry."

Anzo made a face. "*She* was angry?"

Jhared ignored the man's tone and walked out of camp. He picked up the Bearer's trail easily. The extra weight of the basket added depth to her prints and left other signs: a torn leaf where she brushed past a branch, crushed grass where she rested her burden, a bit of broken basket reed. She traveled east, toward the stream, as Lenaro had suggested. Jhared jogged through the forest, the approaching night filling him with disquiet.

Her tracks never reached the water, turning north instead. They led him toward a place where the grand old trees began to thin. Thorny bushes and slender saplings took advantage of the space, creating a prickly border. Jhared pushed through where the priestess had done so before him. Beyond lay a small meadow carpeted in dried grasses and autumn flowers. The priestess sat in the center of the meadow, the basket open at her knee.

Jhared halted sharply.

On the edge of the basket perched one of Cael's creatures. Another sat on the lady's arm. A third darted circles in the mauve sky.

The Bearer of Cael's Blade looked up at him and smiled. The dove on her wrist shook out its wings, exposing feathers of even grey. A small downy plume floated to the ground.

Revulsion washed over Jhared. "Why?"

"Because they've traveled too long in a small box and needed the exercise."

She spoke calmly and softly, as though not to frighten the birds. For some reason, that infuriated Jhared more.

"Why have you brought these cursed creatures among us? Do you wish our mission to fail?"

She owns the secrets of blood. She's searching for the strength to overthrow Riana's order.

A madman had told him that. Perhaps he should have listened.

"Come. Sit beside me, Jhared. I will answer your questions when you've taken a breath and set aside your fear. You'll not hear me as you are now."

She was right, and he knew it, but that didn't make it easier to reach for calm. With an effort of will, he inhaled slowly, held it, and released his emotions in a long, controlled stream. Let her see his body unclench and his breathing steady. He needed answers.

"Hold out your hands," she said when he had lowered himself beside her.

The dove on the basket cooed and bobbed its head, peering sideways with one eye as bright as a drop of blood.

He remembered what it felt like to cradle such a small warm life in his palm. He remembered the sensations of the racing heart, the soft breast, and the smooth feathers. The little neck had made only the smallest *pop* when he snapped it between his fingers. Tierzen and Sarena had told him he must do it and had watched to be sure he did. A creature he had nurtured. A small life ended. His doing. Not his doing. His doing. In that instant, he had hated his Teachers. That was the first time the lesson struck him: *he* was the evil one to hate the only people willing to take him in and risk so much for him.

He looked at the priestess and folded his arms over his chest. "No."

The woman opened her mouth. Jhared saw the argument rising in her eyes, but she only sighed and nodded. "I'll not try to convince you these creatures are other than Cael's messengers, for that's precisely what they are. But they're no curse, Jhared. They allow us access to Paths we'd never reach without them."

"Whatever you may think, I'm no temple scholar," he said tightly. "Tell me plainly what you mean."

She reached into a pocket of her cloak and drew out a wooden capsule about the size of Jhared's thumb. With a twist of her fingers, she pulled the capsule into two pieces, revealing a hollowed inside. The dove on her arm hopped closer to examine a bit of parchment sticking out from one of the ends. Gently, she brushed the creature away, then showed Jhared that the parchment was blank.

"When we reach Brenia, I'll write something of our progress and attach the capsule to little Nambi. I'll release him at dawn, and he'll make his way home, where his mate is waiting."

"To Velantar?"

"Yes," she answered.

"All the way to the high temple?"

She smiled. Her eyes were very large in the half-light. "To those who have made a home for him."

"How can you be certain the demon will not cause such a message to be misread? Some misinterpretations could bring about mischief, or true tragedy. Cael's disorder—"

"Cael's disorder is something we risk every day," she said more severely. "And sometimes even hope for. Tell me, soldier, have you ever lost your way in the wilds only to discover some small gift off the known path—a safe place to rest, a needed source of water, maybe the trail of your prey?"

"Perhaps," he admitted, "but—"

"Have you ever selected a place to ambush your enemy precisely because it was the place where he'd least expect you?"

Jhared pressed his lips together.

"And tonight, when you stand watch again, why should you even hope you'll not raise a false alarm the same as the night before?"

"Because I need not repeat my mistakes! A man learns from his experiences. Is changed."

"Exactly," she said. "The unexpected. The unlooked for. The capacity for change. Aspects of disorder that allow us to grow. Without them, we're stagnant. Do not shun my messengers. They allow me to reach the city with words of hope far faster than any Forest Guard courier, and they're available to me even when I have no courier."

Cael's messengers carrying words of hope to Velantar. Every bit of it felt wrong. Yet Jhared could start to see a pattern in what she was saying. Who was this woman who so easily threw aside the warnings of the temple? Should he close himself to her fearsome thoughts or might she offer something he needed? Would a woman who understood disorder know a way to help him regain his slipping control? Abruptly, he realized something more.

"You knew I would come looking for you. You wanted me to see this. Why?"

She sighed. "Because I hurt you this morning, and I'm sorry for it. I very much want for you to trust me."

He bowed his head and pressed his fingers against his eyelids. "Revealing your use of Cael's creatures is a strange way to try to earn my trust, Lady."

"You hold a secret for me now, as I hold one of yours. Perhaps the balance will help you to understand I mean you no harm."

A balance. If he remained quiet about her unlikely messengers, she wouldn't tell Sevar he had killed a man. The idea of such deceit ate at him, but his only alternative was to admit his crime. If Sevar chose to execute him, all hope of final reparation was lost.

"A balance then," he said heavily.

"Thank you," she murmured. "I hope one day it truly feels like a balance to you and not like a burden." Reaching behind her, she picked up a small clay jug. She shook it in the air, creating a dry rattling sound. The two doves on the ground immediately fluttered into the basket. The third bird darted from where it had perched on a sapling at the edge of the meadow to the basket lid.

The priestess cooed softly to the creatures as she opened the jug and poured a measure of seed into three shallow cups that hung on the basket's edges. When all the birds were eating, she slowly closed and secured the lid.

"We should return to camp," Jhared said, unfolding himself to rise. "Someone may come to see where we've gone."

"Wait, Jhared." She caught his sleeve in her long fingers. "Won't you tell me what happened last night? What did you really see?"

He closed his eyes. The memory of his watch was strangely hazy now, except for the lilt of foreign words and the flash of a knife. "I told you what I saw, Lady. And what I heard. Someone threatened the camp."

"Some*one*? You said before there was a band of men. Jhared, are you certain what you saw was on this Path?"

"It was no dream!" he insisted. "He . . . they were watching us!"

"Easy, soldier. I'm sorry." She looked down at the basket then back up at him. "Truly, I'm sorry."

Her eyes matched the velvet blue of the night sky. Her features glowed: a wide brow and a small, straight nose; cheeks that sloped smoothly toward her gently squared jaw.

He drew away, wondering how she switched so quickly from the formidable goddess to the curious scholar to the quiet woman.

"Come, Lady. It's time to go back to camp."

4.
STRANGERS

The fair weather held for three days more; then the damp wind that had been waiting in the clouds swooped upon the valley, whipping under cloaks and slapping at the horses. Now that Jhared knew the truth, it seemed impossible the others didn't hear the soft calls or the sound of fluttering wings that came from the Bearer's basket when the wind whistled through the woven reeds. Perhaps it was lucky that many of the men had begun to avoid the priestess. When Jhared met his comrades' gazes, he felt the lie between them. It wouldn't go well if the others learned their journey was burdened with creatures touched by Cael. It would be worse if they discovered he knew of it.

For her part, the priestess appeared undisturbed by her secrets or the men's mutterings. She endured the rigors of travel without complaint, growing more eager as the patrol drew closer to Brenia. Her manner with Jhared varied as wildly as the unpredictable autumn skies. Much of the time she was easy and familiar with him, chatting about the villages they passed or asking him questions about tracking and his work as a scout. Sometimes she grew dark and intense. Then he would catch a glint of Cael's Blade at her hip and remember she still owned some objective he couldn't guess.

It was a wet and leaden afternoon when they crossed into the lands of Clan Valador. Clan Manitar's forested vales had surrendered to the rolling trimago fields from which the Valador clansmen produced their famous green dyes. On either side of the road, the tall, bushy trimago plants bent and nodded, their large, yellowish leaves spilling over with rain like broken cups. Rain drenched the horses' coats and dripped off the front of Jhared's hood. He wiped the water from his face and surveyed the road and fields before and behind them.

"Soldier, that's the fourth time in as many minutes you've twisted yourself around to spy behind us," the priestess noted. "Are you worried Anzo and Jase will run off?"

"No, Lady," Jhared replied, more mildly than he felt. Several times since Parnas Pass, he had the uncomfortable sensation that someone observed them on the road. He kept imagining a foreign soldier leaping out of the fields waving a knife and speaking words as soggy as the rain.

"In this wet weather, I wouldn't blame them if they did," the priestess went on, "but they'd miss something lovely in Brenia. How many more days until we reach town? Three?"

Jhared peered at her. She seemed uncowed by the gloom. Droplets scattered in her black hair like tiny gems. "Two. If the roads don't flood."

"Wonderful! I'll be glad to see the glories of Brenia. Although at the moment, I'm not certain whether the most glorious will be the sky tower of Clan Valador or the hot baths at the temple."

Jhared smiled a little at her enthusiasm.

She caught his smile and chuckled. "Lady Esania is a warm hostess. You'd best warn Jase that unless he fancies losing his favorite bits, he'd do well to keep his eyes and hands from wandering."

"Of course, Lady." Jhared didn't remind her that in Brenia Jase and the others would find no shortage of warm welcomes. "Do you know the Lady of Brenia well?"

"Well enough," the Bearer said, one corner of her lip curling upward.

She didn't say more, and Jhared was left to wonder at her distant, thoughtful expression. As they rode in silence, Jhared once again felt eyes on him. He glanced back at the rearguard: Anzo and Jase swayed easily in their saddles, looking wet but relaxed. He surveyed both sides of the road. There he spied it: the disrupted pattern. On the Bearer's side, the trimago stalks swayed farther than the others, as though something hurried through them. Something large headed toward the company—

"Lady, hold! Hold!"

Jhared clapped his heels to Seravina, sending her surging forward. With a squeeze of his calf, he wheeled her a tight quarter turn, cutting off the Bearer completely. The priestess gasped as her horse half-reared. Shorn energy arrowed through Jhared's veins.

A doe burst out of the fields, with a stag just behind her. The deer tore through the patrol, startling the horses and causing the men to pull up. Water splashed as cloven hooves pounded through the puddles. The stag trumpeted and swung his massive horns, scything a path through horses and men. Carn's gelding kicked at the beast. Seravina squealed, but held her ground. Then, with another leap, the wild beasts cleared the road and disappeared, white tails flashing, into the fields on the other side.

The soldiers cheered for the rutting animals. Seravina whinnied and tossed her head. Blood hammered in Jhared's ears as he looked to the priestess, who was bringing her mare under control.

"I'm sorry," he panted. "I saw the stalks parting, and I was afraid it might be . . ." He trailed off. He didn't know exactly what he had feared. "Are you all right?"

Spots of color dotted the Bearer's cheeks. "I'm fine, Patrolman! You prevented any damage."

"Bad omen for a rutting doe to cross our path," Grion muttered, shooting a glance toward the Bearer. "Near as bad as hauling Cael's woman with us."

Anzo laughed. "Old man, is there anything you consider a *good* omen?"

Sevar called for a stop to untangle the packhorses and take a quick meal. The men hunched near their wet mounts, downing flatbread wrapped around cold roasted cabrin. As the patrol started onward again, Jase started a bawdy song about one of Riana's sly Pathguides who fell in love with a doe-eyed maiden. Rather than waiting until the maiden died, when it would become his task to lead her to the Hidden Paths, the Pathguide came to her in the form of a stag and convinced her to run away with him. Their love shone so brightly that Riana forgave her guide for disrupting her order and allowed the pair to leap eternally through the stars. It was the odd song in any musician's repertoire, for the lovers did not pay for their transgressions, but Jhared had always been fond of its lively melody. He sang with the others, chasing back some of the day's dreariness.

They were well into the third verse, Jhared singing the part of the stag with Jase and Esran, when he caught the priestess watching him and tripped over a note. He lost his place and let the others go on.

"I didn't mean to stop you," she said. "You've a lovely voice. Rich as summer."

His face heated. "Thank you, Lady."

"You've the controlled power that comes of training. Someone took the time to teach you?"

"I . . . yes. My mother."

"Ah. I suppose I should have known that. She was a bard, wasn't she?"

Jhared bowed his head. That Mahla Denaban had been a bard was perhaps the only thing he knew of her for certain. He glanced at the priestess sidelong. "Why does that matter to you?"

The Bearer let out an exasperated breath. "By all things unbroken, Jhared Denaban, where did you learn such endless wariness? I've found Tierzen Trianor to be a frank, honest man. Surely, he was a scrupulous Teacher."

"Indeed, Lady. Maybe that's why his rivals try so hard to use his Shorn fosterling against him."

Understanding flickered in her expression and her tone softened. "Soldier, I hope by now you trust I have no wish to harm you. . . ."

Jhared sucked a breath and tugged Seravina to a halt. The other men stopped singing and drew rein. "Oh no."

For most of the morning, the thick foliage of the trimago plants had formed a yellow-green wall on both sides of the road—the kind of cover that made highwaymen smile and caused solitary travelers to hasten their steps. But where the patrol had paused, and for as far to the west as Jhared could see, the field had been crushed. Stalks were stripped of leaves, snapped in two, and torn from the dirt. Even through the rain, Jhared smelled the heavy malty odor of trimago sap. Beyond the field, where iron-colored clouds hung over a low rise, lay piles of wood that looked like the material for a massive bonfire but probably should have been a house and a barn. Several other smaller structures leaned this way and that, like children's blocks tossed in the sand.

The wreckage of the killing winds was unmistakable.

Lieutenant Sevar spat a command and kicked his stallion into a dead run, off the road and across the ruined fields. The patrol tore after. Moving amidst the farm debris were a dozen men and women. Someone must have spotted the racing soldiers, because suddenly the survivors were scurrying into a ragged formation. Six men threw themselves onto horses and started toward the patrol. The others hurried into a half-circle with their backs to the debris and various makeshift weapons in their hands. An archer prepared her arrow.

Sevar pulled up just outside the archer's range, and the patrol formed a neat wedge behind him. Jhared maneuvered Seravina in front of the priestess. He watched as the strangers approached. The leader, a solid, broad-shouldered man, rode a sway-backed beast more suited for the yoke than the saddle. At thirty pac-es, the man yanked the plow horse to a stop. He wiped rain from his chin with a yellow- and brown-stained hand.

"The village'a Obled on the lands'a Clan Valador stand under my protection. Speak your names and your business."

"The lands of Clan Valador and all of Avelos stand under the protection of High Chieftain Adan Rumar. I'm Matio Sevar, Lieutenant of the Forest Guard Fourth. Who are you? And when did the killing winds strike this farm?"

"So the cleansing storms already 'ave a name, eh? Killing winds? Struck two days ago. I'm Belen, commander'a clanguard for Obled. These are my men." He gestured to the riders behind him. "What do you want 'ere?"

"Where are the witnesses who survived the storm?"

The man shrugged. "Not so many witnesses. Storm struck at night. The Erisma estate, mostly. Took all Master Erisma's apprentices and field 'ands. Took Master and Madam Erisma, the lady's father, and their three oldest. Only two'a the little ones got away, Ani and Tomen. Young enough to be innocent'a their family's depravities, I s'pose. Twice I've asked your business. If I ask again, it will be w' my men and 'eir blades 'round you."

A damp breeze gusted across the field, lifting the horses' manes. A muscle flexed in Sevar's jaw. "I know the savagery of the killing winds, Clanguard Belen, so I'm going to allow you've been upset by the deaths here. Let us start again. My men and I are tasked with stopping this evil. I want to speak with the survivors."

Jhared shifted in his saddle, prepared for whatever might happen next. As a rule, the clans couldn't afford to equip a professional guard. Instead, they cobbled together motley forces from local farmers who lacked weapons, and fighting men who lacked discipline. Still, most clans wanted their own force and resented the high chieftain's Forest Guard levy.

The clanguard commander surveyed the patrol. There was a pause as his gaze fell upon Jhared. The ice in his expression turned to something darker. "We don't welcome deceit and corruption in our clan, Lieutenant. Or those who tolerate it. We purge it clean. You and the cursed should be on your way."

Malice burned undisguised in the commander's face and reflected in the eyes of his men. Jhared knew a chill of foreboding. Beside him, Jase's hand twitched toward his sword.

"That is your second threat," Sevar replied with deadly calm. "I won't tolerate a third. Move aside or we will—"

"Commander Belen, we grieve with you for the color that's left the world!" the Bearer said quickly. "Riana's blessing on those who have gone."

"Who's that? A priestess?" Belen's gaze searched through the patrol until he found the Bearer. "How does the Bearer'a Cael's Blade travel w' Forest Guard? With the Shorn?"

"Riana has condoned this mission. It is my place to see all is done according to her order. I am certain the people of Clan Valador won't hinder what the goddess has woven."

Belen stopped short, his expression indignant. "Valador knows all the colors'a the weaving! We follow her order!"

"I have always thought it so," the Bearer agreed. "Speaking to the survivors might be of some help. Please, Commander."

"If these soldiers meant to be any 'elp, Lady, they would'a been 'ere to deal w' the Sa'isten."

Tension vibrated through the patrol. Sevar went still. "*What* Sahisten?"

"We caught 'im sneaking through the rubble the morning we got 'ere. Tried to run, but one of my boys put an arrow through 'im quick as spittin'."

"No one tried to question him?"

"Speak to a stone-licker? Bah! We didn't let 'im say a word in 'is cursed tongue. You can be sure of it."

"Which means I can also be sure you didn't discover how many men were with him or what his purpose was."

Belen's expression steeled. "No. We didn't. We stopped a demon from causing more ill to our clan. That's the most important thing for Valador."

Sevar looked sickened. "Where's the body? We will see it. Now."

Belen opened his mouth, protest written in his eyes.

"Please, Commander," the Bearer said again.

To Jhared's surprise, the man gave her a tight nod, then turned his horse and led them toward the ruined farm. He signaled to the group huddled against what

Jhared realized now was a row of pyres smoking in the rain. Slowly, the archer set down her weapon. A half-dozen grim-faced villagers turned as the company passed. Their loathing arrowed into Jhared as he followed the others to a small stone shed.

He offered the Bearer a hand down from her horse into the slippery mud. She stumbled as she touched his palm and let out a low moan. Jhared tightened his grip.

"Lady?"

"So many doors are open. I've never felt such a thing. So many Paths converging. A spirit could just . . . wander."

Jhared glanced at the closed shed door and frowned at the priestess. "Perhaps you shouldn't go in. A dead body—"

"No. No, I'm all right. It's passing." The priestess drew a deep breath. "Ah, Goddess. That was important, I think." She glanced up at him. "Did you feel it?"

He wasn't certain what she expected him to feel. Instead of answering, he gestured at the shed. She kept her hand on his arm as they filed in with the others.

Inside, it smelled like spoiled beer and death. Jhared gagged on his first breath, then inhaled more cautiously through his teeth. Feeble light crept through two slit windows just beneath the ceiling. A number of hoes and a scythe leaned in one corner near a stack of empty baskets. A rough-woven bag overflowing with wilted trimago clippings squatted in the center of the shed. The body sprawled on the dirt floor as though it had been tossed there with the clippings.

"We didn't know what to do with 'im," Belen said. "Didn't want to honor 'im with the pyre, but don't want 'is spirit lingering 'round 'ere either."

Sevar crouched beside the body and pushed open the dead man's short robe to expose his chest and fatal wound.

A glance told Jhared the foreigner was indeed Sahisten. He was tall and lean, with hawk-sharp features that carved his face and a red-gold braid down his back. The man had been barely into his prime. Dark tattoos of entwined serpents coiled along both sides of his jaw, down his neck, and around his wrists to smooth, elegant hands. The shaft of an arrow was buried deep in the center of his chest.

"Where'd he cross the border and who'd he bring with him?" Jase murmured.

Grion spat. "Curse Sahisten warriors and all their treacherous ways."

"He wasn't a warrior," Jhared said. "He was a priest."

Bevan laughed. "Trust the Shorn boy to know a Sahisten witch."

"Shut it!" Sevar snapped. "All of you."

The lieutenant straightened, piercing Jhared with an iron gaze. "Anyone with his eyes open can see he's no warrior. Why do you think he was a priest, Denaban?"

"He's marked in the same manner as the priest I spied last summer, sir. The only difference is the man at Demonrock also bore true serpents."

Jhared rubbed one hand against his chest, remembering the grisly night when he had failed to stop the Sahisten ritual of poison. Only a day later, the killing winds had slain a company of Forest Guard recruits and almost took General Nadel. No one had proved yet that Sahisten magic conjured the killing winds, but in Jhared's nightmares, the spirits of those boys still blamed him for their deaths.

"A snake binder," Sevar said, staring at the body. "What was he doing here?"

"Could be we're looking at the scourge of Avelos, right there," Carn offered. "Could be this witch and his people called the winds in Velantar and the storm that chased us up the pass."

"Perhaps," the lieutenant answered, but the hard lines in his face said he didn't believe it. "Strange there's no evidence of the winds on him—no slashed skin, no bruises."

"The witch'd know how to guard 'imself from 'is own storm, surely," Carn offered.

Sevar made a derisive sound and turned toward the clanguard. "Strange also, Commander Belen, to see an arrow in the *chest* of a man who died fleeing."

The clanguard lifted his chin. "I won't apologize for protecting my people."

"No. You should apologize for leaving them vulnerable." The lieutenant turned his back on the clanguard. "Carn, take your men to search the grounds and make a thorough patrol of the fields. I want to know how many others were traveling with this one and which way they're heading."

The patrol stirred like a pack of hounds anticipating the hunt. Jhared's blood quickened. Tracking was what he did well. It was the way he would pay his debt. It was the closest thing to freedom he had ever found.

"Denaban, have you forgotten your charge? You stay with the Bearer."

The lieutenant's order dropped around him like a snare. Grion sent him a smug grin. Jhared could only offer Sevar a compliant salute.

As Carn and the others filed out, the priestess looked up from where she had been studying the body. "Where are the children?" she asked Belen.

"What's that, Lady?"

"You said the ones who survived are children. Perhaps they know something about what this man was doing on the farm. I need you to take me to them."

"Not possible, Lady. Not with corruption standing beside you, so tall and shameless." He glared at Jhared. "We've 'ad enough such ones around 'ere. With 'is so-called *Teaching*, Master Erisma brought this down on 'imself. On all 'is Shorn-loving family. On us. Name 'em what you will, those winds cleansed our land. We should'a driven Erisma out long ago. Should'a—"

"Enough!" Sevar grabbed Belen by the shirt and smashed him into the wall. "You've killed our best chance to learn anything about the winds or Sahiste's plans! By the authority of High Chieftain Rumar, Ward of the Council of Clans, you *will* allow the Bearer of Cael's Blade to question the survivors of this attack!"

"Lieutenant," the priestess said quietly, touching Sevar's arm. "I'm sure Commander Belen won't mind if we see the children when he understands I might offer them healing."

Sevar's breaths rasped loudly. He stood with one fist wrapped around the clanguard's throat, a man at the edge of violence. Jhared stood beside the priestess, afraid he would be forced to step between her and his commanding officer. The moment stretched. The Bearer remained a small, steady point of calm. Finally, slowly, Sevar uncurled his fingers from Belen's throat and took a step away from him. "Well?" he growled.

The clanguard watched the lieutenant warily. "Right, Lady. All right. You can talk with 'em. If you do one thing for us."

"If it's within my ability, Commander."

Belen nodded toward the body. "Send this demon on 'is way so 'is spirit won't trouble us."

The clanguard brought the Bearer, with Sevar and Jhared, to a stone hut in the center of the largest trimago field, where the children had been stowed while arrangements were made for their care. The hut served as the stewing rooms for the harvested trim. During the cutting season, a farm hand lived there night and day to make certain the fermentation didn't go too far and spoil the dye. Now the hut held only two grieving children.

"Tell me what else you remember about the storm," the Bearer said.

She was sitting on the floor by a small table where the children perched in wooden chairs. Natiani was a buttercup of a girl, no more than four winters, tow-headed and wide-eyed. The bruises on her face and arms stood out starkly against her pale skin. As the Bearer had started chatting with her about insignificant things, an old silver tomcat prowled into the room and leaped into the girl's lap. Natiani's brother, Tomen, was a thin, freckled boy of about nine winters, who kept a vigilant eye on Jhared and Sevar. At the lady's insistence, the lieutenant sat on the only other chair at the foot of the bed on the far side of the room. Jhared hunkered as inconspicuously as possible by the threshold to the vat room, remembering how hateful strangers were to a boy who had just lost his mother.

"Momma got me out'a bed," Natiani said, anxiously stroking the cat's grizzled shoulders. "Sounded like roaring outside. Was dirt blowing in the windows. Everything blowing off the table and the walls. I put my 'ands over my ears and dropped my Maneca."

" 'Er doll," Tomen translated.

The priestess gave him a smile. "What happened after that?"

"Momma pushed me into the cellar," the girl said. "It's dark and there's *spiders*, but I didn't cry."

"Brave girl. Did your momma wake you, too?" the priestess asked Tomen.

"No. I was awake." The boy crossed his arms over his chest and scowled at the table.

"It was very late and you were awake?"

"I woke up 'cause I 'eard Father go outside. He does . . . did that sometimes to check on the vats. He liked when it was quiet. Before Troi died, he did it every night. Liked to listen to the world growing greener, he said. I must'a fell asleep for a while 'cause I dreamed I 'eard people shouting at each other. Then I woke up and it was like Ani said, 'roaring outside.'"

"Who did you hear shouting?"

Tomen kept his gaze pinned to the table. "I don't know. Was a woman's voice."

"Was she shouting at your father?"

"I told you. It was just a dream."

"Where was your father when the storm began, Tomen?"

"Don't know." The boy shrugged stiffly. "I didn't see 'im till it ended."

Jhared's heart turned over. If Master Erisma had been outside when the winds struck, then he had died in agony, his body shredded. No child should own that image of his father.

"How long did the storm last?" Sevar asked from across the room.

Tomen looked up, his eyes gleaming wetly in the lamplight.

"Forever," Natiani announced, hugging the old cat.

Further questions about the winds and what happened when they ended soon had Ani and Tomen retelling parts of the story Belen had already given them. The priestess raised an inquiring brow at Sevar, and the lieutenant shook his head. She nodded and started to rise.

"Wait." Jhared said. He couldn't stop thinking of the winds' first attack—a cave in Lamirna and the grey feather curse in the hand of his injured general.

"Speak, Denaban," Sevar ordered.

"Sir, you were there at Lamirna. You heard what General Nadel said about the winds. What he saw. Shouldn't we ask of it here?"

"What the general saw came from a mind wracked by pain and wind madness," the lieutenant replied.

"Sir, with respect, pain didn't put a grey feather in General Nadel's hand. And the evidence wasn't only at Lamirna. In Sahiste, the priest invoked darkness. Cael's messenger was tethered there. I *felt* his power."

"Are you challenging my judgment, Patrolman?"

Jhared flinched and felt the sting in his back. "No, sir. I only—"

"Go on, then," Sevar said. "Ask it."

Jhared licked his lips, surprised and suddenly at a loss. How did one ask frightened children if a demon had walked among them? The priestess gave him an encouraging look, but Tomen glared at him as he stepped closer and crouched down to the children's level. "Thank you for your help," he murmured. "I must ask you just one thing more. Before the storm came, did you see anything the others didn't?"

Natiani shrugged and shook her head, but Tomen's eyes narrowed. "What d'you mean?"

Jhared watched the boy. "I mean something that shouldn't have been there. Something unnatural."

"Like what?" the boy pressed.

"Did you see . . . Cael?"

"No! No, no, no!" Tomen leaped from his chair, sending it crashing onto the floor. The silver tom flew out of Ani's lap and skittered under the bed.

"Demons 'ave no reason to come 'ere!" Tomen screamed. "The closest thing to a demon is you! I know what you are! I know what it meant for my brother Troi. Leave me alone. Just leave us alone!"

Tomen charged at Jhared, his fists clenched and his head tucked. Jhared stumbled backward, clumsy with dismay as the Bearer sprang after the boy. Catching him by the shoulders, she spun him around and dropped to her knees to face him.

"Easy, child. Easy. Of course no demons have reason to be here. Cael doesn't torment such brave boys and girls. You're safe, Tomen."

The Bearer locked her gaze upon the boy's. As she drew a long breath, her eyes filled with otherworldly power. Jhared had witnessed that same preternatural look in the high priestess at his Becoming. A languorous thrumming started against his skin and deep in his bones. It recalled to him the holy water enveloping him in Riana's grotto, sunshine melting tension from his shoulders, and Zia's lips against his throat.

He pulled himself straight and dug his nails into his palms to dissuade his body from its undisciplined response. Tomen had stopped struggling and was breathing deeply in a manner that mirrored the priestess.

"Good boy," the woman murmured. "Enough of such troubling talk. More than enough. Tell me a place where you feel safe."

Tomen shrugged loosely. "In the seedling 'ouse, I s'pose. It smells like summer."

"How lovely." The priestess shifted to look the trembling Natiani in the eye. "Tell me, Ani. Where are you safe?"

"Momma's lap," the little girl sniffled.

"Of course, your momma's lap. And what is it like in that place where you're safe?"

"Soft," Ani said, beginning to smile faintly. "Momma sings."

"Things are growing," Tomen added. "I like to 'elp 'em grow."

The priestess crooned over the children with the same care with which she treated her birds. Gradually, Ani and Tomen calmed under her touch.

"It's been a long day," the Bearer said, climbing to her feet. "It's time for rest now."

"When's momma comin' for us?" Ani asked.

"Shhh." The priestess gathered the little girl in her arms and carried her to the bed. "Your momma loves you very much. Close your eyes and see if you can find her in your dreams."

Ani tumbled willingly into the blankets and closed her eyes. Tomen was swaying on his feet when the priestess led him to the bed beside his sister.

"You're both safe now." The Bearer smiled into the boy's half-lidded gaze and stroked his hair.

It wasn't long before the children were snoring lightly. Ani's thumb snuck into her mouth, and Tomen's arm wrapped protectively over his sister. The priestess motioned for Jhared and the lieutenant to follow her from the room.

When they were once more outside in the damp afternoon, the lieutenant bowed his head. The battle-ready tension that had driven him since they discovered the ruined farm had unwound into something more reflective.

"That was a kindness," he said quietly.

"It's a small thing relative to all they've lost," the Bearer answered, pushing strands of hair away from her face. "Only memories that won't last long."

"I didn't mean for them." The lieutenant's grey eyes rested on the woman with an expression that suggested he was seeing her, perhaps for the first time, as something other than baggage the patrol must haul. "Thank you."

The Bearer inclined her head. Jhared caught a gleam of the goddess's mysteries fading from her gaze. "No debt to you, Lieutenant. You've confronted the winds more than any of us. You deserve a bit of peace."

"I wish the children might have given us more." Sevar sighed. "Do you think our dead Sahisten wrought the storm?"

"Why else would a priest of the southern gods risk travel into the heart of Avelos?"

Sevar shook his head. "That's not an answer to my question."

"Ah, Lieutenant, I am but Riana's servant. And I've little enough access to the Lady's power. I cannot speak for all the gods."

"Answer me then as Cael's Bearer."

The priestess looked to be considering. She plucked a broad trimago leaf from where it had been wedged into the stone of the hut and smoothed the pattern of veins between her fingers. "I suspect we've lost so much of our understanding of the power of chaos that Sahiste or Amuria or even little Sona may possess abilities well beyond our own. It would not surprise me to find the

Sahisten priest capable of feats that would baffle us, and yet . . ." She trailed off, her features drawn in thought.

"Yet?" Sevar prompted.

"Yet I wonder, as it seems you do, Lieutenant, if the Sahisten spy called the winds himself, what would make him remain to search through the rubble? This wasn't looting by a victorious army. He was alone after sunrise in his enemy's land. That seems either a sign of spectacular recklessness or a powerful need."

A little of the fevered look crept back into the lieutenant's eyes as he surveyed the ruined field surrounding them. "Recklessness and obsession are but two edges of a fine blade."

"A blade that killed the Sahisten." The Bearer gave Sevar a meaningful glance. "Perhaps you should take it as a warning. It can be dangerous to want something too much, Lieutenant. Even if what you want is to put an end to destruction."

Sevar laughed hollowly. "Be careful, Lady. Don't force a man to surrender his obsession unless you know what new evil will replace it. Doesn't one of your own scholars tell us so?"

The Bearer released the little leaf. It spun slowly to the ground. "Morican was wrong about a great many things. Better to listen to Anarava about desire. It's a worthy goal to seek an end to the killing winds, but don't cling to your desire so tightly it smothers your compassion."

As the priestess and Sevar spoke, Jhared's eye was drawn to the fallen leaf. The veins twisted in a complex pattern. He thought of the dead priest in the shed, King Javahari in Sahiste, and his own patrol here in the lands of Clan Valador. The way their paths intertwined was also complex, and unexpected. Suddenly, he understood something about what that pattern might mean.

"Sir, what if Sahiste doesn't have the winds' power at all, but is looking for it, as we are?"

Sevar and the Bearer turned to him as if they had forgotten he was there.

"What is that, Patrolman?"

"What if the reason King Javahari wants open borders is to search more easily for the source of chaos? That's why we found a priest here, not a soldier. That's why he was examining the wreckage of a recent attack." Jhared glanced at the priestess. "Lady, might Sahiste know about Clan Valador's sky tower?"

The Bearer peered at the fallen trimago leaf, then back at Jhared. "What are you saying?"

"That the Sahisten spy arrived here *after* the winds struck, not before. That he had a reason to be in this part of the country. He's looking for clues to Sabela's temple."

Lieutenant Sevar touched a hand to one of the scars on his cheek, considering. "Not even our own people recall Sabela. How likely could it be that Sahiste holds this piece of our history? Lady?"

"Of course they know our history." The priestess's lips twisted into an ironic line. "The Sahistens were friends of the Avelune, after all. And Sahiste endured none of Tumal's purges. King Javahari may very well know more of our history than we do."

Jhared dared to be heartened. It had been a long while since anything he had done felt like a contribution toward reparation. After a moment, he realized he was holding his breath. He straightened and softly exhaled.

Sevar's flinty gaze immediately fell on him. "Feeling self-satisfied, Denaban?"

"No, sir," Jhared stammered. "That is, I—"

"One bit of insight today, and tomorrow you'll make some new mistake that costs us. I've paid that cost. And I've seen others pay it. I've seen—" Sevar cut himself short. "It doesn't matter how clever you are, Denaban, I'd trade ten of your kind for one dependable man."

Jhared struggled to hold the lieutenant's gaze, though inside he felt like the cursed boy who always managed to cross his Teacher.

"Does that mean you disagree with him?" the Bearer asked.

"No. No, I don't disagree," Sevar growled, "but it doesn't change our course. We must still find the spies traveling with this one before we go on. And word must be sent to Velantar. When Carn picks up the trail, I'll be forced to split the patrol. The closest council courier is almost two days away in Brenia."

The Bearer's couriers were secure in their basket behind her saddle. The priestess said nothing. Jhared didn't have time to decide whether he felt angered or relieved by her silence before the rumble of distant hoofbeats rose from the south.

The lieutenant squinted at the figure galloping along the horizon. "Who?"

Jhared studied the distant form. "It's Anzo, sir. Alone. Unharmed."

Sevar jogged across the field, with Jhared and the priestess following. Anzo galloped up to them and bounced out of the saddle, huffing as hard as his gelding.

"Report, Patrolman," Sevar ordered.

"We found him, sir. The Sahisten's folk. One'a Belen's boys showed us where they killed the priest. We followed his trail back to a glen. Four miles southeast. Found the remains of a small camp concealed in a gully. No more'n two men been there. The second man ran this morning or late last night, earliest. He's on horseback and heading north. Commander's got Jase, Twitch, and Esran after him. The others are waiting for your word."

"North?" Sevar's gaze sparked.

"Toward the Sandien Mountains," the Bearer said. "Toward Sabela."

Sevar stared into the distance. "Perhaps."

Anzo gave Jhared a questioning look. Jhared shook his head.

"Tell Commander Carn catching up with the spy is the patrol's priority," the lieutenant ordered. "Find him, but don't bring him in until you must. I want to know where he's going. I'll catch up with you in a few days, after I send the council courier on to Velantar."

The priestess cleared her throat. "Lieutenant, I—"

"Lady, we've no time! We'll return for the sky tower as soon as we can. *If* we still need it once we have the Sahisten."

"Lieutenant, please slow down. Remember your Anarava: obsessions and recklessness . . ."

"Yes, yes." Sevar hissed out a breath. Then he stopped. After a moment, the lines of his body unclenched a little. "Very well, Lady. What is it?"

"Allow me to carry your message to Brenia. You've no wish to slow your manhunt for my sake, and I've no wish to delay my search for the tower."

"Impossible. I won't have it said I sent the Bearer of Cael's Blade running errands for the Forest Guard."

The Bearer's eyes blazed. "The protection of Avelos isn't only a Forest Guard matter! The day Rumar's soldiers acknowledge the role of the temple our people will be safer."

Jhared bit at the inside of his lip, waiting for the lieutenant to explode. Anzo half-concealed a grin.

Sevar folded his arms across his chest. "You've no fear of traveling alone?"

"Lieutenant, I carry the demon's weapon. The highwaymen are afraid of *me*." She quirked a dark smile. "Besides, I'll not be alone. I've an able guard."

Sevar shot Jhared an ugly look, then glanced back at the priestess. Slowly, his expression shifted, reflecting a feeling Jhared understood—the type of protectiveness he felt toward Branlen, toward Avelos—but had never expected to see in Sevar.

"Lady, that's the second time today you've proved I undervalue you." The lieutenant shook his head. "I expected the Bearer of Cael's Blade to know nothing beyond her books and rituals."

"And I expected a Forest Guard lieutenant to know nothing of either books or rituals," the priestess replied tartly, but her eyes were still smiling. "Tell me where to find the courier."

"At the Pestle and Caldron. Near the center markets. Ride with good speed. We'll meet you at the temple in Brenia when we've brought in the Sahisten."

"Walk steady on the dark Paths, Lieutenant, and never fear the maker of your fate." The Bearer held Sevar in a probing gaze.

Jhared frowned. The odd blessing prodded a vague memory.

The lieutenant nodded once. "Travel safely, Lady."

Something that might have been disappointment flickered across the Bearer's expression, but it was quickly replaced by her starless-sky smile. "Good hunting, Lieutenant.

5.

TRANSGRESSORS

"There's no one else to hear you now, soldier, so out with it."

Jhared turned from where he had been removing the bags from the pack animals. The priestess was rubbing down her mare. It would take another day to reach Brenia, but at least they were free of Obled. "Lady?"

"You look like a man who's been forced to chew bitterbalm and can't spit it out. I know you want to ask why I didn't share my couriers with Lieutenant Sevar. Will it help if I give you permission for it?"

Jhared deposited the packs in a pile and shifted to the struggling fire. Clumps of scrubby trees dotted the hill where they had stopped, but what wood he found was damp. "I don't need to ask. I understand."

"Oh? And what is it you understand?"

He broke a twig into pieces and fed it slowly to the flame. "It would be dangerous for others to know what you carry."

"So you believe I keep my secret out of fear for my own well-being?"

Her expression chilled. Jhared glanced at her hands, still marked by the dirt she had thrown over the Sahisten priest, and stifled a shudder. After Sevar and Anzo had ridden off to join the patrol, she had fulfilled her promise to Belen. The Sahisten had been allowed no pyre to cleanse his body and no mask to identify him to the Pathguides. The priestess made Jhared dig a hole deep into the soil of the trimago field and sent him to fetch the corpse. Cael's Blade had reflected the grey clouds when she drew it from its sheath. Then he had watched her perform a rite he hoped never to witness again.

"Soldier?" She moved closer as the fire licked tentatively at the tinder.

He shrugged away from her. "Fear has no hold on you. But my comrades would have wanted your creatures destroyed. And Lieutenant Sevar isn't easy to predict. I don't know if he would have mollified the men by killing the birds or stirred the contention by allowing you to use them. In either case, I didn't think it was your intent to slow us with conflict." Jhared met her gaze across the flames. "Or was I wrong?"

Something flickered in the woman's features. "Ah. I see."

"Do you? What is it you see, Lady?" A reckless level of acerbity edged Jhared's tone. He found he didn't care.

"I see this is about more than the birds. So speak it."

"Very well. What did you do to the Sahisten?"

The priestess's head came up, and she eyed him anew. "You saw what I did. You helped me do it."

"What I saw wasn't everything. It wasn't just a knife carving flesh, and blood spilling on the earth. There was something more."

"Yes. There was." She leaned toward him, her gaze dark and depthless. "Tell me what you felt."

The memory of rending and loss ached, like the healing wounds across Jhared's back. The ache had nothing to do with the man who had died; he owed no sympathy to a Sahisten spy. But when the priestess had finished with her Blade and smothered the mutilated body with dirt, something had changed in the world, something that hurt endlessly, like losing a limb. Like being Shorn.

"It felt as though his spirit were amputated . . . annihilated."

She made a sound of surprise.

Jhared watched her. "What was it?"

"We name it the Dissolution. The moment the stranger stopped walking the Paths and became a part of them."

"Then it's true. You destroyed his spirit."

"That's a narrow way of expressing it." She crouched beside him, her eyes on the flames. "When I put him into the ground, he joined the Paths, became a component of them as one grain of sand is a component of the shore. For those who are unprepared it can be . . . startling to witness."

"And for those who are prepared?" he challenged.

"I told you before that some must walk the dark Paths, Jhared. It is my place as Bearer to be one of those people. Will you judge me for doing what is required?"

He offered the rest of the tinder to the fire and dusted his hands against his thighs. "Lady, I don't presume to judge you at all."

She tossed her head back and laughed, a sound that raised fleshbumps across his arms. "Why don't we pretend you didn't just lie to the Bearer of Cael's Blade and focus on what you can tell me honestly?"

She stopped laughing and set her gaze on him again. She seemed suddenly very near. The scent of death and incense rose from her clothes.

"Why did you insist I witness the rite? I had no preparation at all. Is this like the birds, another secret for me to carry?"

"No, that was not my intention. Jhared, temple initiates wouldn't sense the rite of Dissolution as you did. I couldn't have predicted it."

He looked down, unsure whether to believe her. "Then why did I?"

The priestess opened her mouth, closed it. She was silent a moment before finally shaking her head. "I'm not certain. Something's amiss among the Paths, but I think it's more than that. Have you felt anything like it before?"

"No. Maybe. I don't know." Unable to bear her intense regard another moment, Jhared leaped to his feet. "The sun is setting, and the hills will be full of game. If you feel safe by the fire, Lady, I'll hunt for dinner."

The flickering firelight made hollows of her eyes. "Go on," she sighed. "Go. It's not my place to stand between a hunter and his prey."

He was already reaching for his bow. "Thank you."

"No debt," she said, then looked up at him with one of her starless-sky glances. "Jhared, a time will come when we must speak of these things."

He said nothing, but left the Bearer behind and stepped eagerly into the evening's embrace. The air smelled sweet and clean. The Valador hills unrolled under a boundless sky. He started walking, a brisk, muscle-warming gait. At the foot of the next rise a dense copse of cottonwood trees stretched along a creek. Small game preferred the borderlands, the fertile spaces between meadow and forest or forest and stream. It would be a good place to hunt.

He shouldn't have been with a priestess tonight discussing mysteries he wasn't meant to understand. He should have been with his comrades hunting the Sahisten. The men in his patrol were skilled soldiers. In the midst of a mission, they relied upon one another, no matter what their status or faction alliances. Working among them, Jhared had found the closest thing to companionship he'd ever known; but since Sevar had made him the priestess's guard, all of his differences seemed to have come to the fore again. He was city-born, Shorn, and Trianor's Folly. Now, as the one who guarded the Bearer and her secrets, the gulf around him seemed impossible to cross. Even Anzo couldn't look at him without scowling.

Without another thought, he began to run.

The land unfurled as he sped over the soft ground. The wind fluttered over his body, teasing more speed from him. All his painful thoughts dropped behind him. He knew only the exhilarating sensation of strong muscles working well. When he reached the copse, the tree branches reached out in welcome. Roots and underbrush created a test of agility. He hurtled over a fallen log and leaped the pit beside it. He was darting around a large tree, when the branches creaked above him.

It was too late to change course. Something heavy struck his back, driving him to the ground. He hit the dirt and rolled sideways. Behind him came a thud and the sound of cursing. As Jhared scrambled to rise, he tangled in his bow, giving his assailant time to tackle him at the knees and fling him back to the ground. A blade skimmed across his flank. Jhared twisted away as his belt deflected the sharp edge. With the side of one hand, he struck his assailant's shoulder at the tender place where it joined the neck. There was a grunt of pain and the knife fell.

Jhared followed with a quick blow to the man's temple, then wrestled them over, jerking free his own blade.

He ended on top, his knife pressed against his attacker's scarred throat. Glittering eyes blinked up at him.

"Now this seems familiar," Alende gasped, amusement rising in his wild gaze. "Hello, soldier. Did you miss me?"

Alende's angular features were scrubbed clean of the waylayer's paint he had flaunted the first time Jhared saw him, and his golden hair was confined in a warrior's club. Rather than bold-colored, fluttering silks, he was dressed plainly, as a woodsman. Jhared rolled off the man, drawing his sword as he stood. "Get up!" he commanded. "Slowly."

"Ah, but it's such a lovely night to lie beneath the stars with someone you love."

"Do you want to die beneath the stars?"

"Oh, that's exactly how I'll die. At least *one* of the ways. There are so very many. It's hard to remember them all." The creature rocked to his feet in a single fluid motion and pushed aside Jhared's sword with one finger. "But none of them tonight."

Jhared circled the madman, his heart hammering out the impossibility of this meeting. Alende should have been dead twice over. A Shorn man who had failed the Becoming nearly ten years ago, Alende had been driven from Velantar to die in the wilds. He had survived then, taking the guise of one of the caelevano, the demon-touched waylayers who considered themselves guides to Riana's Paths. When Jhared left the city with his patrol, he had expected Alende to die as a traitor, this time for attempting to assassinate the Bearer.

"How did you get out of the city?" Jhared demanded. "All the Arionade were hunting you."

"Please! Give a fellow the recognition he's due. It wasn't just the temple's stone-footed white-coats. I confounded the City Guard as well. They were unexpectedly thick in Shorn Circle that last day. I imagine I have you to thank for that." Alende raised an inquiring brow and must have seen what he expected in Jhared's expression, for he nodded and offered a poisonous smile. "I warned Zia you would give us up to your Elder Trianor, but she'd hear nothing of it. She thought you would be a true son to Mahla in the end."

Jhared clenched his jaw. Zia's name cut him with unexpected force and his mother's was a body blow, but he refused to reveal that much to the creature before him. "I didn't give her up. I only told Elder Trianor about you."

"Truly?" The waylayer paced around Jhared, as graceful as falling water. "You kept our little scribe's secrets even after everything she did to you? Fascinating. But no matter. Riana leads me out of harm's way."

"If you've come for the Bearer, Riana won't spare you from my blade."

Alende stopped his prowling. "*Don't* test that belief unless you're ready to bleed." His tone dripped with hatred. With a supple, sideways motion, he ducked under Jhared's sword and leaped, lightly as a hunting cat, onto the tree branch above him.

Jhared swore. The man's speed had earned him a knife in the shoulder at their last encounter. He backed out from under the tree, just far enough to be out of range of a jump. "You *have* come for her, haven't you? You followed us all this way to try to kill her."

"Ah, now you're disappointed." Alende chuckled from the tree. "You thought I came only for you."

"I need to know why," Jhared demanded.

"My, my. Could it be you're starting to wonder if the Bearer of Cael's Blade is as corrupt as the demon whose weapon she carries?"

Jhared wasn't about to tell Alende of the spirit-priestesses he had seen in Parnas Pass or the messenger birds or the Dissolution, but he had no source of information other than the Bearer herself, and he couldn't make himself trust her. He could still see the hungry expression she had turned on him when she spoke of the dark Paths.

"You didn't chase us across the mountains just to taunt me, Alende. And I've seen what you can do with a blade. You could have killed me already, if that were your goal. You think you can win my help. That means you're going to tell me what I want to know."

The waylayer grinned again. "So you're only a fool, not an idiot. Good. Fools can be taught. But why so hasty? You have as many questions for me as I have for you. Questions that pain you on long sleepless nights."

"I hope you don't imagine I spend my nights thinking on you."

"In fact, I think you do." The waylayer fluttered his lashes coquettishly. "You want to know how I survived in the wilds when Avelos sent me out to die. You want to know if Mahla truly committed treason to save me. You want to know why your mother gave me freedom while sending you to be chained—"

"Stop!" Jhared pressed a hand against his heart. "My mother didn't turn against Avelos to save a caelevano. There's nothing you could say about her I would believe."

All the teasing vanished from Alende's features. "Unworthy," he growled. "Mahla Denaban freely risked death for those she loved. She deserves to be remembered for who she was."

Jhared backed another step away from the tree. "Just tell me what I've asked of you. Why should I fear the Bearer?"

There was a silence. As Alende swung down from the branch, he landed poorly, stumbled, and barely managed to stay upright. Jhared realized that the man was injured and exhausted. Fresh wounds crisscrossed the older scars on his throat, and blood stained his shirt. Alende's taunting had disguised the truth as completely as if he were wearing his waylayer's veils. Jhared considered what it would have taken for a traveler on foot to keep up with the patrol all the way from Velantar and felt an unwanted twinge of sympathy.

"Are you going to answer me?" he asked more gently.

Alende leaned against the tree trunk and closed his eyes. "No."

"What? What game are you playing now?"

"I will not allow Mahla Denaban to be remembered as a tool of the Teachers." The man's tone was suddenly intensely sober. "I owe her that. Mahla was a Storyteller and has earned her own place among the tales. You will hear what I have to say about her before I speak to you of the Bearer."

"I've already told you, Alende. I want no lies from a faithless unbound man."

The waylayer sighed and opened his eyes. "You have an interesting understanding of faithlessness, soldier. You assume I failed the Becoming because I couldn't convince Avelos of my loyalty. Perhaps you should consider that *I* was honest enough to face the blade and death in the wilds rather than swear an oath I knew I couldn't keep."

"Is that why you think I won't kill you for treason? Because of my broken oath?"

Alende laughed, a sound so beautiful and bitter it hurt. "Oh my, touched a tender spot, did I? No, that's not it. You won't kill me because you've seen enough of the Bearer by now to worry that what I told you in Velantar is true: she craves chaos. You need to hear what I know before you decide what to do about it."

What to do about it. The implication of those words made Jhared dizzy. "What do you want from me?"

"Not so very much. Let me tell you of Mahla while you keep watch on the Bearer. Ask yourself this question: Does the priestess yearn for chaos? I believe you will see the answer for yourself, but if you return and say she's no danger to our world, I'll tell you all I know of her. Then you can choose."

"How can I trust that you won't try to harm her in the meantime?"

"It's my business to share what Mahla would have taught you."

"No good," Jhared answered. "Tomorrow you'll change your mind again and decide it's your business to slay the Bearer. Swear to me you won't do anything to harm her so long as I come to hear your tales."

"Why would you believe an oath from the deceitful unbound?"

"Because you'll swear it by my mother's spirit."

"Ah, indeed. Not an idiot." Alende looked at him more thoughtfully. "Let it be so. I swear by the spirit of Mahla Denaban, who saved my life, so long as you come to hear my stories, I will not harm the Bearer of Cael's Blade."

The words settled uncomfortably over the pair of them, and Jhared wondered at the tangle of oaths that bound him. If he pulled on the thread of one, how many others would unravel?

"Should you break your vow," he warned Alende, "you need not wait for Cael before you pay the price."

Alende raised one brow. "That eager to do the demon's work, are you?"

"I'll come to you when I can. How should I find you?"

"Where are you headed?" the waylayer asked.

"Brenia."

"Ahhh, Brenia." Alende sighed like a pining lover. "City of a Thousand Colors and Ten Thousand Pleasures. If only the banner of Tumal's Legacy didn't flutter so brightly from your tree."

"What does that mean?"

"It means you had best take care what pleasures you taste. Or the Legacy will shear off your manhood and hang you from an oak branch."

Jhared found his patience fraying. "Valador isn't a Legacy clan. They vote with Clan Manitar or with the northern five. Do you plan to tell me where to find you or shall we be done with this absurdity now?"

"As you will. Don't say I didn't warn you." Alende twirled around Jhared like a banner dancer. "You'll find Brenia's gates guarded like a whore's virtue. A coin in the palm of the clanguard will get you out at night. Or slip through the breach on the south wall near the fountain. I'll be in the forest northwest of the trimago fields. I'll know when you come."

"Right." Jhared tried not to wonder how he would find enough time on his own to sneak out of the city.

"Don't make me wait too long," Alende murmured, giving Jhared a wink.

Jhared ignored him and turned to go. He was nothing like this man. This anathema.

"Good night, my darling," Alende called. "Dream sweetly."

As Jhared strode away, he heard that beautiful, empty laughter again and then the strange, wet-sounding words, "*Sulosan, surma sen.*"

The same foreign words had been whispered in the heart of the night while Jhared kept watch.

"Alende!"

Jhared spun and ran back to the tree. The waylayer was not to be seen: not on the ground or among the branches. Jhared searched for a few urgent moments before realizing Alende had truly fled, and the priestess was on her own. He raced toward camp, running full out by a sliver of moonlight. Before he reached the clearing, a wave of dizziness crashed over him. He stumbled, slammed into a tree, and went down. Blue sparks scattered across his vision and the world rocked beneath him. As he lay stunned, waiting for the land to stop spinning, he caught the gleam of the moonlight from a pair of eyes just above him.

For an instant, he saw Alende's tormented gaze; then he realized it wasn't a man's gaze at all. He climbed unsteadily to his feet and looked more closely. A dead bird had been tucked into the nook where the tree trunk split. She had been a young raven, with feathers not fully grown. Down stuck out softly around her head and neck. Someone had sheared off her wings.

They had been opened and laid with care beside her, a ward against cursed creatures. A warning against the Shorn. Jhared took a breath and choked on the smell of the fledgling's blood. He backed away, not needing to see more.

The priestess was anxiously pacing at the border of firelight when he made it back to the camp. She hurried to his side, touching his arm and searching his face.

"What happened, soldier? You were away so long."

"I'm sorry. You are well? All is quiet here?"

Everything appeared fine, but for Seravina, who whickered and tugged at her picket. Jhared strode over to calm her before the packhorses followed her example.

"Come closer to the fire," the priestess ordered. "You're shivering."

He let her direct him toward the flames. Two mugs were warming by the fire's edge. She handed him one. "If there's something wrong, you must speak with me. Do you understand?"

"I'm fine, Lady. Just . . . fine. I'm sorry I've won nothing for our dinner."

She took a step backward, her critical gaze skimming over him. "Perhaps you're not the tracker I thought you were."

"No doubt of that, Lady." The tea smelled spicy and gave Jhared an excuse to keep his gaze lowered. "It was wrong of me to be gone so long. I promise not to leave you again."

"I've warned you about making such promises." She sighed. She didn't seem angry, only weary and disheartened.

"Some promises must be made." He set down his mug and stood, feeling the weight of all his recent promises bearing down on him. "I'll make something for us to eat."

"You really are all right," she said as he began to pull provisions from their bags.

It wasn't a question, so Jhared gave no response, but he didn't much care for the disappointment in her voice. While he worked, he kept one eye on the darkness. Alende was unlikely to sneak up on them from the open hillside, even if the oath didn't hold him, but Jhared wasn't going to give him the opportunity.

They ate a dull meal of boiled grain and lamb sausage. Afterward, Jhared checked the horses. Seravina treated him with the same contempt as ever, and the packhorses only cared to know if he had apples to offer them. When he returned, the Bearer was preparing for sleep. Jhared went to the packs to retrieve her tent.

"Leave it," she told him. "Without the patrol it will be quiet, and I prefer to sleep under the stars." She looked at the sky and breathed slowly. For several moments, she was still.

"Jhared?"

"Yes, Lady."

"You've been rescuing villagers from the winds all summer. Do you still see the victims in your dreams?"

He set down the bag in his hand. "Yes. Sometimes."

"I think I shall see that little girl's face tonight."

Jhared nodded silently. Amidst all that had happened since Obled, he had almost forgotten about Ani and Tomen. "I understand."

"Within the walls of the temple, it is possible to think of balance as an abstract precept," she said. "One can almost forget how necessary it is. I thought I understood better after the horror in Velantar, but . . . it's so easy to forget that without true balance, chaos can tear through a child's home and destroy everyone she loves."

"That's why we're here now." Jhared shook out his bedroll. "Have you doubted the importance of our mission?"

"No. Never doubted," she said. "I just realize how dire it is if I am wrong."

"Wrong about Sabela's temple?"

"Yes. Among other things."

"You won't be wrong. You mustn't be. You are the Bearer of Cael's Blade."

He meant to be reassuring, but as her expression hardened, Jhared realized he had made a mistake.

"Indeed, I *am* the Bearer. You would do well to remember that next time you consider evading my questions or offering your half-truths. If I am to achieve true balance, I must know what tools are available to me!"

"Lady, I didn't mean—"

"No!" She smacked her palm against her thigh. "I am weary of hearing what you don't mean. From now, you will speak to me only of what you do mean or don't speak at all."

She marched away and said nothing more as she settled into her blankets by the fire. It seemed a long time before her breathing slowed and he knew she was asleep. She lay on her side with her legs drawn close to her chest. One slender hand gripped the blanket to her chin. A dark tendril of her hair curled against her pale cheek. She looked very small.

Somehow he had disappointed her, although he didn't understand exactly how. He thought of Alende alone in the darkness, beset by visions no one else could believe or understand.

Stiffly, he rose from his watch. He scraped the last of their dinner into a bowl, pulled an apple from his pack, and walked a short way down the hill. Night birds cried in the dark. He set the bowl and the apple on a rock.

"*Sulosan, surma sen,*" he called toward the trees.

His boots flattened the grass as he returned to camp. He didn't bother trying to conceal his trail. Alende would know where to find him if he wished it. Jhared took up his duty beside the sleeping priestess, his sword unsheathed beside him.

6.

FORBIDDEN PATHS

The dancers spun in kaleidoscopic patterns, concentric circles of green and scarlet that turned in opposite directions. Their silky banners flashed in the sunlight, and the circles unwound into rows. Like waves, the banners rose and fell and rose again with the sinuous movements of the women. Green and scarlet: the colors of fertility and desire, order and madness. The dancers moved together—twirling, tumbling, and leaping, but never tangling in their streaming flags—to the melody of a Valadorian long-pipe.

When the music stopped, the Brenian banner dancers poured off the stage, their flags snapping in the breeze. Their skirts parted to reveal glimpses of bare feet and strong legs. Men whooped and threw pebbles in acknowledgment of a pleasant moment along their paths. Some grabbed at the women and were deftly evaded or smacked on the head with a banner. Lightheaded and feeling as if he were still spinning, Jhared tried not to be sick.

A stench like stale piss and rotting spinach drifted up the river from the dye houses. The dancers' spirals left blurred traces in his vision. He focused on the blessedly motionless bit of road near the threshold of the main gate, vaguely aware of the audience moving away—men and women heading back to the dye houses and the docks. It was Seravina who forced him back to the moment; she didn't like the crowd. She tossed her head and fretted, until Jhared had to draw rein to keep her from trampling someone. Clamping down on the antics of his innards, he looked back to make certain the packhorses weren't about to cause trouble, then chirruped to get his little caravan moving again. When he glanced ahead, the priestess was already gaining distance on him as she headed toward the city center.

She had released one of her courier doves at dawn before they reached Brenia, and although she refused to speak of it, it had visibly lifted her mood. To Jhared's dismay, she now seemed intent upon wandering. He had already encountered one bad moment that morning when a tall figure veiled in blue and gold danced up to them. The flash he had imagined to be a knife had only been a set of

57

silver finger-bells. The form he had seen as Alende in his waylayer's garb had only been a Shorn harlot hoping to sell her embrace to a soldier. When the girl saw the priestess with him, she had given him a sly smile and twirled off. She couldn't know how close he had come to putting a sword to her breast.

"Lady, please," he called, reaching the shop where the priestess had halted her mare. "The streets aren't safe."

She looked over her shoulder, her gaze deep and lively. In the shop window, bolts of shimmering cloth showed off the work of Brenia's finest dye houses. The priestess smiled. "Soldier, be calm. This is Brenia, not the lower circles of Velantar. No one is going to threaten the Bearer here."

He eyed the crowd. Despite the bustle and the bright colors, the city had a gritty edge to it. "Are you such a judge, Lady? You thought yourself safe in the high temple until a man tried to knife you."

The priestess stiffened a moment before sugaring her smile. "But that is why you're here, isn't it? Because you are adept at catching blades."

"I am, Lady. If that's what's required to keep you from harm."

She sighed and laughed a little. "Jhared, it was a jest. It's too lovely a day for such seriousness. Come. Enjoy the sites. We'll be with Lady Esania soon." She tapped her mare onward, forcing Jhared to hasten after her.

Like Velantar, the ancients had designed Brenia to reflect Riana's circles, but in Brenia the circles were concentric over a single hill rather than interlocked across three. Two main roads dissected every circle from the walls to the center, like the spokes of a wheel, which meant there was no avoiding Brenia's more infamous sites: the herbalists' parlors, the destiny houses, the brawling pits. Jhared and the Bearer cut across the lane known to soldiers and watermen as Clan Row, where it nestled in an elbow of the Verdant River, its proud clan flags waving in front of a line of brothels. Samples of the offerings from each clan's house posed in doorways and leaned out casements: slender, golden daughters of Clan Nadaren; lithe, grey-eyed boys from Clan Manitar; almond-cheeked, soft-hipped girls from Clan Avien. They arranged themselves decoratively and flirted with passersby, the slender chains around their wrists or ankles sparkling in the sunlight. Jhared flinched away from the girls' vapid smiles and overbright gazes. Brenia offered its decadent pleasures unapologetically, perhaps because it was a trade town— Gateway to the Plains and Crossroads to the West. It was a place of transition, not home, for many of the people within its walls. Perhaps that made it easier for some to see only the sparkle and not the chains.

The river unwound ahead of them, carrying with it snatches of song from the watermen unloading goods on the docks. Jhared led the Bearer across the river and into the town center, where shops, city offices, and taverns surround-ed a gathering of busy markets. He scanned the host of banners that fluttered over the rooftops and market stalls—champions in the dye houses' battles for supremacy—looking for the Pestle and Caldron. On one building, flags boasted brilliant gold flowers across a field of scarlet; on another, the flags showed a blue bear dancing over green hills. On a third, a row of flags offered silver stars on black. Most of the banners Jhared didn't recognize and were likely the marks of local craftsmen. Except one. That one stopped his search.

"Lady, hold. There's something going on—"

Too late, he realized the Bearer was already nudging her mare through the crowd. He swore and pushed Seravina forward, hoping none of the pack animals panicked. The priestess stopped at the edge of an audience gathered around a tall tree in the center of the plaza. Her smile had vanished.

The banner that swayed from one of the tree's branches depicted a bloody sword on a field of cerulean, the sigil that Tumal the Just carried into battle when he purged Avelos of the Avelune evil during the Exile War. One hundred fifty years later, Tumal's Legacy had taken up the banner along with the ancient high chieftain's call to keep the borders tight and Shorn Law strong. Two men stood before the banner: one of them, a dark-eyed, dye-stained, earnest-looking young man, perched on a speaker's square addressing the audience; the other, a large scarred man of middle years, hung in chains.

"Where was Adan Rumar to care for the people'a Clan Valador when field-rot attacked the trim and the dyers lost their livelihoods?" cried the speaker. "Why does he steal the traveler's tax from us, money paid by rich merchants for the right to cross *our lands*? Money the people of Clan Valador need and deserve! Where was Adan Rumar when a Sa'isten witch brought the killing winds to Obled?

"Clan Manitar 'as 'eld the staff'a warding in the Council'a Clans for too long. Rumar 'as forgotten that 'is duty lies beyond the walls'a Velantar! Tumal's Legacy hasn't forgotten. Tumal's Legacy 'elped Obled in its need. Tumal's Legacy brought a cursed man to justice!"

The newly healed gash across Jhared's ribs twinged, stirring the memory of Legacy blades on a dark street. Alende had spoken the truth: Clan Valador had opened its gates to those who held most tightly to the memory of Avelune betrayal. Clans Amerre, Makri, and Rehamra at the Sahisten border owned the most reason to cling to Tumal's ways, while the central clans like Valador had always been more interested in keeping the watermen's guild happy to ensure their wheat, wool, and fabrics made it to market. If the Legacy could gain a foothold here, some important balance had shifted.

Reluctantly, Jhared slid his gaze to the other side of the tree. He spotted the faded V-shaped scar on the prisoner's left arm before he saw the parallel weals of ruined skin and bone down the man's back. Shorn. They had stripped him of all modesty but a pair of dirty breeches, and strung him up by looping a rope through his shackles and over a gnarled branch. The bark of the branch was worn smooth, suggesting a long history of such service. With the rope, the prisoner was lifted off his feet until only his toes held his weight. Blood trickled down his wrists where the iron had chewed into his flesh, and around his neck swung a brace of dead blackbirds. From the scratches and puncture wounds across the man's chest, the birds hadn't been dead when they were first hung there.

The world pendulated under Jhared. Any moment he was either going to throw up or fall down.

"For what is this man punished?"

The priestess's clipped question came from a distance as she leaned over her mount's withers to speak with a ruddy-faced matron beside her.

The speaker's tone grew angrier. "Adan Rumar laughs while Sa'istens and Shorn spread their evil across Avelos! While the Shorn breed an army to turn against us! Shorn women seduce righteous men in the darkness. Shorn men force their scarred bodies on clean women, violating them with the spawn of deceit! Shorn children are raised to hate good people. It is an army they want! An army to destroy all that is good!"

"For 'arming a child," the matron answered the priestess. " 'Is own little girl, Goddess curse 'im. Six years ago he got a daughter on a Shorn woman. But the babe was born clean. I don't know 'ow a father could 'arm a defenseless child. It's as the man says!" She nodded her head at the speaker, quivering with rage.

"What did he do to her? To his child," Jhared asked, needing but not wanting to know.

"Corrupted 'er!" spat the woman, glancing in his direction. Her expression narrowed as she took in his uniform and the red border on his cloak. "How many cursed children 'ave you spawned, soldier?"

Heat rose in Jhared's cheeks. "I have no children."

The matron snorted. "As if anyone could believe that. You Forest Guard leave cursed bastards at every town. And then aren't those poor women spoiled for any *good* man. Raising a cursed army, indeed!"

At the woman's accusations, the people around them began to mutter. Jhared shrank into himself. As a Shorn soldier on a tall horse, he stuck out like a weed in a garden, and the rumble of the crowd was growing threatening. "Lady, we must go," he told the priestess, scanning for the quickest way out of the press.

The Bearer's gaze remained fixed on the misery under the tree. "This is the outcome when people forget the meaning of balance. This evil against its own is what Avelos should fear more than foreign invaders or the killing winds themselves."

Under the tree, the prisoner dragged his head up. His sunken green eyes were vacant, as though his spirit sought refuge in some other place. Jhared knew he should feel the same fury at the man the priestess did, but all he could muster was a terrible sense of pity.

He shepherded the Bearer through the crowd to the opposite edge of the plaza, where a flag overhanging a brick façade marked the Pestle and Caldron. The priestess slid from the saddle and tossed the reins into Jhared's hands as she headed for the door.

Jhared opened his mouth to call for her to wait, but closed it again without speaking. No obvious faction sigils marked the inn. It looked like neutral ground for dyers and tradesmen to find food and drink and perhaps discuss business—or as neutral as one might hope in a town where the Legacy was spreading its rhetoric. As the Bearer disappeared into the building, Jhared told himself she was safer without him.

The horses' hooves clopped hollowly as he led the mares down the narrow alley beside the tavern to a small stable. He waited while two men ahead of him negotiated with the skinny stable boy for board and fodder for their mounts. When his turn came, he lingered to unsaddle and groom Seravina and the lady's mare and see them loosed into suitable stalls. He offered the boy a pebble, and warned him to keep a close watch on the belongings of the Forest Guard. The child gave Jhared a wary look, but took the money readily enough.

By the time he made his way to the inn, the Bearer was finishing her business. She caught Jhared's eye as she bustled out of the smoky interior toward the door, her expression satisfied. "The courier leaves within the hour. He has a fast horse and promises to ride hard."

"He'd best ride hard," Jhared muttered.

The priestess lifted a dark eyebrow. "Oh?"

Jhared grimaced. "Nothing. Forgive me. I spoke without thinking."

"Or perhaps you were thinking." She touched his arm gently. "Thinking of a Shorn man's torment. What did you mean to say?"

"Only that the high chieftain needs that message. If the Legacy leaders in Velantar receive news of this new attack before Rumar, they'll use it to make him look uninformed and negligent."

"They could. But that won't happen, Jhared. The courier knows what he's about, and your lieutenant will have written what Rumar needs to know."

The priestess patted his arm and started to walk. "Come along to the temple. We'll find a more hospitable welcome there, for us both."

They left the horses stabled and walked along one of the smaller streets toward the east side of town. As they drew farther from the plaza, the neighborhood quieted. Brothels and gaming houses yielded to well-appointed guild houses and then to clusters of pretty family homes. A breeze across the hill helped to dissipate the reek of the dye houses.

The temple faced the far side of a long parkland. Banners of the five Aye, Riana's Chosen, swayed gently from granite columns across the temple's long portico, with Shira the messenger in her hare on one end, and Trevazio the scout in his wolf at the other. Jhared and the Bearer passed beneath the central banner: Silvien the healer in her shape as Silvaye. The priestess smiled at the lovely banner with its crimson field covered by green tendrils of the ever-blooming vine.

No Arionad greeted them at the entrance to the first circle, but a wizened little priestess with bright eyes and a beaked nose took Jhared's small blades and sword. The heavy weapon caused her to totter, and he feared it would pull her over before she balanced it across her shoulder. When she saw the Bearer's Blade, she squinted and stared, then lowered into a creaky bow, more the challenge for the sword.

"Tell Lady Esania the Bearer of Cael's Blade has come to see if she still walks the proper Path," the Bearer said, a merry lilt in her tone Jhared hadn't heard before.

"A'course, Lady," the woman answered. "A'course! It's been an age since any of the 'igher Circle visited Brenia. Come with me."

She shuffled past the first circle and led them into the sanctuary. The temple was small, but offered the light, airy feeling typical of the ancients' architecture. No carvings adorned the walls with the stories of Avelos, as in Velantar's high temple. Instead, the walls were plastered and painted in bright hues of green and blue. Reminders of the ancients still remained, however, as here and there a stairless doorway or gallery lay high up the wall and near the ceiling.

The old woman led Jhared and the priestess down a wide hall to the library. "Walk steady on the dark Paths," she murmured at the threshold.

The Bearer's gaze grew wide. She leaned forward and kissed the old priestess's cheek. "Never fear the maker of your fate, my sister."

The woman flushed. "Sister Jhema, Lady Bearer. One who longs for true balance. Be comfortable 'ere. I'll take word to Lady Esania." She disappeared down the hall with scuffling footsteps.

Elder Trianor had often spoken of Brenia's library, always with a touch of envy. As Jhared entered the grand room, he understood why. Never had he seen so many books in one place. The chamber formed a spacious cylinder that rose into an elegant dome. Six gilded columns supported the dome, with benches between the columns. All the way around the room, books filled the ample shelves. A series of slender windows just beneath the dome provided enough light to read the inscriptions that labeled the shelves. Jhared eyed them with interest. There were books on everything from the breeding of sheep to the cultivation of dyes, from the training of hounds to the cycles of the stars. Reverently, he touched his fingers to a rare set of volumes of the histories. Beside them sat a collection on the healing arts. He could have spent days exploring the mysteries between those pages.

"They're forbidden to you. The healers' books."

The Bearer set her cloak on a bench and strolled toward him.

"As they must be." Jhared drew back from a volume on the treatment of wounds and fevers, aware that the priestess was watching him.

"Yet they tempt you."

Knowledge had always tempted him. When he began the Teaching, Sarena Trianor had recognized that fact even before he had. She had devised clever ways to expose his weakness. "I would never open them, Lady."

"I'm sure that's true. I wonder what Avelos will lose because of it."

Jhared turned his back and strode away from the shelves. "Did the Lady of Brenia leave Velantar to study here?"

"No. That came later. Esania left the city because she didn't care for the challenges of life in the high temple." The Bearer smiled at Jhared. "You enjoy history. I think you'll find this an intriguing meeting. Lady Esania has knowledge of the ancients that no longer remains in books."

Jhared said nothing. *Enjoy* was a strange word to describe his relationship to the history of Avelos. Nearly everything the Bearer said to him seemed a taunt, something meant to pull him off his proper Path. Another test, perhaps.

As she stared at him, her expression wavered and she rubbed two fingers against her forehead. "Patrolman, tell me truly. Do you feel all right? All . . . here?"

Before he could answer, a *click-clack-clickity* echoed on the stone in the hall and someone coughed. Jhared turned to discover huge brown eyes in a small white face peering around the doorway.

"Oh, *there* you are!" a girl said breathlessly, popping fully into view. "Finally!"

"Finally, indeed," said the priestess. "Were we expected?"

"*Someone* was expected. Days ago. I just didn't know it was you." The girl put her hands on her narrow hips and frowned from the Bearer to Jhared and back, exhaling wetly. "No. I didn't expect anything like you two at all. My name's Delria. I'm a daughter of the temple. Who are you?"

The girl looked as fragile as a new blossom. Her slender wrists poked from the sleeves of her heavy wool gown, and her thin shoulders hid beneath the layers of a lavender shawl. Her hair was as fair and fine as milkweed silk. Jhared tried to guess her age. Her size put her at somewhere near fourteen winters, but her blunt speech better fit an elder matron.

"I'm Leita, the Bearer of Cael's Blade," replied the priestess. "This is Jhared Denaban of the Forest Guard Fourth."

No awe entered the girl's expression at the Bearer's title. "Why have you come to see—oops! *Inalde!*"

Inalde. The word meant *treasure* in ancient Velos. The treasure in question scrambled out from behind Delria's skirts: a honey-colored, curly-eared feist, small and plump as a sausage. Its claws clicked and slipped on the stone as it spun a circle around Jhared then raced back to its mistress, flopping down at her feet as if the burst of excitement had exhausted it.

"Silly creature," Delria scolded fondly, scooping up the little mongrel and settling onto a bench near the Bearer. "What do you want of Lady Esania?" she began again. "Have you come to ask for healing? Strangers often come to ask her to heal them."

"We're on our own mission of healing," the priestess answered frankly. "I believe one of the ancients' sky towers still stands on Valador lands. Finding it may bring us closer to stopping the killing storms. I hope the Lady of Brenia can tell us where it lies."

"If your task is that important," the girl asked, frowning at Jhared, "why are you traveling with a broken boy?"

The Bearer looked at Jhared and back to the girl. "You see that he's broken?"

Delria coughed, a deep, wracking sound that shouldn't have been possible of such a slender frame. "No, I smell it," she said when she could speak again. "He smells like a freshly felled tree. Roots pulled out of the dirt to wither."

"Fascinating," the priestess murmured. "What else do you smell?"

Delria sniffled and wiped her nose with her sleeve. "Oh, most people around here smell of dye and boredom. Sometimes I'll catch a whiff of someone interesting, like when Lady Esania brings a new student to my lessons. The young Arionad who's come smells of spring, but Prefect Fesan reeks of spoiled milk." The girl wrinkled her nose. "Dawnings' Eve has the scent of a meadow at twilight. And I think I smelled one of the ancients' ruins once, from far away. Blood and rot, that was."

"What do I smell like?" the Bearer asked.

The girl grinned. "Wild roses, autumn storms, and charred wood."

"Truly astonishing." The priestess's tone revealed only amazement, but Jhared saw hunger rising in her eyes. "How is it I've never seen you in Velantar?"

Two sets of footsteps from the hall halted at the door. "Greetings, Lady Bearer. Leita my friend, welcome to Brenia. It has been too long."

The warm words were spoken in a tone that would have calmed wild dogs. Jhared turned to face Lady Esania, High Priestess of Brenia. She was taller than the Bearer and rounder at hip and breast. Her hair hung in a thick braid the color of a summer dawn. Her eyes were the rich shade of freshly turned earth. And when she smiled, a weight lifted from Jhared, as though Riana herself welcomed him.

The man looming behind the priestess reflected none of her warmth. His green eyes were as pale and cool as frost on a new leaf. From his shaved head to his bony, unadorned fingers he was a model of severity. Only the traditional white of his Arionad robe—the symbol of pure loyalty—was stained with a border of red. He was Shorn.

Jhared pulled in a startled breath, and the man caught his gaze, answering Jhared's shock with flawless impassivity. Abruptly, Jhared was conscious of his travel-worn uniform, his dusty boots, and the fact that he reeked of horses.

Delria coughed where she had been sitting beside the Bearer. Lady Esania stepped further into the room, dismay flickered in her gaze. "Delria? Why are you here? You should be at lessons."

"Important guests had arrived, Lady. Someone needed to show proper hospitality."

"It is not your place to give hospitality to visitors. Go."

"Yes, Lady." Delria scooped up her pup, lifted a spiral to the Bearer and the Lady of Brenia, and huffed out of the room. Her cough echoed in the passage as she disappeared.

Silence fell. The Bearer stood. A spear of sunlight from the high windows touched the toe of her boot but didn't reach her face. "Esania, for the sake of the friendship we share, tell me you don't know you've a Pathwalker in your midst."

The high priestess didn't speak. The man behind her remained as still as one of the marble columns.

"I see." The Bearer folded her arms across her chest. "Can you explain then why you have broken the Chosen Lady's laws and kept her from Velantar?"

"Because she is no use to you. She was born a frail thing. I've barely kept her alive with what skill I have. She would never survive a sacred journey."

"Esania, she senses the Paths and the people on them as clearly as a hound. She must be given safe knowledge of her own power before she does herself a harm."

The high priestess glanced up. "You think I would allow a child to be endangered by her own talent? She knows enough to keep the Gate shut. That's all she ever need know."

"It's not all," the Bearer insisted. "You don't have the right to prevent the girl from traveling her own road."

"*Her* road has nothing to do with your interest, Lady Bearer. I may not have taken a place in the Higher Circle, but I know the selfish nature of the high temple. And I know you."

"No. You don't, Esania. You turned away from what you might have been to grow trimago and brew dyes. Now you know nothing of the dangers we face. The Higher Circle is fractured. Only Lady Nemiah's strength of will holds the pieces together. If we lose our connection to Riana's ways, we lose our relevance to the world. Another Pathwalker would offer a chance for healing. You of all people must understand the need for healing."

There was a pause. The Lady of Brenia turned her back to her guests and paced toward the shelves. "It grieves me to hear what has befallen Velantar. We've had some news of it, though little enough from the high temple. Some days I wonder if the Chosen Lady has forgotten about us entirely. Then I receive the annual receipt to tell me what we owe in dye and fabric." She caught a breath. "Don't take the child. It will serve no purpose but Cael's when she is lost. I've never asked anything of the Higher Circle. Please, Leita." The woman turned. A line of light from the high windows painted gold at the edges of her hair and gown. "Delria is my daughter."

Jhared's heart turned over. The Arionad kept his frosty gaze on the high priestess. The Bearer looked untouched.

"You know what is required, Esania. The girl is a daughter of Riana, and we need her. She must be sent to Velantar to begin her training."

"If children are needed, let the Lady of Avelos bear her own! Nearly ten years as Lady, yet she has given none of her own gifts to the temple."

"It is a sadness for her and for us all that she has not."

"Is that what you call it? Sadness? Some would call it fear." Esania stepped closer to the Bearer. "Why did you come to Valador, Leita? Surely it was not just to destroy my child."

The Bearer sighed. "We are seeking the ancients' sky towers. You know Clan Valador's ancient spaces better than any other."

"Yes. I do." The high priestess lifted her chin. "Leave Delria in my care and perhaps I will recall where the ruins stand."

"Again you would deny Riana in her need?"

"I have never denied Riana, Leita. Only you."

The Bearer made a sound of frustration. She turned on Jhared. "Soldier, I will be some time here. Remove yourself until I call for you."

Jhared glanced at the High Priestess of Brenia and back to the Bearer. "Lady, I promised you my protection."

"I've no use for a guard now. I said leave us!"

The high priestess nodded at her Arionad. "Enaro, see to the Bearer's guard."

As Jhared followed the man out of the room, Lady Esania's voice rose behind him: "Can the Bearer of Cael's Blade not attract an Arionad that she must keep one of the high chieftain's soldiers for company?"

He didn't hear the Bearer's response.

"How strange it must be to serve such a mistress," the Shorn man observed as they walked toward the opposite wing of the temple.

"Have a care," Jhared muttered. "The Bearer of Cael's Blade deserves reverence."

"I mean no offense. I only find it curious to see you bound to her. You're no Arionad."

Jhared didn't want to hear another word about the Bearer and his binding to her. Was it for the welfare of Avelos she forced a mother to bargain for her daughter's life—or for the sake of her own desires? What would Alende say to that?

He made himself uncurl his fists. "I'm no Arionad, and neither are you. How is it you've not been pushed from the wall for breaking Shorn Law?"

"I've broken no law. I do not serve Riana, and I bear no blade in her temple. I am only an aide to Lady Esania."

"An aide?" Jhared repeated, his inflection a breath away from indecency.

"Her brother," the man answered with infinite patience.

"Ah."

"Forgive me." Enaro smoothed a wrinkle from his robe with one hand. "I've probed farther than I have a right. It was my choice to pay the debt with service to the High Priestess of Brenia. Perhaps your service to the Bearer was not freely given."

"I am honored to pay the debt in whatever way demanded of me!"

"Of course," Enaro said serenely. "I understand."

Enaro ushered Jhared up a staircase and into a chamber with rows of empty bunks. Jhared's boots pounded the wood floor as he escaped to the unglazed windows on the far side of the room. Unlit iron braziers were scattered between the bunks. In the corner, a staircase spiraled downward to the floor below. Jhared caught the odor of hay and horses.

"I intend no mockery," Enaro continued. "The ancients' tower is a dangerous place. The oldest priestesses say it is a bastion of Cael, and all manner of Ael make it their home. No one who cares for the integrity of his flesh and spirit will go there."

"Why do you tell me this?" Jhared asked.

"Because my sister is grieving, and she may not."

Jhared gazed out the window. Below him, the park lapped like a green lake against the street. Travelers flowed toward the center of Brenia and the markets. Jhared could see the top of the dead tree where another Shorn man paid his debt.

Enaro joined him at the casement. "Our road these days is a precarious one," the aide observed. "Those we love make decisions too difficult to trust and old friends treat one another as enemies. It can cause a spirit to wonder what will become of Avelos."

"It will become what we make of it," Jhared said. "We live the consequences of our own actions."

"Interesting you think so. I suppose you learned such things from your Teachers."

"No," Jhared replied, unwilling to discuss the Teaching with a stranger in a town of Legacy supporters. "It is what I learned from the temple. Riana gave Arion the right to choose his own way, and he suffered the rewards and regrets of his choices."

Jhared pointed toward the city center. "The prisoner there. He's paying the consequences for corrupting his daughter. What does that mean?"

Enaro's bland expression wavered. "It's unpleasant. Are you certain you want to know it?"

"I'm a soldier. Do you think I've not seen the evils men are capable of inflicting upon the helpless?"

"Very well, then. Vesarian told his daughter that the Shorn are not cursed. He says that his scars are a transgression against the goddess, and the killing winds are Riana's punishment to those who uphold the Shearing."

Jhared sucked a breath. "The man's no criminal. He's mad!"

"He confessed it before our clan elders."

"And they're going to execute him for it? For not knowing truth from delusion?"

"Not execution. Six days he's required to stand for his crimes. One day for each year of his daughter's blighted life. The sun is setting on his third."

Jhared had seen the prisoner's injuries, his sunken gaze and dried-leaf skin. He wouldn't survive to the sixth night. "What of the child?"

"Fled or hiding. No one has seen her or the mother."

"Riana protect them," Jhared murmured. What would it do to a child to have such terrible tales in her head? How could someone live with the belief that the pain inflicted on those she loved had no just cause? What would it do to her to think that the goddess sought deadly retribution on all her people? Could such a child know anything but fear? Would she grow with anything in her but hatred?

"Riana protects us all," Enaro replied, staring out the window. "It is not for you and me to wonder on it, only to keep the Lady's balance."

The aide's detachment would have made any Teacher glow with pride. Jhared should have admired it. Avelune appetites would find little hold in a man of such ascetic character. But Jhared felt raw: a little girl would lose her father; a mother would lose her child; and a man would lose his life.

"I can't claim to keep anything so perfect," he replied.

Jhared didn't see the Bearer again that day. He managed to get a bath and a meal, for which he was grateful, although he would have traded both to be with his patrol. In the wilds, at least he would have been of some use. The chamber where Enaro had left him served as the Arionade barracks when the men were not overseeing the harvest of the temple's trimago outside of town. The scent of horses came from the stables below. After Jhared had cleaned himself up, Enaro led him to the evening devotion. Jhared was glad for an opportunity to seek some equanimity, but when the candles in the first circle were extinguished and Riana's eye closed, all he could think about was the last evening devotion he had attended in Velantar, when the Bearer had called the darkness with a strength that radiated from her like heat from a sun-warmed rock.

That night, as he lay in the silent barracks waiting for sleep to find him, he thought of Alende, tormented by madness, and of the prisoner—Vesarian, Enaro named him—tormented by Valadorian justice. *He told his daughter the Shorn were not cursed.*

Perhaps Alende and Vesarian were both mad. Wasn't it madness to maintain a belief so contrary to the beliefs of everyone else? Contrary to everything the Teachers taught? Wasn't it madness to share a story no one else accepted?

Mahla Denaban told me that story.

Jhared took a breath, a thought creeping upon him. What if another possibility existed? What if Vesarian wasn't mad? What if he had heard stories few others ever learned? Could it be he had known a Storyteller?

A quiet, rhythmic clicking came from the hall and entered the barracks. Jhared pushed himself up on one elbow and saw a curly tail waving just above the beds. Inalde weaved his way to Jhared's bed and sat, his tail thumping the floor.

"Hello, pup. What're you doing here?"

Taking Jhared's tone for an invitation, the little dog leaped into the bed, rucked up the blankets with his front paws, then turned a circle and threw himself down. Jhared smiled a little and rubbed the creature's silky ears.

"What if Mahla came to Brenia?" Jhared dared to murmur the dangerous thought to the dog. Ziabela had claimed that the Storytellers told their forbidden tales wherever they found welcome. Mahla Denaban had been the last living Storyteller in Velantar. She had been a bard with talent enough to sing for the high chieftain; she would have traveled the bards' circuit. And Velantar was not so far from Brenia, after all.

Jhared realized the risks of considering such a possibility, yet a part of him refused to let it go. What if another man lived who could speak with Jhared about the Storytellers, about Mahla? Someone free of Alende's malice. What if the prisoner in the center of Brenia could share something that would help Jhared to understand what his mother had done and why?

Jhared slept fitfully. In the morning, he was still chasing after small bits of support to feed his faint hope. Wasn't Vesarian of the right age to have known Mahla? Didn't Mahla seek out Shorn men and women with whom to share her stories? Wasn't Brenia an active trade center that could afford talented musicians? After the morning devotion, Jhared sent word to the Bearer, begging time on his own to check on the horses and attend to errands at the markets. He had to wait for her response, which was only to say she would be engaged all day and that she wished him to retrieve a list of things from her bags. It was a relief to have her blessing to go out, and a greater relief to know she would be too busy to wonder if he took his time getting back. As he left the temple, the wizened priestess, Sister Jhema, greeted him from her post at the entrance, her black eyes small and bright.

"Walk steady on the dark paths," she told him.

She had offered the same strange prayer to the Bearer. Jhared wasn't comforted by it. "Lady, I do my best to walk in the light."

She gave a little snort, looking disappointed. Jhared wasn't in the mood to confront her doubt. He offered her a spiral and hurried off.

A close, grey sky dulled the colors of Brenia. The banners on the buildings hung limp. Jhared drew up the hood of his cloak and kept his head down as he stepped into the street. He owned none of Enaro's detachment. He had to see the prisoner again and decide if there was a way to speak with him.

This time, no crowd was gathered around the dead tree. No Legacy speaker shouted for change. From one bare branch, the wretched waste of a man sagged like a carcass hung for gutting. A few people stared at the prisoner as they passed. Some took interest enough to spit, but most didn't even raise their eyes to his agony, inured or perhaps merely apathetic. A Shorn man's dying had no bearing on their own lives.

The street noises became a buzzing in Jhared's ears. Rivulets of fire streamed through his limbs. He had taken a half-dozen strides toward the prisoner before he caught himself. He gulped deep breaths and closed his eyes, willing his body to stop its release of poisonous Shorn energy. There was no one to fight here and nowhere to flee.

Jhared took measured steps to a stone bench and sat. He forced himself to look once again at the stranger in chains. The prisoner's head hung to his chest. Flies competed for space on the bodies of the blackbirds and Vesarian's open wounds. Then something, perhaps a spasm of pain, caused the man's head to twitch upward, and his green eyes met Jhared's.

The prisoner's misery cascaded over him. *'We live the consequences of our own actions,"* Jhared had told Enaro. Tierzen had offered him that precept, and Jhared believed it, but Tierzen would never have condoned this cruelty.

Jhared didn't flinch from Vesarian's gaze. He had nothing else to offer the man but acknowledgment. He would bear witness to Vesarian's suffering, as if by doing so he could give it some meaning. Who had Vesarian been before the Legacy entrapped him? Where had he given his service? Did he have friends who trusted him? Had he known Mahla Denaban and heard her stories?

Had Mahla been the one who set him on the path that led to this torment?

At some point, the rain started, a light mist that beaded across Jhared's skin and veiled the town in silver. A Legacy speaker arrived later. The young spokesman listed the needs of Clan Valador, the failures of the high chieftain, and the strength of Tumal's Legacy. The juxtaposition of the ruined Shorn man and the earnest Legacy supporter was powerful. Anyone could see that the Legacy only meant to protect people from the corruption of the Shorn. Jhared knew it was foolish to linger, but he couldn't turn his back on the dying man. He couldn't shake the sense that what the elders of Clan Valador did here had little to do with justice.

The markets had closed and the lights had risen in the taverns by the time Jhared decided what to do. He rose from the bench, sending water streaming from his shoulders and down the back of his cloak. In the gloom, the unmoving prisoner might have been nothing more than a broken branch dangling from the tree.

Jhared strode past without glancing at the man this time. As he approached the stable where he had stalled Seravina, lanterns on either side of the stable door cast twin coronas against the mist. Inside it was dry and heat from the animals cut the chill. The stable boy greeted him with a friendly halloo.

"S'ere a rush for your mount?" the boy asked as he saddled a fat piebald gelding.

Jhared assured the boy he had just come to see how the horses were faring and to retrieve some things from his packs, but promised if all was well there would be a pebble or two in it for the groom.

"All s'well." The boy offered a gap-toothed grin. "They're happy as hens. All but 'at silver dame. She thinks she's a chieftain's lady, too good for a stall."

Jhared smiled at the description of Seravina, trying to ignore the somersaults his stomach was turning as he strode down the row. No reason existed for alarm. Nothing he did here was suspicious, and the boy wasn't even likely to remember this visit.

The horses looked well, if bored, in their small, clean stalls. Seravina surprised Jhared by poking her head over the half-door to watch him with a lambent gaze. He lifted a hand to stroke her arched neck. She didn't shy or nip, but only turned her head to snuffle at his hair.

It took longer than he expected to find what he wanted from the patrol's provisions and then to decide what he could carry out without arousing questions. He had already made a pack for himself and restored the rest to its place when he recalled the Bearer's list. No use for it now; he couldn't spare more time to dig everything out again. He would find some excuse for it, after.

He thanked the stable boy, gave up the promised pebbles, and stepped back into the street. The mist had become a steady rain. It pelted the roofs with a repetitive chorus of *thip-thip-thips* and washed down the center of the alley. Jhared shouldered his pack and pulled up his damp hood, glad for the excuse to stay bundled. He was lucky; the wet and cold seemed to be keeping the taverns full, and the people still about looked in a hurry to be someplace else.

As he reached the tree and took his first step toward the prisoner, the night nearly rippled out from under him. He halted and waited for the dizziness to pass. This trip should be easy. Traveling unseen on a dark, rainy night was no challenge to a border guard. He knew how to move and where to watch. He knew how to make himself a shadow.

He thought of the Legacy men sent to beat him on Dawnings' Eve. If the Bearer and Bilar hadn't stopped them, he would have died on the street. That was Legacy justice. That was the kind of justice hanging from the tree tonight.

The thought pushed him onward. He edged around the tree trunk until he stood beneath the prisoner's branch.

"Riana, mercy."

Vesarian was slumped in his shackles, his face hidden behind a mat of sodden black hair. The rope that looped through his chains and around the tree branch stretched his arms behind his head at a hideous angle. Where the iron bit into his swollen flesh, blood trickled down his wrists and joined with rivulets of rain. The dead ravens stared with blind eyes.

Wondering if he were too late, Jhared glided the two steps from the trunk to the prisoner. He stretched a hand to Vesarian's throat and felt an irregular pulse beating faintly beneath the skin. The man's body was giving up its struggle. Jhared lifted Vesarian's head and patted his cheek, calling his name. It wasn't a kindness to bring him back to awareness, but this would be easier without dead weight on the rope, and Jhared didn't want to risk the man crying out if he awoke suddenly.

The prisoner's eyelids fluttered. "No," he moaned.

Jhared set a hand on his shoulder. "Easy. I've not come to hurt you."

Vesarian shook his head weakly. "Please. No," he said again and then slumped once more.

Things were going to be more complicated if the man couldn't walk under his own power, but it was too soon to worry over that. Jhared stepped back into the shadow of the tree and slipped the pack from his shoulders. From inside the bag, he pulled out a knife and a blanket. He slung the blanket over his shoulder. The knife wasn't nearly as fine as the one the Bearer had given him, but when he sawed at the bloated rope strung through Vesarian's shackles, the blade chewed determinedly and cut through with a sudden snick.

One end of the rope whipped free. It snaked out of the chains and up the branch, pulled by Vesarian's falling body. The chains rattled and clinked. Jhared dropped the blade and grabbed for the prisoner. Metal clattered onto stone.

From somewhere behind him, a pale light flashed across the tree trunk.

Jhared froze beneath the branch, clutching the unconscious man tightly to his chest. The prisoner's wet, slippery skin made it difficult to hold on. If the townsfolk came for them, Jhared couldn't say whether he would flee or stand and defend a convicted criminal.

Men cursed and laughed, at least three of them, as the cheerful noises of a tavern competed with the rain. Jhared's arms began to shake from the strain. Water streamed down his face.

Finally, the light cut off and footsteps hurried up the street. They were leaving.

Jhared lowered Vesarian to the ground and knelt there, lightheaded with relief. He could barely see through the downpour. Nothing seemed to be quite where it should be. Swiping futilely at the water in his eyes, Jhared focused on the next part of his plan. He felt along the ground under the tree, until he found the rope. Then he shook out the blanket and rolled it like a log—or a body. The rope was only long enough to wrap twice around the blanket-log and hang it from the branch. When the knot was secure, he slung the dead ravens around the top. It would fool no one in daylight, but he hoped that in the gloom the tall, limp shadow would turn away casual glances.

With the blanket hung, Jhared turned to the prisoner. He eased the man's manacled hands into a more natural position. Vesarian groaned as his torn muscles were forced to move. As gently as possible, Jhared pulled him into an upright position, but no amount of encouragement or cajoling would get the half-conscious man to his feet.

"I'm sorry for this," Jhared mumbled, bending to press his shoulder to Vesarian's chest. With a grunt, he heaved the man onto his back. Vesarian struggled feebly. Straightening under the load, Jhared gazed from one edge of the town's center to the other, trying to regain his bearings. Nothing seemed to be steady beneath his feet. He closed his eyes.

The shifting town couldn't be anything but an illusion caused by panic. It was unworthy of a Forest Guard scout. With a deep breath, Jhared searched for stillness within him. It was there, and so was the map of Brenia. With effort, he steadied the prisoner on his back and his feet beneath him and started forward.

It took longer than it should have, but finally he reached an alley where he found a half-collapsed doorway to what might have once been a riverman's hovel. Only as he crouched to squirm through the broken doorframe did he think to pray the storm hadn't chased any others inside.

"Hello?" he said to the darkness.

No one answered. Rain slapped the planks of the roof and pooled across the dirt floor. Beneath the clean scent of the storm, it reeked of cats and fish.

Vesarian stirred. Jhared laid him under what seemed to be the soundest portion of the roof and spread his own cloak over the man. He wished he could dare a fire, but even if he were willing to risk notice, nothing was dry enough to burn. Instead, he pulled a pot of bitterbalm and a small flask of brandy from his pack.

"Hold on," he murmured. "We're going to get those manacles off."

Vesarian's labored breathing was the only response. Jhared crept around the hovel in the dark, feeling for something to use as a hammer. When he found a chunk of broken brick, he pulled the knife from his belt. The manacles were sealed with iron bolts shot through both ends of the cuffs and pounded flat. He set the blade perpendicular to the flat end of one bolt, and as best he could without light, brought the brick down on the knife's pommel. The first strike bent the bolt. The second missed, sending the blade skimming across Vesarian's wrist. With the third strike, Jhared heard a crack. He snapped off the bolt's head, then tugged the opposite end until it slid free of the cuff. The second bolt was more of a challenge, enough to make him glad Vesarian was still unconscious. Once both bolts were removed, Jhared had to dig the cuffs out of the man's swollen flesh before he could open them. He cleaned the injuries, smeared bitterbalm on them, and wrapped them with cloth.

Shorn Law forbade Jhared from serving as a healer, but somehow the small aid he gave Vesarian felt more like reparation than anything he had done since leaving Velantar. He took a swallow of brandy to drown the thought and leaned against one damp wall. No other relief could be had until Vesarian was out of Brenia. Then Alende could care for him.

Jhared didn't doubt Alende would take in a Shorn man punished for treason. But now that the prisoner lay before him, Jhared could no longer deny the significance of what he had done. No one had coerced or enticed him. He had made this choice alone.

He took another drink, then leaned forward and dribbled some of the brandy into Vesarian's mouth. The man coughed and rustled in the dark. Jhared laid a hand on his cheek and felt him stiffen.

"You're in a safe place," Jhared said quietly. "I'm not going to harm you."

" 'O . . . are you?"

Jhared hesitated. "A Forest Guard from Velantar. I need you to tell me some things."

"I told the elders everything." Panic fluttered in the weak voice. "I told 'em I did it all. I . . . corrupted Sancha."

"Who told you?" Jhared asked.

"Told me?" the man echoed.

"Who told you the stories about the Exile and the curse? The ones you told your daughter."

Silence stretched until Jhared wondered if the man had lost consciousness again. Then he heard Vesarian move and realized his mistake. "Please. You needn't fear me. I'm not here to see anyone else punished. I just have to know. Who was the Storyteller?"

"What is this?" Vesarian gasped. "They told me six days and six nights and my ordeal would be over. They told me . . . my Sancha'd be kept safe. Kept clean of all the lies."

"It hasn't been six days. You weren't going to live that long. I cut you free."

Vesarian's howl rang with agony and fear and unmitigated despair. "What 'ave you done? I promised 'em six days. They said they'd let 'er be for six!"

"Who said? The elders?"

"The Legacy." Vesarian gulped for breath. "They said f'I confessed to every crime, they'd see me serve six days and wouldn't touch my Sancha. It 'ad to be six. No pardon. No escape. Or they'd corrupt her. You've doomed my little one!"

Lightning flashed above them, illuminating Vesarian's anguish for one painful heartbeat. Thunder exploded, rattling the walls and shaking plaster from the ceiling. Jhared's brittle boundaries fractured. He cried out as he was sucked like smoke into the storm.

He lays the banner of Avelos at the feet of a Sahisten king.

She dives from the clifftop, crying with the pleasure of the wind over her body.

He sees his own people attack his friends.

Jhared senses each moment as part of a blue and red pattern framed by an arch of infinite blackness. The moments gift him with a fleeting touch, then vanish. He's falling too fast to hold them. From afar, they look like ribbons, beautiful and alluring. They twine through the blackness and around one another, creating a weaving of unfathomable complexity. Someone else falls with him. He senses familiarity and curiosity and dares to call out.

"Do you know me?"

The someone beside him forms a fascinating pattern, woven tightly with intelligence and strength. He cannot see what creature creates such a pattern, and he wants to; he tries to look closer. He calls out again.

"Who are you?"

"Jhared Denaban! You do not belong here!"

Steel impaled his spirit. Jhared gasped at the white-hot force of it. He hung in the blackness, no longer falling, no longer able to move at all. All around him, the weaving of gleaming blue and red faltered. Pieces shattered and fell to ash. Long, lovely swags of brightness disintegrated. Jhared fought to break free, desperate to defend this complex, beautiful world. The bright patterns belonged to him, were a part of him. What would be left of him if they were destroyed?

"Jhared Denaban, Scout in the Forest Guard Fourth, Son of an Elder, Child of a Bard, your place is on *this* Path!"

Steel ripped into him a second time. For an instant, he was torn in two. Then the remains of the intricate weaving vanished and he slammed into a cold, stiff body.

Dull yellow light dirtied the blackness. Jhared lifted his heavy head. The curved Blade hovered above him, shiny red droplets of his own blood quivering at its tip. His assailant bent close, her breath cool against his cheek, chaos glittering in her gaze.

In that instant, he hated her, for what she had taken from him and what she could still take. With a sweeping blow, he knocked the knife out of her hand. It struck stone and splashed into a puddle. He rolled to his feet and reached out to grab her. As she sprang away, his fingers closed on her arm. She yelped as he spun her around and pinned her wrist to her back. With his other hand, he dragged her close, preventing her from using the space against him.

He stood over her, his breathing loud and raw, his blood trickling down his neck. One hand clamped her wrist; his other arm wrapped around her throat. He could feel the sharp ridge of her collarbone and the rapid pounding of her heart.

The sensation of that fragile beat brought his control crashing back into place.

"Oh, no," he moaned, releasing her and staggering backward. "Oh, Goddess, help me."

The Bearer of Cael's Blade scrambled free and turned to face him. She lifted her hands, palms outward. "Easy, soldier. Easy now——"

Cold exploded upward through his body, driving out his life-preserving heat. His last clear image was the Bearer's face brightening with a look of elation; then his muscles convulsed and dropped him to the ground. The side of his face struck something hard as he fell. Dazed and helpless, he shivered in the dirt.

"May you be rewarded for your sacrifice," the priestess said from far away. "Through this sacred ending may you find a new beginning. Rest until the two are one and true balance is restored."

He sensed another rending, another loss; then she was beside him, wrapping her cloak around him and whispering his name.

She was still close when the worst of it had passed, and he lay limp and exhausted on the wet floor. He was ashamed to look at her.

"Here. Drink this." She put the brandy into his hand.

He sat up, afraid to set the world swinging again. The brandy was hot iron at the back of his throat. He coughed, then took another swallow. "It's . . . a madness, Lady. I'm not fit for service. I'm sorry."

The Bearer patted his bruised cheek. "You came near to causing great harm tonight. Avelos would have suffered if we had both been lost. It's my fault. I should have been more careful with you."

He shifted his gaze to her face. "What does that mean?"

"I know what it is that plagues you."

"No. How could you possibly?"

"You're dizzy and sick for no reason, especially at dawn and dusk. At other times or places of transition, the world seems to jump out from under you. Daydreams take you deeper than any nightmare, and fits of strange visions leave you gasping with cold."

He stared at her in bewilderment. "If you know, then why am I not dead?" He touched a hand to his throat; it came away bloody. "Or did you mean to finish this?"

Her eyes widened and she laughed. "Oh Jhared, may it never come to that! I've told you I mean you no harm. You were lost in the weaving, and pain is the surest way to pull your spirit back where it belongs." She leaned forward to touch the wound beneath his jaw. "The healers say the spirit hovers closest to the surface at this point."

"All this time, the daydreams, the dizziness, you knew?"

"I wasn't sure. I didn't dare believe it, and you didn't give me enough evidence." Her expression turned rueful. "You wear a tight mask. Perhaps I should have warned you, despite my uncertainty. I just hoped you would come to me of your own will."

"Lady, please. Tell me how I can be cured of this ailment. I can't fulfill my duty. I'm a danger to my comrades." He glanced toward the corner where Vesarian lay too still. "To everyone near me."

Her smile deepened. On a sunny summer day it might have thrilled him to cause a woman to attend to him so, but on this night, with this woman, he shuddered.

"Ah, Jhared, I once named you an unexpected treasure, and it was truer than I dared hope. There is no cure for what you suffer. You are not mad. You are sensitive to the Paths." She touched her hand to his brow, claiming him. "You are meant to be a Pathwalker."

7.
TRIALS

"Carian Nuello, Daughter of Sianale, you are cast from the Higher Circle. Let all here witness and beware."

The bell sounded from the temple's tower, one low, mournful note that reverberated against the silvered dome and made the candles on the altar tremble. Nemiah sensed Rom, still and forbidding, on her right. On her left, each of the four remaining members of the Higher Circle stood in brooding silence, staring out over the assembly of sisters and Arionade. At her feet, Capalino sat alert, his large head lifted. Nemiah formed Riana's spiral and raised her voice again.

"Carian Nuello, Servant of Riana, on Dawnings' Eve, when all Riana's children are free to choose their ways, you coerced a sister to follow your command. For this offense, you have sacrificed the right to speak your will in any temple for one full turn of the seasons. Let no novice be placed in your care for six turns of the seasons. And till the end of your days, may you never again serve in Riana's high temple."

The bell tolled a second time. Carian stood beneath the dome with her broad shoulders unbowed. Sunlight streamed from the open oculus, setting her red hair afire and sharpening the defiance in her eyes. It had been a mistake to hold the ritual at noon. Leita would have considered the position of the sun over the dome; Lia would have found a way to use it to bring the others to her cause, but Nemiah hadn't done either of those things. The young ones shifting behind the balustrade overhead were reading the light as a sign of Riana's hand on their former Mistress. Through all their years in the novices' quarters, Carian's face was the first they saw in the morning and the last before bed. She taught them the correct prayers for each of the four devotions, how to behave in the sanctuary, and the proper ways to greet the Lady. Many of them looked upon Carian as a second mother. By sending her away, Nemiah was going to lose some of them.

She needed guidance, another high priestess with whom to speak about her decisions. Nemiah thought of Lady Lia. Wherever Lia existed on the Paths, had she ever been forced to scar a member of her own Circle? Nemiah desperately wished to speak with the Pathwalker again.

She forced her focus back to the moment and turned to her Arionad. "Captain Rom, take the ring."

Rom's leather gear creaked as he marched off the dais and snapped out his gloved hand for Carian's ring of service. A small hitch in his gait was the only visible remnant of his Dawnings' Eve battle with four of his own men, but Nemiah knew how deeply the Higher Circle's intrigues had wounded him. The Captain of the Arionade was probably the only one in the hall who held no ambivalence about banishing Carian from Velantar.

Specks of light flickered over the floor as the stone-faced Mistress of Novices pulled the ring from her finger and dropped it into Rom's palm. The Arionad held up the symbol of the Higher Circle so that all might see its perfection before placing it at his feet. With one fierce stomp, he crushed the malleable metal. The flattened silver made a sad *plink* when he set it on the altar before Nemiah.

"The circle is broken," he said.

On Nemiah's left, the young Mistress of Messages tried to stifle a sob. Nemiah pressed her lips together without sympathy. Clemina's testimony had given Nemiah the grounds to charge Carian with profaning the Right of Choice. Nemiah wondered if Clemina realized her words had saved Carian from the more dire charge of defiance against the Lady of Avelos. The Mistress of Novices could have been banned from Riana's service forever. For the deaths of four Arionade and the torment Rom suffered, Nemiah would have taken some satisfaction in that, but she couldn't afford to breed more animosity within the Higher Circle. She had to compromise to keep the temple from crumbling under the weight of its own conflicts. Nemiah understood that; Carian did not.

"Let the transgressor speak one final time before her name is scarred forever in the Book of Circles," Nemiah ordered. "Let her say how she will make reparation to her family and those she has injured."

Carian threw a look of disdain at Nemiah. "Yes, I have failed Riana and my sisters, for I have allowed weakness to prevail. I vow not to fail the Lady so again."

Shocked silence held in the sanctuary. Nemiah wished she could see the reaction of the other Circle members. She needed to know who still sympathized with Carian. The crisis had not passed.

"Bring the Book of Circles."

The acolyte came forward with the ancient book and held it open before Nemiah. The Book of Circles kept the records of each member of each Higher Circle and every Circle's proclamations. Although the book was meticulously kept, it was sadly incomplete. Each time Nemiah opened it, she wondered what she might have read before Lady Amalia conspired with Sahiste to assassinate High Chieftain Tumal. After Tumal executed Amalia and all the members of her

Higher Circle, he appointed his own allies to create a new Circle. They had started their own Book and destroyed all the volumes before it.

Nemiah intoned the blessing as she drew up the green silk ribbon that marked the pages of the twelfth Circle, her Higher Circle. Carian's entry was filled with the densely packed script of several different scribes, for she came from a long line of Riana's servants. Her mother, Sianale, had served as the Bearer of Cael's Blade for Lady Pahlina. Her aunt had been mistress of a chapterhouse for Clan Aglar in the north. Her sister still served near Lake Linde. The scar that marked Carian's name would also mar the names of her offspring and the offspring of all her sisters and cousins. She had proved her line to be flawed.

Nemiah lowered the pen to the inkwell. "With this cursed quill dipped in the ink of transgression, I scar the name of Carian Nuello."

Never forget our own name was scarred. Long ago. The year it most mattered.

It was her mother's voice. Nemiah remembered the warning, but this wasn't just a memory. Blue and red shimmered in the corners of her vision. She reached for the Book. It was too far away.

Never forget, for they will not forget. Every time they look into your green eyes, they will know and wonder how much traitors' blood remains in you. You must be willing to sacrifice.

It was the warning her mother had given on the day Nemiah left home to enter Riana's service. The moment was so sharply familiar it would be an easy Path to fall into. Nemiah squeezed her eyes shut and reached to close the Gate. The voice changed, grew deeper and demanding:

A sacrifice will be required!

Drums pounded in Nemiah's ears. She dug her nails into her palms. If she fell onto the Paths here, all the temple would see her weakness.

She discovered the Gate thrown open at the border between her self and Riana's infinite ways. It blazed with the light of all the spheres, lovely and terrifying. She tried to keep from flinching. Riana had given her the skill to travel, but not the desire. She never yearned to know the boundless secrets that lay along the Paths, although for the sake of Avelos she knew she must seek them. But not like this, not when the Gate was utterly out of her control.

Find the Gate, grasp it, close it. Make the boundary of her self whole once again. Nemiah wrapped her mind around the blue-red flames and dragged them toward her. Fire licked hungrily at her thoughts. There was a shriek, like the protest of a forced hinge. She staggered as the Gate slammed shut and the world realigned itself. The voices went silent.

Beside her, the Mistress of Messages stared with wide eyes.

Nemiah caught her breath. "With this pen . . . I scar the name of Carian Nuello and all of her line. Let the scribes paint the names of her family and fly the banners from the highest balconies of the high temple so that all may witness her shame."

She lifted her eyes to the gathering. Tension crackled throughout the sunlit chamber. "It is done."

Four Arionade marched out of file to flank the Mistress of Novices. Their boots rapped against the stone. Their white coats shone. As they turned in formation to leave the room, Carian tossed her head. Her gaze was sharp and bright. She looked more like a high priestess with her procession than a penitent.

Such a waste. Carian should have been an asset. Nemiah made a staying motion to the guards.

"You could have helped us regain our position as the Guides of Avelos, Carian. Instead, you squandered yourself and violated the sacred rights. Cael smiled upon the day you shattered our Circle. I pray you come to see that. Perhaps then you'll find true reparation."

Carian's expression showed only contempt. "I don't need your prayers. Your family's name was scarred long before you ever stood behind the altar, Nemiah Rustania. What I've done opens the possibility of a Path on which the temple no longer grovels before the council. I don't mourn my loss."

The woman's vehemence pushed Nemiah backward an involuntary step. Rom signaled furiously, and the Arionade prodded the Mistress of Novices away from the altar.

Time spun into a tenuous thread as Carian was marched out of the hall. Nemiah brought the ritual to a close, hoping all the right prayers came out of her mouth. At the end, it was her place to leave the hall with her Arionad, ahead of the sisterhood. Rom knew better than to take her arm while all the temple watched, but he stayed no more than a finger's stretch away. His hard, angry presence was a source of stability. It tethered her to her Path when every infinite possibility in Riana's weaving threatened to break through the Gate and carry her off.

She floated beside her Arionad, past the altar and through the congregation of women and girls who relied upon her. A ray of sunlight flashed over her as she passed under the oculus. What rituals had the ancients performed beneath the open dome before the Exile? What purpose had such a bright, airy chamber served before it became a place of blood and guilt?

Wings strum the air, making a breathy song of the morning. Below her, voices join the melody, soft as a breeze. She felt their joy. They lifted her soul. Lifted her above the crowd. Her first flight—

Murmurs of curiosity filled the halls outside the sanctuary. Strangers stared as Nemiah passed. The temple was filled to bursting with people displaced by the killing winds. Her Arionade pushed the bystanders back.

She hovered above the altar, hardly aware of her own efforts. Below, the music continued as she opened the Paths of her own experiences, one after another, shaping them into the breeze that held her—

"Sit here, my lady. Merisel is heating tea."

Nemiah looked around, startled to find herself in her own apartments in the tower. Capalino patrolled the room, then settled in front of the fire. Somewhere nearby ethereal music played. No. Not nearby. She pinched her brow between her thumb and forefinger. The music could only come from somewhere she didn't belong and some ritual in which she would never take part.

Rom was scowling. "The sooner Carian's away from Velantar, the better. That one thinks too much of herself to ever acknowledge her wrongdoing. She's dangerous."

"She'll be harmless enough in Avarel Forest. Clan Nadaren will keep her busy tattooing blessings and setting wards against the Bloodless."

"Perhaps," Rom grumbled. "But you should add time to her sentence for speaking to you as she did."

Nemiah lowered herself into a chair. "She only spoke the truth. My family name *is* scarred." Nemiah didn't need her mother's warning to be reminded how close she had come to the Avelune curse. All six women of her Higher Circle knew she had an Avelun ancestor who served the temple before the Exile. Only two people knew more.

"I won't punish someone for stating the truth," she added with a sigh.

"I know you won't." Rom motioned to where Merisel was drawing the kettle off the hearth. "The child has boldblood ready. Please drink it. I'll send for Madam Kaliska."

Her observant Arionad watched her steadily. No doubt he had seen her disorientation during the ritual and recognized it for what it was, but he didn't ask what they were both wondering: why couldn't she seal the Gate? Why was she still drifting onto the Paths? She had no answer to satisfy either of them. She had believed her control would return with the passing of the Day of Dawnings, when the Paths no longer converged and Riana took up her order once more, but since the killing winds struck the city, leaving death and chaos behind, her control had slipped further.

"Don't trouble Kaliska, Rom." She accepted the tea Merisel offered, but didn't state the obvious: *nothing ails me a healer can treat.*

The wonder of boldblood was not that it stopped the throbbing in her head, but that it enlivened her body and focused her mind enough that she no longer cared about the pain. As her limbs warmed and thoughts cleared, she sent Rom away and went to her desk to confront the mountain of correspondence that had accumulated since Dawnings' Day. Much of it came from chapterhouses and temples with their harvest reports and accounts of the year's debts, but more recently requests had arrived from clan elders and guild leaders, all of whom needed something from her. Clan Ontera asked to be released from the autumn tithe because the winds in Velantar had destroyed so much of their harvest. Henaro

Delsian inquired whether she had yet spoken to the high chieftain on his behalf and that of Clan Delsio. The head of the wool guild asked for a meeting to renegotiate the terms of a contract his clan could no longer meet, as the winds had decimated their flocks. Clan Nadaren sent another plea for a priestess for their small temple near the Sonan border.

Nemiah sorted the letters into those she must deal with immediately, those that could wait, and those that could be delegated to an assistant. Delsian went into the wait pile—let the oily little clan elder worry whether she had changed her mind about speaking for him. With a twinge of guilt, a letter from Lady Ansa in Panetar also went into the wait pile. She wished she had time to send the old priestess the long letter Ansa deserved. Clan Nadaren's request went into the immediate pile; their needs would soon be answered. Nemiah hoped the wet weather of Avarel Forest would cool Carian's feverish temperament.

Gradually, the disorder resolved itself into three neat stacks. Nemiah sat back and sipped her tea, staring at one final letter that remained unsorted. The familiar mountain-crag seal of the Council of Clans shone blue in the lamplight.

Correspondence from Elders' Hall could mean nothing good. Her allies in the council were few and unlikely to write for anything but more favors. Her enemies knew her vulnerable points and made free with their threats. As she cracked the wax, her imagination created a congregation of unpleasant possibilities. It was almost a relief when she saw the sender was Tierzen Trianor.

Quickly she scanned the letter, skimming over courteous inquiries about her recovery from her fall at Panetar and the welfare of Riana's servants after the killing winds. The elder went on to offer his gratitude to her for allowing the Arionade to contribute to the city cleanup. He lamented briefly about the unrest growing in the clan circles since the winds' attack and provided some details about the council's efforts to calm people's fears. Then abruptly the tone of the letter changed. Nemiah began to read more closely.

Although our trip together proved a perilous one, I don't regret the opportunity it gave me to learn your thoughts about the troubling choices facing Avelos. In what will likely be the dire times to come, I feel certain the historian Morican was wrong: if we hope to resolve our conflicts, we must have more communication between us, not less. In that spirit, I share news of particular relevance to you. The Minister of the Treasury has accused his Shorn scribe of stealing his authority for her own malicious purposes. Among a number of other serious allegations, Elder Abrigado holds Ziabela Marcalo to be responsible for the inflammatory display at Panetar that led to several deaths and your own injury. An initial inquiry will be held at Elders' Hall in three days.

In this matter of alleged betrayals, Abrigado would use the words of Morican for his own ends, but the laws she left us were meant for the benefit of all. I can only hope Riana will oversee the proceedings so we might learn the truth.

Tierzen Trianor
Minister of the Teaching

Nemiah lowered the letter and stared at the fire, considering the implications of the elder's letter. She had expected to despise Tierzen Trianor, but on their ill-fated trip to meet the Sahisten ambassador, she found the elder to be not simply an intelligent, diplomatic man but also a compassionate one. He well knew the enmity that existed between her and Toren Abrigado. He knew the long history of distrust between Adan Rumar and herself. He had gone so far as to challenge her on that point, urging her to consider the high chieftain's actions in a way she never had before. When it came to it, however, she and Tierzen Trianor agreed on very little.

Why then did the elder want her to attend the inquiry?

I can only hope Riana will oversee the proceedings so we might learn the truth.

His invitation was subtle, so subtle she might act as though she hadn't understood it and he might act as though he hadn't requested it. Did Rumar know what his elder had written? It wouldn't have been the first time the high chieftain sent her a covert message through another. But what good could her presence possibly do Rumar, unless he meant to feed her to Abrigado? She shivered at the thought. A treasonous Shorn scribe was fuel to the Legacy's quarrel with the high chieftain. People had died in Panetar. When the clans heard that a Shorn woman had betrayed them, anger and fear would explode. Rumar might just be desperate enough to try to redirect that anger away from himself with reminders of a high priestess's treason.

Nemiah rose from her desk and moved around the room, touching the tapestries, the books, and the piles of correspondence, all the small items that defined her. The complexities of council politics defied her. Leita was always the one she trusted to help her navigate the tortuous way, but Leita was far from Velantar, and no one could say when she would return. Nemiah would have to navigate for herself. Capa twitched one soft ear in her direction and continued to doze. Merisel stirred from her place near the hearth.

"Is there something you need, Lady?" the child asked.

"No, Merisel. Go on and . . ." Nemiah trailed off. She looked again at the letter.

In this matter of alleged betrayals, Abrigado would use the words of Morican for his own ends, but the laws she left us were meant for the benefit of all.

Tierzen Trianor was a deliberate man. Nothing about the unusual phrasing in his letter was accidental. What did he mean to say?

Abrigado would use the words of Morican for his own ends. Nemiah's thoughts on Morican were sharply divided. Her pre-Exile histories were filled with dark assessments of man's nature and a rigid isolationist sentiment that not only promoted the withdrawal of Avelos from all interactions with the border nations, but went so far as to sanction the segregation of men and women for all but the act of procreation. Despite the radical ideas that conflicted with Riana's order, Morican was the only priestess whose writings had survived Tumal's purges from the time when the temple still shaped the country's Path. In fact, one might say Morican represented the last vestige of temple influence on the council, for her examination of the ancient laws offered the only pre-Exile code to which the elders still adhered. Those such as the supporters of Tumal's Legacy, who held traditional views on foreign policy, particularly valued her writings.

"Yes, child. I do need something." Nemiah hesitated, knowing she was stepping onto a tortuous Path and hoping it would take her where she must go. "Hurry to the archive and retrieve Morican's *Deliberations on the Council of First-Clans*. I've some studying to do."

8.
Strange Alliances

The four most powerful men in Avelos stood at the end of the cold, windowless hall with their backs to Nemiah: Tierzen Trianor, Toren Abrigado, Enrian Nadel, and High Chieftain Adan Rumar. None of them could be considered an ally. One of them still owned a piece of her heart.

Enrian didn't look at her when she entered the room alone. Tension drew the lines of his broad back. His gaze was fixed on something or someone within the men's half-circle that Nemiah was too short to see. For a moment, she considered fleeing. She was a mouse among raptors in this chamber. Then Toren Abrigado turned, and it was too late.

As ever, the Minister of the Treasury looked aristocratic and fine that morning. His coat and breeches of blue and silver hugged his graceful figure. His honey-brown hair fell neatly across his smooth brow. Nemiah expected to see some mark of the demon on him; his contempt for the goddess must surely leave its stain, but as hard as she looked, she saw only a model of order. Standing beside Adan Rumar, whose dark copper hair was bound like a soldier's and whose boots were speckled with mud, Abrigado looked more the high chieftain. Rumar might have been his groom.

"Lady Nemiah." Her name from Abrigado's lips was a challenge to her right to exist.

With effort, she ignored him and forced herself further into the lamp-lit chamber. He didn't deserve acknowledgment ahead of the high chieftain, and now that she understood the extent of his ambitions she refused to validate them.

Rumar caught her gaze from across the room and rewarded her with the ironic arch of one well-defined brow. Red marred his grey eyes. His weathered face sagged with exhaustion. Scrapes and bruises marked his large hands. He looked as though he had been on the streets cleaning up the wreckage of the city himself.

"Here's an interesting turn," he said mildly, "the Lady of Avelos at a council inquiry."

"The temple has the right to attend any hearing relevant to the welfare of the people," she answered, trying to sound as though this were exactly where she wanted to be.

"Finding food and shelter is relevant to our people's welfare just now. Figuring out how to defend our borders from likely invasion and stopping the menace that blows apart our cities: these are things that matter. Yet here we are once again, wasting time and effort in a debate chamber." Rumar tugged once on the state seal that hung around his neck and released it with a gesture of disgust. "The council acknowledges your right, Lady Nemiah, for all that earns you. Join us if this is where you think you can best serve."

Nemiah's cheeks burned. She felt like a child scolded for wasting time with dolls. "Uncovering the truth is never useless, Lord Rumar. There will be safety for no one if traitors live in our midst."

"How refreshing," the Minster of the Treasury drawled. "Someone who understands the magnitude of this inquiry."

"Toren, you were preparing to present your evidence," Rumar said. "See to it."

Abrigado uttered a dry comment, and the high chieftain countered, but Nemiah was no longer following their conversation; someone had stepped behind her.

"Welcome, Lady of Avelos."

That dear, familiar voice could still scatter her thoughts and leave an ache of sadness behind. The voice belonged to a man who could only love her on some other Path. After thirteen years, the discovery that Enrian Nadel did not despise her offered little relief. Hatred was the only kind of passion she might ever have from him. His gentle apathy rubbed her heart raw.

"General," she said, pressing a smile to her face. "I thought you would be with the garrison preparing to march south."

"That's where I should be." He cast a look of aspersion toward Abrigado. "I've been warned this inquiry may be a more important battleground than the Sahisten border at the moment."

Like the high chieftain, the general looked as though he had come to Elders' Hall straight from drilling his men. He was clothed not in Forest Guard dress colors but in the plainly cut, deep-green garb of a patrolman. The dark flecks at the edge of one shirt sleeve might have been blood.

He studied Nemiah, his gaze still astute, although the winds had scarred his body. "It's not going to be a safe place for observers. Why have you come?"

She opened her mouth to offer the diplomatic answer, then shook her head. "I'm really not sure."

Elder Trianor cleared his throat. "Lady. General. Your pardon. We're going to begin."

The elder's features revealed only polite welcome when he nodded at Nemiah. If she had been given the chance to speak with him privately, she couldn't say whether she would curse or thank him for turning her attention to Morican's work and opening her eyes to Abrigado's ambitions. She wasn't certain why she had put herself and the temple into this situation. Just what did she expect to accomplish here?

As the men took their seats, Nemiah saw the object of the inquiry for the first time: Toren Abrigado's Shorn scribe Ziabela Marcalo. If Carian had been the picture of arrogant defiance, this woman was the image of submission and despair. Dust and sweat marked the grey tunic and breeches of her scribe's garb. Her curly sable hair hung in tangles to her breasts. The scribe might have possessed a Shorn woman's height, if her shoulders weren't so heavily bowed. Nemiah couldn't see her face, only long dark lashes and the curve of a down-turned cheek that suggested delicate features. A burly City Guard grasped a chain attached to her shackled hands, as though it were within the realm of possibility that she could rebel. The woman was utterly helpless, surrounded by men who controlled her fate. Nemiah felt a swell of empathy toward her.

"Let all present be reminded this is an initial inquiry." Elder Trianor opened a large, age-stained volume and wrote the date on an empty page. "It is not mandatory that a sentence be rendered today. Whatever occurs here may be brought to the full council for further investigation."

Abrigado waved a hand impatiently. "There's no cause to delay. Ziabela Marcalo has used the seal of the treasury to forge official documents and letters in my name." The elder pointed to a sheaf of letters spread across the table. All bore a cracked blue council seal and the mark of the treasury. "She has stolen food and supplies, incited men to riot, and caused the death of innocents. Look for yourself. She is damned by her own hand."

Rumar picked up a letter, examining the seal before reading. "It's a requisition for supplies for three Forest Guard companies. To be delivered to Lieutenants Dirdan, Sevar, and Ren. What's wrong with it?"

Enrian glanced at the letter, and a red scar twitched across his jaw. "We have no Lieutenant Ren." He looked up. "Why do you believe it was this scribe, Toren?"

"Because I caught her at it."

The woman lifted her bound hands, a small nervous gesture to tuck a curl behind her ear. With the motion, her loose sleeves slid up her arms, exposing bruises around her wrists, ugly brown fingerprints on her smooth skin.

The general sat forward, a haunted expression descending over his features. Nemiah could imagine what he was seeing: his own Shorn daughter would have served as a scribe had she lived. Nemiah saw more: the gingerly way the prisoner held herself and the careful way she moved. Nemiah knew what it meant and she seethed over it.

Elder Trianor studied another letter. "What's the purpose of stealing supplies? What's she doing with them?"

Abrigado started to speak, but Rumar waved him to silence. "The accused has the right to answer for herself. Ziabela Marcalo, did you write these letters and requisitions?"

"Yes, sir," she murmured in the ghost of a voice.

Abrigado gloated. "See? She admits her treason readily enough. Perfidy is an art among her kind."

"For what purpose did you write them?" Rumar demanded.

The scribe's head remained bowed. Other than the rapid rise and fall of her chest, she was motionless. Nemiah had the impression she was coming to some decision. After a silence, the woman looked up at the high chieftain. "For the welfare of Avelos."

"What?" Toren's self-satisfied expression evaporated. "You stole provisions from our soldiers for the good of Avelos? You planned riots and planted rumors—"

"We already know the accusations, Elder," Rumar interjected. "I want to know why a Shorn woman would convince Legacy men to spread rumors about the insubordination of Shorn soldiers. Why would she desire to incite Legacy sympathies? Explain what you mean, scribe."

The woman's gaze darted in Abrigado's direction. "I cannot, sir."

"You are accused of a crime for which the sentence is death," said the high chieftain. "I believe you can."

"Tell him," Abrigado growled.

A delicate shudder shook the scribe's shoulders. Her gaze flicked again toward her minister. Her fear of him was palpable. "Forgive me, Lord Rumar. I cannot."

Abrigado exploded out of his seat. "Tell him the truth, you little serpent! You've stolen for your allies in Shorn Circle, haven't you? You've planned to destroy the council. To destroy Avelos! How many Shorn soldiers are a part of your plans? Tell us!"

Red fury mottled the minister's fair features. With each accusation, he took another angry step toward the woman. She shrank from him until she was almost in the arms of the guard behind her.

Elder Trianor's expression filled with dismay. Enrian's lip rose from his teeth in a snarl. Rumar watched with a shrewd eye and remained silent.

"Be certain you will make reparation for your betrayal." Abrigado took another step toward the cowering woman.

Nemiah pounded one hand against the table. "Stop! Leave her be! Fear and torment will not yield the truth."

The Minister of the Treasury turned. Nemiah sensed his rage and the astonishment of the others, but she didn't release Abrigado from her gaze. He must not see her dread or he would finish her.

"Torment will not yield truth," she repeated more calmly. "It yields nothing but the lies you want to hear. You have claimed this inquiry to be a matter of uncovering truth, Elder Abrigado."

The minister hesitated, but must have decided he couldn't win by attacking the Lady of Avelos in front of the others. He offered a condescending smile. "So it is. Only tell me, Lady Nemiah, when you find a serpent in your bed, do you ask it gently why and how it will strike you?"

Cold iron weighted Nemiah's words. "Keep the serpent out of your bed, Elder Abrigado, and you needn't worry about being bitten."

How many ways had he used the woman? Had he gone so far as to force her to write the letters that condemned her? Revealing a traitor among the Shorn scribes would throw the council into disorder and give him a reason to invoke the Law of Integrity. Morican's words rang in Nemiah's head:

> *When the Goddess removes Her Favor from the High Chieftain of the Council of First-Clans, he will know it is time to surrender his rule to one who is more able. However, if he is such a man who is blinded by arrogance or shielded by cunning, the elders of the first-clans may come together—for ever there is more wisdom in the hearts of many men joined than the heart of one man—and they must give their witness to the High Chieftain of his poor leadership. After an open accounting, the High Chieftain shall be cast out and each of the elders must give their vote for the new leader from among themselves. So shall Avelos be guarded from the rule of evil or ignorant men. This is the Law of Integrity.*

Abrigado desired Rumar's place as Warden of the Council of Clans, and he would use the Law to do it. Had Ziabela Marcalo played any part in this game beyond her misfortune to be a scribe for the leader of the Legacy?

Rumar cleared his throat. "Will the accused make any statement in her defense?"

The Minister of the Treasury glowered at the trembling scribe. She shook her head.

"Very well then. Remove her." The high chieftain gestured to the City Guard. "We've had enough of this play."

As the woman was led from the chamber, her gaze drifted upward, landing on Nemiah as lightly and briefly as a moth. Her eyes glistened as green as Nemiah's own. In that instant, Nemiah thought she caught a hint of animation concealed behind the woman's devastated expression.

"If that's all you have, Toren," Rumar began.

"No!" The Minister of the Treasury rocked forward. "Oh no, there's a good deal more. Some of the supplies requisitioned by the false commanders in these letters were retrieved. I've spoken to the merchants myself. Forest Guard patrolmen retrieved them. Shorn patrolmen."

"Indeed." Rumar scrubbed one hand over his eyes. "General?"

"If it's true, it's easy enough to confirm," Enrian said. "Good records are kept when soldiers retrieve garrison supplies. If the records support the elder's allegations, I expect there will be tribunals."

"You think we have time to check records and hold tribunals?" Abrigado looked incredulous. "In days you're marching south—into the very heart of my people's lands in Clan Amerre. Would you lead our armies into Sahiste with conspirators among them? Who knows what other Shorn scribes have dared? Who knows what's taking place in Shorn Circle? We must act! Shorn soldiers must be pulled from the ranks. Every Shorn scribe should be questioned—"

"Do not dictate to me, Toren. I will not move rashly in this."

Abrigado smoothed his hands down his fine coat. He had become bolder than ever since the killing winds struck Velantar. The Legacy's influence swelled as terrified clansmen flocked to that banner with its promise of security. He gave the high chieftain a look of strained patience.

"What would be rash is *not* to move. The Shorn are turning. The Teaching has failed. Shorn patrolmen may very well have used my scribe to garner supplies for their own militia." His frigid gaze fixed on Rumar. "I ask you to think it through, Adan. What will happen when the city learns of this?"

Elder Trianor startled. "You can't start that kind of panic! If the people hear about a Shorn scribe's treason, we'll have clansmen seeking retaliation against innocent Shorn citizens. Shorn Circle will grow treacherous."

"Shorn Circle *is* treacherous! Wasn't it you, Elder Trianor, who told us of the abominations who have survived their failed Becomings and returned to Velantar?"

"Sir, restricting Shorn soldiers means stabling more than five hundred men." Enrian looked grim. "I've already left General Orn with a skeleton force at Aglar Tower in the north and I've reassigned half the companies in the west to bolster the towers at Ravia and Makri. Still, it will be a close thing should Javahari decide to cross the border. I cannot afford to lose able soldiers."

"How can we afford to keep them?" Abrigado asked. "What if they turn on Avelos at the border? What if they resurrect their old alliance with Sahiste in the midst of war?"

"Alliance?" Enrian scoffed. "Elder, do you know what happens to a Shorn soldier if he falls into the hands of Sahisten forces? His scars are an affront to their gods, so the skin is flayed from his back. Then they geld him and cut out his tongue, so he can't despoil their lands with word or seed. After, if he's fortunate, they give him the chance to fall on his sword before they stake what remains of his body to the desert floor as a gift to their creator." Enrian waved a hand over the letters. "I see no evidence of treason here. All I see is evidence of theft and the dissemination of Legacy propaganda in the hands of a man who has a considerable amount to gain from such things."

Abrigado smiled in a slow, sly way that made Nemiah shiver. "To gain?" he replied. "You're right, General. I have everything to gain. The safety of Avelos is at stake. Perhaps we should speak instead of what *you* have to lose. They are your men we're discussing, after all. What have you been teaching them?"

Disbelief shot through Elder Trianor's expression. "Are you accusing the General of the Southern Towers of treason?"

"Interpret it as you will," Abrigado said. "I've been assured this inquiry is about truth, and I'm merely asking questions no one else has dared to ask. For instance, have any explored your part in this, Minister? Ziabela Marcalo is a product of the Teachers you trained. In fact, each one of the Shorn patrolmen who stole supplies would have come from your cadre. And don't let us forget the boy you yourself raised, with all your grand notions of redemption through insight. Tell us, Minister, through what *insight* did your Shorn son learn that men who failed the Becoming are running free in Velantar?"

Rumar strangled the arms of his chair. Abrigado had twisted him into an untenable position. The high chieftain couldn't afford to be seen as offering favor at the expense of the country's safety, yet he must secure the people's safety without appearing to be a puppet of the Legacy. He must deal with accusations against the Shorn while still supporting his Minister of the Teaching, but if it were determined that treachery existed, he would lose the minister, his general, and quite possibly his rule.

"Enough!" Rumar roared. "The scope of these accusations goes well beyond any individual's interests and *I will not act rashly in this!*" He scooped together the letters and shoved them toward Abrigado. "I want all the requisitions, the names of the merchants involved, the records of Forest Guard supply deliveries, and the names of every Legacy man who received a letter at Ravia and Panetar. I want everything you have, Elder Abrigado. Don't think to keep anything back or I'll hold you as culpable as your scribe. General Nadel, I want someone looking into the activities of the *real* lieutenants on these requisitions."

Rumar leaned toward Abrigado, and his face bore a look of such ferocity a wise man would have put some distance between them. "Isn't it remarkable, Toren, that you came upon this evidence just now, when we've so little time to act before our troops move out?"

Abrigado flicked a puff of lint from his sleeve and met the high chieftain's eyes coolly. "Indeed, Adan. I'm relieved I learned of this danger before our armies left for the border."

Nemiah had an image of Rumar balancing on a frail bridge over a violent river. "Very well," he growled. "I'll not be goaded to panic, but neither will I risk the integrity of our defenses. While the council investigates further, Shorn soldiers are relieved of duty. I'll not restrict them to the barracks—not yet—but they're prohibited from carrying weapons within the city walls. I'm extending the ban on

Shorn scribes as well. No one Shorn may enter Elders' Hall or continue to work where there is access to council activities."

Enrian's face remained impassive, but the muscles in his arms flexed, as if beneath the table he clenched his fists.

Elder Trianor looked troubled. "What do we do with the girl in the meantime?"

"She remains in the custody of the City Guard at Aelend Prison," Abrigado said. "She must be kept safe from those who would slay a traitor out of hand. And she must be properly interrogated if we're to learn the entirety of her plans."

Enrian made a sound of protest. "She'll confess to the burning of Altan Mar if you allow the City Guard to interrogate her."

Rumar shook his head. "What alternative is there? Elder Abrigado is correct about one thing: she must be kept alive."

"If I may," Elder Trianor began, "there are other issues to consider. You might recall her family—"

"Those things are of no matter! No traitors shall be shown favor. Regardless of *what family* raised them." Abrigado threw Tierzen a pointed glance.

"Is there no other situation in which she can be securely held?" Tierzen's gaze captured Nemiah's from across the table. She frowned at him. What did he possibly imagine she could do? She was powerless in Elders' Hall among men who disdained Riana's ways.

Riana's ways, but not always her servants. Abruptly, Nemiah recalled that even the leader of the Legacy still found at least one of Riana's priestesses useful.

The laws she left us were meant for the benefit of all.

Elder Trianor hadn't been referring only to the Law of Integrity after all. Morican offered a legal alternative, a dangerous alternative, to the problem of the scribe. Nemiah wondered if at last she had found the reason Tierzen had invited her to this inquiry. Rumar had much to lose if Ziabela Marcalo confessed to participating in a Shorn conspiracy, but the high chieftain couldn't keep the woman safe from Abrigado's reach without appearing to impede the council's investigation. Had Rumar planned all along to use the Lady of Avelos for this purpose? She would be a fool to allow herself to be manipulated. Speaking for the scribe would be declaring open war against Abrigado, and the deadly-clever elder might very well direct the strength of his followers—at least three clans and all the Legacy—against her. It could cost her, and it could cost the temple.

Yet Ziabela Marcalo was traveling toward a sad fate not all of her own making. Nemiah thought of the bruises that marred golden skin, and a spirit cowed by the brutality of powerful men. Nemiah understood that kind of soul-deep dread. It could force a person to take one step and then another off her Path until she traveled a road she never intended to walk.

Nemiah drew herself straight. The back of her chair pressed against her shoulder blades. "By right of the Law of Advocacy, Riana claims custody of the accused."

"Unacceptable!" Abrigado cried. "We cannot set a traitor into a nest of—"

"Watch your tongue," Enrian warned.

"It's not your decision, Toren. It is council law. Ancient law." Rumar's grey eyes probed Nemiah with a look of wary surprise. "Speak your claim, Lady."

"According to Morican's deliberations on council code, any woman named to stand before the high chieftain's chair may claim an advocate from among Riana's servants. In return, that advocate has the right to require compensation be made through service, service that can include personal custody as determined at the discretion of the Lady of Avelos."

"Just so," Elder Trianor said more brightly. "I believe the Minister of the Treasury is quite familiar with Morican's *Deliberations*."

Rumar dusted his hands together. "Good then. Let it be done. The Lady of Avelos has claimed the Right of Advocacy. We are finished here."

Abrigado shot Nemiah a venomous glare. The world rippled, circles within circles in an infinitely expanding pattern. She steadied herself against the table.

"Lady?" Enrian whispered.

She shook her head. She had created a point of influence; her decision was undulating through the Paths, altering the weaving. Perhaps safe from Abrigado's abuses, the woman would answer the questions she so feared to answer in the elder's presence. Perhaps she would find Riana's balance and discover some healing within the temple.

Of course, if Abrigado manufactured a link between the temple and his allegations of treason, nothing more would matter to Nemiah or to Ziabela Marcalo. Traitors were pushed off the city wall.

"You look unwell, Lady. Let me help you."

Steel fingers closed around Nemiah's elbow, startling her from her dark thoughts. Rumar and Elder Trianor were disappearing down the busy corridor, speaking in hushed voices. She had lost track of Abrigado as soon as he left the debate room. That was unwise.

But it was Enrian staring down at her. His eyes, grim and hard in his scarred face, reflected nothing of the concern suggested by his words. She tried to reclaim her arm, but he held her firmly.

"General, I'm quite well—"

"Here's a quiet room," he said, pulling her toward one of the chambers along the hall. "A place for you to gather yourself."

He opened the door and herded her toward the threshold. A group of brown-robed scribes glanced her way. A harried clerk passed by, scrambling to balance an armload of records. Nemiah bit her tongue on a cry for aid. No powerless clerk would step between her and the General of the Southern Towers, and tales of an undignified struggle in Elders' Hall would do her no good.

"How solicitous." She glanced up at the looming soldier to let him see she wasn't cowed. She wished she weren't so painfully conscious of his large hand still wrapped around her arm as she stepped into the chamber.

Cloud-filtered light from a northern window dipped the room in grey. In the center of the room sat a round table with an unlit lamp, a reed with ink, and a decanter of auburn liquor. A small fireplace on the eastern wall held a few dying embers that offered no warmth. The room smelled of pipe smoke and men.

Enrian pulled the door closed behind them and latched it, only then did he release her. "Brandy?" he asked, striding toward the table.

A time had been when she found pleasure in watching him move. He was one of those breed of men with the particular grace that marked all wild creatures, as fluid as one of his Clan Everen stallions. The killing winds had stolen much of that from him. There was strength in him still, but less of grace.

"No brandy. Just tell me why you've brought me here."

He poured a glass for himself, swallowed it in one long draught, and refilled the glass. "I don't think you realize what you've just done."

"I have offered a woman necessary protection."

Enrian shook his head. "Abrigado has too many secrets locked within that girl to let her go."

"Ah, so this is to be a lecture on political strategies?" Nemiah spoke mildly, although her heart was pounding.

"You'd best listen. There are things you need to understand."

"But of course, General Nadel. Shall I kneel at your feet like a novice? Would that please you?"

His glass of brandy smashed against the table and exploded in a fountain of red-gold fragments. Shards scattered across the table, overturning the bottle of ink and threatening the lamp.

"Not now, Nemiah! Not today! Don't you understand what happened in there? Don't you realize what happens next?"

She gaped at him, suddenly uncertain she understood anything.

"Abrigado *wants* war!" He struck the table with one fist, heedless of the broken glass. "Not just war. He wants a war *Rumar can't win*."

"No." Nemiah heard the strain in her tone. "No, there's no order in such a foolish thought. His own clan takes the brunt of any conflict with Sahiste."

"No order?" Enrian laughed, a caustic sound. "You dangerously underestimate the Minister of the Treasury if you think so."

Blood creased Enrian's palm where the glass had cut him. He was not a man easily driven by anger, but helplessness he could not endure. Nemiah remembered that.

"Abrigado wants Rumar crippled. In the council and on the battlefield. He plans to be the one who puts the pieces back together to save us all and earn himself the high chieftain's seat."

"Rumar's a fox, Enrian. If this is true, he must know."

"He can't see it. Not truly. No matter the rivalry between them, Rumar believes Abrigado loves Avelos too well to do her harm. His father had the same blind spot. It seems a flaw of Clan Manitar's line that they must find a reason for trust at the core of any man."

But not any woman, Nemiah thought bitterly. She held her tongue. Enrian was suffering the consequences of Rumar's final judgment and she dared not press him further. Whether removing Shorn soldiers from duty would save Avelos or doom her, Nemiah couldn't guess, but she could guess what it meant to the general for his men to be accused of treason. "They have decimated your forces before you've even reached the battle."

Enrian nodded, a muscle bulging at the corner of his jaw. He halted near the table again, his body poised just at the edge of balance, the stance of a man in combat or a man about to fall.

Nemiah stilled her trembling hands against the soft wool of her dress, finally recognizing why he wanted her here. She knew what he needed: not futile words of comfort or explications on Riana's ways, but only a safe heart that could bear what he revealed. It was an unimagined gift that he still trusted her with so much.

Without speaking, she went to the table and rescued the decanter and two of the remaining glasses from the sticky, inky pool spreading across the wood. The mantel served well enough to hold the glasses as she poured. She took one for herself and went to the window to stare at the blanket of clouds over the city, offering him privacy without solitude.

She knew she had been right to wait when he finally drew a long breath and exhaled softly. His boots drummed across the stone. Chair legs screeched against the floor. She turned to find him sitting with a glass in his hand, watching her.

"I'm sorry, Lady. That was never intended for you. Will you forgive me?"

His expression was open, guileless; he appeared to genuinely care what she felt. She didn't indulge herself with hopeless interpretations of that fact. She glanced toward the mess on the table.

"It's no wonder you can't convince Madam Nadel to move to Velantar with you, Enrian. No doubt she's tired of cleaning up the wreckage after you explain council affairs."

He stared at her, and she held her breath, uncertain whether she had spoken too sharply or made a mistake in mentioning his wife. Then his expression changed and he tilted his head back to laugh.

For a brief moment, she heard amusement in the warm, full sound. She smiled a little and took another drink. Then they faced one another in a quiet that held too many recollections to be entirely companionable. The brandy slid down Nemiah's throat like smooth fire.

"War is inevitable, then?"

Enrian drained his own glass and set it aside. "Rumar says not. He believes a show of strength in the south will convince King Javahari not to take offense at our rejection of his bid for open borders."

"I know what Rumar believes. You're not convinced."

He made a gesture of frustration. "Five years ago, I would have advised against such a show. Javahari would have perceived the increase in our border defenses as a challenge to prove himself. Sahiste was easy to predict when retribution was the primary goal. Javahari's tactics have changed. There are others influencing him now: the nephew-heir, Prince Ashani; his new allies in Laebek. Javahari's grown subtler, more complex." Enrian paused and shook his head.

Nemiah hadn't considered Sahiste's new alliance; the union with Laebek had been so unexpected. "If it comes to war, we'll be battling the Laebeki army as well?"

"Probably. The border nations are slipping free of the chains of the past. Not just Sahiste and Laebek. I've had reports that even little Sona is sending smugglers into Avarel Forest. We're the only ones who haven't changed. The others have grown stronger with new connections, while we remain alone. They won't let us stay that way. If it's not Sahiste this fall, then one or more of the others will come for us. Soon."

The Paths undulated under Nemiah. She leaned against the casement. "And when they come, will Rumar have enough votes in the council to hold his seat against the Legacy?"

"Ah. Now I'm afraid you've mistaken me for a statesman." Enrian offered her his detached smile. "I don't have Rumar's or Trianor's ability to predict the council's actions. All I can offer is a soldier's guess."

"I would bet on your guess against most men's certainty. Can Rumar unite the clans around our common enemy?"

"Unite them, Lady? When in history has our council ever been united . . .?"

She saw him think of it just as she did, and his eyes filled with regret. The last time the council had been united in purpose, Marinen Tumal was the high chieftain and the enemy had been the Avelune. Hundreds of Riana's servants had been murdered for fear they were part of Lady Amalia's conspiracy. Nemiah sometimes thought she heard their screams echoing along empty temple corridors.

"Rumar is not Lord Tumal," Enrian murmured. "For better or worse. The central clans will stay with him. They're tied to Clan Manitar by the waterman's guild. But he's already lost the south, and the west is probably too small to make a difference. It's going to come down to the northern five."

Nemiah sipped her brandy, thinking. "That doesn't bode well. Aglar and Lasla are furious at Rumar for his push to limit clan rights."

"None of the five are happy with Rumar, but they don't trust Abrigado's centralist tendencies, either. And they resent northern silver going into southern garrisons. It's impossible to tell which way they'll turn."

"I'm sure they spare no love for you for baring their defenses."

"They hate me," Enrian admitted. "And I can hardly blame them. They're afraid of Amurian opportunists raiding their unprotected villages. They've a right to be afraid. I fear it myself. If we have to fight on three fronts, we're done."

His chair creaked as he leaned back and scrubbed his hands over his face. Nemiah wondered when he'd last slept. Even now, she might have crossed the room, laid a hand on his shoulder, and offered him Riana's peace. Even now, she knew he would reject her.

He straightened and opened his eyes. "You've endured more than I've had the right to ask of you, Nemiah. I wonder, do you have it in your heart to grant me one more favor?"

She flushed, overwhelmed by the sense that he had read her thoughts. What was this perverse need that kept her longing for things so far from her proper Path? It was a dangerous way to deal with Enrian Nadel. "If I'm able."

"Go to Rumar. Speak with him. He's in need of what gifts you might offer."

The sound of bitter surprise that escaped her throat could hardly have been called laughter. "You want me to walk into the bear's den and offer myself as his dinner?"

"Oh, Nemiah," Enrian sighed. "You can't deceive me by playing the persecuted. If you despise him so, why haven't you tried to organize your allies against him? You could do it. The west would go with you, and maybe even a few from the north. With the Legacy holding the south, you could enact the Law of Integrity yourself. Right now."

"I'm not fool enough to believe Toren Abrigado would serve Avelos or Riana any better than Rumar."

"That's not it. You might have found a man to stand for you in the council. Someone you could control. Whatever you've been doing since last spring to strengthen your alliances, it's paid off. I hear that Elder Nadro of Nadaren is so devoted he's petitioned the council to lift the ban on the Tests of Rona. Clan Ontera's elder would fall on his sword for you if you but smiled at him."

"You've spent quite a bit of time thinking on men I could make my own, Enrian."

He didn't rise to her taunt. "You know the truth, Nemiah. You play at this show of mutual animosity with Rumar, but you know he's given himself to Avelos no less than you have."

"Play? Is that what you see? I've contended with threats against the temple since the hour I was Chosen. Last spring, Rumar accused me of conspiring with the Legacy! You yourself warned he would use me as a scapegoat if we failed to stop the killing winds. Now I should risk going to him? Let him seek Riana in the first circle like anyone else."

"The temple and Riana offer nothing he needs," the general said, still calm. "He needs someone who will truly listen. I admit, he's a difficult man, but you've the strength and spirit to match him." Enrian paused. His voice grew quieter. "I have cause to know. It was a gift you gave me all those years ago. You have a talent for recognizing a man's need and an honest heart to hear it. Whatever the machinations of Lady Pahlina, I know what you offered me was true."

He went silent. Nemiah wondered if he could see her spirit breaking apart. "Is this a game, Enrian? Some bet with Elder Trianor to see how far you can force the temple to bend?"

"It's about balance, Lady. Adan is brilliant, but he has no patience and he moves too fast for the clans. If his Aviya had lived, she might have steadied him. If he had taken another consort and gotten an heir—"

Blood suffused her face. "You dare too much!"

The general held up his hands to ward off her protest. "I'm only saying that so much conflict in the council might have been avoided if he had stepped more carefully. I know you see the cliff edge he's walking. With the threat of war, it's going to grow narrower. He needs someone with the grace he lacks to keep him from falling."

Enrian was telling her things he shouldn't now, giving her words she could use against him. She had often hoped for such trust. She never dreamed it could hurt so deeply. "He has you as advisor and friend. You offer what he needs."

"I don't. I'm no asset to him with the clans. The north and south openly despise me. Clan Everen and the other central clans I might deliver are already his."

She set her glass down on the casement. "You started by warning me about Abrigado. That wasn't the warning I needed."

He winced at that, but she knew he wouldn't withdraw. For thirteen years, she had watched him sacrifice his own heart for Avelos; it would never occur to him to shelter hers. "Will you do it, Lady?"

She turned toward the window and the gloomy light falling across the broken city. She was no longer a new priestess under the order of Lady Pahlina; she could make decisions for herself. Despite the heartache and fear, a part of her wondered what would happen if she tried once more to offer Rumar the wisdom of a Pathwalker. For a moment, it felt as if Leita was with her, encouraging her to leap beyond the short portion of the Path she could see toward the possibilities of the unknown. Then Nemiah was alone again, and the man who would forever own a part of her spirit was waiting for her to say she would seek the confidence of another.

It began to rain. Drops struck the windows and slipped down the glass.

"I'll go to him," she heard herself answer. "I don't know what might possibly come of it, but I'll go."

"When?"

She turned to face him. "I don't know, Enrian. Not today. I've only just taken in a Shorn prisoner accused of treason. One deadly step at a time."

He opened his mouth, closed it, then let out a breath. "Don't wait too long, Nemiah. Even if my men can hold off Sahiste, I don't know that Avelos will survive the destruction of the council."

Nemiah nodded, staring beyond him at the shattered glass on the table. She thought of the killing winds, the fractious council, and the threat of war. They had entered a time of destruction. She wondered whether unity between the high chieftain and the Chosen Lady was possible in such a time, or if she had just made a promise that would break her into pieces.

9.
MIRROR OF NIGHT

"You're back, Lady. Finally. Come inside. I've news." The silver-haired, grey-eyed Keeper of the Shadow Guards shifted restively at the doorway to Nemiah's apartments. "By the goddess, we must get you out of that damp cloak. You're pale as death."

"A moment, Kaliska. A moment. Badgering won't make the spheres turn faster." Nemiah wasn't certain the old saying was true of the tall sturdy woman before her. Kaliska often found ways to chivvy others into doing what she wanted of them. The skill served her well in her disparate duties as spy keeper, temple healer, and Mistress of Guardians, who cared for women in childbirth and named those who must be Shorn.

A hint of woodsmoke and incense drifted up as Nemiah opened the door to her tower. In the dusky haven of her private receiving room, she shrugged out of her cloak and handed it to Merisel, who scampered up the spiral stairs with it. Capalino hurried over to offer a slobbery greeting and lean his large body against her legs. Nemiah balanced against him for a moment, still stunned by the inquiry and by Enrian Nadel. Rom was on his way to retrieve Ziabela Marcalo from the City Guard at Aelend Prison. Her Arionad had taken the order with less reluctance than Nemiah had predicted, perhaps because he'd been too upset over Abrigado's veiled threats. She hadn't told him of her meeting with the general.

Kaliska uttered a quiet sound. "Are you all right, Lady?"

"Yes, yes." Nemiah blinked and drew back to prevent Capa from knocking her over. The spy keeper had turned up the lamps and was holding out a shawl. Nemiah pulled the summer-green wool around her shoulders. "What have you to report?"

"It can wait a little longer," Kaliska said, although her tight expression suggested otherwise. "Sit first. Merisel will bring something for you to eat."

"Don't bother with food. All I need is a cup of boldblood."

"You've had enough boldblood from the looks of it." The healer reached into her satchel and withdrew a small vial of thick, dark liquid. She handed it to

Nemiah. "Drink this. Merisel tells me you're hardly sleeping, and she hasn't seen you eat a full meal since before Dawnings' Eve."

Nemiah looked at the restorative and set it aside. "Hasn't she? Well, it's not something little girls need worry over. Neither should you. Your news?"

The older woman inclined her head, but let the issue go. "Lady, things are bad in the city. It may be time to consider leaving Velantar."

"Unnecessary and impossible. I've a temple full of homeless families to care for and a city full of fear." *And a promise to Enrian Nadel.*

"Nemiah, now that people have had time to realize how much they've lost to the killing winds, it's not just Rumar who's the target of hostility."

"The temple too? Well, that's no surprise, I suppose. People never see what's being done to help them, only what's not being done. We'll endure."

The spy keeper sat down beside her. "There's been rioting in the lower circles. It's more than just angry, grieving clansmen or Legacy propaganda. It's . . ." The older woman's clear gaze held Nemiah's own. "Lady, last night Riana's fountain in Shorn Circle was filled with blood."

The room lurched into a slow spin.

Starlight reflected from the glossy black surface of the fountain's basin. The rich, fertile scent of blood filled her head. At her feet, a man in white lay pale and still.

Nemiah leaped back from the Gate and the terrible vision faded. Kaliska narrowed her eyes.

"It's nothing," Nemiah croaked, waving off the woman's questions before she could voice them. "Tell me of the fountain. It was a new moon last night."

"Yes. It was." Kaliska looked Nemiah up and down and frowned. "When I report what information I have, perhaps then you'll share what it is that ails you. What you'd rather your healer not know."

Despite the lingering image of death, or perhaps because of it, Nemiah found Kaliska's concern precious. She smiled a little. "You know, I've never wondered why Pahlina made you the Keeper of the Shadow Guards."

The silver-haired woman gave a snort. "No one else was foolish enough to take up the job."

"What I mean is that I've held nothing back from you of concern to the Shadows. With Carian's exile, there are too many sisters I dare not trust. You are not one of them. I trust you as Pahlina did."

The woman who wore so many faces in the service of Riana turned away from Nemiah and picked up a poker to rouse the fire. "The day you lose that trust, Lady, you must release me from my duties. I cannot serve you otherwise." She stabbed hard at a glowing log and it rolled over with a thud. A vine of flame sprouted up from the wood.

"Then see I never have reason for it," Nemiah said. "I cannot afford to lose my healer, spy keeper, and Mistress of Guardians all at once, maddening as she may be." As tendrils of warmth unfurled into the room, Nemiah leaned into them. "Tell me of the fountain. Was it . . .?"

"A Mirror of Night." Kaliska wiped her sooty hands on a cloth. "At least the start of one. Someone is trying to tap the demon's power."

"Ah Goddess. Cael's followers haven't dared to raise their heads for years. The Bearers have kept such careful guard."

"Cael's people are never driven out, only driven deeper," Kaliska replied. "Even during their waning days, they still had a frightening reach."

"The death of Pahlina's sister?"

"The slaying. Cael's people poisoned Pahlina's sister and her Arionad."

"Do you know who dared the Mirror?"

"Not yet." Kaliska shook her head. "We've a possibility. There have been a number of recent thefts in the homes of elders known for the quality of their libraries. I wouldn't have taken much note of it, but for a strange piece of knowledge from one of my Shadows in the Circles of the Lost. Do you know Efren Iyal?"

"By name only. He's a clan elder from one of the northern five. Clan Avien?"

"Aglar," Kaliska said. "Clan Aglar didn't attend the fall gathering in Velantar, yet this man was seen wandering in the Circles of the Lost. A bit far from home, yes?"

"Not only in miles." An elder of the northern five wouldn't deign to walk among those who had lost their clans.

"Iyal met with a young man we identified only by chance. He studied for a time at the temple in Ravia. He would have been an Arionad, but was driven out for blasphemy a year ago. His name is Ranz. He serves the Clan Amerre clanguard now."

"An elder of Clan Aglar and a clanguard of Clan Amerre?" Nemiah thought of Enrian's prediction about the importance of the north. "The north and south have no use for one another; their political interests are as distant as their lands. What were they doing?"

"Iyal presented Ranz with a small crate of books," Kaliska said.

"The stolen texts?"

"Perhaps." The spy keeper formed a perfect spiral. "There are those in the world who believe Cael, not Arion, should be Riana's consort. There are others who believe Cael should rule alone. They may see this time of chaos as an opportunity to call the demon's strength."

"First, they must have the prayers and skills to do it. You think these men are searching for magics not cleansed by Tumal's purges?"

Few priestesses still lived who had witnessed the hatred Cael's cults could manifest against the goddess. Kaliska was one. Nemiah knew it the way she also knew what the cults would do to a priestess on a festival night and what uses they had for the body of an Arionad: the stories had been passed to her by Lady Pahlina, who was Chosen before her.

"Someone discovered how to begin a Mirror of Night," Kaliska said. "They must possess some source of knowledge that escaped the purges."

"I miss you, little dove."

Nemiah gasped and bit the inside of her lip to push back the lurid flames of the Gate.

"I know," Kaliska murmured, mistaking her distress. "I have Shadows working to learn who's involved. With such disorder in the city, most of our chains of information have been destroyed. I'd like you to consider leaving. Just *think* on it." She lifted a hand as Nemiah began to protest. "You could go to Lady Ansa in Panetar. She would welcome you, and Clan Delsio is only half a day's ride, after all."

It would be good to see Ansa. Nemiah had promised to visit Panetar before winter, and there was comfort to be found with the sharp-tongued, quick-witted old woman. Ansa had learned much in her years, but she never begrudged Nemiah's inexperience, not like Mistress of Maps Bena. It took effort for Nemiah to shake her head. "I can't leave. What message would it send if order fled before the threat of chaos? More practically, what do you think would happen to my seat here in Velantar should I abandon it?"

The spy mistress ran a hand over her straight silver hair, frowning. Nemiah could see her formulating another argument.

"Does Abrigado have anything to do with this, Kaliska? It's his clanguard that may be meddling with the demon."

Kaliska sighed and let herself be redirected. "I wish I could answer you better. We have no evidence for it yet. How would you judge the man? Is it in him to associate with Cael's followers?"

Nemiah considered the Minister of the Treasury. He was cold enough to torment a powerless woman and cunning enough to worry men of such strength as Enrian Nadel and Tierzen Trianor, yet no stain of disorder showed in him. He had no care for Riana, yet Nemiah had seen his face when he accused Ziabela Marcalo of treason: he truly feared for Avelos. "He believes his cause is just. He can be cruel, but I don't believe he is evil."

Kaliska nodded. "I promise to bring news to you as soon as we have it."

A loud knock on the outer door prevented Nemiah from replying. As Rom's gruff voice announced his return, relief washed over her with unexpected intensity. She called for him to enter.

The Captain of the Arionade pushed back the cowl of his cloak as he offered a spiral to Nemiah and then to the healer. The scent of leather and wet wool filled the space around him. Raindrops sparkled like silver beads across his shoulders and in his dark beard.

"We've brought back the scribe, my lady. We found some space in the travelers' quarters for her. Two of my best guard the door."

"Was there trouble with the City Guard?" Nemiah asked.

"They weren't overeager to give her up. Their captain calls himself a friend to Elder Abrigado and strutted about as if it would please him to test us. Word came from the high chieftain just after our arrival. They let her go quick enough then."

"Good. There's sufficient enmity between us without my Arionade brawling with the City Guard. Did the woman speak?"

"Only to beg me to bring her music—a flute. I saw no harm in it, and she clutched it like a talisman all the way across town, poor thing." Rom shook his head. "Whatever she's done, they've made her pay."

"She needs our care. I would have her know the temple will protect her from unjust torments."

Kaliska peered intently at Rom. "Did the City Guard say what they'd learned from her during their interrogation? Anything of her letter writing or alleged conspirators?"

"Later for your questions, Kaliska." Nemiah laid a hand on the healer's shoulder. "Go care for the girl. She needs peace first."

"Very well, Lady. With your permission."

"If she speaks to you," added Nemiah, "I want to hear of it. It won't serve us to forget she has been charged with crimes nearly as grave as those of her ancestors."

The healer paused. "It was a generous thing you did, Lady, taking the woman out of Abrigado's hands. Not everyone in the temple will be pleased by it. They're going to say you've brought danger to our door."

Nemiah's lip twisted. "They will be correct."

"But Riana knows the balance in it. We must endure some risk to ourselves in order to stop the suffering of others."

"Indeed, Madam Healer. Which is exactly why the Lady of Avelos will stay where she belongs, here in Velantar."

"As you say." Kaliska bowed her head.

"Good night, my lady." Rom turned to follow the healer.

"Stay, Captain. I must speak with you."

Her Arionad raised a granite-colored brow. "Of course."

He closed the door after Kaliska, and the room grew quiet. Rain pattered against the windows. Nemiah tried to order her thoughts. She must tell Rom about Kaliska's report. Because of his devotion to the Lady, he and his men were likely to become targets for those who worshipped disorder. The cults despised the Arionade as much as they despised Riana herself. Their hatred dragged at Nemiah. She swayed.

Rom began to move, his fingers reaching for his dagger, alarm written on his face. "My lady, what is it? Are you slipping?"

"No, Captain," she sighed. "It's not the Gate. Put away your blade."

He stared at her unhappily. "Oh, my lady. What did they do to you? I should have been with you at Elders' Hall."

"I told you I needed to go alone. I made my own choice."

"Abrigado wouldn't have dared to threaten you if I had been there."

Her Arionad stood before her, stalwart and righteous. More than anything, Nemiah wanted to lean against his solid form and let his strength support her. She was so small: how could she possibly battle the hatred growing in Avelos? She longed to release her fear in a place where it would not be used against her, where someone might reassure her that her inadequacy was an illusion. Instead, with one well-intended sentence, Rom had proved it true.

"Is it so very clear the Lady of Avelos has no authority without her Arionad's sword behind her?"

"What?" The captain's fierce expression faltered. "No. That's not what I—"

"And if Carian were Chosen, would she need an Arionad to help her stand straight before the men of Avelos?"

"If Carian were Chosen she would have refused Elder Trianor's invitation as a point of unbending pride," Rom said. "My lady, what are you doing?"

"Carian owns the strength to say no to the council. She would not be a pawn for Adan Rumar."

"Carian is a fool who would have given up a girl to torture and thrown away a chance to build an alliance with the high chieftain!" Rom crossed the final steps to reach her, so close Nemiah could feel the cold still lifting off his cloak and smell the salt of the day's labors on him. "Nemiah Gabriana, do you dare to question the choice I made on Dawnings' Eve?"

She released a sharp breath, her anger draining from her. Rom's choice to remain loyal had forced him to kill four of his own men. "No. I have no right. None at all."

"My lady, what is it? Riana herself did not fight Cael alone. Why do you insist that you must?"

She closed her eyes. Where she should have found serenity and strength inside her, only darkness waited. Rom had bound himself to her, to this growing abyss. "I am sorry, Captain."

"Nemiah, will you not even look at me and give me an answer?"

Oh, my Arionad, if you fight beside me, I will be your ruin.

The thought formed with sudden, perfect clarity in Nemiah's mind. It was no gift of knowledge from Riana or vision from beyond the Gate, but only a moment of understanding. Rom's devotion to her would be the end of him, and she was obliged to allow him to follow his chosen Path.

With a trembling finger, she traced Riana's spiral over his heart. "Your place is at my side, even as Lord Arion stood at the side of the Lady, shielding her from the demon. Let this affirmation of your oath be answer enough."

"Forgive me, my lady, I cannot." He reached for her hand and reverently touched her fingers to his lips. "I must know why my service grieves you. Riana did not mourn her captain's loyalty."

"And I am not the Great Lady!" She pulled her hand free and stood. "Leave it be, Rom! We've no time to indulge our doubts and fears. The demon is in our midst."

She marched away from his shocked expression and up the twisting staircase to her bedchamber and study. It was a relief to find that Merisel had already stirred the fire in the upper hearth; the rising heat made it warmer than the receiving room. Nemiah paced past her bed and desk to the window overlooking the inner courtyard. Rom would follow, because he was bound to the Lady of Avelos and because he loved her. He would always follow, yet her heart would never be quite where it should be, but wandering toward one who could offer her nothing. How did that possibly fit Riana's order? After several moments, Rom's footsteps echoed on the stairs. She continued to stare at the withered garden as he shed his cloak and weapons.

"Sit," she ordered him. "There is news from the Shadows."

He complied, his brittle silence betraying his frustration and hurt. Nemiah kept her eyes on the dead Ulaye tree at the courtyard's heart. She told him of the spy keeper's report, all they didn't yet know and all they suspected. Then she shared what she knew of Cael's cults. Pahlina had given her no written knowledge of the cults; no Chosen Lady since the Exile had dared to validate the ugly works of Cael's disciples by setting them to paper. Pahlina had passed on the whispered stories of horrible crimes and terrible power. Despite Nemiah's intention to remain hard and distant, her voice began to quaver. She stopped.

"It will be well, my lady. I do not fear their darkness."

"Ah, Rom, but I do." She turned and found him standing an arm's length away, his eyes filled with concern.

Perhaps if she were stronger, she could find a way to reject his oath and send him away. But Goddess forgive her, she was not strong or brave. She needed his courage.

She moved toward him and his arms opened for her. His body was warm and unyielding as she stretched to kiss him. It was a full moon past Dawnings' Eve; no sacrifice was required of her Arionad before he could touch her. Yet it was no gift she offered him. She would take everything. His mouth lowered to hers, gentle and reassuring. As his hands gathered her close, she was certain he didn't yet know what these moments would cost him.

They did not kindle the urgent passion of Dawnings' Eve. Nemiah created a prayer of each bittersweet caress that she might keep Rom safe from Cael. Rom moved carefully, seeking consent in her gaze before he led her to the bed, before he roused her body with his lips and calloused hands. He entered her with the reverence of a man breaching the surface of a sacred pool, and for a moment, the chill inside her surrendered to a small flame of hope.

After, Nemiah lay with Rom's arm around her, while his fingers lazily twirled a strand of her hair. They had woven a precious moment of peace, and she held herself from sleep to appreciate it.

"I haven't had the chance to tell you," Rom murmured, his voice drowsy, "Dree has sent a gift to the temple."

She shifted to smile at him. "Your niece is generous. What has she sent?"

Rom flushed. Speaking of his family, a loud and cheerful bunch who differed from him in all ways but perhaps their capacity for loyalty, was one of the few things Nemiah had ever seen discomfit him. "It is, in fact, a gift for Capalino."

Nemiah's smile turned to a laugh. Last spring, Rom's young niece Dree had traveled down from the village of Murita near Parnas Pass to visit family in the city and spend several days in the temple. During that time, she had come to adore the temple hounds, particularly Capa, who had been only too pleased to take whatever treats the girl offered. "Capa's certain to be grateful, especially if it includes a shank of Murita lamb."

Rom's black eyes caught the candlelight and he tugged at the strand of her hair wound around his fingers. "It's a collar of silver link. The first she's forged. She's showing the family's skill with metals. Although I think her calling is to fine work rather than to the anvil." His tone warmed with pride. "I will leave it for you tomorrow."

Nemiah kissed his cheek and tucked her head against his shoulder. "Thank you. Truly, Rom. Your family brightens the Path."

It could be like that sometimes. In rare moments they shaped for themselves, they would speak of their kin or share tales from childhood and laugh about small things. In that simple warmth, Rom was more than Captain of the Arionade and Nemiah felt right and strong on her Path. She sometimes wondered whether those few perfect moments brought more healing to the weaving than all her days struggling as high priestess.

Rom kissed her forehead and held her close until she finally drifted to sleep. She dreamed of nothing more significant than sleek hounds wearing silver chains, chasing hares across the valley.

When she awoke, she was alone again. She slid up in bed, shivering in the darkness, the blanket clutched to her breast. Rom's gear and cloak were gone. Only his scent lingered faintly on her skin. A pang ran through her, as though she had already lost him.

"Enough!" she chided herself aloud. She pushed away the covers and climbed out of bed. "Don't create a Path by dwelling on what need not be."

Naked and trembling, she hurried to the clothes chest on the other side of the room. She pulled a thick wool shift over her head and drew on heavy stockings. She tied her green wrap around her shoulders and took her cloak, mostly dry, from where Merisel had spread it near the hearth.

In the receiving room, a single lamp cast its glow across the rugs and the heavy furniture. Capa awoke, and with a guilty look in his amber eyes, slunk off her chair.

"A walk?" she suggested.

The big, brindled hound shook himself from soft ears to thick tail; then turned a quick circle and looked up at her with a wide-mouthed grin.

She laughed. "I thought so."

They left the tower and traveled along the arched passage to the east wing. Other than the tap of her slippers and the click of Capalino's claws, silence blanketed the stone halls. A few hanging lamps shed wan light over the carved walls and the doors to the priestesses' quarters. All the novices were long in their beds and the sisters asleep or studying in their cells. The three Arionade on the east-wing nightwatch straightened as Nemiah passed. Their sober expressions spoke of the burden of their brethren's recent infidelity. Near the archive, one man made a proper spiral.

Other than the first circle, the archive was the only temple entrance eternally under guard, for within the hall lay the map room, which held the surviving maps of every sacred journey from every Pathwalker since the Exile. The maps were as precious as the Mapmaker, Mistress Bena. Without them, the sisters couldn't begin to understand the complex relationships among Riana's infinite ways, and without that knowledge, the Lady of Avelos couldn't make decisions about how to change the course of any Path. The stocky old guard held his spiral as Nemiah approached.

"Good evening, Arnas."

"Good even t'ya, Lady."

"A quiet watch, I hope."

He eyed Capalino and glanced back at Nemiah. "It's a damp night. No one wants t'be in the halls who has no need t'be."

"No fear, all is well." Nemiah gifted him with the answer to his unasked question. A man of the old guard, Arnas wouldn't ask for anything of the Lady. Nemiah had known him since she came to the temple. He had been kind when she was only an awkward, homesick child. "Capa wanted a walk and I wanted a moment with Lord Arion. We're going to the inner courtyard."

The guard nodded gravely. "A'course, Lady. The lord's not shining bright t'night, but he's up there all the same. He knows what care you've taken t'respect the choices of his brothers—even when their choices were poor ones."

Not an ounce of irony or accusation hid in the man's tone. He meant it. Despite Carian's efforts to turn the Arionade, Arnas was one who remained loyal.

"Thank you, Lord Arionad."

"Riana bless your ways, Lady."

From the archive, Nemiah turned into the narrower hall leading to the loggia that encircled the courtyard. Cold air, heavy with the sweet scent of autumn rot, breezed down the passage. Capa's ears pricked forward. Tail whipping, he trotted ahead, then disappeared between the massive columns into the hedges.

Nemiah followed more slowly along the path that formed an elegant spiral to the center of the garden. In spring and summer, cobalt jeminy and crimson houndspaw grew in the shade of the thick, glossy hedges that defined the spiral. Each path was so densely bounded that fifteen priestesses could walk the garden at once and never encounter one another. The clarity and simplicity of it could hold Nemiah together even when she gazed up at the vastness of the sacred skies.

Tonight, the spiral was thin and ragged from the bite of the cold and the razors of the killing winds. She reached the garden's heart, the dead Ulaye tree, and lifted one hand to stroke the grey trunk. Pieces of bark flaked away under her fingers. Ularian no longer sheltered here or guarded this garden, not since the Exile. The immortal spirit of Riana's Aye archer had been extinguished from this place on the day the Avelune temple leaders betrayed their people.

Nemiah's fingers curled against the tree trunk. If Lady Amalia and her Higher Circle had known how their treachery would rip through the Paths, would they still have allowed greed to move them? If Carian had known four men would die here, would she still have tried to oust Nemiah from her place? So much bloodshed and hatred—so much to feed Cael's hungers—all for the weaknesses of Riana's servants. Sometimes Nemiah could very well understand the Legacy's contempt for the temple. The Lady's priestesses had not taken care with her people.

Something beat the air above her. Nemiah glanced up to see a raven alighting on a branch, its wings arching for balance. Swiftly, she drew a spiral to ward against Cael's messenger. The bird only shifted its weight from foot to foot and cocked its head thoughtfully. Its silver eyes gleamed. A serpent dangled from its beak.

"I've always found this courtyard too confining to be comfortable, but it still saddens me to see it withering away."

Nemiah yelped and spun around. White flashed among the hedges—hedges drooping with wilted summer foliage.

"Who's there?" The sense of a warm smile blossomed in her head and she caught the scent of herbs.

"Hello, my dove."

"Lady?" Nemiah thrilled at the wonder of returning to this woman, a woman with the power and compassion of the goddess. But her delight drowned in a wave of apprehension as she realized what had happened: she had fallen onto the

Paths, again. The Gate had opened, unbidden and uncontrolled, and she couldn't even remember just when or where she had left her body.

"Lia?"

"Yes, it's me. You heard me calling, you clever thing."

"I . . . don't think so." Nemiah glanced up at the Ulaye tree. The raven was gone. Had it existed on this Path or her own Path or another Path altogether?

"Didn't you sense my will and come to answer me?" Lia asked. "Or was it your guide who showed you the way? There's no shame in that. I just thought since opening doors gives you trouble, your skill must be tracking. You seem to have a strength for it."

"No, I don't have the strength for it! I'm not clever or strong. Something's wrong with me. I can't keep the Gate closed anymore. I fall to the Paths without control, and when I do . . . I usually end up finding you." Nemiah wrapped her arms around herself and huddled there, desperately wishing she could close the right door to prevent Lia from witnessing her humiliation.

"Oh no, little one. Please don't wish such things. Don't wish me away."

Nemiah looked around the garden, straining to see the woman. "I despise that you must know the truth of me."

"Here, dove. Hush now. You've no need to hide yourself."

The ethereal impression of a tall, straight figure moved out of the hedges. Nemiah saw only flashes and shadows of her. Moonlight from some other Path gleamed on black hair and shone in eyes the color of shadows on snow. More shadows fluttered behind her. Quiet footsteps approached Nemiah and stopped.

"Tell me what's happening, little one. Is your Path nearing Dawnings' Eve?"

Nemiah bowed her head. Beside the tall, elegant woman she felt small and absurd. "One moon past. I blamed my weakness on the converging Paths for a long while, but in truth, the first time I fell was in the prime of spring."

A light puff of air brushed Nemiah's face, as though someone had settled beside her. "What of the other Pathwalkers on your road? Have they suffered too?"

"The Bearer isn't permitted to travel her own journeys, but she has never fallen uncontrolled."

"And the others?" Lia asked.

"There are no others."

"I mean among the clan temples and chapterhouses."

Nemiah bit her lip and shook her head.

"None?" Lia breathed. "How can that be?"

A leaf fell from somewhere above to land at Nemiah's feet. It was yellowed and desperate for water. "Riana is withdrawing her touch from my Path. When I am gone, it is likely there will be none who can reach her."

The other priestess was quiet, but deep concern radiated from the space she occupied.

"What is it?" Nemiah asked. "Please share what you know. So much knowledge has already been lost to me."

Nemiah sensed the other woman's frown. "The infinite weaving connects all Paths, dove. When one strand is torn, all of us feel the shift to different degrees. I start to wonder what it means that you have come to me over and again. I start to wonder why we both battle against the devastation of Avelos. What point of influence has been crossed that causes Pathwalkers to vanish?"

"Lia, it's past time."

A low voice tickled Nemiah's ear like a soft breath.

"Soon, Ambri," the other priestess whispered. *"I promise."*

"Someone else is here!" Nemiah darted a glance around the garden.

"No fear," Lia murmured. "My guide hovers like a mother hen. Dove, I must think on what you've told me. In the meantime, promise me you will take greater care with the Paths. Falling is dangerous."

"I do know that." Nemiah looked down. "I know I've been lucky not to lose myself."

"I don't mean only for you, little one. I mean for the weaving. We aren't meant to go tumbling about without care and planning. It's like knocking your hand through a spider's web. Destructive."

"Come, my love," the new voice whispered. *"You've traveled too long and your trail grows cold."*

Lia smiled faintly. *"But what barrier a cold trail to the one who guides Riana's Chosen?"*

Despite the woman's light tone, Nemiah began to sense her weariness and anxiety. "I did not mean to burden you with my troubles. What of your own search for Sabela's temple? Have you had any word?"

A hand stroked Nemiah's hair. "Not yet. People are still dying and unrest grows. If we find no way to stop the suffering, I fear Avelos will tear itself apart. Your news is . . . Well, we have much to think about, you and I."

"I must see you again," Nemiah said. "You are the truest source of knowledge I have. We must speak—"

"My lady, please!"

"Calm, Captain. I am coming. It will be well."

"Carry yourself safely home, little one." Soft lips pressed against Nemiah's brow.

Lia's presence winked out like the last star at sunrise. Nemiah didn't wait to be thrown among the Paths; she found the blue flames of the Gate and leaped through. Reeling, she forced herself to turn and lock it with the skills Lady Pahlina had given her. She prayed that, at least for the moment, they would be enough.

10.
STORIES AND SONGS

"When is she, Mapmaker? When is my Lia? And when could an Arionad possibly serve as a guide?"

Nemiah lay against the wall of the east passageway. Arnas had retrieved Bena to record her sacred journey. Now the ancient Mapmaker glowered down at her. "That's a quick way to sloppy mapmaking," the woman snapped. "You've given me nothing to prove Ambri is an Arionad."

Not until Nemiah related the journey aloud had she realized why Lia and Ambri's interactions felt so familiar. "He's not only an Arionad. He is *her* Arionad. The Path belongs to Lady Lia and her sworn. That should tell you something about Time, as well as Perspective and Parallel."

Bena gave a dismissive snort. "Don't tell me my business. I've been mapping for more years than you've walked this Path."

"I'll not argue your mapping skills, Mistress, but you're not a Pathwalker. There are elements your transcription cannot capture. Use what I've given you. Everything I've given you. Then show me the map you've drawn and what repetitions exist for Lia's Path."

"Repetitions! Come, Lady, even you know better. The Paths are infinite. We're as likely to find a brown hair on a black sheep as find another map of this Lia."

Nemiah drew a calming breath, surprised to feel anger when not so long ago the Mapmaker's derision would have caused only shame. "On Lia's Path, Riana's servants possess skills and knowledge we've either lost or never owned. Lia has already given us direction in our hunt for Sabela's temple. We could learn much more from her, perhaps even where to find the point of influence that caused the killing winds. It might save us months of merely waiting and praying for the Bearer's success. Do not tell me why you cannot do what I ask. Find a way to do it."

Bena huffed and looked astonished, but her tone lost some of its sarcastic edge. "As you say, Lady."

As she left the hall, the Mapmaker glanced back at Nemiah. "If you're right about Ambri, Lady, then he's committing a sacrilege that will kill him. Riana won't tolerate men's chaos jostling about her infinite Paths."

"If I am right about Ambri, then somewhere, sometime the Paths were not threatened by the chaos of men."

The days that followed were filled with the myriad duties neglected and tasks created since Dawnings' Eve. Nemiah hadn't realized all the ways in which the killing winds had disrupted life until she concentrated on trying to set things right. Harvests had been delayed or destroyed in villages as far south as Clan Rehamra and as far north as Clan Manitar. Nemiah pored over harvest reports and met with her Mistress of the Provender to determine how the temples and chapterhouses across those regions would be fed through the winter. With so many displaced families quartered in the high temple itself, their own stores were disappearing at an alarming rate. Nemiah reviewed the examinations of the Arionade and the novices who had been meant to take their final vows on Dawnings' Day. She met with the young ones to calm their fears and to assess their hostility since Carian's departure, and met with the Higher Circle to assess the same. The Mistress of Messengers remained remorseful for her decision to side with Carian, although Nemiah was uncertain whether Clemina most regretted trying to unseat the Chosen Lady or being caught at it. Kaliska remained ever a reliable ally. Bena and Maita both despised Nemiah, and they had no compunction about showing it.

No matter how overwhelming Nemiah's days became, each night when she led the evening devotion and saw the angry, frightened people of Velantar, she realized she wasn't doing enough. She thought often of her conversation with Lia and wondered whether the woman was right—that some cataclysmic event had disordered Paths all over the weaving—or whether it was only years of neglect on this Path that had weakened Riana, leaving her vulnerable to Cael.

When Bena arrived one night with the scrolled map of Nemiah's sacred journey clutched in a gnarled hand, Nemiah invited her into the tower. Together, they unrolled the map on the table and weighted it at the corners with books, a small alabaster bowl, and a smooth, black rock from Merisel's collection.

The best maps showed the context of a Path within Riana's weaving—revealing all four Principles of Time, Place, Perspective, and Parallel—and appeared as a many-branched tree connecting over and over to other trees, other Paths discovered on other journeys. This map was a spindly, sickly looking thing, with no other Paths to support it. The lonely lines didn't begin to illustrate all Nemiah knew of Lia.

"What have you determined of the Principles?" she asked the Mapmaker, trying to mask her disappointment.

Bena grumbled. "You haven't asked your Lia the right questions to get to the Principles. I've done what I could with what I was given. Begin with Place: you've met her three times now, always in or near Velantar. We don't have any other Pathwalker's confirmation, but as the woman told you explicitly she's from the city, I am willing to call it a verification."

Nemiah nodded. "Very good."

"Bah! Without knowing Perspective, Place is nothing. All the information you've given me is colored by the Perspective of the woman who spoke to you, but what can I say of her? You've seen her in the high temple, yes. In your first journey, she was officiating the evening devotion, yes. And she's introduced herself as Lady, yes." Bena pointed to three different points on the map where she had noted the information. "I am willing to submit that she's a priestess of the high temple, probably a member of the Higher Circle. No more."

"She has a sworn Arionad!" Nemiah protested. "She's not just a member of the Higher Circle, she's Chosen."

"I am talking about what we can verify. Wishful thinking we cannot confirm will remain in the notes. I will *not* risk creating an invalid map."

Nemiah pressed her lips on her frustration. "What of Time and Parallel?"

"I can say nothing of Time. The woman has skills you do not; that seems certain. She could come from a Path near the age of Alende Isan, perhaps as far back as the golden ages. Or she could live in a distant future, where the temple has regained something of what was lost." Bena shrugged. "If I had been given better information, I could offer a better picture."

Nemiah ignored the jab. "Then you agree the Parallel is close to ours. It is a matter of finding Lia on some past or future branching from our own Path, rather than on an unrelated strand of the weaving?"

Bena shrugged again. "Your priestess knows Alende's history and the stories of Altan Mar. You say her people have suffered the killing winds and that they're looking for a way to control the sacred skies. Yes, I'll record the Parallel as related to ours."

"Good then. That's something." Knowing Lia existed somewhere along the same twisting road made Nemiah feel a little less alone.

"You should seek her out, Lady. With another journey we might learn what we're missing. If you think she has more knowledge of use to us, go after it."

It was a challenge. Bena knew better than most what a poor Pathwalker Nemiah was. She also knew that if a walk stole Nemiah's spirit, the way would be open for Carian to return.

"Be careful what you hope for, Mapmaker. With the Bearer gone, no priestess other than myself can access Riana's power. Without the goddess's touch, Carian would not find the Chosen's seat as comfortable as she dreams it."

Bena waved a hand over the skeletal map. "If this is what you call access to Riana's power, Lady, then I'd just as soon trade it for a woman who would not put her sisters at risk by sheltering a Shorn traitor."

Nemiah straightened. "You're treading very near the edge, Bena."

"I've only a few steps left on this road," the old woman retorted. "I don't believe the goddess will punish me for speaking what I see, and you have no one yet skilled enough to take my place. Pay attention, Nemiah Gabriana. I am speaking with the weight of my years. The Chosen can only truly serve through sacrifice. Carian has made her sacrifice. We are all still waiting for yours."

Bena took up the map and, without waiting for Nemiah to dismiss her, left the room.

For a long while after the Mapmaker departed, Nemiah stood by the fire, her arms wrapped around her chest, her anger tempered by the truth Bena spoke: her access to power was insufficient and unreliable. She longed to find Lia again, but years had passed since she directed a journey with any accuracy, and even then her trips had been short ones to well-known Paths. With the Bearer away, the only person she could rely upon to retrieve her should she stumble was Rom, with his blade. Despite Lia's warning about the damage she might cause to the weaving, Nemiah couldn't help but nurture a faint hope the Gate would swallow her up again and deliver her to her distant friend.

She would never admit as much to her Arionad, who already worried over her frenetic days and sleepless nights, or to Kaliska, who hounded her about eating properly and plied her with foul-tasting restoratives. Instead, Nemiah began to pick through the meager temple archive, hoping to find some historical reference to the Lady Lia or her Arionad Ambri. If Nemiah could determine the pair's Time on the Paths, it might be enough to allow her to track them. She rarely found a free moment for her research, however. Tension continued to rise in the city as Rumar announced his new restrictions on the Shorn. At the same time, merchants had increasing trouble obtaining goods to fill their shops. The watermen's guild had lost a fleet of barges to the killing winds, and shipping fees had surged. Rumors that the winds had struck Clan Valador near Obled, not far from Parnas Pass, made the supply routes even more uncertain.

News confirming the rumors arrived unexpectedly, placed into Nemiah's hand by a palace messenger as she hurried toward a meeting with her priestesses in the city's clan circles. It was a note with Elder Trianor's name on it, but so brief and blunt it hardly looked like a message from the eloquent elder. Lieutenant Sevar had sent word: The winds had indeed struck Obled, just before the Forest Guard and Leita reached the village. Amidst the ruin, a Sahisten spy had been discovered and slain, and the Forest Guard pursued a second man northward. The Bearer of Cael's Blade had traveled on to Brenia in hopes of learning more about the location of Sabela's temple.

Sahistens in Avelos and the winds pushing northward. Nemiah clung to what small relief she could find in the letter: Leita was well and by now would have met with Lady Esania in Brenia. Esania was a clever scholar of ancient architecture and a gentle spirit; too gentle, it turned out, for the intrigues of Velantar and the high temple, but she would give Leita whatever aid she could. By now, the company might very well be on its way again toward the Sandien Mountains.

As riots broke out in the city's lower circles, Nemiah continued to hope for Leita's success. She visited each of the neighborhood temples, trying to reassure her people that chaos wouldn't prevail. Wherever she traveled, children orphaned by the winds massed around the horses and dragged at the coats of the Arionade, begging for food and protection. Nemiah brought in the youngest and the ill, but for the rest she could offer little more than her blessing. The high temple's halls were already crowded with families who had lost everything.

To escape the bitterness of her days, Nemiah began taking midnight walks with Capa in the inner courtyard. Her night wanderings became the only times she could claim for herself, and she looked forward to them. Whenever she passed Arnas's post near the archive entrance, he offered a grandfatherly smile and a spiral tucked close to his broad chest. He was a man of faith like few others she knew.

It was while speaking with Arnas one night that Nemiah thought to extend her search for information to the map room. She had found nothing of use in the archive, but hadn't dared to cross the boundary into Bena's domain. It took Arnas's simple respect to give her the confidence to explore what was hers by right.

The map room had no windows or chimney, but Arnas lit a brazier to chase out the late night's cold. Nemiah tiptoed into the chamber, feeling the bare stone floor through her slippers. A long, heavy table of age-darkened wood consumed the center of the room, balanced by an oak and iron-bound chest at the room's far end. The maps filled a long bank of open cupboards against one of the walls. Their rolled ends poked out to create mounds of small circles. Many of the cupboards were sadly empty, and smoke stains and scorch marks across the wood reminded Nemiah how much had been lost during Tumal's purges.

For now she turned her back to the cupboards, reasonably certain what she wanted wouldn't be found among the maps. Bena was meticulous. No matter her malice, if any existing journeys connected to Nemiah's, the old woman would have found them. It was the map notes Nemiah sought, where Mapmakers recorded their more tenuous interpretations.

She went to the large chest at the end of the room. Raising the lid released a puff of dust and the scent of old leather. Nemiah sneezed as she peered at the treasures within: three stacks of bound volumes, with loose pages shoved between. Kneeling on the floor, she lifted each volume out and set it beside her, making a neat pile of the unbound pages. At the bottom of the chest lay a crusty leather bag with several deteriorating scrolls inside. She wondered when anyone had last touched them.

After a cursory examination of her treasures, she selected what seemed to be the oldest of the books. Age and abuse had cracked the leather binding that at one time would have been richly burnished and beautifully engraved with Riana's spirals. Nemiah lugged the book to the table and, by the soft glow of the lamplight, began to carefully turn through the pages. With such a rich binding, it surprised her to find only simple script within; there were no illuminations or illustrations, and the hand changed from entry to entry. But this was no treatise on the Paths or history of the Great Wars. It was the most ancient collection of map notes she had ever touched.

Her heart beat faster at the realization that she held a remnant of the time very close to the Exile War, perhaps close enough to have been singed by the flames of Tumal's purges. Some of the comments within referred to single maps; others seemed to make arguments based on a collection of related maps or repetitions. Nemiah struggled with the ancient Velos—more archaic than even Morican's writing—as Capa snored beneath the table.

Note copied from Jhemira's translation of Casani [original Jhemira damaged; Casani lost]:

> *Others have argued, cogently, that the series of maps given us by the Lady [name illegible: Dor-xxx?] and her guide, Casani, are a simple warning against excess and only became important because of certain political pressures of the day. Another, I say stronger, argument is that the maps represent access to a Path and a belief far older than Casani herself, and are therefore important in their essence, for Casani writes this about her Lady's journey:*
>
> *Determining the Time and Perspective of the journey was impossible, for no longer did day and night change places on the Path according to Riana's Order; nor did day rule only or night rule only, as in the times of the Great Wars. No longer did spring follow winter and summer follow spring, but rather . . . [fragment lost]. Do not mistake: this Path was not under the rule of Cael, for Cael looks back to the Beginning, and thus, is the reason for all Creation, just as Riana looks forward to the End and the return to all Order. This Path was ruled by neither Creation nor Order but by True Chaos. It is True Chaos that awaits if the Light and Dark do not reconcile. It is True Chaos that will bring an end to the Weaving. Only in the merging are we made individuals once more. Only in the merging will we find True Balance.*

Nemiah pinched the bridge of her nose, weary and disheartened. Only half of what she read was even comprehensible. The last passage disturbed her most for its treatment of Cael as an equal to Riana. No, worse than that— *Cael looks back to the Beginning, and thus, is the reason for all Creation, just as Riana looks forward to the End and the return to all Order*—Casani wrote as though Riana and Cael were both only pieces, two pieces of something greater: Creation and Order. Was the idea an ancient heresy or merely the truth from an unrelated strand of the weaving? Nemiah sensed something here she should understand. Had a time truly existed when the temple was willing to call the demon of destruction the reason for creation? She should have known that. She cursed Lady Amalia once more for the treachery that caused so much to be lost. It was likely that the knowledge Nemiah needed to turn the Path had been destroyed long ago.

Not until she heard footsteps and the exchange of voices in the corridor did Nemiah realize how time had run away. The guard was changing, and Arnas was explaining her presence to the morning watch.

She rose and rubbed the blur from her eyes. The experiences and attitudes of decades of Pathwalkers filled her head in a way that made the rest of the world seem distant and unimportant. Capa nudged her down the east wing toward her tower.

"Another night without sleep, Lady? Your spirit is uneasy. You must do more to find comfort or you'll make yourself ill."

Nemiah looked up and saw a woman waiting by her door. It took a moment before she recognized who it was. "Kaliska," she murmured, trying out the name to see if it was relevant.

"I'm only sorry I have no comfort for you myself," the healer said. She held out a letter. It bore the council's mountain seal and the treasury's mark. Not another letter from Elder Trianor, then. Something darker. "This just came. Shall we go inside?"

The immediacy of Nemiah's own Path descended heavily. She drew a deep breath of the chilly air to clear her head. "I wonder what took him so long," she sighed, clutching the folded parchment between her fingers. "By now I expected Abrigado would be climbing the walls of the sanctuary to reach her."

The Arionad on watch at her tower gave Nemiah a nod and pushed the door open. Capa trotted to the corner of the room to lap water from his bowl. Nemiah lit a lamp with an ember from the banked hearth and sat down to read.

Lady Nemiah,
Please heed me: although you do not see it yet, you have taken the serpent into your house. Ziabela Marcalo will cozen you for protection, and in the end she and her kind will tear apart our country. She is soulless. She has sacrificed her own

people to further her cause, and she would see you or any of your women placed in harm's way with equal ease.

You hold this letter warily, as well you might. I will not mourn if the temple should fall. However, the shining gem of Avelos I will defend to my last breath, whether from the spears of Sahiste, the decisions of fools, or the treachery of the cursed. Be as wary of the scribe as you are of me and it will serve us both.

Toren Abrigado, Edr of Clan Amerre, Minister of the Treasury

Nemiah passed the note to Kaliska. "Nothing terrifies me so much as a man devoid of self-doubt."

Kaliska scanned the letter and tossed it onto the table. "There was a time no man would dare to write such things about Riana's temple."

"A time long before either of us. Have you found what we need to discredit him?"

The spy keeper shook her head. "I'm sorry, Lady. We've had no luck catching up with Cael's followers. And we've found no association between Abrigado and the stolen books."

"Leave it be, Kaliska. Look at that letter. Abrigado's fear of Cael isn't feigned. I think it unlikely he has turned to the demon's disciples." Nemiah fingered the edge of the vellum. "Elder Trianor believes Abrigado will use the Law of Integrity to unseat Rumar."

"That does seem to be where he's headed." The spy mistress tilted her head. "I suppose it's a good thing Abrigado cannot invoke the Law himself."

Nemiah hadn't actually considered it before. She frowned. "Ah. I see it. Too many elders would refuse to support him for high chieftain if he invoked the Law."

"Precisely. Abrigado needs someone with no commitments in the south to invoke the Law for him."

"Then is Ziabela Marcalo merely a part of his plan to undermine Rumar? Or is she the threat to Avelos that he makes her?"

Kaliska glanced down. "Whatever she is, the Minister of the Treasury wants her pushed from traitors' wall. What will you do, Lady?"

"First, I suppose I'd better speak with the scribe. I've let it go for too long." Nemiah hadn't seen Ziabela Marcalo since the day of the inquiry. She had told herself it was for lack of time, but a part of her didn't own the will to face the cursed woman.

Kaliska nodded. "Shall I call for Captain Rom?"

"No, the woman is well-guarded, and even if she is the soulless serpent Abrigado claims her to be, it would serve her no purpose to sting me."

"I'll go with you, then."

"No. I'll go alone. I stood for her at the inquiry. Perhaps she'll reveal something of herself to me."

"Lady, are you certain?"

Nemiah frowned, and the healer lifted her hands in retreat. "As you will. Of course."

The Arionad at the door of the scribe's chamber looked distinctly uncomfortable as Nemiah approached. Avjay was a long-limbed, black-haired man in his middle years. Although his easy temperament contrasted Rom's gruffness, by looks alone they might have passed for brothers.

Nemiah smiled to let him know she meant no trouble. "I've come to speak with our guest, Avjay. Has she been difficult?"

The guard ducked his head. "Ah no, Lady. She's an easy little thing. Quiet mostly."

"Mostly?" Nemiah said.

"Well, she has more than a bit of skill with that flute. Spends much of her time playing. Almost makes a man forget she's cursed, if you know what I mean."

"I see." Nemiah's smile flattened. The level of warmth in the Arionad's voice disturbed her. She waited. He didn't move from the door. "Avjay, step aside. I mean to speak with her."

"Uh, well, Lady, you see . . . she's not in her room at this very moment." He glanced down in chagrin. "She's not on her own, of course. The nightwatch boys are with her. They offered to take her after the morning devotion, since I couldn't very well leave my post. I didn't think it'd be any harm."

"Take her *where?*" Nemiah's heart sank. If Carian still had allies among the Arionade, what would they do to the woman to damage Nemiah before the council? Free her? Would they dare to harm her?

Avjay looked increasingly wretched. "She asked to see a bit of sky. They went to the inner courtyard. I thought it would be all right. She seemed so heartsick all locked up. She's not the kind of creature who fares well behind walls, you know. I just thought—"

Nemiah heard no more. She was already running down the corridor. The travelers' quarters where the scribe had been installed were nestled between one of the public receiving rooms and the petitioner's hall on the north side of the temple. Nemiah hurried to the end of the corridor, around the corner, and toward the courtyard entrance. A group of novices walking arm-in-arm on their way to lessons scattered with gasps and whispers. Nemiah didn't pause until she reached the narrow hall that led to the courtyard's loggia, where she was forced to stop to catch her breath.

"Just let her be safe," she prayed.

The first notes from the flute might have been the whisper of a breeze through leafy branches or the sound of a lover's murmur: low and soft and exquisitely gentle. They wafted out from the garden and hung in the air.

Nemiah followed the sound into the loggia, where a lanky, red-headed Arionad stood on guard between the columns. Nemiah glowered at him and saw him flinch a little when she made a gesture for him to stay silent. The lovely notes gathered into a song. Nemiah listened closer as they twined around her. It was an old, rarely heard song, a lament for the death of the high temple's Ulaye tree and the loss of Ularian.

Ziabela Marcalo was sitting on a blanket beneath the tree, the flute to her lips, her eyes closed and her body swaying slowly to the perfect, painful melody. Sunlight fell in pools around her. A second Arionad, stocky and fair, leaned against the tree trunk, a wistful expression softening his plain features.

Nemiah should have been furious, but the beauty of the music made it impossible to reach her anger. Perhaps it was the tranquility of the ancient courtyard or the voices of generations of Pathwalkers in her head that helped her to recognize the depth of grief in the song: grief not just for the loss of Ularian, but for Riana's servants murdered by Tumal, for the knowledge destroyed in the purges, and for the loss of honor and freedom and the touch of the sky.

The melody ended on a long, sad note, and the scribe looked up. As her gaze fell upon Nemiah, her expression shifted and she leaped to her feet. Belatedly, the Arionad leaning against the tree came to attention and drew a hasty spiral.

"Lady Nemiah! I didn't hear you!"

"I imagine not, Commander Evorales. You were quite decidedly elsewhere."

The fair-featured Arionad turned red, and Nemiah grimaced. Had the woman charmed even the most stolid of the temple's men?

"I'm sorry, Lady."

Nemiah waved off his apology. "Do you know the meaning of your music?" she demanded of the scribe.

The woman blinked her large green eyes. She was disconcertingly tall, even for her kind, taller than Evorales. "Lady, I'm not sure what you mean?"

"Don't be coy. Do you know the story in what you just played?"

With one long hand, the scribe caressed the trunk of the dead Ulaye. "Yes. I know it."

"It's not a song many have heard. Certainly not many of the cursed."

"That may be true, Lady, but I thought it a fitting tribute for this lovely space. I hope I haven't erred."

Nemiah gazed up at the woman more critically. Her hair hung in shining sable curls around her pretty face and set off the sparkle in her gaze. The simple grey dress she wore fit well, too well, from the glances Evorales was giving her. She hardly looked like the broken woman Toren Abrigado had put before the inquiry.

"Where did you learn it?" Nemiah asked.

"From a bard, when I was a girl. I loved her music and convinced her she should teach me."

"And did you also convince her to provide you with an Ulaye flute? That's a sacred instrument you hold."

The scribe lifted the flute so that it caught the sunlight. It was exquisite, as black and sleek as a living Ulaye tree, with keys of silver and bone. "Ularian gifted me with the materials. A flute maker created the magic of it. I never thought I'd be so honored as to play it in the high temple. Would you hear something for yourself, Lady?"

Evorales was observing the interaction with a half smile not particularly appropriate to the situation. Nemiah decided it was time to find their talented prisoner a way to spend her days other than enthralling the Arionade.

"Yes," Nemiah said. "I'd like to hear more from such a magical instrument."

The scribe smiled, a lovely, compelling expression that brightened her whole face. "Of course, Lady. I'm yours to command."

Nemiah had a feeling this charming, vital woman wasn't entirely anyone's to command, but decided it would be worth spending some time to see what could be learned about her. She sent off the two Arionade with orders to have an attendant bring food before they reported to their captain. Nemiah felt a momentary stir of sympathy for the men; Rom would not be easy on them for their transgression. Since Carian's mischief, he couldn't be.

A breeze gently rattled the hedges. The Ulaye creaked. Nemiah glanced through the tree's dead branches toward the brilliant sky. From the map notes, she had learned that many Pathwalkers had chosen the garden as the location from which to begin their journeys. It warmed her to know others had treasured the space as she did.

"It's a beautiful place to pray to the sacred skies."

Nemiah turned to find the scribe watching her and drew in her wandering thoughts. To survive in Toren Abrigado's world, Ziabela Marcalo must be clever and resilient, but was she treacherous?

"Some people find it too confining," Nemiah said.

The Shorn woman turned a little circle to take in the garden, her skirts flaring gently around her legs. She moved gracefully, with an energy that made it seem she might become airborne at any moment. "I don't see it so. It's a safe place for dreaming and planning. Centuries of Ladies plotted for the temple here." She flashed a smile at Nemiah. "Shall I select a song for you?"

A little taken aback by the woman's frank observations, Nemiah sat down on the blanket and invited the scribe to do the same, if only to keep from feeling so small standing beside her.

"That seems a challenge, selecting a song for the Lady of Avelos," Nemiah said. "There are many holy songs you might choose. If you choose well, you might please me and show yourself to be pious, but if your performance is poor, you'll look irreverent and disrespectful."

Ziabela folded her long legs beneath her and laid her flute across her lap. "I've been told I have a gift for knowing what a person needs to hear. Perhaps what you need isn't something holy at all." She winked at Nemiah. "Will you trust me?"

"To choose the music," Nemiah answered.

"That's a start." Green eyes sparkling, the Shorn woman set the Ulaye flute to her mouth. After a moment of pause and a drawn breath, a playful melody came spilling out. Notes chased each other like impish children. The pure, high sounds filled the garden and danced among the hedges. The woman's fingers fluttered like butterflies over the keys. Nemiah's heart beat more quickly, and before she knew it, her feet were keeping the rhythm. She thought of fall days running with her family's hounds and the childish pranks she played on her older sisters when young men from the village began to court them. The mischievous melody only slowed as the tune became a bold, indignant voice—like a father's reprimand—then quickened once more before tumbling to a close.

" 'Lusian's Children.' " Nemiah found herself smiling. "I haven't heard anyone play out the pranks of the stars since I was a girl."

"Lusian is long out of favor on the bards' circuit," Ziabela said with an answering smile, "but I find grace in his stories. Would you have another, Lady?"

"I would, but take your ease first. It's past midday." Nemiah gestured to the platters one of the novices had spread for them. Thin slices of roast lamb rubbed with herbs alternated between wedges of apples and dried berries; a warm loaf of bread peeked out from a white cloth; and a pot of fragrant tea steamed in the cool air.

Ziabela's tongue flicked over her lips as she began to fill a plate. "You're too kind to a cursed prisoner. It will take more than one lifetime of service to repay you."

Nemiah sipped her tea, wishing it were boldblood. "Then start by telling me of this bard who sparked your love of music. She was your Teacher?"

"She was someone who cared about the old songs," the scribe answered. "She feared they would be lost, so she taught them to those who would cherish them."

"Too much has been lost." First the Exile War and later Tumal's purges had decimated the temple's archives, but songs were not so easily destroyed. Nemiah began to wonder.

The Shorn woman took a bite of bread and made a sound of appreciation. "You're wise to see it, Lady. Something of our history lives in those songs."

"What's your repertoire, scribe? Do you know the *Songs of Praise*?"

"Of course."

"The *Alende Cycle*?"

"Yes."

"What can you play that I wouldn't know?"

The scribe's face lit up; then a startled expression flashed in her eyes. She sat back with the look of a pup in a new kennel, still uncertain of the rules. "I can't claim to hold knowledge the Chosen Lady does not."

The world began to sway. Nemiah slipped one hand over the other and pinched the tender skin of her wrist to tie herself to the Path. "Don't be foolish," she said hoarsely. "I'm no musician. You must know hundreds of songs I haven't heard. Show me."

Still looking guarded, Ziabela stroked her flute and looked up into the stark branches of the Ulaye. "Very well, Lady. Let's try this one. I think it might do you good."

A slow, lush tune caressed the air. It lent warmth to the sunlight and evoked the scents of summer: fertile earth and new growth. Nemiah melted into it. Enrian had nearly touched her once, beneath this Ulaye tree. That summer they had spent so many hours together she had known what he desired, although he wouldn't speak of it. Before ever seeking Lady Pahlina's permission, she had leaned close and brushed her body against his, knowing what it would do to him, longing for him to take what she offered . . .

Nemiah straightened, realizing suddenly where the music was pulling her. She gestured for the scribe to stop.

"That's 'The Rape of Shira'! The tale of an Ael's unholy desire is not what I intended from you."

The scribe's caramel-toned features knit in consternation. "Forgive me. I know the work as 'Shira's Dance.' I thought a quieter melody would suit. You seem in need of some peace."

Nemiah sighed. Deep within her, the Gate pulsed in time to her own heart. "Yes. Well. Have a care for what's proper in Riana's temple. I'll give you leave to try another."

The Shorn woman bowed her head. "You're gracious, Lady. Perhaps, this."

The piece began with a combination of sounds so foreign that Nemiah winced and nearly told Ziabela again to stop, but as she listened, the melody slowly started to make sense. It was like growing accustomed to the rhythms of a strange accent. Her untrained ear couldn't possibly appreciate all the nuances, but oh the complexity and depth of it. Joy and grief entwined through the movements, opposing each other, then merging into the same, poignant theme. It was a song of death and renewal, sacrifice and love. Nemiah felt herself torn in two and made whole again.

"What was that?" she whispered as silence returned to the garden.

Ziabela set down her flute. " 'Lady Elia's Gift.' "

Nemiah let out a wondering breath. "I know the story. Lady Elia gave up her place as Chosen of Avelos to wed the Amurian duke and prevent an invasion in the north. But what is this gift?"

The scribe bowed her head. "The song tells how the Lady left Avelos to marry a cruel stranger in the hope she could stop the attacks against her people. The sacrifice cost her everything she loved, yet in the midst of her grief, she found a cause for joy. When she gave birth to the duke's son, she realized the child was Riana's gift to her and her gift to Avelos. An heir of Avelonian lines would be less eager to spill Avelonian blood."

"A gift and a sacrifice." Nemiah knew a rush of hope as the story came suddenly, beautifully clear. " 'Lady Elia's Gift.' It's her. I think it must be her. My Lia."

"Lady?"

"She hasn't yet committed to Amuria. Her people are dying in the raids and threatened by the killing winds." Nemiah came to her feet, and grabbed the tree trunk to steady herself.

Ziabela rose beside her, looking uncertain. "What is it, Lady? Shall I call for help?"

Nemiah laughed, feeling giddy. "Oh no, Ziabela Marcalo. It's your help I need. Your songs may hold clues to treasures too long hidden. Come, you're getting back to work as a scribe. We'll set you up with ink and paper. Then I must see Captain Rom."

11.
ASSASSINS

Rom tossed his sword belt onto the table. His dagger followed with a clatter. "I'll not stand watch for you now, my lady."

"Captain, I've no patience for argument tonight. Lady Elia is my Lia. I'm sure of it. I could find her!"

"And you will find her. After you've slept and gathered your strength. Look in the mirror, Nemiah. The Gate burns like danger in your eyes. I'm not the Bearer. I have only steel to cut you free if the web entangles you." He straightened and pressed his fists to his sides. "I beg you: do not order me to do this."

Nemiah laid her hand on her Arionad's forearm, surprised by the tension in him. "It's no order," she said gently, "only a request. Stand by me and bring me home should I falter. I don't fear your blade at my throat."

He scowled. "You plan to go whether I stand for you or no."

"It's close, Rom. The Gate shines so brightly I can nearly feel the heat of it. I dare not wait." She couldn't bear to tell him that waiting would cause her to lose what little courage she possessed.

"You know when to find her, then? Your Lia?"

"Within a span of some years. The precise date is not so important as the context." He gave her a skeptical stare.

"We know Velantar was a young city when Lady Elia led the temple. We know the first-clans ruled themselves—and fought bitterly. We're not sure who the high chieftain might have been, but it was near enough to Alende's time that likely Clan Amerre still held the seat. Amuria was a collection of aggressive duchies battering our western border." Nemiah met her Arionad's black gaze. "I'm not setting off in ignorance. If I can create the context of Lia's world clearly enough, I should reach her Parallel in the weaving. I must believe the connection I've formed with her is enough to do the rest. Do we have so many other possibilities we can shun this hope?"

"I despise you going where I cannot keep you safe!" Rom growled. "It isn't Riana's way to separate Lord Arion from his Lady."

Nemiah sighed, thinking more of Lia and Ambri than her own worries. What if the Arionade truly had served as guides once? As priests in their own right who could guard their Ladies even onto the Paths? *"Come, my love,"* Ambri had whispered. He didn't yet know Lia must leave him for a duke who had earned his rule by torturing and slaying their people.

"Lia sacrificed everything for Avelos, Rom. Is it so much to ask that I take this small risk? I'll make the sacred journey without you, if I must, but I ask you not to turn from me while we still have the time to share."

The captain drew back to look at her. She saw the subtle changes in his expression as he considered it, saw him push aside his own fears.

"Where will you begin?"

"In the inner garden." Nemiah squeezed his arm and smiled. "Don't worry. It will be well."

"It will be cold," he grumbled. "The sun is setting. Take your heavy cloak."

She exchanged her fine green cloak for the grey one she wore when she ran the hounds outside the walls. Rom's rough concern was enough to warm her on its own. "Come, we've a long trek ahead."

Pale starlight lit the courtyard. Nemiah wrapped the cloak around her and settled on the ground under the Ulaye. Twice now she had fallen through the Gate beneath the tree's bare black branches. She hoped the association might once more draw her to Lia.

Rom stood behind her, his body a spot of heat at her back. "The blade is your last recourse," she reminded him, "I'll return on my own if I can."

"By the holy ways may you travel, my lady."

She drew up her hood and closed her eyes. "And by the ways I will return."

She had no time to focus herself. As she relaxed her hold on her own Path, the Gate flared up to consume her. Blue flames crackled over her body for a searing instant. Then she was pitched into mind-stealing darkness.

Hastily, she set up her boundaries, trying to steer her way through the Paths. "Nemiah Gabriana. I am Nemiah Gabriana, Chosen Lady of Avelos. I serve Riana of the Spheres. By her will, I walk the Paths. With her knowledge, I seek my sister, Lady Elia."

Long blue and red strands began to light the emptiness, one by one at first, then in numbers too great to understand. Each strand was a Path, and each Path wove through the others in a pattern of infinite complexity. The glory of it staggered her. Each moment, as lives were lived, countless new Paths were born, creating new patterns endlessly.

Nemiah's purpose faded beside the overwhelming wonder of the infinite. Her attention darted across every strand as she struggled to comprehend the incomprehensible. Her thoughts fluttered like a little bird.

Little dove.

Lia.

Nemiah clutched the name close, filling her head with all she knew about Lady Elia. She imagined a young Velantar. A new temple. The bitter, bloody rivalries between the clans, and the threat of invasion from Amuria. She thought of the woman, Elia, who would give up her home and sacrifice her heart for the love of her people.

Flashes of Paths revealed themselves, and Nemiah sorted them as best she could, pushing some aside, grasping hold of others.

Hounds bay on the trail of their quarry and find broken bodies abandoned in a gully.

Clan Amerre banners wave over Velantar's walls as armies collide in the fog.

A child plays at the foot of a foreign throne.

A woman moans softly in her sleep. Open windows welcome the sounds of summer. A crescent moon throws pearly light across the tower chamber.

Nemiah recognized the high arches in the ceiling and the pattern of light across the flagstone in the woman's chamber. It was the high temple, the Lady's own rooms. Lia's rooms? She turned herself toward that Path, fumbling with the last doors—the transitions that kept each Path distinct from the rest of the weaving. The doors fought her, resistant to invasion by someone who didn't belong. The key was to convince them she did belong. Nemiah drew upon her knowledge of the tower. She knew the shape of the shadows on the walls when the moon was high. She knew the feel of stone beneath bare feet and the way that voices echoed if one stood just so under the arch. She thought of Lady Elia and the terrible decision before her. She thought of Avelonian blood spilled by Amurian pirates. The next door slammed open.

With a graceless tumble, she landed on the Path.

Panting and dizzy, Nemiah pulled herself up. From the tower window, she saw the inner courtyard. Wind blew through the leaves of the great black Ulaye tree as she had only seen it once before, lush and vibrant with Ularian's spirit.

"Lia!" Nemiah approached the figure sleeping in the large bed. "Lady Elia, I've come for you!"

The figure shoved aside the blankets and sprang out of bed. Nemiah caught glimpses of long limbs, a girl's waist, and arching brown shadows over her shoulders. Then fury flew toward her, fast and vicious as a raptor. It crashed against her mind, knocking her backward. Doors slammed shut and the world went dark.

"J'ya think I'd be lying defenseless!" a girl's voice hissed. "J'ya think a little groundling like yourself could kill me when all the others failed?"

Nemiah struggled to see, struggled to move, but someone with inconceivable strength had wrapped herself around Nemiah's presence, holding her at the edge of the Path, the final doors once more locked between them.

"Lia, it's me," she gasped. "Your sister of the Paths. Don't you know me?"

"No sister'a mine steals onto m'Path without the words'a trust," growled the girl. "Who are ya?"

Nemiah reeled, uncertain what had gone wrong. Elia's voice sounded young, so young, but her speech was odd and soft, nearer to ancient Velos than Nemiah's tongue. Had she entered the Path too early? "Lia, it's Nemiah Gabriana."

"Gabriana," the girl spat. "That tells me nothing but that you've the support'a the temple. What clan claims ya? Why j'ya speak like a stranger?"

"Darnios is my clan," Nemiah said. "But I've come from farther—"

"Liar!" the woman howled. Without warning, the grip that held Nemiah opened. She hadn't realized just how close she was to the edge until she tumbled off the Path entirely and spun toward the flames. After hovering so long in the dark, the blue flames blinded her. With a skill Nemiah couldn't dream of, the girl forced her into their heat. And held her there.

She was submerged within the Gate.

It was the last coherent thought Nemiah managed before the flames ran up her body and chewed at her flesh. They burned her with an intensity that could give birth to stars and destroy the spheres. She writhed to break free until the pain ate into her mind and she forgot everything else. Forgot how to struggle or why.

Abruptly, she was jerked out of the fire and flung back onto the Path.

"Liar," the girl said again, her tone all deadly control now. "The Clan Darnios temple was razed by Clan Valador on Dawnings' Eve. You've come from Amuria."

The air whistled in Nemiah's seared lungs. She opened her eyes to find the girl glaring over her. Elia had barely enough years to be a woman, but her small face was already twisted with distrust and her green eyes held fear as well as fury.

"Oh . . . Lia," Nemiah groaned, remembering her Lia's eyes the blue-grey of shadows on snow and realizing she had both succeeded and failed.

"Stop saying my friend-name, mage! The duke wants the gifts my line offers. If he has me, Avelos will have peace. I'll let no Amurian lordling destroy it. Tell me whose pawn ya are."

Nemiah tried to catch a breath. "I'm not Amurian. I'm not . . . of your Path."

The girl made a derisive sound. "You're no Pathwalker, groundling. You've not the skill of my youngest novice. Speak truth or I'll bath ya again in holy fire."

Nemiah struggled to throw herself back into her body, but Lady Elia gripped her mind with Riana's own strength. Nemiah closed her eyes. Truth was all she had.

"There will be a child. Your son . . . will be a duke."

Elia's laughter slashed the air like shattered glass. "For promising myself to a foreigner, m'family has cursed me. M'own brothers have tried to slay me. And with such a farewell, I go to a country that hates me to give m'body to a man I despise. Ya can't weaken me with hope, stranger." The grip on Nemiah tightened, and she felt herself lifted. "Pray to what gods ya will. I can't let ya live to try again."

"Riana bless your ways," Nemiah whispered.

She sensed an instant of shock from the girl, but she was already tumbling from the Path into the blinding beauty of the Gate.

The blue fire gnawed hungrily at the meaning of her life. Flames blazed through her fears and wishes. Heat burnt away her memories, leaving only cinders behind. She heard herself murmuring a pair of names over and over, as though they could keep her intact, but they had lost all significance. When the fire consumed its fill, she was blown out, like a speck of ash. Blackness enveloped her, and she floated in nothingness.

It might have been centuries later when voices crept into the nothingness. A woman wept, and a man murmured consolingly beside her.

"*Come to me, my love. Lia, I do not fear your grief.*"

"*Dead,*" choked the woman, "*All dead. How could I have failed them so completely?*"

"*They knew the search for Sabela's temple would take them into the wilds.*"

"*It wasn't the wilds that killed them, Ambri. Our hounds found the bodies. They were slain before they ever cleared Parnas Pass. I should have realized he wouldn't let us succeed, but I never believed he'd go so far.*"

Nemiah felt a vague stir of curiosity as the voices flowed past. "*Lia and Ambri,*" she murmured again, wondering if the names should have meaning.

A hard gaze fell upon her, picking her out of the dark. A man growled. "*Who's there? Speak or risk death.*"

"*What is it?*" the woman asked, then gasped. "*Stand down, Ambri! It's Lady Nemiah. Catch her! Before she floats away.*"

Nemiah felt herself plucked up like a pup in its mother's mouth. She struggled, terrified of being tossed into the fires again.

"*Hold still, you,*" the man said more gently as he set her down. The blackness remained, but she was no longer drifting. "*She's unfeathered,*" he said with a tone of surprise. "*I thought you said she was Chosen.*"

"*Hush. Her Path is far from ours. Such things may no longer matter.*" The woman's voice seemed familiar now. "*Oh, my sister, what's brought you to this?*"

"*She's been charred, Lia. The flames have made a husk of her. Perhaps it would be a kindness to let her go.*"

"*No.*" Iron entered the woman's tone. "*I'll not lose another friend today. If I can reach her, I can heal her.*"

"*Lia, you've not the strength to spare.*"

"He murdered them, Ambri."

There was a moment of heavy silence, then the man spoke again. *"Be careful. I'll be close if you need me."*

The man's presence faded, but Nemiah sensed movement around her and heard someone whispering. "Little dove, it's Lia. Do you know me? Can you show me there's some will left in you?"

Lia and Ambri. Nemiah felt longing and warmth as she thought of them. She tried to call out, but ash filled her mouth. Fine, bitter particles clogged her throat. A tendril of blue flame curled around her thoughts, burning away another memory.

"Wait!" the woman cried. "You're still too close to the Gate."

The flames flared behind Nemiah's eyelids. Lia's voice grew distant again.

"Dove, listen now. Too many doors remain closed between us. You must come fully onto my Path so I can help you. Reach for me, and I'll pull you through. Reach now. Hurry!"

Nemiah imagined reaching. She felt like she was swimming in sand, but she imagined pushing her arms above her head and grasping a strong hand. She sensed the doors between them as the hand began to drag her through. They tore at her ragged thoughts, ripping what remained of her. But Lia whispered to them, wheedling them with sweet words, convincing them with her own strength of will to let Nemiah pass. Slowly, the doors swung open.

Clean air poured into her lungs. Nemiah felt herself tumbling; then arms caught her and pulled her close. She looked into the eyes of the woman who held her: a beautiful, fathomless gaze of blue-grey, with the strength of the goddess reflected within. She knew those eyes and remembered the power of the woman, but for the first time, no doors remained closed between them. Nemiah looked up to see Lia fully, and recoiled with a faint mew of shock.

"Easy," the woman murmured. "You've been badly burned. It will be some time before the world makes sense again."

Perhaps that was it. Nemiah's jangled thoughts and memories were painting the world all wrong. That a cursed woman embraced her with the warmth of massive wings made no sense at all. Exhausted, she laid her head on her friend's shoulder and closed her eyes.

She slept, perhaps for days or maybe for weeks. When she opened her eyes, the world was grey and distant. She stared at the grey, feeling no reason to move and little reason to speak. Lia always seemed to be with her, working at a desk beside the bed, surrounded by piles of correspondence and numerous books, or holding Nemiah's hand and whispering to her, telling her stories of the weaving of the Paths and the Great Wars of Riana and Cael, as though the images of battle and creation would help Nemiah fight her way back into the world.

Sometimes Ambri was there as well, a tall man with eyes the soft green of new apples and hair glossy and black as a stallion's mane. Nothing about him was impassive or grey. Nemiah liked the Arionad's straightforward manner and easy laugh. She discovered that she knew unexpected things about him: that he came to Velantar from Clan Makri after his father died; that his favorite hound was a temple-bred hunter named Vorian; that he loved the taste of Lia's kisses when they embraced beneath the Ulaye tree at the full moon.

A well of strength existed in Ambri's love. Lia's spirit glowed with it. The night air brushed across her heated skin. Strong hands gripped her waist, and lips nibbled at her ear. She wrapped her arms around him and ran her hands over his smooth back, so different from hers. His was a different type of strength, but treasured, so dearly treasured. Her eyes closed and she released her cares for one rare moment.

"Come to me, my love."

Nemiah lifted her head to meet his lips. He tasted pleasantly of fennel. She sighed and sank into his embrace, her body awakening.

Ambri paused, then drew back, chuckling softly. *"A man should not complain for being gifted with the passion of two beautiful women, but I fear what will happen should one of you be jealous. Lia, love, it seems we're not alone."*

There was more gentle laughter and flustered movements as bodies drew apart and clothes were straightened.

"Careful now, little one, or you'll forget who you are."

Nemiah flushed. *"I'm sorry! I had no idea. What . . . happened?"*

"Wait. Don't continue to speak this way. It saps your strength. I'll come to you."

It was only a short time before Lia entered, bright-eyed and smiling. "It's all right, little one. I brought you through the doors of this Path, and you're traveling from my perspective. It's natural you'd slip so close to my thoughts. No cause for shame. How do you feel?"

Nemiah looked around the room and realized, for the first time in un-countable days, that the grey had vanished. She truly did feel. She gazed upon Lia and knew a clash of emotions, like the pleasure-pain of leaping into an icy stream on a hot day. Her first perception had been no illusion: Lia was Avelun. Her wings rose in two bold arches from her strong shoulders. Her feathers were the color of shadows on snow, the same remarkable shade of blue-grey as her eyes. They were glorious and horrifying. They reminded Nemiah of the shame of her own heritage and everything the temple had lost. Yet she had *seen* Ambri. Just a moment ago she had put her hands on his back.

"Ambri. He's not Avelun."

Lia laughed and shook her head. "No, dove. Of course not. He's my guide. I'm the one who opens the doors."

"I didn't know."

"There's so much you don't know. I will always wonder what catastrophe shaped your Path." Lia stroked Nemiah's hair. The Avelun smelled pleasantly of herbs—tarragon and sweet basil. "Sometime we'll speak of all the marvels that are possible for a Pathwalker. We must keep you out of danger when you travel. I worry for you with all this falling, and fear what damage it does to the weaving. Ah, little dove, I worry for us all. But rest now. Your scars still require time to heal."

As Lia brushed her fingers across Nemiah's brow, Nemiah drifted back to sleep. Sweet lips tasted her mouth. Eyes the color of new apples peered kindly into her spirit. Warm laughter faded in her ears.

More days fled. Although Nemiah began to track them more clearly, she still found it a struggle to maintain awareness for longer than a few hours at a time. She wandered into the halfworld too easily. Sometimes as she wandered, Nemiah caught glimpses of Lia surrounded by grim faces or in the midst of heated discussions. Her friend looked haggard. But Lia put her off when Nemiah asked after her, saying it was too soon to talk about such things. It was only as Nemiah's memories began to return, crinkled and brittle, that she recalled the destruction spreading across Avelos. She awoke with a start one afternoon with the recollection that she had come in search of Lia, hoping the woman had found some answer to the chaos encroaching on both their Paths. With a shiver, Nemiah realized how close a thing it had been. She had crossed the Gate in search of hope and had almost lost herself.

"*. . . and I've just had the report from the chapterhouse commander. All the young ones are accounted for and safe.*"

Nemiah stirred. It was Ambri's voice, but he wasn't in the room.

"*Good,*" Lia replied. "*Lend the Mistress of Novices one or two of your men, if you can spare them. She'll have her hands full with all the little ones restricted to the dormitory while the ambassador is here.*"

"*Have you thought of sending the children home?*" Ambri asked.

"*I've thought on it. It's not possible. Too many of them have lost their families to drought and fever.*"

There was a considering pause. "*Send them west, then. The temple at Clan Ontera could take them. At least while the ambassador—*"

"*Clan Ontera has its own troubles. The chapterhouse will have to do. It's only for a short time.*"

"*It may not be so short, Lia. What will you do when our guests have departed and you're alone again? He's already dared to kill within the Higher Circle. You can no longer doubt he'll come for you.*"

"*Oh, I know he'll come,*" Lia sighed, "*but not in any way you expect. He's too cunning to attack me directly.*"

"He couldn't attack us at all if his Path were to end."

"Stop!" Lia's voice whipped the air. *"I cannot hear such sacrilege."*

"And I refuse to call it sacrilege! It is my place to keep you safe. We must speak of it."

A soft *whoosh* beat the darkness, once, twice. *"All right,"* Lia said more quietly, *"but not now. We've woken Lady Nemiah."*

"Tonight?" Ambri pressed.

"If she's resting, I'll come to you."

"It cannot wait any longer, my love. I'll find you as soon as I'm back inside the walls."

When Ambri's farewell had faded, Lia rose from the desk beside Nemiah's bed and stretched wearily. Her great wings opened, filling the space between the bed and the wall. They trembled, then furled against her shoulders.

Nemiah stared, afterimages of feathers rustling in her vision. It took several breaths to find her voice. "Ambri speaks to you from the Paths as though he were standing beside you. How? Is it the same as when I slip into your thoughts accidentally?"

Lia turned from her desk and gave Nemiah a tired smile. "It's the blessing and curse of being sworn to a talented guide. He always knows exactly where to find me."

"I didn't know it was possible to track the four Principles with such accuracy."

"How else would my guide direct me?" Lia came over and sat on the bed. Her black hair slid unbound over her shoulder as she leaned forward to brush Nemiah's cheek. "I told you we would speak more of the Paths and travel. I'm sorry I've had no time for it. Things are not well here, dove."

Nemiah shivered and tugged at the coverlet. Lia slid closer and put an arm around her, an unguarded, sisterly comfort.

"I set out to find you," Nemiah murmured. "I hoped you had discovered some way I could turn my Path, but you've found no answers either, have you?"

"No. I haven't. And I don't much care for the directions left to me."

Nemiah tried to sit up. The Avelun helped her to lean against the headboard. "What's happened?"

"Oh dove, I don't know if you are well enough for this."

"Please, tell me."

Lia's shoulders rose and fell with her careful breath. "The women I sent to find Sabela's temple were slain. My closest advisors. Friends."

"I'm so sorry." Nemiah glanced up and saw steel in the other priestess's expression. "You know who killed them. It's the one Ambri said would come for you."

"Yes. The craven who calls himself high chieftain. He has no answer to this drought himself, but more than anything he fears I'll find the answer. Then all the vitriol he's spouted about me and my kind will be proved false."

A chill ran through Nemiah. "Drought?"

"Four summers of it. Three since the first time you came to me." With a sigh, Lia leaned her head against Nemiah's.

"And the council? What have they done?"

Lia made a sound of disgust. "The elders remain adamant we must not reveal our weakness to the border nations by asking for help. Of course, it won't matter if we're safe from Amuria when civil war rends us to pieces. Which is why I must take the risk myself."

Nemiah felt faint. "What risk?"

"To bring in an ambassador who can speak knowledgeably about how to survive where water is scarce."

"But . . . what of the killing winds?"

Lia gave her a puzzled look.

"The storms that tear apart cities and slice flesh like glass."

"I've not heard of such a terrible thing, dove."

"The killing winds," Nemiah insisted. "They're flattening Avelos. Did you not send your women to find Sabela's secrets to control the sacred skies? You said Sabela was our hope."

"Indeed. I hoped we could learn to bring the rains, as Lady Sabela did to quench the fires at Altan Mar. As we both hoped." Lia gripped Nemiah's hand. "Dove, what's wrong? You're trembling."

Nemiah shook so badly she could hardly speak. Surely, the terrible thought in her head must be wrong; the Gate had burned her mind so that nonsense seemed almost sensible.

"Who leads the council?" she whispered. "Who is your high chieftain?"

Lia's face contorted with revulsion. "Lord Marinen Tumal."

A cry of despair tore from Nemiah's throat.

"What is it?" The Avelun reached for her, but Nemiah pulled away.

Lia looked stricken. The ground lurched.

"Careful, dove. I can't hold you here if you fight me. What's wrong?"

"I thought I was seeking a way out of chaos for my people," Nemiah cried. "Instead, I've led them into the very heart of betrayal!"

Lia went pale. "Why do you speak so? You are a sister of my heart. I could never do you harm."

"You are Amalia. Lady Amalia!"

"Yes. Yes, of course." The Avelun's wings mantled like an agitated raptor. "What does that mean to you?"

Nemiah closed her eyes, unable to look at her friend's expression. "You are the serpent who brought the goddess to her knees. The traitor who cost us everything."

"What are you saying?" Lia's voice fell to a strangled whisper. "That's not who I am. You've seen my true self."

The world began to fracture. Doors along the Paths slammed open. Without willing it, Nemiah slid toward them.

"Reach for me," Lia begged. *"You're not yet strong enough to cross the Gate."*

Nemiah could not make herself reach out. *"There was so much I could have learned from you. You are the last high priestess to know the stories and hold the maps of the ancients. Tumal will destroy them all. Then he will kill you and every woman and girl sworn to you."*

The inevitability of that horror would rip Nemiah into fragments. No mortal owned the strength to unravel what was already woven. Riana's Chosen Lady could only change the Paths ahead. No matter that Nemiah had found a sister on this Path. No matter that she had come to love a woman whose name she cursed.

"I must not seek you again."

The first lick of the blue flames burned her vision.

"Ambri, help me! She's falling!"

Lia's cry was still echoing in Nemiah's head when a man's thoughts roared onto the Path. Nemiah sensed him searching for her, but his grip closed on nothing. She plummeted once more into blackness.

Nemiah lay motionless for a long time before anything about the world seemed familiar. The first things she recognized were the softness of a bed and the acrid-sweet scent of temple incense. She didn't move; the image of blue flames still seared her mind. She was afraid to turn and find herself tumbling again, afraid she might once more see Lia's heartbroken expression.

Amalia. Nemiah forced herself to shape the name.

Slowly, the garbled noises around her resolved into the sound of voices and the whisper of music. Kaliska. And the Shorn scribe with her flute. Her own Path. A rough hand encircled hers, but when a knock came from a distance, the hand squeezed gently and turned her loose.

"She will not see you," a man said flatly. Rom. It was Rom.

"You cannot keep me out," Bena grumped. "I'm a Lady of the Higher Circle. I have the right to know who leads us."

"You serve the Lady of Avelos," Rom said, "and she has not bid you enter."

Bena huffed. "You're the only one who's bound to Nemiah Gabriana. I serve our Lady Riana. Let me through. I'll not be put off any longer."

A rustling came from below, then the painful steps of the old Mapmaker up the stairs. Nemiah tried to open her eyes and sit up. *"Rom?"* The name sounded in her mind, but no one seemed to hear. *"Rom? Kaliska?"* She couldn't move. Nascent panic fluttered in her breast.

"Great Mother of Order!" Bena gasped.

"Peace, Mistress Bena." Kaliska's voice. "The Lady took injury on a sacred journey. Her spirit has retreated to heal."

"Heal? Look at her! She's long gone. Has she spoken? Given any sign at all?"

Nemiah pounded at the doors that kept her from her Path. Lia had been right; she was too weak. She didn't exist enough in her world to have meaning, and the final doors that separated her from where she belonged remained locked. She shouted until she was hoarse, but only silence blanketed the room.

"A sign will come when she's ready to return," Kaliska replied.

Bena snorted near Nemiah's ear. "Madam Healer, you know what this is. You know as well as I. She's lost."

"You are no Pathwalker!" Rom barked. "Nor a healer!"

"When Riana takes one so young," Bena said, her tone softening, "she has a purpose for it. Nemiah Gabriana's time as Chosen has passed, Arionad. You must let her go."

"Hush, Bena," Kaliska said. "We'll not discuss such things here and now."

The old woman sighed as though it caused her pain to continue. Nemiah could well imagine her smirk. "Come now. The poor child is either so far gone she knows nothing or she's wandering somewhere and suffering. It would be a mercy to her and the best thing for the temple if—"

Metal hissed against leather. There was the sound of a swift step. "Speak that thought, Mapmaker," Rom snarled, "and I'll spill your life on these stones to pay for your sacrilege."

"My Arionad, no! Do not stain yourself with a Lady's blood!"

The doors to the Path trembled. Nemiah had never possessed the brute strength to break through those transitions or the skill to wheedle them open. She only ever had faith she would end where she was meant to be. She grasped the edge of the first door.

"By the holy ways I travel. Lady Riana, end my Path if that's your will, but please don't leave me in this Nowhere."

"Captain!" Kaliska cried. "Consider your oath!"

"Oh, he is," Bena said. "The Arionad's purpose lives and dies with his Lady. I don't expect a man to see farther than his own desires, but you, Madam Healer, must think on how best to serve Riana."

Nemiah dove through the slender breach in the door. Too small. It was too small. Ragged edges caught at her wishes and dreams, still raw from the flames. She clutched them as best she could and dragged herself forward. Pain ripped through her as she passed another door. A cluster of memories tore free and fell into the void, but she didn't turn to see what she had lost. She passed another door and another. Finally, she staggered across the last threshold, and the world righted itself with a thunderous crash.

"Mapmaker. You are not as subtle as you once were." Nemiah pushed herself straight in the bed.

Every face turned in her direction. Kaliska's even features broke into a magnificent smile as she hurried over to Nemiah. "Thank the Lady and her Holy Consort!"

Bena's eyes went hard with disappointment. "You had the chance to do one thing right, Nemiah Gabriana. You left this Path. You shouldn't have spoiled it by coming back."

The Mapmaker's hatred struck Nemiah like a blow. "Why this endless animosity? What does it gain you? I returned for our people! I've only ever tried to help our people."

"Bah! The best thing you could do for our people is to accept Cael's Escape and let someone with true strength fill your seat!"

Nemiah sensed Rom's body coiling an instant before he lunged. Steel gleamed in the lamplight as his sword rose. Bena's gaze went wide in a caricature of surprise. She staggered backward and fell.

"No!" Nemiah gasped. "Rom, I forbid it!"

The blade was already descending toward the old woman. With visible effort, the Arionad wrenched the blow away from her. His sword tip caught the edge of a water pitcher instead and smashed it to the floor. Shards of pottery scattered around Bena where she had fallen.

"Beast!" the Mapmaker spat at him. "Only a hound could give his loyalty so blindly."

"It's loyalty that just saved your life," Kaliska said, putting herself between the Arionad's sword and the old woman on the ground. "Mapmaker, it's time for you to leave this room."

Bena shook off the healer's offered hand. "The Higher Circle will know what goes on here. How Nemiah Gabriana is an invalid barely present on our Path. How the Captain of the Arionade tried to kill a Lady."

Nemiah braced herself against the bedpost and stood, hoping her deliberate movements looked like composure rather than frailty. "Say what you will, if you think it will set our Path aright. If your years of study have proved that conflict in the Circle serves us well."

Bena's expression was black. "You were never meant to be Chosen."

You are the serpent who brought the goddess to her knees.

Ah, Lia, of all the infinite Paths, why was I ever drawn to yours?

Nemiah held herself upright with an act of will. "Madam Healer, see the Mapmaker back to her duties."

Kaliska gave Nemiah an uncertain glance before moving to Bena's side. The old woman's shoulders were stiff and straight as she turned away, though she limped as she walked out of the room. Nemiah heard them reach the bottom of the stairs and then a door slam.

She sank down onto the blankets. "How long?"

"Five days," Rom replied, sheathing his sword.

She nodded. She would have believed it if he had said five years.

"I begged you to wait before seeking the Gate, Nemiah. I begged you!"

She looked up at her Arionad. "Be content, then. You were right."

"You didn't find her? After all this?"

"No. I found her. I found them both." She glanced away again, unable to face the judgment in his gaze.

"Won't you tell me of it?"

"Not yet. I cannot . . . yet." More fear waited in the telling than she had expected, fear at what her errors meant for Avelos and what her Arionad would see in her when he learned the truth. "I tried, Rom. I undertook this journey only for the sake of . . ." She trailed off. It was a hollow declaration even to her own ears.

Rom didn't miss it. "Perhaps your mysterious Lia has so ensorcelled you that you'd rather be with her than on the Path where you belong?"

Nemiah flinched.

"I waited most of the night before I dared to use the blade," he went on, his voice tight. "Your body was cold. So cold. You were farther away than you've ever been before. When I finally set my knife to your throat and watched your blood flow, it did nothing to bring you back. I thought I had killed you."

"No one would have faulted you if you had." She touched the bandages under her ear. "Bena would have named you a savior."

"Nemiah! Have you considered what it would have meant if you hadn't returned? The temple would have fallen to chaos. And I . . ."

He grimaced and held up a hand, as though to grab back his words. "I'm sorry. It's too soon for this talk. Your journey has taken its toll. I'll send for some supper and we can speak of lighter things. Or of nothing at all."

He was raw with unspent anger and days of worry. She knew it, although he wouldn't speak of it. They had shared too much of themselves to hide anything for long. If he stayed tonight, Nemiah knew she would lose her will to keep Lia's secret, and she couldn't speak of it. Not until she had decided what to do.

"Not now," she whispered. "Please."

A muscle moved in his throat. "You wish me to leave?"

She nodded, watching the vulnerable place below his jaw where his pulse beat.

"I see." Hurt darkened his gaze as he stepped backward, away from her. "Of course, my lady."

"Rom, wait."

The flicker of hope that crossed his face made her heart ache. "Rom, have a care. Bena will see to it you pay for this."

He lifted one shoulder. "I did not intend to harm her. She needed to be frightened."

Nemiah stared. "You knew I would stop you."

"Of course."

"And now Bena believes you are willing to shed her blood. For me."

The captain nodded.

"Goddess, Rom. It was a risk. Too great a risk."

"It is my place to keep you safe," he said simply.

The echo of Ambri's words. They sent a shiver of foreboding through Nemiah. "No, my Arionad. Order must come first. My life isn't worth such a sacrilege. Promise you'll not lift a hand against the women of the Higher Circle, no matter what their threats against me."

"Impossible, my lady. My oath is already given."

His spiral was precise and formal, a message in that. She didn't have the strength to argue further; she let him go. His footsteps echoed heavily on the stairs as he disappeared.

Nemiah flopped against the pillows and heaved a shaky breath.

"You are much more to him than Riana's Chosen Lady."

Nemiah yelped and bolted upright. The Shorn scribe was sitting in the shadowed corner of the room, her flute on her lap, forgotten by all of them.

"Ziabela! You should have made yourself known!"

"Forgive me." The scribe peered up through her lowered lashes. "It didn't seem an opportune time to interrupt."

Nemiah sighed acknowledgment and pressed two fingers against the side of her pounding head. "Very well. Call for Merisel. She'll have one of the Arionade on watch take you to your room."

"The child isn't here. She was so distraught by your illness she wouldn't leave your side. Kalisk . . . Madam Healer finally sent her to the infirmary for rest." Ziabela stood and crossed the room with her long stride. "Don't send me away, Lady. You set out on this journey because of what you heard in my song. You thought you would find someone to help you control the killing winds, but something went wrong. The need to speak of it is in your eyes."

Nemiah let her tone go cold. "I've no need to speak to a Shorn scribe."

Ziabela approached the bed, undeterred. "I can't begin to imagine what such a journey must mean. What is it like to escape your own boundaries?"

Escape? The woman's odd perception made Nemiah pause. She had no desire for escape. Boundaries meant order and definition; to cross them, even in Riana's service, was to risk chaos. Nemiah had proved that tonight, if nothing else. "Have you ever lain in bed and felt the world drop out from under you as you touched the edge of sleep?"

Ziabela nodded.

"Imagine that instead of catching up with the ground, you fall through a wall of fire before landing in some place as familiar as a winter night in your childhood home or so strange you don't even know what country you are in."

The scribe made a sound of fascination, and without seeking permission, folded herself at the foot of the bed. "Then what is it I feel when I'm falling asleep? Am I—?"

"You're no Pathwalker, Ziabela. You are Shorn. Such power would be anathema."

"Then what is it I feel?"

Nemiah waved a weary hand. "The same thing everyone with a hair of sensitivity to the Paths feels from time to time, a point of influence. A point where the Paths have split and turned in new directions. Most people experience only the sharpest turns at times when their minds are quiet. A Pathwalker senses much more subtle shifts."

"So you could travel to a point of influence in our past and change things that have happened? Perhaps prevent the killing winds from ever reaching us?"

"No." Nemiah plucked at the blanket, sadness filling her. "Only Riana can unravel her own weaving."

"Ah." The scribe folded her arms across her knees, her eyes crinkling in thought. "A point of influence is a moment of causation. The reason one thing happens instead of another."

"Something like that. Ziabela, these things are not for your ears."

"When you took me out of Elder Abrigado's hands, that was a point of influence, wasn't it?"

She was indeed a clever creature. Nemiah nodded reluctantly. "Yes. Likely a significant one."

"If you hadn't claimed me, I would never have been playing for the Arionade. You wouldn't have heard my songs. Perhaps you wouldn't have set out on the journey."

Perhaps I wouldn't have learned it was Lia's betrayal that made you Shorn. Nemiah closed her eyes.

"Lady," Ziabela murmured. "If a point of influence is the point of causation, then you must find the point that caused the killing winds to learn the source of their power."

Nemiah's eyes snapped open. "Enough! You make it sound as easy as opening a book to the right page. The Paths are infinite, and we have lost all the maps that might have helped us find the way. Enough! It's time for you to go."

The scribe's bright eyes clouded. "Please don't send me away. I didn't mean to press. I really just . . ." She glanced down shyly. "I've nothing to repay the debt I owe you, Lady, but I thought music might ease your spirit."

"I can't imagine any music that would comfort me tonight."

"You trusted me to choose for you before. Would you do so again?"

The scribe's apparent earnestness took Nemiah by surprise, and when it came to it, Nemiah wasn't prepared to be left alone with her thoughts. What more appropriate company for her now than a woman already accused of treachery? "Very well. Choose something. But carefully, Ziabela."

The melody to which the woman gave breath was at once fragile and enduring, sculpted from the air like softly falling snowflakes. Nemiah recognized "Morning's Kiss" from the *Songs of Praise*, and it filled her with images of her life in the temple: entering the sunlit sanctuary to welcome Riana to the morning devotion; witnessing the transition from child to novice as a young girl sang to the goddess for the first time; singing the songs herself, just for the joy of it. Every note from the flute bound her more securely to her own Path.

She hardly noticed as Ziabela's song led to another and a third, and then became the full cycle of the *Songs of Praise*. Nemiah let go of sadness just long enough to find her way to an honest, dreamless sleep.

12.
CAEL'S FOLLOWERS

"Where are you, dove? Please speak to me. I need to know you're safe."

"Lia?"

Nemiah awoke disoriented and shaking. Moonlight slid through latched shutters, cutting everything in the chamber with narrow blades of light: an ancient desk and matching table, bookshelves under faded tapestries, a high-arched ceiling over a large, soft bed. It might have been Amalia's tower or even Elia's. Nemiah twisted in the blankets, seeking some sign of herself, some sign that this was her place. Ziabela and the flute were gone. No broken pottery remained on the floor. On the bedside table sat two vials of brownish-green liquid. Nemiah grabbed one up and sniffed it. Immediately, her eyes watered at the sharp stench. She laughed a little through her tears. Kaliska's restoratives.

When she caught her breath, Nemiah slid out of bed, grateful someone had built up the fire. A platter of cold biscuits sat on the table. She took one, nibbling at it as she moved around the room in the near dark. She felt a disturbing strangeness, a sense her life no longer fit within the pattern demanded of her. The patterns of past generations remained here, witnessed by the ancient walls: Elia who had been a hero, Amalia who had been a traitor, and countless others long forgotten. They pressed on her.

She didn't know where she was going, but she knew she had to get out. She dug to the bottom of her clothes chest for the wool breeches and tunic she wore hunting with Capa. It took some time to find her thick grey cloak. It was downstairs crumpled by the hearth, likely just where Rom had dropped it when he carried her into the tower. Blood darkened the collar and most of the left shoulder. Looking at it, Nemiah realized just how near she had come to her own ending. She slipped into the stained wool; she must consider another ending now.

Only as she started for the door did she catch sight of the figure in the darkness. She drew up sharply to see Ziabela sleeping upright in one of the receiving room's leather chairs. Annoyance prickled through Nemiah as she strode over to wake the scribe, but she saw something else then, and stopped in the middle of the room. The woman had turned the chair so that she faced the door, a self-appointed guard. Nemiah thought of the well-tended fire and the swept pottery upstairs. She took another step toward the chair. In sleep, Ziabela's bright features were tightly knit, and her long hands twitched and wrung at her wrists, as though recalling the weight of chains. Nemiah's heart turned over.

"Serenity on your Path," she whispered. If Ziabela felt safe enough to sleep in the high priestess's chamber, let her rest. If she had begun to feel some connection to Riana, even better.

As Nemiah left, she said nothing to the Arionad on watch at her door, but drifted silently along the corridor. The hall was quiet; her own conflicts had not disturbed the sleeping sisters. She paused at the entrance to the archive, but Arnas wasn't on duty and she had no mind to deal with the histories just now. What she needed was to go beyond the temple walls; a different kind of boundary, those. Since she had come to the temple, the ancient stone had encompassed the important aspects of her world. Within the walls; she understood her role, even if she had never been quite clever or skilled enough to do what was expected of her. With slowly growing insight, she realized that her only hope of finding a Path for Avelos beyond doom and treachery was to break free of the constraining boundary of others' expectations. She must escape.

Turning away from the archive, Nemiah tucked the length of her unbound hair into her hood and headed for the kitchens; less likely there she would have to deal with an Arionad who would insist on accompanying her. Warm, yeasty smells greeted her as she pushed open the door into the kitchen chamber. Although the fire was banked, a lamp still burned, throwing friendly light upon the broad-shouldered figure of the baker bent over a table and kneading the morning's bread.

Nemiah hesitated at the doorway, reconsidering, but the matron glanced in her direction. Flour dusted her greying hair.

"Girl, if Mistress Maita's sent you to fetch a sampling of the fresh rolls, she'll have to wait. I can hardly keep up with all the extra mouths to feed, and now both my assistants are in bed with a cough."

Nemiah opened her mouth to announce herself, but on second thought pulled her hood farther forward and kept walking toward the door to the yards. "No, madam. Mistress Maita didn't send me."

The baker turned. Nemiah knew Linisi a little: a devout woman, not shy, strong opinions on the proper proportions of flour to butter in a peach cake. Ample proof of the importance of Riana's order could be found in a good cake, Linisi once told her.

"Where you off to so late, then?"

Nemiah chose her words carefully. "To give care to a woman in need of it."

"Ah, Healer Kaliska sending you out then, eh? Goddess keep mother and babe. And may no curse mark the child." The baker made a floury spiral in the air. It was a common thing, girls going out at all hours for Kaliska, and convenient; no one had to know whether they went out for the Guardians or the Shadow Guards.

"You keep an eye out," the baker added. "Streets turned nasty since the killing winds."

Nemiah nodded. "Yes, madam. Riana keep you."

The door to the yards was unbarred. She tugged it open, stepped into the cold, and closed it tight on the comforts behind her. Beyond the sputtering light of a single torch, lay the kitchen garden and the straw-strewn yard. The stables and goat shed were low, black blocks on the right, behind them, the peaked roof and open runs of the kennels. Mingled odors of animals and decaying vegetation tinged the night air.

Standing in that familiar place, something new stirred in Nemiah's chest, something freeing. In the moment when she had slipped loose of her identity, she had crossed another boundary. Although the thought unsettled her, she realized it might not be the last such crossing of the night.

Nemiah walked out of the yard, around the stables, and into the circular city plaza. Quiet filled the city's center at the crown of Travitar Hill. The sporadic riots and looting that battered the lower circles didn't climb this far—perhaps deterred by the imagined threat of guards from the palace or her own Arionade. It wasn't widely known that she had given up many of her men to help with the city cleanup. It was such a small gesture, the lending of strong backs and willing hearts. She hadn't been able to do any of the things that most mattered.

If the point of influence is causation, then you must find the point that caused the killing winds to learn the source of their power.

Even a Shorn scribe could name solutions, but it was the Lady's place to shift the Path toward answers. She had sent Leita with a patrol of Forest Guard to hunt for Sabela's temple, but she could no longer say whether Sabela's treasures might include the secret of the winds. Lia had expected to find the power to ease drought. Had Leita been sent on a fool's errand, after all? Nemiah paused in front of the high temple and looked up. The gold dome gleamed dully in the moonlight. Below the dome, beside the wide staircase that led to the sanctuary door, one lamp illuminated Riana's blessed, the Aye, carved in gorgeous detail in an incomplete circle on the wall. Nemiah ran her eyes over each of the Aye and murmured their names like a prayer—*Ularian, Silvien, Trevazio, Shira, Mavias.* In the past, their beauty had lent her a sense of peace. Tonight, she could only focus on the lower half of the carving, where the stone had been shattered by Tumal the Just. She had never known what images completed the circle. She wondered if Lia had been forced to witness the destruction of it or if the high priestess had been executed first.

Sickened by the thought, Nemiah turned away from the temple, wandering past the high chieftain's palace, Riana's fountain—silenced by the killing winds—and the library. By the time she reached the statue of Alende Isan towering in front of Elders' Hall, she was lightheaded and breathing hard. She wrapped her cloak close about her and folded to the ground to rest.

She faced the monument rather than leaning against it, unable to take comfort there. Alende's figure dominated the plaza, dwarfing Riana's fountain. The hero was depicted with no sign of his guide, Lady Sabela, but only his hound. He bore a staff in one hand, and beneath his heel, he crushed one of Cael's messengers—as though a mortal man alone could possibly possess the strength and wisdom to defeat the demon. Commissioned by Lord Tumal, the monument was another sign that Riana's servants had been found irrelevant. It was a mark of endings, and Nemiah had been thinking on endings since she returned from her journey.

You were not meant to be Chosen. Bena's words again. Nemiah had never convinced herself she was a leader. The authority of the Chosen had never felt quite right in her hands. So many of her rituals lacked power; so many of her choices seemed futile. Her own fault, she had long ago decided. She had clung to the belief that her devotion to Riana would make up for her meager skills and help her to shift this Path away from chaos, but her friendship with Lia proved she had been wrong.

Her Path must change now. In the end, she would traverse a boundary she had never expected. Bena was right: a stronger Lady must be Chosen. It must be Leita. It should always have been Leita. When the Bearer returned, Nemiah would step down and Leita would be purified of Cael's taint so she might travel the Paths. Nemiah's heart ached. She would miss studying the histories and arguing interpretations of the maps, greeting the goddess at each devotion, and working with the young ones. By stepping down as Chosen Lady, she would surrender her life's purpose, but that loss she would somehow master. What tore her heart and threatened to undo her choice was the fact that by Rom's Dawnings' Eve oath, her decision to give up Riana's service must be his as well.

"Hello, little temple mouse," said a woman's voice in the dark. "You look pensive. What wisdom have you found in Alende Isan?"

Nemiah jumped to her feet as an elongated shadow stretched up before her: a tall, hooded figure.

"Perhaps she's dreaming of that wisdom Riana's girls so rarely find," answered a male voice, "the wisdom a man offers a woman in the night."

A second figure, broader and strong-looking, parted from the shadows of the monument and strolled behind Nemiah.

"Not so," continued the woman, her voice amused. "The girls of Riana need no such wisdom. Don't you know? They drop babes from their fingertips, like acorns from the oak tree."

"I have nothing of value," Nemiah said, darting a glance to the man behind her and back to the woman.

The man snickered. "I think we should be insulted, Yarla. We've just been taken for thieves."

"I doubt she understands the irony of one of Riana's servants naming us thieves. Do you know what you steal from the world, temple mouse? Do you know all that was lost when Riana came into being? Do you know how to walk steady on the dark Paths?"

The woman's words fell like a stone into a pool, sending ripples through the Paths. Kaliska had begged Nemiah to leave Velantar to escape the danger of Cael's cults. If these two had come for a priestess's blood, it was too late to tell Kaliska she'd been right.

Nemiah pulled herself straight. "I will walk steadily wherever Riana's order takes me."

No City Guards were on patrol to call for help. What need for City Guards with the high temple and the palace so close? But Nemiah had sent most of her Arionade into the circles of the city. It had seemed such a small thing.

"As bravely and ignorantly spoken as I might expect from the high temple," the woman muttered, less amused now. "Riana was not meant to rule this Path. She cannot achieve True Balance on her own any more than you can get an heir without your Arionad."

"Yarla, no time for teaching. It's not why we've come."

The woman started to say something more, but the man cut her off. "Look at her. The girl's no fool. She might be one of the Shadows."

"Perhaps." The woman's eyes gleamed within her cowl. "Are you out collecting seeds for your spy mistress, mouse?"

Nemiah looked toward the temple. The entrance was impossibly far, and she was weak from blood loss and days of journeying. She hadn't intended that her service to Riana end this way, but then no one is permitted to see the twists at the end of her own Path.

"Now, now, let's not play chase," Yarla purred, guessing her thoughts. "No Arionade are waiting at the temple door. We know it as well as you. And besides, we have a gift for you." The woman moved forward. As her cloak fluttered back, the hilt of a short sword shone in the moonlight.

Nemiah threw a prayer to the night and ran.

She fled toward the center of the plaza, hoping to evade the man behind her, but her boots slipped on the smooth cobbles, making a mockery of her effort. Before she had gone nine steps, a strong arm caught her around the shoulders and swung her about until she was again in front of Alende's monument. The man shoved her into the stone of the pedestal.

Stone scraped her cheek and forehead. Her heart raced. "You may take my blood, but you'll not have my spirit!"

The woman chuckled, but it was the man who restrained Nemiah against the stone.

"Oh, brave mouse! Let none doubt your stout heart. We have no need for your blood tonight. We only need to know if you can take a message to your Chosen Lady."

"A message from whom?"

The woman *tsked*. "Not your turn for questions. Will the Lady of Avelos hear it if I give the message to you?"

Mad laughter caught in Nemiah's throat. She nodded.

"These words come from the Bearer of Cael's Blade who has given us her trust."

Nemiah stiffened. Alende's monument cut into her cheek.

"That means something to her," the man said, shifting his grip.

"Good. It will help her to remember."

"Why?" Nemiah choked. Not *how*. The first question should have been how did the Bearer send a message? But fear and loss already overfilled her heart. Nemiah had to know *why* followers of Cael had a message from her closest friend.

"Don't ask me why the Holy Bearer bothers with a message for a woman so rigid and ignorant," Yarla snapped. "It's not my place to question, or yours. Are you listening?"

Nemiah could only nod again.

"Too many open doors may explain uncontrolled journeys. Traveling is perilous without a guide. Do not cross the Gate alone."

A warning. A warning not to travel the Paths. Why would Cael's followers want her to have it? "What proof this comes from the Bearer?"

"Proof? You've just been given a gift. It doesn't matter to us if your Lady chooses not to accept it."

"Wrong. It does matter," the man said gruffly. "Or the Bearer wouldn't have sent it." He leaned closer to Nemiah. She caught the scent of ashes. "How's this for proof? We know of the Lady's Avelun ancestor."

Nemiah tried to sink further into her cowl. "Anyone who looks in her eyes knows the Lady has the curse in her line."

The man snorted. "But not everyone knows that her ancestor served the high temple at the time of the Exile. Or that she died at Tumal's hand."

The words stabbed through Nemiah. Among her advisors and friends, only Leita and Rom knew her cursed ancestor had been among the first of the priestesses executed by Tumal. No one in her family would even utter the woman's name. It might have been Amalia herself, Nemiah thought dizzily; blood calls to blood across the Paths, after all. Rom would die before he told her secret. Nemiah had never believed Leita could possibly expose her.

From somewhere in the distance, footsteps echoed against stone. It must be her Pathguide coming to claim her spirit, for betrayal had cut her open. Nemiah cried out to the goddess. Let none believe she too had chosen the demon at the end.

The Pathguide answered her cry with a roar of warning. The footsteps accelerated.

Yarla hissed a command. The arm that grasped Nemiah disappeared. Abruptly freed, she took an unsteady step away from the monument, but her feet found nothing solid beneath them. She flailed for balance as the world tipped forward. The plaza slid away down a long, steep road into darkness.

She was still lying on the ground when awareness crept back to her. Hands were moving over her body, turning her gently. She tried to pull away.

"Easy, child. They've gone. Are you hurt?"

The rough voice was at once familiar and strange. Nemiah opened her eyes. She licked her lips and tasted dirt. A man knelt beside her, not a Pathguide at all. From beyond the edge of her hood, Nemiah saw breeches and boots and a belt with no sword. His hands felt down her limbs, but she lacked the strength to escape the indignity. Fingers moved across the left collar of her cloak and paused. The man swore.

"Be still now." His arm came around her, lifting her easily.

As he cradled her against his chest, her hood fell back, letting the length of her hair tumble free. She lifted her gaze to see a wind-lined face with sharp grey eyes peering down at her. Moonlight gleamed on his tousled copper mane.

"Oh, Goddess."

His eyes widened and his mouth opened. For an instant, she thought he would drop her. She had never seen Adan Rumar startled to speechlessness.

"I'm all right," she managed.

Not exactly true, but he couldn't see the wounds they had dealt her. *Oh, Leita.* She braced against the cry that was working its way from deep within her heart. Two betrayals so close together, twin blades: the two women to whom she had entrusted her spirit.

"You've taken a blow," Rumar said, unexpectedly perceptive. "Come with me, Lady Nemiah."

He didn't give her the option to refuse and didn't put her down, but carried her into Elders' Hall. Nemiah was aware of the warmth and clean scent of his body as they traveled dark, empty corridors. Rumar stopped at a door in a narrow hall and elbowed his way into a small room. Lamplight threw shadows across a cluttered desk, several shelves of scrolls, a low table, and a small bed with rumpled blankets. The chamber smelled faintly of smoke from a smoldering brazier and the remnants of a meal that had been pushed to one side on the desk.

He laid her upon the bed and took a step backward. "I've no attendant here. I must run to the temple for your healer."

"No." Nemiah struggled to sit up. She could imagine the panic that would take the temple if the high chieftain appeared calling for Kaliska. She couldn't afford to reveal to Bena and the others just how weak she was. "No," she said again. "I'm not injured."

"You are. Unless that blood on your cloak belongs to someone else."

"That was different. My Arionad. It was . . . necessary."

Rumar's brow rose. Nemiah lifted her hand to her scraped cheek. "Tonight they didn't use a blade."

His eyes didn't release her. "Who were they?"

She realized why his voice had sounded so strange at first; it had been filled with concern and tenderness, tenderness for an injured stranger on the street. Now that he knew her, his voice had returned to its formal, unyielding timbre.

"Followers of Cael," she said. "Do you know what that means?"

"That they wanted a priestess's blood. Did they know who you are?"

Nemiah hadn't expected him to understand so quickly. She hadn't been certain he would acknowledge Cael's disciples at all. Not every elder believed the demon's followers were responsible for the horrors that took place in the shadows of the city. Cael had many uses for the blood of Riana's Chosen Lady, but the woman named Yarla had only given her a message. From Leita. Nemiah began to shiver.

"Do not cross the Gate without a guide," the message said.

Leita, my heart, what have you done?

Without speaking, Rumar took a bottle from the desk, drained the half-empty glass beside it, and refilled the glass. Yellow liquor trembled precariously at the rim when he placed it into her hand.

"They didn't know you," he concluded on his own. "Else they wouldn't have lingered in the plaza to be caught. They would have taken you with them. What were you doing out in the depth of night with no Arionade?"

Her head was spinning from spent fear and Rumar's arrow-swift pace, but she refused to let him open her like this, pulling whatever information he wanted. She tried to gather her wits. "That's two questions, Lord Rumar. Are you more interested in what intrigues brought me out or why my guards didn't join me?"

Rumar's expression darkened. He had remained standing near the bed and his broad frame seemed to fill the tiny room. "Pardon my tone, Lady. I am trying to avoid a war while leading a council too divided to agree upon the color of the sky. With your sway over the western clans, you could give Abrigado nearly a majority in the council if you chose to. I'd be a fool not to be wary."

Nemiah stared, anger steadying her a little. "Taking Abrigado's Shorn scribe out of his reach—making the Legacy an open enemy—wasn't enough to assure you I'm not with them?"

"You make Abrigado's mistake if you think me unable to play a deeper game than that." Rumar looked unmoved. "You and he are both dissatisfied with my rule, and not all your ideals are opposing, after all. I expected you would use the Shorn scribe as leverage to pull favors from me or the Legacy.

"And *I* haven't heard from you," he added pointedly.

"I didn't claim the Right of Advocacy for political gain, Lord Rumar! I did it to save a woman from torture!"

There was a silence. An uncertain expression wiped the antagonism from the high chieftain's face. He lowered himself into the only chair and glanced at a stack of letters on the desk before returning his gaze to Nemiah's. "I cannot tell you how very much I want to believe that."

Years of conflict had formed a chasm between them. Perhaps if his wife and child had lived, Adan Rumar might have been a different man, but what happens on the Paths—a moment of deep sorrow or remembered joy—shapes a man and pushes him toward places he might not otherwise go. On this Path, Adan Rumar sacrificed order and balance to achieve his goals. Nemiah had always known him to be harsh, irreverent, and uncompromising.

Tonight he had run into the street unarmed to rescue a stranger.

She looked at him again, the High Chieftain of Avelos. In some ways, he reminded her of Enrian: both were broadly built and physically powerful men, both keenly intelligent and clear thinking, but Rumar owned none of Enrian's cultivated objectivity. The high chieftain's face was a complex architecture of shrewdness and impatience; his hands were calloused like a soldier's and ink-stained like a scribe's. He ruled a country of clans defined by their kinship ties, yet he had never brought himself to take another wife or produce heirs. Too many contradictions existed in him for Rumar to know peace. In the uncertainty shadowing his eyes now, Nemiah saw an isolated leader searching for a reason to trust. She wondered that he allowed her to see such a vulnerability, but perhaps she only recognized it because it resonated with her own feelings tonight. She lifted a hand, unable to continue the subtle game.

"I left the temple without Arionade because I needed to escape. To think."

He looked at her skeptically.

"You wanted to know why I was out alone," she said. "I needed to think without the demands of centuries of priestesses and my own advisors crowding me."

"I see," Rumar muttered.

Nemiah took a sip of the liquor. It was potent and sour-sweet, with a scent that reminded her of sunshine. It seemed meant for celebrations and summer evenings, not dangerous nights and the games of power.

"I'm not mocking you," the high chieftain went on. "I know what it's like to have to dig through others' expectations to find your own thoughts. The ghosts of my father and grandfathers and a palace full of sycophants hound me." His tone lost some of its crafted quality, dropping lower with candor.

Nemiah's gaze roamed the little room: only one chair, a rumpled bed, a single glass, no attendants. This wasn't a place to which Rumar readily brought others. It was a place to work alone and undisturbed, his small escape.

"I'm grateful you felt the need to flee your own ghosts tonight," she said. "That is why you came out, isn't it?"

He smiled in response, a quick, vibrant expression that offered a glimpse of a younger, less burdened man. Nemiah thought she caught a flash of something else in that smile, something astonishing that made her flush. Then his smile vanished. He picked up the bottle and leaned forward to refill her glass.

"The drink is *vavaneh*," he said. "It's Sahisten."

She waved away the bottle. "I didn't know that."

"Prince Ashani gave it to me at Velanhan. His people drink it at important gatherings—weddings, funerals, business negotiations—to remember that life ever offers sweetness and sorrow."

"A ritual of balance," she said. "Unexpected."

"They're not the vicious brutes we'd have them be, Nemiah. The prince and I spoke of many things in Velanhan—not only the weighty matters between our nations. I saw something of who he is." Rumar took the glass from her and filled it for himself. His eyes closed as he sipped. "It's difficult to hate a man when you've heard him speak lovingly of his children and seen his worry for their future."

Nemiah remained quiet, feeling the ebb and flow of the Path beneath her like a tide. She wondered if something positive might be carved from this moment, something to keep the bitterness of the night at bay. *Sweetness and sorrow.* She had meant to step down as Chosen Lady, to see Leita selected, but Leita had gone beyond her reach, perhaps even beyond the reach of the goddess.

"Two letters arrived from Sahiste today," the high chieftain said at length.

Nemiah startled from her reflection. "Two?" All of Avelos had been waiting for a response from Sahiste: King Javahari's response to the council's refusal to open the border. But it only took one letter to start a war.

"The first letter we anticipated. It's from Javahari. It's—" Rumar frowned. "Forgive me. You're weary, and you needn't be burdened tonight. I must address the council in the morning. The temple has the right to be there."

Nemiah pulled herself straighter from where she had leaned against the wall. She *was* weary, desperately so, but something important was shaping the Path here, and she could see how badly Rumar wished to speak. "Please, go on. No one should have to bear such tidings alone."

"Very well, then. Javahari's letter is what I would have expected from him five years ago. It's blunt and aggressive, with none of the restraint he's shown in recent years. He berates us for turning our backs on the potential for mutual gain. He warns against incursions into his lands and says that an overwhelming Forest Guard presence in Maren's Burn will be viewed as an imminent threat." Rumar paused, finished the *vavaneh* and set down the glass. "He closes by addressing me specifically as a coward as foolish as my father and the leaders before him."

"He wrote that of you?" An outrageous taunt. Rumar was the first high chieftain since the Exile War willing to consider Sahiste as anything other than a foe to be destroyed.

The high chieftain's smile this time was sharp and thin. "Perhaps he meant to be ironic, but I think not."

"And the second letter?"

"From Prince Ashani." Rumar lifted the page under his hand and held it out to her. "What do you notice?"

She took the letter, feeling a spot of warmth on the vellum from Rumar's hand, quickly gone. The calligraphy was accomplished, and the Velos was fluent, if somewhat old fashioned. Clearly, the note hadn't been written in haste. Nemiah's hands grew clammy as she scanned the page.

King Javahari's key advisors in the *Camril Fi* opposed peace with Avelos, the heir wrote, and while his uncle did not wish for war, in the face of Avelonian rejection, Javahari looked weak if he did not show his teeth. The prince urged Rumar not to respond impulsively to the king's threats, reminding the high chieftain that neither of their countries would benefit from more years of bloodshed. He closed with an appeal to some foreign god, words not vastly different from Nemiah's own prayer to Riana as she finished reading:

"May Lumati's eyes help us to see our way through darkness."

As she dropped the letter into her lap, the seal caught her eye. It wasn't the royal seal of Sahiste—three crowns above entwined serpents—but a single snake coiled around a nest of eggs, fangs presented. She looked up.

"Ashani's family seal," the high chieftain replied to her unasked question. "This note didn't come through a court scribe. The prince wrote it himself."

"Of course. Discovery of such a letter would surely cost him something."

Rumar set down his drink. "Nemiah, he reveals internal politics and speaks of his king's weakness. It could cost him the throne."

"Unless it's a ploy. The two letters together to weaken our commitment to the border."

Rumar took the letter from her and tossed it back onto the desk. He looked disheartened. "Not with Ashani a part of it. He's no callow boy to be manipulated by the court, and he's not alone. The priests are with him. The Favored of Lumati, he calls them. Their temple holds significant influence in Sahiste, not like

. . ." Rumar grimaced and shook his head. "It's more than that, though. Ashani's ready for peace. I saw it. It's our bad fortune he's not yet wielding the power of the crown."

"What will you do?"

"The only thing I can do, defend Avelos as best I might. Our increased military presence at the border may force Javahari to war, but at least we'll be prepared. If I don't fortify the south, the war-mongering factions in the Sahisten court are likely to push the king to take advantage of the opening and invade. With Laebek to back them, that kind of opening could be catastrophic."

War in Avelos. All of Velantar had been buzzing with the possibility for weeks. Now that it seemed a promise, Nemiah found herself unable to accept it. War meant hardship, violence, and death for men and women she knew, for the people she loved. So long as it had not yet come to pass, surely some way existed to avoid it. "Slow down, Adan. Please. What does General Nadel advise?"

"I don't know yet. He's four days on the road to Ravia. The courier must have passed the troops on the way."

"Oh." She hadn't known Enrian was gone. He had left while she traveled with Lia. His absence shouldn't have mattered, but she felt the loss. He was marching to face an army of Sahisten spears, and she had promised him she would meet with Adan Rumar. Another of Riana's spirals spinning them.

She straightened again, abruptly aware of Rumar's eyes on her, aware her hair was unbound and she was sitting in his bed. She cleared her throat and reached for her ritual tone. "You should send an ambassador to Sahiste."

"Certainly," the high chieftain replied dryly. "Perhaps Toren Abrigado. That way I might rid myself of two problems at once."

"I don't mean it in jest. Send someone of rank who can continue the discussion about the border and reassure Javahari you don't intend to attack pre-emptively. At best, it will calm the factions and perhaps pave the way for further negotiations. If not, it will at least win us more time to prepare for an attack."

"Any men I send would be little more than hostages. And targets for assassination by those who fear peace."

"Javahari sent us his heir," she observed.

Frustration flashed over the high chieftain's features. "And I would have opened the borders for him! If only the killing winds hadn't ripped apart the city. Even then, I would have done it. A new trade partner would go far to recovering the wealth the winds destroyed. We *need* new markets! It took Trianor and Nadel to convince me the council would fracture if I did it." With a look of disgust, he dropped back into his chair. "No doubt they were right."

Nemiah saw something intriguing then. Rumar was too accustomed to using his power to herd people where he wanted them. When dealing with a man he couldn't overwhelm with his own personality and strength, he found himself at an impasse. By contrast, Nemiah had long engaged in political battles in which she possessed little power at all. She had survived by discovering two truths: that men define themselves through the reflections they see in others' eyes, and that most men have a need to see themselves reflected well. She understood what Javahari had done and how it must be answered.

"Opening the border isn't the only way you can respond, Rumar. Javahari made himself and all Sahiste vulnerable when he sent his heir. He needs to believe we understand and respect his gift or else we hold ourselves above him and he's humiliated. We *must* show some vulnerability in return. You must send someone."

The high chieftain grimaced. "Not easily done."

She frowned. "How many soldiers did you just dispatch to the border?"

"Perhaps you think that putting another handful of men at risk shouldn't matter. But it does."

Genuine pain thickened his voice. As so many other things this night, it surprised her to realize that sending men into harm's way wasn't merely something Rumar did by right; he regretted the need for it and mourned the losses. Nemiah thought of something Enrian had told her: *He's given himself to Avelos no less than you have.*

She hadn't believed it then.

The entire night had been about endings, since she had learned that she had befriended a traitor. Grief made it difficult to remember that endings were only illusions. Though a man might die too soon on one Path, somewhere else in Riana's infinite weaving he lived a full life. Though Avelos might fall to foreign armies, on another Path her people would continue to tell their stories. Though a Chosen Lady might give up her home and safety and all she loved, somewhere her heart was sated. Endings had no truth to them. Nemiah knew that. As she began to see the direction her Path must take, she wouldn't allow the perception of endings to paralyze her.

"I'm the one who must go."

Astonishment lit Rumar's grey eyes. "Nemiah, how could you possibly? You despise Sahiste. You see our destruction in our dealings with them. Has that changed?"

Her fear hadn't changed, but her understanding had: a necessary symmetry existed here. She had loved Amalia, who had first betrayed Avelos with Sahiste; now her life ran like a mirror of Amalia's. Perhaps that meant building trust where the Avelun had torn it apart. Perhaps it meant seeking new connections in foreign lands when her dearest friends had become strangers.

It wasn't wholly absurd to imagine she might do this thing. She possessed some skills after all, not the boldness and strength a Chosen Lady should have, but gentler gifts, the ability to recognize the form of a man's need and the ability to listen with an honest heart.

"It should be me," she repeated. "Think on it. Sahiste will want an accounting for the past. Those who most oppose peace will put the treachery of Lady Amalia before us as evidence of our dishonor. Who else but the high priestess can give answer for that?" She didn't drop her gaze from Rumar's, but under her cloak, her hands trembled. "It's a chance to avoid war, Adan."

Rumar looked perplexed. "You do love Avelos, don't you? The people, not just the distant goddess. Nadel tried to tell me that."

It gave her a moment of pause to realize Enrian had spoken to each of them about the other. She wondered what else the general had told Rumar about her. "Have you truly believed my heart so small it could hold only one love?"

"I've long assumed Riana demands everything from her Chosen Lady. I've seen little from you in nine years to suggest otherwise."

"Perhaps because for nine years I've been forced to defend her so fiercely!"

"Perhaps," he admitted without venom. He pushed both hands through his hair, shoving the dark copper strands into further disarray.

She sighed. So many years of conflict had made her anger reflexive. "How much of what we've come to despise in one another is merely the shadow of our own fears, Lord Rumar?"

He leaned back in his chair. "That is a question I would very much like the chance to answer."

This time, the warmth in his expression was unmistakable. Nemiah glanced away. "Do you agree I must go to Sahiste?"

"It is a larger sacrifice than I would ask."

"You could not ask it. This is something I must give."

He nodded, and she saw he understood: her offer was for Avelos not for him. "It is truly a wise idea to send someone, Nemiah. I should have seen it myself."

"You will send word to King Javahari that I'm coming?"

"The courier will leave in the morning." His fingers drummed across Ashani's letter; then he looked back at her. "I would offer something to Riana in return."

She looked at him warily, at the intensity in his eyes.

"I want to lift the ban on the Tests of Rona."

She gaped, then startled beyond all wisdom blurted, "The Legacy would never allow it!"

For such words, he might have been furious, but he laughed instead. It was the first time she had heard him laugh so artlessly. It brightened his eyes, like sunlight on a storm cloud. "Allow a man *some* pride. Abrigado does not rule the council yet. Nor do I intend to hand him my seat by acting foolishly. The western clans have been clamoring to lift the ban for some time, and one or two of the northern five might rejoice at it as well. I could use their good will."

What Rumar offered was no mere token. For generations, the Tests of Rona had intimately connected the goddess to the soldiers who defended Avelos. Men seeking promotion were required to first pass rigorous trials of body and spirit to earn consecration by Riana's servants. The Tests had not only allowed the temple to influence the appointment of Forest Guard officers; through the ritual blessing, they had also bred children for Riana from the most able men in Avelos. When Adan's father banned the Tests, the temple had lost its last significant share of power in the council. Lifting the ban could help to bring Riana out of the shadows.

"It is a worthy gesture, Lord Rumar." Nemiah's voice slipped from her control to waver slightly.

He looked pleased. "I'm glad you see it so. I begin to suspect I've undervalued *your* good will, Lady."

She liked the frank tone of his voice just then. A breeze flowed across her shoulders and played with her hair, as though someone had opened two doors in a hall at the same time. She had a sudden sense of vital moments passing by, opportunities for change here and gone. Close, too close, she sensed the tumult of chaos. She drew a calming breath.

And inhaled Rumar's warm scent. She thought to pull away, but relaxed into his embrace instead. Something sacred flared between them. Riana's power filled her, a blessing to be offered. She stood on tiptoe and brushed her lips across Rumar's. He tasted of vavaneh. It was he who ended the kiss, drawing back to study her, his eyes serious and tender, a question manifest there.

"You are the body of Avelos as I am the spirit," she answered. *"Let us heal the discord between us and end the suffering in our land."*

Rumar smiled, a lifting of his features that was at once knowing and shy. She laughed a little at the contradiction, then pressed herself closer to the strength of him. Truly, it was a sacred thing they wrought here. He bore her backward toward the bed, and willingly she drew him down to her. A needful sound escaped his throat as she opened herself to him.

Nemiah slapped a hand against the bandaged wound beneath her jaw and gasped at the pain. The heat of intimacy faded. She glared around the room in confusion.

"You're safe in Elders' Hall," Rumar murmured. "You only drifted off for a moment."

Drifted off, indeed. *Too many doors are open,* Leita had warned. Nemiah didn't understand how that could be or why the Bearer knew such a thing. Perhaps she would never find out. Leita had betrayed her for Cael's disciples.

Nemiah rose from the bed, bracing one hand against the wall to steady herself. "It's time I return to the temple."

Rumar offered her his arm. "Allow me to see you there."

She nodded a cool thanks, then stepped carefully toward the door without taking his arm. She didn't dare risk reaching out to him. On some other Path, she had offered him Riana's blessing.

On this Path, he came up beside her. "It's all right, Nemiah. We've both revealed some vulnerability tonight. Let us not regret it. Perhaps it can be a small step toward better understanding between us."

"Perhaps." Again, she sensed opportunities passing, perhaps a point of influence waiting to be grasped—but where would that point lead them? Adan Rumar was yet a clever, powerful man. By his own admission he had given her nothing that would cost him with the council, while she had agreed to go to Sahiste, leaving Riana's servants leaderless. She mustn't be lulled. There was a history of blood between them. The deeds of Lady Amalia and Tumal the Just could not be forgotten in a night.

"You are the body of Avelos as I am the spirit."

"Lady, you're not well. Won't you let me seek your healer? Nemiah?"

He repeated her name with soft uncertainty, like a prayer from a man who did not pray.

She took another step away from him, difficult to do in the small room. "No. It's no illness you witness, only a part of what Riana requires."

Rumar drew back a little at her tone. Easy for him to speak of vulnerability when he still had faith in his own strength. "I understand."

He couldn't possibly understand, but Nemiah's body betrayed her attempt to rally her anger, flooding her with a flash from that other Path: Adan's weight and warmth above her, the unlooked for tenderness in his gaze. In that other place, she had offered him Riana's gift, and he had accepted.

Without another word, she hurried from the room, past the point of trusting even herself.

13.
SPREADING POISON

Linisi was too busy preparing breakfast to acknowledge Nemiah when she slipped through the door from the kitchen yards. Two sleepy novices brushed past, offering distracted good-mornings on their way to milk the goats. No one else paid Nemiah any mind. With her hood pulled up, she was only a slight figure heading for some morning duty with the other girls. She might have been any novice. She might have been anyone.

At the door to her tower, the curly-haired night guard Jhesco did at least bend to see her face before allowing her to pass. A reliable Arionad, Jhesco. Nemiah tottered into her receiving room and gazed the long way across the chamber to the stairs that spiraled up to her bed.

She had forgotten about the Shorn scribe.

"Lady Nemiah, I'm so relieved to see you!"

Ziabela stood from where she had been seated at the table, wiped the reed she held, and stoppered the ink. Her slippers made no noise on the thick wool rug as she hurried over. With slender fingers, she unfastened the clasp on Nemiah's cloak and exchanged the soiled grey wool for the green wrap that had been waiting by the fire.

"Oh, Lady, you're icy! It's a cold night to walk in the city. Sit here near the hearth."

Half-stunned by the warmth and attention, Nemiah sank into the chair as the scribe brought her a steaming mug of tea. She cupped her fingers around the heat.

"Ziabela, how did you know?"

"That you've been outside the temple?" The scribe crouched by Nemiah's chair. "You took your heavy cloak. Jhesco said you left no orders about where you were going or when you'd return. I guessed you sought a bit of peace where the others wouldn't find you."

"And what have you been doing all this while?" Nemiah looked around her receiving room, wondering what correspondence might have been accessible to an intelligent Shorn woman accused of treason.

"Waiting for you." The woman smiled prettily. "I started working on the task you gave me."

Nemiah struggled to recall what task the scribe was talking about. "You've been . . . writing songs?"

Ziabela smiled again and brought Nemiah a piece of new vellum half-filled with neat, small lines of text, a scribe's hand. As Nemiah read the poetry, Ziabela made herself busy at the fire.

"This is lovely. It's Elia's story, isn't it? The one you played in the garden."

"Lady Elia seemed important to you. I thought I would start with that one. It's been a long time since I recalled the words to her full cycle."

Ziabela returned to the chair carrying a bowl of steaming water and a piece of folded cloth.

Nemiah frowned. "What's this?"

"Lady, if you wish to keep the story of your wandering to yourself, it would be wise to clean the blood from your face."

"Ah. I suppose so."

Ziabela balanced the bowl on the arm of the chair and Nemiah took the cloth from her. She dipped it into the hot water and wrung it out. Her cheek was tender, but the heat felt good.

When she finished, the scribe looked closely. "There will be a small bruise. Here on your forehead there's still . . ." Ziabela took up the cloth. "May I?"

Nemiah hesitated, then nodded. "Tend to it."

Gently, the Shorn woman dabbed the cloth over Nemiah's brow where Yarla's man had pushed her into the stone. He had smelled of ashes. Nemiah had thought they meant to kill her. She drew a tremulous breath.

Ziabela set down the cloth, her green eyes glittering. "May those who dared to harm you find their punishment long and painful."

Nemiah glanced up in surprise. "You are presuming, Ziabela."

"Am I? Forgive me then." The Shorn scribe carried the bowl back to the hearth.

Nemiah studied the woman's stiff back. Ziabela had been at the mercy of the City Guard for nearly the turn of a moon. She had been shackled and tortured. She still clutched her wrists in her sleep.

"Forgiven," Nemiah replied.

The scribe inclined her head in acknowledgment.

Nemiah leaned into the chair, not quite stifling a groan. Dawn was creeping upon them, and she had decisions to make. She was leaving Avelos to cross a border that she had never imagined crossing, into the land of the serpent. Who would she risk to bring with her? Who would keep the temple in order while she was gone? What must be done to protect Riana's servants before she left? After those questions were answered, there would be the most difficult, heartrending thing to decide: what must be done about Leita?

A knock jerked her up from the well of contemplation.

"I'll answer it." Ziabela started toward the antechamber. "Shall I send them away?"

"Yes. Please." Nemiah was in no state to greet anyone or to tell others all the things she must.

"Zia? What are you doing here?" The healer's voice at the door was sharp with surprise.

The scribe spoke quietly. "Only . . . to be of use and . . ."

"No. I understand well enough what you hope for, and I won't allow it. Lady Nemiah has risked enough for you. Let me in."

" . . . very sorry. The Chosen Lady is not . . ."

"You test a spirit's patience, Ziabela. Move aside."

Something thudded against the wall—the door being pushed wide, Nemiah thought. Then Kaliska appeared in the receiving room, the scribe at her heels.

The spy keeper could be difficult to read, her grey eyes as clear and calm as a sacred pool, but as she gazed upon Nemiah sagging in the chair, bruises on her cheek, and wearing clothes soiled from her encounters, Kaliska's expression opened into an improbable landscape of urgency and dismay.

"I'm afraid you must tell me about it later. Bena's on her way to the tower. The rest of the Higher Circle is behind her."

Nemiah blinked. "What do they expect to find?"

"Bena hopes to prove you too incapacitated to lead. It seems she's decided that if she cannot unseat you fully, she'll start by appointing a Lady Interim."

"Oh, Goddess guide us." Nemiah sank deeper into the chair. She had only ever known the position of Lady Interim to be appointed at the death of the Chosen of Avelos while the Higher Circle debated the selection of the next Lady. It was a position meant to maintain order. Nemiah bridled that Bena would use it to create turmoil.

"As your healer, I can keep them from the room and delay their vote," Kaliska said, "but if the Circle does not speak with you and find your mind intact, I fear they will go forward with the appointment."

"You truly think they have so little faith in me?"

The healer looked aside. "They will be here very soon. You might want to dress more suitably if you wish to face them."

Nemiah touched the back of her hand to her cheek, uncertain and heartsore. Would it be so terrible to let the Circle appoint a woman they trusted? Even now, she didn't truly blame Bena or the others; she had led them wrong in so many ways. But she had told the high chieftain she would travel to Sahiste, as though she might balance Lady Amalia's treachery. If she were meant for such a balancing, it mattered that she remain Chosen Lady. Nemiah gazed at the vellum where the scribe had written part of the story of the other Lia, Lady Elia who had sacrificed her happiness for Avelos. With a sudden intensity, Nemiah sensed that who she was now did indeed matter. She could not allow Bena to make her irrelevant.

Footsteps clicked on the spiral stairs. Ziabela descended from Nemiah's bedchamber carrying her green dress, along with slippers, a brush, and a handful of ribbons.

"May I help dress your hair, Lady? I've been told I have nimble fingers for such things."

Kaliska gave the Shorn woman a look that could have melted glass.

Nemiah smiled a little queasily. "Hurry then. We've not much time."

The Shorn scribe and the keeper of the Shadow Guards made unlikely handmaids, but they helped Nemiah to shed her boots and stained clothes and to pull her dress over her head. As Ziabela's deft fingers tamed the length of Nemiah's hair into a braid, Kaliska tilted Nemiah's chin toward the lamplight, frowning as she examined the wound at her throat.

"Bena's not going to make this easy, Nemiah. Can you manage it?"

"I hope so. I'd rather not support her argument by fainting in front of her."

The healer nodded, her lips pressed together. Her gaze went to the scribe. "We must get this one out of here. It's unwise for her to be seen so close to you."

Three loud raps at the door halted the healer's words.

Nemiah stood. "Ziabela, go into Merisel's room and shut the door. Don't step out until Kaliska comes for you."

The scribe gave a small, eager bow. Nemiah heard the outer door open and braced herself, but only Rom rushed in. His black gaze flew from Nemiah to the healer to the disappearing scribe.

"You know then."

Nemiah nodded. "I told you Bena wouldn't let it go." A quick breath, then the necessary words: "You can't stay, Rom. Bena will use you to detour from what I must tell the Circle. I can't allow it."

Her Arionad stiffened. His coat was fresh and spotless; his boots gleamed, but his red-rimmed eyes suggested he had slept no better than she had.

Women's voices echoed in the outer hall. No time remained for explanations.

"Into Merisel's chamber, Captain. Try not to frighten the scribe." Kaliska gave Rom's shoulder a little shove.

"Wait!" The others halted, staring at Nemiah. "Wait," she said again. "This is absurd. If I am to maintain any authority, I can't let Bena bully me. I've had enough. Stay here."

Nemiah turned her back on her Arionad and healer and strode through the antechamber, thinking quickly. She must not let Bena goad her into anger or submission. Her advisors had the right to be concerned by her absence; she would not dismiss their fears, but she must not let them goad her. The latch pressed against her palm as she opened the door. Four women were clustered around an unhappy-looking Jhesco, snapping at him like an angry flock of gulls. As Nemiah stepped out, they all jumped a little, their gazes filled with surprise, all but Bena's. Frustration flooded the Mapmaker's desiccated features as she looked Nemiah up and down.

Nemiah schooled her features to calm. "Riana light your ways, Mistresses. Bena, Clemina, Maita, Isa: all my Higher Circle has leaped early from bed, it seems."

There was a silence. They had not expected her to greet them. While the women peered at one another, trying to decide who would speak, Nemiah folded her hands at her waist and forced herself to breathe. She had scored the first point merely by being awake and coherent.

Pretty, anxious Maita, Mistress of Ritual and Bena's closest ally, pursed her lips. "We've come to hear about your sacred journey. Why has it not been properly recorded? We want to know where you've traveled. Why do you dare not share it?"

"Reasonable questions," Nemiah replied. "Though surely not so dire as to cause you to race to me like untrained puppies. The Higher Circle is the model of Riana's order for all of Avelos. Yet here you stand in disarray."

The women paused again. Nemiah watched their faces: sweet, simple Clemina glanced at Bena, as though needing permission to say anything; Isa was intelligent and thoughtful, but too new to the Circle to speak out.

Bena took four halting steps, her cane thumping against the floor, and stopped in front of the others. "Even my own eyes, clouded with years, can see the crisis that gives reason to our haste. The devastation of our city, the rise of Tumal's Legacy, and the spread of the killing winds are the direst circumstances the temple has faced since the Exile War!"

"And only Cael rejoices to see us discarding all proper order in the face of the dangers he's wrought," Nemiah replied. "We must hold together in the darkness. If we mistake one another for the monsters we fear, we will only end by clawing ourselves apart."

"You would say so? You who allowed an Arionad to raise his blade to a Lady?"

Nemiah closed her eyes and rubbed one hand over her brow: *neither anger nor submission*. "Mistress Bena, the captain's blade was not the first threat to be wielded last night, but I am willing to forgive what was said and done that we might move ahead." She raised her hands to forestall another retort. "The Higher Circle will meet at midday, as is proper. I will answer your questions then. I will even offer some new reasons for hope. If you cannot find order in your hearts before that time, do not join us."

Nemiah looked upon each of the others, then set her gaze back on Bena. "Press me only if you wish to join Carian in the depths of Avarel Forest."

Without waiting to observe their responses, Nemiah shut the door and latched it. She marched back into the receiving room to find Rom and Kaliska looking equally astonished. Ziabela poked her head out the door of the attendant's chamber.

"I'm not certain that last was wise," Kaliska said.

"It was necessary."

The healer made a face. "At least now you can steal a moment's rest. Midday won't make Bena or the others any easier to manage."

Nemiah wiped her sweaty palms against her hips. "Rest will wait. I must speak with you and the captain."

Kaliska raised a brow. "Nemiah, truly. You must take care."

"Now."

"Very well." The healer's gaze went to the scribe. "Just as soon as we send the Shorn prisoner back to her chamber."

Shorn prisoner. The label gave Nemiah an unpleasant chill. Earlier she thought Kaliska had called the woman "Zia" but now she couldn't imagine so much familiarity between the two.

The scribe stepped forward, eyes downcast. "Madam Healer, you judge me wrong if you think I hold any loyalty to Minister Abrigado."

"Perhaps that's so," Kaliska answered, "but Abrigado isn't the only one who could harm the temple. And you gamble too readily with your own life. I won't see you gamble with my Lady's."

Nemiah shook her head. "Let her be, Kaliska. She's been a help to me. If she troubles you so, have Jhesco see her back."

Ziabela smiled faintly and offered Nemiah a spiral. "Gracious Lady, I thank you for your tolerance. I hope another time will come when I might offer you music."

When the woman had gone, Nemiah sent to the kitchen for food and a pot of steaming boldblood tea for the three of them. A young girl arrived with a basket of Linisi's fresh brown bread, a small pad of cheese, sliced apples, and a crock of dark, fragrant honey. While the others ate, Nemiah hugged a brimming mug of the boldblood to her chest, ignoring Kaliska's looks of disapproval. Rom was hardly more subtle, slipping a piece of bread, glossy with honey, onto a plate before her.

She took a bite of the bread, then pushed the plate aside. "I need to tell you both what befell me on the sacred journey. You need to know why I feared to speak of it, and what I've come to understand about it since."

Only as she began to speak did she realize how much she still dreaded for them to learn of her friendship with the traitor, but the truth was the only way she might balance Amalia's deceit. She drew herself straight and began the tale of her search for Lia and how, in the end, she had found two Lias. She told them of the staggering power of the young Lady Elia, who believed Nemiah to be an assassin. She spoke, hesitantly, of the searing fire and the great black nothing that held her until she had awoken in her Lia's arms. Her voice grew faint and she had to take gulps of the boldblood before she could say how she had learned her Lia was the Avelun who had started the Exile War. She remembered Ambri's fearless love for his Chosen. She wished she could forget the look of despair in Amalia's eyes when Nemiah had told her who she would become.

Kaliska's expression remained thoughtful and detached, but Nemiah knew that under the smooth mask she was full of questions. Rom sat rigidly, his arms folded over his chest, scowling.

Nemiah turned away from his disappointment and forced herself to go on, telling them how Cael's followers had accosted her and how Rumar had spared her. When her Arionad drew a choked breath, Nemiah only stared at the fire, unable to face him. She hurried to reveal her decision to travel to Sahiste and why she believed it was necessary to balance Amalia's evil. Finally, like a tonic to ease all the madness before it, she told them that Rumar was lifting the ban on the Tests of Rona.

When she stopped, the only sounds in the room were the crackle of the fire, and through the shuttered windows, the sounds of early morning in the city. Kaliska shifted in her seat, toying with a piece of cheese, her gaze contemplative. Rom's hands were fists on the table.

"What do you think Cael's people wanted of you?" Kaliska asked.

"What do such demons ever want?" Rom snapped. "Her blood! Her spirit!"

Nemiah hadn't spoken of Leita's warning. It was the one stone she hadn't yet dared to place on the Path.

Kaliska tilted her head, looking unconvinced.

Rom cast a fierce glance around the room, as if searching for somewhere to aim his anger. "I'll call my men back from the lower circles. We'll have a watch on the main steps day and night. I'll brook no dispute in this, my lady. During the day, the women must travel in groups of no fewer than three. No one leaves the grounds after dark without an Arionad." He gave Nemiah a stony glare. "No one."

"I wonder if we should consider sending the young ones home," Kaliska mused. *"Have you thought of sending them home?"*

"It's not possible."

Nemiah shook her head and poured herself more boldblood. "Releasing them to their ruined homes in the city isn't safer, and some of the girls have already lost their families to the winds. No. The captain will take what steps he deems necessary to secure the temple. For now, the young ones stay."

A mirror of Amalia, Nemiah had named herself. She felt the certainty of it with every word she spoke.

"At least this boon from Rumar—returning the Tests—may give us some protection from the Legacy," Kaliska observed. "Abrigado will be less likely to attack us if we make an ally of the soldiers. He hasn't enough support within the Forest Guard, and none of his friends on the council is eager to make enemies of the generals. Not since General Nadel defeated their attempt to unseat him."

"Is that boon a worthy exchange for facing Sahiste?" Restrained fury drew every taut line of Rom's stance. Nemiah had never seen him in such a mood, and no wonder, now that he knew how reckless she had been.

"The journey to Sahiste will bear its own gifts," Kaliska said. "It may save Avelos from war."

"*Save* Avelos? Do you believe the serpents of the south will hear words of peace from Riana's Chosen?" This question Rom flung at Nemiah. "You know how they hate the Shorn. How they break the Shorn soldiers they capture. What do you think they will do when they learn you are our Chosen Lady, just as Lady Amalia?"

Nemiah snapped her gaze to his. "I understand the danger well enough, Captain. Sahiste may use me to take its retribution. I have no doubt my end in that case will not be pleasant."

Rom paled, and Nemiah regretted her words. She went on more quietly. "I can only hope the Sahistens recall we treated their prince with respect."

She wished she and Rom were alone so she didn't have to hold back the words she most wanted to say—that she understood why he would doubt her; that she too mourned the talents she would never be able to offer as Chosen, that she too mourned her mistakes—but Kaliska sat between them, attentive as ever. From the misery brilliant in her Arionad's black eyes, Nemiah could see he was holding back as well. She leaned her head on her hand.

It was Kaliska who pulled away from the table, giving Rom's arm a tug as she rose. "Lady, the first thing that must be done is to see your body whole and one with your spirit, else there can be no Higher Circle and no new journeys. You've shown little enough inclination to listen to your healer. Perhaps if I say it as a friend you might consider it: *please rest.*"

Nemiah rubbed her bleary eyes and nodded.

"Good. I'll send Merisel back to you. She's been wild with worry. Let her be a help."

Rom formed a sharp, lean shadow at Nemiah's elbow. "My lady, is there any way I can ease you?"

She gazed up at her Arionad, wanting so badly to smooth away his scowl and find a means to relieve his doubts, but she had not enough focus left to give him the explanations he would need, and she didn't think she could bear his anger.

"Not now," she sighed. "See to the changes in the watch. We must speak about Sahiste . . . and other things. Later."

"As you say, my lady."

Nemiah hoped he might recognize the regret in her, might see it as a kind of apology, but he didn't meet her gaze when he followed the healer from the room.

Although Nemiah held her ground amidst the Higher Circle sufficiently that her advisors could not call her undone, her revelations, even Rumar's promise to lift the ban, did nothing to warm Bena's attitude. The Mapmaker remained civil enough not to earn a reprimand, but within days, ugly rumors were creeping through the temple.

"It's Bena's venom," the spy keeper told Nemiah. "Even among the novices they're muttering that Riana's Lady has become Rumar's puppet. They say this trip to Sahiste is proof you're headed for doom. We must do something to counter her malice."

"Probably. Yes." Nemiah waved a dismissive hand. "Do whatever you think best. I don't have time for it. I must review the land maps with the captain and argue with him about how many men will accompany me south."

She left Kaliska in the tower and hurried toward the archive. She was coming to realize how consuming a task it was to prepare her people for a trek into foreign lands. She had never before considered the effort it took to move a company with horses and supplies across so many miles. Hours of studying land maps and planning with Rom gave her a deeper appreciation for General Nadel's ability to move an army of soldiers while keeping them organized, sheltered, and fed. Even if she made no error in her calculations regarding their supplies or the time necessary to travel from one village to another, her men were still house guards, not soldiers. She trusted their discipline, but worried about their lack of experience when it came to facing the challenges of travel beyond their own borders.

As she approached the archive, Arnas offered her a proper spiral. "Good afternoon, Lady. The captain waits within."

"Thank you, Arnas."

The old guard bobbed his head. His eyes sparkled.

Nemiah wondered what rumors he had heard. "Is something wrong, Arnas?"

"Not at all, my lady. It's only that Captain has selected me for the journey south. I'm honored t'be found worthy t'bear my sword as part of your guard."

Nemiah blinked. "You don't fear leaving Avelos? Entering the realm of the Sahisten king?"

The guard smiled broadly. "An Arionad has no need t'fear what Riana unwinds before him."

Nemiah answered his smile. Small joys did sometimes hide along the Path. "I'm glad you'll be with us."

Small joys. They allowed a spirit to keep twisting through a Path, even when other moments threatened to rend her heart. She held onto her smile the best she could as she entered the archive to find Rom already leaning over a map of southeastern Avelos. One hand tugged absently at his beard, while the other hand drummed an invisible line from Velantar into Sahiste. Since she had told him of Amalia, they had found no time for anything but duty. Rom seemed ever in three places at once as he prepared for their travel and strived to see the temple well guarded. Nemiah could have ordered him to speak of the things he was keeping from her, but his carefully neutral expression—so at odds with his habitual gruff candor—suggested the distance between them was something he felt necessary. The best thing she could do was to respect that barrier. She didn't seek his company during his free hours and extended no evening invitations he would need to refuse. For his part, Rom attended to every duty in a way that left no room for complaint. If she but stepped into the outer courtyard, one of his men was at her side. Two guards stood at her tower day and night. When Rom was in her presence, he curbed his surliness and said nothing that might disturb Riana's order. Perversely, she found his flawless compliance the hardest to bear. It had little to do with who he truly was.

At the sound of her footsteps, he glanced over his shoulder. For a heartbeat, Nemiah saw devotion in the depths of his black eyes, and it warmed her. Then misgivings shuttered his gaze again. As he straightened and made his spiral, she could see he was going to renew his press to bring a full complement of Arionade into Sahiste. He wasn't willing to admit that forty men would hardly have a better chance of surviving than twenty or ten if their enemies proved to be dishonorable. Nemiah was unwilling to leave the high temple stripped of defenses. She shoved the loose strands of hair back from her face and prepared herself for a long afternoon.

At the end of each demanding day, Nemiah found the cost of her sacred journey had caught up with her again. Returning to her tower after the evening devotion, the ground shook, making her footing precarious. Just turning a corner too quickly caused the world to blur as her Path splintered into myriad new directions. She walked slowly, offering blessings to the novices she passed so they wouldn't notice her need to put out an arm for balance. Finally in her tower, secure from curious eyes, she dropped into a chair. Instead of facing whatever grim news

Kaliska had to share, Nemiah often ordered Ziabela's guards, Avjay and Fen, to bring the scribe and her flute.

The Shorn woman's gratitude lit the chamber. "Lady, you've given purpose to my confinement!" she said one night. "I'm thankful for any chance to serve you. Shall I play one of the ancient melodies?"

Nemiah smiled vaguely at the pretty language. "Not just yet. My head's too full of the day's troubles to appreciate music. Talk with me."

The scribe's brightness faded a little and she gave Nemiah a sidelong glance. "Of what would you have me speak?"

"I don't know. Anything, so long as it has nothing to do with the weighing of grain for a company of horses or speculation about the motives of Sahisten courtiers. Tell me something more about yourself. How did you come to love music so?"

The woman relaxed and smiled again. "Of course."

Nemiah sat near the hearth and Ziabela folded gracefully to the floor at her feet. The scribe fell into her storytelling easily, sharing tales of herself as an outgoing child who could not be kept away from the inns and drinking houses where musicians earned their livelihood. The tales were artful and amusing, although Nemiah quickly grew aware that the woman offered no details that might connect her to others, no names of people or places, no dates of specific events. Nemiah couldn't fault her for it. Ziabela had been accused of treason; what else could she do but try to shield those she loved?

They talked for a long while. The guard at the tower door had already changed to the nightwatch when quiet fell between them. Merisel had been sent to bed. Ziabela rose and refilled their cups with Makri ruby from a decanter on the table. The wine helped to dull the boldblood Nemiah had been drinking since morning. Tonight perhaps it would allow her to sleep.

Ziabela returned the decanter to its place and sat. The room had darkened as the fire burned low. The scribe's easy manner seemed to have burned away with it. She rubbed at her wrists; then, as though becoming aware of what she was doing, she dropped her hands into her lap.

"Lady, I would ask you a question. If you'll hear it."

Nemiah sank back in her chair. "I would. What is it?"

"After all this time, why haven't you asked me what you want to know? About Abrigado and the letters?"

"Because if you were ready to tell the truth, there would be no need for me to ask for it. And if you can't speak the truth, I prefer you to keep silent. We're near enough to the edge of chaos without more lies."

Ziabela frowned, causing a crease to form between her brows. "I see."

Nemiah waited, giving the other woman the space to make her own decisions. Finally, Ziabela began again. "You'll be leaving for Sahiste soon. What will you do with me before you go?"

"Do?" Nemiah peered at the scribe.

"Abrigado would reward you well if you were to let him reach me. Rumar would likely offer more if you found a way to make me disappear. He fears what I might say."

Nemiah let out a troubled breath, despising the world in which a woman's life was a coin to be exchanged for favor. "Ziabela, whatever intrigues you've stepped into or have been forced into, the temple takes no part in them. I won't plot with your life."

The scribe's expression hardened. She glared down at her wine. "Lady, there needn't be any pretense. I'm bound for traitors' wall. I would just like to know what's coming before then."

"Ziabela!" Nemiah's tone yanked the other woman's gaze back to her. "I have never lied to you. I am not lying now. I will not give you up to torture."

The scribe made a sound of confusion. Her expression filled with an uncertainty Nemiah hadn't seen since the council inquiry. Ziabela held secrets that might ignite violence against her own kind, might condemn Elder Abrigado or shatter what confidence the clans still had in Adan Rumar. She had already been tortured for those secrets and hadn't spoken them. Who did such a woman trust?

"I truly don't know what will happen," Nemiah said more gently. "Just now, the high chieftain is occupied by worries far greater than you, although I suspect Abrigado won't let him forget you for long. When the councilors call to sentence you, unless I am given some cause to do otherwise, the temple must offer you over. I have no intention of allowing Abrigado—or any other member of the council—to reach you before then."

"You are more generous than I deserve," Ziabela said softly.

"That I cannot judge. If you think so, perhaps you'll take steps to balance it. For order's sake."

Again, silence descended. The Shorn scribe didn't fill it, and Nemiah allowed the moment to pass. To push the woman would be of no use. Whatever she had done or not done, Ziabela seemed willing to pay the price for it.

Gradually, Nemiah fell into an unlikely routine with the scribe. Ziabela transcribed songs, while Nemiah prepared for the journey to Sahiste or read map notes in the archive. After, Zia would play her flute and they would talk. At times, it was difficult to remember that the woman was a prisoner.

Little one, what's happened? The weaving writhes like a tormented spirit. Do you feel it?

The stone walls twirled. A lamp traced a circle of light in the air. Nemiah grasped at the Gate.

"Lady Nemiah?"

"Ah, dove, please don't keep me out!"

Worry weighted Lia's voice. Her friend. Her sister. Nemiah peered at the blue flames within her. She longed to speak with someone who could understand a Pathwalker's fears.

"Lady, do you hear me?"

"All you need do is reach for me and you will find my Path."

"Lia?" Nemiah took a deep, wavering breath and felt the thickness of long sobbing in her throat. Someone stood over her with a worried expression. Nothing in the world seemed quite right. Her friends were dead. She had failed Avelos.

"Should I call Madam Kaliska, Lady?"

"Oh, Zia. Ziabela." Nemiah shook her head and felt doors banging shut all around her. She breathed slowly as her own Path snapped back into clarity. "I'm all right. Just tired." She suddenly realized it was true. Her body felt heavy with grief.

Ziabela looked dubious. "Perhaps you'd like to go back to the tower?"

Nemiah glanced around the room. She had been examining a land map of Avelos on which Rom had marked their planned route, but her thoughts had drifted to Sahiste, and then to the Sahisten ambassador Lia and Ambri had secreted into Avelos. *"To learn how to survive the drought,"* Lia had said. Sadness flooded Nemiah.

Oh, Lia, what happened? How did you come to such a place?

The scribe was still watching her.

"That's fine," Nemiah said, hoping it answered whatever Ziabela's last question had been. "I'm done here. Help me put away the map."

Ziabela took great care rolling the scroll and sliding it back into its cabinet. Nemiah used the time to secure herself to her Path.

Arnas hadn't yet taken up the nightwatch at the entrance to the archives, so it couldn't be so very late, but the east wing was as still as midnight. Ziabela opened the door to the tower and waited while Nemiah entered.

Her tower rooms were chilly and dark. Only embers glowed in the hearth. Ziabela hurried to stir the flames. "Lady, perhaps a cup of wine would do you well."

"Yes. Good. Lovely." Nemiah picked up her shawl from the arm of her chair. On the table sat the dinner of roasted carrots and meat pie she hadn't touched. Capa padded from Merisel's room to offer a greeting. Nemiah gave him a carrot.

When the fire was licking hungrily over the logs, Ziabela poured the wine and offered it to Nemiah. "Will you send for Fen to escort me back to my room?"

Nemiah looked around the ancient tower. It had been home for Elia and Amalia, and centuries of other Ladies. Tonight it felt full of ghosts. "Eat something first." She pushed the plate of food in Ziabela's direction. "It will only go to waste otherwise."

Ziabela gave her a curious look, but perched on a chair and plucked up a pie. "Would you like me to play for you?"

"I don't think so." With her cup cradled in one hand, Nemiah made her way to her chair by the fire. In truth, music would have been a pleasant escape, but Ziabela's songs awakened memories. Memories were keys to the Gate, keys Nemiah couldn't necessarily control.

She closed her eyes. *Too many doors are open,* Leita had warned. What did that imply? Did it explain her uncontrolled falls? What else might pass through the doors? Could the thoughts and emotions that filled one Path leak into another? Is that why she felt this grief that wasn't quite her own?

"Are you still thinking about Elder Abrigado's letter?"

"Hmm?" Nemiah looked up to find herself the object of the scribe's scrutiny.

"He's worried about what you have given the high chieftain in return for lifting the ban on the Tests of Rona, you know."

"I do know." Nemiah pressed her palms against her thighs, as though she could press herself firmly into her own place. Abrigado's recent note had followed several others from elders offering congratulations about the Tests of Rona. Abrigado was courteous, but even his congratulations were filled with hints of malice. He had requested a meeting with Nemiah.

The Shorn woman finished eating and joined Nemiah near the hearth. "He fears you'll let Rumar question me. He'll also want to know if you've promised Rumar the support of the western clans."

Nemiah shook her head. "Abrigado has no reason to care about the only two clans willing to follow my lead. With the north still uncommitted, the west isn't enough to shift the balance."

Enrian had helped her to see that. It would be the north that mattered. Nemiah sighed. "In exchange for the Tests, I'm afraid Abrigado and his supporters will make us pay."

"Don't let him shape your life, Lady. Toren Abrigado is only a man."

"A man with more skills and resources than I'll ever possess."

There was a pause as Ziabela took a long sip of her wine. She set down her cup and looked back at Nemiah. "Is it shame that makes you deride your own talents, Lady?"

Nemiah's mouth opened. "Ziabela!"

The Shorn woman gestured toward her own green eyes and Nemiah's. "You've the curse in your family. It makes you overcautious and conservative when you deal with others in power."

Nemiah sucked a breath. "Scribe, I've been tolerant, but you push too far."

"I know. It's ever been my downfall to push too far." The woman gave a small, rueful smile. "Lady Nemiah, you've helped me when you should not have. When it's done nothing but weaken you in the eyes of your Circle. There's little I can do to repay such a debt, but I am beginning to think Riana intends me to help you too."

The Paths rippled around Nemiah. She tried to laugh but the sound came out an uncertain thing. "How do you fathom that?"

"I've watched you struggle against rivals inside and outside the temple. You're determined, so determined, Lady, that you've exhausted yourself with your efforts. Yet for all your work, how many elders would call themselves allies of the Lady of Avelos? How many sisters support the Mistress of Maps in her bid to see you out?"

Nemiah stared, stunned by the woman's cutting observations.

Ziabela went on. "You don't think beyond the walls that others have erected for you. It makes your solutions predictable and leaves you vulnerable to manipulation."

"If all that were true," Nemiah cried, "I wouldn't be here now! No other woman with the taint of the curse has served as Lady since the Exile."

"It *is* true. Think on it. How else would a Shorn woman accused of treason have slid her way into your confidence?"

A wave rolled and crested under Nemiah as the Paths divided and multiplied. There was honesty here. It was a moment on the border between order and chaos. "Ziabela, what are you saying?"

"I am saying that you do not choose your allies with care. Tell me, when you face so many of the same threats as Adan Rumar, why have you not drawn him close to you? I don't mean just a surreptitious meeting in the middle of the night, but a true joining of strength."

"You are the body of Avelos as I am the spirit. Let us heal the discord between us and end the suffering in our land."

Nemiah gasped. "If I had time to write a volume on the issue, you'd have your reasons."

"Reasons your enemies gave you," Zia pressed. "Do you know how the Legacy dreads what would happen if you and Rumar came to terms?"

Another wave crashed over Nemiah. She grasped her wineglass just in time to keep from dropping it. The Paths were scattering in new directions. She stared at the scribe. "That's foolishness. Abrigado's too clever to fear something he knows will never happen."

"Lady, I've served the Minister of the Treasury for nearly as long as you've been high priestess. A woman comes to know what the man beside her most fears. Abrigado knows he lacks the support to overcome both you and Rumar at once. If you never reconcile, it's because he's done his best to prevent it."

"What are you . . . Wait. Let me think." Nemiah took a careful breath, afraid to do anything to drive the Path in the wrong direction when things suddenly looked so strange. "Last spring. Abrigado used a difficult Becoming to lead Rumar to believe I was colluding with the Legacy."

"That's right. The Becoming of Elder Trianor's fosterling." A new note entered Ziabela's voice.

Nemiah tried to concentrate on what she was saying now, rather than letting the Gate pull her somewhere else. "At the time, I saw only that Abrigado endangered the temple by subverting a sacred rite. It wasn't until later I realized he meant for it to appear as though I was attacking Elder Trianor."

"Oh, yes. The Minister was quite proud of himself for that one. In one elegant move, he heightened Rumar's distrust of you and gave you more reason to stay clear of the council."

"He shared all this with you?"

The Shorn woman shrugged stiffly. "Elder Abrigado has particular ways he likes to celebrate when his plots succeed. It leaves him . . . talkative. Lady, you must recognize he has kept you from even imagining a path where you and Adan Rumar rule together."

"Perhaps. Will I regret it if I answer his request and meet with him?"

Ziabela straightened with a look of surprise. Nemiah was surprised herself; she hadn't planned to ask the question.

"Abrigado has nothing in mind to your benefit," the scribe answered. "And you have nothing to gain from such a meeting. You should avoid it—"

"Lady Nemiah! Open the door!"

Nemiah jumped at the urgent cry. Someone pounded on the door.

"Lady, are you there? We're coming in!"

The outer door crashed open. Footsteps rushed through the antechamber. Before Nemiah could rise, the inner door flew wide and three Arionade stormed into the room, swords drawn. Capalino leaped up from the rug, growling a warning.

Nemiah forced her fear toward anger. "What outrage is this?"

Commander Evorales charged across the room and backhanded her cup out of her hand. Wine arched into the air in a crimson stream. The cup struck stone and shattered.

"Beast!" cried Ziabela. "Get away from the Lady!"

She flung herself at Evorales, wrapping her arms around his neck. Red welts sprang up where her nails scored his throat and face.

"Be still, woman! Someone get hold'a her!" The brawny commander wrestled Ziabela off him and shoved her toward the other men.

Avjay leveled his sword at Ziabela's breast. Red-headed Fen stood behind her.

Kaliska hurried into the room after them. "How do you feel, Lady? Is there tingling in your fingers and toes? Is your vision blurred or your head light?"

"No. That is . . . only what the Gate brings." Nemiah ordered Capa to her side with a sharp gesture. "What is this?"

"Poison," Evorales said as Kaliska set to examining Nemiah. "We found Ilias unconscious in the barracks. Four or five'a the others are sick." Evorales paused, looked down, and wiped a hand over his face. "Arnas is dead, Lady."

"What . . . No. Oh, no." A loud buzzing started in Nemiah's ears. Not kind, steadfast Arnas. The one who always had a smile and an encouraging word. "Who? Who dared to attack the temple?"

"Lady, look at me," Kaliska commanded. "Open your mouth and breathe."

Dazedly, Nemiah did as she was told. Kaliska sniffed, then picked up the bottom of the broken wine cup and sniffed the remaining contents before dipping her finger and tasting it.

"The wine is clean. What of dinner?"

Loyal Arnas, why have they taken you? We needed your true spirit on this Path.

"It's the act of a traitor," Avjay growled, jutting his blade toward Ziabela. "You played so prettily for us. You played and smiled and we forgot what you are."

"I didn't!" Ziabela's green eyes went wide. "I've done no harm to any Arionad. I swear it!"

"Lady, what did you eat tonight?" Kaliska demanded as she examined a left-over meat pie.

"Nothing. I ate nothing." Nemiah looked at the scribe, who had blanched behind Avjay's sword. "Only Ziabela ate."

Kaliska looked directly at the Shorn woman for the first time since she had entered the room. "The meat's too spiced to detect poison. How do you feel, scribe?"

"Commander, in Riana's name, stand down your men and let the healer to her!"

"Avjay! Fen!" Evorales snapped. "You heard Lady Nemiah."

"She's been with me for hours," Nemiah said as Kaliska began to examine Ziabela. "She couldn't have delivered the poison. She didn't have a chance to reach the men. She wouldn't have—" Nemiah cut herself off. "Where's the captain? Why didn't he deliver this news?"

Evorales looked at her unhappily. "Can't say, Lady. I haven't seen him since muster just after midday."

The room was suddenly too hot, the Path beneath her too uncertain. Nemiah felt insubstantial as a dried leaf. Her hands shook. Her legs barely held her upright. They had reached the point of influence at last. Was she turning toward inevitable loss?

"How many men are looking for him?"

"None yet," the commander said. "Lady, we don't—"

"None? Then we've wasted too much time already!" Nemiah headed toward the door. "Capa and I will lead the search. I know him. I know where he goes."

"Whoa, Lady!" Evorales barred her way. "The snake that poisoned us wanted the temple unguarded. I have to guess they want to get to you."

"Lord Arionad, stand down!" Nemiah ordered. "In Riana's name!"

The plain-faced commander didn't budge. "In Riana's name, I've sworn to keep you whole. Until we know more, you stay behind a bolted door. I've a detail of men in the hall between the sisters' quarters and the tower, and men at each outer entrance. We'll get someone searching for the captain as soon as we can."

Nemiah bit her lip to keep from shouting her frustration. She was beginning to realize the implications of what he was telling her. "You don't know the source of the poison, do you? How many men are ill? What of the sisters and all our guests?"

Kaliska glanced over her shoulder. "I don't know the worst of it yet. So far, only Arionade have been stricken. I suspect the poison contaminated the barracks mess at lunch or dinner. I haven't had time to question anyone, but with so many strangers in the temple, it wouldn't have been a trick for someone to get into the kitchens." The healer shook her head. "It could be hours before we know how many will take sick."

"We can't wait that long. Isn't there something you can give them to drive out the poison before it takes hold?"

"Yes. There is." Kaliska looked bleak. "In fact, the best chance of surviving is to take the antidote before the poison invades the spirit."

"Well and good. Every man must take the antidote immediately! Commander, surely you and your men have taken it already."

Evorales shifted his weight. "No, Lady. We can't. The thing is . . ."

"What is it?"

Kaliska gave her a pained look. "Nemiah, the antidote is just another type of poison. It causes the body to reject everything recently consumed. The process is violent and incapacitating. Some don't survive the cure. The commander and his men won't take it because . . ."

Nemiah felt a wash of weariness. "Because they won't be able to guard us if they do."

Kaliska nodded.

"Ah, Goddess." Nemiah turned away from the others. She could order the men to take the remedy and leave the temple unprotected. Or she could order them to do their duty and serve Riana unto death. Whatever she did, she was condemning some of them to the end of their Paths. She faced Evorales.

"Commander, select twelve men to guard the sisters and six to search for the captain. Choose first from those who didn't eat in the mess today. If you don't have enough, ask for volunteers. Use your judgment to select the remaining. Every other man will take the antidote, starting with those who show signs of poisoning, until the healer's supply is exhausted."

"Twelve isn't enough for the temple," Evorales protested. "We don't know who or what's going to attack next."

"It will have to be enough. I won't risk more."

The commander looked as though he would protest again, but he bowed his head. "As you wish, Lady."

"One last thing," Nemiah said. "When you find the captain, bring him directly to the healer. No matter how he objects. Do you understand?"

"Yes, Lady." Evorales smiled grimly. "What about the scribe? Should we throw her back in her chamber?"

Ziabela was seated at the edge of the hearth, pale and composed. Nemiah had promised the woman she would be safe in the temple. "Ziabela is under the healer's care. Leave her and get to your work."

"Yes, Lady."

"Riana guide you and Lord Arion guard you, Commander."

Evorales gave Nemiah a hasty spiral and hurried off with his men. Nemiah bolted the door behind him.

"The cults," Kaliska muttered.

"Likely." Nemiah returned to the hearth. "How is Ziabela?"

"I'm well," the scribe piped with forced confidence.

"If she's taken poison, we're likely soon enough to do something about it." Kaliska removed a small jug from her satchel and poured some of the contents into a cup. She offered it to the Shorn woman. "You heard what I told the Lady. This will make you very ill. It's a dangerous antidote, and if you've taken no poison, an unnecessary risk, but it's the best I have."

The scribe took the cup with a tight smile. "Very well. But if I'm going to die, there are things I must—"

"Hush," Kaliska said. "You'll need your strength to survive the cure. Drink it. Then I want you to rest."

"Make her comfortable in Merisel's room. Merisel can sleep upstairs in my bed." Nemiah touched Ziabela's cheek. "You took on an Arionad for me, brave one. Don't think I didn't notice. I am so sorry I couldn't keep you safe."

Ziabela leaned her head briefly against Nemiah's hand. "No one else has ever tried, my lady."

Once the Shorn woman was made as comfortable as she could be, little remained to be done but wait. Kaliska hurried off to the infirmary, but Nemiah was locked in her tower like a holed rabbit, with a detail of nervous Arionade at the door.

Kaliska or her assistants brought reports when they could. Three more men fell ill, then seven, then ten, including one of the men on watch in the hall. Nemiah commanded him to take the antidote. The rest were already incapacitated by the cure. At midnight, there was still no sign of Rom, and another Arionad was found dead: Nemiah's night watchman, Jhesco. The only sister who showed signs of poisoning had shared a meal with Jhesco when he had carried lunch to her in the outer gardens. They had been lovers for less than a year.

Nemiah sat at her desk and pulled out a small piece of parchment. Her reed scratched over the surface as she wrote.

"Who?" Kaliska asked, coming out of Merisel's room where Ziabela was growing delirious. The healer hadn't exaggerated the potency of the antidote. Nemiah feared the scribe's body would fling itself inside out.

"Ansa," Nemiah replied. "She'll send what Arionade she can spare from Panetar."

Kaliska took a sip of the tea that had gone cold hours ago. "It will be all over by the time they reach Velantar."

"I don't think so. This is only the first move against us."

Kaliska considered a moment. "The second. You were the first."

Nemiah gave the sealed letter to one of the guards with orders for it to go out with their best rider. As the grizzled man took the letter, his expression flickered with sadness. The realization struck Nemiah at the same time: Arnas had been their best, and Arnas was gone.

With tears burning at the back of her eyes, Nemiah wandered through her tower. She drew her hand across the ancient stone walls, the aged volumes of temple records, and the wool tapestries: objects that helped define Avelos for centuries and now defined her. Tonight she took no comfort from her ritual. The years of tradition around her were not reassuring; she could think only of how faded the tapestries were, how worn the stones had grown, and how empty the temple records had become. Only endings lay ahead, after all. She climbed the stairs to check on Merisel. The little girl was sleeping with the easy peace of the young. Her head barely peeked out from under a pile of blankets in Nemiah's large bed. Nemiah brushed the child's butter-colored hair from her round cheek and murmured a prayer.

A few hours before dawn, Evorales pounded on the door and spoke the entry word. Nemiah threw back the bolt and opened the door. The Arionad was alone.

"Commander, where's the captain? Has he refused you?"

Evorales was grey with exhaustion. "We don't have him, Lady. One'a the stable hands saw him head into the city late this afternoon, but no one's seen him since. His colt's still missing."

"The city?" Nemiah's heart sank. Six men weren't near enough to search all of Velantar. It would take too long to find him. It had already been too long.

"Lady, I swear if I had the men, I'd send 'em lane by lane. We've got the hounds out now, but we just don't have the men."

"I know, Commander." Nemiah bit the inside of her lip until she tasted blood. Before the killing winds, she would have known all the likely places Rom would go—to his cousins' home in the clan circles; to the peaceful trails along the river; to a favorite tavern. But the winds had destroyed his cousins' house and the family had left the city to shelter with an uncle in the mountains. The riverbanks were flooded and the tavern closed. "You must be able to focus the search," she said. "Wait a minute. Let me think."

She tried not to think of how long it had been since she and Rom had ridden together along those peaceful trails. Instead, she thought of the places he might still visit—one of the small clan temples or perhaps the lower circles where they had only just pulled her guards from the cleanup efforts. She had approved the order that brought the Arionade back to the temple. That decision had killed men tonight. When she sent the commander away again and closed the door, she sank onto the edge of a chair and tried not to think at all.

Kaliska found her there when next she came to tend to Ziabela.

"Will she survive?" Nemiah asked.

"Oh, that one will always find a way to survive."

Nemiah gave the healer a look.

Kaliska attempted an apologetic gesture, but it dissolved into a tired shrug.

The shadows haunting Kaliska's gaze reminded Nemiah that the healer had faced temple poisonings before. It was Kaliska who told Lady Pahlina her sister and Arionad were dead. Nemiah had been too young then to fully understand what such losses had meant to Pahlina. Now she couldn't stop imagining her Arionad on the ground in some dark corner of the city, crying out in pain and dying alone.

Lord Arion, guard your brother.

"Lady, we must consider what to tell the high chieftain about why you cannot leave for Sahiste," the healer said gently.

Nemiah looked up. They were meant to depart in a very few days. Too soon. With a sigh, she leaned her head in her hands.

Perhaps Ziabela had spoken truly: she must think beyond the expectations of her enemies. What would Cael's followers assume she would do—the small, ineffectual Lady of Avelos? Hide in fear, waiting for the next attack? What would Abrigado assume—that she would be isolated, too distrustful to seek help? What would she gain by staying locked in the temple? She could do nothing for the Arionade on her own. Nothing for Rom. If Kaliska was right, he was already dead.

"I must meet with Rumar."

The older woman's expression filled with dismay. "Is it wise to let him see how vulnerable we are?"

"A time must come when we suspend our distrust, Kaliska. Either we reach out for help or face destruction alone."

"Very well, Lady. I'll go with you."

"No. You're the only one who can keep Riana's order while I'm gone. And if they find Rom . . ." Impossible to think on that now. If Nemiah considered it further, she would lose herself to grief. "Stay to care for the others. Let me do what small things I can."

The healer consented with visible reluctance. "While you're gone, the Mistress of Ritual will begin preparing our fallen. Do you have any instructions for her?"

Our fallen. Like soldiers fighting a war. But they weren't soldiers. Jhesco was only a young man carrying lunch to his beloved. Arnas had only ever unwaveringly served the goddess he adored. *We were not prepared for this kind of battle. We knew the enemy would come, but we were not prepared.*

"Lady?"

Nemiah made a weary spiral as she rose. "Tell the Mistress of Ritual to leave Arnas's death mask to me."

14.
DECEPTIONS

Vesarian's mutilated body half rolled, half slid down the muddy bank. At the bottom, it collided with a small log and stopped. One arm flopped into the black water rushing under the bridge.

Jhared wiped his hands on the tall weeds, but his fingers still felt sticky with blood. "This is wrong," he murmured to the dead man's spirit. "I'm sorry. I will pray for the Pathguides to find you."

The Bearer turned. "You wanted to save the child. The Legacy might leave her alone if they think someone freed their prisoner only to slay him."

Jhared doubted that men willing to threaten a father with the welfare of his little girl would care about such details, but he didn't have it in him to argue.

"You are sensitive to the Paths," she had told him.

He was demon-touched. Caelevano.

As they scrambled back up the hill, Jhared held out his arm to aid the priestess. She gripped him tightly and didn't let go as they returned to the wet streets. Jhared knew his way back to the temple, but he could no longer tell who was leading whom.

"How did you find me?" he asked flatly.

She steered him toward higher ground. "When the Gate opens, it causes the Paths to shift. A person treading those shifting Paths has a very distinct footstep. Some Pathwalkers can track those steps."

"Have you done that before? Tracked me?"

"Yes. Although I wasn't sure it was you at the time."

"When?"

"That's not important now, Jhared. What you must—"

"When?" he insisted.

She blew out a breath. "In Velantar, the night the Legacy attacked you. In the high temple, when you encountered the unbound Shorn man."

"And since we left the city?"

"I thought I felt a shift the day the winds chased us in the pass, the night you saw an intruder in camp, and—"

"The evening after Obled," he finished.

"Yes."

He closed his eyes. *"Why?"* he whispered to the rain.

"Jhared, don't drift off." She jostled his arm. "You're in a dangerous position right now."

"Not yet." He laughed grimly. "I'll be in a dangerous position when Lieutenant Sevar learns I'm demon-touched."

She stopped abruptly. "You mustn't tell the lieutenant. He'll send you back to the garrison."

"No, he won't. Most likely he'll find a wall and push me. This goes well beyond your courier doves, Lady. I won't risk my comrades' lives to keep it secret."

"Jhared, slow down. You don't understand what's happening to you, but you needn't give up hope. I can teach you to keep the Gate shut."

In the darkness, Jhared could hardly make out the raindrops slipping down her white cheeks, but he could hear the anxiety in her voice. "I wouldn't ask you to endanger yourself by defying Shorn Law. I could never repay such a debt."

"It's not for you. It's . . ." She paused and tried again. "You're still spinning from your fall. It's no time to be making such decisions. When we reach the temple, I'll give you something to let you sleep safely. Tomorrow, you'll face this new road with a clearer head."

To roads yet untraveled I must be on my way,
The roads yet untraveled are calling me away.

"Jhared?"

He tilted his head, uncertain whether what he heard was a song or only the sad music of the rain reflecting his thoughts.

A soldier they have made me, love, and given me a spear,
But I'll come back before the snow so don't you shed a tear.

"Someone's singing," he murmured.

The Bearer renewed her grip on him. "I don't hear anything. Look at me. Do you feel off balance?"

He chuckled, letting the rain pelt his face. "I've never felt so off balance in all my life, but I know when I hear a man singing. It's Jase. My patrol is back."

To roads yet untraveled I must be on my way,
The roads yet untraveled are calling me away.
I'll bring you back a comb of gold and silks and diamonds, too,
I'll bring you back the stars and sun and build a house for you.
But greater treasure waits for us when all the war is won,
When we are wed in summertime and you will have my son.

"I do hear it," the priestess said. "Faintly. Where are they?"

"Not far ahead. The park in front of the temple, I think." Jhared started to jog toward the sound. The priestess hurried to keep up.

> *But now the snow is falling, love, summertime is past,*
> *Still I know you will wait for me 'til I come home at last.*
> *And if I cannot find my way beneath the starry sky,*
> *Still promise me that you'll be mine and promise not t'cry.*

The singer's voice was thready and gilded with fading hope, as the soldier in the ballad.

Jhared hailed the patrol and saw his comrades turn. The horses' heads hung low, and the men sat their mounts wearily. No Sahisten prisoner rode among them. The singing came from a figure huddled in a sodden cloak swaying drunkenly in the saddle. Jhared could see nothing recognizable of the man, but he knew Jase's untrained tenor.

"What's going on?" the Bearer demanded. "Why haven't you taken shelter?"

Some of the men raised their heads; others looked too tired to care. Grion scowled. "It seems soldiers loyal to Avelos aren't welcome in Riana's house."

"Did you not tell them you're traveling with me?"

Grion snorted. "That's when they turned us out."

The Bearer's expression hardened. "Where's the lieutenant?"

Anzo gestured toward the temple portico. "There, Lady."

Lieutenant Sevar stood at the entrance, hunched sideways to avoid the water pouring in a curtain from the roof. Lamplight from inside the building cut sharp angles across his face as he argued with a tall silhouette. Enaro.

"No. Oh no," the priestess said angrily. "No one in need is turned away. Not while the Bearer of Cael's Blade is in Brenia. Wait here."

Jhared stepped after her, but she motioned him back. "Stay with the others. This won't be long."

> *To roads yet untraveled . . . I must be on my way,*
> *The roads yet untraveled . . .*

Jase's singing trailed off into a delirious murmur and he leaned precariously over his colt's neck. Jhared hurried over to steady him. The Clan Nadaren man dragged his head up. "Denaban, my friend! Where have you been? We had need of your golden bow and shining wings!"

"What's wrong with him?" Jhared whispered to Esran.

"Snake bite," Esran said bleakly.

Jhared grimaced. "Where's the Sahisten?"

Esran shook his head and made a warning gesture in Sevar's direction. "Later."

"Not right for a good soldier to die from a snake," Twitch muttered. "Not right at all."

Commander Carn gave a bark. "Shut it! Men of the Fourth don't go so easy."

The Bearer spoke to Enaro and Sevar briefly before disappearing into the temple. Jhared waited in the rain, wondering if her appeal would help or hinder them. Eventually, Enaro returned alone. His frosty features revealed little as he granted permission for the patrol to enter. He waved them all toward the stable. Jhared picked up Jase's reins. The injured man hummed morosely as he was led onward.

The stable was small and dimly lit with lamps hanging from the massive beams between the stalls. At the far end of the alley, a brown mare stuck her head over a stall door and peered inquisitively at the newcomers. The rest of the stalls were empty. Enaro appeared at the top of the spiral staircase that connected the stable to the barracks.

"Lady Esania welcomes the men of the Forest Guard Fourth and offers her skills as a healer to your wounded. The temple of Brenia is, as ever, an ally to High Chieftain Rumar."

So the Lady of Brenia had come to realize rejecting the patrol was more than just an insult to the Bearer. Jhared wondered what the Bearer had done to make that point.

"The welcome is appreciated, if somewhat belated," Sevar replied. "Perhaps the lady confused us for one of the hosts of Legacy supporters that fill Brenia's streets of late."

A row of small furrows creased Enaro's shaved head. "It's true some of our clan have turned their Paths toward the irreverent Legacy. I assure you the lady is dismayed to see it."

Grion snorted. Jhared felt a surge of annoyance at the lieutenant for flaunting his Legacy sympathies.

Sevar waved away Enaro's pretty words. "Tell the lady we're grateful for her aid. This man is a good soldier. We need him more than Riana does."

"If it would ease you, come tell her for yourself." Enaro stepped back from the stair landing in a gesture of invitation.

Sevar nodded and shouldered Jhared out of the way to help Jase from the saddle. The delirious soldier staggered heavily, but Anzo moved to assist. Together, Anzo and the lieutenant negotiated Jase up the stairs.

Esran made a spiral. "Goddess keep him."

"So much for his Nadaren blessing," Grion muttered.

As the lieutenant vanished and the door closed, Jhared turned to his patrolmates. "What happened?"

The story came out in pieces, mostly from Esran, but with Twitch and the others interrupting to add their commentaries. They had hunted the Sahisten spy northward toward the Sandien Mountains. Their prey had a half-day lead and forced the patrol to move at speed for two days without rest.

"He rode like he was fleeing Cael. Must'a had some magic to bewitch his horse," Esran claimed. "He didn't stop. Not even through the night. And him in unfamiliar territory!"

"He was running for his life," Jhared muttered. "Did he make it to the mountains?"

"Naw. Lieutenant knows what he's about. Split us into two parties. By the morning, we flanked the man. Then it was just a matter'a herding him toward Lake Linde. He didn't know the land well enough t'keep clear'a the water."

"We had him!" Twitch burst out. "Could'a smelled a fart, he was that close."

"It's true enough what Jase said. We could'a used your bow and keen eyes." Esran inclined his chin toward Jhared. "Maybe you could'a stopped him."

"Nothing would'a stopped him." Lenaro pushed a hand through his red hair wearily. "He didn't want to be taken."

Esran nodded again. "Before we moved on him, he threw his bag into the fire and turned his knife to his own throat."

Jhared hissed. "He didn't fight?"

"He wasn't even carrying a sword. I've never seen anything like it. Not in a Sahisten."

Had the spies discovered Sabela's secret? Was that why the man had killed himself rather than risk revealing the key to the killing winds to his enemies? "I wish we could know what he threw on the fire."

"Goddess bless Jase for that," Esran said. "The fool jumped in and pulled the bag from the flames."

"Then he shoved his hand inside and found more than just scrolls," Twitch added.

Jhared winced. "The priest's vipers."

The others nodded.

A silence descended. The men looked tired and glum.

"All right," Commander Carn bellowed. "What are you waiting for? Get your beasts put up and your gear stowed. No host of pretty priestesses is gonna come down here and do your work for you."

When the animals had been cleaned, watered, and bedded down, Jhared led his comrades upstairs to the unoccupied Arionade barracks. The braziers between the bunks had been lit, and bread and cheese had been set on the table with a flask of dyers' brew. The men descended on the food, grabbing up bread and pouring drinks while peeling off their dripping clothes. They crouched, half-dressed, over the braziers and commiserated about the hunt as they ate. In the light, Jhared realized with a start that not only was he stained with Vesarian's blood, but his own blood had trickled from his neck down the collar of his shirt. He sidled away to wash up and couldn't make himself rejoin his patrolmates for fear someone would think to ask why he and the lady had been out in the storm. Instead, he leaned against the window casement and stared at the bleak night.

The rain slowed. Water splashed and gurgled from the rooftops into the streets below. The men finished eating and dropped into bunks. Gradually, the sounds of sleep filled the chamber. For a long while, Jhared lay awake, waiting to catch some sign of the Bearer, uncertain whether he hoped or feared she would return. In the small hours, he finally gave up and fell into a restless sleep.

He didn't know how much time had passed when he awoke, heart thudding. He sat up and glanced around. No one else in the barracks was stirring. In the street, a crier rang the third bell of the morning. From the floor below came the sound that had awakened him: a familiar, irritated whinny. Jhared rose, pulled on his breeches and boots, and hurried toward the stable.

A breeze brushed his face as he circled down the stairs. Lamplight writhed against the stable walls. Several steps from the bottom, Jhared heard a hoof crack against wood and saw the Bearer back away from a stall door. Inside the stall, Seravina tossed her head and thrashed the air with her silky tail, the picture of silver-coated haughtiness.

"Lady?"

The Bearer looked up at him with a smile. "I thought you might hear us. I'm afraid your Lady Mare doesn't much care for her new quarters."

"You should have sent for me if you wanted the animals moved." Jhared took the final steps to the straw-strewn floor. Not only Seravina but the Bearer's mare and the packhorses had been brought from the tavern stable.

"You needed sleep. Enaro and I managed just fine."

Seravina turned a circle in her stall and kicked again at the door. Jhared approached her and made a sharp, disapproving sound. The mare paused to consider him.

"Does this mean you've reconciled with Lady Esania?"

"We've come to an agreement. I'm not sure we'll ever reconcile."

"I'm sorry," Jhared said, and meant it. The women had seemed to have an old bond.

The Bearer waved away his concern. "Esania's choices have led her down a different Path from the one she might have walked. A shame, but nothing to be done for it."

Seravina stopped circling. As Jhared leaned against the half door of her stall, she approached, stretching her neck to blow into his hand. He held very still and allowed her to bump him with her velvet muzzle. It was the first time she had come to him of her own will for any purpose but to snap or show contempt.

"Come away from the doorway," warned the Bearer.

"It's all right. She's calming. See?" The mare had swung around to nibble at her hay; her ears twitched in the direction of his voice.

The priestess made an exasperated sound. "Soldier, we are well beyond the point when you can afford to evade me. If I tell you to do something, there's a reason for it. Now, come away from there."

He peered over his shoulder, feeling a stir of useless irritation. She waited, frowning, until he did what she demanded.

"From now on, you mustn't linger in doorways, on bridges, near gates, or on stairways. The Paths are always multiplying, but they're most lively at the thresholds—the places of transition. That's the reason you feel dizzy from time to time. When so many Paths are in your way, your mind can't decide where to focus."

"Lady, what are you doing? You've proved I'm demon-touched, and you've twice seen me defy Shorn Law. What could you possibly want of me?"

Her expression softened. "Right now, all I want is for you to be safe."

"Safe from what?"

She settled on a bale of straw in the empty stall across from Seravina's. "From losing yourself among trails so complex and wondrous no human mind can comprehend them."

He lifted one shoulder. "I'm a scout. I can always find my way."

"Don't be flippant! Your skill may be more important than you know. And don't call yourself demon-touched again. You don't understand the meaning of that name. Pray you never do."

"What would the temple name me?"

"You think you're being clever, but the truth is the answer depends on who you ask. For tonight, it doesn't matter. Have you felt lightheaded since I left you? Disoriented? Nauseous?"

He shook his head.

"Good. Then stop pacing and sit down. I'm going to give you a few strategies to help you avoid that lightheadedness. You must remember and make use of them."

Reluctantly, he came back and sat beside her, with the sense that once again he had lost a battle.

"That's better," she said, her tone gentling.

"There are other transitions to avoid besides the structural ones, Jhared. You'll need to stay alert at sunrise and sunset. In fact, as we shift from autumn to winter and the Paths grow more turbulent, you'll likely start to feel ill more often."

"There's not much I can do to avoid the change of seasons."

"Some would disagree with you, but that's a story for another time. If you feel the dizziness coming on, pinch the flesh of your wrist or bite your lip hard. Moderate pain will often anchor you to the present, but only if you catch yourself soon enough. Be careful of prolonged or intense pain. It can separate your spirit from your body and make it too easy to fall. The key is to keep yourself in the moment. Don't daydream. Avoid exhaustion and illness. Intense pleasure causes some people to lose themselves, so no—"

"Lady!" he hissed. "I don't even know exactly what I'm trying to prevent."

She blinked at him, then suddenly started laughing. The low, gravelly sound blended irony and hints of genuine mirth. "Forgive me. I've been waiting so long for someone who can sense the Paths that I forgot you don't even have the training of a novice. Do you know *anything* about sacred journeys? You've read Anarava, haven't you?"

"Only her histories. The sacred journeys aren't proper topics for a Shorn man."

"They would have been proper for you." She stared at him, tapping a finger against her lips, as though he were a riddle in need of a solution. Finally, she sighed. "There's not much choice. I'll simply have to give you what knowledge you need as I teach you the skills."

Jhared folded his arms across his chest in a manner he hoped seemed self-assured. "Lady, the only skill I need is the one to stop me from having another spell."

"Of course." Her lip curled upward. "For now, we'll only teach you how to control the Gate."

For now. Jhared wasn't so foolish as to think he understood her plans, but he would deal with the rest as it came. He did need to learn. "The Gate . . . it controls the way to Riana's Paths?"

"To everything," she said reverently. "The Gate is the boundary between you and every possible moment of every possible past, present, and future. Each Path has its own doors. A 'walker must know how to open those doors, but the Gate is the passage to all." She turned a transcendent expression on him. "When you cross through the Gate, you step out of the world and look upon the map of all creation. For a skilled Pathwalker, the possibilities are infinite."

Her words resonated in his head. She spoke of the sacred. Jhared recalled blue-red flames and a sense of freedom he had never before experienced. A dozen questions rose in his mind, but he needed the answer to only one.

"How do I keep the Gate closed?"

"How do you close a door? It's no more difficult than that. The natural state of things is for a person to remain on her own Path. It takes effort to push through the Gate. Those spells you've had, we call them 'falling,' but in truth, you must either exert your own strength or some other force must shake you from your proper Path in order to travel Riana's weaving."

"Very well. Then tell me where to begin."

"I'm going to present you with an idea," she said. "An image, really. You won't be able to make use of it until you find the Gate again, but that's all right. I want you to practice just by imagining it. After all, you don't have to be standing by a door to think about how to close one."

Jhared nodded. "It sounds very like imagining the steps of a combat drill. Rehearsing the maneuvers in your head helps train the body how to move. General Nadel starts the youngest recruits with such exercises even before they're given a sword."

"That's it exactly." She looked pleased. "This drill will help train you to stay on the Path where you belong. Are you ready?"

He nodded again, hoping he was.

She slid off the straw bale and reached up to lower the lamps until they offered no more than an amber glow. "I want you to prepare yourself. You must come to this practice undistracted. Close your eyes. Make your breathing slow and deep."

Jhared shifted into a more balanced position. He set his hands, palms down, over his knees and closed his eyes. He'd been schooled to find the still center of himself. It was a place to escape his own chaos.

"Good," the Bearer murmured. "Very good. Remember to breathe."

He took another long, mind-clearing breath. Gradually, the tension in his muscles began to drip out of him and his racing thoughts slowed. He grew aware of the small noises of the horses stirring in their stalls, the texture of the straw under his body, and the scent of the woman beside him. He noted those sensations and let them drift away. The strong, steady rhythm of his heart drew him deeper into himself. Finally, at the core of his being, beyond fear and anger and shame, he found stillness. He floated there, unburdened.

"Excellent. When you're ready, I want you to imagine a gate," the priestess whispered. "It doesn't matter what it looks like. It's only a representation of something much greater. What matters is that *you* construct it, so that you can control it."

Jhared considered a moment, then began to build his image of the Gate: stone and iron between two mighty towers. He fashioned it with a scholar's knowledge of construction and a soldier's experience of fortifications. Brick settled firmly upon brick. Unyielding iron formed hinges and massive locks on an entrance of seasoned oak. No part of him would pass through to the wonders beyond. He would not allow his flaws to pollute Riana's infinite Paths. Never would he look upon the extraordinary map of all creation.

He hadn't considered the tendrils of blue flame, but somehow they made sense amidst his construction. They were a natural extension of himself that skimmed up the stone of his towers and twisted like ivy around the locks. They burned with a dazzling force that sped his heart and made his muscles hum. They ruptured his careful building.

Bright fire lashed at his face. He staggered backward, blinded. Blue flames burned his imagined Gate to ash and encircled him, crackling like untapped passion.

Somewhere outside of himself, Seravina whinnied and kicked at the stall door. The Bearer gasped. "Whoa, soldier! What are you doing?"

"It's beautiful," he breathed. "Glorious. Scorching. Like whips of sunlight."

She made a startled sound. "By the One, you found it. You shouldn't have found it. Stop!"

Her words held no meaning next to the magnificence around him. He discovered an unearthly rhythm in the crackling of the fire. A resonant melody sang in his blood. The music burned through him, destroyed his flesh, then healed all his wounds.

"That's enough, Jhared! Open your eyes."

He laughed. The woman was far away and so small she had no power to command him. The Gate sang of the marvels hidden behind its blue flames. He had been wrong to barricade himself from them. Beyond, he would find the strength to overcome his flaws and make final reparation for all his kind. As he yearned toward the heat, his self began to melt into something new and pure.

A massive presence rose before him, towering as high as the flames and seething with need.

"Jhared Denaban! You are not fit for this place! Leave it!"

The command struck him as sure and sharp as an arrow. He tumbled, uncertain when or where he might land. With his last fragment of awareness, he thought he saw the gleam of a curved blade; then he fell into the blackness.

He returned to the stable with an ache in his chest and a stomach-lurching view of twirling ceiling beams above him. It took several moments to realize he had fallen off the straw bale. With effort, he levered himself into a sitting position and untangled his feet from the straw. So much movement was a mistake. He swallowed back bile.

The priestess no longer sat beside him. She was crouched near the wall, her head drooping over her knees. In response to his rustling, she lifted her face to reveal strained features.

"All right, soldier," she said, dragging each word like a bag of stones. "Let us begin again. I asked what you knew about sacred journeys. And you said . . ."

"Nothing. Nothing more than anyone learns during the devotions."

She pushed herself upright and came to stand over him. "You endanger yourself by lying to me. If you've read forbidden texts, come clean of it now."

"Lady, I haven't read anything about journeys. I swear it!"

"Someone taught you, then. Perhaps you didn't realize what you were learning. When you were a child, someone told you about drawing the Paths together and calling the flames."

"I know nothing of the flames! I can't say it any other way. If you think me false, tell Lieutenant Sevar. Then you won't have to worry ever again about whether I've lied."

Something flickered in the woman's expression. She closed her eyes and hugged her arms around herself as a shudder rippled through her slender frame.

Jhared shrank backward, pulling his anger under wraps. "Lady, I only tried to do what you asked of me. I don't know what happened."

She let out a breath that seemed to steady her and opened her eyes. "You're treading much closer to the edge of your Path than I expected. I never thought you would find the Gate. I couldn't have you falling again, so I tracked you to the border."

Jhared rubbed at his chest. "Something ordered me away from the flames. That was you?"

"We were lucky you didn't end up floating through the Gate this time. You're not ready to travel, Jhared."

"I don't want to travel. I mustn't," he added quickly.

She pressed her lips into a dubious half smile. He forced himself not to glance away.

"Tell me what I need to do. I'm ready to try again."

"Again?" She pushed strands of dark hair from her face and looked him over. "You're too dizzy to know which way is up. A child could push you off your Path."

"Lady, I can't wait. I'm a danger—"

She cut him off with a wave of her hand. "You're done, Jhared. For now, you must use the tricks I've given you to anchor yourself. We'll find more time for this soon."

He wanted to argue further. How could he bear this new burden and still serve his patrol? It wasn't only that he feared doing harm to his comrades should he fall at the wrong moment—with a drawn bow in his hand or perhaps while he gripped a rope; the blue flames terrified him. They felt so horribly familiar and so terribly enticing.

She didn't give him another chance to protest, but reached out a hand to help him up. He met her gaze and saw with a start that his self-focus had kept him from recognizing her own weariness. In the amber light, her skin looked sallow and the hand she offered trembled. He'd not even paused to consider how much she was risking for his sake. Tentatively, half expecting her to withdraw it, he took her hand and came to his feet. "I fear I'll never be able to repay the debt for what you're trying to give me."

"We'll speak of debts later," she said, reaching up to sweep a bit of straw from his hair. "Go find what rest you can before the night is gone."

She drew her cool fingers across his brow and patted his cheek. He had a disconcerting sense of himself as some exotic creature she had caught and hoped to train.

"Here." She reached into the pouch at her belt and handed him a thumb-sized packet. "It's best to take this in tea, but it will serve you well enough to chew it."

Through a layer of cloth, he smelled a peppery herb he didn't recognize. "What is it?"

"Something to send you safely to sleep. The border between wakefulness and dreaming is a dangerous place for an untrained Pathwalker."

"Ah. No, thank you." He offered the packet back to her. "I can ill afford to be drugged to unconsciousness."

She didn't take it from him. "You can less afford to fall through the Gate when I can't reach you. The drug will wear off. If you fall, Jhared, don't mistake me, you will be lost. It's an ugly way to die."

The truth was he had no idea of all the unpleasant effects his affliction might produce—for himself or those near him. Reluctantly, he closed his fingers around the packet. The herbs made an uncomfortable lump inside his fist.

"Good," she murmured, as though he had done something worthy rather than just compounded the layers of his deceit.

He sighed. "Come, Lady. If we're done here, I'll escort you back to the sanctuary."

"Go on ahead," she said. "You're free. I've some things to think on."

He watched her, unmoving. "I am not free, Lady. I'm bound to ensure your safety. It is the one thing still within my ability to accomplish. Will you allow me that?"

She paused. For the first time that night, she seemed to look at him, not through him. "Jhared, what's happening to you doesn't have to be about loss. It means change, to be sure, but you might remember that good can come out of the darkness: rest and healing; passion for some; and for the very lucky, love."

He looked down, thinking of Zia and the brief moments they had shared in the darkness; those moments had had very little to do with healing or love. "If there's any hope buried in this loss, I'll have to trust you to see it, Lady."

"You will," she replied, her expression more thoughtful. "Now, walk with me back to the first circle. If you please."

They left the stable by the outer door and walked toward the portico along the gravel footpath at the edge of the park. Although the rain had stopped, a cold fog had climbed up from the river and crept across the city, making it impossible to see one's feet much less the puddles that dotted the path. The priestess laughed in surprise as she splashed into one of the deeper pools, sending a spray of water over them both. The cushion of fog made her low laughter less resonant, smaller. Jhared thought it offered more of the woman and less of the goddess. He preferred it.

They slipped through the portico entrance back into the sanctuary. The Bearer parted from him to go to the first circle for prayer. Rather than picking once more through the water, Jhared used the temple corridors to return to the barracks. A stern-looking priestess on duty at the bottom of the stairs to the living quarters gave him a skeptical nod, then watched to be certain he entered the Arionade wing. Small lamps lit each end of the corridor, leaving a long stretch of silent dusk between. He strode quietly, already dreaming of the comfort of bed.

The rustling in the window niche just ahead alerted him. He halted, all his drowsiness gone, as a tall figure moved out of the shadow to block his passage. For an irrational moment, Jhared feared an elder or some Legacy supporter had learned what he had done with Vesarian and had come to confront him. Then he realized it was Enaro and had another sober thought.

"Is it Jase?"

The slender man's features lifted in surprise, as though he had expected a different question. "Lady Esania was able to help him. Your comrade will be well."

Jhared let out a relieved breath. He had come to respect Jase's skill on the trail, and the man's lighthearted manner evoked a protective fondness in him. Enaro's manner, however, had nothing lighthearted about it. "I imagine that's not what you've accosted me in a dark hallway to tell me."

"Come," Enaro said, heading back the way Jhared had just walked. "And keep quiet."

He didn't wait for Jhared, but strode toward a door at the darkest part of the passage. He glanced up, checking the empty hall before lifting the latch.

As the door swung open, damp cold air gusted into the corridor. Fog-shrouded moonlight from an unglazed window threw shadows across a small room with a neat bed on one wall and a desk in the opposite corner. Jhared paused at the threshold, listening for the telltale sounds of someone concealed beside the doorway.

"If I had cause to ambush you, there would have been better opportunities tonight than inside the temple, don't you think?" Enaro brushed past him into the room.

Jhared swayed as the floor rippled beneath him. Belatedly, he remembered the Bearer's warning about thresholds and moved several steps farther into the chamber. Enaro closed the door. The aide's face in the milky light was as flat and dispassionate as ever. It occurred to Jhared that had he not been so determined to escort the Bearer back to the sanctuary, he would be in bed now, with the woman's drug working in him, safely out of reach of anyone.

"Opportunities?" Jhared repeated, as though he didn't understand the aide's meaning. "Should I be distressed you were considering such a thing?"

"Don't bother with pretense," Enaro replied. "We had men watching the tree. I know what you did with our Kin."

The blood drained from Jhared's face. "What do you—"

Enaro put a finger to his own lips. "We needn't speak of it. You tried to ease his pain. For that, I am grateful."

"Your kin?"

"As all of us who bear the scars are Kin."

Hope and despair rose in Jhared with such dual intensity they choked his reply: hope for a world in which others cared enough to free an innocent man from torture; despair that it must ever be the Shorn at the heart of conspiracy.

"I know," Enaro murmured, mistaking his silence. "You can't say anything that might confirm what I've told you for fear I mean to entrap you. That leaves precious little for you to say, doesn't it?"

"Why have you said anything at all?" Jhared managed.

"Because I have a warning for you, and I wanted you to be clear of two things. First, I have reason to wish you well, and second, these words have more strength than I could give them alone. Understand?"

"Not yet," Jhared replied. "Speak your warning."

"My sister has given the Bearer the location of the ancients' sky tower. You must not let your people go there."

"And give up the possibility of finding a clue to Sabela's temple? Not if an army of Sahisten spearmen guarded it."

"You must not go there," Enaro repeated.

"You'll have to give me more than that." Jhared stepped closer to the man, trying to read his impassive features. "Who was watching the tree? What are they afraid we'll find at the tower?"

The Shorn aide sighed. "I wish I could throw aside my mask entirely, but I'm no freer to do that than you are. I can tell you we are Kin who care what becomes of our country and who mean to stop such suffering as Vesarian's. I don't always know all the reasons for the things I'm asked to do, but I've learned to trust those who work with me. It could go badly for you and your comrades if you don't do the same."

"Are you threatening the Bearer of Cael's Blade and the High Chieftain's Forest Guard?"

"I don't know," Enaro said patiently. "I told you, I don't know why you're being warned away."

Anger and frustration warred within Jhared. "You've never known someone slain by the killing winds, have you? You've never seen what's left of a village after the winds have demolished it."

"No, I haven't." Enaro didn't waiver, didn't own the grace to appear so much as chagrined.

"Go to Obled," Jhared said. "Speak with an orphaned child named Tomen and his little sister. Then tell me to hinder our search for an answer to that horror."

"Soldier, you make a grave mistake if you think me heartless, but you seem to believe only one danger threatens Avelos. Have you forgotten Sahiste grumbling at our border? Do you not see the signs of unrest within our own lands? We're not so far from the north here in Brenia that we can't feel the cold as the northern five turn their backs on Rumar's council. And we're close enough to the south, as you have witnessed, that Tumal's Legacy can still twist a man's life for its own purposes."

Jhared hesitated. He hadn't expected a temple aide from Clan Valador to be so aware. In truth, it had been a long while since Jhared thought much beyond his own fears and the threat of the killing winds.

Enaro sat on the thin bed tick and gestured to the chair near the desk. There was no rug, no tapestry, no brazier, nothing to soften the stone or muffle the cold. The ascetic chamber made an odd contrast to Brenia's excesses. As Jhared sat, he realized it was Enaro's own room.

"I'm sorry I don't have wine," the Shorn aide said. "My sister would tell me a conversation such as this calls for wine."

"Is your sister . . . ?"

"No. I can give you that much. Lady Esania has no part in it." Enaro looked down at his smooth, bony fingers and said more softly, "Although I like to believe she would be glad, if she knew."

It was a small admission, but meant something in this impassive man. The downward glance, the subdued voice, and the quiet hope signaled a need for acceptance from his family. It was the first indication Enaro cared what anyone else thought of him or had any attachments at all.

Jhared rubbed a hand across his eyes. The night had already held too many warnings and too much death. "Give me something, anything, to explain why I should do this."

"I've given all I can," Enaro said, looking up again. "The choice is yours now."

"Then I'm afraid there is no choice." Jhared rose, keeping his eye on the expressionless figure across from him. "Did you truly think it could be otherwise?"

"I wasn't certain what to think, Jhared Denaban. I'm still not. When we met, I wouldn't have taken you for someone willing to risk his life and his oath to succor a man named a criminal. Your sense of duty appears to be . . . fluid."

Jhared winced, but couldn't argue. He wondered, here in the temple, at the heart of Riana's order, how Enaro faced his own deceit. Then Jhared gazed around at the cold, ugly room, empty of all but the barest comfort, and thought maybe he knew at least a part of it.

"Perhaps you'll answer a question before you go," Enaro suggested quietly.

"A question of yours?"

"No. As it happens, it is a question Lady Esania put to the Bearer."

"Ask then."

"Had the choice been yours, what path would you have taken out of childhood? Would you be a soldier, still?"

Jhared stiffened in surprise. For no reason he could understand, he thought of the night the winds struck Velantar and what it had meant to him to comfort a young mother and tend his brother's injuries. Then he thought of Vesarian's agony, and the way the man's lifeless body slid down the muddy bank in the rain.

An old, painful taunt returned to him.

Killing is what Shorn men were born for.

He looked at Enaro. "How did the Bearer answer for me?"

"She said more talent exists among the men of the Forest Guard than among many clan prefects. And that you have a strong singing voice, well-suited to the complex themes of *Lord Arion's Choice.*"

Jhared laughed. "Well, there it is," he said with a shrug. "I might have tried my luck as a bard."

He opened the door to the corridor and paused. "Warn your fellows it will cost them if they try to thwart my patrol. The killing winds and the Legacy have shed enough blood. Vesarian is dead. If they care for Avelos and the Shorn, tell them not to add to our grief."

He didn't really expect an answer, and Enaro didn't give him one. Jhared walked out and shut the door.

The night was deep enough yet that the barracks remained quiet. Twitch mumbled in his sleep. Grion snored. Jhared sat on his bunk near one of the glowing braziers and unwrapped the packet the Bearer had given him. A russet-colored plug of leaves the size of his thumb rolled across his palm. He hesitated, wondering if he dared risk the blue flames instead. The Bearer had warned him the flames would consume him, but perhaps losing himself on the Paths would be a relief.

He picked up the plug, ashamed of his thoughts of escape. Deciding to be cautious, he bit off just half the leaves and tucked the other half back into his belt pouch. Tart, peppery juices ran down his throat. His mouth and tongue began to tingle. He tried to lie down, but his body insisted on floating somewhere above the bed. Like a falling leaf, he twirled and drifted in midair. It wasn't unpleasant. He recalled there were things he ought to worry over, but he no longer felt capable of worrying. Soon he felt nothing but a lovely warmth through his limbs and a gentle breeze across his body. From some distance, wings rustled against the wind and a soft voice hummed an unfamiliar melody. He listened to the peaceful song until he floated away.

15.

FAILED WARNINGS

Light scuttled back and forth behind Jhared's eyelids like tiny red spiders. He made an effort to move and found his limbs formed of brittle wood. Quite definitely he was no longer floating. With effort, he opened his eyes, blinking his sticky lashes. Sunlight poured in from opened windows, pounding against his head in an ugly rhythm. He saw a rectangle of blue sky and neat, empty bunks.

Abruptly, he remembered where he was and scrambled upright, searching for some sign of his patrol. He spied Anzo at the table, his bandied legs stretched in front of him and his bare toes warming near a brazier. The veteran was eating something that smelled sweet. Too sweet, Jhared's stomach warned him.

"Where's everyone?" Jhared croaked.

"Ah, the slumbering soldier returns," Anzo said genially. "Lieutenant gave us a day's leave to spend in town. The others wasted no time getting out'a here. Though to be fair, Twitch thought they should wake you, and Lenaro actually poked at you just to be sure you weren't dead."

Jhared swung his legs over the edge of the bed to discover himself still wearing pants and one boot. The last thing he remembered clearly was leaving Enaro's room. Despite a second warning from his stomach, he leaned over to pull off the boot, then navigated the room to take a seat across from Anzo. A bowl of roast yams, a jar of cream, and a pitcher of water sat on the table. The other patrolman pushed the pitcher toward him.

"I can't say as you don't look dead," Anzo muttered.

Jhared poured a cup of water and drank. "How's Jase?"

"Complaining 'bout missing Brenia's pleasures, so I think he's gonna be just fine."

"Good. You stayed?"

"For now. Perhaps I'll go out later." Anzo chewed on a piece of yam. "I don't have the stamina'a you young men. A day'a what Brenia offers is like to end me."

Jhared doubted the truth of that, but didn't press. Anzo likely had some private reason for staying behind. "Where's the Bearer?" he asked instead.

Anzo chuckled. "Four questions in ten words. I guess you're well enough. Despite how you look."

"Ah. Sorry." Jhared filled his glass again. He wasn't convinced the effects of the priestess's drug were better than falling through the Gate. "The Bearer?"

"Yes, yes, the Bearer, indeed. She came by to see the others on their way. Something 'bout her duty to keep honorable soldiers on the right path. I think she mostly came to check on you. Seemed glad to know you were sleeping." Anzo cleared his throat and gave Jhared an inquiring look.

"I wish I were sleeping still."

"So you're not gonna tell me what she's up to? You've had a lot'a things you won't tell since our darkling lady took you as her guard."

Jhared peered sideways at Anzo. "I didn't know you were paying such close attention."

"No one could miss the odd way she treats you, boy. She keeps her eye on you like she thinks you might turn into a magpie and fly off."

Anzo *had* been paying attention. Jhared wondered what else the man might have noticed. He tried a shrug. "I'm her protection in the wilds. Of course she wants me close. She's nervous."

"Naw. That one walks in Cael's shadow. She isn't nervous 'bout anything."

Jhared's cup thudded onto the table. "You're wrong. She fears for Avelos! Don't speak such things about her."

Anzo lifted his hands, surprise on his open features. "Easy, boy. It's not Grion you're talking to. I *like* her. But I don't have to tell you Cael's no friend to a soldier. The woman who holds the demon's Blade shouldn't have rights over a man'a the Fourth."

"Speak with the lieutenant, then," Jhared said, more bitterly than he intended. He stared at the table, knowing Anzo was too sharp for lies, and afraid of where the conversation was heading. Anzo had always been kinder to him than he deserved. More than once he had been tempted to confide in the man, but the story was no longer his own. He couldn't share it without putting the priestess at risk, and that wasn't something he'd consider.

Anzo pushed away his plate and pulled his pipe from his pocket. "You can't blame the lieutenant for this one. She asked for you. We all heard her in Velantar. I'm not the only one who's wondered on it. And I'm not the only one to notice you've been struggling since she came."

As Jhared considered the implications of that, he had an unsettling thought. "You stayed here to speak with me, didn't you? Did the others put you up to it?"

"No one put me up to anything," Anzo said gently. "I decided it was past time to say something after seeing you come out of a blowing storm spattered in blood, with the Bearer clutching at you like she owned you."

Jhared's hand lifted reflexively to the gash concealed beneath his collar. By the time he checked himself, Anzo had already noted it.

The little veteran whistled softly. "What has she gotten you into, boy?"

Jhared pulled his hand into his lap, miserable and silent.

"There's a name for those who seek power in others' blood," Anzo whispered.

"That's not the way of it, Anzo. She's a priestess of Riana, the same as any other woman in the temple."

How many times had he made that argument already—to Alende, to Enaro, and to himself?

Anzo set down his pipe and bent his grey head closer. "Well, I've never known any other woman in the temple who used blood magic. And I've never heard of a priestess who carries birds."

Jhared sat back in his chair. All his secrets seemed to be unraveling at once. For a giddy moment, he expected Alende to stride into the barracks and denounce the woman as the demon's consort.

"Does the lieutenant or any of the others know about the birds?" he asked in a strangled tone.

"Probably the lieutenant. I don't think any'a the others. Not Grion, for certain, or we'd all have heard about it. You'd best hope he and Bevan don't find out."

Jhared closed his eyes and tried to gather himself. He drew a breath. "It's not her, Anzo. It's not her. I'm the cursed one."

From the hallway came the sound of skittering on stone. Jhared looked up just as Inalde burst into the room, a large bone clamped between his jaws. The curly-eared feist zipped down one aisle of bunks as fast as his short legs would carry him, then scampered back up the second aisle. He ended at Jhared's feet, where he dropped his bone and offered a canine bow.

Jhared laughed with pent anxiety. Anzo was looking over his shoulder toward the door, an expression of concern on his weathered features.

"Delria was right. Her pup quite likes you."

Jhared jumped out of his seat as the Bearer appeared in the doorway. Dressed all in deepest blue the same shade as her eyes, with her black braid drawn over one shoulder, she was a lovely image of midnight.

"I'm glad I found you before you decided to escape into the city," she said, smiling. "I'm on my way to take Inalde for a run in the park. Would you indulge me with your company?"

Jhared wondered how much of the conversation with Anzo she'd heard. He shifted his weight, feeling frustrated and irritable. All he wanted was to serve his patrol without the need for warnings or secrets. "You needn't ask it, Lady. It's my duty."

Her smile faded, and Jhared instantly regretted his chilly response. "Just let me clean up," he added more amiably. "I'm not fit for your company as I am."

He agreed to meet the priestess in front of the temple. Anzo puffed contemplatively on his pipe as Jhared washed up, put on his cleaner shirt, and tugged a comb through his hair. As he threw his cloak across his shoulders, the other soldier halted him.

"I'm just an old man, with plenty of veils between me and the truth. I'm willing to admit I might not see her clearly. I'll only say this: you're a good soldier, Jhared. A good man, I think, in spite'a the curse. Don't let her lead you where you don't want to go."

Jhared found the Bearer in the open parklands, where she was throwing Inalde's bone and watching the little dog tear across the grass after it. Water droplets sprayed up from the soft ground as the pup ran. Inalde pounced on the bone and sped back with it, dropping it at the priestess's feet and wriggling with excitement as he waited for her to toss it again.

The woman laughed in delight. Jhared decided she couldn't have overheard his conversation with Anzo. She wouldn't be so carefree otherwise.

Children played in the meadow. The rain-washed air carried only the faintest hint of the dye houses' stench. As Jhared strode up to the Bearer, she turned and held out the bone. He took it and waved it over the twirling dog before throwing it almost as far as the patch of trees on the other side of the park. He watched as Inalde galloped off.

"Do you know my friend name, Jhared?"

"What?" His gaze snapped back to the priestess. She was watching him, not the dog.

"Do you know my name?" she repeated.

He had never even thought of her by her friend name; that was a privilege for peers and confidantes. He tried to recall his time in the high temple in Velantar. Surely he'd heard someone call to her. Then it came to him that he had heard it here, in the warm voice of the Lady of Brenia. "Yes," he answered.

She tilted her head. Sunlight revealed delicate blue veins along her jaw. "Novices in training as Pathwalkers are allowed to use their mentor's name, without title. It's one of the ways we foster trust. What we do together creates an intimate bond. That cannot happen if we don't trust one another. I want you to say my name."

He recoiled. A boundary lay between them that was not his to cross. Her name represented a part of her to which he owned no right. He would no more say it aloud than watch her slip into the creek to bathe. "Lady, please. I won't—"

"I'm not playing, Jhared Denaban. Look at me and tell me who I am."

Sweat slicked his palms. For no reason he could say, an image of Zia flashed into his head. "The Lady of Brenia called you Leita."

"Almost," she replied with a frown. "Now *you* must call me Leita. Try again."

Inalde returned with his bone and bounced merry circles around them. Jhared held the woman's fathomless gaze. "Some of my comrades know about your birds, Leita."

He couldn't have said what he expected to happen. He should have known by now that crossing forbidden boundaries rarely heralded immediate chaos. It only ever left him feeling less certain who he was.

"That's a fair start," the woman said softly. "Thank you. Come, I know a place we can work undisturbed. Then we'll talk about the rest."

She took him to a small, tired-looking inn, the Ash and Kettle, not so far from the bridge where they had abandoned Vesarian's body. On the street, travelers and tradesmen went about their business. Jhared wondered if anyone had bothered to notice the Shorn prisoner was gone.

An assessing glance about the inn's smoky common room revealed mostly dye-house workers: old, rough-featured men and women who kept their heads bowed over their cups, and some younger dyers who ate with fingers burned raw by the mordants. In a corner of the room sat the only two drinkers bearing swords, a skinny, long-limbed man with a red beak of a nose, and a well-knit, tawny-haired man. Their coarse woolens and unkempt beards gave them the look of dye-house thugs. The skinnier swordsman scowled as Jhared and the Bearer walked through the common room. Jhared met the man's gaze just long enough to warn he was no likely mark.

Inalde sniffed at the floor around the Bearer's feet, while the Bearer spoke to the innkeeper. The man frowned at Jhared, but shrugged as the priestess pushed several coins in his direction. When she led Jhared down a narrow hall to the back of the inn, he didn't ask what she had said to the man to win them a private room.

The tiny chamber offered just enough space to squeeze a bed and a side table within it. It had no windows and one lamp. The Bearer sat on the bed; Inalde immediately joined her. Jhared remained standing near the door.

"Before we leave here today, you're going to learn to shut the Gate," she said. "Tomorrow we travel to the sky tower. The Paths will be turbulent at a place with such blood and conflict in its history. It won't be safe for you if you don't have some control."

"Tomorrow?" He had hoped to have more time to decide what to do about Enaro's threats.

She must have heard the concern in his tone, for she looked at him more sharply. "Aren't you pleased? We'll be another step closer to Sabela."

He thought quickly for a way to warn her without revealing Enaro's secrets. "I imagine some clansmen will be unhappy to have the spirits of a traitors' tower disturbed."

"I've no fear of angry clansmen while I'm among the Chosen's soldiers," she said, "and with the Bearer among you, none need fear the Ael." She patted the hilt of the Blade.

She was right, of course. A ragtag group of clansmen couldn't hope to hold their own against a Forest Guard patrol. Enaro's friends wouldn't be so foolish as to attack them. When it came to it, Jhared didn't really believe anyone would be so ignorant as to impede a mission to stop the killing winds.

"Are you ready to focus, Jhared? We've work ahead of us."

"Very well, Lady."

She raised a brow.

"Leita," he said with difficulty.

"Good. We're going to try something different this time. Last night I treated you as a novice, a child who's seen nothing of the world. That was wrong. You're a border guard, accustomed to walking others' Paths and through the in-between spaces. I think that's the reason you find the Gate so readily."

"You *think?*" he asked, frowning.

She nodded unapologetically. "Don't mistake me, Jhared, I know more about sacred journeys than anyone in Avelos, but the Paths are infinite and we've lost too much. There are limits to what a Pathwalker can learn on her own."

Jhared sensed something unspoken in her sharp words. "That's not all," he dared. "You believe there's something else."

She drew an audible breath. As her gaze came back to him, dread shone unmasked in her eyes. He realized with a pang of apprehension that she *wanted* him to see it, to know how deeply this unspoken thing disturbed her. "It's not yet time to make you understand what I fear," she said. "All you need remember for now is that you're in no danger from the Gate so long as I am close. I will always pull you back when you fall."

It was the type of enigmatic non-answer he had come to expect from her, but he closed his fist around his frustration. *I will always pull you back.* . . . "How many other Shorn men have you known who bear this burden?"

This time, she didn't flinch or show any change in expression at all. "None living."

In the hallway, men were arguing in low voices. The world retreated to an unreachable distance, leaving Jhared alone. "What happened to them?"

"You know what happened," she said more gently.

He thought about it and realized he did know. "They failed the Becoming."

"That's right."

"I should have failed too."

She nodded silently.

"Then why didn't I?"

"Why isn't important," she said. "Nothing can be done about 'why.' We can only look to the problem at hand."

To him "why" did matter. It mattered a great deal. According to her, he should have died on the day of his Becoming, taking his curse with him. Nothing he had done since that spring day should have happened. He felt unreal, detached. Perhaps it was the reason he never seemed to be in quite the right place.

"Jhared!"

Inalde gave a startled yip and leaped off the bed. The Bearer's features had gone hard. "If you don't learn to control the Gate, you'll be of no use to me. Or to your patrol. I need your attention here."

He straightened and nodded. She was risking her own status to help him. "What do you want me to do?"

"I want you to do whatever it was you did last night to reach the Gate."

He shuddered. He could no longer deny that he yearned for the blue flames with the same futile ache that made him long to throw himself from the mountain cliffs, even though the flames would destroy him just as surely. "Is that wise?"

"You needn't worry." She slid off the bed and motioned for him to join her on the floor. "I'll be here."

"How do I avoid the Gate once I've found it?"

"You don't. I want you to pass through and return."

"No. Not that." He scowled down at her. "It's too much. I won't flaunt the law."

She reached up, took his hand, and drew him down beside her. "Jhared, a thing may be forbidden because respect for it has been replaced by fear, and knowledge has been replaced by ignorance."

"Or because innocence has been replaced by corruption," he countered. "It's not right."

"I am the Bearer of Cael's Blade. Are you questioning my ability to keep you on the proper Path?"

She squeezed his hand. He smelled sweet, smoky incense in her hair. Although her fingers felt soft and small in his, she possessed a strength he had no power to defy.

"Of course not. It's merely . . ." He closed his eyes. Anzo's caution seemed no longer relevant. She demanded only that he do the very thing he longed to do. And he owed her, after all. He opened his eyes.

"Very well . . . Leita."

She smiled. "Excellent. Prepare yourself. I want to learn if you can find your own way back. I'll guide you home should you need it."

His body already anticipated the kiss of flame and the freedom of infinite Paths. Shorn energy heated his blood like sparks flashing through kindling.

He lowered himself to the floor and sat cross-legged, startlingly aware when his knee brushed the Bearer's. Leita's. He coughed and reined in his focus. Deep within him a calm point existed, a place where he could open himself to the incomprehensible. He steadied his breathing, drawing his awareness into himself and imagining a blazing Gate full of possibility.

"Traitorous child! What are you doing?"

"Stop! Stop this instant!"

The two voices screamed in tandem. Jhared jerked backward, slamming his head against the corner of the table. Stars exploded behind his eyelids.

He hadn't spoken with his inner Teachers since the day one of them had told him to die.

"I'm cursed with sensitivity to the Paths," he explained hastily. *"I'm learning to maintain control."*

"Open to the Paths? You? You're an abomination! A half-man!"

"We leave you to your own thoughts and this *is how you repay us?"*

The voices weren't at all the same—the first voice was a masculine growl that put Jhared in mind of a wild boar; the second was a woman's angry shriek—but the inner Teachers had always guided him as if they spoke from one mind. In all the years they had come to him, Jhared had never considered them as individuals, not until the shrill one had told him to let the killing winds destroy him and the boar had told him to live.

"Soldier, look at me," the priestess ordered. He felt her hands on his shoulders.

"I'm doing all I can," he told the Teachers. *"I didn't ask for this."*

"Don't whine," the boar scolded. *"At least have courage enough to take responsibility for your own perversion."*

Anger flashed to life in Jhared, an unexpected thing fueled by Shorn energy. *"The curse is my own. I blame no one else! But you left me alone with it, and the priestess agreed to help me. I've only done what she required. Go now! I won't speak to you further."*

From far away, he heard a *pop*, like a rope snapping apart. He knew he had dared too much, but a part of him reveled in the sudden freedom of it.

"Insolent boy!" the shrill one spat. *"You've been too long without the nightmares. Perhaps tonight, when I show you all the horrors concealed within you, you'll remember why you need us."*

"Don't search for the Gate again," the boar demanded. *"You're a blight on Riana's bright weaving."*

They went silent. Jhared reached toward their corner of his mind, but felt only emptiness. Since they had come to him, on the day of his mother's funeral, they had done their best to keep him within Shorn law. They had guided him when Elder and Madam Trianor couldn't reach him. He wondered if other inner Teachers loathed their Shorn charges with as much passion.

"Jhared Denaban. Please open your eyes."

He did. Inalde sniffed his face and gave him a consoling lick. Leita hovered over him with the Blade in her hand, her expression strained and indecisive. As his eyes met hers, she sighed and sheathed the knife.

"What in all the sacred skies happened? I felt no shift. You didn't fall. But you're so open, too open. The Gate is close."

He sat up and touched the lump on the back of his head. "My Teachers don't approve," he muttered. *Half-man. Abomination.* He should have been accustomed to their lashings by now.

She frowned, looking puzzled. "Well, no. I imagine they wouldn't approve. Only because they wouldn't understand the importance of what we do."

"I tried to explain it to them."

Her puzzled frown deepened. "Jhared, where did you go?"

"I don't know," he said flatly. "Where am I ever?"

"All right. You'll be all right." She leaned forward to pat his check. "Take a few moments to gather yourself. Then we'll try again."

"Again? Lady, don't you see I cannot?" Need drove him to his feet. He strode the three steps to the far wall and came up short. The little room closed on him. He was trapped between the priestess and his Teachers, torn by what he should do, what she wanted him to do, and what every part of his being ached to do. His heart hammered against his ribs and he couldn't catch his breath. He wanted to run.

"Come sit," Leita said softly.

Her cool hand on his made him jump. He didn't realize he had ground his fists against the stone wall until she pulled him away and bright bruises bloomed across his knuckles. She led him to the bed. Unwillingly, he sat. She knelt on the floor in front of him.

"It's not rare for a Pathwalker to be pushed to the edge," she murmured. "Not just the edge of her own Path, but the edge of reason. I don't fear for you, Jhared. You passed the Becoming with your self intact. I know you'll find the strength to give me what I need."

How could she look at him so intently and not see him? Why couldn't she see he wasn't intact at all? Pieces of his self had been tearing away since the day he shot an arrow into the breast of a hawk and had fallen out of the sky.

Leita's blue-black eyes consumed the light and consumed him. She was solid and still, while he stood swaying on the clifftop. He couldn't say what finally made him leap; he only knew he was tumbling. He reached for her. His hands found a slender shoulder, the gentle slope of her back. He clutched her to him, burying his face in the curve of her throat. Her skin smelled of incense and spring water.

The room somersaulted. Motion made the world a blur as he tumbled. He didn't know when he stopped falling, but the wind caught suddenly in the arch of his wings, tugging hard against the muscles of his back and slowing his descent. Tavia tightened her arms around his neck and settled her bare legs around his hips. Her strong, sable wings arched over her shoulders, a mirror of his. Steam streamed from her fevered skin into the twilight. Their bodies moved in synchrony, wings stroking the air. The wind rose with their desire, buoying them above the forest. Entwined as one creature, they strove for the first stars in the lavender sky.

"There will be a child," she whispered next to his ear.

The warmth in her voice caused his body to shudder, but he held onto the sweet ache of unspent passion. Wonder made him wait. With drought withering the grapes on the vine and conflict in the council pushing the clans toward civil war, she had been reluctant to bear a child, but the uncertainty only made him yearn for offspring, someone to learn his family's songs and share their stories. He pressed his brow to hers and looked into her green eyes. "You would do this for me?"

"For us," she murmured, drawing him deeper inside her.

Jhared gasped, overwhelmed by a mix of emotions he hadn't known could fit into one moment: unbridled desire and deep respect, gentle affection and fierce protectiveness. He grieved that the moment didn't belong to him.

As he came to that awareness, the moment ripped apart. Jhared tumbled away, through a black nowhere and across blue and red gleaming paths that branched like veins beneath pale skin. He left behind peace and fell into a smoke-filled sky echoing with screams. Orange and gold flames streamed through the trees, lighting the grim faces of the soldiers below—men he once claimed to know—and the bodies of his friends falling to their deaths. Tavia had been slow to break away, the child within her making her too heavy for speed. He had dragged her higher, their wings scraping the sky as they struggled to gain distance. He had heard a man give the order, heard the quiet thrum as two lines of General Maren's archers drew and fired. Tavia's body jerked and she cried his name as the arrow struck her breast. Jhared clutched her to him now, although he knew she was already gone. He was losing altitude, his strength spent. An arrow struck his shoulder. Another pierced his left wing. He smelled his own burned flesh.

The forest blazed beneath him. Long before his first flight, he had known those trees; they were the last bit of lush green before the red rocks of Sahiste. Now the forest was only another dying friend. Jhared kissed his beloved and touched the swell of her belly. With effort, he folded his wings against his shoulders and plummeted toward the pyre.

Orange flames reached for him, then blue ones. They scorched his mind and burned away his memories. He groaned in pain as he collided into a cold, stiff figure.

"Lady Riana of the Journey, the sun you gave to us, and the stars, and the flame for the darkest nights. Because of these we seek to find balance to your order. Now, by the light of this soldier, Jhared Denaban, illuminate for us the steps along your Paths."

Jhared Denaban. It was the name that defined and constrained him.

"Don't move or open your eyes," the Bearer ordered. "Just tell me what you remember."

Grief was what he remembered. A grief so crushing he could scarcely draw a breath. But he was a scout. For years he had been recalling details and recognizing patterns. He distanced himself from the waves of emotion.

"The forest is in flames," he murmured. "It's a battle. No. It's a massacre. An Avelonian army. One hundred cavalry, nearly five hundred foot, two lines of archers. General Maren's archers—"

He opened his eyes and sat bolt upright. "Ah, Goddess, it was Maren's Burn! They were shooting down the Exiles. I was *there.*" He clutched a hand to his shoulder, but found no injury. Then he remembered something else and reached around to touch his back.

"Easy, Jhared. You're here and safe. None of it happened on this Path."

None of it. Not the glorious feel of wind through his feathers. Not the exhilaration of discovering himself to be whole. None of it on this Path. Not a woman in his arms, strong and giving. A woman who smelled of incense . . . .

He gaped at the priestess in horror and thought he saw tension in the set of her shoulders, caution in the darkness of her gaze. "Oh Lady, what have I done? Please, tell me."

"None of it on this Path," she whispered, spreading the bedcover over him. "Hang on, Jhared, you traveled far. The Gate must claim its toll."

The heat drained from his body in an instant, as though someone had opened his veins and poured out his spirit. For an uncertain heartbeat, he lay emptied, nothing more than a husk. Then ice rushed in to fill the void. His jaws clenched hard and his limbs jerked out of control. He struggled to hold himself together, ashamed of his helplessness. He was aware of Leita not far away.

When the tremors finally ceased and he leaned against the headboard, panting for breath, he found her studying him, like a hunter might study a fascinating, potentially dangerous animal.

"By Riana's ways you travel and by her ways may you return," she whispered.

"I'm sorry," he said murmured, miserable. Lieutenant Sevar had once called him a rabid dog. Perhaps the lieutenant had seen the truth.

"Jhared, you just journeyed farther than I did in my first two years of 'walking. That's remarkable. The doors to the Paths fly open for you."

He closed his eyes. The memories were slipping away, and he wanted to clutch them close, both the wonders and the horrors. A woman had loved him. He had known himself to be Avelun and felt, not his own wickedness, but balance and well-being. How many times could he bear for those things to be torn from him?

"That's right," the priestess said. "Hold onto the journey as completely as you can. It's important you remember your travels. Another time, I'll teach you about the four Principles and about mapping them. You have the ability to journey with the ancestors. Goddess, what I might learn from that."

"What I felt then, was it the true past?"

"Yes. For someone. Probably someone in our own history. Maybe someone in *your* history. Blood can bind us across the Paths."

"I don't think I can do that again."

"Don't think on it now." She smiled down at him. "You're worn out. You've just survived the hardest part of journeying."

Perhaps he had survived, but he still had no control over the Gate, and his Teachers would return tonight to punish him for his transgressions. "What if I never learn to keep the Gate shut?"

"You will," she said.

"What if?" he insisted.

"Then you'd best get used to the traveling. If the doors open so easily for you, you will fall often and far. And then you will be lost."

A smart rap on the door snapped Jhared back to the present. Inalde gave a little growl and trotted over to scratch at the doorframe. Irritated surprise flickered in Leita's expression.

"Who knocks?" she called.

"Your pardon, Lady. It's Neb, innkeeper. I've a message for you."

Leita frowned. "A message from whom?"

"From a Forest Guard patrolman, Lady. Will you open so I can share it?"

Jhared hissed in dismay. Leita pressed her lips together and reached for the latch.

A soft rustling sound came through the door. Another voice muttered, then Jhared caught the hiss of steel on leather.

"Wait, Lady! I'll do it!"

He threw aside the blanket and lunged for the door. Too late. As Leita clicked the latch, the door was knocked from her grasp and two men strode in, the swordsmen from the common room. Inalde leaped onto the bed, barking wildly. The skinny man with a red nose wielded a dagger. The tawny-haired man looked strong and solid enough to make a naked blade redundant. With no introduction, the tawny one closed on Jhared. Reflexively, Jhared slid into a defensive stance in front of the Bearer, but in the heartbeat he had to consider it, he realized how dangerous it would be for her if fists and blades started swinging in the tiny room.

"Smart," the tawny man said, grabbing him by the elbow and shoving him toward the doorway. "S'needn't be a struggle.

"He the one you saw, Nian?"

The young innkeeper stood in the hallway, fists on his hips, looking annoyed. But Jhared's assailant was addressing a third swordsman, a nervous looking, ginger-haired youth who didn't look directly at Jhared.

"Stop!" the priestess demanded, her gravelly voice cold as a frozen pool. "Who dares offer aggression against the Bearer of Cael's Blade and her guard?"

"Commander Imil, Clanguard of Valador," the man holding Jhared responded. "Your soldier s'been accused of interfering with clan justice. Nian?"

"It could'a been 'im, Commander," the ginger-haired boy said. "Maybe. It was pretty dark."

Inalde yipped at the intruders and paced nervously at the edge of the bed.

"Someone quiet that beast before I do!" spat the red-nosed guard, slicing the air in front of his throat with the dagger. "Nian, you told me s'morning you saw a tall soldier with a Shorn stripe to 'is cloak. This shouldn't be a 'ard task."

The Bearer set a restraining hand on Inalde. "Jhared Denaban travels under Riana's protection. If he's being accused of something, it must be done before the Lady of Brenia."

The commander didn't loosen his grip on Jhared, but as he turned, he glanced from the rucked-up bed to the priestess and smiled unpleasantly. "Under Riana's *protection*, eh? Wish all of us could get s'lucky."

"Take care," Jhared said through gritted teeth. "You're speaking to the Bearer of Cael's Blade."

"Settle down, Forest Guard. We're only 'ere to see justice served. Nian, tell me we 'ave 'im, and we'll be away. S'not a good idea to let Emen get restless with a knife in 'is 'ands." The commander gestured to the red-nosed guard. "And Master Neb's starting to worry we'll spill blood on 'is floors."

"For certain, Commander," Nian sputtered, nodding. "Looks just like the soldier I saw at the tree."

Jhared didn't think Nian had actually looked at him. Likely the boy had no need; Enaro or one of the Kin had probably given him the information. This was the consequence for defying their warning.

"I tell you again, you cannot take this man into custody without the leave of Lady Esania!" The Bearer's eyes darkened as power crept into her gaze. Jhared thought of the blood and rending of the Dissolution. If this confrontation didn't end quickly, it could spiral toward chaos.

To his surprise, the commander responded to Leita with a calm shrug. "F'it's gonna make you come along quicker, fine. We'll 'ave the temple charge 'im before we take 'im to the elders. The Lady of Brenia's no threat to clan justice."

The knife wielder, Emen, looked aghast. "Commander, Riana's 'ores are Shorn lovers—"

Commander Imil shot Emen a dangerous look. Emen shut his mouth. Nian studied the floor.

"I'm not an unreasonable man," the commander told the priestess. "My duty's to do what's right for Valador. Will you lead on, Lady?"

Leita scooped up Inalde and marched out. Imil and Nian escorted Jhared, with Emen taking rearguard. No one in the common room turned to watch the odd procession of priestess, soldier, and clanguards, although a few people peered vaguely over the rims of their cups. On the streets, it was the same: people hurried along, focused on their daily tasks. Jhared felt strangely invisible. No matter the enormity of what happened to him in the next few hours, none of these strangers would notice any ripple from it. He thought of the apathy that had surrounded Vesarian's suffering.

"Where'd you put 'im?" the commander asked, breaking into Jhared's chilly thoughts.

"Put who?" Leita responded.

"Not you. I'm speaking t'the soldier. Where'd you put the Shorn wretch after you freed 'im?"

The priestess glanced over her shoulder. Jhared said nothing.

"You should answer the questions," Emen said. "Commander's the reasonable one. I'm the one our elders say can take confessions. I got that animal Vesarian to tell 'is crimes. Don't think you'll be any challenge."

"Shut it," Imil ordered. "We do what's necessary and don't boast."

The guard gave his commander a petulant glance. "I'm only letting 'im know I can deal with a Shorn traitor, soldier or no."

"I said *shut it*."

Jhared didn't need Emen's intimations to imagine the grim outcomes of this disaster. He had given the Legacy a gift. They would see him hanging from the tree; then they would point to him and accuse the high chieftain of using soldiers to undermine clan authority.

At the temple portico, beneath the banner of the Silvaye, Leita stopped and faced Imil. "Commander, you and the boy are welcome in the temple, but that one is filled with malice." She gestured at Emen. "Riana has no tolerance for such irreverence. He must wait here."

Emen swore aloud. "The goddess doesn't rule in Brenia. I'm a Valador clanguard. I go where I like."

"Wrong!" Imil barked, swinging around. "You go where *I* tell you. I've 'ad enough from you. You'll wait 'ere and you'll do it like a man keeping watch for 'is clan, not a street bully."

Emen stared with a defiant, incredulous look no disciplined patrolman would ever give his superior.

"What'd you say, clanguard?" Imil snapped.

"Yes, sir."

"What?"

"Yes, sir!"

"Damn right! Don't move from this spot or you'll be sharing the soldier's chains." The commander tipped his head to the Bearer and prodded Jhared up the step.

Leita led them into the temple, where they were greeted by Sister Jhema. The withered little priestess offered a spiral to the Bearer and took the squirming Inalde before requesting the others' unsanctified blades.

Imil sent an evaluating gaze around the sanctuary. "All your temple guards are out in the fields bringing in the trim, eh?"

"That's right, Commander," Leita answered coolly.

Imil nodded and gave up his sword and Nian's. "No matter. The Lady 'as my respect, same as ever."

"Good man," Sister Jhema said, squinting up at him and patting his hand.

The Bearer escorted the clanguards to the library and left Jhared in their custody while she went to request an audience of the Lady of Brenia. Nian peered around the elegant room uneasily, sat on a bench, then rose and looked behind him, as though afraid he'd left a dust trail. Commander Imil planted himself on the lovely carpet with his dirty boots, examining books Jhared doubted he could read.

"Before the end, I will 'ave to know where you put Vesarian," Imil said offhandedly. "You could tell me now. I don't like Emen's ways, but I use 'im when I must."

Jhared didn't answer. Looking up at the bookshelves, he discovered himself beneath Lady Esania's volumes on the healing arts. Could he have saved Vesarian had he been allowed to know their secrets? This arrest would seem less absurd if he had at least spared the man.

Imil stomped over and looked him in the eye. "What is it makes a Shorn soldier s'arrogant as to free a criminal in someone else's clan?"

"What if he was innocent?" Jhared said, holding his ground.

"S'at what 'e told you?"

"The Legacy has many reasons to want a Shorn man to appear corrupt," Jhared answered.

"S'you think Vesarian was just painted as a menace for political gain?"

"Isn't it possible? Your man Emen, the one who took the confession, he's Legacy."

"True enough, soldier. And s'am I."

Jhared opened his mouth in surprise.

"What?" Imil demanded. "Don't I fit your picture of a goddess-hating Legacy supporter? You damned 'igh chieftain's men color us Legacy boys as if we're all from the same bolt of cloth. You want to know what gets a Shorn man on the tree in Brenia? That bastard Vesarian kept 'is little girl locked in the cellar like a rat. To keep 'er safe from the Teachers' lies, 'e said. S'at the kind of man the Forest Guard names innocent?"

Jhared stared in frozen silence.

"Maybe I don't agree with all the Legacy stands for," Imil continued, "but I'll tell you this, the Legacy'll let the clans decide what's best for the clans. You Forest Guard rush onto our lands like you're saving the world when you know nothing of who we are."

"I serve all of Avelos," Jhared murmured, as though it could explain something. Instead, he found he was no longer certain what that meant.

"Commander, the Lady of Brenia will hear your petition."

Crows cawing in the distance. That was the quality of Leita's low voice. The first time Jhared heard it she had worn the shape of Cael. Now she stood in the doorway, only a mortal woman, looking pale and resolute.

"Good!" Imil said heartily. "Your soldier is in need of a lesson about 'ow we take care of our own in Clan Valador."

"Jhared Denaban patrols the most dangerous borders of Avelos so that your children are safe and your clanguards can stay close to home," Leita replied. "Don't speak to me of lessons. Shall we go?"

Her tone was grim. Jhared heard nothing of salvation in it. He wondered what Lady Esania had told her.

Imil looked unabashed. "As you say, Lady."

The Bearer avoided Jhared's gaze as she turned to lead them down the corridor with its stone columns and high archways. As they passed the inner courtyard, three women in green glanced up from where they sat reading in the sunlight. Ahead lay the stairway to the Arionade barracks, the priestess's living quarters, and Lady Esania's personal receiving room. Leita hesitated at the stairs for a heartbeat before continuing on.

The world careened like a boat on rough waters. Jhared lurched sideways, flinging his hands wide to catch his balance. Imil grabbed him, scowling. He stumbled several more steps before the ground evened out. Leita didn't look back. She continued to the end of the corridor and stopped at a door painted crimson with tendrils of deep green Silvaye along its border. She knocked on the door, then opened it and stepped inside. The sharp scent of herbs drifted into the hall. Nian followed the priestess, then Jhared, with Imil on his heels.

Jhared caught a fleeting host of impressions as the door closed: neat shelves filled with jars and jugs, a long table laden with bowls and tools for grinding, a desk, a lamp, an array of unlit candles. A healer's workroom. He only had time to register one more thing: Esania wasn't present. Then he sensed the Bearer changing.

"May you be rewarded for your sacrifice," she murmured. "May you see the day the two are made one and true balance is restored."

Her eyes were large and dark. Her long fingers had closed around the black grip of the demon's weapon. It slid free of its sheath with a whisper. The Blade gleamed as she dove for Nian's throat.

She moved swiftly, with surprise on her side. Nian backed up so fast, he knocked into the table. A bowl fell to the floor and shattered.

"No!" Imil roared, but no time remained for warning. He launched himself at the priestess, his right arm swinging toward her knife hand with a force that could break bone. Jhared had an instant to see the desperation in the commander's expression, an instant to despise the inevitability of what would happen next. Then Shorn fire ignited his blood and he moved to protect the Bearer, as he had sworn to do.

Intent upon stopping Leita, Imil had left his flank exposed. Jhared moved in unhindered and kicked the man's supporting leg out from under him. With an outraged cry, the clanguard crashed to one knee. Instruments tumbled to the stone where Nian and Leita struggled, but Jhared couldn't spare the instant to look up. He closed on Imil, striking the clanguard twice in the head. As the commander tried to clamber to his feet, Jhared wrapped his right arm around the big man's throat, grabbed his own fist with his left hand and squeezed.

Imil made his second error, the same mistake most men make when they're caught by the throat: in the last seconds of awareness, he punched at Jhared's forearm and scrabbled at his shoulder, futilely trying to break his grip. Jhared braced himself and hung on. In a handful of heartbeats, the tawny-haired clanguard sagged in his arms. Cautiously, Jhared loosened his hold, and Imil slid to the floor. Jhared let the man go and looked for Leita.

The Bearer had pinned Nian against the wall, the Blade pressed against his throat. The boy was wide-eyed and furious. Blood stained the front of his shirt.

"Lady, enough! You mustn't kill him!"

"I'd rather hoped not to," Leita replied crisply, "but I could use your help."

Jhared grabbed the boy by the collar, dragged him out of reach of the Blade, and twisted him into a secure hold.

"Speak the truth," Jhared ordered. "You didn't see me at the tree, did you?"

Leita glanced up in surprise. "What?"

"Until now," Jhared went on, "your commander had nothing against me but your false word."

"Until now," Nian sputtered. "Now it doesn't matter what *I* saw. You're bound for the tree for certain."

"Who told you to give me up?"

Nian stared ahead stonily.

Jhared growled in frustration. "Very well. I'd say our debts are balanced. Wouldn't you?"

"There's no more time," the Bearer hissed. "You have to end it, Jhared."

Nian struggled. In three years, he might have been a challenge for a Forest Guard, but now his broad frame was still a boy's, all bony angles and awkwardness. Jhared felt sick as he wrestled the young clanguard into submission. He felt the boy's panic as he wrapped an arm around his throat. When Nian went slack, he laid him beside the commander.

The Bearer descended over the guards and began to shove something into their mouths.

Jhared watched, aghast. "What are you doing?"

She held up a russet-colored plug of leaves, the same potent sleeping drug she had given him the night before.

"Ah, Goddess. Why?"

"Because I need to delay their waking. I've not the power to protect you and I can't let them take you."

"Lady Esania?"

"She refuses to put the temple at odds with the clan elders by speaking for a Shorn soldier. Your lieutenant might be made to see reason, but I don't trust him to keep you out of their hands in the meantime."

"Lady, I would have gone with them! I'm not afraid to pay the price for my actions."

"Don't be a fool, Patrolman. They'd torture you as they tortured Vesarian. You'd be thrown through the Gate, and I'd have no way to keep you from being lost. There's no other choice. You must flee."

"Run away?" He gaped at her. Abandon his comrades? Escape his duty? "That's not possible."

"Your Path has turned, Jhared. Turn with it or tumble off. Wait for the patrol beyond the walls and follow us when we ride out. It won't be long; we won't be able to linger in Brenia with this affront to the elders. I'll come to find you when I've spoken with Sevar."

"Lady, don't you understand? You set your Blade against a clanguard. I must stay and see that you're safe."

She smiled up at him. No matter what happened next, he would always remember that patient smile, like a mother explaining a complex truth to her child.

"You're the one who doesn't understand. You are beloved by Cael. You travel in his shadow. No one who stands beside you is safe."

Jhared felt the blood leave his face. "That's not true. Please, Leita."

"Go, soldier. Go now!"

He couldn't look at her, couldn't bear to see that patient expression again. Without another word, he fled down the hall, up the stairs, and through the Arionade's corridor, pausing only when he reached the barracks entrance. For a small gift, the chamber was empty. Jhared grabbed up his pack, his bow and quiver, and the two roast yams remaining on the table. He sent his gaze around the room, wishing for a sword, but the temple held all the men's blades. As he headed for the stable stairs, he spied a cloak where it had been tossed over the railing by one of his patrolmates. Jhared stared at the length of pure green wool, then plucked at his own cloak with the bright red border that marked him as Shorn. He needed more anonymity than that red mark would allow him; still, he hesitated. The border was the indisputable reminder of who he was.

"Idiot," he muttered. He had just flung aside duty for survival. The Bearer had named him Cael's beloved. It made no sense to shrink from necessity now. With a shrug of his shoulders, he dropped his own cloak to the floor and snapped up the unmarked one.

Swiftly, he padded down the spiral stairs into the stable. The patrol's border horses nickered greetings. Seravina snorted and danced as he saddled her. She wanted to run.

He led her into the sunlight and swung onto her back, keeping a tight rein as they trotted into the park and away from where Emen waited. No one followed. Jhared didn't bother to avoid the main streets; he only wanted to be free of the walls as quickly as possible. Every moment he expected a stranger to call him out for trying to disguise himself. When a pair of swordsmen ran toward him, he prepared to kick Seravina into a gallop through the crowded street, but the men breezed past him and disappeared down an alley on the other side of the road.

He was sweat-soaked by the time he reached the city gate. The drowsy-looking guard on duty paid no particular attention to the hooded soldier leaving Brenia amidst a caravan of wool merchants.

Once beyond the eye of the watch, Jhared threw off his hood and kept up a steady pace along the road back to Obled. Several times he deliberately met the eyes of travelers heading toward Brenia. When he paused to rest Seravina, he nodded to a gentleman wearing the crest of the weavers' guild. Let them note the Shorn man on the tall silver mare. Let his pursuers believe he had fled south toward familiar territory.

Only after several hours, as the sun came to nest at the horizon, did he find a quiet place to turn Seravina off the road and back toward the northwest. Only when he was far from curious eyes did he give the mare her head. She responded joyfully, stretching her long legs into a ground-eating gallop and snorting plumes of steam into the crisp evening air. They skirted farmhouses and the black squares of harvested trimago fields. Jhared turned her toward the forestland west of Brenia, and for a change she didn't fight him. Her mane whipped into his face as he leaned over her neck. Her hooves barely seemed to hit the ground as she conquered the softly rolling hills.

For a long while, Jhared thought on nothing but the perfect, balanced motion of the mare and the way his body thrilled to the touch of the wind.

16.

BLUE FLAMES

When they reached the edge of the forest, where moonlight threw skeletal shadows of the trees against the earth, Seravina refused to go on. She halted with an angry whinny, twisting her neck away from the bit. With his eyes on the trees, Jhared retrieved his bow from behind the saddle. He'd learned well enough that the granddaughter of the Mavaye didn't shy at shadows. Wolves sometimes ranged this close to the cities and a variety of wild cats thrived in the borders where forests met farms.

"We *are* going in," he told the mare. "Trust me. Tonight the predators outside the forest are worse than the ones within."

He guided her farther north along the forest's edge, sticking to the fields and attempting to leave behind whatever distressed her. The night air began to grow cold. At his left, the autumn leaves whispered a lonely song. A song of lost spirits, Jase would have called it. When Jhared was almost directly north of Brenia, he again asked Seravina to enter the trees. She tossed her head, as though to say she thought it a poor idea, but complied.

They picked their way along a game trail that wound into the densest part of the woods. Jhared doubted the clanguard would search for him so close to the city, but after the trouble he had taken to distract pursuers, he didn't care to give himself away by crossing the path of some farmer collecting firewood. For a time, he kept a hand on his bow, as vigilant as Seravina, but as they continued on, the forest gave no cause for alarm and he began to relax. The skittering of creatures among the leaves and the creaking branches were a part of the normal night rhythms, rhythms he knew.

At the base of a small, wooded bowl, he came upon a tall hedge of brambles and vines. He slowed Seravina to investigate. Riding around the boundary of the hedge, he discovered that it hid what had once been a small cottage. No door remained on the squat structure, most of the roof had fallen in, and a hickory tree poked its branches out from the dark eye of one window, but it offered shelter enough for a night.

Jhared slid out of the saddle. As his boots touched the ground, the stars swung sideways. He grabbed at Seravina's neck, breathing deeply to dispel the dizziness. He cursed the endless hungers of his Shorn body. The yams he had devoured hours ago weren't nearly enough to hold him, but food would have to wait.

He rolled his shoulders, heavy with weariness; there was to be no reparation this day. He had started by violating Shorn law and ended by leaving the Bearer in danger and his patrol in disgrace. From a memory that shouldn't have been his, he recalled the stench of charred wood and burning flesh. He thought of Maren's Burn and the woman named Tavia.

Seravina balked as he tried to lead her through the cottage door.

"Perhaps you want to be discovered," he grumbled at her. "Perhaps you'd rather serve a clanguard who doesn't know a plow horse from the Chosen?"

Before he could nudge her forward again, an eerie, high-pitched squeal rang out from within the vines. Jhared grabbed his bow and nocked an arrow. The squeal came again. Cautiously, he approached the hedge.

What he saw nearly made him drop the bow. Out of the shadows toddled a small child with long black hair. As the toddler swayed on unsteady feet, she gave a high-pitched giggle and spread little wings to catch her balance.

Jhared could hardly breathe. "Wait!" he croaked, as the child disappeared into the cottage.

He hurried in after her. Someone bumped his arm. He turned to find a slender, brown-haired man with merry eyes stirring bean soup over the hearth, while a young woman at a table sorted herbs and various healer's notions into the drawers of a red box. Ruddy firelight and thick rugs made the room cozy, even though the floor was only packed earth and the space was small and mean. The woman smiled and glanced to where the toddler played on a blanket at her feet. Perfect little feathers lay smoothly against the child's shoulders. Their color was a captivating shade of sand with fine black speckles. Jhared stretched out a hand, needing more than anything to touch them.

Pounding shook the door. The woman bent hastily to scoop up the child. Her smile fled. The young man grabbed a knife from the hearth as the door flew open and three guards in white coats crashed into the room. He shouted and ran at them, waving his knife. Not a soldier, this man, or a fighter, but his wild flailing distracted the white-coats long enough for the woman and child to escape out the door. They disappeared into darkness as a guard's sword pierced flesh. The determination in the young man's eyes turned into terrible surprise. He collapsed on the hearth, overturning the kettle. Blood and soup pooled in the dirt. The Arionade ran after the woman and her Avelun daughter as the man they had left behind died on the floor. A sand and black-speckled feather floated on a draft from the open door and came to rest beside him.

Jhared reeled. His boot caught on the edge of a root, and he tripped, smacking his head against the table. The pain threw a ray of clarity over him, like sunlight cutting through clouds. He understood what was happening. Leita had warned him that too many Paths in his perception at once could feel like madness, but understanding came too late. Blue flames reached for him, and all he could do was open his arms and embrace them.

Stillness and peace. No blood or screaming. For that, he was grateful. A breeze puffed across a lake like a long-held breath, releasing the day's heat and infusing the air with the delicate scent of water roses. A girl peered out the door of an odd-looking house lifted above the bank on stilts and secured with wide shutters locked over the windows. She scurried down the ladder that leaned against the house, then turned her face to the sky. Her smile was all warmth and openness. Jhared imagined he saw something familiar in it, although she was not familiar. Her features were severe for her youth: her smooth brow rose above a sharp, straight nose and her cheekbones angled steeply toward a slightly narrow chin. As she tilted her head, unbound waves of dark hair rippled down her back to her waist. She lifted the weight of it off her neck and made a face, as if it annoyed her. Then, casting one glance back at the house, she returned her gaze to what lay ahead, her eyes bright with a desire Jhared understood.

Her bare feet slapped against the cool mud as she skirted the lake. It struck Jhared that he couldn't hear her footsteps; he felt them. She passed a garden, with neat rows of vegetables and berry bushes, and on the lakeside, a small dock with a rowboat tied to it. As soon as she reached the point where the shore curved away from the house, she paused. In one fluid motion, she pulled her shift over her head and tossed it aside. It took more effort to unknot the strips of cloth that bound her. When the last one fell away, she sighed in relief and unfurled her glossy wings. They began at her shoulder the color of frost and grew darker as they curved toward her ankles, until at the tips of the primaries, they gleamed true black, the shades of twilight slipping into night. Jhared's heart sped with anticipation that wasn't completely his own.

She shot out along the shore, propelled by strong legs. The wind caught in her primary feathers and tried to slow her, but she fought it. She fought, as she could not fight during the day, against those who would slay her with their good intentions. They expected her to find a place here, but she was not meant to be tied to the land. Wings beating, she leaped, seeking the lift that could carry her above the mud, over the water, and away from this nowhere. As ever, only her spirit soared. Her body returned heavily to the ground.

Large hands closed over the ridge of one wing as she landed, dragging her to a painful halt. The girl squirmed around to face an older woman with features that echoed hers. The woman was strong and capable looking, but panting hard; the girl had been difficult to catch. Fear and rage gleamed in the woman's eyes, and something more, an intention the girl did not see.

"Watch out!"

Jhared thought they heard him. The girl twitched her head sideways, and the woman flinched. Then the instant passed, and the woman's hand flew. The slap made Jhared's ears ring. Wings fluttered. The girl fell to the ground. The woman drew back her arm a second time.

Jhared threw himself forward, as though he could insert himself between the two. It was a mistake. As the woman struck at the girl again, the world heaved beneath him.

The summer night began to crumble. Pieces of the Path tumbled free like a broken puzzle—a piece of lakeshore, a cutout of sky, a fragment of garden—revealing blackness behind. Blue flames roared up through the blackness. A piece of muddy ground disintegrated under Jhared's feet. As he fell toward the Gate, he imagined that his hand brushed against feathers. The girl's eyes went wide. Jhared saw they were the gentle grey-green of the mountain meadows where he used to love to run.

The smells and sounds of the forest returned. The Avelun was gone. As Leita had demanded, Jhared rehearsed every part of the journey he could recall: the way the moon illuminated the curve of the girl's breasts; the perfect arch of her wings; the black stream of her hair as she ran.

He groaned. What was he doing? Why, even among the infinite Paths, did he find the traitors? He tried to sit up, but the ice of the journey fell upon him, and he could no longer think about anything but trying to keep his body and mind in one piece.

Sometime later a warm breeze ruffled his hair. He opened his eyes to find Seravina blowing in his face. Grassy horse-breath tickled his cheek. He reached up to grasp her bridle, and she tolerated his effort to haul himself to his feet. If he had heeded her warning, he wouldn't have entered the cottage at all. He flung one hand across her withers for support, stumbling beyond the threshold and back into the open air.

"Too many stories here," a voice moaned. "Too many bloody stories."

Jhared whipped around and jammed his fist into a tree trunk, praying the pain would keep him out of reach of the Gate this time. Nothing seemed to happen. Then Alende glided out from among the trees. Jhared swore aloud.

"I thought you were a scout," the waylayer said with a grimace. "How did you ever choose such a horrid place to wait for me?"

Jhared rubbed his fist against his thigh. "I wasn't waiting for you."

"And now you break my heart as well? If you haven't come to fulfill our bargain, why do you linger here? Have you finally thrown off your chains and escaped the Forest Guard?"

"I'm no deserter," Jhared answered coldly.

"No. No, of course not." The waylayer turned thoughtful. "Wait! Could it be you and your dark lady quarreled? Did she send you away?"

That hit too close to the truth to be comfortable. Jhared glowered. "Go back to the darkness that spawned you, caelevano, and leave me be."

Alende laughed, his eyes glittering in the starlight. "It's lovely to see you show a bit of spirit, my darling, but you should take care how you speak to me. I have friends in this forest."

Jhared studied the trees and saw no one. He didn't trust the madman's raving.

"Never mind," Alende said, scratching at his throat. "We'll get to the rest soon. Goddess, I need a drink. Come along."

"I don't think so."

Alende rolled his eyes. "Don't be dense. Even someone as tamed as you couldn't possibly find a moment of peace in this violent place. You promised to listen to my stories of Mahla. So, come."

Jhared had promised. If not for Vesarian, he might have found a way to meet Alende already. The waylayer was no fool in the woods and had even more reason than Jhared to stay out of reach of the clanguard, so what did he really fear about going with the man?

Mahla Denaban saved my life.

Jhared shivered as he realized the reason for his fear was exactly the reason he must go: Alende knew things he didn't, about his mother and about the Bearer. "Very well."

"Excellent! I should have known you couldn't disregard a command. Very obedient. General Nadel would be proud."

Jhared didn't respond to the man's baiting. He took up Seravina's lead. "Which way?"

"Whichever way is the fastest out of here," Alende said, seesawing drunkenly. "The smell of blood is ruining my appetite."

Jhared turned in disgust and started walking northward, away from the cottage. Alende fell in beside him, humming a familiar melody, one Jhared's mother had written, "Alende's Flight."

"That way," the caelevano said after a while, cutting westward through a thicket of mature varenut trees. He seemed to have regained his feral energy, for Jhared had to lengthen his gait to keep up. "Now that your lieutenant thinks he's discovered the location of Sabela's temple, I may just make myself an honorary member of the Forest Guard to keep a closer eye on the Bearer. What do you think of that?"

"What are you saying about Sabela's temple?"

"Ah, you haven't heard? How marvelous! That Sahisten spy of yours was carrying copies of two ancient maps. Lady Esania has helped your lieutenant to interpret them. She thinks one marks the temple."

"Sabela on a map?" Jhared's elation was quickly balanced by the disturbing realization that it supported his guess: Sahiste was also searching for the source of the killing winds.

A second, more immediate, realization caused Jhared to straighten and glare at Alende. "How can you know? When I left Brenia, not even the Bearer knew." He stopped dead. "You're one of the Kin. Enaro told you."

"My, you are a bright one." Alende smiled generously.

"Then you're the one who ordered Enaro to warn me away from the tower."

"Not me directly. I can only be in a dozen places at once, you know, but I've people in Brenia just as in Velantar. As in most places where Shorn men still live who reject the debt."

Jhared's anger gathered strength. "Did your people tell Nian to give me up?"

Alende shrugged. "You didn't imagine I would let the Bearer of Cael's Blade wander into such an ancient space as a sky tower, did you? Who knows what she might find? I didn't know about the maps yet. I just thought the clanguard might slow you down."

"Slow me down? Not only have you put Leita and my comrades at risk, you've given the Legacy a treasure! They'll blame Elder Trianor and the high chieftain for my actions!"

Below one raised brow, Alende's gaze steeled. "*Leita*, is it? So she's given you her friend name? What else has she given you? Has Cael's whore taught you to crave the chaos between her thighs?"

Days of pent emotion roared through Jhared, exploding free of the barriers that contained them. He flung himself at Alende, unsure in that instant whether or not he meant to kill the man. He made it close enough to see the pattern of scars crisscrossing the waylayer's throat before something cracked him hard across the back of the knees. The same trick he'd used on Imil. The irony wasn't lost on him as he slammed to the ground. Beside him, Seravina half-reared, bugling in fury. Alende reached out to grab her lead, but she was the granddaughter of the spirit of Captain Mavias and owned the Mavaye's instinct for battle. She struck the air with her forelegs and snapped her strong jaws. A short, lean man swathed in dun garb and wielding a staff appeared at Alende's shoulder. He took control of the mare, crooning wordlessly to her.

"I did warn you to be careful," the waylayer murmured to Jhared, backing away from the horse to look down at him.

"You are the essence of what Avelos fears in the Shorn," Jhared panted. "You are the worst of us. Undisciplined, self-centered, and full of malice!"

"Is that so?" Alende mused. "Perhaps that's why I have such trouble with the ladies."

The caelevano gestured with his hand and four more men with staves stepped out of the forest, quelling Jhared's temptation to try again.

"You're here because the clanguard hunts you," Alende said, uncommonly sober. "I suppose that makes you irritable and gives you some cause for anger. Now, I want to know if you fled of your own will or someone pushed you to it."

Jhared watched the warriors surrounding him. Small and neatly built, none of them would have reached his collar bone, but they moved like seasoned men. As they shifted around him, he caught the scent of pungent herbs, mint maybe, and something else. Their faces were thin and angular and their hair the brown-grey of tree bark. Their pale eyes gave away nothing of their intent. He arrowed his gaze back to Alende.

"What does it matter why or who? I've run from my duty either way."

In the starlight, Alende's expression changed from sober to one Jhared could have called regret. "I'm afraid it matters a great deal. If you had chosen for yourself, it would say something very different about the man you are becoming. You would claim it proudly and exalt in your freedom. No. No matter how far you flee from them, you will still be wearing their chains." The caelevano sighed. "Goddess of the Skies, I really do need a drink."

"Enough of this, Alende!" Jhared surged to his feet. The stranger holding Seravina startled and barked one word. From the edge of his vision, Jhared saw another man dart forward.

"Hold!" Alende cried.

Jhared was already turning when the staff caught him solidly on the side of the head. The forest flashed with summer-day brilliance. In the last moment before day turned to darkness, Jhared imagined he saw sorrow in Alende's green gaze.

17.
UNCHAINED

The smell of roasting lamb made Jhared's mouth water. He could hear the fat sizzling as it dripped into the fire. The meat would be melting-off-the-bone tender, and Neta's herb dressing would soak up the flavorful juices. She always cooked his favorite meal when he came home. He was grateful; he couldn't even remember the last time he'd eaten.

"Wake up," his Teacher prodded. *"You must find out what's happening."* It was the Boar. Now that Jhared recognized the Teachers were of different minds, he found he had to name them.

"What's happening is I'm about to taste one of Neta's dinners. I'm famished. Come back later."

"You haven't even opened your eyes," the Boar reported dourly. *"I can't see a thing. Come along now. He didn't hit you that hard."*

"What? But the roast . . . ?"

"I grew tired of waiting for you to stir. I thought it might rouse you."

Jhared recalled Alende and a staff smashed against his skull. *"Don't do that! Ever! How can I be a scout if I can't trust my senses?"*

"Calm yourself," his Teacher said. *"It was hardly more than a dream. And you're in no position to negotiate. Wake. Up."*

For a moment, Jhared considered defying the Boar, but knew it would win him nothing. Reluctantly, he turned away from the memory of good food. He found the outer world much less appealing. His head throbbed in time with his heartbeat. Although the stones and roots digging into his side said he lay on the ground, someone had thrown a blanket over him. The cold air on his face smelled of dusk.

Footsteps and low voices came from a short distance away. He caught the scent of herbs again—rosemary and mint—and dared to open his eyes. Above him, vines and branches had been woven into a clever shelter. Embers glowed in a firepit dug into the ground beside him. Among the trees, mist muted the twilight. It curled around two silhouettes: Alende bent in conversation with one of the dun-clad men. As they spoke, Alende took a book out of a bulging satchel. The shorter man opened the cover and flipped carelessly through the pages. Jhared cringed to hear ancient vellum crackle in complaint. With a shrug and a nod, the man closed the book and returned it. He peered into the satchel as Alende slipped the book back into place, then took the satchel from Alende and swung it over his own shoulder.

With a low whistle, the man signaled. The others melted out of the trees as silently as the best scouts of the Fourth. He touched three fingers to his forehead and flicked them at Alende.

"Losa medres, se'yo. Wurs muk," he said, nodding unhappily in Jhared's direction.

Alende chuckled. *"Losin medres, Mursa Vin,"* he answered.

The man shrugged again, in a way that seemed to acknowledge Alende's madness and suggest there was nothing to be done about it. Then he and his companions started southward, vanishing as silently as they had appeared, leaving only the fading scent of mint.

Losa medres. Alien words, but familiar sounding. So familiar.

Jhared scrambled to his feet, searching for Seravina. "Must I be cursed again and again?"

Alende turned, blinking at him owlishly. He reeked of bad liquor, but something in a kettle on the fire smelled nearly as good as one of Neta's roasts. "Don't fear, Mahla's son! You've no curse but the old one. And we have stew!"

Jhared spied Seravina munching grass under a tree and strode after her. "You did this, Alende. My patrol is a day on the road while I've slept. I'll have to ride the night through to catch them."

"Ever the dutiful soldier," Alende sighed. He took a swig from his flask and wiped his mouth. "How much is it worth to you to know exactly where your patrol is right now?"

Jhared frowned, thinking of Leita's courier birds and wondering. "You've no informants so fast as that."

"Is it worth a year of your life?"

"It's worth Seravina's speed and my own fortitude. If I take the main road north, I'll find them by morning."

"Unless you take the wrong road when you reach the fork at Aven Plains," Alende observed. "You don't know if they're heading west for High Road Pass or taking the low road east. You could spend days backtracking. If they make it into the mountains ahead of you, you may never catch them."

Jhared paused. There was some truth in the waylayer's assessment. He wouldn't make good time in the dark, while Sevar would be driving the men hard with the promise of Sabela's temple ahead of them. Without knowing anything of the maps they'd found, Jhared couldn't guess which route they would take into the Sandien Mountains. It was early enough in the year that both passes would be open.

"Is it worth a *season* of your life?" Alende asked, green eyes glittering.

"Right," Jhared said in exasperation. "A season. Where are they?"

"In the High Temple of Brenia, probably packing provisions and daydreaming of the pleasures they found during their day of leave. They'll set off tomorrow."

Jhared scrubbed both hands over his face and groaned. He needed to take better care. Alende was caelevano, but no less intelligent or dangerous for it.

The waylayer laughed. "I see I've angered you again. Perhaps this time I can go some way to make up for it?"

Alende turned from the firepit to a spot where the underbrush grew thick and tall. Pushing bushes aside, he revealed a tattered pack and a trio of blades. Jhared saw they included his sword, the small knife Tierzen had given him, and the lovely fish-and-palm-frond hunting blade from Leita.

"Enaro didn't think the sisters would have much use for these."

Jhared frowned, wary. "You're returning my weapons?"

"It's not as though you've plans to kill me," Alende replied lightly. "Not yet, anyway."

As Jhared reached for the blades, Alende snatched up the fish-and-palm. "This one belongs to me."

"As I recall, it was fairly taken after you tried to kill a woman."

Alende smiled. "I may need it again."

"You would harm the Bearer and be foresworn on my mother's name?"

"Ah, my darling, don't you see? We make the perfect tale for a song." The waylayer spun in a graceful circle and floated to the ground. "I must follow the Bearer to stop her and you must follow to protect her. Our paths are entwined in a most epic manner. I am ever so curious to discover how the song will end, aren't you?"

Jhared opened his mouth to say he knew exactly how he intended the song to end. Then, deciding not to be baited again, he accepted his sword and sat down.

Alende nodded, grinning, and held the flask out to him. After a moment's hesitation, Jhared took it. The liquor scraped his throat like a wedge of glass.

"That's poisonous," he coughed.

"Almost. Some of the farmers here distill the dyers' brew. They call it dyers' bane. It's easier to find than brandy."

Jhared stared at the flask in distaste, then threw back another swallow.

The waylayer stirred the bubbling contents in the kettle, sending up the rich scent of wild goat and sweet onion in a steamy cloud. Jhared's hunger rushed over him so suddenly that a small sound escaped his throat.

"Well, look at that," Alende chuckled. "Not all desire's been driven out of him. The tamed man hungers, after all."

Jhared was past the point when such a taunt could provoke him. He sat silently, appreciating the way the liquor cut to his head and blurred the ache in his chest. Risky, he knew, but he didn't surrender the flask.

Alende stared at him from across the fire. The dancing flames reflected in the waylayer's eyes, as wild as the man himself, yet in the depths of Alende's gaze, Jhared saw something painfully lucid.

"There's food enough for you here," Alende muttered. "That is, unless Shorn Law requires you to starve rather than share a meal with me."

"After this day, my dinner company will hardly be the thing that condemns me." Jhared hunched into himself. No Path he could ever have imagined included running from clanguards for freeing a criminal or sharing a fire with the man who wanted to kill the Bearer. This couldn't truly be his life. Was it ever possible that a man might return to the wrong Path after one of his journeys through the Gate? He needed to ask Leita. For now, he must endure one more night of this absurdity. Tomorrow, he would go after his patrol. With Leita's help, he would rejoin them by sunset.

He wiped the back of his hand across his eyes and sighed. Alende passed him a bowl heaping with meat, onions, and chunks of the wild tubers that flourished under the trees.

"Thank you." Jhared took the meal gratefully. With Tierzen's knife, he skewered a piece of steaming meat. He burned his mouth and didn't care. Not even Neta's roasts had ever tasted so good. Alende willingly filled his bowl a second time. Strength returned to his limbs and he felt less likely to float away.

"Thank you," Jhared said again, meeting the waylayer's gaze.

"Don't mistake it for a kindness, Mahla's son. You're not the reason I do it."

"I know." Whatever strange connection Alende had to his mother, Jhared understood it had likely saved his life.

He rose and walked away to check on Seravina. The mare blew at him in greeting and watched him with a limpid gaze. Someone had unsaddled her and tethered her in a spot with good foraging. Her tack and his gear were neatly piled beside the tree. Jhared was surprised; he hadn't really imagined Alende capable of tending to any creature but himself, and barely that. He watered the mare at a creek not far from the shelter. As they returned, she halted and laid back her ears. Her tail switched a warning. Jhared paused to eye the forest and listen. His own senses detected no danger, but that meant nothing. The previous night she had offered a warning, and shortly after he had been face-down in the dirt and wandering through the Gate. Who knew what a granddaughter of the Chosen sensed that he could not? He waited, but felt no dizziness; the ground remained stable beneath his feet. Jhared urged the mare back to the camp. She went, but continued to fret and stamp.

Jhared found the waylayer staring into the flames. In one hand, Alende griped the fish-and-palm hunting blade; in the other hand, he held the dyers' bane.

"You haven't yet told me about your staff-wielding companions," Jhared said.

Alende startled. He looked at an empty space across the fire, then darted his gaze to Jhared, confusion flickering across his features. He squeezed his eyes shut and shook his head. "Ah, yes. The fish herders, you would call them. Have you never seen a Sonan?"

Jhared hadn't. What he knew of them included only the sparse attention they received from the historians during the Amurian occupation and the stories told by soldiers who patrolled the southwest border. Mostly marshland, Sona bred little but swamp eels and disease. Amuria had held the country for half a century, until the Amurian duke decided Sona owned nothing worth wasting his money and men on.

"I didn't think Sonans ever traveled so far across the border. What are they doing with you? And with books?"

"They're avid scholars of the ancients, Sonans. I imagine they'd like to see where we went wrong. Sadly for them, Sona has a remarkable lack of texts, but happily for us. We give them books. They show their gratitude by lending us aid."

"Us? You mean the unbound?"

Alende stiffened. "I mean those whose scars aren't deep enough to make Avelos willing to claim us. No matter how much we bleed, the only scar of significance to Avelos is that one." With the tip of the hunting knife, the waylayer pointed to Jhared's left shoulder, where his sleeve covered the scar of his binding.

Jhared shrugged out of reach of the blade. "Enaro's stealing the books for you?"

"Perhaps." Alende smiled faintly and took another drink. "Perhaps Lady Esania has so many volumes in that fine library she doesn't miss a few."

"Where are the other un . . . the others who follow you?"

"You may call them Kin or unchained Kin. They are wherever I want them to be. In this story, soldier, I don't tell you all my secrets."

The waylayer staggered precariously close to the firepit. He no longer appeared merely drunk. His skin shone with sweat in the cool evening and his eyes had a feverish gleam. He began to tap the hunting blade against his collarbone listlessly.

Jhared frowned. "I owe you for the meal. Let me take the watch. Why don't you get some sleep?"

"Sleep? Now there's a question!" Alende laughed bitterly. With exaggerated care, he paced over to Jhared. "As it has much to do with Cael's Bearer, I'll tell you why I don't sleep: because only chaos waits in the darkness. Because I live so many lives and die so many times in my dreams that sleep exhausts me. Because I'm bored of watching the world come to its end."

Silence fell. Alende took another swallow from the flask. Jhared tried to make sense of the waylayer's pained words; he feared he almost could. "I know the nightmares," he said softly. "I know what they're like—"

"Quiet!" The waylayer rocked with the force of his outcry. "Don't waste your sloppy, empty sentiment. A man of duty and order like you can't possibly understand!"

"Then tell me! What does the Bearer have to do with it? You've given me nothing but nonsense, yet you know what's happening. I can see you do!"

"Not tonight," Alende growled, clutching at the blade. "I've already dealt with too many of you tonight. I won't tell this story again." He turned from Jhared and began to stagger off.

"You needn't bother with the watch," he called as he disappeared into the trees. "More evil lurks in the dark than your clouded eyes will ever see. The only thing you can do is hope it doesn't want you."

For a moment, Jhared contemplated following, but the waylayer's words had held such raw vulnerability he refused to violate the man's solitude. He wasn't such a fool as to neglect the watch, however. He took up his bow, slung his quiver across his back, and set out to walk a wide perimeter. The first thing he did was determine just where in the woods Alende's Sonans had dragged him. The waylayer had selected an isolated position well north of the city and west of the road. It would be easy enough to watch for the patrol in the morning. Next, Jhared cleaned up the signs of their dinner and checked on the mare. She had calmed since Alende's departure. He stroked her silver coat and she swiveled her ears to catch his quiet murmurs. He smiled to see it. Her response to him seemed to be changing, as though she had decided he might be worth consideration after all. He laughed a little at the thought of that.

Intent upon keeping his mind in the present, he settled near the fire. The voices of the forest provided familiar company, and he occupied himself by translating them. When a squeal tore the darkness as a small creature died under the teeth or talons of a predator, Jhared shuddered; he had never realized before how much death sounded like the squeal of a young child.

The moon rose, but Alende did not return. Jhared drew up the hood of his cloak and allowed himself to drowse. The Sahisten war drums started sometime later, booming through the forest. Their ominous rhythm reverberated in his chest, telling him the enemy approached. Seravina whinnied frantically. He snapped fully awake and rolled to his feet. The ground bobbed beneath him as he reached for his sword.

Alende appeared, moving like an old man and breathing through clenched teeth.

"What's happening?" Jhared demanded.

"The world is ending," the waylayer answered dully. He pushed past Jhared and crumpled to the ground by the firepit.

Jhared stared into the trees. "Is someone out there?"

"No one you can fight, soldier. Dreams and visions don't fear the sword."

Jhared turned toward Alende, and the ground shifted beneath him. The shift reverberated deep in his chest. He took another step and felt it again, although the feeling was beginning to fade. Not drums at all. More like footsteps.

"How did you find me?" he had asked the Bearer.

"When the Gate opens, it causes the Paths to shift. A person treading those shifting Paths has a very distinct footstep."

Was that what he felt? The footsteps of someone on the Paths? Alende lay on his back, staring blankly at the stars. After another moment, Jhared sheathed his sword. With a sigh, he crouched to stir the embers and feed a log to the fire.

"Are you injured?"

The waylayer lifted his right fist and dropped the hunting knife into the dirt. Blood blackened the blade. Blood trickled down his neck as well, tracing the ridges of his scars.

Jhared put a hand to his own collar and felt the sting of the wound beneath it.

"Did *she* teach you how to do that?"

No answer came from the other side of the fire. Alende's eyes had closed, though he wasn't asleep. After a long silence, Jhared rose and covered him with the blanket.

Jhared waited to leave until just before dawn, when the first birds began cursing the day. Seravina stood so patiently for the saddle that he had the impression she wanted to be free of the place as much as he did.

Alende stirred as Jhared adjusted the buckles on his saddle packs. "Where are you going?" the waylayer rasped.

"I'm going to find my patrol," Jhared replied. "Then I'm going to Sabela's temple."

"But you can't ride without me." The waylayer attempted his ironic grin. "We have a song to write together. You've still Mahla and the Bearer to learn about."

"I tried asking for what I needed last night. You refused to speak with me. So be it. You have nothing more to tell me, and I have nothing more I want to know from you."

Jhared slipped the bridle over Seravina's head and she opened her mouth for the bit. He sensed Alende's gaze on his back, but he didn't turn before gathering the reins and swinging into the saddle.

"Wait!"

The single word tore raggedly from Alende's lips. Jhared wasn't surprised to hear the hatred in it; he was surprised to hear the need.

The waylayer climbed to his feet. "I first met Mahla because of you. Did you know that? It's one of the few stories I'm still certain belongs to me on this Path."

Jhared looked aside, wishing the words meant nothing to him.

"I was fifteen winters," Alende continued. "The Minister of the Teaching had just brought me to Velantar from Clan Delsio. He knew that I sang and thought music might help me to . . . settle into a new city. It happened that a child named Jhared Denaban had recently come to his household for the Teaching. That child's mother was a bard."

"Tierzen introduced you?" Jhared frowned. "I thought you met my mother through Ziabela."

"Ah, lovely Ziabela." Alende smiled wistfully. "No. It was Mahla who introduced me to Zia. I imagine she thought such a charming singing partner would distract me from some less pleasant things. I daresay Mahla came to regret the decision. I'm sorry for that." The waylayer trailed off, rubbing one hand against his heart.

Jhared had never heard Alende speak with such clarity. "What happened?"

The waylayer shook his head. "I can't. You spoke the truth, soldier. I have no right to hold you. Go to your patrol. I'll meet you again at the end of our song."

The increasingly familiar urge to throttle the man burned through Jhared. Instead, he kept his composure and smiled thinly. "Did my mother find your endless games endearing?"

The waylayer glanced up, his eyes bright with surprise. "No," he admitted. "She had no tolerance for them. She always knew which story was mine. Even when I didn't."

"Then I offer this. I'll ride with you today, but only if you commit to speaking with me as you would have spoken with my mother."

"Ah, cruel heart!" Alende protested. "Don't you understand that my stories no longer travel like your arrows? They make loops and double back and spiral around—"

Jhared tapped Seravina's sides and she started forward. "Farewell then. I'll be waiting at the end of our song."

"Very well. Very well!" Alende cried. "You're a hard one, my darling. Hard and cruel."

Jhared sank into the saddle and Seravina halted. Unexpectedly, he felt a little less trapped. He smiled as he dismounted.

It was a small task to break camp. Alende traveled with only such provisions as fit into a worn leather pack. They scuffed dirt over the firepit and dismantled the shelter. A mushroom of grey light was rising in the east as they started for the road. Alende strode easily beside Seravina, his predatory grace returned. All Jhared saw of the previous night's anguish were the blue shadows beneath the waylayer's eyes and a new gash across his throat. Jhared tugged at his own collar.

"Now, tell me what happened."

"*What happened* includes far more stories than time allows, my darling. Pick a place we might start and I'll do my best to go forward from there."

"Very well. What did you do to Zia that caused my mother to regret your meeting?"

The waylayer glanced up. "Ah, yes," he chuckled bitterly. "I suppose you would see it that way."

Jhared inclined his head. "I know how Zia despises you."

"Here's a lesson for you, soldier. Don't ever *need* a creature like our Zia. Desire she requires. Jealousy she thrives upon. But don't depend upon her, don't trust her, and don't . . ." Alende plucked a purple lily as he passed it and shredded the petals between his fingers. "Ah, Zia. Even when the world is ending I can still smell her, still taste the wine on her lips, still feel her—"

"Mahla!" Jhared said urgently. "You are telling my mother's story."

Alende uttered a deep-throated sigh. "Of course. A story that deserves better attention." He tossed the lily away. "Mahla Denaban was selfless where Zia is only selfish. Mahla brought me back from my nightmares with tales about the gifts of our ancestors. After she died, I even began to see some of those stories." The waylayer hesitated and seemed in danger of drifting away, but he drew himself up and his gaze cleared. "I wonder what the Minister of the Teaching would have thought had he known he introduced me to a Storyteller?"

Something altered in the waylayer when he talked of Mahla. He seemed less feral, more present, as though speaking of her made him remember something about himself. Jhared recalled how much it had meant to him to share stories of his mother with Zia after so many years of silence. It had given him a connection he desperately needed. He couldn't hate Alende for needing the same.

Sunrise kissed the horizon and poured red-gold light through the trees. Jhared nudged Seravina up a low ridge overlooking the road while the waylayer continued his story. As Alende spoke, Jhared began to imagine the youth his mother might have known. Alende had been fifteen, a boy still struggling toward his Becoming. Mahla had cared enough about him to introduce him to Zia. She had trusted him enough to tell him forbidden stories, perhaps the stories she hoped to share with her own son someday. And then Alende had gone to the Becoming to prove himself, and he had failed.

Jhared's perception of a vulnerable boy fit awkwardly next to the spiteful, demon-touched man who strode beside him, but Jhared pushed aside his dislike to ponder the new idea. He thought he almost understood. "Why did my mother risk so much to save a boy who couldn't demonstrate his loyalty? The truth, Alende."

They stood at the top of the ridge gazing down through the trees at the road. A few hearty travelers were already heading north. The sounds of their horses' hooves and cart wheels disrupted the quiet morning.

"All I know is *my* truth," the waylayer said. "And I warn you, it won't match your view of things."

Jhared's hands tightened on the reins. "Tell me."

"Mahla sent me to the Becoming with my head full of the forbidden history of our people. History she gave to me. She blamed herself when I failed."

It fit. Better than any of the devastating reasons Jhared had imagined. It helped to explain why a respected bard had been willing to commit treason and why Mahla had been so very fearful that Jhared would fail the Becoming. It explained why the only story she had ever shared with him was the story of final reparation and why she had never offered him any of her dreams for the future. Jhared pulled in a lungful of air, like a man who realizes he's escaped a killing blow.

Beside him, Alende stood coiled with feline tension. "So, my darling, will you assail me with sword and fist for marring Mahla's name?" He bared his brittle grin. "I've no Sonans to step between us, and there are no Arionade this time."

Jhared looked down at the waylayer. "I thought what you had to tell me would destroy the small part I knew of my mother. Instead, I think you've returned her to me."

Alende drew back, wariness gleaming in his green eyes. "Don't turn her into something tamed," he growled. "She was fearless, and no slave to the Teaching."

That assessment was at least partially wrong, Jhared thought. He remembered his mother filled with worry. It struck Jhared that she must have truly loved the boy Alende. The thought sparked a lonely jealousy, but it no longer horrified him. Alende hadn't always been caelevano.

He opened his mouth with a reply, but the older man had wandered several paces away and was grinning in the direction of the road. "Now there's a sight to see! The Bearer of Cael's Blade rides like the Dark Queen of Winter. And doesn't Lieutenant Sevar look dashing beside her?"

Jhared peered over Alende's shoulder. Indeed, Leita and Sevar could have acted as the moon and sun in one of the old plays. They led at a trot, with all the others in perfect formation behind them. A cheerful marching song floated up the hill, "Lord Arion's Victory." Esran and Twitch made a solid effort with the melody. Anzo was woefully off beat, as ever. Jase's right hand was wrapped in bandages, but he sat upright and sang in his fine tenor.

"What a sharp little troupe," Alende said brightly. "Don't they realize they're missing their best scout?"

Jhared turned Seravina northward along the ridge without saying anything. He wasn't certain which bothered him more, his comrades' good humor or Leita's serene expression as she rode beside the lieutenant.

Alende called out behind him. "You'll need to stay off the road, my darling. Take the wooded trails. I'll follow the patrol. We can meet tonight at the fork before Aven Plains."

Jhared looked back at the waylayer. In truth, with his golden hair and simple woodsman's garb, Alende could blend in among the villagers, traders, and farmers better than Jhared could. "That's an easy way to be rid of me while you reach the Bearer."

The unbound man grinned. "Not as easy as it would have been to let my Sonans dump your unconscious body into the river."

No denying that fact. Still, Jhared had witnessed too much chaos in the man to trust him. "I'll take my chances on the road. You have more to tell me about Mahla."

They traveled all day. Jhared found himself almost hoping Commander Carn would send the rear guard to watch for him, but no one came. He and Alende reached the fork as scattered rays of late sunlight fell across the two roads: Linde Way, which curled toward Lake Linde and the eastern edge of the Sandien Mountains; and the High Pass Road, which rolled north across the plains before winding into the foothills to Alende's Pass in the west. Jhared and Alende watched as the patrol selected the High Pass Road and moved into the forest for the night. With a secretive grin, Alende led Jhared a distance farther, toward a ruined tower that was just visible where it sagged over the trees.

The tower stood in a clearing littered with stones the size of Seravina's head. Jhared let the mare pick her way. It was remarkable that such valuable building materials remained untouched. Aven Plains had its brick yards, but offered little decent lumber, and good stone must be hauled from the mountains. Then he gazed up at the ruins of the tall, slender tower, and understood why no one wanted these stones.

He dismounted at the arched doorway and let Seravina tell him what to expect. She flared her nostrils wide, but allowed him to lead her inside. Her hooves rang against cracked flagstone. Breezes whistled like unsettled spirits through the crumbling mortar. From years of enforced habit more than any belief in its protective quality, Jhared made a warding sign as bats darted out from the open roof. No stairs circled the tower. In the dark, it was impossible to say if they had rotted away or maybe burned, but Jhared guessed they had never existed at all. Unreachable galleries ringed the interior at three levels. The tower had belonged to the Avelune.

Alende dropped his pack and pulled his flask from it. He leaned against the niche of an arrow loop, eying Jhared. "There's a small copse near the river. Your people will have camped there. Good ground for a company unwilling to hazard the ruins of the traitors."

"Thank you."

Alende's stare was unblinking. "You're going to her now?"

"Yes," Jhared said. "Will you tell me why you hate her before I go?"

"I don't think so. I haven't had enough to drink yet. When you return."

"Alende, I'm going back to my duty. I'm not going to return."

The waylayer looked up with a sad smile. "No fear, Mahla's son. We will meet again."

Something in the man's expression reminded Jhared disturbingly of Leita. There was an otherworldliness about him, a sense he had seen more than any mortal could understand.

"Don't come for her, Alende. Please. I don't want your blood on my hands, but I will defend her if you come."

"Be careful of the rocks on your way out, soldier. It'd be a shame to lame that beautiful mare."

Jhared shook his head as he left. By the time he had Seravina on the road again, eagerness and anxiety had blown Alende's fey words away. It wasn't difficult to locate the Forest Guard camp. Laughter drifted into the trees from a good way off, and Jhared smelled fresh meat roasting. He left Seravina just outside the perimeter and crept toward the river. After dinner, Leita would walk to the water; it was part of her evening ritual. He need only wait.

Near the riverbank, he picked a sycamore with thick branches. It felt good to leap for the tree and swing himself up. He had just found his balance when the rustle of underbrush announced Leita's approach. Her light, unwary steps could never be mistaken for a soldier's. As she reached the water's edge, she held her arms out wide, palms up, and lifted her eyes to the bank of clouds in the north.

"To Lady Riana, who looks forward to the end and signifies the return to order, I give my heart. To Lord Cael, who looks back to the beginning, and signifies the birth of all creation, I give my spirit. Let what was split asunder be merged again, for only in the merging will we find True Balance. For the one who was and will be unbroken, let me be your good servant on this Path."

Jhared watched in dismayed fascination as she completed the strange prayer with a gesture that wasn't quite Riana's spiral, then slid out of her cloak. Her long fingers gripped the hem of her tunic and lifted it.

"Lady!" Jhared hissed, dropping out of the tree behind her. He landed in a crouch and sprang upright, a little afraid to turn his gaze in her direction.

"Who?" she demanded angrily. He heard the Blade drawn free, then a gasp. "Jhared? Oh, thank the One. Come here, Patrolman!" She grabbed him by the arm and looked him up and down. "I've been so worried. So many times I thought I felt the Gate swing open, but it was too faint to be certain. Are you well?"

"I'm fine."

She must have caught the edge in his voice, for concern creased her features as she returned the Blade to its sheath. "It was you I felt, wasn't it? How many journeys?"

Memories that never should have been his came rushing into his head: a babe with wings of speckled sand; a man bleeding to death on a cottage floor; a young woman with desires that running couldn't sate. "I don't know. How do you count them? Each journey holds so many stories." He trailed off, chilled to hear something of Alende in his words.

"You found your way back," she said gently. "That's the most important thing. Have you had no luck at all holding the Gate shut?"

"No. At least, it doesn't seem so." He tried to recall the hazy moments of his journeys. "What does it mean that sometimes I catch only fleeting images of a place or a person, sometimes I can see people but can't hear them or reach them, and other times it's as though I've dropped fully into another's life; I've become them?"

"That's Perspective," she said. "It's one of the four Principles of a sacred journey. The Perspective you have of a Path depends on which doors you open. It takes training to open doors, but also strength. You've true skill, though dear Goddess, you lack training. You must learn how to note not only Perspective, but Time, Place, and Parallel, as well. You must learn to map. We just don't have time!" She went quiet, her gaze distraught.

"Another night," he said. "Let's return to the others now. I really just need to be a patrolman again. Whatever the consequences."

The Bearer didn't release him. "Record your journeys whenever you can. You have links to the ancestors I don't. We will learn from what you see."

"Leita, I've spent all my life trying to sever those links. Please let's not talk about their usefulness tonight—" He broke off as he caught the scent of incense in her hair and remembered the feel of her silky braid against his cheek, the smoothness of her slender throat beneath his lips. More memories that shouldn't have been his. He choked and pushed them aside. "I'll retrieve Seravina, then I would ask you to walk back with me to face Sevar. It's not going to be pleasant."

"Jhared. There's something I must tell you."

Her tone had turned grave. Something about her expression drove a blade into his middle. It took him a moment to realize what it was: she had never before refused to meet his gaze.

"Leita?"

"You can't return to the patrol. Lieutenant Sevar has declared you a deserter."

The ground lurched out from under him, and Jhared grabbed for a tree. He knew now it was his Path twisting, but the knowledge was no consolation. "No. No, it can't be that bad. Even Sevar knows me better than that. What did you tell him?"

"I tried my best," the priestess murmured. "His rage rose beyond anything I had expected."

"All right. It's all right," Jhared said breathlessly. "I'll just turn myself in. Then it's only illicit leave, not desertion. I'll take the lashes that come with it. I'm not afraid of the lash."

Leita grabbed his arms, her expression urgent as she gazed up at him. "You're not understanding me. If you show yourself, the lieutenant is likely to have you killed. He took your flight as a personal blow. I never expected that. If not for the map and Sabela's temple to put his mind elsewhere, I think he would have come after you himself."

Jhared gaped. "What did you *tell* him?"

"The truth," she said simply.

What had he imagined? The truth was enough to condemn him to a traitor's death, and Sevar had ever wanted to be rid of him. Why had he looked into Leita's eyes and believed her when she told him all would be well? He drew an unsteady breath, struggling to quiet the roar in his ears. Somewhere in that roar, his Teachers railed at him.

"Return to camp," he told her. "Or they'll come looking for you."

"Jhared, please understand—"

"Stay close to Anzo or Esran on the road," he continued flatly. "Jase and Lenaro would never mean you harm, but Jase is too forward, and Commander keeps Lenaro too busy to help you. Some of the men know about the birds. That puts you in a risky position. Don't trust Grion or Bevan for anything. Don't trust the lieutenant."

"Jhared, you needn't fear for me."

He pulled out of her grip. "Dangers exist in these wilds you can't know. Don't leave camp alone again."

"Wait," she said. "This isn't the end of our work together. We'll merely have to be more careful. Follow us, and I'll come to you."

Jhared stared at her. He reached into his pouch and held up Branlen's stone. "Only look for me if you find this talisman behind your tent and only during Anzo's watch."

"I'm sorry," she murmured.

I'm sorry. The words floated into the air as meaningful as dust. He had been named a deserter. The worst kind of coward. A *deserter.* His mind kept rejecting the word. This wasn't his Path.

"Are they watching for me?"

She shook her head. "The rear guard rode close today. I've heard no unusual orders for tonight. Sevar is more interested in moving forward than looking back."

"Toward Sabela's temple?"

"We're truly going to find it!" She smiled, unable to hide her delight. "I'm truly going to have the chance to understand the killing winds' power."

Jhared had imagined himself a part of that discovery. He had once imagined making final reparation and earning forgiveness for the Shorn. He had gone too far now to even imagine forgiveness for himself.

"The lieutenant has you riding toward Alende's Pass. Where to after that?"

"Clan Aglar," she answered. "Sevar and I believe the temple is in the western most portion of the mountains."

Sevar and I. He couldn't linger over that thought. "Near Aglar Tower?"

She nodded.

"Very well. Go now, Lady. I'll shadow you back to camp."

She patted his arm and gave him a mild look that he supposed was meant to be consoling. "Be well, Jhared. I won't be far away."

He followed her until he could see the flames from the campfire and catch glimpses of his patrolmates through the trees. As she rejoined them, he heard Jase's unencumbered laughter and saw Twitch grin and thump Esran on the back.

Jhared turned away, drawing up the hood of his cloak against the growing cold. As he wandered into the night alone, he wished he knew what had made them laugh.

18.

EXILED

Jhared found his way back to Seravina, flung himself into the saddle, and clapped his heels against her sides. She reared, thrashing the air with black hooves, and came down running. It was reckless. He knew it. Horses broke their legs and men broke their necks tearing through the trees in the dark. But he needed to escape. The wolves of despair chased after him, and they hungered for his heart.

Seravina's long gait consumed the small copse and hurtled them into the open fields. A chilly wind lashed Jhared's face, but it wasn't enough to cool his need. His body buzzed with desire. The tortured muscles in his shoulders tightened painfully, as though to lift invisible wings. He needed to be airborne. He pulled the mare to a halt and dropped to the ground. He didn't tie her. She was the granddaughter of the Chosen, immortal spirits forever trapped in mortal form. She understood his need.

As he ran through the darkness, his sense of the world narrowed to the feel of the terrain beneath his feet and the blur of the stars above. On the Paths, he had tasted the sky. He yearned for that sense of wholeness once more. If he couldn't have it, he wanted to feel nothing at all. By the time he returned to the tower, he was blown and panting. He sank down in the grass where the moon crafted a long shadow of the Avelune's ruin. His hand landed on something cold and soggy. Glancing down, he saw the body of a bird. Shorn. Just like the creature he had encountered outside Obled. In the dark, he couldn't judge the color of the body or the mutilated wings spread on either side of it, but he thought it a lark or a scarlet. Another warning. He supposed the local farmers wanted no one to doubt the tower had once belonged to the cursed.

Jhared left the tortured body and trudged toward Seravina. Mercifully, she allowed him to gather her reins without a chase. He wondered if Alende had already finished the dyers' bane.

The tower door creaked open at his touch. As he crossed the threshold, his gaze went to the niche in the wall where he had left the waylayer. It was empty.

245

A swift step tapped the flagstone. Air rushed past Jhared's shoulder. Before he could react, a blade pricked his throat just below his ear.

"Alende?"

"Which story is this?" the waylayer demanded, his liquor-laced breath caressing Jhared's cheek.

"It's me. Jhar . . . Mahla's son."

"I know *who* you are, soldier. Which story are we? Is the Bearer alive?"

"Of course."

"Don't be arrogant!" Alende growled. "Nothing is so certain. Has the war ended?"

"We're not at war. The high chieftain is trying to prevent it."

"No war yet. The Bearer's still alive." The waylayer slid the blade slightly and Jhared felt it sting. "Where did you come from just now?"

"From speaking with the Bearer. Alende, I'm no threat to you."

"Are you not? Did she order you to kill me?"

Jhared let out a breath. "She doesn't even know you made it out of the city."

There was a silence. Jhared wondered what Leita would think if he never appeared to meet her again.

"*Ah,*" Alende finally sighed. "*That* story." He lowered the blade and took a step backward. "I'm sorry, my darling. I didn't expect you back this soon. You're supposed to be celebrating with your patrol."

Jhared moved away from the knife and drew Seravina into the tower. The waylayer's confusion was beginning to make sense. That probably should have terrified him, but he felt only emptiness. "They're done with me."

"What? They opened your cage and you flew back here? I'm touched!"

Jhared dragged the saddle from Seravina's back and dropped it against the wall. "Just a moment ago, you were wondering whether to put your knife through my throat."

Alende smiled archly. "And a moment ago, you were wondering whether you cared if I did."

"I only came back for the liquor," Jhared muttered.

Alende gave his musical laugh, snatched something from his pack, and pushed it into Jhared's hand. It was a new flask, larger than the last, of smooth, oiled wood. "How fortunate for you I managed to acquire something magnificent from an obliging trader."

Jhared pulled out the stopper and sniffed the contents: scents of warm honey, toasted almonds, and ripe figs filled his head. Not dyers' bane, it was Melandrien, a particularly fine sample. The flask would have easily cost him two months' wages. "You didn't steal this in town, did you?"

"Don't be absurd. I rescued it on the road. From a fool who wouldn't recognize good brandy if he drowned in it."

Jhared despised the thieving, but just now he wanted the liquor more than he cared about reparation. He took a long swallow. The Melandrien rolled smoothly down his throat and filled the hollowness in his chest with a lovely heat.

Alende grinned evilly. "Seeking a better escape than running, are you?"

"No need." Jhared pushed the stopper into the flask and tossed it back to the waylayer more forcefully than required. "There's no one left to run from."

"Oh, my darling, don't fret. Their chains did not become you. By returning to me, you've reached well beyond what I imaged possible of a tamed man."

"Then you've a limited imagination," Jhared replied.

"Wrong, my darling. I've seen your kind so many times in so many places I know very well what you're capable of. It gives me hope you can still surprise me."

Jhared turned from the waylayer's nonsense to finish with Seravina, brushing the sweat and dust from her coat and picking stones from her hooves. When he had done the best he could for her, he turned her loose in the tower and settled under one of the galleries.

Alende didn't settle at all. He paced around the tower, one hand clutching the flask while his other hand scratched at the scabs across his throat. Seravina whickered nervously.

The waylayer's madness—his flights from the present, his confusion, his need for self-destruction—no longer seemed so foreign to Jhared. "Does the liquor let you escape the blue flames?" he asked.

Alende spun to face him, his expression wary. "What did you say?"

"When the flames come, does the brandy keep you out of reach?"

"Nothing stops the flames. The liquor only makes me care less."

"Oh." Jhared touched a hand to his throat.

The waylayer eyed him suspiciously. "How did you . . . ? Ah, wait. The Bearer told you about Pathwalkers. She told you what to look for, didn't she?"

Jhared nodded and pulled his fingers away from his own healing scar.

Alende growled. "I should have guessed. That's why she's wanted you with her. Who better than the Shorn son of an elder to twist to her bidding, a boy so dutiful he wouldn't dare to question her? She's recruited you to help her search for us."

"Is that why you hate her?" Jhared asked. "Because she wants your kind?"

"I've tried to explain it to you, but you can't possibly understand. No one understands! I've seen the end of the world. Not merely *our* world, all the infinite Paths!"

The waylayer was breathing hard, his gaze drifting to some distant place or moment. "You can't imagine what it's like to witness every instant of the past and future torn apart. You've never suffered the agony of an annihilated spirit. How can I possibly explain what it is to feel millions of spirits explode into nothingness?"

Jhared *had* witnessed the destruction of a spirit, and he prayed never again to suffer something so horrifying. "You mean the Dissolution. Is that what you fear?"

Alende's expression intensified. "Not that. There are stories of catastrophes vaster than the destruction of Altan Mar. Stories of pain. Of endings. They will all become our story."

"Why, Alende? Why do you think the Bearer has anything to do with this? Tell me what you know."

The waylayer shuddered. "I've seen the stories of her power. She is cruel!"

"Stories? You mean you've seen it on a Path? Who knows what that means? You could be traveling in a place that has nothing to do with us. You can't condemn her for your own chaos!"

"Can't I? Where do you think her birds fly when she sets them loose with her messages?"

"To Velantar," Jhared said.

"Velantar indeed. To dark temples in the oldest parts of the Shorn Circle, where Cael's power is treasured. She leads those who love the demon!"

Jhared was silent, wondering what grains of truth could be harvested from Alende's raving. The man seemed to confuse the events he had experienced on his journeys with what he knew about his own Path, but Jhared couldn't deny some truth at the heart of his words.. If Leita had been committed to Riana's order, after all, she would never have set about training him to travel the sacred ways.

"What did the Bearer do to free you from Brenia?" Alende continued. "Lie to those who trusted her? Poison the guards? Kill with Cael's Blade?"

"She only acted as she did because she feared for me."

"She feared so much for you she managed to have you condemned as a deserter, didn't she?"

Jhared scrubbed a hand over his face. "All right. Enough. I understand your point."

"I doubt it," Alende said. "I doubt very much you understand. But I've done what I could. Now I must follow my own Path. Name me caelevano if you will. I won't let her end Riana's ways."

"And I won't let you kill a woman because you look through your own veils and call her evil."

"Well then, it seems we're back where we started." Alende sank down against the wall.

"With your knife at my throat?"

"No. In the high temple garden, with the Bearer of Cael's Blade running to claim you while I beg you to hear me."

Jhared shook his head. "Alende, do you remember that moment happened weeks ago?"

"When it happened doesn't matter, only that it did. I hope you think about it often, soldier. It was the moment you shifted the course of our world. The moment you joined with destruction."

Perhaps the exile from his duty made Jhared vulnerable to the waylayer's dramatics, but he found the man's words disturbingly earnest. He leaned against the stone, weary and heartsore. "Do you plan to correct that shift? Should I fear falling asleep?"

Alende looked at him from across the tower. It was the second time Jhared could remember seeing regret in the man's expression. "Not tonight, Mahla's son. The only thing you need fear tonight are your own nightmares."

The nightmares didn't come, but Jhared's Teachers did. The Boar and Shrill took turns castigating him for once again defying Shorn Law, questioning him for remaining with the waylayer, and exhorting him to pay the new debts he owed to Avelos. Jhared awoke feeling bruised and bad tempered.

He climbed to his feet and shook the dirt from his damp cloak. A dull grey sky showed through the opening in the tower roof, holding the promise of rain. Alende was nowhere to be seen, but his pack remained propped near the arrow loop.

Seravina ambled over and looked at Jhared expectantly. He laughed a little and bent to retrieve her grain. As he measured out a ration, his own stomach gurgled. What few provisions he had taken from Brenia wouldn't last much longer, and they were riding too hard for the mare to be sustained by grazing. As much as he dreaded the thought, he would soon have to stop in a village.

The door squeaked and Jhared whipped around. Alende entered, his arms laden with a small jug and several irregularly shaped bundles. His gaze went immediately to Jhared.

"You look terrible!" the waylayer declared cheerfully. "It seems I've arrived just in time to save you from starvation."

He tossed one of the bundles across the chamber. Jhared caught it, a soft sphere wrapped in coarse brown cloth. Drawing back the cloth, Jhared discovered a lump of creamy cheese. He pinched off a piece and put it into his mouth.

Alende unwrapped another cheese and several pieces of flatbread. Then he opened the jug, took a drink, and offered it to Jhared, who waved it away. The liquor was becoming more important than he cared to admit.

The waylayer laughed. "Go on. Take it."

Hesitantly, Jhared lifted the jug and tilted it to his lips. His eyes widened as warm, frothy sheep's milk filled his mouth.

"I thought so," Alende said. "You preferred it as a child, too."

Jhared set the jug down, savoring the earthy richness that lingered on his tongue. "Thank you."

"The debt's not mine. Thank the farmer who leaves his dairy house poorly tended." Alende grinned as he took a big bite of bread smeared with cheese.

The waylayer always seemed at his most lucid and good humored in the mornings. Jhared wondered if that had something to do with the way the Paths progressed during a day. If each new decision spawned a multitude of new Paths, by the end of a day a new rat's nest of possibilities would exist. Perhaps that tangle played a part in Alende's confusion and madness; he sensed so many Paths he could no longer keep any of them straight. Jhared's thought was followed by a chillier one: was Alende a picture of what would happen to him if he didn't find a way to control the Gate?

"Shall we go?" the waylayer asked, taking another bite of food and wandering over to pick up his pack.

Jhared glanced up. "Are we continuing together?"

"What's the point of separating? We're tracking the same prey."

"Well, to start, I don't consider them prey." Jhared shrugged as he said it. His Path and the waylayer's had been linked since long before his mother died. Jhared thought he was beginning to glimpse generosity behind the man's bitterness, perhaps a part of the boy his mother had known.

"Don't fool yourself," Alende answered. "You've enough anger in you to be a hunter. One day you'll have the chance to face Matio Sevar with a naked blade in your hands. Then we'll see who's prey."

Jhared sighed. "Enough, Alende. Let's go."

They tracked back to the Forest Guard camp and waited until the patrol was well on its way before returning to the main road. From Clan Valador's lands they passed into Clan Darnios and entered the heart of Aven Plains, where the land turned flat as a book's cover. Jhared's gaze stretched across fields of long pale grasses and autumn flowers in shades of plum and gold. Villages built of russet and yellow brick blended into the fields so naturally they seemed to have grown out of the soil with the flowers. In fact, that wasn't so far from the truth; the brick yards of Aven Plains were well known. From a distance, Jhared spied mud-covered Shorn men cutting into the ground to win the heavy clay, while others prepared it with charcoal and water to be fit into molds. Stacks of bricks sat drying under covered pavilions, waiting to be fired in the pyramid-shaped kilns, which loomed in the background like strange, small fortresses.

Had he been raised on the plains, Jhared would likely have become one of those brickmakers, working off the Avelune debt through monotonous routine, and living on the flat, featureless land. Could he have served more honorably in such a position, removed from all sources of power and temptation, or would the weakness in his blood simply have manifested itself in some other way? Jhared was still considering it when the Sandien Mountains rose into view on the northern horizon. With an indrawn breath, he pulled Seravina to a halt.

Jagged peaks of grey-green and lavender stretched their granite arms east and west for as far as Jhared could see. Taller than any other work of goddess or man, they reached boldly for the sky, where the clouds embraced them. Endless crags and clifftops promised seductive views and the temptation of breezes that could encircle a body and make one believe he was weightless. The Sandien

Mountains were the fierce sentinels of the north, the barrier that set the northern clans apart from the rest of Avelos. By comparison, the Parnas Mountains were slump-shouldered old men.

Jhared had only ever seen the Sandien once, on a training expedition. He had forgotten how they set his heart to pounding and caused his back to ache, even from a distance.

"Now there's a view to heat a man," Alende choked, rolling his shoulders. "We'll be climbing through those beauties in a couple days."

Jhared nodded, trying to steady his breathing as desire vibrated through his body. "You want to ride for a while?"

Alende glanced up. "You'd trust me with your silver lady?"

"We'll move faster if we spell one another, and I . . . I need to run."

The waylayer chuckled. "Running does serve better than a dunk in cold water, but not so well as a good woman. When Zia and I—"

Jhared held up a restraining hand. "Yes or no?"

"Why not?" Alende replied with a shrug.

Jhared swung down and held the reins, uncertain what Seravina would think about the new arrangement. Alende patted the mare and allowed her to snuffle his hands before leaping into the saddle. Seravina snorted and danced, but the waylayer handled her with skill. It was cause enough to remember that before the Becoming Alende also had been trained for the Forest Guard.

All day they trekked toward the mountains, switching riders each time they paused to rest. They camped that night amidst the tall grass of an open field between villages. Jhared hated the lack of cover, but the flat land offered nothing better without moving closer to his patrol, camped just on the other side of the next town. He had no hope of speaking with Leita; there was no safe place for them to meet. The only positive thing about their location was that the hearty grasses made decent grazing for the mare.

The next day progressed much the same. Jhared took turns with Alende riding and running. Although the mountains drew ever nearer, the plains seemed endless. As darkness fell, Jhared stood beside the road gazing at the spots of orange firelight scattered across the plains like fireflies, where travelers with no means to go to an inn or no interest in sharing a bed with strangers made their places. Their music drifted on the air—whistles, flutes, and voices—an argument at one fire, passion at another. Sound carried all too well.

Jhared strode back to his own place and set himself to dealing with the tasks he would have completed had he been traveling with his patrol. The discipline was habit, but mostly he wanted to stay busy enough to avoid thinking about the Bearer.

Long after Jhared threw himself down by their little fire, the waylayer still prowled restively. Tonight, Jhared's efforts to draw him into conversation only provoked incoherent stories about doors that wouldn't close and spirits blown to pieces. Alende swallowed enough liquor to drop an ox before he finally collapsed.

"You know, I've met death so many times, I can hardly remember the one she spared me." The waylayer's voice rose sadly from where he had sprawled in the grass.

A log popped and settled deeper into the flames. Seravina sighed in her sleep.

"Who?" Jhared asked, propping himself on one elbow.

"Mahla Denaban. Savior of the unworthy," Alende mumbled. "I remember the priestess. So young then. After I made a mess of the council's questioning, she wielded the blade with great precision. A Shorn man who fails the Becoming mustn't die too quickly, you see. He must have time to consider his faithlessness while he awaits the wolves."

The waylayer trailed off, rubbing a hand against his left thigh. Jhared shuddered. He could imagine the pain and fear too well. According to Leita, he should have failed. As he considered that truth, part of Alende's story came clear.

"It was the Bearer, wasn't it? The priestess who maimed you."

"Ah, yes. That's what they call her now," Alende drawled. "Not then. Not yet. I remember the tears in her eyes. Tears, but still she cut me. There's something unnatural about a woman who can kill even when her heart tells her no. I cursed her for it. After, I was alone in the wilds. I think I heard water flowing. They must have thrown my body near a stream. Then . . . only music."

Alende began to hum softly. Jhared had to lean forward to hear. It was "Alende's Flight," a bittersweet melody full of changing moods. Jhared knew it for his mother's composition. For the first time, he realized it had nothing to do with the hero Alende Isan or the escape from Altan Mar.

"Mahla wrote that song for you, didn't she?"

"I think so," the waylayer replied.

Jhared was silent. "I'm glad," he said finally.

Alende didn't answer. Jhared thought him asleep or passed out at last. With a sigh, he leaned back and closed his eyes.

"*Sulosan, surma sen,*" Alende murmured.

Jhared opened his eyes. "What does it mean?"

"Brother, our scars are the same."

As Jhared finally floated down into sleep, the words echoed softly over and over in his ears. *"Brother, our scars are the same. Same. Brother, our scars. Brother . . ."*

The third afternoon, they reached the lands of Clan Hilera, the only clan of the northern five with territory south of the Sandien Mountains. Jhared breathed easier as they entered the forest, terrain that made sense to him. Above the tree line, the mountains rose invitingly out of the foothills. The patrol stopped early, just outside the town of Isantar at the base of Alende's Pass. From a safe distance, Jhared watched the Bearer ride into town with Commander Carn and the packhorses, probably to reprovision and equip the patrol for the cold. Tomorrow they would enter the mountains. The highest peaks already wore lacey caps of snow.

Forest meant a more secure place to rest. It also meant Jhared could finally go to Leita. He hurried to groom Seravina and feed her the last of the grain. Then he collected firewood while he considered what to tell Alende. He wasn't certain what he would say until it fell out of his mouth.

"I'm going to speak with the Bearer."

"Be careful," the waylayer replied, his attention on striking sparks into the kindling.

Jhared glanced sidelong at the man. "Is that all?"

Alende paused and looked up from where he crouched. "What did you want, my darling? Were you hoping I would tell you not to go?"

"Of course not. I only expected that you would."

"The more you learn of her the better," the waylayer said. "Lies stretch thinner over time."

"Very well." Jhared started to turn, then looked at Alende again. "If I were to leave Sera—"

"Madam Silver will be safe. It will be a pleasure to spend an evening with someone who doesn't drink all my brandy."

"I'm in your debt."

Alende put two fingers to the center of his forehead and flicked them toward Jhared in the same salute the Sonans had used. It struck Jhared how many times in the past few days he had trusted the waylayer. It wasn't a comfortable feeling. He told himself it was necessity that drove him to it and turned his thoughts to Leita.

Once he slid into the patrol's camp, he hid among the trees just a few feet from the back of the Bearer's tent. Lenaro was cooking. Twitch and Esran sang as they cared for the horses. The men's easy banter was so familiar: Grion said something unpleasant, Jase laughed, and Anzo made a smart reply. Jhared wanted to call out to them, to rise and enter their circle. Instead, he crouched at the border between existence and invisibility, watching them like some lost spirit.

"Don't just sit there! Get to the water before they catch you. That's where she'll go."

Jhared pressed his lips on a gasp. *"You're the one who'll get me captured speaking out like that!"* he told the Boar. *"I thought you didn't approve of my work with her."*

"We don't. But you won't find a way to repair your errors if you're executed as a deserter."

"You believe I could still make reparation?" Jhared hadn't dared to own that much hope.

Boar made a noncommittal sound. *"Perhaps."*

Jhared reached into his pouch and took out Branlen's little talisman, with its winking face like an old man's toothless grin. The grey stone was cool and smooth against his palm. It drew him home to Velantar. He wondered how his brother had recovered from his injuries and whether Tierzen was surviving the turmoil in the council. What had become of Zia since Abrigado ordered her arrest? Jhared wondered if he would see any of them again.

"Go!" the Boar demanded.

Jhared tossed the talisman toward Leita's tent, where it landed with a soft *plunk*. He paused to be certain the sound hadn't drawn the attention of the men, then silently slipped back into the trees.

Not far from camp, the hills had captured some of the mountain runoff to form a small lake. In the failing light, the water was a black caldron surrounded by silver-blue giants, great Hileran firs. Jhared climbed into one of the big trees, the shaggy bark crumbling in his hands; then he settled in to wait.

Night bruised the sky to shades of plum. Wind gusted off the mountains, causing the trees to whisper of the coming winter. Jhared shrugged deeper into his cloak and watched the clouds churn over the water, willing Leita to appear. An hour passed. Raindrops plopped against Jhared's hands, slowly at first and then with growing intensity. He waited for Leita until the rain became a steady curtain, driving him out of the tree. Still, he didn't go back to Alende. He hurried along the lakeshore, searching for Leita in case she had somehow gotten past him. Wind whipped his cloak sideways. Lightning seared the darkness into colorless day.

She wasn't coming and he knew it, but he couldn't bear to leave. He strode along the trail toward his patrol, trying to convince himself it was only to be sure she hadn't fallen on the slippery hill. Without intending it, he found himself peering into the camp again. Rain had extinguished the fire. His comrades had brought the horses in close. Men and beasts huddled under the shelter of the old fir trees. The priestess was not among them; she was inside her tent.

So near. She was almost reachable. With another two steps, Jhared could touch the tent's wet fabric. If he could loosen the rear pin, he could lift the flap and roll inside. The number of boundaries he would have to cross to do it made him giddy, but ah Goddess, how long could he live in this place of nonexistence? He needed to do something besides wait for Alende to try to kill the Bearer.

He crept the short distance from the trees to the tent. When lightning flared, he froze. The tent obscured him from the men, but it also meant he couldn't keep his eye on them. As he lay on his belly and worked his fingers along the bottom edge, water streamed into his eyes. He wiped them clear and kept working.

Lightning struck again, closer. For a split second, Jhared lay eye to eye with the grinning face of Branlen's talisman. He grinned back at it, feeling all of Branlen's good wishes washing over him, and paused to shove it into a pocket.

The trickiest part of the business came next: to slip the rear pin, which would give him enough slack in the tarp to creep inside. His outstretched hand touched the wet iron. From his prone position, he wrapped his fingers around it and took a deep breath before pulling with a slow, steady force. It refused to come loose. Jhared scrambled to his knees for better leverage and swiped his hands against his shirt to dry them a bit. This was Anzo's good work. The pin was sunk deep into the ground. He tugged hard.

The pin broke free suddenly, sending the tent flap whipping upward. Jhared grabbed for it, but the wind snapped it out of reach. A strong gust caught the underside of the tent and tore it nearly inside out. He heard the priestess yelp as the rear pole collapsed, then the forward pole, bringing down the tarp amidst a tangle of rope. It looked like the closing scene of some players' farce. Jhared would have laughed, if it hadn't been so horrible.

His comrades were laughing. He could see them now across the fallen tent. Some of them saw him.

"Who's there?" cried the watchman from behind Jhared. "Turn before I warm my steel between your ribs."

Jhared had a wild memory of wings arched against the wind, lifting himself and his beloved Tavia toward escape. Escape wasn't possible, then or now. He turned slowly, keeping his hands well away from his sword.

"You," Grion snarled. "Shorn deserter filth. I could kill you and not a man would question me."

The others were running now. Someone chased after the flapping tarp. Someone helped the priestess. The rest encircled Jhared. Several besides Grion had drawn swords. They stood in the pounding rain, looking uncertain what should happen next.

"Selfish, foolish, cursed excuse for a soldier!" Lieutenant Sevar growled.

He blasted away the uncertainty, striding through the circle and shoving Jhared backward with both hands. "Do you know what harm you caused with your games in Brenia? Do you? Or are you that blind to your destructiveness?"

The questions took Jhared off guard. He sensed one slim chance to explain himself. "Sir!" he gasped, catching his balance. "It was inhuman what they had done to the man. You should have seen him on the tree. It was worse than any traitor's death. I couldn't ignore his suffering. Haven't I sworn to save each citizen before my own life?"

Lightning revealed incredulousness across Sevar's scarred face. "You dare to hide behind your oath? You're a Shorn soldier! Not a council elder. If for one moment you could think beyond your own impulses, you might remember you have no right and no ability to make such judgments. You might see the harm you do. But I know your kind. Oh, I know you too well. You make us pay. You make any who stand close to you pay dearly."

Jhared stared at the lieutenant in stunned silence, understanding stirring in a place he couldn't fully access. With blue-edged clarity, he spied the moments that had shaped Matio Sevar: a youth studying intently under an elder's supervision; a golden boy singing to the sweet sounds of a flute; a young man told that his dream of serving as elder had been shattered; a defiant son seeking to prove himself in the Forest Guard. There were other moments, so many others. Some of them Jhared had heard as rumor; some of them he had never known, couldn't know. They unrolled before him: Sevar facing the horror of the killing winds to save his general; standing in the hall of the high temple, devastated by news from Elder Trianor; sitting among the rocks of a cavern, a flute crushed and broken in his hand, an expression of loss in his eyes.

Jhared felt weightless as insight lifted a burden. Sevar's fury wasn't only about him. Each of those moments revealed a different veil through which the lieutenant viewed the world. Every moment of his present was distorted by the past. It was the truth of every person on Riana's Path. In that sparkling instant, Jhared knew it, could see the blue and red Paths of his own past twisting his future.

"Through what veil do you see me?" he asked the lieutenant, his voice strange and distant. "Is it even me you see at all?"

From miles away, his comrades murmured uneasily.

Sevar cocked his head. "Denaban, what in the name—"

"Jhared, don't go! Not now! You must stay *here!*"

Leita's voice cut through the fog twining around Jhared's thoughts. He turned his attention inward, reeling as he discovered the flames crackling hungrily at his center. Panic swallowed him up. *Goddess, I beg you. Spare me this journey!*

Pain was what he needed. Pain would anchor him. It was the one thing he knew would. He reached for the blade at his belt, slid it free, and saw Sevar's expression fly into surprised outrage. As the lieutenant closed on him, Jhared realized that once more he had failed to consider all the consequences of his actions. Someone cried his name as he fell toward blue flames.

19.
CAEL'S CHOSEN

Wind played quiet music through the reeds along the shore and chased the waves across the water. A tall, hooded figure knelt beside the lake, scrubbing clothes against a rock. Charms of copper and silver caught the light as the figure lifted a wrist and pushed back the hood, revealing the familiar features of a woman Jhared couldn't have known. Her black hair was cropped to her chin. Her cheeks were rough and red from sun and wind. It was her eyes he imagined he knew: they shone with the tranquil grey-green of a mountain meadow just before dawn.

She jerked her head upward, tranquility vanished. "Who are you?" she demanded. "What are you doing here?"

"I don't know," he whispered, feeling the Path already falling out beneath him.

Her expression shifted again, into something unanticipated. "Wait! You're not well. Do you need help?"

He opened his mouth to ask where he was, but discovered he was somewhere else.

"*Sulosan, surma sen,*" the waylayer murmured. "Our scars are the same." Alende's laughter followed Jhared as he plummeted through the blue.

Jhared awoke with his teeth chattering, feeling as though he had spent the night at the bottom of a well. His clothes were damp, his head ached, and his body was leaden. Warmth pressed against his chest, though, and he felt a familiar jarring beneath him. He tried to stretch and started to slide backward. It startled him to awareness.

"Don't fidget or you'll have us both in the mud," Anzo muttered.

Jhared had been tied to the saddle of Anzo's grey gelding, and his wrists were bound around the patrolman's thick middle. Steel-colored sunlight lent little heat to the morning as they scrambled up a steep incline. The mountains swept up and away from either side of the road. They had entered the pass.

Anzo's back was stiff and unyielding. Jhared realized that the smaller soldier was bearing much of his weight. He tried to straighten, but the bonds made it difficult.

"Why am I still alive?"

"Likely because Lieutenant doesn't want Elder Trianor burdening the high chieftain with an inquiry if you're executed out of hand. We're less than two days from Aglar Tower. You'll have a formal tribunal there. Everything done proper and well documented, I'd wager."

"And then?"

"Then they're going to push you off the wall or hang you for a deserter," Anzo said flatly.

Of all the men in his patrol, it was Anzo's regard Jhared most valued. He wasn't surprised to lose it; he was just surprised how much the loss hurt. He bowed his head, which inadvertently set his forehead against Anzo's shoulder. Again, he straightened. "I'm sorry."

Anzo only cleared his throat and stared at the riders in front of him.

"Deserter. Deserter. Hang you. Deserter."

The words echoed softly on the air. Jhared didn't know if they came from beyond the Gate or from his own imagination.

" . . . to leave behind your pretty filly," Anzo was muttering.

Jhared shook his head. "What?"

"What'd you do with the mare?"

"I left her with an unbound Shorn man who wants to kill the Bearer."

Anzo snorted. "It's talk like that will get you lashed before we even reach the garrison. What happened to you, Denaban? I've heard plenty of speculation, but I want it from you."

"I can't, Anzo. My life is forfeit. I'll not risk yours."

He glanced over his shoulder at the empty road. Not so far behind them, Alende would be following on Seravina. The waylayer wouldn't give up his purpose just because Jhared hadn't returned. Jhared wondered if Alende had been disappointed by his disappearance, then realized it was foolish to imagine such a wild creature could care what a tamed man did.

"This all has something to do with the dark lady, doesn't it?"

Jhared brought his attention back to Anzo. "Why do you say so?"

"Leave off the subtlety, boy. I don't have enough time left on this path to play games. You spent all morning with her in Brenia. Next thing I hear, you're gone and she's explaining to Lieutenant how you attacked two unarmed clanguards."

"She said that? What else did she say?"

"That you feared imprisonment too much to let them take you. It didn't sound right to me, but then I saw you draw a knife on the lieutenant. Wouldn't have believed it if I hadn't seen it myself. Cael's cock! What were you thinking?"

"Ah. That." Jhared slumped against his bonds. "I didn't intend to attack him. Truly, Anzo. It was only . . ." *Only that the Gate to Riana's Paths called me with a voice I couldn't refuse.*

At the front of the patrol, Leita rode beside Sevar, her dark head beside his golden one. Jhared could understand why she had blamed him for what happened in Brenia: he was already a fugitive and she had to keep her ties to the Forest Guard. He understood that. But why had she lied to him about it?

"What did you tell the lieutenant?" he had asked her.

"The truth."

"What is it?" Anzo glanced back with a look of concern.

"I'm not sure. I just wonder . . . why would she . . . ?" Jhared stammered back to silence, trying to ignore the sick feeling in his stomach.

"What are you trying to say, boy?"

"Nothing. Nothing that makes any difference now."

The pass led them upward and ever upward, until the sky burned a blue so pure and deep it pained the eye. The air grew thin and sharp. By the end of the day, only Jhared wasn't panting; even the doughty border horses were winded. Still, Sevar wouldn't allow Jhared to help set camp. The lieutenant had taken his sword and ordered his hands to remain bound. Only then did Jhared realize he truly was a prisoner, not just a soldier in disgrace.

Within his patrol, he discovered himself more isolated than he'd ever been on the outside. With the exception of Anzo, his comrades avoided speaking to him or even looking at him. Only Bevan approached. The raw-boned soldier marched up with a murderous expression and threw a muddy, smelly bundle at his feet.

"That belongs to you, thief," he snarled, ripping the cloak off Jhared's back.

As the other men stared, Jhared unrolled the bundle: it was the cloak he had abandoned. The red border had been partially hacked from the hem, leaving holes and a frayed edge. It smelled as though it had been used to clean the horses.

At dinner, he sat alone, eating what Anzo brought him. The veteran seemed to have been burdened with the role of prison guard. Leita hadn't dared to talk with him, but the devastated look she gave him across the fire was an arrow in his heart. He turned away, trying to hide his confusion and hurt. As he did, he accidentally caught Jase's eye. The lighthearted soldier gave Jhared the unexpected gift of a half smile and tapped the blessing tattooed on his cheek in a gesture that meant good luck.

It was a relief when the patrol finally settled for the night, quieting the whispered speculations and muttered curses. Anzo ambled over, looking unhappy.

"Lieutenant says you have a choice. You can learn to sleep bound to a tree or he'll leave you with only your hands tied and what remains of his trust."

"He'd leave me free? What if I were to run?"

"I take your place."

Jhared swallowed. "I'd never do that to you, Anzo."

"I know. Try to get some sleep."

Jhared didn't want to sleep. In one more day, the freedom of forest and sky would be replaced with stone walls and barred doors, and the rope around his wrists would be replaced with iron. He wasn't sure how he would bear it, knowing how it would end. With some struggle, he slipped his fingers into his pouch and grasped Branlen's talisman. He clenched it in one fist, feeling the stone warm as it absorbed his own heat. The thing that most tormented him wasn't his broken oath or even his failure to make reparation; it was knowing that Branlen would hear he had been executed for desertion and would never understand why.

Jhared stretched out under a cluster of aspen trees. Breezes from the mountain slopes caused the leaves to chatter quietly. The sky had cleared, and a crescent moon filtered cold light through the aspens' branches. Distantly, he watched blue-black shadows flutter across his body like moths.

"Sulosan, surma sen," a voice barked softly.

"Brother, our scars are the same. Same! Same!"

Jhared sat bolt upright, darting his gaze around the camp. All was still, no watchman in sight. It was Twitch's watch, and the man liked to wander.

"Sulosan, surma sen. Sen! Sen!"

"Alende?" Jhared whispered, getting to his feet and reaching for a sword that wasn't there.

Drums reverberated against his breastbone. Jhared's breath caught. Not drums, footsteps. In the distance, the Paths were shifting and someone was staggering across them.

The priestess hurried out of her tent, her hair unbound and shirt half-laced. "Jhared?" she murmured, tiptoeing toward him. "Are you drifting?" She grabbed his hand, and her expression changed to one of astonishment. "It's not you."

He shook his head mutely.

"Then someone else is approaching the Gate. Another 'walker. Somewhere close!"

Before Jhared could stop her, she darted into the woods.

"No, Lady!" he hissed, dashing after. This was the moment Alende needed. If the waylayer still owned the awareness to draw his blade, Leita would be dead.

"A pleasure to spend an evening, my darling, darling."

Jhared shook his head at the mocking voice. Leita was fleet, but as he closed on her, he sensed the shifts inside himself with growing clarity, like a map unfolding a few steps at a time. The Bearer stopped in a rocky clearing, casting her gaze back and forth. Jhared spied Seravina first, no tack and no ties, pacing at the edge of the trees. Then he found Alende.

The waylayer was sprawled face down beside his gear, a flask not far from his hand. His body twitched and shook, and he moaned like a wounded animal. Nausea roiled through Jhared. Was this what he looked like when he fell through the Gate? Lightheaded, he leaned against a boulder, his hands still bound. The Paths twirled seductively around him.

Leita dropped to her knees beside Alende. "Riana and Cael," she breathed. "What gift have you given me now?" With effort, she rolled the waylayer onto his back and brushed the dirt from his face. She gasped. "I've seen this man before."

"Yes," Jhared agreed, moving to Alende's side. "You tried to kill him once."

Her brow wrinkled in thought, then understanding smoothed her features. "A failed Becoming! Goddess, that was so long ago." She trailed off, frowning. "This is the waylayer from the high temple. The one who attacked us. He followed us all this way?"

Jhared looked down at her. "He still wants you dead."

"I see." Her expression steeled. "You know him quite well, it seems. Did you hope to help him, after all?"

"No! I've only ever tried to keep you safe!"

She stood, grabbed Jhared's chin in her hand, and stared into his eyes. He felt her power soaring, dark and fierce and wild. His longing grew with it. He need-ed to plunge into that power, to spend his strength traveling infinite Paths. He clutched tightly to control.

"Do not believe you can hide your desire from me," she warned. "What is it you want?"

"Tell me you don't worship the darkness!" he gasped. "Tell me you're not a leader of Cael's disciples. That you wish no destruction upon the Paths."

Her expression went wide in astonishment. Then she laughed, the sound of rising storms.

"Oh Jhared, is that what you fear? You truly believe I'm demon-touched? You poor, poor boy!"

He yanked free of her grasp. "You violated Shorn law. You attacked unarmed men. You lied to Sevar and to me!"

"I know." She straightened and held up a hand. "I owe you explanations, but not now. Not right now." She looked at the waylayer writhing in the dirt, and the hunger returned to her eyes.

"No, not now," Jhared agreed, bending toward the knife at Alende's belt.

"What are you doing?"

Jhared shifted the blade into his bound hand. "Bringing him back."

"No! I want his journey! The unbound will travel places we wouldn't dare."

"They travel places you *shouldn't* dare!" Jhared set the knife's edge to Alende's throat. "It's destroying him. Hardly enough of him remains to call him a man."

"Jhared, don't go! Gooooo!" Leita's voice howled from the direction of the camp.

"What veil . . . ? Veil, veil, veil!" Jhared's voice panted in answer.

Seravina screamed a challenge to the voices and raced around the clearing.

Jhared watched the galloping horse, cold dread filling his veins. "Goddess, mercy. Goddess, have mercy, I've been a fool." With a swift, decisive motion, he cut the waylayer at the point where the man's jaw swept down to his throat.

"Come back, Alende! You must come back now! This is where you belong."

The waylayer groaned. His eyelids fluttered.

"Through what veil do you see! Seeeee!" howled Jhared's voice.

Jhared pitched to his feet. "Cut my bonds, Lady. Quickly!" He handed her Alende's knife.

Leita took it, looking around in puzzlement, as though she heard a familiar song but couldn't remember the words. "I think I know who makes those sounds. They're stirring the Paths."

"Cut me free!" Jhared demanded. "They've been following us for days. They've got our voices. It means they're ready to attack."

"Oh, but they feel so lovely. What *are* they?" the priestess said, sawing at the knots.

As the rope fell to the ground, Jhared grabbed the knife back from her and snatched up his bow and quiver from among the gear. "Verael." He bent over the waylayer and shook him hard. "Alende, please come back! Your Path is here!"

Leita's eyes darkened at the name of Cael's Chosen. "Ah, Verilen! I've always hoped to meet that trickster." She pulled her gaze from the forest to glance again at the waylayer. "It's no good, Jhared. He's too far away for the knife. I must go after him." She started to fold to her knees.

"No!" Jhared dragged her bodily to her feet. "I can't have you gone as well. We must get back to the others."

Jhared scanned the clearing for some form of shelter for the unconscious waylayer. He couldn't leave the man to be mauled and eaten by Cael's servants, no matter what his crimes. Scrubby little trees clustered at the edge of the clearing where Seravina stood sentinel. Dropping aside his bow, Jhared hoisted Alende to his shoulder and carried him to the closest tree. The first branches weren't higher than Seravina's withers, but Alende was as long-limbed as Jhared, making it a challenge to wrestle his body into a position where he wouldn't fall.

"Mother, as you saved him once, please guard him now." Jhared turned away from the tree. Riana, it seemed, had abandoned Alende long ago. The only spirit Jhared thought might care for him was Mahla Denaban.

He returned the hunting knife to Alende's belt and set a hand on the man's brow. "Forgive me, Brother."

Swiftly, he retrieved his gear. For a heartbeat, he contemplated trying to capture Seravina, but the horse was white-eyed and unbiddable; he'd only lose more time. Reluctantly, he let her be and grabbed the priestess. "Come, Lady. We have to run!"

As he pulled Leita along, new voices called out ahead of them. Some were the familiar sounds of his comrades, others the voices of strangers. Some spoke in languages he didn't know. He counted at least thirty distinct voices before he lost track.

He skidded into camp, nearly dragging the Bearer. It relieved him to see the men already roused, weapons in hand. His relief vanished as those weapons turned on him.

"Can't decide if he wants to live as a deserter or die as a deserter," someone muttered.

"What about her? She's always in the thick of his trouble, isn't she?"

Anzo was silent. The old man looked tired and grim.

"Patrolman," Sevar said, shaking his head at Jhared in angry amazement, "do you truly care so little for your life?"

"Verael!" Jhared panted. "A big pack, sir. They're about to attack. Listen!"

The name of the Chosen was enough to make every man shut his mouth and tighten a hand on his sword. Silence dropped over the camp.

The quiet lengthened. Nothing stirred among the trees. Dismay heated Jhared's face. The voices couldn't have been a creation from beyond the Gate. Surely, he wasn't so far gone.

"Denaban," Sevar snarled.

"Veraeel! Veraeeeel!" a host of voices bayed all at once.

"Denaban! Ban, ban, ban!" barked beasts just north of camp.

Out of the trees to the south came the phrase of a song Anzo favored. The cheerful melody was just as off-tempo as when the veteran sang it, but at the end, it twisted into a chilling howl. The horses whinnied and yanked at their ties.

Anzo whistled softly. "At least twenty of 'em out there. It's a queen's pack."

"So we grab torches and chase 'em off," Grion said with a shrug. "I've seen wolves before."

"Fool!" Twitch spat. "Verael are twice as smart as wolves and not so skittish. They use the voices of their prey to lure it out."

"If we separate, they'll take us apart one by one," Anzo added.

"Shut it! All of you!" the commander snapped. "Orders, Lieutenant?"

"Orders! Orders! Shut it! Orders!"

"Defensive formation around the horses," Sevar growled. "Lady, get behind our swords and stay there."

Leita caught Sevar's arm as the men hurried into position, "Lieutenant, Verael are Cael's Chosen. They should listen to me."

"Perfect," Sevar replied. "Tell them if they don't flee, the Fourth will make winter cloaks of them, but do it from behind our swords. Denaban!"

Jhared stepped up, heart pounding. "Sir?"

The lieutenant gazed down at Jhared's unbound wrists and smiled darkly. "Since you've claimed yourself to be a soldier once more, see what you can do about evening the odds. Put that bow to use in front of the defensive line."

Jhared stiffened. Sevar saw it. "Problem, Patrolman?"

"No, sir. As you say."

Sevar knew very well what it meant to put a single archer outside the defenses in a close fight. It was likely Branlen would never need to know that Jhared had been meant for execution.

Jhared was turning away when Jase raced up, waving something in one hand. Jhared's sword belt. "Lieutenant! We can't afford to be short a sword arm."

Sevar gave the Clan Nadaren man a dry look, but he returned the weapon to Jhared. "No, we wouldn't want to be short a reliable man."

Jhared accepted the belt gratefully. Jase grinned, tapped the blessing on his cheek, and ran back to the others.

"Get ready, boys!" Commander Carn called. "They're coming!"

All around the camp, the forest came to life with the sounds of angry beasts. The Verael's guttural growls were interspersed bizarrely with human expletives.

Anzo made a sound of amazement. "I was wrong. Closer to thirty. Must be four or five small packs."

"Don't meet their eyes," Sevar ordered. "Keep the line tight."

Jhared had never seen more than three or four beasts at a time in one of the small, male-led Verael packs. Stories held that when a female united several of the small packs into a queen's pack, they grew fearless and cunning. He stepped slowly backward until he stood in front and slightly to the side of the others' defensive circle, an arrow already on the string. Behind his comrades, the horses headed toward panic. Somewhere in the midst of it all, Leita murmured a low, rumbling prayer. Jhared couldn't think on her now. His mind narrowed to battle readiness, his single focus the danger before him. He lifted the bow and let out a slow breath, slipping into that space where he understood everything the air would say to the arrow and exactly how the arrow would respond.

Through the trees, he caught a glimpse of powerful jaws, a deep chest, and large paws. He chose his mark, held his breath, and released. The arrow hissed through the darkness, borne on the breeze and steadied by feathers. It vanished into the forest, but Jhared sensed the thud of impact half a heartbeat before the animal's wail.

"Darlingggg!" A broad-shouldered beast staggered into the firelight and collapsed on its side, Jhared's arrow embedded in its neck.

Leita cried out in horror, but her cry drowned beneath the men's roar of approval. In that instant, Cael claimed the Path. The Verael charged, their bestial howls and human curses rending the air. Dark bodies hurtled into the camp from all sides. They bounded on long, sturdy legs, triangle ears pointed forward, heavy jaws exposing serrated teeth. Gorgeous creatures, Jhared thought incongruously. He let fly at a lanky male, heard a howl cut short even as he nocked his third arrow. A smaller beast fell with a shaft in its shoulder.

Two more Verael went down, then the wave of battle broke around him and all his skill as an archer was worthless. A lean grey leaped for his throat. Jhared smacked the beast across the muzzle with his bow. The creature yelped and shook its head in surprise, a disconcertingly human gesture. It gave Jhared an instant to draw his sword. As the Verael rushed in again, he slashed at its head. This time, the cagey creature dropped to its belly and rolled in under the blow, nearly tripping Jhared. The beast took the advantage and leaped into his face. Jhared wrenched himself backward as jaws snapped inches in front of his nose.

He flung himself another several steps away to gain the space to swing. As the grey sprang once more, Jhared's sword came around to meet it. The blade bit deep into the creature's neck. It stumbled, howling in blind fury. Another swing and it fell silent.

Gasping for breath, Jhared turned around to find the battle had charged past him. His comrades were besieged. Cael's Chosen the Verael might be, but they fought with terrible orderliness. Squads of two and three beasts covered each man. As a result, the defensive circle had fragmented and the horses were under attack.

Jhared searched for the Bearer. She stood twenty feet away, between Esran and Anzo, Cael's Blade in her outstretched hand. Her eyes were closed, and her face was lifted toward the sky. At her left, Esran fought three Verael as they tried to reach the horses, while Anzo slashed at a pair of brindled beasts. Neither man saw the regal white loping toward Leita.

"Anzo, behind you!" Jhared grabbed a log near the fire and whipped it. The log spun end over end and bounced against the white's skull. The Verael stumbled and halted. Jhared ran to finish it.

Before he could reach the beast, the ground opened before him. He pulled to a halt at the edge of a chasm and looked down. Cael's messenger stared up at him from the threshold of the Gate, beak agape, midnight wings mantled.

"Leave me be!" Jhared cried, clutching urgently to the present.

"Don't fear, soldier. I'm not here for you," the raven said in its low, beguiling voice. *"You have many more years to find your way alone. Now, go back to those who need you and let me do my work!"*

The raven flapped its powerful wings against the night. A preternatural wind flung Jhared away. He struck the ground hard, and his sword clattered out of his hand. Instantly, the white Verael was on him, slavering jaws reaching for his throat.

Jhared flung an arm upward to protect his face and struggled to contain the furious mass of teeth and muscle. With his opposite fist, he clouted the beast's wet nose. The creature only cursed at him in some foreign tongue and renewed its efforts.

"Verael, Chosen of Cael, these men are not for you!"

The command echoed in the rich, rumbling voice of the raven. Jhared wasn't certain whether it came from within him or from the chaos around him.

"Verilen, wise trickster who bides inside these beasts, see I bear his Blade and honor his name. Obey me and be gone!"

With a conflicted snarl, the creature on top of Jhared glanced toward the Bearer. It was all the opening Jhared needed. He hugged the Verael close with one arm and shoved his other arm under the creature's chin to keep its jaws from his face, then he threw himself over and started them rolling. The beast kicked with its back legs to slash Jhared's belly. Jhared slid sideways, gasping as one clawed foot found purchase, and kept going. Heat from the fire licked his arm. Gathering his strength, he flung himself and the beast through the flames. Pain seared his hands as he rolled himself free and came out the other side. His sword gleamed not far from the fire. He dived for it. Frantic, the white beast flipped onto its feet, flames dancing across its thick coat.

"Brother! Brother! Our scars!" it howled.

Jhared choked back a cry. Must Cael's creatures always be destructive? Must their intelligence and beauty ever be tainted? They were immortal spirits trapped in fallible bodies—living, breeding, killing, dying, over and over. Was it any wonder they had gone mad?

The Verael streaked toward him, uncoiling in a powerful leap. Its golden eyes glowed like the flames limning its face. At the last instant, Jhared dropped into a crouch and yanked his sword upward. With a terrible wail, the white sank onto his blade, nearly wrenching it from his hand. As he tore his sword free, the animal tumbled lifelessly into the dirt.

Jhared surged to his feet, Shorn energy burning in his blood, and searched for the source of the next onslaught. It took several moments to realize the battle had ended.

Dead and dying Verael littered the forest. The rest had turned and fled. Soldiers leaned against trees or stood panting over the bodies. One of the packhorses lay on its side, entrails spilling from a hideous wound in its flank. Every few moments it strained its head upward and squealed. Some mounts milled around in fear; the others had vanished. The stench of blood and burning fur choked the night.

Jhared spotted the priestess huddled on the ground, head on her knees, arms wrapped about her trembling body. He hurried to her side. "Lady, you're injured?"

Leita lifted her head; her face was bloodless, her teeth chattering. "I am not."

"The Gate?"

She nodded.

"Then you're the one who sent them off. You spoke to them?"

She sucked a breath. "You heard me?"

"*. . . see I bear his Blade and honor his name.*"

Jhared's tone hardened. "I heard you. And I saw the raven. I don't know if you saved us or doomed us, Lady. You laughed at me for fearing your devotion to the demon, but I have the feeling you've been laughing at me since the beginning."

Leita's eyes went wide. "Jhared, please don't."

He picked up a torn blanket and set it across her shoulders. "I understand. Now is not the time for explanations. You knew my only choice was to trust you. Now it seems I have no choice at all."

As he turned away, someone caught him by the arm. He peered down to find Anzo blinking up at him. A long scratch crossed the old patrolman's forehead and blood smeared his cheek. Even in the dim light, Jhared saw the grief that filled his eyes.

"Oh no, Anzo. Who?"

The man gestured toward a tree where the others were beginning to gather. Jhared glimpsed a prone soldier on the ground and the lieutenant at his side.

"Jase. We've lost him."

"Ah, Goddess."

Jase, who loved his Path so dearly. Jhared thought of the Clan Nadaren man's mischievous smile, so like Branlen's. When Jhared first came to the patrol, Jase seemed to take pleasure in taunting him, but over months of scouting and fighting beside one another, Jhared had found the man utterly without rancor. He simply took all of life with a grin and a wink. He possessed a gift for lifting the most sober moments with his impish manner. Men and women alike loved him for it. Jhared rubbed a hand across his eyes.

"He's got to be cursing that he missed his last day of pleasure in Brenia," Anzo said, a sad smile carving his bloodied face. "He's probably sidling up to his Pathguide and giving her his best smile."

Jhared laughed softly. "No doubt."

Sevar rose from beside the dead soldier and limped across the camp. Tight composure masked his features, although his right boot was mangled with teeth marks and he held his left arm close to his side. Bending over the mortally wounded horse, he drew his sword and plunged it into the animal's heart, silencing its squeals.

"All right, Forest Guard," he said, straightening. "I want a detail of four to go after the horses. Nevia, assist the commander with the wounded. The rest of you get these demon corpses out of my sight."

20.
COLD WELCOME

Despite his own injuries, Lieutenant Sevar took it on himself to prepare Jase's body for the pyre. It surprised Jhared, as did Sevar's visible grief. Commander Carn and Anzo offered what skills they had to care for the rest of the patrol. Anzo grimaced over the burns on the back of Jhared's hands and the deep punctures on his left forearm that marked a bite Jhared hadn't known he'd taken. Nothing could be done for the wounds other than to clean them, smear them with bitterbalm, and bandage them. More would have to wait until they reached the garrison at Aglar Tower. Jhared at least was fortunate that the four parallel scratches across his belly hadn't pierced his gut.

As the grisly cleanup began, Jhared's thoughts went to Alende. Nearly fifteen Verael bodies lay among the ruins of the camp. That meant nearly half the beasts had survived. Had they turned to more quiescent prey or merely run to ground to lick their wounds? Had Alende returned from his journey or did he remain lost and tormented?

"Planning on leaving us again, Denaban?"

Jhared startled. Sevar had caught him gazing into the forest. "No, sir."

"Good. See you don't. Relki saved your life before this battle began. You owe him your honorable service."

"Yes, sir. I'll make sure of it."

A flicker of weary disbelief passed across Sevar's gaze. "I've had enough of Shorn promises for two lifetimes. Don't bother to say it. Just do it."

As the lieutenant limped away, Jhared hurried back to work. He supposed Sevar only allowed him his freedom because the crippled patrol couldn't afford to drag a prisoner, but it was a relief not to be in ties. He prayed he could do what he claimed. When Leita caught his eye and gestured in the direction of the clearing, he shook his head and turned his back. Nothing good could come from pairing the Bearer and the waylayer, for either of them.

Eventually Leita gave up on Jhared's help and went with Esran to gather materials to prepare the death mask. In her absence, a good deal of speculation arose about her part in the battle. Many of the men thought Cael's Blade had drawn Cael's Chosen to them. A few described experiencing the uncanny sensation that the beasts had listened to the Bearer, as she said they would. Bevan observed how reluctant she had been to watch Cael's creatures die. The other men frowned and considered that. Jhared stayed silent.

When it came time to light the pyre for Jase, no one voiced objection to Leita saying the prayers. As Forest Guard tradition required, Lieutenant Sevar named the fallen and placed the mask over Jase's face, but the priestess spoke the holy words to call the Pathguide, her expression taking on the otherworldliness that signified her rising power. Jhared swayed as the Path gently twisted. The Bearer's eyes filled, not with the hunger he had seen so often, but with a deep stillness, as though she had opened the Gate onto the Hidden Paths themselves, the part of the weaving to which every man and woman must one day be exiled. In the shifting pyre flames, Jhared saw a woman take shape; she was young and lovely, with hair as red-orange as the fire. She leaned forward to kiss Jase's brow, and when she looked up, Jhared saw that her eyes were the slanted amber eyes of a fox.

She smiled at him, and her wise gaze said that death held much more than he could understand. In spite of his ambivalence, Jhared was grateful to be given such insight. It made him think about the interconnectedness of Riana's great weaving. If each Path eventually connected to all the others, as Leita told him they did, could a Pathwalker travel the roads of the dead? Could a spirit survive walking the Hidden Paths before its ordered time?

He spoke the last prayers with his patrolmates, and smoke carried the fox-woman and the dead soldier's spirit up through the trees. With a tremulous breath, Leita shrank back into herself.

The men returned to the task of preparing to move out. Two of the pack-horses had been slain and the third was lame. Sevar ordered the provisions divided among the mounts, and Jhared was given Jase's colt. Leita remained by the pyre. She no longer appeared the avatar, but only a small, tired woman.

"I'm going for a walk up the hill," she told Sevar. "A few minutes for myself before we leave."

"I'm sorry, Lady. I can't allow it. The Verael have a sense of vengeance like none other but man. They'll hunt again."

"Perhaps. But not for us." She wiped ash from her cheek. "I'll take my guard if it will ease you."

Jhared thought nothing would ease Sevar less, but there was an unexpected look of concern in the lieutenant's eyes as he gazed at Leita. "As quickly as you can. We've a long road to reach the garrison."

"Thank you, Lieutenant." She turned and looked blankly at Jhared, then without a word she walked out of camp.

He sensed the others watching as he picked up his bow and followed. She didn't head in the direction of Alende's clearing, as he expected. Instead, she wandered to a place where a narrow game trail wound steeply into the mountainside, and began to climb. Tracks and scat revealed that bighorn sheep and little wild cabrin used the trail. Jhared remained vigilant for predators, but he imagined the priestess was right when she said the Verael would not return for her.

She didn't speak or even glance back at him again. She scrambled up the trail, over rocks and across patches of slippery mud, until she was panting clouds of steam into the cold, thin air. Her foot skidded over gravel. Jhared caught her arm.

"Lady, rest a moment?"

She nodded and moved away from him to sit on a flat-topped rock. Her cloak swirled around her and she buried her hands within it. Below, grey smoke from the pyre rose toward the sky. Jhared could see his patrolmates moving around the horses.

"That should never have happened last night," she said without looking at him.

"What is that, Lady?" *The death of a good soldier? The crippling of my patrol? Or the revelation that you serve Cael?*

She glanced up at his tone. "Do not mistake me, soldier. The death of your comrade was a holy sacrifice, a creative act. I cannot grieve it as you do. No. I mean the way the Paths slipped from my grasp. It was wrong. I called to the beasts before you loosed the first arrow. I commanded them to leave us. I should have been able to reach them. I should have been able to open the right doors without calling on . . . what you saw."

Jhared leaned against a tree trunk, wincing as he unthinkingly tucked a blistered hand behind him. How had he arrived at a point where he worried for the well-being of a waylayer and dreaded the lies of a priestess?

"If I ask you what I saw, will you tell me truthfully? Or give me more false reassurances?"

Her answering stare was as cold as starlight. "You presume much to speak to me so."

He shrugged. "I've nothing to gain with subtlety. I've followed your guidance as best I might. It's led me to be named a deserter and brought me an arrow's edge away from execution. I've seen the raven and I've heard you call the demon's name. Give me a reason I should let you teach me further."

She looked startled by his words, and Jhared thought bitterly of what Alende had told him: she wanted his aid because he wouldn't question her.

Silence fell between them. Wind puffed across the mountain, sending a shower of dead leaves whirling into the air. Leita shivered and tucked her chin into her cloak. When she spoke, her voice had gone quiet. "You poor boy. You have so many boundaries to cross before you can understand what I need. You are constrained by what you believe is right—for a man, a soldier, the Shorn. I knew

I would frighten you. I had hoped to progress more gradually, but you've already seen too much and traveled too far. I'm sorry."

"Lady, I don't care to be coddled like a stray kitten or a child afraid of the dark. Tell me or don't. Either way, I must make my own decision."

Her expression darkened. Shadows slinked over the rock, as though creatures moved there he couldn't see. Jhared sensed her building anger and knew he had demanded something he didn't truly want.

"Only two priestesses living can participate in the mystery you witnessed," she said. "To my knowledge, no man has ever experienced it before his time on the pyre."

Jhared thought of the raven's dark strength. *"You have many more years to find your way alone,"* it had told him. Something impossible and terrifying suddenly came clear. "It was a Pathguide. You called a Pathguide to be rid of the Verael."

Leita's brow rose. "Then you truly did feel it."

He nodded. "It wasn't anything like the spirit I saw at Jase's pyre."

"I'm not Riana to order about the Pathguides. I can summon them, but the guide who answers is the one most suited to the task."

"The raven. Cael's messenger to speak with Cael's Chosen. That's a dangerous gambit."

She blew out a loud breath. "Jhared, you may let yourself be hobbled by the narrow perceptions of ignorant men, but do not impose your limits on me! You must understand the magnitude of our peril. What went wrong last night had little to do with hungry Verael. Things have gone awry on our Path. The war, the winds, the imminent destruction of the council—the failure of Cael's Chosen to listen to the Bearer of his Blade—they're all signs we've tilted woefully out of balance. This Path is rushing toward its end."

The warning rang familiar. Jhared opened his mouth, but she lifted a hand.

"Wait. You wanted this; now you must listen. You and I are nothing. Avelos is nothing. Even the destruction of our Path, by itself, would be nothing, only the loss of a few slender threads in the great weaving. What terrifies me is a horror greater than you can comprehend. The weaving itself is unraveling. Threads all around us are snapping like spider's silk in the wind. Others are snagged and tangling. I must find a way to achieve true balance and stop the unraveling. Whatever face you've seen me wear, whatever Pathguides I summon, look at me and know I do it to *heal* the weaving. If I do not, I believe we will face—"

"Every instant of the past and future torn apart. Every spirit exploded into nothingness."

Her eyes widened. "How do you possibly know?"

"Alende has seen it. He says you are its cause."

Her face went white. She pressed her hands flat against the rock. Jhared had never seen such intense fear in her.

"Leita? What does that mean to you?"

"Too many things to tell you now." She scrambled to her feet.

"Leita, *please!*"

She turned slowly toward him. "It means that the man is a marvel, for he's seen what I only pieced together through years of observation and study. It means the Paths have predicted their own destruction, which frightens me more than I have words to say. It means I might be . . ." She squeezed her eyes shut and shook her head. "I must find the waylayer."

"Alende," Jhared told her. "If he's alive, he'll find you."

"Of course." She laughed mirthlessly. "His passion for my death makes sense now." She shook her head again. "The infinite Paths are unraveling, and it took the unbound to see it. Had he died at his Becoming, his vision would have been lost. How many others died and took their secrets with them? Ah, Avelos, how much has your hatred cost you?"

Jhared paced away from her, arranging the pieces she had given him, fitting them to other things he knew or guessed. She claimed she meant to heal the rupture in Riana's weaving, but she hungered for Cael's darkness as certainly as the Verael hungered for human flesh. He didn't know what to do with those competing truths. She said she must restore the balance. No, "achieve true balance," is what she had said. True balance?

He turned with that question on his lips, but a bobbing motion near the bottom of the hill caught his eye. Riders. He looked closer. A neat file of ten men was cantering in the direction of the camp. A farmer and his neighbors investigating the smoke, perhaps? As Jhared watched, the cantering line split, each half moving as briskly as any Forest Guard company to flank his patrol. Sunlight reflected on steel. One of the riders glanced up.

Jhared bounded the single step to Leita, clapped a hand over her mouth and dragged her to the ground. With a muffled cry, she struggled to break free. He threw his weight over her, stifling a curse as her teeth closed on the tender flesh of his burned hand.

"Lady, be still!" he hissed. "Mischief below."

For an instant, the only sounds were Leita's rapid breaths and the angry chitter of a squirrel overhead. Jhared set his mouth near her ear. "Armed men circling," he whispered. "I need to look. Understand?"

She nodded, glaring at him. Slowly, he lifted his hand from her lips and raised himself just enough to peer down the hill.

Glimpses through the brown and gold leaves revealed the riders in formation around the camp. His comrades had been caught in the midst of their preparations. They were scattered, with nothing like the protection of a defensive line.

Sevar stood two feet in front of a bearded horseman on a shaggy red mount. They seemed to be talking. The lieutenant hadn't drawn his sword, but his posture was tense and unwelcoming.

Leita pounded a fist against Jhared's chest. Abruptly, he was conscious of her body beneath his. He rolled onto his side to free her.

"Who?" she mouthed.

"Don't know," he admitted. The party was too well equipped and organized for bandits. The Amurian border was spitting distance, but raiders wouldn't be so bold as to attack soldiers in daylight less than a day's ride from the garrison. Northerners possessed no love for the Forest Guard, but villagers had no cause and no skill to attack. And they were talking, after all. His hand closed reflexively on his bow. He could pick off half of them before they knew what happened, but his comrades hadn't drawn weapons.

"I'm going down. Stay here."

"No. I'm coming."

He gritted his teeth. "Leita, please don't."

She smiled and patted the Blade at her hip. "Fear is a potent weapon. Come on."

He kept her behind him as they crept back down the trail. Each time her step sent a stone rattling across the hill, he held his breath, but his comrades and their assailants seemed to be fixed upon one another. The riders were northerners certain enough, big and broad with curly hair and heavy beards. Their shaggy mountain ponies were as stocky as the riders were. The man speaking to Sevar owned the stern, handsome features usually carved into sculptures of Lord Arion or Alende Isan. His polished black boots fit over grey breeches, and instead of a cloak, he wore a fine black vest of boiled wool lined with a silky grey fur. On his breast and on the shoulders of his men shone the triple streak-of-lightning sigil. The sign of Clan Aglar. A warning thudded in Jhared's ears.

Leita set a hand on his shoulder. He glanced back to see his own questions reflected in her eyes. Surely these men, as well turned out as palace guards and as organized as soldiers, couldn't be Aglar's clanguard. But if not, who were they? Jhared moved silently through the underbrush until he crouched behind Sevar, where he could see the northern leader's face. The rider closest to Jhared was on his right, a dour looking man on a dirt-colored horse.

". . . saw the smoke from the end'a the pass and thought it must be raiders," the leader was saying, stroking a hand along the soft grey lining of his vest. "What a surprise for us ta find Forest Guard riding through Clan Aglar lands, eh? Sorry for the loss'a your man. Nasty business the Verael."

He sounded more annoyed than sorry, and his riders still encircled the patrol. Sevar ignored the false courtesies. "When did the clanguard take up the watch of the high pass, Commander Ciam? The road from the pass to the sea is the province of the General of the Northern Towers."

"Ay, for what Rumar steals from us in silver, ya'd think we'd get at least one company'a soldiers from General Orn ta man the pass. But no, sir. Your General Nadel has near emptied the barracks ta deal with southern concerns. Always the south, eh? The north must care for the north. And we mean ta do so."

The lieutenant gazed pointedly at the clanguards' fine livery, strong horses, and sparkling gear. "Considering such tough conditions, it is astonishing Prefect Aglar has managed to cobble together a guard at all," he said mildly.

Commander Ciam's eyes turned flinty. "Just what's your business with Clan Aglar, Lieutenant? We didn't expect ta see troops heading north again till spring."

"High chieftain's business," Sevar answered. "Business I'll share first with General Orn at the garrison."

"Prefect's not gonna like this," the man beside Jhared whispered to his companion. His companion hushed him sharply.

Ciam's mouth worked as though he were chewing on Sevar's words and found them foul. Slowly, he leaned back so that his vest pulled open, again revealing the lining. The grey fur fluttered on the breeze.

Jhared sucked a breath in sudden recognition. Not fur, *feathers*. The commander's vest was lined with downy feathers. The down of young birds or . . . Jhared squeezed his eyes shut, but that was no good. It left him alone with a vivid picture of the maimed and bleeding babes. Leita touched his arm anxiously. He fought to bring his focus around. A sense of danger roared in his head.

"Commander, we're losing the light, and I intend to get my men to the tower tonight," Sevar was saying. "We'll hold no grudge for your mistake. But we'll be on our way."

Standing in place for so long must have stiffened Sevar's injuries, for as he pivoted away from Ciam onto his right foot, he staggered and just barely caught himself. Ciam leaned forward, his expression predatory.

"Lieutenant, your men and horses are injured and beat. Let us take ya ta Ebilan at the base'a the pass. It's hours closer than the garrison."

"Unnecessary," Sevar replied coldly. "My men have managed far worse than Verael bites."

"No doubt. But no need ta suffer so tonight. The Storm and Bluster is a clean inn, and I know a good healer. When ya've eaten and rested, we'll give ya an honor guard up ta the tower. After taking ya for raiders, we owe it, eh?"

In the silence that fell, Ciam's hand drifted casually, almost someone might believe inadvertently, toward his sword. The rider above Jhared had gone still, a soldier waiting for the word to be given. Sevar was not going to be allowed to refuse. Careful not to tangle in the underbrush, Jhared brought his bow around and took a step closer to the Bearer. His insides churned. It wouldn't be a pretty fight. And unless they killed the clanguard, they would face a long, hard flight to the tower, after. Jhared tried not to think about sending arrows through his countrymen. Instead, he watched the lieutenant for some indication.

He didn't hear Leita until she breezed past him. He gasped and reached out to grab her, but his fingers closed on air. She was already stepping into the circle of men.

"An inn sounds like a gift from the goddess," she said brightly, smiling up at Ciam. "If you tell me there's something other than lamb sausage to eat and the hope of a real bath, I must follow you anywhere."

The northern commander startled and looked Leita up and down. Several other riders muttered in surprise. Jhared's comrades looked aghast.

"Lady Bearer?" the commander said uncertainly, drawing a lazy spiral in the air.

"Yes. I am the Bearer of Cael's Blade." Leita pushed back her cloak to touch the hilt of the knife. "I'm well pleased to meet a devoted man of the north, Commander Ciam."

"My honor, Lady. But how do you come ta travel in such rough company, eh?"

"I hope you'll forgive me for saving that story until we've taken some rest, Commander. And I hope the good lieutenant will forgive me for begging a place for us in town. I'm not so hearty as the Forest Guard, I fear." She turned her too-sweet smile on Sevar. If Jhared weren't so breathless with worry, he would have given a lot to see the lieutenant's expression.

"What can a poor soldier do against the will of the goddess?" Sevar said dryly. "I won't disappoint Riana's servant. We'll accept your hospitality at Ebilan, Commander."

"Do ya have any other surprises for us?" Ciam said, narrowing his eyes at the patrol. "Perhaps the Lady'a Avelos herself?"

"We had a Shorn soldier among us," Sevar answered, gesturing to Jase's pyre, "but he can no longer surprise anyone."

Commander Ciam glanced at the pyre and back to Sevar. "Just as well. Cursed soldiers have no place in the north."

A chill shivered through Jhared. Sevar had just cut him free. *He can no longer surprise anyone.* It was a message from the man who believed Jhared had nothing but grief to offer any of them. *Surprise me: prove me wrong,* it challenged.

Jhared's comrades made a sober party riding out of the forest and back to the road. The arrangement of guards on either side of them made it clear who was escorting whom. As Leita brought her horse into line, she smiled again at Ciam, and the commander's brown eyes gleamed in a way Jhared was certain had nothing to do with devotion to Riana.

He waited in hiding long enough to be sure Ciam wouldn't send outriders back to watch the road, then set off after them.

The town of Ebilan jutted out of the mountainside at the northern entrance to the pass. Its stone towers and walls scowled down at travelers with the same superior air as its clansmen. Jhared knew a moment of panic when he saw the gate watchmen diligently questioning his patrol and other travelers. He owned no good story that would get him through. Fortunately, ages of wind and snow had scoured dimples into the walls, creating decent footholds. Careful to avoid the view of the gatemen, he pulled himself up the wall and swung over the edge. At the top, he lay flat on his belly to catch his breath and observe the layout of the town before dropping lightly down on the inside. Hunkered next to the stone, Jhared used Tierzen's knife to slice the last of the red border from his cloak. He was achingly aware he cut a part of himself away with it.

Dusk brought a new wind that carried the crisp, metallic scent of snow. Jhared drew up his hood and hurried along the steep, narrow streets. Among the big northerners, his height wasn't quite as conspicuous, but he still felt painfully out of place. Clan Aglar wasn't friendly to a city man at the best of times, and this town had a particularly unwelcoming air. Locked shutters on shops and houses seemed to guard secrets. A group of frayed old men with the Shorn red on their coats shoveled dung from the road. Two dull-eyed Shorn women in thin dresses tried to entice passersby to pay for a bony grope. Jhared wondered where the younger Shorn men had gone; then he recalled the silver mines.

He strode across town, searching for the inn where Ciam had taken his patrol. Cold stone sculptures marked the shops. Granite swords tall as a man stood at the end of the smiths' lane. A pair of black stone boots marked a cobbler. Men and women in various stages of undress announced the brothels. Finally, Jhared spied a two-story building set back a bit from the drinking houses around it. In front, a choleric-looking stone man stood with hands on his hips and his cheeks puffed out. The Storm and Bluster.

Two of Ciam's clanguard lazed on the front step, trying to appear as though they merely had no better place to be. Jhared turned on his heel and strode down the alley between the inn and the tavern beside it. He hadn't expected a watch. Why in all the sacred skies was Clan Aglar so threatened by nine weary patrolmen? He crept to the back of the inn and found the stable, a low building cut into the rock. Leita's mare and Sevar's stallion stood tied to posts in the yard, until a curly-haired stable boy came and led them into stalls.

Jhared sank down onto a mounting block and studied the inn. The front entrance opened to the street, but the back leaned against the mountain. On the second floor, a row of tall, shuttered windows opened onto a balcony and the bare hills. Occupants' assorted laundry hung from several of the shutters, fluttering as the breeze lifted. It wouldn't be impossible to find a way in around the guards, but then what?

He rested his chin in his hands and his eyes closed of their own accord. The rawness of his wounds and the gurgle in his belly reminded him it had been a long two days. Would it have been so bad to go with the rest of his patrol to a respectable inn where he might eat a meal, take a bath, and sleep in a bed? He sighed and shook his head. His comrades and Leita were prisoners; there was no other way to see it. Commander Ciam didn't want Sevar at the garrison. Jhared just didn't understand why. Could Clan Aglar have some reason to prevent the Forest Guard from stopping the killing winds?

"Ya waiting on a horse?"

Jhared blinked at the stable boy staring down at him and bemoaned his clumsiness. "I need a mount for hire," he said, gathering himself. "What about that bay mare you just took in? She has a spirited look about her."

The boy put his hands on his hips and glared at Jhared in a fair imitation of the stone man in front. "She's not for hire. Belongs to a lady, she does. And what kind'a groom would I be ta send a poor, tired beast like that back ta the road?"

"Good boy," Jhared said, with genuine feeling. "You care for your charges. Do you have a mount that's ready to stretch its legs?"

"Don't know." The boy peered closer at Jhared, wrinkling his brow. "We don't hire ta the cursed."

Jhared froze, hearing Ciam's words: *"Cursed soldiers have no place in the north."* They'd likely throw him off the mountain if they caught him. Swiftly, before he could change his mind or his Teachers could protest, he surged to his feet.

"Cursed?" he cried, towering over the boy. "So every man who comes from the other side of the Sandien is cursed, eh? Is that the way it is in Ebilan?"

The stable hand shrank back a step, eyes wide. He really wasn't more than a child. "No. No, 'course not. It's just ya have—"

"What is it you think I have? Eh, boy? I don't need to stay here to be affronted. What I have is money to spend, and I need a horse!" He glowered and turned to stomp off.

"Wait!" the boy squeaked. "Don't go. It's sore trouble for me if I let business walk away."

"Why should I care about that?" Jhared huffed in a way he'd seen often enough growing up in Elders' Circle.

"I've a good horse for ya. A willing beast at a fair price. Ya couldn't get better down the hill. Just don't go."

The boy scurried off and returned quickly leading a lanky, brown and white gelding. *Riva*, the boy called him, a short name for *Rivaliren*. "Strong Magic" it meant in ancient Velos. Jhared couldn't say if the name was portentous, but the beast was sound and had an honest eye. Jhared haggled over the price, grumbling sufficiently. Finally, he counted out his coins. It left him with nothing more than a few pebbles.

As the boy turned away, looking relieved, Jhared called out offhandedly. "I hope the lady's mare has time enough to rest before she's back on the road."

"Oh, certain enough. She's a guest'a Commander Ciam. She'll be well attended for as long as she likes." The boy offered a crooked grin, looking happy to atone for his previous mistake. "The lady and the mare both, if I know the commander."

Jhared managed some reply and swung into the saddle. When he returned to the street, he knew exactly what he intended. He held the horse to a walk down the slippery lanes. As soon as they escaped the walls, they began to run.

21.
ENDING PATHS

The gelding had an ugly gait, but it galloped with a good will up and down the rocky hills. Jhared pressed harder than he should have over unfamiliar roads. General Orn would know what to make of the threat from the clanguard, and once the garrison knew the patrol was in Ebilan, Commander Ciam couldn't further delay them. Jhared rode with a hopeful heart. It was the first time in a long while he knew he had chosen the right Path.

Traveling in the dark always made the journey seem longer. Jhared could see the tower's watch fires pricking the crystalline sky for hours before he finally came down the last ridge. He was following the river toward the gate, when Riva pulled up hard, pinning his ears and backing on his haunches. Jhared caught the stench a moment later. It drifted down the hill from the direction of the tower, smoke that tainted the night with the memory of death. It was smoke from pyres. A great many of them.

Jhared had only ever known three causes of so much death: battle, illness, and the killing winds. Rampant illness would be a good reason to keep his patrol away, but if that were the cause, why would Ciam not have said so? Jhared paused at the river to calm the gelding. While the beast drank, Jhared dipped his hands into the icy water, relieving some of the heat creeping from under the bandages. Then he hurried back to the road. A sickle moon had risen by the time he reached the final ascent to the fortress. Wary now, he led Riva into the trees and tied him, then went on foot to get a closer look.

Aglar Tower, the north's primary defense against Amuria, straddled a ridge at the northwestern edge of the Sandien Mountains. Along the southern walls of the keep, the Yavra River rushed noisily, swollen with the recent rains. Moonlight silvered the battlements, whose height rivaled the rocky peaks beside them. The star-shaped curtain wall was fortified with towers at each of the star's five points, but the towers were unlike any other defense Jhared had seen, for open platforms jutted out from them at several places along their height, like fungus jutting from the trunk of a tree.

This close, there was no mistaking the clouds of smoke that rose from the inner yard. Dread told Jhared to run to the main gate to learn what had happened, but Sevar's reprimands rang in his head. He would not charge in impulsively; he would skirt the wall and see what he could puzzle out before he faced the general.

He crept around the hill to the east side of the fortress and crouched in the grass. Against the starry sky, it was easy to detect movement on the battlements. He spied only one guard walking between the eastern towers. The guard scanned the road and hills, then turned to the inner yard, where the clang of metal echoed intermittently. Jhared ticked out the moments it took the man to pace between the two towers, marveling at the sheer length of defenses the star fortress presented. The ancients who built it must have had three times the soldiers to fortify it than now served all the northern Forest Guard.

When the guard marched off once more toward the opposite tower, Jhared rose from cover and headed for the wall. He was moving uphill now and in the open. He leaned into the slope, pausing at intervals to make his movement arrhythmic, the less likely to draw attention. As he reached the wall, he spied many signs of deterioration—the berm had disintegrated into little more than a gentle rise; vines shot like a parasite across the stones—but no signs of recent attack. Slowly, Jhared crept around the north-facing fold of the star and under the first of the western towers. The watch was heaviest here: two men walked the wall and lights bobbled from the embrasures. Across the border, Amuria would see the garrison still fortified against her. Nothing seemed amiss but for the dearth of men.

Finally, Jhared reached the southern side of the fortress, facing the mountains once more. One last tower separated him from the gatehouse. Below, the river gurgled toward the sea. He moved carefully; only a few feet of sloped rock separated the wall from the drop to the water. A breeze carried a cloud of smoke into his face, and the greasy odor set him coughing. He put a hand over his mouth and stumbled deeper into the shadow. There, in the southern fold of the star, lay the men.

Two of them sprawled amid a pile of offal, as though they, like the refuse, had been dumped over the wall and hadn't quite reached the water. A third body was crumpled closer to the tower, across the threshold of a narrow archway where steps led into the wall.

"Riana keep you," Jhared whispered as he leaned to examine the closest body. It was a soldier, about his own years. The man's head was twisted at an inhuman angle. Overhead, an owl screeched.

Pain exploded at the base of Jhared's spine, sending him staggering over the dead man. As he flung out his hands to catch himself, another blow knocked his arms out from under him. His chin smacked the stone, making his vision swim. Before he could move, his assailant dropped onto his back, jamming the air from his lungs.

"I'm dead already," hissed a voice in fluid Velos, as a blade pricked Jhared's throat. "Cry out to the watch and I'll take ya with me."

Jhared's blades were trapped beneath him and his arms pinned by the man on his back. "Killing me will gain you nothing," he gasped. "I own nothing of value."

"Shut up, traitor. Your blood is the only thing I value." The blade bit deeper. "Where's the rest'a your patrol? How many are still searching for me?"

Anger kindled in Jhared's veins. "Murderer! Back-stabbing men in the dark? You're worse than Shorn!"

The pressure of the blade eased abruptly. Jhared didn't wait to learn why. He lurched onto his knees, bucking his attacker off him. The man fell backward and hit the ground with a grunt. Jhared clambered to his feet and scrambled toward the archway. A small landing recessed into the wall before the stairway continued up. Jhared backed against the stairs, drew his sword, and braced for another attack.

The man lay as still as the corpse beside him. Wind whistled in the crevice and ruffled the fabric of his shirt. Jhared took a step closer and kicked the knife out of reach. It slid down the stone and splashed quietly into the water. With dismay, he saw his assailant was a soldier. His uniform was filthy and torn. Jhared guessed the man past his middle years, but blood and muck masked his face. The grey in his hair might have been only dirt. Whatever his age, the man had been broken. His left shoulder was bloody and badly twisted; his arm lay useless at his side.

The soldier opened his eyes and blinked. When he saw Jhared in the archway, his gaze hardened. "Finish it, boy," he growled. "Or should I roll over so it's easier for ya to slide your sword into my back?"

Jhared straightened in shock. "It's not my place to bring sentence against you. What's your name? I'll see you to the healer. General Orn is the one who will deal with you."

The man pushed himself up on one arm to squint at Jhared. "You're no northerner. A Shorn boy, eh? I thought they finished ya off."

"I'm Patrolman Denaban of the Forest Guard Fourth under Lieutenant Sevar." Jhared stepped back and gestured with his sword for the stranger to rise. "Who are you?"

The soldier growled a curse as he tried to get up. It took several moments to gather his feet beneath him. He glanced up at the battlements, then staggered into the hidden recess and crouched against the wall opposite Jhared. "You're a liar. A bad one. Sevar's at Ravia. If they're using ya ta smoke out the others, it's no good. They're all dead."

"I'm General Nadel's man from the south," Jhared repeated, less patiently. "I was sent north with my patrol on the high chieftain's business. You're sick and in pain. Let me help you to the healer. Whatever you've done, they'll see your suffering eased." Nodding toward the bodies, he added coldly: "I imagine you'll find a better end than the ones you killed."

"Cael's demons," the soldier said slowly. "Cael's long, cold cock. You're telling the truth. Ya really just arrived." He slid back against the wall, hissing as his broken shoulder met the stone. "Enrian Nadel. That old hound might've seen this coming. But he's too busy in the south, isn't he? They're all so worried about Sahiste."

The feverish glitter in the soldier's eyes made Jhared shift uneasily. "What happened here? What about the pyres? Was it Amuria?"

The man spat into the dark. "Amuria? Those pirates fight more honorably than what we faced. It was the clans, boy. The northern five. They *turned* on us. Took the garrison. I'm General Orn. Or was," he said bitterly. "For they've made a ghost'a me, and ghosts'a all my men."

Stunned silence greeted the soldier's words. The sound of wings whispered in the passage as bats flew about in the dark.

Disbelief and horror warred within Jhared. "Grey feather find them."

"And all their kin for six on six generations," added the man. "Avelos is going to lose the north."

Jhared sank onto a stair. "How could they? Their own people."

"Rumar should've known it would come," muttered the general. "It's been years in the making. Once the bulk'a my forces marched south, I didn't have the men ta stand against them. Two days ago, clanguard from Aglar, Lasla, and Avien put any who opposed them to the sword and claimed the garrison for themselves."

The general stopped and a grimace of pain twisted his features. Jhared reached for his water skin, pulled out the stopper, and handed it to the soldier. Orn took the flask with his good hand and drank.

"Then everyone's dead?"

The general coughed and set down the skin. Flecks of blood darkened his lips. "So far, those who threw down their weapons are hostages. The rest'a us tried ta fight our way out. A damned few made it over the wall. If anyone made it farther than me, they've been rounded up by now. Likely I'm only still here because Commander Avien doesn't think anyone is stupid enough ta hide in the wall." Orn groaned as he shifted. "Damn Rumar for being too stubborn ta give the north its due. He'll pay in blood now."

Jhared stared at the wounded officer. "You're a northerner. What are you doing on this side of the wall?"

"Because even when he's a fool, Rumar's still the high chieftain, and I'm still sworn ta him! Where I was born doesn't make me a traitor. And it's still *general* ta you, Patrolman!"

Jhared glanced away. "Forgive me, General. What are your orders, sir?"

"Tell Rumar not ta hesitate. These traitors will use every day they get ta strengthen their defenses. The garrison leader is a commander by the name'a Simavir Avien. My bet is his orders come from his father, the prefect. The son's too impulsive to manage this by himself. Though he's no idiot. He knew me well enough ta keep me out'a their plotting."

"Sir, I came to the garrison for aid. My patrol was taken by Clan Aglar."

"I'm sorry for that, boy. Prefect Aglar's in this up ta his grey beard. You're on your own. I'll add your people to my prayers for the fallen."

Jhared's chest tightened. "No need for that, sir. They're not dead. Now let me help you up. We need to be moving to beat the dawn."

"No." Orn lifted one hand, a gesture somewhere between resignation and resolution. "There's no help for me. If Cael loves chaos, he'll leave my spirit on these walls ta torment them."

"General, I can take you out of here." Jhared knelt by the injured man. "I will."

"You have an order, Patrolman. Get ta Rumar before the snows cut off the north from Velantar, or come spring, Amuria will fall on this fractured country and claim it one piece at a time."

"Yes, sir. Understood." Jhared rose. He did understand. The injured general could do nothing against a fortress of traitors. The man's sacrifice was larger than that. Orn refused to slow the message from reaching Rumar. After a moment, Jhared pulled Tierzen's knife from his belt and set it beside the general's good hand. "If the time comes," he said. "Is there any message you would like me to take?"

General Orn considered that and gave a ghoulish grin. "If you see 'im, tell Matio Sevar it looks like he owes me for our last wager."

Jhared nodded. "Anything else, sir?"

"No. When they say I betrayed my country, at least a few will know the truth. It's more than I expected." The soldier let out a wheezing breath and wrapped his fingers around Jhared's knife. "Go now. Run for the south and don't stop to look behind ya till ya've crossed the Sandien."

Jhared saluted the general and left before he could think further about the fate that awaited the man.

Riva galloped over the rough roads with a stout heart, but he couldn't swallow distance like Seravina could. Jhared pushed the horse, hoping the beast's strength would hold. No wonder Command Ciam saw Sevar as a threat. The northern five wanted no word of their betrayal to reach the high chieftain while there was still a chance for Rumar to react before winter. The clanguard had killed loyal Forest Guard, their own people. Jhared trembled with a deep-rooted fury fueled by more than a century of shame. Had Avelos learned nothing from the betrayals of the Avelune? Only suffering came from such treachery. With his anger for company, Jhared galloped on, goading the horse to its limits.

When he reached the fork where the road split, leading into the pass or up the hill to Ebilan, he drew in his flagging mount. He had orders: Take the news to Rumar. Don't stop until you've crossed the Sandien. But his comrades were in the hands of traitors. Leita had smiled at Commander Ciam, hoping that flattery and Cael's Blade might keep them safe.

Nausea rolled over Jhared and blue stars burst across the hills. He gripped the gelding's mane to keep from sliding out of the saddle. The Bearer's warning came back to him too late; he was standing at the center of the fork, the heart of transition. The Paths churned, waiting for a decision that would shape his life and the lives of uncountable others. He dug his fingers into the enflamed skin of his forearm to free himself from the Gate. Pain brightened the night. He cursed his helplessness. What good was it to sense the movement of the Paths without the ability to see where they would lead?

Straightening, he retrieved the reins and kicked Riva back into motion. As he made his decision and left the fork behind, the Paths settled a little. Ebilan's inhospitable stone stared down at him like a challenge. He would bring his comrades out; then they would run for Velantar. All they needed was to make it back through the pass and out of Clan Hilera's forest. They would find friends in Clan Darnios.

The tired gelding made no protest when Jhared tied it outside the walls. He climbed back into town unnoticed. It was late enough that even the drinking houses were quiet. A single lamp flickered in the window of the Storm and Bluster. After his uphill trek, Jhared was forced to pause in the alley to catch his breath and blink back the points of light floating in his vision. No guards stood at the door, but he took care to hug the shadows as he slipped into the stable yard.

The yard looked deserted, and a lantern beside the door burned low. Somewhere in the hills, a wild dog barked. Inside the stable, a horse whinnied in response.

Jhared crept to the wall of the stable, raised his arms above his head, and grasped the edge of the roof. With a deep breath, he leaped and dragged himself onto his stomach. The roof creaked under his weight, and for an uncomfortable moment, his legs dangled down. Then he pulled himself to his knees and into a crouch. He climbed onto the hillside at the point where the stable roof met the rock. From there, it was a sharp, slippery scramble over boulders and thorny bushes to reach the second floor of the inn.

He found himself on the balcony staring at the row of shuttered windows and drying laundry and wondering how in all Riana's skies he was going to know where his patrol slept.

When the answer struck him, he laughed softly. He slinked closer to the windows and reached out a hand, just to be certain. Hanging from the shutters of the corner room was a soft, finely woven tunic the size of a slender woman. Around the collar and cuffs, ornate embroidery depicted chains of complex spirals. He knew that shirt. He knew the scent of it: incense and spring water. Something domestic and comforting lay in the touch of the fabric. He thought of Leita on her knees near the lake, scrubbing clothes against a rock, a tranquil look in her grey-green eyes. Light danced over the charms on her wrists. She paused and looked up from her task.

Not Leita.

Jhared leaped up, sucking breaths of icy night air, as if the cold might quench the blue flames. *Please, Lady, not now!*

Without waiting for the Gate to take him, he threw himself back into the moment, putting his hands to the shutters and pushing inward. The shutters tented together with just enough of a gap between them that he could work one finger down their length until he bumped the latch. It took more effort than he expected to wriggle his swollen finger around the hook closure. As splinters pricked his flesh, he lost his hold on the hook and had to start again. It occurred to him that Alende's skills would have come in handy just then. With fraying patience, he found the latch, twisted his finger to reach the hook and pushed upward, away from the eye. Finally, the hook popped free. He swung his legs over the casement and was in.

A large shadow lunged at him from the left. Jhared threw his right arm upward to block a blow. He knocked his assailant's arm wide and drew back his own fist. Then his eyes met his attacker's. Firelight reflected in a steely gaze.

"Lieutenant!" he gasped, dropping his hands and hurrying back a step.

"Denaban," Sevar said, echoing Jhared's astonishment.

Jhared darted a glance around the little room. "Where are the others? The Bearer?"

Leita stepped out of a niche on the far side of the fireplace, Cael's Blade in her hand. "Thank the Lady it's you. The others are asleep in the next room. All's well. What took you so long?"

Jhared rubbed a hand over his eyes. The chamber was warm and he was standing on a plush sheepskin rug. Across the room, a bed was piled high with blankets, and on a table sat two glasses of wine and a half-eaten meal of roasted pork and buttered potatoes. He licked his lips. "I went to Aglar Tower."

Sevar choked in disbelief. "You rode all the way to the fortress and back?"

"Yes, sir. And, ah sir, it's worse than—"

"You're not a raw trainee, Denaban. Where's your proper report?"

"Sir! Yes, sir!"

Leita closed and locked the shutters as Jhared began to report every terrible detail. When his throat grew hoarse, the Bearer brought him a cup of water, but Sevar lifted a hand to stay her. The lieutenant's expression had gone hard and dangerous. He pummeled Jhared with questions. Jhared answered until he had nothing useful left to give.

"Curse their duplicity and short-sighted arrogance!" the lieutenant growled. "They've done our enemy's work and turned imminent war into a diversion for their own treachery. Do they truly believe the mountains will save them when all the border nations come to claim our broken lands?"

"This will finish Rumar," Leita said quietly, handing Jhared the water. "With the northern five gone from the council, the Legacy will almost certainly carry the vote."

Jhared hadn't considered that. He narrowed his eyes at Sevar. "How convenient for Toren Abrigado. The north has done his work and he doesn't even have to dirty his hands."

Sevar didn't appear to notice Jhared's appraising stare as he paced the room. His left arm was bandaged, and he still favored his right leg. "Nothing can be done about Abrigado now. General Orn says the garrison's holding hostages. That means they intend to ask for something." The lieutenant stopped in the middle of the room and bowed his head. "Damn it, Orn. You shouldn't have ended this way."

Jhared made a sound. He had almost forgotten. "Sir, the general sent a message for you."

Sevar lifted his head. "Yes?"

"He said to tell you . . . you owe him for your last wager."

The lieutenant closed his eyes, the color drained from his face. "I never expected I would owe him this." The shifting light softened Sevar's features. Since the night Jhared had glimpsed the numerous faces of the Matio Sevar who walked this Path, Jhared couldn't quite see the invulnerable, disloyal Legacy man he had believed the lieutenant to be.

"What does that mean?" Leita asked gently.

Sevar stared into the fire. "Orn believed Aglar Tower would be his last commission. I said not. He was too skilled a soldier to be wasted as a watchman for the silver mines." The lieutenant paused. "I had just refused the post. He took it in my place."

"I'm sorry, Matio."

The lieutenant didn't respond. A familiar, impassive mask tightened his expression.

Jhared straightened. "Sir, give me my orders. We must get out of Ebilan. I can saddle the horses while you rouse the others."

"Jhared, slow down. You must eat and rest before anything else." Leita gave him a meaningful look. "You can't go on without rest."

"The lady is right," Sevar replied. "Irony of ironies, it seems we need our cursed soldier. Sit down. We must plan this carefully."

Leita nudged Jhared toward the table and he fell into a seat. She moved aside an open scroll—a map, *the* map, Jhared realized—then pushed the platter of food in front of him. The aroma made him lightheaded. He snatched up a wedge of potato. Leita frowned, and Jhared followed her gaze to his hands. What remained of his bandages was black with dirt and dried blood.

"We'll only have one chance to escape," Sevar said, joining them. "Once Ciam realizes we know what's happened, there'll be no more pretense of hospitality."

"He'll use us as leverage against Velantar." Leita's voice remained as steady and rich as ever, but Jhared saw apprehension in her eyes.

"That's why we must wait," Sevar said. "I don't like it, but this night is nearly gone. And the horses and men need rest if we're to outrun fresh, hungry clanguard."

Jhared swallowed and set down the food in his hand. "The high chieftain can't afford the delay. With our troops in the south, it'll take time to organize a response. He needs to move while he still might be able to surprise the northern prefects." Jhared looked from Sevar to Leita and decided what had long ago ceased to be secret must be spoken aloud. "I think we've another possibility. Don't we, Lady?"

Leita raised a brow at Jhared's boldness but she turned to Sevar. "It's true, Lieutenant. My couriers can carry a small bit of information to the city. They're fast and faithful. And I won't deny it, they're Cael's messengers."

"Ah, yes. The birds." Sevar folded his arms across his chest and leaned back to glower at the Bearer. "Had I known what you carried when we set off, I would have gladly left you and your creatures on the temple stairs. Now they offer a hope for our country's survival? I'm not sure why I'm even surprised. Riana enjoys toying with men's understanding of the world. In that, Lady, you're her true servant."

Jhared made a sound of agreement.

"They're not a certainty," Leita warned. "Across so many miles, a thousand dangers can keep a dove from returning home. And they've never been tested this far."

"They're what we have," Sevar answered. "With any fortune, we'll be just behind them."

The Bearer nodded. "I'll release them at dawn, then. Two remain. We'll send them both and hope at least one makes it."

The knock on the door was soft, but it could have been a hammer on an anvil for the way it pounded through Jhared.

"Lady Bearer, can I speak with ya? It's Commander Ciam."

Jhared came to his feet.

"Send him off," the lieutenant hissed at Leita. To Jhared he indicated the window. "Two days. The stables at high moon watch."

Jhared nodded.

"Lady, are ya well? Did I hear someone in with ya?" The door latch began to wiggle.

"Commander," Leita called sleepily. "I'm preparing for the morning devotions. I'll see you at temple soon."

"Well now, Lady. We've plenty'a time yet till dawn." Jhared heard metal clink against metal and hurried to the window. Ciam was working the lock. "Perhaps ya have some wisdom ta share with a devout man'a the north, eh?"

Sevar walked calmly to the door, shaking his head. Jhared popped open the shutters. Two clanguards went wide-eyed with surprise.

"Whoa, now! You're not the commander's lady."

"Just who in the name'a darkness are ya?"

Jhared froze in dismay. Both men were heavily built. One was short with a boyish face; the other stood nearly as tall as a Shorn man and had scars twisting down his neck. If Jhared lifted a hand against them, any chance Sevar had to talk their way out of the situation was gone. But how could Sevar explain a Shorn soldier who was supposed to be dead? Ciam would figure out that he'd been fooled and what it meant. Jhared saw the Path laid before him as clearly as if the Gate had been thrown open. Everything had twisted away from what it had been only a moment ago. He was already diving across the casement when the lieutenant's voice rang out:

"Run, Denaban! Don't wait for anything. Remember what you owe to Avelos."

Jhared skimmed headfirst between the two clanguards and hit the balcony with outstretched arms, gasping as his hands took his weight. He fell awkwardly into a roll and staggered to his feet. Steps away, the hills beckoned, but he paused, glancing back toward the room. Ciam had entered and was staring out the window at him. In the depths of the commander's cold gaze, Jhared saw a concept of order that included only power and submission. Here was a man for whom all others existed only in so far as he must yield to them or could force them to yield. Beside him, Leita stood slender and straight. She offered Jhared her starless-sky smile and formed five silent words: *Keep to your own Path.*

His heart tore in two as the woman he had sworn to protect turned her back on him to face the traitor. The two clanguards flanked Jhared. He had lingered too long.

"Commander thought a city lady might need someone ta warm her in the cold north, eh? But looks like she's already found some company."

As Jhared reached for his sword, the scarred man caught his right wrist and shoulder in a steel grip. The guard behind him threw an arm around his chest, trapping his left hand and hauling him half off his feet. Jhared's exhausted body refused to respond.

"At'a boy. No need for violence, eh? Commander'll want ta talk with ya. Where'd ya come from and where've ya been?"

In that moment, Jhared realized, he could truly fail. Failure no longer meant a thing so small as his own shame; it meant the end of Avelos. It meant Sevar and Leita and all his comrades could disappear and no one in Velantar would know how or why. Anger bolted up from deep within him, kindling illicit strength. He opened himself wide to it and felt the heat racing through his veins. As the Shorn energy reached his muscles, he felt boundaries exploding outward; doors to the Paths slammed open.

He dropped into a crouch, dragging the guard behind him off balance. As the man began to tumble, Jhared threw his head backward. Bone crunched as his skull connected with the other's nose. The guard grunted and flailed backward, freeing Jhared's left arm. Jhared leaped to his feet, whirling toward the clanguard on his right. He threw a punch that contacted hard with flesh. The scarred man roared and went down. Jhared jumped over the balcony rail and landed in the scrubby bushes of the hill.

The ground lurched beneath him. His body vibrated with the forbidden strength of his cursed ancestors. The night had become too small to hold him. If he desired it, he might slay the men behind him. He might force Ciam pay the price for his betrayal. He might launch himself into the sacred skies.

He groaned in dismay, drunk on the energy that had poured into his blood. He sucked deep breaths to clear his head as best he might. The image of Leita's composed smile brought him back. She and Sevar were surrendering themselves into Ciam's hands so that Jhared might reach Velantar.

He didn't head back to the streets, where the clanguard would have all the advantage of familiarity. Instead, he scrambled up the rocky hillside above Ebilan. The guards pursued him clumsily. He could hear them cursing the night and the rough terrain. All their shiny gear was no exchange for his long experience treading foreign borders in the dark. Jhared waited until he was certain he'd lost them before cutting back around the walls toward the woods where Riva was tied.

Only as he pelted through the trees did he sense the prickling at the base of his spine. Only then did he notice the wind rising out of the east to lick his cheek and cool his fever.

"No, Lady! It is enough!"

He leaped onto the branch of a juniper tree, climbing to the highest point that would bear him. He couldn't see the cloud yet, but the low roar thrummed against his breastbone. The killing winds had reached the north.

He gazed across the hill where he had abandoned Leita and the lieutenant. The Storm and Bluster was constructed of ancient stone. They stood a better chance of surviving the winds than surviving the clanguard. For a long moment, Jhared stood poised between running back and running south, but he could do nothing now to help them. With a strange, terrible insight, he knew that everything he had left behind was already a part of his past.

He flung himself the rest of the way to the clump of trees where he had left the gelding. The horse fretted, head up and ears twitching in the direction of the storm. It rolled a wild eye as Jhared tightened the girth.

"I'm sorry," he muttered to the poor beast, "but staying isn't a better choice." He wondered if any Path existed where the gelding lived a long, pleasant life, petted and pampered by a farmer's child. He swung into the saddle and squeezed the beast's sides. The horse wheeled into the pass.

They galloped up the empty road, trees and hills only a blur, the gelding's hooves loud against the stone. The storm was traveling east to west. If they fled south through the pass swiftly enough, perhaps they would break past the boundary of the chaos before it reached them.

Jhared leaned low over Riva's neck, grimacing into the bristly mane as the storm howled and keened. It rolled faster than he'd ever known it; almost it seemed that it followed them. From the next hill came the grinding sound of trees and stones being torn from the mountain.

And then it fell upon them, death in the darkness, slicing with invisible knives and scouring with grit. The gelding screamed in terror and threw himself sideways, bucking and twisting. Jhared clung tightly and worked to pull the horse under control, but the creature was no seasoned Forest Guard mount. It arched its back and crow-hopped, then reared onto its haunches. Jhared narrowly missed being smashed in the face by the muscular neck. He ducked aside, but the maneuver cost him his balance. When the gelding flung its head down and its hindquarters rose into the air, Jhared sailed over its neck.

He hit the ground with his shoulder and rolled, fetching up hard against a rock. As he jumped to his feet, the winds nearly knocked him flat again. Already, the horse had become no more than a blur fleeing back toward town. One useless attempt to call out earned Jhared a throat full of dust. He had no choice but to give up the beast.

Nothing remained of the world but roaring darkness. As Jhared staggered from the road, the winds tore at him like anger and loss. They shredded his spirit as well as his flesh. Before the Bearer's teaching, he had never understood what that meant: the storm ripped at the infinite weaving itself with a power that burned like vengeance.

It ripped him apart and scattered his spirit across the mountains. Jhared hardly noticed when his hands found rock. Only some small core of him knew to press forward along the cliff face. With his eyes squeezed shut, he pushed at the folds of stone, struggling for every breath. There would be shelter here. Little finger canyons cut through the pass. He remembered rows of irregular holes and larger caverns lining the stone.

He didn't know how long he had been stumbling along the rock face when he came upon the woman at the lake. She was on her knees, humming as she scrubbed her clothes against the stones in the water. Her grey cloak was draped over her shoulders, and about her neck she wore a scarf the rich blues and purples of a raven's wing. Copper and silver sparkled at her wrist. All was still and blessedly quiet. Jhared sat down a bit away from the woman and enjoyed breathing the pure air.

She looked up. "Back again? You don't have much respect for a person's privacy, do you?"

"I'm sorry," he said. "I didn't know you were here."

She narrowed her grey-green eyes. "You're very odd."

He had been called far worse. He shrugged and leaned back on his elbows. His left shoulder ached, but he couldn't remember why. "You've an unusual lilt to your speech, Lady. What clan are you from?"

She gave a snort. "I hope you don't think that's funny." She slapped the wet fabric of a shirt against the stone with more force. Jhared didn't think it funny or difficult to answer, but he didn't feel like arguing. He closed his eyes, glad for the rest.

"You're different from the ones I've spoken with before," she said eventually. "Are there others like you?"

He opened his eyes. Men? Soldiers? Shorn? He didn't know which she meant, but the answer to all three was the same: "Yes."

This produced a thoughtful expression in her, which he liked far more than the cross one. A lock of short black hair fell against her cheek. She frowned faintly. "You seem rather battered. Are you all right?"

He considered. "I think so. It's very pleasant here."

She made a face. "Indeed. It is here. But where are *you?*"

He had to think about that for quite some time. When he finally remembered, he let out a groan. Would he know if his body had died on his proper Path or would his spirit simply wander the weaving forever?"

"Keep to your own Path," Leita had warned him.

"I have to go," he said, rising hastily.

"Yes, I think you'd better," the woman agreed, returning to her work.

Her tone made him hesitate, but he had no time to figure out just what she meant. He glanced one last time at the peaceful scene before turning away.

He wasn't certain how to find his way back to his own Path, but he knew he had done it before. Leita had said it was a matter of opening doors. He thought of the place he belonged and tried to bridle his instinctive aversion to the storm. He recalled all he could of pain and suffocation and blindness, forcing himself to imagine the sting against his skin, the ache in his lungs. He threw open his arms and welcomed them.

They struck all at once as he fell back into his body. He lay gasping for breath, trying to orient himself. Who knew how long he had laid there, the wind tearing into him? His feet still toed the ground, but his body was bent over some kind of low barrier. His chest pressed against something rough and solid. He had fallen across the threshold of a tunnel or cave.

A cave. Stone. Shelter. He drew his knees beneath him and crept into the darkness. He used his elbows to avoid putting pressure on his hands. He couldn't tell how deep the cavern was, but the ceiling brushed the top of his head. He kept crawling: one arm up and forward; one knee forward; another arm up. His left shoulder protested as he set weight on it. With gritted teeth, he kept going. When the cold of the Paths claimed him, he shuddered helplessly in the dark, thinking that bears or mountain lions or even Verael might find this cave to be a perfect shelter, too. At the moment, however, even an angry Verael seemed a more manageable opponent than the killing winds.

Eventually, he gathered himself and continued on. It grew warmer as he crawled, and quieter. Dust no longer poisoned the air, and the cave seemed to become brighter. The roof of the cavern began to lift. Ahead he could see flickering light.

Without warning, he tumbled out of the tunnel. The floor of the cavern was lower than he expected, and his left shoulder gave way, dropping him headfirst in a heap.

"*Shifa! Qen i suvan?*" cried a startled voice.

Jhared blinked, afraid the killing winds had beaten understanding from him. Then he realized the voice wasn't speaking Velos. He untangled himself and forced his legs to push him upright.

And saw the woman from the lake. Dust coated her face and made her black hair mud-colored, but Jhared recognized her eyes, grey-green like a meadow in shadow or the sage at the Sahisten border. It wasn't her eyes that transfixed him, though. She no longer wore a cloak, and her great grey wings stretched toward the cavern walls, slapping angrily at the air.

Avelun. She was Avelun.

"*What? What is this? No, it can't be! Kill it! Kill it! KILL IT NOW!*"

His Teachers' command drove Jhared to his knees.

"*What are you doing?*" he panted.

"*Hurry! If you don't kill it, it will bind you until you have no will of your own!*"

Too late. The woman snatched up a blade and leaped across the fire. As her dagger pricked Jhared's chest, his eyes found hers, and for countless seconds he knelt before her, motionless, like the tableau of some ancient sacrificial rite: the Demon and the Soldier.

The heart pounding in his chest didn't seem to be his own. He knew rage and fear and a thread of curiosity, but all from a distance. The winged woman rippled like water. Perhaps she wasn't even real, just another vision on another Path. Perhaps his body still lay on the high pass road where the horse had thrown him.

He looked into her eyes and understood that he was falling. "I know you," he murmured.

As he hit the stone, he realized he had wasted his single chance to save himself, with words that were entirely absurd.

22.

THE UNBROKEN ONE

The four pyres pushed heat against Nemiah's face, drying the tears in her eyes unshed. The funeral prayers were complete; she had nothing left to offer, not to the men who had died in her service or to the crowd of onlookers who had followed the temple procession beyond the city walls and into the meadow.

A smoky breeze swirled Nemiah's gown around her legs. The dark grey wool matched the dusky sky. Grey was the color of transition, of endings and beginnings both. It was said that the empty place between the Paths of the living and the Hidden Paths of the dead was as grey as twilight and as life without love. Today not only the acolytes but all the priestesses wore grey. Behind Nemiah they watched in silence as fingers of fire claimed the bodies of Arnas and Jhesco and the two other Arionade felled by the poison.

They were truly only bodies now, empty husks burning to ash as their Pathguides led their spirits to a new place in the weaving. Nemiah had been able to give them that comfort, at least. She had drained herself to call the Pathguides, and despite her fears, they had come. One of them, a great bear-woman, had gifted her with a glance of acknowledgment, revealing an immortal's sadness in her limpid eyes and in the tears on her grizzled cheeks. With great tenderness, the bear-woman had removed Arnas's death mask and kissed him before leading the Arionad's spirit away.

That much peace Nemiah had provided to four men, but only four. Somewhere Rom had died alone. On an empty lane or a secluded trail, her Arionad's body lay untended.

"Lady, will you come away? There's no one left here for us."

She turned and looked up. Evorales stood at her shoulder, his features tight with strain. "Did you see them go, Commander? Our men and their Pathguides?"

"I didn't see the guides, Lady, but I think . . . I think I saw Riana's touch upon you when you called them." Surprise and doubt shadowed his tone. How not? He wasn't accustomed to seeing her wield power.

Nemiah couldn't allow his doubt to remain. If she were to do anything more than lay down in surrender to her sadness, she would need him to command the Arionade for her. With a pang, something Rom once told her came back: "A good commander, Evorales, but never for captain. He's a hound who doesn't like running ahead of the pack." Rom had trusted Evorales, even after Carian's attempt to turn the Arionade against her, but the commander had lost his captain and had watched his brothers fall to treachery. The Higher Circle was in a tangle and rumors were flying about Nemiah's capacity to lead. If there was any hope that Evorales could hold the Arionade together, he needed to trust her strength. She straightened and pulled the resonance of ritual back into her voice.

"Riana still lends her power to her Chosen Lady, Commander. Don't allow others to make you think otherwise. Now help Bena and the rest of my Circle into the litter. We must return to care for the living."

Evorales's fair head lifted, like a horse responding to the rein. "Will you join them in the litter, Lady?"

She shook her head. "I must travel this Path with my feet on the ground. The men who served Riana deserve no less."

She walked alone at the head of the procession, as Riana had walked when Lord Arion fell in battle against Cael. As the procession turned toward the city gates, the commander strode a pace behind her. After him came the litter and the rest of the priestesses, flanked by two short files of Arionade.

They reentered the city and wound their way through the clan circles, where the acrid scent of char still lingered from the fires set by the killing winds. As Nemiah began the climb up Travitar Hill, she found herself sinking into a weary rhythm. By the time she reached the shattered walls of Shorn Circle, every step dragged her downward, as if shackles weighted her legs. She had a vague awareness of people turning to watch her, their faces hostile. She sensed the potential for violence and felt as if she were marching toward death.

"Ah, my lady, they have killed your Arionad! They are coming for you now. They are coming!"

Nemiah jerked herself back from the Gate. The sea of hostile faces vanished, leaving the street busy with people moving about their days or standing to gawk at the procession.

"See how Riana has abandoned her own servants," a woman said coldly. "She lacks the power even to save the Arionade who adore her."

The voice pierced Nemiah's fog. It was familiar, a memory of danger.

"The Lady of Avelos cannot see beyond the narrow canyon she names order," the woman went on. "She cannot see how she dooms us with her notions of purity. Where is the balance you claim is the gift of the goddess, Nemiah Gabriana?"

The faces of the passersby held a mix of curiosity and apathy, all but that of the tall woman wrapped in a dark cloak and standing merely ten paces away. Her long yellow hair shone as brightly as Nemiah's own. Anger hardened her blue gaze.

Nemiah had not seen the faces of the two heretics who had accosted her in the dark, but she would not forget the scornful tone of the woman called Yarla, a woman who worshipped the demon and hated the Arionade.

"Ah Goddess, that's her!" Nemiah gasped. It came out on a breath that no one heard. No one but Yarla, who was watching her. One bright eyebrow rose mockingly. Nemiah drew a deeper breath. She would not stand broken before one of Cael's followers, perhaps the very one who had killed her men. Fire burned through her, but not the fire of death and pyres. Without realizing it, she had reached for Riana's gift. It rushed with the heat and light of a thousand summer days to fill the hollowness inside her. She caught the woman's gaze and held it. Her voice echoed with Riana's strength.

"Tell me, Yarla, what do you know of sorrow?"

The doors of the Paths slammed open, Yarla's Paths. Every Path on which the woman knew sorrow began to merge, like streams rushing out of the mountains to flood a valley. The force of that sorrow should have been overwhelming. The woman should have been crushed beneath it, should have collapsed on the street sobbing in despair, but Yarla stood tall and firm. Her lips curled upward in what might have been called a smile, if it had held anything other than contempt.

"Lady, the power I worship is so much greater than your goddess that she has no hold over me."

Nemiah staggered in bewilderment. It was impossible. Unbearable! If Cael had grown so strong, the balance was lost. Without thinking, she closed her eyes. Instantly, her connection to Yarla was torn away. Riana's power abandoned her, and all the doors slammed shut once again.

"Commander Evorales, hold that woman! She belongs to Cael!"

The procession lurched to a halt. Someone in the Higher Circle yelped as an Arionad lost his grip on the litter and one corner dipped toward the ground. A moment of confusion took the men as some looked around to confront the uncertain threat and others moved defensively in front of the priestesses. Evorales barked commands, urgently trying to restore order. Yarla offered Nemiah an amused glance, then turned and fled into the crowd.

"Commander, after her!"

Evorales hovered at Nemiah's side, his sword drawn, his eyes darting up and down the street. Men and women shouted and tripped over one another, trying to put distance between themselves and the Arionade's blades.

"Can't, Lady. Look where she stopped us. Narrow, crowded street. No room to swing a blade. A perfect cage. And us that far from the temple. They could give us a hard fight here."

"Two men, Commander. Just two. I order it!"

He opened his mouth, then nodded. A sharp gesture pulled two Arionade from the line. Another command sent them pushing through the crowd after Yarla.

"Come now, Lady. Please! Captain would flay me alive for halting on such ground."

The procession turned from a mourning rite into a hasty military retreat. Nemiah trembled with frustration. What part did Yarla play in this? Cael's followers sought power through the goddess's destruction. Had it been Yarla and her people who poisoned the Arionade and sent Rom to his death?

The palace guards on the temple stairs snapped to attention as Nemiah returned, drawing her thoughts to other bleak truths. It was a different kind of hurt to see the fierce-featured young men, with their spotless green and grey livery, standing where the Arionade should be. Rumar had not gloated when she sought his help, though he could have. He could have made a spectacle of bestowing his protection upon her, or worse, he might have refused. Instead, when she told him about the poisoning, she had seen anger in him. When she asked that he lend her men from the palace rather than City Guards, his keen gaze said he understood why. The palace guards were men of Clan Manitar under Rumar's command. The City Guard belonged to the council, with its complex connections to the Legacy. She had put herself in the high chieftain's debt, and she might yet regret that, but it had saved her from being forced into the hands of Toren Abrigado.

She marched up the temple stairs with her Arionade and priestesses in a sober parade of white and grey. She didn't see Kaliska hurrying down against the flow until Evorales noted it.

Nemiah took one look at the healer's pale face and closed her eyes in denial. "Who? Who else have we lost?"

"No, not that." Kaliska halted on the stair. "A message arrived from Elders' Hall just after you left. Something important's happened. There's been a courier from the north. The high chieftain sent you something."

Something from the north. Nemiah rubbed a hand against her forehead, not daring to hope. "Perhaps there's been word about Sabela's temple. About the winds."

Kaliska's weary features didn't brighten. "It could be. Whatever it is, Rumar wanted it kept from prying eyes. He sent it with a kinsman not a council messenger."

"Very well. Show me."

Nemiah's acquiescence jumped along the Path like a fish jumping in a pool, rippling new possibilities into existence. She swayed with those ripples.

The healer frowned. "Lady? Are you well?"

"Fine. Fine. We've just made a significant decision on this Path." Nemiah ignored Kaliska's inquiring look. "Commander, I fear I must keep you from your rest a while longer."

Evorales bobbed his head. "My place is where you most need me, Lady."

A good man, Evorales. He would do his best to keep her safe. Rom might even have been wrong about his ability to lead. As Nemiah followed Kaliska into the temple and into her small receiving room, it finally struck her: the boundary that had been Rom's love would no longer be there to keep her intact or draw her back when she fell, not now or ever again. The secure chains of their oaths to one another had been snapped by his death. She was wide open now and as vulnerable as the temple itself.

"Here, Lady. No one has touched them since they arrived."

Kaliska gestured to a narrow box of polished wood and a sealed missive on one of the receiving room tables. Nemiah marched over to the box, grasped the latch, and pushed it open.

Kaliska and Evorales both gasped. The world swung. Nemiah clutched the table for support.

Oh, Leita.

Cradled upon a fold of soft cloth lay the dark beauty of Cael's Blade. Its black hilt and dangerous curve of steel absorbed the light of the room, making the weapon seem larger and denser than it should have been. Nemiah had believed she had gained a safe distance from the place in her spirit that belonged to Leita. This moment proved her terribly wrong. She snatched up the missive, cracked the seal, and read.

"What's happened? Where's the Bearer?" Kaliska looked as if she wanted to pull the letter from Nemiah's hands to read it.

Nemiah moved carefully, laying the letter down, drawing herself together, as if somehow she might change the Path that had already been woven. "Rumar says Clan Aglar sent men to Velantar on behalf of the northern five. Clanguard. The prefects of the northern five have requested a meeting with the council and the high chieftain to discuss certain grievances."

"I'm not certain what part of that statement is the most bizarre." Kaliska scowled. "Why were these grievances not raised in council?"

"Why did the request not come through the northerners' council elders?" Evorales added. "And what has this to do with the Bearer?"

Nemiah raised her hands to slow the barrage of questions. "Apparently, the five's elders have not appeared in council for some weeks. Rumar also says the northern prefects have reclaimed their titles as chieftains. They have declared it was never within his right to strip them of what Alende Isan gave to all the heads of the first-clans."

"And the Bearer?" Kaliska pressed.

Nemiah shook her head. "The messengers told Rumar that the Bearer's company was attacked by a pack of Verael. Clan Aglar provided the survivors with aid." She swallowed and forced herself to continue. "Reportedly, the Bearer offered the Blade as a sign of her gratitude and her support for the northerners' petition."

"Lies," Kaliska muttered.

Nemiah only nodded. She needn't say it. They all knew the Bearer of Cael's Blade would never willingly surrender the symbol of her authority. Either she was forced to it or she was dead. This one thing Nemiah did not doubt. Leita was bound to the Blade as she herself had been bound to Rom. Only death could break those chains.

Kaliska picked up the letter, her expression deeply considering. "If Prefect Aglar has in some way impeded Lieutenant Sevar's mission and harmed the Bearer, we are speaking of treason."

"Surely, he would never!" Evorales blurted, his horrified gaze darting from Kaliska to Nemiah. "It was a mission to stop the killing winds. Why would the north quarrel with that?"

"This isn't about the killing winds." Nemiah rested her eyes on the dark beauty of Cael's Blade, a symbol of disorder meant to be a warning. The northerners were closer to Riana's ways than most; they understood its purpose. "This has to do with an older anger. The north has been fighting Rumar since he took up his father's staff. This is a warning for us."

Kaliska glanced at the letter. "What does Rumar intend to do?"

"He and the rest of the council are going to meet with the prefects at Parnas Pass. The northerners refuse to meet in Velantar."

"Of course they do." Kaliska's tone dripped with disgust. "They won't hand Rumar another advantage."

Evorales turned to Nemiah. "What are *we* going to do, Lady?"

"We're going with Rumar. I must. The Bearer of Cael's Blade stands under Riana's protection and my own. I must find out what's happened to her."

Nemiah's words rang hollowly in her own ears. What protection had she given to her Arionade? Leita was gone. Amalia was gone. Arnas was gone. And Rom. She left off counting her losses. A spirit could only endure so much.

She sent Kaliska back to the infirmary and headed toward her tower with Evorales. The halls were uncomfortably empty. The women and girls had been restricted to their cells until more Arionade could return to duty. Once Nemiah had washed the scent of smoke from her skin, she would join Kaliska in the infirmary to visit the men still struggling there. They had lost brothers, but illness had denied them even the comfort of standing at the pyres. Nemiah glanced at Evorales, who coughed to cover a yawn. It had been two days since the man had seen a bed.

"Commander, once we reach the tower, you're relieved."

Evorales glanced at her, but the sound of running feet cut off his reply. A figure plunged around the corner of the dimly lit passageway and dashed toward them. Nemiah was tumbling into the stone wall before she even realized that Evorales had shoved her there. Steel rang in the hall as he drew his sword.

"Halt! Declare yourself if you value your life!"

Nemiah's breath caught as the figure drew closer and Rom's ghost, long-limbed and black-haired, flew toward her. Then the figure went wide-eyed with a very mortal look of shock and slid to a halt. He made an urgent spiral. "Commander! Lady Nemiah! Forgive me. It's Avjay."

"Goddess, man," Evorales growled, studying Avjay closely before sheathing his sword. "Don't ever do that again or I'll chop you into pieces and feed you to the hounds."

Nemiah pulled herself from the wall. "What is it?"

"She's here! The woman from the street. She's waiting to speak with you."

"The heretic? You mean the men caught her?"

"No, Lady. She came on her own. She's in the first circle."

Exhaustion dropped away from Nemiah and her blood pounded in her ears. "That demon-follower is in the high temple? In Riana's sanctuary?" She spun around and started back down the passage. "Come with me, Commander."

Evorales gasped. "Lady Nemiah, wait! If this is the woman responsible for the poisoning, you mustn't go near her!"

Nemiah did not wait. She hurried down the corridor, her shoes tapping on the stone, and entered the first circle behind the altar. The chamber looked empty. Before the massive granite of the altar, bare white walls swept up into graceful arches. From high above the entrance, Riana's eye threw blue and green shadows onto the stones. Then, tall and dark beside a column, one of the shadows moved, and Nemiah realized it was a cloaked figure. The two Arionade who guarded the exits tracked that tall figure like hounds on a deer. They had heard who the woman might be.

Nemiah strode through the center of the circle, Evorales at her back.

If Yarla felt any trepidation, she didn't reveal it. She looked Nemiah up and down, then smiled a little, her same contemptuous expression.

"Well, well, little mouse. You fooled us, didn't you? We never imagined the Lady of Avelos wandered the streets alone at night."

"Detain her," Nemiah ordered Evorales. "Then call for the City Guard."

"Really?" Yarla said, with infuriating calm. "For a small bruise and a scare in the dark you would have me arrested? You truly are constrained by order, aren't you? It will destroy you, you know."

Nemiah ignored the taunt. "Detain her for attacking Riana's temple and murdering four Arionade."

At last, surprise registered in the woman's eyes. "Ah, now *that's* an interesting conclusion." As the commander approached, Yarla stepped back and held up a hand. "No. No, I think not, Evorales. You see, I have your captain."

The commander froze. Nemiah drew a sharp breath.

Starlight reflected from the glossy black surface of the fountain's basin. The rich, fertile scent of blood filled her head. At her feet, a man in white lay pale and still.

Cael's followers had unholy uses for the blood of an Arionad.

"If you have defiled his body, I will curse you wherever Lord Arion's light falls!" Nemiah hissed.

Yarla offered a wicked smile. "I rather think he hasn't the energy to be defiled right now. Not that most of my women and some of my men haven't thought on it."

"What are you saying?"

"Your Captain Rom is alive, Nemiah Gabriana."

Hope could be a dangerous thing. Nemiah tried to gain control of her racing heart. "Impossible. The followers of Cael cannot abide the Arionade."

"Order serves you poorly once again," Yarla replied. "It makes you so anxious to label me. Yet the only label you have is 'Cael's follower.' That name places so many veils between your understanding and the truth of who I am that it would be better not to label me at all." Yarla reached into her cloak and pulled out a fold of beige cloth. She offered it to Nemiah. Evorales stopped her, his blade tapping her wrist.

"Open it yourself," he commanded. "If you make another move toward the Lady, you will lose your hand."

Unfazed, the woman opened the cloth. Inside was a lock of black hair. Nemiah realized that the cloth was not truly beige, but was stained. At one time, it had been white. It was almost certainly a piece torn from an Arionad's coat.

Heedless of the risk, Nemiah snatched up the lock of hair. It curled into a C on her palm. The black was shot with threads of silver. The coarse texture was familiar and dear. She brought it to her face and caught just the faintest scent of her Arionad. It was not proof he lived, but that they had him. And now they had her.

She glared up at the woman. "What do you want from us?"

"I only wish to speak with you. To offer my knowledge in exchange for some knowledge of your own." The bright-haired woman glanced disdainfully at Evorales. "Preferably without the threat of losing a limb."

"Commander, wait by the entrance with the others." Nemiah glanced at Yarla. "We will speak there." She indicated the step below Riana's altar.

Yarla gave a short laugh, strode up to the altar, and sank down directly in the blue-green shadows of Riana's eye. "The goddess's sacred spaces do not unsettle me, Lady. She too has her role."

"If you're not one of Cael's, then who are you?" Nemiah remained standing beside the step.

"Soon," Yarla said. "Tell me, have you learned who poisoned your Arionade?"

Blunt, demanding, and arrogant. Nemiah bit the edge of her lip to bridle her anger. Her heart lay vulnerable in this woman's hands now. "I believe it to be someone among Cael's disciples. They've been stirring in the city. We discovered an attempt at creating a Mirror of Night.

"Yes, yes, my people know about that. The cults are taking advantage of the chaos in the lower circles, but they're disorganized and have no competent leaders. They're more like petty thugs than the bloodthirsty packs of Lady Pahlina's time."

Nemiah made a sound of surprise. "How do you——?"

"Know anything of temple history? I've heard Storytellers with decades of lore, and read more history than you even know exists, Lady. It wasn't Cael's cults who attacked you."

"You've not yet told me that you and your people are not responsible."

"Don't be foolish!" Yarla's outcry made Evorales take a step across the room. Nemiah shook her head at him. "We are not responsible for harming any of Riana's servants, though you are foolish and unbending." The woman lifted both hands. "Does the winter begrudge the spring? Would the left hand cut off the right?"

"Then tell me now what you are."

"So, you need a label even to have this conversation?" Yarla blew out another breath. "Very well. We seek no name for ourselves, but I suppose you might call us the Ones Who Remember or the Healers of the Broken. We are the ones who know of that which came before Lady Riana and Lord Cael." As she spoke, some of her hardness slid away and her eyes shone as clear and blue as an alpine lake. "What was split asunder must be merged again, for only in the merging will we avert True Chaos."

Terrifying words. Terrifying because they reached toward a time and a perspective that the priestesses of Riana had never been able to see—that time before the goddess. Terrifying because Nemiah heard something familiar in their rhythm, though she couldn't remember from where it came. One of Zia's songs? The map notes? Yes. The pieces came back to her.

For Cael looks back to the Beginning, and thus is the reason for all Creation. Riana looks forward to the End and the return to all Order. It is True Chaos that awaits if the light and dark do not reconcile. In the merging will we find True Balance.

It was heresy.

"You dare to set Cael as an equal beside Riana? You would bring the demon out of darkness and worship him as one of a . . . a holy dyad?"

"No," Yarla answered. "My people see farther than that. Cael and Riana are not twins or consorts to rule beside one another. Not as the Amurians say of the seas and the land or the ancient Laebeki said of the sun and the moon. Riana and Cael have little import alone. They are merely segments of a greater deity, the Unbroken One, who was sacrificed so that the light and the darkness might exist."

Nemiah pressed her fingers against her forehead. "Why have you taken Rom? Why have you come with teachings I cannot accept?"

"We did not *take* your captain. Two of our number followed him from the high temple into the lower circles. They saw him fall from his horse. They might have left him to die, but instead they carried him to one of our shelters and brought a healer."

Nemiah stared. "How long have you been following my people?"

"Ah. I see gratitude is not permitted of the Chosen Lady."

"You've not yet proved I have reason to be grateful. Tell me the rest of this heresy."

"Can you not see the truth for yourself? The infinite weaving cannot continue to exist while Cael and Riana remain divided. Since the moment the Unbroken One was sundered, we have been traveling toward True Chaos. Now it looms close. I know you have felt the Paths writhing beneath you. The Bearer has tried to warn you of it."

"I feel them. I could not say what it means."

Yarla sighed, a softer note in her voice. "I suppose it's too much to expect that you'll believe what I'm telling you. If your loyalty is half that of the Arionad bound to you, you'll not find it easy to accept that the goddess must be destroyed in order to save her weaving."

"No. It is not something I accept. Riana has battled Cael for the sake of order since the first dawn. Battled and survived."

"Very well then, don't accept. Hold tight to the beliefs that comfort you, like a blanket or a favorite toy. That's what a child does when she's scared of the dark, isn't it?"

Nemiah pressed her lips together. "Why weren't you overwhelmed? Out on the street when I called on the goddess's power? You should have been drowned in sorrow."

"I told you why. Riana is a broken thing."

"Ah, Lady." Nemiah squeezed her eyes closed, then opened them. She didn't accept. This was heresy. Still, she couldn't deny that Yarla dealt with significant power. She must try to understand. "Continue. I'm listening."

"Listening is not the same as hearing."

Nemiah only glared.

Yarla began again. "Ancient writings of Avelos are being stolen from temple libraries and private collections. We fear those responsible seek True Chaos. If you were wise, Lady, you would fear it too. Those who hunger for True Chaos shape despair as Cael's followers could not do in their grimmest nightmares. We fear the thieves are searching for the means to prevent us from reaching True Balance. And without True Balance, the weaving will tear itself apart. Every Path will be flung into blackness."

"Who are they? The thieves?"

Yarla shivered, the first hint of apprehension she had revealed. "We don't know for certain. Some of us think they are the unbound."

The woman's spies truly were exceptional. Few even knew the unbound existed. Then again, an unbound man had tried to kill the Bearer before she left the city, and the Bearer was working with the heretics. An ache arose in Nemiah's heart that she couldn't address now. She must focus on this new thing: ancient writings had been stolen. She already knew something about that.

"My people discovered that Clan Aglar is providing stolen books to the guard of Clan Amerre. Do you know of it?"

Yarla's expression altered. She had not known.

"What does it mean?" Nemiah asked.

The other woman sat frowning for a long, thoughtful stretch. "The north giving secrets to the south? I don't know. It may mean the clans themselves are making evil choices, or perhaps it only means some resourceful smuggler has found a collector interested in the histories. It's worth exploring, I suppose. I'll bring it to the others."

"Others?" Something in Yarla's tone sparked a disturbing thought. "How many people believe in your . . . Unbroken One? Are there elders among you? Prefects?"

"Elders are only men, as capable of choosing the truth as any other." Yarla shook her head dismissively. "That's not where your concern should lie. I must know, Lady, what did the attackers steal from your archive?"

"Steal? We've found no reason to suspect the attackers had any purpose but murder. I've not been in the archive since the attack. I doubt anyone has."

Yarla came to her feet. "Take me there. We must find out."

Nemiah hesitated.

"By light and darkness!" the woman cried. "Bring the whole contingent of your Arionade if you doubt my intentions, but *please*, let us look!"

"If I do this for you," Nemiah said, "you must release Captain Rom."

"Of course! Of course, we will. When he is well enough to move."

"If you'll not release him now, then you must let me see him. Today."

Yarla narrowed her eyes, as though in deliberation. After a moment, she shook her head. "I cannot."

The woman's need to see the archive was evident in every line of her expression. Nemiah had not expected refusal. "You lie, then. He is dead."

"So much doubt in Riana's Lady," Yarla said with irony. "I will not allow you to see him because his spirit is bound to yours. Close as he walks toward the Hidden Paths, he would still rather risk death at your side than allow himself to heal. If he were to see you now, he would only fight us the more. I fear he would not survive it."

Nemiah wanted to argue that her presence would reassure and calm her Arionad, but somehow Yarla had guessed the truth of him. "Very well. I won't insist on seeing him, but I must have more than words to prove he's alive."

"Yes, yes. Let your healer come to him. She can best judge his condition, and he will trust what she tells him of you."

"Good then. She will go with you when you leave the temple."

"Yes, she can go with me." Yarla smiled slightly, smoothing her sharp edges a little. "You are stouter than I've credited you, Lady Nemiah. Come. We must check the archive."

Nemiah signaled to Commander Evorales and the three of them walked in silence through the sanctuary. For the first time in Nemiah's memory, no Arionad stood watch at the archive's entrance. She hurried inside, Yarla striding behind her. Evorales carried a lamp.

Murmuring a prayer, Nemiah scanned the open shelves, trailing her fingers gently along the aged leather bindings lined up one after another. Old friends, these. She had known them for years. None were missing. Evorales pulled open cabinets and slid out drawers.

"All is well here," he reported.

Nemiah let out a breath in relief.

Yarla stepped up to the shelves, frowning over the titles. "Morican? Anarava? Iradios? Where are the important writings? Where are your ancient works?"

"That Morican volume is older than Tumal the Just," Evorales said indignantly.

"This is what we have," Nemiah said.

Yarla lifted one slender volume between two fingers, staring at it scornfully. "I suppose I never quite believed the Bearer when she told me no power remained here. It's no wonder nothing was taken."

"Do not mock us!" Nemiah yanked the volume out of Yarla's hand, a book of poems she had loved as a girl. "Tumal destroyed more than vellum and history in the purges. The blood of priestesses and Arionade has watered these stones."

"Lady?" Evorales jerked his head toward the entrance to the map room. The door was unsealed.

Nemiah swallowed, brushed past Yarla, and shoved the map room door inward on silent hinges. A chill crept out and wound around her ankles.

"Commander, the lamp please."

Pale light writhed across the stone floor, the massive oak table in the center of the room, and the bank of open cupboards. Nemiah lifted her eyes to where the maps belonged in the cupboards, to where their rolled ends should poke out to create little hills of circles. Dark emptiness glared back at her.

Emptiness. Nemiah felt it like a yawning pit inside her chest. She hurried to the cupboards, sliding her arm into the closest of them. Every sacred journey since the purges had been stored here. She covered her mouth with both hands. Two scrolls had rolled into a corner. Two out of dozens. Another, partially opened, lay discarded on the table.

Nemiah ran to the far end of the room, to the oak and iron trunk. The oldest treasures had hidden there, the map notes from before the Exile War. Dust puffed up as she shoved open the lid. Only a decaying leather bag remained at the bottom of the trunk.

Even the most recent maps of her journeys with Lia. Gone.

Nemiah felt untethered, as light as a dead leaf. She grasped the edge of the great table and sank onto the bench to keep from blowing away.

The sacred maps were the taproot of the temple, connecting each Pathwalker's journey to the infinite weaving and feeding Riana's servants with the knowledge of where they belonged in the world. The maps offered the truest picture of where Avelos fit in relation to the goddess's complex weaving; not only where Avelos fit, but where the temple fit, where Nemiah herself fit.

"It would have taken planning and effort for this," she said hoarsely. "There was so much to carry. They poisoned the Arionade so they could slip in and out of the temple. They needed to be sure Arnas would not be on watch that night. They needed him dead."

Beneath the table, her foot bumped a scroll that had escaped the theft. She bent over and scooped it up. It was of no particular note: one of Lady Pahlina's journeys, a short one, with only Perspective and Place identified. Nemiah clutched it to her chest.

"Evorales, see this room sealed. Speak of it to no one."

"Yes, Lady," the Arionad said, subdued.

"This will kill Bena. Her life's work and more." Nemiah drew a strangled breath. "Ah, Goddess, where have you left us? If we had little guidance before, we have none now."

"Tell me! What is it that's lost?" Yarla demanded.

Nemiah met the woman's gaze. "Everything."

<h1 style="text-align:center">23.</h1>

GREY FEATHER FIND YOU

The sound of singing resonated against the walls.

When Jhared had been small and the nightmares woke him, his mother's songs had slowed his dream-falls and provided a safe space to land. The voice he heard now offered no comfort. It was raw, an open wound. It competed with the howl of the killing winds, singing the despair of Alende Isan when he looked upon the destruction of Altan Mar.

Gradually, Jhared realized that he was the one singing. He stopped and forced himself to awareness of his surroundings. He smelled fresh grass, mint, and burning wood. Beneath him was something much softer than stone. He tried to stretch out a hand to learn what it was, and felt rope tug at his wrists. His hands were bound. He shifted and discovered that his sword was gone. With a surge of dismay, he rolled and lurched upright, pushing to his feet.

"*Shifa!*" the woman cried out. "You don't want to do that—"

His knees folded like soft wax. Darkness crowded the corners of his vision. He found himself once again on the cavern floor. He struggled to rise, panting with the effort. "What . . . have you done to me?"

"Calm yourself," she said wryly. "Another maneuver like that and you'll bash your head open on the stone. Look at your hands."

He did. The filthy bandages had been removed, exposing swollen, angry flesh. Red streaks bullied up his forearm from where the Verael had bitten him. Each of the wounds had been cleaned and a cool, greasy ointment that smelled of green grass coated the burns.

"I bound you to keep you from scraping your hands against the rocks while you slept." She rose and crossed the cavern to him. "It looks as if you chose a fire demon and a wolf for your dance partners, and you've a wicked fever to go with that festered bite. The weakness, however, is mostly the fault of the Silvaye."

Silvaye. Riana's Chosen in the hands of an Avelun? He frowned. "Why are you doing this?"

"You ask a lot of questions for a dying man." She knelt beside him and reached for the rope.

"I've been told that," he muttered. She smelled of berries and dust. As she worked at the knot, he noticed her hands were as callused as a soldier's. "Why are you helping a Forest Guard?"

"Well, if you'd been a cabrin or a hare and dropped at my feet so, I could have made a meal of you. As you're not any creature nearly so useful . . ." She shrugged, a sinuous movement that involved her shoulders and her wings. "Maybe I've seen enough dead bodies not to want to deal with yours."

She slipped the rope free, careful not to drag it across his injuries. Her eyes said her words were truthful, but the tension in her voice suggested they were a partial truth. She wanted something from him. She was Avelun; it was her nature to desire and take.

"My sword?" he asked.

She gestured to a large leather pack on the other side of the cavern. Beside it lay a staff of glossy black wood, a lovely longbow, and a full quiver. Peeking out of the pack was one edge of his scabbard. "I think I'll just keep that until I can see what you've decided about trying to kill me."

His mouth opened. Had she somehow heard his Teachers' command? "Lady, you've given me shelter. I don't intend—"

"Stop. You're a soldier. I am the bane of Avelos. You'll have to decide whether to do your duty. I've no intention of dying when you do."

Her candor shocked him, but he couldn't deny anything she said. "Understood, Lady."

"Stop calling me 'lady.' I'm no priestess, and I've no use for Riana's servants."

Avelun. How was it even possible such a creature existed? She had donned her cloak, but now that he knew what she concealed, the intriguing contour curving over her shoulders and tapering down her back was unmistakable. He tried to remember the glimpse he had seen: sleek feathers the color of ashes; powerful wings that could lift a body over the mountain heights. He hoped and dreaded he might catch another look. "Who *are* you?"

"My name is Mayavana, but I don't think that's what you're asking. Is it, Jhared Denaban?"

"Mayavana. How do you know my name?"

"You introduced yourself in some detail before you started singing."

Jhared felt the heat rise in his face. "Oh."

"Silvien is more of a trickster than most credit her. She speeds healing, but only by sapping your own strength to do it." The Avelun smiled a little. "I imagine she enjoys the stories men tell once she's stolen their defenses."

Jhared lifted a hand to rub it across his face, remembered the greasy ointment and thought better of it. "What else did I say?"

"Do you truly want to know?"

Her tone was gentle. Was she offering him pity? "Yes. I do."

"You said you are beloved by Cael, and no one who stands beside you is safe. That someone named Tavia is dead, and probably Ziabela as well. That you abandoned Leita to the whims of a wicked man and left your comrades to face the enemy alone. I could understand why a man might run away after all that."

Jhared swallowed. "I'm not running away. I didn't want to leave them. I have orders to reach Velantar. If not for the winds . . ." He stopped. What did he think he was doing blurting out his mission? It must be the Silvaye. "Did I say more?"

She tilted her head with a familiar thoughtful expression that did something to Jhared's insides. "Yes," she said finally. "You said you know me."

"Oh yes, we know it," growled the Boar. *"The demon. The cursed. An Avelun who escaped reparation."*

"Why haven't you done away with it?" Shrill cried.

"Leave me be!"

The woman recoiled a step. "Whoa, soldier. You asked."

Jhared looked up. He was losing track of which voices were inside his head and which were outside. "Not you. It was just . . . not you."

His Teachers groused and fumed. Jhared ignored them and tried to keep his attention outside of himself. Inside, there was too much confusion to manage.

"Gods of seas and skies, what an odd creature has come to my fire." The woman shook her head. She added a log to the flames from a small pile against the wall. The charms dangling from her wrist clinked and danced in the golden light. Jhared saw a wolf, a tree, and a vine—symbols of the Aye, he realized—but he also glimpsed a heron, an owl, and a calf. He wondered at their significance.

The cave was clearly more to the woman than fortuitous shelter from the winds. In addition to the store of wood, a small shelf held several large jugs. Where he had been sleeping lay a pile of skins scented with dried herbs. Another such bed lay on her side of the fire. Farther back in the cavern was a necessary pot.

"This cave is home to you?" he asked.

"Home? In this wretched country?" She blew out a breath. "Not likely. It's just a space to sleep when I pass through. I was damned lucky to be close when the winds struck. I planned to hole up at dawn anyway." She looked toward the tunnel where the storm moaned, and shook her wrist, jingling the charms like a warding sign. "Evil work for an evil land," she muttered.

Jhared didn't much like her outlook. "You've seen the winds before?"

"Once. In the south. A close call, that one. I didn't think they had reached this far north or I wouldn't have lingered."

"They hadn't reached the north," he said. A breeze whined through the crevices in the ceiling, swirling the smoke into a funnel. Jhared shivered. "My company was searching for a way to stop them."

"Was?"

He nodded. Somewhere within him, blue flames crackled. He wasn't sure that enough of him remained in the moment to keep from falling through the Gate again.

The Avelun reached for a jug and a small cooking pot. "Will you drink something? It will help to drive the fever off."

He nodded once more and leaned back against the pile of skins to see if he could keep his head where it should be.

She heated water in the little pot, then drew out a red wooden box from her pack. She pondered herbs from different drawers in the box, then added pinches from three different compartments to the water. When it had steeped, she crossed the chamber to offer Jhared a brimming mug. He sniffed it: some type of mint and two herbs that were foreign to him. He watched her, waiting.

She caught his look. "Ah, I see. Wouldn't it be just like the Avelun to use poison when a blade would suffice?" She sighed and sipped from her own mug.

He followed her lead. The tea had a tart-sweet taste that wasn't unpleasant, much better than Kaliska's restoratives. In a few minutes, he began to feel a little more substantial. "You haven't yet told me what you're doing in Avelos."

She shrugged. "Buying secrets. Summoning the winds. Causing chaos wherever I may."

The fascinating motion of her wings beneath her cloak was almost enough to distract Jhared from her sarcasm. Almost.

She met his gaze unflinching. "Well, that's what you expect, isn't it? What you're hoping to hear to keep everything in your world in its proper order."

"Nothing in my world has been in order for some time," he answered. If he were honest, the collapse had started as far back as Velantar, when he had tried to kill a man and the Bearer had saved his life. Since then, the beliefs he held about himself and the world had cracked, like a bad foundation under an unsteady building. He had become caelevano, been declared a deserter, and allowed Leita to send him onto the forbidden Paths. His patrol had been attacked by demons and the northern clans had betrayed Avelos. Perhaps order didn't exist at all. Perhaps it was no more than a wishful thought men imposed on the world in a desperate attempt to win some sense of control over their lives.

"Ah, there's a fine excuse," Shrill said in disgust. *"Throw away order and you no longer have reason even to try to do your duty or follow the laws."*

Jhared pressed two fingers against his temple. The Avelun was watching him and nibbling the corner of her lip. While he slept, she had scrubbed the dirt from her face and brushed her hair into a tail. Her features were too severe to be beautiful, but they captivated him. The complex expressions shifting there were familiar in a way they shouldn't have been.

"I'm a guide," she said eventually. "I lead travelers across Avelos."

Something inside him twisted. "You mean you're a smuggler."

"If the people I lead carry goods for their own profit that's their business. I have no part in it. I know the wilds and I know how to cross these lands quickly. That's what I'm paid for."

"Where do they come from, these travelers? Laebek? Amuria?"

"Some of them. Yes."

Jhared groaned. "Ah, Goddess. Sahiste? You're leading Sahistens into Avelos?"

"They're not here for trouble," she snapped. "They're here for profit. And most want to get out as fast as possible, believe me." She drew the edges of her cloak more closely around her. "You needn't fear, soldier. No army of strangers is pouring in to threaten your way of life."

Jhared opened his mouth to retort, but when he glanced at her, a wave of loneliness took him. He thought of his mother, long dead, and the father he had never known who refused to claim him. He thought of Tierzen and Sarena and their fine home in the Elder's circle. In so many ways, he was a stranger even to those who raised him. The Avelun's eyes gleamed, a reflection of his loneliness. Abruptly, he realized he was staring at her; he looked away.

"You're between trips, then?" he said more tentatively.

She peered at the bottom of her mug and poured herself more tea. "No. I'm done for the season. Snow will be filling the passes soon. I'm heading south, to someplace where the winds aren't bent on blowing every tree and village into the sea."

"Sahiste?"

"Eeee, gods, no. I'm no high desert creature. I need the touch of water." She fingered the heron charm on her bracelet.

In an unbidden memory, Jhared saw a girl running beside a moonlit lake and silver light kissing bare skin. He coughed and hid his face behind another swallow of tea. He thought to ask where she had come from and how she had escaped what she owed, but he wasn't certain he wanted to hear it.

She reached into her pack and brought out a sack of dried apples and sticks of what looked to be salted meat. "You might try some food," she suggested, taking a bite of one of the sticks before tossing it to him. "Silvien will burn away your flesh in her eagerness to heal you."

He caught the stick in his left hand, and was acutely reminded of the way his shoulder had connected with rock when the horse threw him. "I . . . thank you."

She offered him a handful of apples, laughing. "You needn't sound so apprehensive, soldier. I don't require blood or flesh in payment."

"Nevertheless, I cover my debts."

The stick turned out to be some kind of dried fish and not particularly appetizing, but he was famished. When he had subdued the worst of his hunger, he tried flexing his shoulder to assess the extent of the injury. With his right hand, he reached around to feel the joint and blade. His fingers encountered the lumpy weal of his scarred flesh, and he winced.

"That looks painful."

He turned to find her watching him again, her expression reflective. "It's not broken," he answered, pulling his hand away.

"You're one of the Shorn, aren't you?" she murmured. "You've been—"

"Yes!" he said quickly. "I've balanced that part of the debt."

"Ah." She shuddered and tugged her cloak around her wings. "Well, I have ointments for bruised joints. If you let me look at your shoulder."

"No." He was mortified by the thought she might see his shame. "It is well enough."

"As you wish." Her tone remained neutral, but a tightness settled over her features that hadn't been visible before. She grew quiet. Jhared supposed he had disgusted her with the idea of his scars. He finished his food without speaking, listening to the winds cry and flail against the mountain.

The Avelun ate her own meal, then rose and dragged several skins and blankets closer to the fire, shaping a small bed. She curled onto her side and propped her head on her pack. With one hand, she toyed with a small leather pouch that dangled from a cord around her neck. Jhared's gaze followed the cord along the contours of deep muscle in her shoulders and chest. While he looked at her, he had the sense she was studying him. Even when her eyes weren't on him, she had an animal watchfulness that suggested she was aware of him.

Eventually, she tucked the mass of her wings around her shoulders, pulled the blankets over her, and closed her eyes. Jhared looked toward where his scabbard stuck out from her pack. Even if he could slip it away, he had nowhere to run. The winds would beat him down before he took ten steps. He must restrain his impatience and use this time to gather his strength. It was a long way to Velantar. He thought of Leita, recalling her calm smile before she turned to face Commander Ciam. *"Keep to your own Path,"* she had begged. The memory made Jhared's chest ache; he hadn't even been able to do that. He drew up his knees and dropped his head onto his arms. "Riana, shelter your lady."

Silvien soon had her way with him, tugging him into dreams. Leita turned toward danger and he could never reach her; men beat him in the street and left him helpless; a Verael laughed and called him "Brother." He startled awake, panting from a wild struggle with a beast he couldn't see. He wiped cold sweat from his face and surveyed the cave in the red-gold light of embers. The winds still growled and moaned outside. He crept over and placed another log into the hot center of the coals.

The woman sighed in her sleep. He looked over to where she lay with her head pillowed on her arm. Her blanket had slid away, exposing one glorious wing to the firelight. Jhared's eyes traveled along the entire tempting curve of feathers, from her shoulders to her ankles. The wings were not an even grey, as he had thought, but ran from pale to dark, with covert feathers of the finest frost, secondaries the color of storms, and primaries that ended in the black of a moonless night.

Jhared crept closer until he was crouched beside her. He had to look. Her long, strong flight feathers lay lustrous and smooth, all in perfect order. Faint black speckles were scattered across the grey of her covert feathers. His hand twitched forward of its own accord, fingers aching to know the feel of the wing. What were they like, those feathers? Warm and soft? Or firm and cool, a thin cover over muscle and bone? His hand trembled with his daring and his need. He stretched. Just a little closer and he could slide a finger over a covert feather. He was so near now he could feel the warmth rising from her body. He inched forward again, his heart pounding. His straining fingers brushed softness—

A gust of wind screeched through the tunnel. The Avelun stirred. Jhared snatched his hand away and stumbled backward. He hunched in the corner, confusion and shame holding him fast. Moments passed. The woman settled her wings around herself and let out a long, deep breath. Finally, Jhared retreated to his side of the fire and sank down against the wall.

"Ah, Cael," he muttered.

He wasn't certain whether he meant it as a curse or a confirmation.

The second time he awoke, it was the silence that stirred him. Quiet filled the cavern. He sat up and looked around. The Avelun was gone.

"Lady?"

No answer. Jhared flexed the fingers of his left hand experimentally. They were less swollen, but remained hot and stiff. Silvien had done what she could. He wondered what it had cost him. Cautiously, he tried standing. Black bees swarmed in his vision and whined in his ears. He gripped the wall, determined not to go down. The winds had stilled. He must be on his way to Velantar.

"Lady?" he called again. "Mayavana?"

Nothing. On the other side of the cavern, her pack lay half open. He could see his sword sticking out from among her belongings. Slowly, he made his way across the space. He wrapped his hands around his scabbard, dismayed by the effort it required to heft the familiar weight. As the weapon slid free, two cloth bundles escaped from the pack and tumbled to the ground. He set aside the sword and scooped up the smaller of the bundles.

His hands sank into the softest wool he had ever touched. Lush folds of it dripped through his fingers. It was a long scarf knitted from a yarn of such intense colors they could compete with the best of Valador dyes. Pale lavenders shifted to deep purples, then slid gradually from every shade of aqua to rich teal. The colors might have been stolen from a starling's wing or the gleam of a raven—offering all the colors of the sun on feathers. Worked down the center of the scarf was a pattern of interlocked feathers. He ran his fingers over them, wondering if it had been a gift or something the woman created herself. The scarf smelled faintly of autumn berries. Her scent. Quickly, he shoved it back into the bag.

The second bundle was a small rectangular shape wrapped in undyed wool. As he lifted it, the cloth slipped a little, exposing one silver edge. He pulled the rest of the cover away. In his hand sat a box crafted of silver with a small stone owl inlaid in the top. The owl's outstretched wings were formed of iridescent white shell. Lapis served for its wide eyes. Jhared had never seen such silver work. Two tiny clasps the shape of the owl's talons curved over the lid. He rubbed his thumbs over the clasps, curious what lay inside.

He was trampling boundaries, disregarding the kindness she had done him. For a moment, he hesitated. Then he remembered the unremorseful look on her face when she told him that she led Sahistens into Avelos, and he pushed open the lid.

Inside, on a lining of dark velvet, lay three feathers, each a different color and size, bound together with grey silk ribbon, as a mother might bind locks of her child's hair. The smallest feather was a bit of cream-colored down that fluttered under Jhared's breath. The longest feather was tapered and glossy, shifting from deep grey to black, the color of one of the Avelun's flight feathers. Given to a man with the right invocations, it would serve for a grey feather curse. It wasn't the curse that caused Jhared's heart to pound, however. It was the last feather: a short, rounded plume a lovely shade of sand with fine black speckles.

Jhared sagged to his knees as blue flames flared up in the darkness and grasped for his spirit.

A man stirred soup over the hearth, while a young woman sorted herbs and healer's supplies into the drawers of a red box. Ruddy firelight and thick rugs made the room cozy, even though the floor was only packed earth. With a warm smile, the woman glanced to where a toddler played at her feet. Small, perfect feathers lay against the child's shoulders.

The door burst open and four guards in white coats crashed into the room. The child gave a startled yelp. The man grabbed a knife from the hearth.

"*Shifa!*" someone cried in dismay.

A sharp blow reverberated from Jhared's shoulder across his drifting spirit and through the fog surrounding him. The vision burst into gleaming particles. Jhared tumbled from the Path and landed on the ground, his eyes level with the Avelun's boots.

"Thief! *Mus'nilor!* I should have known that even a soldier who can barely stand would still be a heartless treasure stealer."

The woman's staff whistled through the air. Jhared grunted as it smacked his left shoulder a second time.

"Enough!" He rolled onto his back and showing his empty palms. "I wasn't stealing."

She clutched her staff in a two-handed grip, one end under his chin in such a way that one good thrust would crush his throat. "Why do you lie when I've caught you at it? I may have been a fool for wasting my Silvaye on you, but I'll not be fooled again."

Every line of her was drawn with fury, but when her gaze met his, Jhared flinched at the weight of sadness that struck him. *A sand-colored, black-speckled feather floated to the ground beside a man in a pool of blood.*

"I'm sorry," he gasped. "I only wanted my sword. Then I saw the box, and it was beautiful. I didn't intend to steal it. I just wanted to know . . . . Let me go and I'll be out of your way. I must get to Velantar."

The end of the staff bumped his chin. "You wanted to know what?" she growled.

He couldn't afford to die here, and what he had seen was so unlikely she would probably think it another lie, but the image of a slain man and a small feather compelled him. "Where you came from." He sighed. "You truly are a child of Avelos."

"I consider myself a child of Avelos no more than a child of the moon," she said, but her eyes said he had touched something genuine.

He took a chance and slid out from under her staff, keeping his palms up. She allowed it. "The feathers in the box. They're yours, aren't they? At different ages?"

A muscle tightened in her jaw. "That can mean nothing to you."

"It means you came from Clan Valador. Not far from Brenia, I think. Your family must have thought their small cottage well hidden." He looked down at his hands then back to her face. "It wasn't hidden well enough."

Her breath caught, and the staff wavered. "How do you dare to tell my story? You're a soldier. A Forest Guard. Had you the strength and a company of men, you'd see me nailed to a tree."

Jhared had no good answer. If he had been faithful to his oath, he would have done as his Teachers demanded and killed her, but his Path no longer moved with any kind of order. Leita had warned him that the infinite weaving was unraveling. Perhaps he must cling to the threads dangling before him to keep from falling.

He took a deep breath. "I found a ruined cottage in the woods outside Brenia. I saw a child from another Path. An Avelun child, with wings of sand and black, living with her family."

The woman was staring at him, her eyes round. She didn't stop him, so he went on. "The Arionade came for the child. I don't know what happened to her or her mother, but the man with her was slain."

"What did he look like, the man?"

Jhared thought back to his journey. "In his prime. Dark-haired. Black-eyed. Slender. Not the build of a woodsman or farmer. Maybe a tradesman. When the guards came, he was cooking—"

"Blue bean soup," she said hoarsely. "Gods of seas and skies." She turned away and bent to retrieve the silver box from where Jhared had dropped it. She held up the feathers, examining them, before stowing them in the box. With one finger, she caressed the stone owl. Jhared couldn't see her face.

He climbed to his feet. "Was he your father?"

"My uncle." Her head was bowed over the box, her staff discarded several feet away. Jhared could snatch up his sword and flee. He was nearly certain she would let him. He didn't move.

"I barely remember him," she went on, "but my mother saw to it I would never forget the story. Uncle held off the Arionade long enough for us to reach friends. They helped us escape to Sona. She never knew for certain what had happened to her brother."

She had escaped the country, escaped the debt, and escaped the knife. A man had died to help her do it.

The silver box disappeared into her bag and she turned to face Jhared. "You're a Traveler," she said with a tone of wonder. "I thought . . . I thought I'd only imagined it. You journey through others' stories."

"I'm nothing so balanced. My spirit sometimes tumbles from my own Path into places it shouldn't."

"*Shifa*," she murmured. "I didn't know the Shorn were permitted to touch the Paths. What teachers allowed you such recklessness?"

He gave a pained laugh. "We're not permitted. If someone had guessed what I was, I wouldn't have lived long enough to reach the Becoming. The one person who dared to tell me about Pathwalkers found me a poor student." He thought of Leita and his heart turned over. What was happening to her in Ciam's custody? He leaned down to grab his sword.

Feathers rustled as the Avelun stiffened. Her staff lay out of her reach on his far side. He shifted to pluck it up and hand it to her before reaching once more for his blade. Surprise showed in her grey-green gaze.

Just how many times had he met that gaze on the Paths? She was a creature who shouldn't exist. The incarnation of corruption. So why did the thought of walking away from her make it difficult to breathe?

"Because she's bound you," Shrill told him. *"We tried to warn you, but you seem to think yourself beyond need of your Teachers' guidance."*

"I have to be moving," he said aloud. "I've already lost a day. You've given me my life. I owe you the same."

The Avelun shook her head. "Your fever has cost you two days, I'm afraid. The winds ended yesterday evening, and the sun is already sinking." She looked him up and down. "You know you'll never make it to Velantar alone."

His lip twisted. He had poured out his failures to her in the grip of the Silvaye. He imagined what she must be thinking: He was Shorn. Broken. A soldier who abandoned his duties and left his comrades in trouble. "Well, then it's good you have no stake in my success."

"No, what I meant is that you're still healing, and the Silvaye has taken her toll. You have no provisions and no mount. The winds have left the pass a mess. Just getting out of the mountains will be a trial."

"Do you *wish* my failure?" he asked. "Is that what this is about?"

"No," she said again, sighing. Under her cloak, her feathers rustled once more. "We're traveling in the same direction. You could . . . journey with me."

Here it was then: the reason she had spent her time and resources caring for a Shorn soldier. Jhared frowned at her. "There's nothing I can do for you. I might be a useless soldier, but I'm not so far gone as to betray Avelos."

"*Do* for me?" Her black brows lifted, and she uttered an artless laugh. "You still think I have some dark designs upon this country? Perhaps I'm trying to subvert the Forest Guard one soldier at a time, eh?"

In fact, he hadn't decided that she wasn't a spy. "If there's nothing you want, why would you travel with me?"

She shrugged a shoulder. "I don't know. Perhaps because it's a long, dull trek to the south. Or maybe because I've never known one of the Shorn, and when it comes to it, I am as foolish as my mother accused me of being."

Jhared had grown accustomed to conversations with Leita in which he had to plead for every explanation, and in the end, was left feeling like an insignificant piece in her secret game. The Avelun's apparent frankness was a relief.

In the face of his silence, her expression faltered and a flush rose to her almond skin. "Never mind. It *was* a foolish thought," she said. "I'm the bane of Avelos. I've no wish to tempt your sword to my throat."

She was a creature who should not have existed, yet she did: a single surviving Avelun in the country that cursed her. They shared a common history and tainted blood. He wondered what stories she knew of their ancestors. What could she tell him of the scent of the air over the mountains and the sensation of soaring into the clouds?

"Wait," he heard himself say.

She looked at him dubiously.

"I just didn't expect that. You're right. I have nothing."

"Don't mistake me," she said, narrowing her eyes. "I won't be your trophy for the Forest Guard to raise you from disgrace."

He shook his head quickly. "The truth is I can't afford to shun any aid. I must reach the city."

She stared at him, then with one hand, reached around her body and under her cloak. Jhared saw her tug gently. She withdrew her fingers holding a small, oblong feather the color of cracked ice. "Hold out your hand," she told him.

He hesitated. With the grey feather, she could curse him to wander the undefined twilight beyond the Paths, forever out of reach of the Pathguides. Still, he had spoken truly: he did need her help, and he had just claimed that he was willing to trust her. He offered his hand. She set the feather into his palm.

"I gift you with this heart feather as a pledge you may sleep safely by my fire," she said solemnly.

As he closed his fist around the feather, the soft vanes tickled his fingers. He searched for the right words to answer her gift without binding himself to another promise he couldn't keep. "I accept the debt of your hospitality. So long as we share a fire, I will not lift my hand against you."

The words seemed to please her well enough. She smiled a little, then ruffled her wings and let them settle around her shoulders. Jhared's ruined muscles twitched in pathetic imitation.

"I must warn you: I only travel at night and I don't follow the roads."

"That suits me," he replied, slipping the feather into his belt pouch. Now that the storm had abated, he had to assume that Ciam's clanguards were hunting for him.

She gave him a curious look, but didn't ask the question he saw in her eyes. "Well, if you've the strength for it, we should make the most of the dark and set out."

"Let's go." As he buckled his sword belt, heat surged in his blood that wasn't entirely due to his fever.

"Undisciplined beast," his Teachers spat as he followed her. *"You'll not be so smug when she leads you off a cliff."*

24.

THIEVES AND HEALERS

Each time Jhared walked amidst the silent wreckage of the killing winds, he felt as though the world had taken its final breath, ending every living creature but himself. It was the perception of isolation more than the broken trees and the landslides that left a lonely ache in his gut.

"I hate the stillness," the Avelun breathed, climbing around a tangle of fallen aspens. "It seems as if every other living thing has perished, and we've been left behind."

Jhared glanced sidelong at her, startled by the way her thoughts echoed his. Moonlight silvered her figure as she wove gracefully over and around the devastated forest. He, on the other hand, was already breathing hard. His arms trembled from pulling himself over the mounds of debris and dragging branches out of the way. It was going to be a long night.

"I wonder how far down the pass this goes on." She kicked aside a small branch, sending it rolling down the slope.

"I suppose we'll find out soon enough." He wondered why she didn't just fly ahead and find out. Couldn't she soar in the darkness? Or was she holding herself back because of him? A humiliating thought.

They pressed on through wooded trails that the Avelun seemed to know well. The destruction was the worst in the forest, and travel became a struggle even for her, as she had to take care not to entangle her feathers. After several hours of laboring, they had covered little ground. When Jhared gazed northward, he could still catch a glimmer of light from Ebilan.

"This is no good. I have to travel faster." He halted to survey what lay ahead. Snowflakes had begun to float from the slate-colored sky.

"I suppose we could go back to the road," the woman replied, reclaiming the tail of her cloak from a greedy root. "It'll be in better shape. We're getting nowhere here."

"Such open travel doesn't frighten you?"

She shrugged. "It's the dead of night and we're the only ones left in the world. What's to fear?"

321

The road remained mostly free of trees and they made better time. Jhared had just recognized the point where his patrol had been attacked by the Verael when he and the Avelun finally crossed the border of the winds' devastation. Beyond, the forest stood intact and the road was only the rocky, rutted thing it had ever been. The Avelun paused, and he pulled up beside her, sucking air through his teeth. He was sweat-soaked, but the climb was no longer enough to stop his shivering. Snowflakes, which earlier were light enough to ignore, now began to collect in the crooks of the trees and on top of the rocks. Jhared gulped water from his flask and scowled at the snow, maddened by the way the land and his injuries conspired to slow him.

"In Sona, the healers say to give the body the tax it asks of you," the woman said, watching him. "The price grows larger each time you refuse."

He offered her the flask. "Whatever I pay goes to fulfill the debt. I give it gladly."

He thought she rolled her eyes, but couldn't be certain in the dark. She dug into her bag, pulled out two sticks of dried fish, and handed him one. "From the looks of it, you've denied your body too often. Allow yourself time to recover."

"I have no time," he answered. "The only price I fear is the one my companions are paying for my delay."

"And if you march until you drop, what happens to them then?" She shook her head. "Come on. It's not so long until dawn. We should stop anyway."

Before he could protest, she turned off the road up a slope toward a long, striated ridge. About halfway around the ridge, she came to a deep crease in the rock, partially hidden by brush. She touched her fingers to her lips, then reached out reverently to touch the stone.

"Honor to those who came before me," she murmured as she stepped inside.

For about fifty paces, the crease was so narrow Jhared had to edge sideways, and the Avelun's cloak scraped along the stone. Here the snow had accumulated deep enough to cover the toes of his boots. Gradually, the passage expanded, until he stood in what looked like a circular courtyard, a space as wide as five men standing shoulder to shoulder and half again as deep. Six smooth columns formed a hexagon in the center of the courtyard, as though they might once have supported a roof. Now moonlight streamed in, lighting three arched openings in the ridge. It only took a moment to realize the openings were too symmetrical to be anything but manmade. Mayavana chose the middle archway. She touched the stone again before entering.

Jhared followed her into a yawning cavern far larger than the one in which he had first found her. As his eyes adjusted to the loss of starlight, wonder wiped away his weariness. It seemed he had wandered into an ice-frosted forest. Columns of crystal that stretched up from the floor had been carved into trees with gnarled branches; overhead, crystals from the cave's ceiling were formed into birds in flight: hawks, owls, jaybirds, and very close to the ceiling, a little silver finch. Some of the birds had become deformed—wings dripping into crippled lumps—as the rock formations continued to grow, heedless of the creatures existing within them. They were fascinating, astonishing, heartbreaking.

He turned slowly to take in all of it. In the walls surrounding the rock forest, artisans had worked a mountain landscape with villages in the valleys and clouds over the mountain tops. Jhared lifted his hand to touch the wall. Much of the scene was damaged. Several villages were nearly erased. Only torsos or sometimes a leg or a foot remained of the human figures. He laid a finger on the defaced figure of a girl hovering over a mountain.

"What is this place?" he whispered. He'd only ever seen such carvings in the high temple. Was that why the cavern felt sacred?

"It's a spot to pray. And to remember." The Avelun's voice carried a strange intensity. "You've seen such carvings before?"

"In the city. The high temple's walls are rich with them, but they've been shattered as well."

"Of course they have. Tumal the Just was thorough in his destruction." She started a slow circle around the chamber, touching each carving as though in greeting.

"They left the trees," Jhared wondered aloud.

She glanced over her shoulder, her expression sharp. "Because they told no stories of the Avelune! They offered Avelos no threat!"

She wanted to be free of his company. He could see it. He reached out for her water skin. "I'll fetch water."

She sighed and her wings rustled in a way he realized signaled aggravation. "You needn't. I didn't mean to drive you off."

"I'll be back. It's only water."

She untied the skin from her belt and held it out. "The stream is at the bottom of the ridge."

As he reached for the flask, his fingers brushed hers inadvertently. A crackle of flame traveled from his hand along his arm all the way to his chest. He swallowed and pulled away.

She frowned, her gaze following to where his hand had pressed against his heart. "Do you feel the ancestors? They've lingered here."

Was that what he felt? The unsettled spirits of the traitors? "I'll be back," he stammered again, hurrying from the grotto.

His boots crunched the dry snow. Flakes landed on his forehead, melted, and dribbled down his cheeks. As he picked his way down the ridge, it occurred to him that the ancients were not the only ones who had walked these trails. How many Sahistens had sneaked into the cave at the Avelun's direction? How many Amurians had sheltered with her here?

At the bottom of the ridge, a stream flowed south with runoff from the hills. With his boot heel he smashed the thin plate of ice that clung to the bank, then crouched to fill the flasks. After, with a bit of foraging, he uncovered a patch of creek potatoes. The purple tubers were sweet and filling when roasted.

As he returned to the courtyard, a quiet tune floated out from the cavern. The Avelun's voice was warm and lush, untrained but unabashed. He paused between the rock walls to listen. It was a foreign melody, Sonan perhaps. His first inclination was to wonder what songs she must know, songs he had never heard and would like to learn. At his Teachers' warning, he shoved that thought aside. She didn't belong here. She represented the deceit and weakness Avelos had tried to grow beyond. Yet Jhared was painfully aware that he had been torn from his comrades and was fleeing for the city, not because of a stranger, but because once more Avelos had turned against itself.

The woman worked with her back to the cave entrance. He hunkered down and crept behind a scrubby bush to watch her, wondering what he might witness in an unguarded moment. The fire danced as she fed it dried leaves and twigs. Her staff and bow leaned against the rock, far enough from the heat to be safe, close enough to be reached in a few quick steps. She drew out her box of herbs, measuring them into the pot for tea. He expected to see the mark of corruption in her, some slyness of manner that would help him to remember why she was anathema. But her song was gentle and she moved with the easy, open manner of someone confident of her place on the Paths.

As Jhared watched, she paused in her singing. Dusting her hands on her breeches, she straightened and turned toward the courtyard. Her eyes landed squarely on the bush that concealed him.

"The fire's warmer at this distance," she observed mildly.

He shrank in disbelief, certain he had made no sound. Slowly he stood, his face burning. "I'm sorry. I meant no harm." He forced himself to meet her gaze.

"Do you always slink up to watch people when they're unaware?"

He shrugged helplessly. "Well . . . I am a scout."

To his surprise, her shoulders relaxed and she laughed. "So you're bound by duty to be sneaky, yet you're too honest to hide it. I wonder if you're in the right job, soldier."

"My lieutenant often wonders the same." He handed her one of the water skins, then held up the roots. "Shall I prepare these?"

She smiled. "Thank you. The contribution is appreciated."

They worked in efficient silence. As he settled the potatoes to roast among the embers at the edge of the fire, she heated water for tea, then dropped dried apples into the remaining water with a pinch of spices from her precious herb box. The aroma of roasted roots and stewed apples soon filled the chamber, reminding Jhared of suppers in the Trianor household.

The meal was quiet. The Avelun kept to her own thoughts, and Jhared didn't know how to draw her out. As the sun crept over the mountains, rosy light filtered into the cavern, striking the edge of the crystal forest. After they had eaten, Jhared helped the Avelun to clean up. Then he settled against one of the crystal trees. Without thinking about it, he slipped his hand into his belt pouch and pulled out Branlen's talisman.

The glossy obsidian sparkled, its face beaming with an old man's gap-toothed grin. He rolled the stone between his thumb and forefinger and held it up to the light. It had always brought him safely back to Velantar and to Bran. Perhaps it would see him to the city one more time.

"Muvanhi ri Lumati!"

The Avelun's startled declaration wrenched Jhared back. Realizing how strange he must look staring at a pebble, he closed his fist around it and sat up. "That was Sahine, wasn't it?"

"It was. Life and light to you, son of Lumati," she said. "A greeting you should know if you're so lucky to hold one of the god's blessings. Did you steal that stone from the body of a Sahisten soldier?"

Jhared glanced at the talisman. The ancient face seemed to be laughing at him. "I don't rob from the Pathguides. I found it years ago. Near the Laebeki border."

"You found the Old Man in Avelos?" She looked disbelieving.

"Perhaps one of your smugglers dropped it," he said dryly.

"Unlikely. Most of them could never earn such a gift. Lumati doesn't concern himself with mortal wealth."

The little stone was beginning to feel uncomfortable in Jhared's palm. Over all the years he and Branlen had shared it, had they been feeding a Sahisten god? "The only power I've ever known in this stone comes from the good wishes of my little brother. I gave it to him as a gift. But he gives it back to me when I leave the city. It's just a game."

It was somewhat more than a game, Jhared knew. It was a way to ease the fear of loss neither he nor Bran wanted to speak aloud whenever he returned to duty.

The Avelun's face lit. "It's a symbol of affection and loyalty to you then. I think you have met Lumati. Whatever you might say." She leaned to her right and drew her left wing forward.

Jhared watched her, puzzled by her motions. "Who is Lumati?"

She laughed gently. "What a question to ask of a god. Could you tell me who Riana *is*? I can only tell you names I've heard for the faces he wears. Sahistens call him the Old Man in the Mountains, the Warrior Who Weeps for the World, and the Great Owl Who Guards His Children."

Jhared ran one finger over the face of the stone. "The warrior who weeps for the world?"

"Lumati guards our sorrows. He is the one who understands and mourns our pains and fears. I carry him for luck." She shook the charms on her bangles, where a small copper owl swung among the many others. As her wing curled all the way around her, storm-colored feathers gleamed in the early light. Jhared had to remind himself to breathe.

"I've never known a Sahisten god who didn't demand blood," he said, a little hoarsely.

Mayavana set both hands over her wing and began to stroke her feathers. Her fingers glided methodically along the primaries and then moved to the secondaries, laying each one smooth. Now and again she gave a little tug until a worn or broken feather came free; those went into a pile beside her. She nodded over her work. "But you have. Lumati left his own lands to give you his blessing."

Jhared didn't answer. He drank in Mayavana's every movement. She was preening. It was a gorgeous, graceful act, yet so unguarded and revealing he felt embarrassed watching.

She raised her head, both hands full of shiny wing. A loose feather clung to her sleeve. "What is it?"

"Nothing." He looked at his boots. "It's just . . . no. Nothing."

She glanced at her feathers as though just now conscious of what she was doing. "Oh." Her expression turned to dismay, and the wing slid out of her hand to fold under her cloak. Jhared watched it disappear along with her contentment. "I'm sorry. I don't do this in front of others. That is . . ." She trailed off, offering him a troubled gaze. "I keep forgetting what you are."

Shorn. Maimed. Broken. He looked down. "I see."

"No. I don't think you do. Soldiers mean death for me. As soon as I could walk, I was taught to flee. When I could hold a knife . . ." She paused until he raised his eyes to hers. "Avelos will never take what my mother and uncle gave up their futures to protect."

In the filtered light, her gaze heated to molten gold. Something wild and powerful arose from their depths; it reminded Jhared of the Verael, regal and deadly. She did what she must to survive. Boundaries began to give way and suddenly he was pouring out of himself, moving beyond his own Path.

With a curse, he tore his gaze away from her. His right hand clamped onto his left, and he dug into the tender flesh.

"Soldier?"

Keep to your own Path, Leita had begged him.

He grasped for a hold on the moment. Images slid across his awareness: stories in which he was whole and soared through the sacred skies; stories of the ancestors who studied and prayed in this cavern. He fought against desire. He mustn't lose himself now. His comrades needed him. Leita needed him.

Keep to your own Path.

"Jhared, what's wrong?"

There was rustling and footsteps. Then the Avelun was bending over him. The Gate reached for his thoughts with seductive beauty, inviting him to search for what he had lost. Urgently, he immersed his senses in the immediacy of the woman above him—the subtle nuances in her voice, the layers of her scent, the complex curves of her body. She became his moment. He forced his awareness to know nothing else.

"You're burning up," she said, her voice an intriguing composition of concern for him, a need to reduce suffering, and confidence in her skill. "I have a bit of Silvaye left, but I'm not sure—"

"No," he croaked. "Don't touch me!" He scrambled back from her. If she touched him with Silvaye, it would steal the last of his strength. He would have no will to resist the Gate and nothing left to keep moving toward Velantar.

"Of course, soldier. You needn't fear me touching you."

Still drowning in his awareness of her, Jhared heard brittle anger and loneliness edge her words, and had no idea why. She shifted her weight and looked ready to take wing.

"Don't go. Please. It's just that . . ." He sighed and tried a smile. "You really don't want me to sing again."

"Or perhaps you still think I care about the secrets you carry," She folded her arms across her chest. "You needn't worry. There's nothing in this cursed country I care about."

The Gate's flames licked at Jhared's memories. He didn't take his eyes from the Avelun. He drew a deep breath: she smelled of fall berries, mountain wind, and clean sweat. "You were singing before. A melody I've never heard. What was it?"

She snorted. "No doubt you've never heard it. It doesn't come from Avelos. It's a Sonan lullaby."

"It was lovely."

Her mouth twitched a little, but she didn't turn away. Jhared thought he sensed surprise and a hesitant openness, a waiting to see what he would do next.

"I have a favor to ask. Although I have no right to ask more of you. I just need to stay on this Path, and I've no kind of control. It seems to help when I can focus on the moment. Do you think you could sing again?"

Shock shone clear in her expression this time. "You meant it when you said no one has taught you about traveling."

He shrugged. "I was too dense a student to learn what little was given me."

"*Shifa*," she muttered, shaking her head in disgust. But to his astonishment, she lowered herself beside him, careful to prevent her cloak or feathers from brushing him.

"You truly want to hear something from Sona?"

"I think the novelty might help to keep me with the song."

"Very well." She went quiet and looked at her hands in her lap. Jhared thought she was thinking about the music, but when she raised her head, he saw the dark flush on her cheeks and realized she was self-conscious. She was no performer like Zia. He took unexpected comfort from that.

"Lef ri Vanik," she named the song: "Over the Water." It was beautiful and strange. Although her voice was untrained, it had a natural expressive quality that fit the foreign scale. Even without understanding the words, Jhared heard the soft lapping of the tide against the shore, the cry of the gulls, and the rush of a breeze through the reeds.

He didn't let himself wander far with the images. Drawing close to the fire, he lay down on his cloak where he could keep his gaze on the Avelun. As she sang, her eyes brightened to the color of a lake in the sunlight. A soft weight slowly pushed Jhared toward darkness. He felt no flames or greedy Gate, so he didn't question it. He kept his mind on the music and let his body gradually sink. When the lullaby ended, she glanced at him and caught him watching her through slitted eyelids. Whatever she saw in his expression, she stayed beside him and started a second song.

Jhared didn't know when the music became a dream, but at some point the woman stopped singing. Emotion shifted across her features as she peered into his face. He felt grief in her and old rage. He wondered if perhaps she would try to kill him after all. Finally, her deadly heat cooled and she let out a long sigh. She whispered in a barely audible voice, "Lumati lend you strength," and leaned forward to brush a hand across his brow. He realized then that he was asleep.

They set off again the following evening, marching into powdery snow that cloaked the ridge and deadened Jhared's steps. Stars hung in an icy sky, their light glittering off the snow in a million blue-white facets.

"How beautiful," the Avelun breathed, her eyes glittering as brightly as the snow.

It was beautiful. The forest was all gentle curves and feathery surfaces. The cold, clean air felt good in Jhared's chest. It drove back his fever and sharpened his thoughts. Perhaps that was why he finally recognized how close they stood to the place where he had abandoned Alende and Seravina.

"Which way?" he asked the woman.

She pointed southwest. "The snow's not heavy. The hill trail should still be reliable."

Jhared nodded. "There's a bit of meadow on the tableland slightly farther west. I need to stop there."

"Looking for something?" she said, one brow rising.

"Someone," Jhared replied. Then, in response to her startled look, he added, "He won't be there. I just need to see if I can figure out—"

"If he's alive?"

He nodded again, a shiver running through him at how effortlessly she completed his thoughts.

"I know the meadow," she said. "If we head north around the ridge, we'll come to it sooner than if we go south and backtrack."

Jhared let her lead. They approached the tableland from the opposite direction he had come with Leita, climbing a stony hill that bordered the black gulf of a wide ravine. Jhared turned his face up the hill and tried to ignore the mischievous breezes that swirled snow out of the ravine and kissed his left cheek. The very real challenge of climbing in the near dark helped. He scanned for stable footholds, shifted his weight cautiously, and didn't overreach his balance on the slippery rocks.

The Avelun skipped ahead of him and soon disappeared over the top, nimble as a mountain goat.

"What're you looking for?" she asked, as he joined her at the top.

"Verael attacked my patrol. An injured man was left behind. I want to know if he escaped."

It really didn't explain anything, but she didn't question it, just as she hadn't questioned his need to reach the city. She had respected the boundary of things he couldn't share.

No doubt working with smugglers teaches discretion," Boar smirked.

"I'll search the ledges over the ravine." She nodded to the left.

"Thank you," Jhared replied, offering his Teacher no response.

Three nights had passed since the Verael attack. Although the killing winds hadn't come this far, the snow likely had done as thorough a job erasing any signs of the waylayer. Still, Jhared couldn't give up the possibility of piecing together his fate. He owed Alende, if not for the man's own sake, then for the memory of Mahla.

He prowled across the tableland before coming to study the tree where he had left Alende, heartened by what he *didn't* find: no remains of man or horse and no claw marks on the tree. What he did find at the edge of the meadow was the battered carcass of a single Verael. Its ribs had been staved in and the skull cracked. A crescent shape cut cleanly into the space between the beast's eyes: a hoof mark. Jhared stood, smiling grimly, grateful to Seravina.

He turned and spied the top of a dark head just above the edge of the table on the ravine side of the meadow. The Avelun had climbed partway down the hill to investigate one of the ledges. He strode to the edge, and without thinking, peered down to where she stood. A rush of vertigo nearly carried him over the cliff.

The rocky outcrop jutted scarcely ten feet from the hill, then fell away into a sheer drop. Jhared swayed and flung out both hands for balance. Beyond the ravine, the snow-frosted mountains sparkled like sapphires amid layers of black velvet. Jhared turned from that dangerous vista to see the Avelun's cloak and gear discarded on the ground beside him. He stared at it, drawing a steadying breath before daring to look at the wonder of her.

She stood at the very edge of the chasm, her wings stretched to their full, magnificent span. A soft moan rose from her throat as she beat the air with deep, measured strokes that stirred Jhared's cloak and fingered through his hair. She raised her arms and leaned into the wind. Her body extended partially over the edge. Over nothing.

"Soar," a voice whispered.

Jhared slammed himself backward and struck a boulder. The hard edges dug into his flesh, reminding him of the truth of his maimed body, but the pain wasn't enough to dull his need. His heart raced and his spirit begged for the sky.

The Avelun sighed with pleasure and leaned farther, hovering like a fledgling at the rim of the nest. "Gods of the sky. For this, it's almost worth living in Avelos," she purred.

"Let go," the voice commanded Jhared. Not his Teachers, just his own undisciplined thought.

He clutched the rock. It would be so much easier to throw himself into the velvet sky than to stand, trembling like a child, trying to hold himself back. The Avelun looked over her shoulder. Her delirious smile melted away.

"You're panting like a hound, soldier. Are you all right?"

"Perfect." Slowly, cautiously, he forced himself farther from the edge.

"Did you find something of your lost man? There's no sign among the rocks." Her wings *whooshed* against the darkness. "Gods, what a glorious night!"

"I found enough," he said, his hands still grasping the stone. "It's time to move on."

She peered at him again, seeming puzzled. Then amazement filled her expression. "Oh! Oh, I see it! You're afraid of heights! But how did you learn such a *ridiculous* thing?"

She didn't understand. Not at all. The irony wasn't that he feared heights, but that he loved them. Craved them. He squeezed his eyes closed and tried to find the litany of Shorn Law that had always fortified him. He couldn't remember it.

"I'll help you," she called. "Come to me. You needn't fear this."

Come to me. It would be so easy. "Mayavana, let me be! I *must* make it to the city. This one thing, at least, I cannot fail!" He ripped his gaze from the sky and threw himself in the opposite direction of the cliff.

The strength of his longing gave him new energy. He made it down the hill and back to the forest, not daring to examine the feelings roiling in him as he left the woman behind. The surge of relief he felt when he heard her hurrying after was damning enough.

"Wait, soldier."

He pushed himself to keep marching and didn't turn.

She jogged up beside him, her wings folded and cloaked once more. "What was that? What happened?"

His hands clenched. It was another bitter irony that an Avelun should taunt him with his own weakness. He glanced at her and saw the bewilderment in her expression. Abruptly, it came to him that she truly didn't know.

He rolled his shoulders, feeling the tug of his scars.

"I need to make better time," he muttered, without looking at her. "We need horses."

She didn't speak. From the corner of his eye, he saw her frowning. "All right," she said eventually. "One horse. I'm no rider."

He laughed thinly. "Of course you're not. Why should you be?" He imagined what she would have looked like if she had taken the last step off the ledge, her wings carrying her toward the stars.

Her head snapped up, and her eyes flashed. Jhared thought he had said something to anger her. Then he heard the hoofbeats.

She set a finger to her lips. He nodded and jogged toward the road. He could hear four or five horsemen cantering hard down the pass. In the dark. Along snow-slick precipices. Whose need was so urgent they risked a deadly fall? Could it be his own people escaped from Ciam? Loyal soldiers running from the garrison?

In the still night, the horses' hooves echoed from a long distance. Jhared scrambled along the crest of the hill and down, his boots sliding over the scree. He threw himself into the shadow of a big fir tree overlooking the road just as the riders pounded past.

Five. The horses were stocky northern beasts, and the men the same. Starlight shone on their pale faces, disappeared in their thick beards, then reflected again from the silver lightning sigils on their vests. Even if Jhared hadn't seen the livery, he would still have recognized the men from Ciam's patrol.

His escape from the clanguard had set something in motion. Would the riders lay for him at the other end of the pass? Were they carrying a warning to Clan Hilera? Or did they have some other role in the north's betrayal? Five of them. Where was the other half of the patrol?

"Looks as though you know what that's about."

Jhared whirled. The Avelun was standing on the opposite side of the tree. "Not as much as I need to."

"Was that truly Clan Aglar's guard? When did that ratty bunch equip itself so fine? I wonder what they're up to."

Jhared scrubbed a hand over his face. The most dangerous thing for Avelos just now would be for the border nations to learn of the internal conflict that weakened her. The Avelun crossed borders with less concern than crossing a road. She took money from both Sahiste and Amuria. What would he do with her if she figured out something of Clan Aglar's treachery?

"Please don't," he said. "Don't wonder."

She tilted her head. "I offer no loyalties to your enemies, you know."

Jhared hadn't yet heard anyone to whom she did offer loyalty; she even collected gods from every country. "I *don't* know. Please don't make me have to consider it."

"Ah." Her expression sobered. "I understand."

He shook his head. "Mayavana, I must tell you this much: those men are likely searching for me or warning others to do so. Traveling with me isn't safe."

No one who stands beside you is safe.

The Avelun lifted her chin. In the green fire of her gaze, Jhared glimpsed the girl who snuck out at night and revealed the dangerous truth of her wings just for the freedom of running bare beside a moonlit lake. "No place I travel is safe for me," she said. "I have never allowed fear to narrow my world."

Courage echoed in her tone. Jhared couldn't deny his respect for it, but he recalled too well the strength and beauty of a hawk gliding over the valley as he nocked an arrow and took aim. Cold dread shivered through him. "Onward then?"

They ran through most of the night. Jhared pushed himself forward with thoughts of what Leita and his patrolmates were paying, and what General Orn and the garrison soldiers had already paid. Despite the breath-stealing pace, dawn beat them to the southern end of the pass. The Avelun pressed him to stop, and Jhared had to admit he couldn't continue without rest.

"Just for a few hours," he panted. "We're close enough to Isantar now that there'll be more traffic in the pass. A chance to find a horse."

"How do you mean to obtain that horse?" she asked, glancing at him.

"I'm not entirely sure yet."

She had no grotto to show him this time. They climbed into the heights, well off the road, and tucked into a gully where a tree had fallen across it, creating a small hide. They didn't dare a fire, and the ground was cold and damp from the snow. Without hesitation or complaint, the Avelun again shared her provisions. As Jhared ate her pressed fish and flatbread, he added it to his growing debt.

Mayavana took care not to touch him in the cramped space as she wrapped herself in her wings and cloak. "Sleep while you can. You're still trying to regain the strength Silvien borrowed from you. Several more days before you've caught up. At least you'll keep your hands, though."

Jhared glanced at his hands. It was true: in only two days, the dangerous swelling had disappeared, and dead skin had begun to flake away, revealing shiny flesh beneath. He flexed his fingers, stretching the new scars. It was no wonder he was so drained; Silvien had forced his body to repair itself faster than any man could heal on his own. "I owe you for that. More than I can repay."

"Owe?" She frowned, as though the word made no sense to her. "For a decision I made of my own will? What a strange one you are."

With a shrug, she leaned against the rock and tucked her head against her shoulder. Very soon her breathing turned deep and even. Jhared surprised himself by drifting off easily beside her.

It was past midday when he awoke once more and peered up at a colorless sky, unwilling to return to his nightmares. More snow was coming. He hoped the mountains would be far behind him before it arrived. He arched his back and shifted his legs, trying not to disturb the Avelun. He wondered where Ciam's clanguards were now.

For the first time, he had the clarity of thought to seriously consider what the north had done. Tierzen had always said, only half jokingly, that two mountain ranges and a mountain of arrogance separated the northern clans from Velantar. The northerners named themselves the hardiest and purest of the fifteen first-clans and viewed High Chieftain Rumar from the central lands as weak. Repeatedly they had clashed with Rumar as he sought to empower the council and reduce individual clans' influences on trade and diplomacy. Interference with the north's own sovereignty was met with resentment, and perceptions of favoritism to the south were met with fury. Pride was only the kindling for the fire, however; silver was the true fuel. Much of the wealth of Avelos lay in the silver mines in the Sandien Mountains, and the northern clans despised Rumar for maintaining control of the mines.

When it came to it, the northern prefects had planned their treachery well. As Avelos waited to see if Sahiste would press its demands with open war, Rumar could ill afford to pull soldiers off the southeastern border. Once winter made the mountain passes impossible, no one would reach Aglar Tower until spring. This was no impulsive act of rebellion; it had taken time and funds to prepare the northern clanguards. Just how those funds had been raised was an important question. Had the prefects been siphoning silver into their own coffers? Wouldn't the Minister of the Treasury have brought it to the council if the northern levies hadn't arrived as expected? How had the northern five earned enough coin to raise its own army? An army that was killing loyal men.

Jhared didn't realize how much rein he had given his anger until he looked down at his clenched fists. He hissed out a breath. Dead leaves rattled as his head grazed the roof of the shelter. The Avelun opened her eyes. Like a wild creature, she shifted from sleep to wide-eyed awareness in one breath.

"It's too early to move on," she said.

"I know. I'm going down to watch the road."

She stretched languorously and shivered her feathers into place. "I suspect you won't find clanguard, if that's what you're looking for. They seemed in a great hurry to be somewhere else."

"Not clanguard. I'm hoping to find a horse."

"*Find*, eh?" She smiled knowingly.

He didn't much care for that smile. In truth, the idea of commandeering another man's property turned his stomach. He climbed out of the gully and shook the snow from his cloak.

"I'll come with you," she said, climbing up beside him.

"In the light of day? That doesn't seem wise."

"Don't worry. I know how to stay out of your way."

He worried more about whether she could stay out of the way of hostile blades, but he discovered he wanted the company, and she seemed able to take care of herself.

"Very well. Come on."

They found a ledge overhanging the road where he and the Avelun could stretch out flat and spy on travelers as they trotted down into a slight depression below. The pass narrowed here, and the opposite side of the road ended in a steep drop into a gorge. It would give him the advantage if it came to a struggle.

"Now here's a thing I never imagined," the woman murmured, peering over the road in amusement. "I've never spied *with* a Forest Guard."

Jhared didn't laugh. "I suppose you've learned the border patrols quite well in all your travels."

"Well enough. The patrols are stretched so thin that most days it's not a trick to avoid trouble."

He nodded. She was proof enough that the country's defenses were crumbling.

Time crept along, but few travelers. Over several hours they saw four men leading pack mules loaded with grain; a boy with three dogs and a herd of goats that came out of the hills and went south; and an escorted wagon of wine from Clan Makri lumbering north. Then nothing. The wind sifted snow across the road in grey and white patterns. Mayavana drowsed for a time, head on her arms. Angled sunlight painted shadows across her face, lengthening her dark lashes and creating bold slopes of her wind-roughened cheeks. Even in repose, a faint crease marked the center of her brow, as though she were pondering something troubling. Jhared had thought her a few winters his senior, but in sleep she looked very young. He wondered how many years she had spent traveling across Avelos, knowing that every moment within the border her life was at risk. The thought of what would happen if anyone caught her stirred a feeling Jhared couldn't consider too closely. He breathed in the fall-berry scent of her and slid as far to the other side of the ledge as he could, suddenly grateful for the cold that seeped from the stone through his clothing.

The sun slipped toward the west. Jhared began to fear he would lose another night of travel to his own slow pace when he caught sight of a new party.

"That's what I've been waiting for."

Mayavana lifted her head. Riding south on a tall bay horse was a tired-looking Shorn woman with a dark-haired little girl clinging to her waist. A tow-headed boy in a threadbare cloak walked beside them. The boy, who was probably eight or nine winters, whistled as he walked and poked at lumps of snow with a sturdy stick. Jhared couldn't have hoped for a better find. The horse was no beauty and could have used a few more meals, but looked sound.

"That's too sad even for a jest," the Avelun said, frowning at the little family. "Leave them be. Find yourself a merchant or tradesman."

Jhared gave her an incredulous look. "This is a gift: a healthy mount and no weapons. We won't have this kind of luck again tonight."

"You can't steal from a family," she insisted. "Those poor children don't even have proper boots."

Wind whipped over Jhared's body. Hours had already been lost, and the light was dying. His patience shredded. "Steal? Is that what you think of me? Of course I'm not going to *steal* from them."

"But I thought you said—"

"The woman is Shorn. She'll give us all we need and be happy to do it. It will go toward repayment of her debt."

Mayavana's expression darkened. "By the looks of it, she's paid and more."

"What would you know of it?" Jhared hissed. "You can't begin to understand what it means to pay. I can't lose this chance. I'm going after them." Heart thudding, he leaped off the ledge and slipped through the trees toward the road.

The horse shied to a halt as Jhared stepped into its path. Fear flashed across the woman's gaunt features. The little girl peered anxiously around her, but the boy with the walking stick glared.

Jhared held out his hands, palms up. He guessed he had only a moment to convince the woman not to grab up her son and wheel them back up the pass.

"Don't fear, madam. I'm Patrolman Denaban of the Forest Guard Fourth. I mean you no harm, but by High Chieftain Rumar who wards our land, I need that horse."

Standing so close in the fading light, Jhared saw that she was young, though cares had bowed her shoulders and resignation flattened her green gaze. No spark of anger seemed to kindle in her, even the fear had vanished.

"Have what ya like'a me," she said dully, "but not in front'a my children. Please."

Several heartbeats passed before Jhared understood what she meant, and a wave of horror washed over him. "I'm not going to hurt you! I only need the horse."

He took a step toward her, and she cringed. The girl clinging to her began to whimper. They should have fled by now, but the woman only stared at him with empty eyes, unwilling to aid him and unable to save herself. Jhared stifled the desire to shake her.

"Come, madam. Take comfort that your sacrifice will go toward reparation." He strode forward once more.

"Don't touch her!"

With a sudden blur of motion, wood smashed against the left side of Jhared's face, making his ears ring. He drew his sword as he turned, and found the boy brandishing the walking stick in front of him. With one swing of his blade, Jhared sent the stick flying. The child yelped and stumbled backward toward the rim of the pass. He tripped and sat down hard on the snowy ground. Jhared prepared to swing again.

"You're no Forest Guard!" the boy shouted. "You're a thief and a bully! Leave us alone!"

Jhared looked at the child, not even as old as Branlen, a little boy defending his mother. With a dizzying lurch, he saw himself from the child's eyes: an icy-eyed beast wielding the threat of death. It nearly dropped him to his knees when he realized what he had been about to do. Could a child really owe so much?

His blade tip dipped toward the ground. "You're right," he gasped. "It's not you who should make this sacrifice. Not you."

The boy popped to his feet and raised his small fists. He barely reached as high as Jhared's waist. The sight would have been comical if it hadn't been so sad. "Off with ya, thief!"

Everything Jhared understood was suddenly twisted inside out. Just a moment ago, he had been fulfilling his duty. Now . . . He stared at the child another moment, then sheathed his sword, turned his back on all of them, and walked into the hills.

The Avelun had gone. Her prints led into the woods and south along the road. Jhared drifted along the same track. The ache in his chest felt like grief, although he wasn't certain what he was mourning.

A booted step broke the stillness. Jhared flung himself to the ground, hands sinking into the snow as something heavy whistled overhead. He rolled sideways to see the Avelun's staff beat the air exactly where his head had been. She stood over him, cursing in Sonan and Velos.

"Lumati's shriveled balls! I took you for a clanguard. What are you doing tracking me?"

"I'm not sure," he muttered.

She frowned and gazed up the empty trail. "What happened to your not-stolen horse?"

Jhared came to his feet. Snow clung to his clothes and face. It felt good against the bruise blooming over his cheek. "I left it."

She peered more closely at him. "That's quite a lump. I guess the woman wasn't so happy to pay the debt after all."

He stared at the Avelun, yearning for that moment of recognition he had experienced before, when he sensed how deeply he knew her. He needed that connection. He needed someone to tell him why he ached as he hadn't since the day last spring when he sent a hawk spiraling to her death.

"I don't think the woman had that much will left in her. It was the boy."

"You attacked the child? Gods of seas and skies." Maya thumped her staff against the ground. "What did Avelos do to you, Jhared? What did they do to convince you this was just?"

He felt the sting as though she had slapped him, hurt and smoldering anger. He said nothing, but turned away and started running. The sharp wind burned his eyes and blurred his vision. His boots fountained snow behind him. Curse the woman. Curse her smugness. How did she dare to mock Avelos, to deride laws she didn't understand and never had to face? From her safe place outside every boundary meant for her, she threw her daggers at his country, at his upbringing, and at him.

For the second time that day, he found himself resorting to escape. What was it about her that drove him so hard he couldn't even face it? She was Avelun, the demon's messenger; she was supposed to be greedy, deceitful, and cruel. He kept trying to convince himself she was those things, but so far he couldn't see them. She had been only generous, compassionate, and forthright.

He stopped dead, gulping breaths of cold air. That was the most terrifying thing about her: she *didn't* match what she should have been; instead, she tore through his veils and challenged everything he knew.

"Soldier?"

He tensed. She stood not ten paces behind him. Her cloak had fallen back from her wings, and a breeze ruffled the feathers above her shoulders.

"I didn't harm the child," he said. "I didn't touch any of them."

Shadows hid her expression, but the lines of her body relaxed a little, and she moved closer.

"I'm glad." She looked at the ground, twisting her staff into the snow. "What you said before is true, you know. I learned very little of what Avelos wants of me."

He glanced at her. "Your mother never told you?"

Mayavana shrugged. "She told me who I am, not what I escaped."

A silence fell. She bit the corner of her lip. "Would you tell me?" she asked finally. "Would you tell me what it is to be Shorn?"

He blinked at her, uncertain.

"Jhared?"

"I don't understand what you want."

"I would like to know something of your story. If you'll share it with me."

He sank down onto a fallen log, his heart pounding.

"Are you all right?"

His Teachers ranted at him, ordering him to doubt her, but in that moment he couldn't. In her reserved, earnest expression, he sensed a willingness to understand. It was a treasure he had never known. As his gaze met hers, he realized the emotion cascading through him was relief.

"What is it you want to know?"

25.
UNRAVELING STORIES

"*What is it you want to know?*" Jhared heard himself say.

"It took more than a knife to make you Shorn," Mayavana replied softly. "Tell me what shaped you."

Jhared stood up and shook the snow from his cloak. It wouldn't be easy what she wanted. "I will tell you. But we've got to keep moving while we talk."

They set off at a quick march, and Jhared tried not to think about how much more ground he could have covered had he taken the horse. Instead, he spent several miles figuring out where to start with Mayavana's request. He stretched his thoughts to the hazy years before his mother's death, when as a child of five winters, he had been proud to go to Elder and Madam Trianor to begin the Teaching.

Once he started talking, it was as though he had thrown open a trunk filled with blackbirds. The stories flew free. The words came painlessly at first. In the early years of the Teaching, his lessons had focused on gaining the basic tools of knowledge—reading, scribing, manipulating numbers. He recalled the smiles and sweets Sarena bestowed upon him for successfully copying part of Shorn Law or some bit of history from the Exile War. She was generous with her praise when he behaved well or answered correctly. But reading came effortlessly, and he had soon mastered it. After that had come the tests.

"Madam Trianor is a clever Teacher," Jhared said, watching the road in front of him. "She understands that learning happens best through experience. To reveal my weaknesses, she would leave temptations within my reach when she knew I was too undisciplined to resist them."

Forbidden books had been her favorite. Once he learned how to read, he had never been able to restrain himself from opening the cover of a volume to see what secrets it held.

"She laid traps for you," the Avelun said, a frown in her tone.

"She taught me," he corrected. "A man must know his own flaws before he can hope to overcome them."

"But you weren't a man, you were a child. What happened when you didn't learn well enough?"

Jhared grimaced. Of course the Avelun would want to know about his failures. He shrugged aside memories of the nights he had been prohibited from sleep and the days he had been required to keep his mouth shut, unable to speak or eat. "What should happen if you haven't mastered a skill? More practice. My Teachers gave me exercises in self-control."

Mayavana made a dubious sound.

"Elder Trianor was more straightforward," Jhared said, shifting the conversation away from Sarena. "He allowed me to read broadly and encouraged my questions. He believed reason and insight would help me to control the weaknesses in my tainted blood. If not for Tierzen, I wouldn't have survived the first of the urges."

Maya glanced at him. "Urges?"

Jhared's face heated. "You know, the need to . . ." He made a little leaping and falling motion with his hand.

She tilted her head inquisitively; then understanding lit her eyes. "Oh, I see. Oh! The cliff edge. Jhared, it never occurred to me you would still feel that need. It just never occurred to me."

He gave another little shrug. "There's no reason it should."

The telling grew painful as he spoke of his mother's death and Tierzen's battle with the council to keep him. For the first time in his life, he told another person about Boar and Shrill, the Teachers within him who strived to keep him within Shorn Law. He took a drink of water and wished it were Alende's brandy.

"How did they come to you?" Mayavana peered at him as if she might see Shrill and Boar peering back.

"I can't really say," he admitted. "It's hard to remember a time without them. They arrived after my mother's death, so I've always thought they somehow knew I needed them. But perhaps that's just the age when every Shorn child receives the Teachers within. Since then, they've been just one more part of my education."

"How do you stand it? Having someone groping about in your head every moment?"

Jhared went still, afraid of awakening Boar or Shrill with the conversation. "They're not," he said more quietly. "Not every moment. They sleep sometimes, especially after a long night." In response to her curious look, he sighed. "When it's necessary, they create nightmares. To remind me of my duty."

She made a face of disgust. "Do they torment all Shorn in the same way or do they particularly dislike you?"

"I don't know. No one has ever trusted me enough to speak of them."

He glanced away as he went on, describing each part of his training for her to see both the joy and the ache of it. The Avelun began to grow quiet. With each story, she seemed to shrink, hugging her arms around herself like armor. Fleetingly, he wondered if he should stop, but discovered he could not.

More came out than he ever intended. He told her about the night he had been attacked by the Legacy, the revelation he was a Pathwalker, and Vesarian's torture and death. His desire to reach her carried him far, too far.

"The Becoming is only held in the spring," he said softly. "Riana commands that a bird of prey be slain in the prime of spring."

Mayavana gasped, but Jhared was standing in Parnas Valley again, his bow clutched in one hand. Sunlight limned the mountains and brightened a meadow of wildflowers. Against a flawless blue sky, a hawk wheeled and soared. The perfection of her flight hummed through his body. "She was so lovely," he whispered. "I never expected to find beauty in a creature Riana cursed."

The temple had demanded her death, and he had sent an arrow plunging into her breast. He had tumbled with her out of the sky and crashed into oblivion, leaving her chicks to starve.

Jhared staggered against a tree, hot pain stabbing through his heart.

"You killed her?" The Avelun gripped the branch beside him, her eyes round with horror. "And they told you it was for Riana? How did you ever survive it? How did you survive the Becoming?"

He heard the condemnation in her voice and knew she saw him as the faithless man who lacked the strength to save his comrades or the courage to pass the Becoming.

"The hunt was a test of loyalty," he said, rubbing his chest. "Avelos must know me willing to complete any task she asks of me. I survived because I was . . . *am* loyal."

"A test of loyalty? Is that what you think? Oh, Jhared." Revulsion lay stark across her face. Even in the dusky light he could see her shoulders trembling.

"What is it?" he demanded.

"It's too much. I never imagined they would dare to steal so much. Look what they made of you."

He lifted his head, prepared to tell her that what they made of him was what he was meant to be, but as his gaze caught hers, the world went heavy with grief. For an instant, he was plummeting into that grief, as though it were his own. Then she tore her gaze away and turned her back on him, leaving him gasping.

"There's not much darkness left," she said tightly. "We should keep going if you want to be free of the mountains."

"Mayavana, what happened? Are you . . . ?"

He didn't know how to finish the sentiment. Sadness clung to her in a way that said he had hurt her. He had revealed who he was. He should have known his failures would repulse her.

They cleared the pass and entered Clan Hilera's lands. Jhared's relief at leaving Clan Aglar's territory was dampened by the Avelun's silent figure marching ahead of him. The air smelled of morning by the time they found a suitable place to rest, a partially concealed hollow at the base of a hill. Jhared went for water while Mayavana collected firewood. They worked together with little need for words.

Once the flames were crackling, the Avelun picked up her staff and tucked the ends of her scarf into her cloak. "I'll be back before the sun's fully risen."

He frowned. They were uncomfortably close to Isantar and the traffic that went along with a busy crossroads town. "I'll come with you."

"No!" she said sharply. When he drew back in surprise, she shook her head. "There are things I must think on," she said more quietly. "Sleep now, soldier. When I return, I have something I must share with you."

The grimness of her tone put a chill in his heart. He opened his mouth to ask what she meant, but she was already vanishing into the trees.

It was too warm for snow below the pass, but as the false dawn spilled through the woods, the clouds loosed a slow drizzle. Jhared walked a perimeter around the camp as rain pattered against the leaves and plinked into the little streams that flowed in the creases of the foothills. Isantar lay about four miles to the west, but within a mile, the trees began to thin and the game trails showed the tracks of recent hunters. Mayavana had gone in the opposite direction, deeper into the wilds. Jhared stayed clear of her tracks.

By the time he had completed a circuit, he was wet through. He returned to the camp and dropped down by the fire. With a boulder at his back, he stared at the flames and tried to order the chaos in his mind. It was no good; he only ended up thinking of the Avelun. The truth of her thrummed in his middle like the promise of a drawn bow, thrilling and dangerous. She was whole, marked by the curse but unscathed by the debt. She had asked for his story, then condemned him for what he was. So why did a glimpse of her storm-grey feathers make him dizzy? Why did he come so close to losing himself whenever his gaze caught hers? She was, truly, the bane of Avelos. He couldn't conjure a word terrible enough to describe what that made him.

Jhared tugged up his hood against the rain and rested his head on his arms. When the fingers of his dreams reached out, he let them pull him down.

Daylight caught him soaring above the valley floor. The sun had burned through the clouds and blazed across his body, warming his golden wings. For the pure pleasure of it, he wheeled in an effortless arch toward the cliffs. He flirted with the mountain thermals, dropping lower over the valley. On one green hill there was movement. He dismissed it. The man was too large to be prey.

With a sudden low hum, a predator shot toward him, swift as an eagle. Too fast to flee. He shrieked as the shaft penetrated his feathers and shattered his breast. With a great battering of wings, he tried to break free, but the predator had embedded in his flesh. Unable to breathe, unable to move, he crumpled, and his body began to spiral toward the ground. Grey cliffs, blue sky, and green trees streamed into a long tail of color as he tumbled over and over toward oblivion.

One last, desperate thought filled his mind as death enfolded him: *fledglings.*

The raptor's shriek tore through the forest. Jhared woke with a start, gasping for breath, one hand clutching at his chest. Pain radiated from the place the arrow had pierced him. He lurched to his feet, sweat soaked and shuddering, trying to shake free of the death-terrors. It hadn't been the Gate, he told himself, only a nightmare of the Becoming.

As he stomped around the fire, trying to convince his body he was no longer a dying hawk, the shriek ripped apart the day once more. With a new kind of horror, Jhared realized it was no dream and no raptor. It was a woman.

Mayavana.

Although the rain had ceased, silver mist wreathed the trees, making sound a slippery thing. Jhared wasted precious heartbeats orienting himself to the direction of the cry. Southeast, he decided. The way she had set out. His sword slid free of its sheath with a hiss. He knew where to find her tracks. He had deliberately turned away from them on his patrol. He had been so careful to respect her need for solitude.

The weight of her wings made her prints distinctive, and the soft ground made them easy to find. He hurried along her path, seeing how at first she had wandered this way and that, like someone not fully attuned to her surroundings. Jhared knew the thoughtful expression that would have wrinkled her features as she walked. She had climbed a hill and sat on a rock at the crown, then wandered down the south side into a narrow gap. Jhared saw where she had grown wary, her prints revealing a sudden pause and a change in direction. By then, the ambush must have been in place, for only a few steps farther, near the end of the gap, new footprints collided with her own: two men had leaped in front of her and three behind. As the assailants tried to close, she had held them off with her staff, catching at least one of them. A still figure lay on the trail. Jhared recognized him as the smaller of the two clanguards who had tried to stop him in Ebilan. Dead. An evil black bruise discolored his temple and one side of his face.

Jhared ran on. Beyond the gap lay a small clearing. Through the trees, he found the rest of the guards and saw where they had finally run the Avelun to ground. She was face down, blood soaking the dirt beneath her.

It took three men to keep her there, and even so, she struggled against their grip, cursing them in two languages. One wing flapped wildly, sending pale feathers into the air. The guard at her head had a hand knotted in her hair and a knee on the back of her neck. The second man threw his weight across her legs. The third gripped her right wing in both hands, yanking it until she screamed. Jhared knew the fourth man; he was the scarred guard from Ebilan. He stood over Maya, swinging his sword across her back, inches from her wings, and taunting her with foul names. Jhared froze, unable to breathe. They meant to make her Shorn.

"Ah, Avelos, no!"

It was a prayer. A plea for someone to say that what was about to happen was evil, was prohibited. No one gave answer: Riana perhaps unwilling to speak for Cael's creature and Avelos uncaring. Jhared knew what he must do and knew something of what would happen afterward, but he didn't allow fear to halt him. Silent as the mist, he glided into the clearing. The guards had their backs to him and eyes for nothing but their captive. As the scarred man swung his blade high, preparing to hack through Mayavana's wing, Jhared's sword slid between his ribs under his left arm and into his heart.

The man toppled without a gasp. Cries of shock and rage burst from the others as they leaped up and grabbed for their weapons. The guard at Mayavana's feet had no time to reach his sword before Jhared's blade flashed across his throat. Suddenly, a second man lay dying in the grass. Men of Avelos. Jhared had sworn two oaths to protect them. He faltered.

Not citizens, traitors.

The thought steadied him a little, but his delay allowed the last two clanguards to flank him. The burly man on his right swung an underhanded cut that forced Jhared to parry downward, opening his left side. As the clash of metal vibrated along the blade through Jhared's hands, he knew he would be too slow to protect his left, knew that in a heartbeat, steel would part his flesh. Urgently, he untangled from the parry and spun outward, distancing himself from the second blade and putting the man on his right into the center. Before either guard could turn, Jhared had dispatched his third man with a thrust through the back.

By the time he tore his sword free, the final guard was already falling to his knees, his eyes rolling back in his head. Mayavana stood behind him. She brought her staff crashing down once more, and Jhared heard the skull give way. The guard fell face-first into the mud. Then it was over.

Jhared stared at the Avelun across the bodies, at the cold, flat hatred in her eyes. She gripped her staff defensively in both hands. Blood trickled from her lip and ran freely from a gash that spanned the inside of her left forearm.

He had killed for her. Three of his own people. He didn't know where to begin unraveling the emotions twining through him. He didn't know how to reach her as she stood defended by a wall of hatred.

One end of her staff slipped from her fingers and thudded against the dirt. Suddenly, none of the complexities mattered. Jhared crossed the distance between them and caught her elbow as her legs began to fold.

"It's done," he said softly.

She nodded, her breath rasping between her clenched teeth. He helped her to the edge of the clearing, where she sank down beneath a tree, cradling her left arm against her body.

"Gods of seas and skies," she hissed. "What a fool I was. A careless fool. I should've heard them. Or noticed the tracks in the gap."

"They didn't want to be noticed," Jhared said, kneeling beside her. Blood had soaked the sleeve of her tunic. "Can I?" He gestured to her injury.

She let him take her left arm. The gash was long and ugly.

"One of the bastards thought he'd have my head," she muttered. "His blade glanced off my staff and slipped down my arm. I would've taken another of them otherwise."

The life-vein hadn't been severed, but her bracelet was deeply scored on the inside of her wrist. Her collection of god-charms had deflected the blade and likely saved her life.

She didn't protest as Jhared unwound the raven's wing scarf from around her neck. The fabric was soft and clean. She watched him as he made a bandage of it.

"A Forest Guard and the bane of Avelos fighting together," she said with a weak laugh. "I've too little wit just now to savor that irony."

"You needn't." He was trying hard not to think about the clanguard bodies behind him or their blood spattered over him. Yet a question slid into his head, a question about the thing that could have spared Mayavana from injury and spared him the necessity of killing.

Why hadn't she flown away?

It wasn't a question he could ask now. As gently as he could, he bound her wound and tied the bandage at the crook of her elbow. Then he raised her arm and directed her to keep it above her head in the way he'd seen Forest Guard healers do, moving the injury as far above the heart as possible. He could do better when they made it back to camp. Now he just wanted the bleeding to stop. With a little searching, he found her cloak in the clearing and helped her to draw it over her wings and shoulders.

"You've a healer's way about you," she sighed. "Perhaps you missed your true path."

The unbidden image of Vesarian's lifeless body rolling into the river flashed in his head. "There's a good reason the Shorn are prohibited from serving as healers," he said.

With her right hand, she pushed herself straighter and fixed her gaze on him. "There's nothing good about what Avelos has done, Jhared."

The reflexive impulse to rail at her surged up in him, but he swallowed it. The clanguard would have cut her apart and watched her die; she had earned the right to her anger. "I'm going to backtrack the guards to see if we should expect pursuit." He stood and stepped away from the tree. "I won't be long. You'll stay here?"

She only nodded.

"I won't be long," he repeated.

He returned to the site of the ambush and followed the guards' trail to a ridge that overlooked the hills. Little signs—bits of grass torn up in boredom, a pile of arranged stones, discarded apple cores—showed that the men had been there for some hours before the Avelun arrived; they'd probably kept watch through the night, waiting for him. A half-mile farther, he found their horses tethered in the woods. They weren't the five he and Mayavana had seen galloping through the pass. This party had been the other half of the patrol; the half Ciam would have ordered to hunt him. The Avelun hadn't been their target at all, just a stunning distraction they couldn't resist. By nightfall, she and Jhared would almost certainly have traveled this way together. Taken by surprise in the dark, they might very well both have been slain. Instead, here he stood before five sound horses and half a patrol's worth of provisions. He should have thanked Riana for the fortunate twist that would help him to reach Velantar, but he could only think of Mayavana struggling beneath three men, her blood watering the ground.

He searched the saddlebags, gathering food—including a silver flask of apple brandy—some warmer clothing, and a purse with a handful of coins. He selected two of the horses, a stolid-looking dun gelding and a black mare with an inquisitive eye, and cut the others loose. The mare turned to look at him as he lengthened her stirrups, but she made no objection when he swung onto her back. With the gelding's reins in one hand, Jhared kicked her into a trot and hastened back to the clearing.

Mayavana had vanished. The sight of the empty place beneath the tree set Jhared's heart racing. He pulled up the horses and threw himself out of the saddle. Then suddenly, silently, she was at his side, a dagger in her hand and that dead expression in her eyes.

"Just me," he said, showing his open palms.

Slowly, she lowered the dagger. Her gaze went toward the horses, not him. "The clanguards were camped, then? They were waiting for you?"

"I'm afraid so."

"How soon before the other half of the patrol comes after us?"

He blinked at how quickly she put the pieces together. "It depends how soon these men are missed. I wouldn't stake our lives on a guess. If you can ride, we should move on. Unless . . ." He paused, both hoping and fearing he might see her spread her wings and rise into the sky. "Unless you have it in you to travel faster on your own."

"No," she replied with a bitter laugh. "No, I don't have it in me. I'll try the horse, if you truly think it necessary."

He answered by bringing the gelding around to her. The horse gave a nervous whicker and fixed the Avelun with a white-rimmed gaze.

Mayavana looked equally uneasy. "They've never liked me any more than I like them."

"I suppose you confuse them." Jhared stroked the gelding's neck. "They're not sure if you're a predator. Just move slowly. They'll get used to you." He laced his fingers and stepped forward to give her a leg up.

A soft grunt of pain escaped her as she clambered into the saddle. Jhared kept a tight hand on the gelding and murmured to it until both the Avelun and the horse seemed settled. Then he slipped the reins over his own saddle horn, picked up her staff, and led them back through the gap to the little hollow where they had camped.

Rain had snuffed out the fire, but their belongings remained undisturbed. Jhared glanced back at Mayavana; she was pale and tight lipped. Her good hand grasped the gelding's mane, and blood soaked the bandage around her arm. Jhared was tempted to call a halt to let her rest and wait for darkness to travel, but he had no idea whether it would be days or hours before the rest of Ciam's clanguard came after him. If they found him with the Avelun, he had no veils about what would happen.

He retrieved Mayavana's pack and stowed it behind the saddle of the mare. Then he did his best to confuse the signs around the camp for the hunters who followed them. There was little else he could do; he hoped for more rain.

Before mounting again, he handed Mayavana a water skin, and she drank as though it had been days since she had seen water. Her face had gone a frightening grey. "Maya, if you still have Silvaye, you must use it. You need the healing."

"I can't." She sat rigidly in the saddle, her gaze somewhere beyond Jhared's shoulder. "I couldn't bear that helplessness. Not now."

He could see her clinging to composure. "I'm sorry," he murmured.

She snorted. "Sorry doesn't get me a hot meal or a dry place to sleep. Let's be on our way. Before this beast decides he's had enough of me."

They headed south, through the gap once more, then across the foothills, working their way lower toward Aven Plains. The mist remained thick throughout the morning, deadening the horses' hoofbeats and drifting like a host of wraiths among the giant Hileran fir trees. Mayavana rode without complaint, though Jhared could sense her discomfort. He was genuinely relieved when she pointed them in the direction of one of her shelters.

"It's been a long while since I've stopped on Clan Hilera's lands," she said. "No promises as to what we'll find."

Jhared turned his mount toward the hills she had indicated. "How far?"

"Half a day if my feet were on the ground."

They reached the hide by afternoon without incident and no evidence of pursuit. As sunlight cut through the mist in blue shafts, they crested a hill overgrown with thorn bushes. Jhared glanced questioningly at the Avelun, but she only nodded him onward, something that wasn't a smile curling one corner of her swollen lip. Thorns grabbed at Jhared and the horses. The black mare spooked when her tail became entangled. Quickly, Jhared kneed her sideways, to prevent her from kicking the gelding, and leaned back to free her. They continued, descending the other side of the hill toward what appeared to be an impenetrable hedge of vines and brambles. Only when they were directly above it could Jhared see a narrow break between the hedge and the hill. He eased the mare through the break and turned to be certain the gelding navigated it successfully. There was just enough room for both horses to stand shoulder to shoulder in a small bowl created by the bushes that grew on all sides of them. Behind Jhared, a rotting doorframe provided access into the earth itself. With a soft whistle of appreciation, he realized they had just climbed over the roof of an old hill cottage.

"I'll take a look," he told Mayavana, dismounting and handing her the reins.

He waited for his eyes to adjust to the dim light before stepping into the cottage. Cold, damp air settled on his face and hands. The scent of earth enveloped him, a scent that took him back to the cellar in Elder Trianor's home, with its shelves lined with jars of lindaberry jam and barrels of winter apples. The cottage had two rooms separated by a waist-high wall. In the first room, a fire pit, a wooden pallet, and a table with two chairs took up the space. The walls held niches dug into the earth and framed with timber. Within the niches, Jhared spied a cache of firewood and two jugs. The second room had been meant as a byre. A hayrack still hung on the wall, and bits of moldy straw covered the ground. There was no sign of recent use and no occupants other than the numerous brown spiders that clung to the timbers.

He offered Mayavana a hand to dismount. She didn't touch him, but slid down alone. Although she turned her gaze from him and kept her face carefully neutral, he could sense her pain and weariness, almost as if it were his own. He thought of boundaries shifting and the merging of Paths, one into the other, and wondered.

He led the horses into the byre, unsaddled and fed them, and returned with the saddlebags. Mayavana was sniffing the contents of the jugs.

"Stale water and bad wine," she announced, then half-turned to Jhared, her right hand extended to take her pack from him.

As he transferred the weight of the bag to her, her face blanched and she staggered heavily. The pack hit the floor. Her right wing fell free of her cloak, brushing the ground at an unnatural angle. He reached out to support her, but she drew back, cursing in Sonan.

He stared at the distance she had put between them and the pain now sharp and hard in her eyes. In an instant, two terrible images filled his head: the doves that huddled in the alleys of the city, wings shattered by children's well-aimed stones; and Mayavana on the ground, one man tearing at her wing so hard she screamed.

"You should have told me," he breathed.

"To what end? So you might say it's a way to balance my debt? That it's what I owe to Avelos?"

Jhared choked, aghast. He couldn't deny he once had those thoughts, but they seemed so removed from what he meant now, they might only have existed on another Path. A larger thing was happening to him here. His grasp on the truths of the world had begun to tear loose when he threatened a child with naked steel, and tore again when he told Mayavana his story. Now he was plummeting toward some new truth, just as he plummeted over and over in his nightmares. But while he waited to crash against the rocks, in this falling time when belief in the laws and the boundaries of Avelos could no longer save him, he had taken action.

"I killed for you. Have you thought on what that means?"

Color was returning to her face. Even as her injured left arm curled around her right wing, her eyes gleamed fiercely. "What it means, soldier, is that you slaked your own anger in blood. How long have you waited for a reason to slay those who've spent so many years slaying you?"

The question arrowed into him cruelly. All the more in that her accusation was wrong. He knew why he hadn't hesitated before rushing into the clearing. Even now, his heart beat out the fact of what he had begun to feel for her: a thing that could also only exist outside the laws, outside the definition of who he was. She would have been revolted to hear it.

"I think our paths have been too different to assume we understand one another," he said, swallowing very different words. "I only wish to ease your pain, as you eased mine. Will you allow me that?"

Emotions shifted in her eyes, changing their color like clouds shifting over the surface of a lake. Amid those emotions, Jhared caught a flash of something that gave him hope: a flash, he thought, of trust.

"I'm sorry." She sighed and shook her head. "Truly. I've been unfair." She paused before adding more softly. "I do know what you spared me, Jhared."

"No debt between us," he answered, suddenly needing someplace other than her steady gaze to set his focus. He turned to the saddlebags and pulled out the silver flask of brandy. The Avelun took it.

"It'll be better than the wine for dulling pain."

She smelled the contents, took a swallow, and made a face. "Or it might just give me such a headache I won't notice the rest."

He smiled a little, glad she could jest. "That gash on your arm needs to be cleaned properly. And then . . ." He gestured toward the sad angle of her wing.

"The arm first," she said, looking uneasy again.

"Very well. Do you carry bitterbalm?"

While he started the fire and heated water, she told him what medicines she kept in her herb box: many names were familiar to him; some were Sonan names and plants he'd never seen. Years among fighting men had given him numerous opportunities to watch healers at work, but it was a limited source of knowledge and one he hadn't dared to use. He let Mayavana tell him which herbs to blend with some of the oats and the boiled water to make a drawing salve. While the paste cooled, he unwound the blood-stained scarf from her arm.

"Zin will scold me for the scarf," she muttered, pulling the ruined wool into her lap.

Jhared focused on her injury, cleaning it thoroughly before spreading the salve between two pieces of boiled cloth. When he pinched the edges of the wound together and wrapped the warm paste over it, she hissed and reached for the flask. A significant amount of brandy disappeared as he bound the wound in a clean, dry bandage.

When he finished, she reclaimed her arm, as though his touch pained her as much as the injury. He drew his hands away from her, calloused hands, scarred from weapons practice and combat, and now from the burns earned while killing the Verael.

Killing is what Shorn men are born for.

The bitter accusation came easily to mind. He picked up the flask for himself and tossed back a long swallow of brandy, glad for its uncompromising fire.

He and the Avelun sat across from one another in silence, sharing the liquor. The flames crackled beside them, pushing back some of the dank chill. In the hedges outside the cottage, birds twittered and gossiped as the day began to fade.

Slowly, Mayavana rose from the table. The firelight gilded her figure as she stood before him. She wasn't small and delicate like Leita or softly curved like Ziabela. She was nearly as tall as Jhared, long-limbed and formed of lean muscle. Her strong, competent hands were curled at her waist now, as though she would have been more comfortable gripping her staff or her bow. The sharp angles of her face were softened by the ever-changing grey-green of her eyes and the smile that often shaped her lips. She spent her days trekking across a country that promised her nothing but curses and death, and despite the malice aimed at her, she preserved a place in her spirit for laughter and kindness. It struck Jhared how much courage that must take.

She wasn't smiling now, though; she looked uncertain as she freed the bronze clasp that held her cloak. The grey wool slid from her shoulders and puddled at her feet. She stepped free of it and turned her back to him, revealing her glory and pain.

Her left wing was furled neatly against her back, while her right hung crookedly, like a door from a broken hinge, until the black tips of her flight feathers bent against the ground. Jhared's palms grew sweaty and his insides churned. What did he know of easing suffering? If it weren't for him, she wouldn't have come to harm in the first place.

His chair creaked as he rose. She startled and checked a step forward.

"I'm sorry," he murmured. He took a breath and gathered himself. "Can you move it at all?"

She bowed her head. Her shoulders hunched with effort, and she seemed to be holding her breath. As her right wing twitched slowly toward her back, she groaned. "Gods of seas and skies. I don't know what happened. It hardly hurt at all just after."

"You needed not to feel it then. To have the chance to escape. I've seen men walk away from battle on a torn ankle or a broken leg and not realize it until after the crisis passed." He shook his head. "I'll need . . . to touch you."

She nodded wordlessly.

He swallowed and lifted his hands. For several moments he froze there, his fingers inches away from her feathers, her heat radiating against his palms. He couldn't have said just why touching her wings seemed so desperately intimate: perhaps because it was her wings for which Avelos cursed her, or perhaps because they represented the lost part of himself. Whatever the reason, what he was about to do felt very different from the way he had cared for her arm, and he could tell from the tension in her body she felt it too.

With a silent prayer to Riana for guidance, he began with the place where her torso joined her wing and the flesh became feathers. As he stared at the lovely shades of frost that gradually darkened to ash and then to ebony, the thought struck him that his body had once been shaped this way, with long ridges of muscle under almond skin that gave way to fans of feather and bone. He wondered what color his feathers had been. Swiftly, he shoved the thought aside.

Her tunic was a softly woven fabric the pale green of spring leaves, with three separate panels in the back tied loosely at her hips. Nudging the fabric aside, he slipped his fingers beneath to gently probe the fascinating muscles that ran down either side of her spine from the center of her shoulders to her supple waist. Those muscles would do much of the work to position her wings. Slowly, he stroked their length as he would the leg of a lame horse. He knew when he touched the first injury. Mayavana gasped, and Jhared felt a spasm in the hot, swollen flesh beneath his hand. He winced in sympathy.

"No wonder it's so difficult to lift. The muscle's badly strained." He didn't possess the skill to tell exactly how badly. Soldiers who tore the insides of their knees often ended up unable to run, and sometimes unable to walk. At the least, she would be grounded for a time. He kept those thoughts to himself as he drew his hands away and gave her space to catch her breath.

"Are you all right?"

"Well enough for another drink of that brandy," she panted, leaning over the table for the flask. When she had taken a long swallow, she showed her back to him again. "Please, finish. Is it broken?"

This time he set his hands over the leading edge of her wing. Warmth and softness greeted his fingers. The feathers gave slightly, enough that his fingertips slipped through to the first knuckle, and he could feel the strength beneath. Gentle exploration of the segments of the wing revealed a single bone closest to the back with a joint connecting it to two longer bones, rather like the bones of an arm, he realized.

As he worked, he took care not to let his rough fingers snag the silky vanes. The feathers had a clean, chalky scent that mingled with the berry scent of Maya's skin. He leaned a little closer and it filled his head, painting images of mountain crags under summer sun, lush green hills, and unbound vistas of perfect blue. With one hand, he brushed aside the loose strands of her black hair so he could better reach the covert feathers above her shoulders. He began to smooth the coverts, then the secondaries and primaries, as he had seen her do, drawing his hands unhurriedly along each feather, letting his fingertips learn their shapes. How must it feel to carry this glorious weight? He imagined the way it would tug back his balance. Every movement would be different—running, climbing, lifting his bow. Rather than the pathetic, painful twitching of his severed muscles, with wings he could shape the wind itself. His pulse pounded. He had been airborne once, soaring near the stars with a woman in his embrace. A warm breeze had buoyed them, and they had shared their love in the sacred skies—

Jhared stopped, abruptly realizing where his thoughts had gone and how shallow Mayavana's breathing had become. Filled with shame, he released her and took a backward step. She uttered a little strangled sound as he drew his hand away.

"Ah, Goddess. I didn't mean to hurt you," he said. "I just started imagining . . . that is, I've never touched . . ."

"The very mark of the curse?" she said hoarsely. She bent to grab her cloak and struggled to throw it over her wings. Jhared moved toward her, his hands out to help, but she pulled away. Her color was high as she turned from him.

He was furious at himself for being such a beast. She had dared to trust him and this was how he repaid her? "I'm sorry. I never meant to . . ." He shook his head. The truth would only do more harm. "You need something cold for that muscle strain. I'll be back. I'll be right back."

Afraid to look at her and see the anger in her expression, he grabbed up the water skins and fled. He was glad, at first, for the thorns that tore at him as he climbed the hill. Their sting overlaid the lingering sensation of softness against his hands, but his traitorous body took that ache and joined it with the ache of his longing until need overwhelmed him.

He ran, then, until he reached an arm of the Shiran River where it tumbled, white and frothy, through a cleft between the hills. His sword belt landed on the grassy bank where he tossed it. He stripped off his boots and clothes and dove into the depths of the icy water. He welcomed the shock of it and swam hard against the current, not rising until his lungs cried for air. He came up gasping, water streaming into his eyes. With handfuls of sand from the river bottom, he scrubbed his skin clean of blood and sweat and thoughts of the caress of feathers.

By the time he climbed out of the river and tugged on his clothes, the bronze light of sunset burnished the trees. He trudged back to the thorn-covered hill, hesitant to face her, but drawn by ties beyond his comprehension.

As he walked into the cottage, Jhared caught the aroma of food. A wedge of hard cheese and several sausages from the clanguards' provisions sat on the table. Mayavana had stretched out on the pallet on her stomach, one of the saddle blankets beneath her and her cloak and a blanket partially covering her wings. Her bandaged left arm stuck out awkwardly from her side. Jhared set down the water skins and quietly padded over to check on her. Her eyes were closed, but no peace dwelt in her expression. The bruise at the corner of her lip lent a blue tinge to her cheeks. The lonely ache Jhared thought he had chased away returned.

She opened her eyes and stared up at him. For several heartbeats, she held him with a gaze of intense appraisal, as though he might be an old friend she didn't quite recognize. Then she blinked, and the sense of connection disappeared.

"Did you have a thought to *swim* back to Velantar?" she asked mildly.

He looked down. His wet hair had soaked through his shirt and was dripping onto the floor. "No. I just didn't like smelling stronger than the horses."

Her subdued smile sent a trickle of relief through him.

"Mayavana, forgive me," he began. "I didn't intend—"

"Don't," she said quickly. "You said it yourself: we travel different paths. You are a Forest Guard sworn to Avelos. You can't see me as anything other than what Avelos has told you to see."

The hurt in her tone made Jhared take a tight hold of his undisciplined thoughts and promise himself not to press her trust in such a way again. He plucked up a remnant of the cloth he had used to bind her arm, poured some of the icy river water into a bowl, and brought it to her.

"It will ease the swelling," he said, showing her the bowl. "Unless you'd reconsider the Silvaye."

"No Silvaye. Not unless I'm forced to it." She sighed and nodded at the wet cloth. "In lieu of a swim, I suppose this will have to do."

Once Jhared had settled the cloth on Mayavana's back, he retrieved some of the cheese and sausage from the table, then sank down beside her, his back to the wall and his legs stretched in front of him. Gradually, the fire dried his hair and brushed the chill from his skin. As the fever in Mayavana's muscles warmed the cloth, he soaked it again. She made a tiny breathless squeak as he returned it, cold and dripping, to her back.

"Sorry," he murmured.

"It's all right," she said, not bothering to look up.

In the quiet, Jhared's thoughts began to drift. The sounds of his own breathing grew deep and distant. In that dream-laden, undefended place, a question returned. After the attack, he had tucked it away, but now it hung before him, begging for an answer that might say why he had been forced to kill his own countrymen. It whispered in his head, and before he could think to stop it, he whispered it aloud.

"Mayavana, why didn't you fly away when the clanguards came?"

Beside him, she stiffened. Her silence was absolute.

"What is it? Did they fall on you too swiftly?"

She twisted her head to look up at him, storms gathering in her eyes. "Are you mocking me? After everything?"

"Mocking? Of course not!"

She laughed bleakly. "Seas and skies. Is it possible you truly don't know? I'm afraid I must disappoint you, then."

He tilted his head. "How?"

"I'm just as land-bound as you," she said flatly. "My wings are useless. I can hover a bit, but injured or not, I cannot fly."

Disbelief flooded him, a wild, raging river of denial. Then a deep sadness touched him, and finally, a measure of understanding, as several of the odd moments of the past days began to make sense. "What happened?"

"War and exile and the destruction of our stories, that's what happened!" she said, waving off his budding questions. "It's more complicated than I can face tonight."

Only then did he remember that before the attack she had intended to share something with him. Just this morning that had been, although it seemed an age ago. "It's part of my legacy, too, isn't it? Will you tell me?"

"I will. I promise. Just not now."

Heartbreak echoed in her voice. Jhared realized something he should have figured out much sooner.

"Maya, you aren't traveling through Avelos for the sake of the smugglers, are you?"

"Oh, they're my livelihood, certain enough. But smuggling isn't why I risk my life here, no." She laid her head back down on her arm.

The ever-present yearning for the sky burned through him, and he didn't know if it was her desire or his own. He felt as though some part of their Paths had overlapped so completely they had experienced the same moment.

A girl runs bare beside the lake, struggling to lift herself above the water. A boy paces in a small room, desperate to climb into the heights and fling himself into the wind's embrace.

He had never even guessed at what she suffered. He had been blinded by his desire to see her as whole. He never guessed they shared this grief.

She lay still and tense. He longed to bridge the chasm between them, but words felt too clumsy to do more than grate against the raw wound. Hesitantly, he lifted his hand and very lightly let his fingers touch her hair. He paused, waiting for her to pull away. When she did not, he drew his fingers along the short, soft strands. It was a thing he had sometimes done for Branlen long ago when the small boy was afraid on stormy nights. A rare, gentle contact. A comfort. A gift of connection.

She didn't say anything or even open her eyes, but very gradually, her body relaxed. That was a gift, too. For the moment, Jhared need not be the lethal soldier Avelos expected him to be or face the flaws that made him a danger. As she lay beside him, injured and weary, something very different stirred within him, a part of his spirit that longed to nurture and heal. A part he had almost forgotten existed.

Softly, he began to sing, a ballad he hadn't dared to recall since his mother's death: "Heart of Stars." It was a love song to the sacred skies—to endless arches of cerulean under a honeyed sun and swathes of velvet night graced with silver stars. His mother had made the song his lullaby long before he could understand why it filled his heart and answered the need in his spirit. Now, in the dark, musty cottage, he shaped the melody as the only bit of healing he had to offer.

Eventually, Mayavana's breathing slowed and deepened. Jhared brought the song to its close and sat in silence, allowing himself to cherish both the beauty and the loss. As he floated into sleep, his hand slid from Mayavana's head to rest upon her shoulder.

26.

TEACHERS

*T*he wind gusts sideways, driving rain into the hedges. He shifts his grip on the thorny branch to keep from blowing away. Above him, just out of reach amid the tangled vines, hangs a withered purple berry. It would be easier to feed after the storm passes; the vines are dense and thorns can do damage, but he's hungry now. He's never been any good at waiting when he's hungry, although it's gotten him into trouble on occasion. This time, he decides, the risk is worth it. The berry is such a tempting shade of purple. And he's a clever one, if not patient. With one eye on the berry, he stretches his neck and stands on tiptoe. The fruit brushes his beak, teasing him. He's not yet high enough to snap it up. The wind blows again, rocking his branch and setting the berry swinging. He squawks in frustration. Then, quicker than a fox, he leaps with a flutter of wings, grabs the fruit, and swallows it down even as he regains his hold on the branch. Clever. Very clever. He squawks again—proudly—fluffs himself until he's round as a plum, and squats to warm his feet. The thorn bush is good shelter. He already sees other berries. Perhaps the storm is not so terrible, after all.

Jhared grins, sharing a feeling of satisfaction that is his, yet not his. He enjoys a sense of simplicity and contentment unlike anything else he can recall. It's pleasant to drift along this Path, unburdened.

A new presence catches his attention with its complex weaving of emotion and thought. This presence has nothing to do with the simple, drowsy awareness surrounding him. His heart begins to race even before he can fully articulate who has come.

"Jhared?" Her voice is soft, careful.

"Mayavana!" Joy lights his spirit with an intensity that takes him by surprise. "How did you reach me?"

"Not now," she says, low and tight. "Take my hand. Before I lose you."

He can't see her, but now that he's attuned to her presence, he feels the tension vibrating through her. Puzzled by her urgency, he tries to remember what it is to have hands and how to use them. Something Leita once said returns: "The perspective you have on a Path depends on which doors you open." He thinks about doors and putting himself in the same place as Mayavana. He thinks of tracking her, as if they were still in the wilds. What tracks does someone make on the Paths? What signs would Mayavana leave behind? With concentration,

357

he can feel them, like memories she discarded: signs of her self. He follows a trail created of her courage and honesty, her generous smile and gentle songs. He flows through a narrow cleft in the blackness and sees starlight and a sliver of green lake. He imagines the arch of her wings and the thoughtful expression that draws her brow. The opening widens further, and Jhared scrambles through.

In the starlight, Mayavana stands at the lakeshore. Behind her is a funny little lodge raised above the damp ground on stilts. She holds out one hand to him. He looks around at this new Path curiously. He's seen this place before; it is a home to her.

"Hurry!" she says, her face contorting with effort. "I don't know how long I can hold us here."

He takes the final step and clasps her outstretched hand in both of his. Her presence rushes through him and he gasps at the force of it. Then she takes a backward step, and without warning, draws him someplace else.

A gentle wind swirled around him, as mild as a summer evening and carrying the scent of a lake. Cool, clear water lapped at his awareness; then Maya drew back and collapsed beside him, and he realized they were on the dirt floor of the hill cottage.

"What was that?" he murmured in amazement. "What did you do to me?"

"*Do* to you?" she panted. "You were traveling with one of the cousins as though you'd decided to take up residence. One of the cousins, Jhared. I had no idea." She trailed off and leaned back to catch her breath.

He frowned. The fingers he touched to his throat found only the scar where Leita had stabbed him, no blood or new cuts, and the Paths didn't come to claim their toll. Traveling with Maya, he had felt a strength and a warmth that seemed a part of him and at the same time more than him. A sense of well-being still flowed through his limbs: *the scent of the lake, a tranquil wind.* It was like nothing he had felt under Leita's Blade. "What I meant is how did you bring me back without blood?"

"Blood?" She made a face. Careful not to lean on her left arm, she leveraged herself into a sitting position. "When the cousins stirred, I awoke and found you traveling. When you didn't return, I feared you didn't know the danger." She shrugged one shoulder. "I followed you and called to you from a Path I thought would hold me."

"Cousins? Do you mean . . . ?" He sat up beside her, pulling images from the haze of the Path: a thorn bush in the storm. Berries. Tasty berries. "You're saying that I was on the Path of a bird?"

"It's easy to grow comfortable drifting with them. If you're not careful, you'll forget your own story."

"Cousins." He tried the word again and thought of what it signified: the connection between himself and Cael's messengers. He thought of the pain of a hawk spinning out of the sky with an arrow in its breast, and shuddered reflexively.

Maya's expression hardened. "Does it repulse you so much to consider your-self touched by a beast?"

"No." He bowed his head. "But perhaps it explains why I'm haunted by a raptor."

Something flickered in her eyes, and she went still. "Jhared, do you understand you shouldn't be able to reach them at all? Not after what Avelos did to you."

She said it as though it were somehow the fault of Avelos that he had been born cursed and in need of Teaching. His anger should have been ready to hand, but this time it was only a small thing. He knuckled his eyelids. "I think you have a lot to tell me."

She glanced toward the open doorway. Night pressed around the cottage, and the rain had returned, drumming steadily over the hill. Every few moments, wind gusted through the hedges, driving a chill into the chamber that cowed their little fire.

He saw the question in her eyes and shook his head. "We're not moving on tonight. We'd never make it through the hills with the storm and the dark against us." What he didn't say was that he knew she wasn't fit to ride, and he didn't in-tend to leave her alone.

"I could use some tea and something to eat," she said, beginning to unfold stiffly from the floor. "Then I'm willing to share what you've asked of me."

Jhared came to his feet, picking up the bowl of water. "If you'll begin your story, I'll see to the food."

She nodded thanks and moved to a chair, where her injured wing wasn't forced to bend so much when she sat. Jhared made tea, hers steeped with willow-bark. She didn't protest when he added a measure of brandy to her mug.

Mayavana watched him from across the table as he dug through the saddle-bags. In addition to the cheese and sausages, from the clanguard he had taken several rounds of black bread, a bag of oats, and fresh apples. He cut thick slices of the bread, layered them with cheese, and set them near the flames to toast.

"Have you ever wondered what the Becoming required of us before the Exile?" she asked.

His knife rapped the table as he cut an apple into quarters. "I didn't think the Becoming existed before." He offered her a piece of fruit from the end of his blade. "After all, if the Avelune had been required to prove their loyalty, war might have been avoided."

"Ah, Jhared. The Becoming has nothing to do with loyalty. Not then or now." She stopped and gently took the knife from him. "Are you certain you want to know this? I would have forced it upon you once, when your story cut through me and I felt my own losses too heavily. Now, I realize what it will mean to you. I have no right to drag you away from your own truths. Sometimes clinging to what is familiar is the only way to keep moving."

He set his hands upon the table, his fingers nearly touching hers. He thought of Zia telling him forbidden stories about the Exile and Leita sharing secrets about Pathwalkers. Neither of them had ever considered that the choice to accept or reject those burdens should be his.

He smiled at Mayavana. "Thank you for the choice, but I am still a Forest Guard scout. I was taught to observe a road from different perspectives. Please, go on."

She set down her mug, but her fingers remained wrapped around the lacquered wood. "Before the Exile, the Becoming was the rite in which our people proved themselves ready to enter the skies."

Jhared felt something shift and wasn't sure whether it was within or outside of him. "Do you mean their first flight?"

"The first alone, I believe."

"I see." It took effort for him to maintain a detached tone. "I never considered there might be any ritual about it. I always supposed learning to fly would be as uneventful as learning to walk."

"If you think learning to walk is uneventful, you've never seen how a parent celebrates her child's first step. Flying isn't simple, Jhared. If it were, I wouldn't have had my feet on the ground when the clanguard came."

"After the war, then, when Tumal created the Shorn, the Becoming became meaningless?"

She shook her head. "Not meaningless. Tumal used it to tear us away from the cousins and from the wonders of the Paths. I didn't know exactly what that meant until you told me about the hawk."

"Riana commands that a bird of prey be slain in the prime of spring," Jhared whispered. A trembling started deep inside him; despite his bravado, he feared her next words.

"That command has nothing to do with Riana," Maya said. "Do you know what Tumal did to the temple?"

"He executed the priestesses who tried to assassinate him."

"*Perhaps* Lady Amalia attempted to assassinate him or perhaps not. My own kin weren't certain, even then." Maya made a dismissive gesture, as though the difference no longer mattered. "What's certain is that he killed every true servant of Riana he could find and installed his own false priestesses—women loyal to him—in positions of power. They altered the rites of the goddess at his command. Your Becoming was no sacred thing."

Jhared leaped up to grab the bread from the fire and almost knocked over his chair. "How can I possibly believe you? By your own admission, you despise Avelos."

She shrugged without rancor. "Most of what I know I gleaned from a book of memoirs kept by the women in my family since before the Exile. It was the only thing my mother carried out of Avelos, other than me. It was meant to tell the story of my kin, not the history of Avelos. But think on it: you've seen the evidence of the purges in the high temple itself. Do you believe Tumal did such a methodical job of destroying our stories, our history, our art, and allowed our rituals to remain intact?"

Wind hissed around the cottage. Thunder shook the doorframe. Mayavana's uninjured wing wrapped closely around her shoulder. "The Becoming was never about loyalty, Jhared. It is a means to force you to slay a part of yourself."

"Because we proved ourselves evil," he whispered desperately. "Because they have reason to fear us."

"They took everything that defined you. What cause have they for fear?"

Jhared turned away. One hand pressed against the pain in his chest. He stumbled to the doorway to gulp lungfuls of night air. *Riana commands that a bird of prey be slain in the prime of spring.* He had always held tight to the knowledge that the goddess blessed what he had done at his Becoming and what he had sworn to Avelos. It was the goddess who would acknowledge it when final reparation had been made and the Shorn could be forgiven. But if the debt was nothing of Riana's creation, then how could it ever be balanced?

When would an Avelun child ever be safe from the knife?

"They only did what they had to," he said. "The temple, the council, the Teachers. They only did what they must to protect Avelos from creatures full of deceit and unholy desires."

"Is that what I am, Jhared? Am I the unholy creature from which Avelos must be defended?"

She had come up behind him and was staring now, unblinking, into the rain. One wing fanned the air gently, and her tone was so mild she might have been asking the chance for clearer weather, but even as the rest of the world collapsed around him, Jhared couldn't help but see the way she braced herself, like someone expecting a blow.

"No," he whispered, bending toward her. His shivering body was drawn to her, as he had been drawn to her on the Paths even before he stumbled into her cave, as he was drawn to the open sky. "No, Mayavana. I cannot see you so."

Tentatively, his lips brushed the corner of her mouth, dry and soft. His head spun as her scent enveloped him, and desire arrowed through his body. Her hand touched his shoulder, steadying him. Grey-green eyes met his, and in her gaze, he found a familiar ghost: a need to be known. With a smile, she entered the circle of his arms. Danger waited here: a part of his mind still knew it. Then all thought fled as her lips tasted the edge of his jaw and her warm breath drifted against his ear. "*Goddess,*" he breathed helplessly as she leaned into him.

They reached for one another, his hands slipping down the column of her throat to the swell of her breasts; her fingers twining around his neck, caressing his shoulders, sliding down his back—

"Oh, no. No!" With a cry of anguished shock, she tore free of his embrace and knocked into the table behind her. "I'm sorry," she gasped, her expression pale and distraught. "I'm so sorry."

Jhared's lucidity returned in a rush. With painful deliberation he straightened, took a long breath, and stepped away from her. Bitterness etched his tone. "It's not your fault. You asked what it is to be Shorn. Now you've touched the scarred heart of it."

"Oh, Jhared. Please don't," she whispered.

His jaw clenched so hard he felt the joints pop. He closed his eyes as he realized with sharp certainty he would never truly know her. How could he have imagined otherwise? He was a half-man. Broken. Shorn.

"When I touched you I . . . *felt* them," she stammered. "Your wings. The knife." Her face shone with cold sweat. "Lumati help me, I felt the Shearing. As though I were with you on that Path."

"I told you I have no control of the Gate," he said flatly.

"Gods of seas and skies, this isn't about you falling through the Gate. It's as though you're throwing open doors to the Paths around you. I very nearly slipped through. Don't you feel it?"

With effort, he turned his focus inward. His body clamored for completion. Released by his desire, Shorn energy bolted through him. And deep in his center, the Gate pulsed—not violently, as he'd often felt it, but steadily, as though it were as natural a part of him as his heartbeat. "I feel the blue flames. I'm sorry I hurt you."

Mayavana stretched out a hand as if she would touch him again, but she glanced at his expression and didn't move. Apprehension carved lines in her brow. "It's a hazardous thing, being so open."

He drew another breath and nodded; he had long expected something like this. In a way, it was a relief that it had finally come and he no longer need dread its arrival. *No one who stands beside you is safe.* "I understand. I'll leave you the gelding and the provisions. Use him to carry your packs, if you won't ride. I'll gather my things—"

Her frown deepened. "What are you talking about?"

"You're right. I'm a danger to you. I won't linger."

"I didn't mean for you to go! I meant we must find a way for you to travel more safely." She added more quietly. "I might help you with what little I know. If you'd allow me."

He peered at her uncertainly; her expression was guileless. "I haven't proved to be a very good student of the Paths in the past."

"Well, I've never been a teacher," she said. "So perhaps we'll be right for one another."

"I would be indebted to you."

Her tone turned crisp. "Friendship has nothing to do with debts. Sit down."

"You mean to start now?"

She cleared her throat and tugged her clothing back in order. "I don't quite feel like sleeping just now," she said wryly. "Do you?"

He ducked his head, his face heating. "Now is fine."

She sat down at the table. He splashed water over his face, trying to regain calm before sitting across from her. The toasted cheese and bread had remained uneaten. She took a piece and pushed another in his direction.

"You do realize how unsafe it is to go wandering among the Paths, don't you?" She took a bite of the bread and glanced up at him. "It's not something you do by choice, is it?"

He worried at the food with one hand. "I'm not trying to lose myself, if that's what you mean. Tempting as the Paths may be, I've no desire for madness."

She nodded, looking more than a little relieved. A crumb sat on her lips and she licked it away. "Tell me how you get yourself home when you travel. You seemed terribly comfortable with our cousin just a bit ago. How would you have returned if I hadn't interfered?"

"Sometimes I fall back to my own place," he said with a shrug. "More often it takes pain to anchor me. The Bearer used her knife."

Maya made a face of disgust. "I suppose it shouldn't surprise me that Avelos has turned even traveling into a rite of suffering."

"How do *you* keep from falling?" he challenged.

"It's different for me. It takes me a lot of work to find the Gate." She dipped her head as though in apology. "I've never fallen."

"Ah."

She touched his hand lightly. "Don't despair. They tore you, Jhared. They tore you inside as surely as that ox of a clanguard tore me. Perhaps that's why you've had so much trouble. You need time to heal."

It was an uncomfortable thought that he couldn't keep the Gate shut because of a wound earned at his Becoming. Was it an inner scar to match the ones on his back and shoulder? Elder Trianor might have appreciated the irony, for if Maya was correct, the Becoming was intended to *seal* the Gate.

"It's as though you're throwing open doors to Paths all around you." Had Leita felt that strangeness in him?

"Jhared?"

He sighed and pushed a hand through his hair. "I'm sorry. That idea doesn't sit easily."

"All right, then. Let's start with something else." She considered for a moment. "Where have you had success? If we find what skills you possess, perhaps we can find a way for you to use them to keep yourself in one place."

"I've never had success with the Paths."

"That's not true! You found me when I called to you. It's no small feat to cross to a Time and Place that have nothing to do with your own. How did you do it?"

He pondered it; the recollection was dream-hazy. "I thought about opening the doors that would lead to you, and I thought of what it would mean to track you." He leaned back and closed his eyes in concentration. "The Paths hold memories and I followed them, like footsteps. I set myself to track after your strength, your smile, your songs: who you *are*. I could sense—"

Mayavana's hand hit the table with a *thunk*.

Jhared opened his eyes, cursing inwardly. Could he not keep himself in check for five minutes at a time? "Forgive me. I didn't mean to embarrass you."

A lopsided smile curled her lips. "You lovely man, you don't even realize your own ingenuity. You've brought a scout's talents to the Paths. Listen to your own words: you tracked me by *knowing who I am*. Perhaps that's your anchor: to track your way home you must know who you are and where you belong."

He groaned at the deceptive simplicity of it.

She turned. "What's wrong?"

"The truth is I thought I knew exactly who I was until I shot a nesting hawk."

"That wasn't your doing," she said softly. "If Avelos hadn't forced you—"

He lifted a hand to stop her. One more bitter word about his country would finish him. He couldn't trust his response. "No more tonight. Please."

She studied him. With two fingers she tugged at a strand of her hair, then dropped her hands into her lap. "No more," she agreed with a tired sigh. "Perhaps later."

"Maya, thank you for . . ." *Your tolerance, you kindness, your courage.* He opened his palms in front of him, unable to select the right words.

She seemed to understand, smiling faintly as she rose from her chair and went to the pallet. "Gods, I feel like I've been trampled by an Amurian blood bull."

She folded onto the makeshift bed and wrestled, one armed, with her blankets. Jhared knelt to help her spread them across her shoulders. His fingers inadvertently brushed her feathers, and he drew a breath.

"There's room," she suggested, indicating the blanket beside her. "A space for comfort and warmth, if nothing more."

"I think I'm not yet fit for sleep," he said, pretending to misunderstand.

She nodded, a hint of sadness in her eyes, and turned away.

Jhared stirred the fire and checked the horses. They were drowsing, the mare with her head stretched across the gelding's back. He drank some of the brandy and said a prayer for Leita and his comrades. Eventually, he sank onto one of the chairs and stretched his legs under the table. He listened to the rain playing a song to the night and wondered, if he were tracking his own way back along the Paths, who was it he would find.

27.

LOOSED DESIRES

Jhared hunkered in the cottage with Maya through another day of rain and then another, taking some badly needed rest. The storm lingered, washing away their tracks and confounding potential pursuit with muddy trails and mist-shrouded hills. Maya slept soundly through the rest of the night and through the following day, waking only long enough to eat a bit and drink more willowbark tea before burrowing back into her blankets. Accustomed to interrupted sleep, Jhared drowsed sporadically, but what rest he caught he welcomed.

By the end of the second day, he felt much renewed, and the plight of his patrolmates pressed on him. He had finished changing the bandages on Mayavana's arm, relieved to find only a low fever in her flesh and no worse swelling. He went to the door, judging the weather for the coming night.

"Are you up to riding?" he asked, glancing over his shoulder at her.

"Riding, no," she snorted. "But I can sit like a sack of potatoes in the saddle."

"Well enough." He smiled a little at her annoyed expression.

"You shouldn't feel reluctant about going on without me, you know. I slow you now."

His heart skipped against his ribs. He came back to the table. "I can't afford to leave you. I need your smuggler's knowledge to cross Aven Plains."

"Rather, you can't bear to leave her," Shrill sneered.

Jhared twitched at the voice. He had begun to entertain the perverse hope that his Teachers had abandoned him.

"Say what you will," he told Shrill. *"Without her aid, I wouldn't have survived the mountains. She's been nothing you've named her. I won't leave her undefended."*

"She's Avelun. Do you think her incapable of wearing a subtle mask and playing on your desires? Did you learn nothing about traitorous women from Ziabela? You'll see, boy. I'm very much afraid that you will see."

Shrill withdrew into silence. Jhared flipped his awareness back to the outer world to find Maya staring at him.

"I'm well enough to travel," she said, raising a brow. "Are you?"

He picked up the bowl and water skins from the table without looking at her. "Let's be on our way."

Night made a cold cloak as they left the forest to enter the flat, boundless grasslands. Jhared truly was glad for Mayavana's knowledge. Her experience on the plains let her choose the best routes to avoid the villages and the most heavily traveled game trails. When he would have stopped to let her rest, she pushed them on.

"We won't pause on the Plains so long as we still have some darkness left." she said, kicking the gelding to a faster pace, then grabbing for the saddle when he broke into a canter.

For hours they rode, with Lord Arion's star a bright guide in the south and the Sandien Mountains a dense shadow growing smaller behind them. The tall grasses parted with a crackle and a hiss as the horses swept through. Wolves called to one another in the dark, and once Jhared caught a glimpse of a plains cat slinking off with a limp form in its mouth. Jhared began to relax as they cantered through lands unclaimed by towns and cultivated fields. It reminded him of the true wilderness that existed at the borders; he had missed it.

When tawny light began to streak the sky, Maya led them down the bank of a river onto a grassy flat, where a line of willow trees collaborated with the slope to form a small, natural fortress. The Avelun dismounted awkwardly. Her wings sagged to the ground, leaving twin trails behind her as she drew her horse under the trees and gave the reins to Jhared.

"We made good time tonight," he said. "With your guidance."

She blew out a tired breath. "I wasn't meant to be a rider."

Frustration filled her tone that Jhared knew now had nothing to do with her horsemanship. He could only nod in sympathy as he led both animals toward the water.

Dawn light filtered through the remains of the willow leaves, turning them gold-green. Maya pulled her hood over her head and curled against the bank, falling asleep almost instantly. Jhared couldn't slow his thoughts enough to sleep. After a moment of consideration, he took her bow and quiver and strode off along the bank.

The bow felt good in his hands and fit him well; he and Maya were nearly of a height. The arrows were fine, footed shafts with heads of steel, costly and well made. He startled, then flushed, when he realized that Maya's own feathers made the fletching. Best not to think too much on that. Game was plentiful this close to the river, but he didn't rush, slipping with easy, silent steps along the water, spying out the signs left by a variety of predators and prey. The work unwound his muscles and steadied his thoughts. It was ever a joy to explore the complex patterns the wilds offered. When he finally sighted his quarry, a young male cabrin wandering too far from the herd, he sent the arrow from the bow with a perfect arc that shot a rill of pleasure through his body.

He returned with his catch to find that Maya had already awoken and started a fire. She smiled and shrugged at his questioning look. "You had my bow. I never took you for a hunter who would return empty handed."

Jhared returned her smile as he set down the meat and picked up her kettle to fetch water. They worked well together, each anticipating the step of the other. The realization gave him more pleasure than it should have.

By the end of the next night, they left the grasslands, riding close enough to the Aven Plains fork that Jhared saw starlight gleaming off the Avelune tower where he and Alende had sheltered. Brenia would be another night's ride. Obled two after that. Perhaps three more to Parnas Pass. He counted out the days, recognizing he was no longer just counting how long it would be before aid could be sent to Aglar Garrison; he was counting how much time remained before he must say goodbye to Maya.

"Where will you go when we reach Velantar?" he asked her one night as they walked to rest the horses.

"I won't travel so far as the city." She twisted the gelding's lead between her fingers. "I'm heading for Sona. I'll turn southwest when we come through the pass."

So soon, Jhared wanted to say, but he had no right even to think such a thing. "You're going home?" he asked instead.

"It's not truly home, but it's a place to wait out the winter until I can begin my search again."

"For the means to fly?"

She nodded. "Somewhere artifacts of the ancients still exist that hold the secret."

"Are your smugglers helpful in that?"

"Sometimes," she said, ignoring his tone. "In Sona, of late, a taste has developed for ancient texts. When the market is good, men are interested in finding more of the books and artifacts Avelos has to offer. They hire me to guide them, and I have the chance to see what they uncover."

He couldn't help but wince at the image of smugglers crawling through Avelos. "An ideal situation for everyone, then."

"Jhared, I must take what I can find," she said more heatedly. "It's not as though the High Priestess of Avelos will give me leave to study the temple's carvings. You can't imagine how many hours I spent studying the art in the cavern at Alende's Pass before finally giving up."

"I *can* imagine," he said. Had he possessed any hope at all for flight, he would have spent his life pursuing it.

A yearning he hadn't meant to reveal slipped into his tone, and Maya gave him a look too close to pity for him to bear. He tugged his mare's lead and turned away.

They made steady progress, riding through the lengthening nights and catching sleep where they could during the day. Maya's injuries slowly improved, although Jhared observed her favoring her arm more frequently than he liked. When he tried to tend to her, she drew away from his touch and engaged him instead with questions about his life in the city, talk about archery and fletching, or discussions of herb lore. She offered to teach him about the collection in her precious healer's box. He refused her the first time, certain it was more knowledge than a Shorn man was meant to possess. The second time she offered, he pushed past the complaints of his Teachers and yielded to his longing to learn.

"That's goatsbane. Don't sniff it." She pointed to a chalky, pale-blue power at the bottom of one of the little drawers. "When the root is ground so fine as this, inhaling it increases the potency. It can speed a failing heart, lift a man's courage, or keep him running when he's at the end of his strength, but the aftereffects aren't pleasant."

It sounded rather like a powdered form of Shorn energy. Jhared peered at it curiously. "Where does it grow?"

"In the west. Near water. In sandy soil usually."

"West?"

"It likes the riverlands of Amuria," she said with a shrug.

He nodded without comment and pointed to a vial holding dirty yellow crumbs that looked like dried moss. "Catspad," he said. "To absorb the poison of insect and serpent bites." It was something he had seen used often at the Sahisten border, where the sting of the local scorpions could cause a man to lose a limb.

"Yes." Maya smiled. "And this?"

She pulled open another drawer, this one lined with a black cloth. Lifting the edges of the cloth itself, she set it reverently in his hand. On top lay a single, silvery leaf. He studied it, fascinated and more than a little wary. "Silvaye."

"Lovely, isn't she?"

The leaf was a perfect tear shape and soft as a kitten's ear. He didn't stroke it, but only held it flat on his palm. It wasn't merely that the Silvaye could kill a man as quickly as heal him. What he held contained a part of the spirit Silvien, who once had been Riana's healer. "It doesn't trouble you to work with the Chosen?"

"The most precious gifts are often as dangerous as they are valuable," Maya said.

"Someone else said almost the same to me once." It had been Kaliska, the temple healer and Ziabela's friend. He hadn't been fully reassured then, either.

With care, Maya lifted the cloth from his palm and returned it with the leaf to the drawer. He let out a breath, surprised to realize he was sweating. She gave him a look of concern. "It truly disturbs you."

"That's not just another dried herb with the potential to be poisonous. It's a wild power. A mad spirit. Such things are deadly and . . ." He licked his lips and looked aside.

"And?" she asked archly.

"Not meant to lie in the hands of the Shorn."

"Ah." With a sigh, she closed all the little drawers of the red box, wiped her hands carefully on a clean cloth, and stowed the box in her pack.

Jhared didn't protest, although watching the healer's notions disappear left a hollow in his middle.

Sometimes as they walked, Maya talked about the Paths, describing her own experiences as a Traveler. He hoped he might learn from her a reliable way to keep the Gate closed. When he pressed her, however, she grew flustered and uncertain.

"It's like trying to explain how to fall asleep," she said helplessly. "I can tell you to lay down and close your eyes, but that's not sleeping. Perhaps if I observe what happens when you cross the Gate, I could sense what's going wrong."

With some effort, she convinced him to seek the Paths one morning while she studied him. Almost immediately, he fell onto the Path of a cousin, and she was forced to pull him back. The exercise left him sprawled at her feet, exhausted and disheartened, as she frowned in bemusement.

"You can chivy open doors as well as any smuggler. Why can't you close them?"

"Why does she care so much about your travel?" the Boar asked dourly as Jhared picked himself off the ground.

"It's sacrilege she's encouraging," Shrill said. *"When do you plan to do away with her?"*

Jhared didn't bother trying to answer any of them.

As they crossed into Clan Manitar's territory, the landscape grew more familiar. Old forests crested rolling hills. The crisp breeze carried the scent of flowing water, rotting leaves, and the anticipation of snow. He was almost home. The Parnas Mountains curved above the trees like giant tortoise shells in shades of evergreen, gold, and plum. Already, the trail twisted upward toward the pass. Velantar was close, no more than a handful of days if the weather held.

The closer they drew to the city, the more Jhared's Teachers prodded him with nightmares and hostile grumbling. They hadn't forgiven him for Maya, and now he was returning to Velantar without the means to stop the killing winds. In the depths of the night, when Shrill and the Boar took turns picking him apart like hungry crows, he began to ask his own questions.

"Did you know the true purpose of the Becoming?" he demanded of them. *"And how Lord Tumal altered the rite after the Exile?"*

"Do you trust your Avelun's lies?" they responded.

"That's not an answer."

"We've always known the truth, and so have you: you're a danger. The Becoming was meant to make you safe."

"But it didn't. I can still sense the Paths. Why?"

Silence.

"Please! Speak to me! Don't blame me for seeking answers elsewhere if you won't tell me what you know."

Jhared felt an uncomfortable rustling in his mind.

"We don't know why," Shrill finally admitted.

"What of the unbound?" he asked. *"Like Alende. Are they all Pathwalkers?"*

Silence again, and then the Boar's deep voice: *"Doubtful. Look how few priestesses are born Pathwalkers. It's a rare ability."*

"You don't know that for certain," Jhared pressed.

The Boar's voice turned hard and unexpectedly caustic. *"No. We don't know. It's been too long and Tumal was too thorough in his purges!"*

"Jhared, wait!"

A hand clamped onto his forearm, and Jhared jerked his head up, discovering that he had drifted toward the Gate. From outside a blanket of fog, Maya's eyes were wide with alarm.

"Shifa!" she hissed. "Don't wander now!"

Through the trees ahead, firelight limned the shapes of men. Low voices and drunken laughter reached Jhared through the haze.

The blue flames rose within him, ravenous. He was dropping away from the moment. "Leave me, Maya! Flee!"

For an instant, he saw the desperate indecision in her, but he had already drifted into the in-between; it wasn't very far to fall.

The chains that bound Jhared's wrists chimed out a strange, sad music as he climbed the stairs to the top of the city wall. A breeze kissed his cheek, crisp with the promise of snow. He shivered, not from the cold, and looked away from the sprawling valley below. He would be soaring over it soon, for a handful of moments, at least. The executioner waited to push him to a traitor's death.

He understood this end. He had violated his oath and rejected the laws his Teachers had given him. It was an expected end, but not one free of regret.

On the city side of the wall, the crowd jeered and hissed. Someone had hung a dead pigeon on a tether and was swinging it in circles. Five elders stood at the front of the crowd, the required witnesses. Jhared couldn't look at them, then forced himself to do so. Tierzen Trianor stood with his family, staring stiffly at the wall but not at his condemned Folly. Madam Trianor clung to her husband, her face pressed into his shoulder. She had always feared what Jhared's ruin would mean to the family. Only Branlen looked directly at Jhared. The boy clenched one fist against his heart. Confusion and grief darkened his gaze. Jhared staggered as if struck. Why had Tierzen allowed Branlen to be here? To watch his brother fall and break? Reflexively, Jhared twisted that thought to what it should be: Tierzen wasn't to blame. *He* was the one who had betrayed his brother's love.

The guards prodded Jhared across the battlement. He stopped at the edge, with his boots toeing off the stone. The executioner stepped behind him, his baton swinging at his side. Jhared gritted his teeth and tried to control his breathing. One more moment of sunlight and bright autumn skies. One more moment before the fall. His gaze went a last time to Branlen.

The boy's head tilted upward and his lips formed brokenhearted words: "You were going to save us, Brother." Bran held up his fist and uncurled his fingers. On his palm lay the silvery stone with its carved face, their talisman.

The executioner coughed and spat. City Guard drums beat a final staccato. Silence dropped over the crowd. Jhared drew a slow breath—

The baton slammed against his back, hammering him over the lip of the wall. He cried out in futile protest. Wind blasted into his face as he flew toward the ground.

Blue flames roared up around him. He tumbled off the Path. Off all Paths. He fell past the moment of his execution, past the killing winds that roared through Avelos, past the Sonan men armed with staves and garbed in dun, past the Avelune who soared in circles above a burning city. Each Path became only another distant thread of gleaming blue and red entwined through the weaving, while he fell through the blackness.

How could any man choose the right direction from among an infinite number of roads? Where might he find a Path where choices remained to him and he needn't end on the wall? Jhared swallowed back panic. Maya had said he possessed a skill. He might track his own way by knowing who he was. He tried to focus on an image of himself: *Cursed. Half-man. Shorn.*

The weaving twisted in the blackness, expanding with every decision made on every Path, but he sensed nothing that belonged to him.

He tried again: *Abomination. Anathema. Demon-touched.*

"Absurd, boy! Is that what *you* say you are or what they say?"

The voice echoed all around him; it quavered like an old man's, yet somehow it was far greater than a man's.

"It is who I am," Jhared answered

"Bah," the ancient voice spat. "If that's true, you might as well stay in this Nowhere forever, for no one will miss you. Try again."

Jhared struggled to find other names he might claim: *Soldier? Scholar?*

One edge of the weaving drew closer. Faintly, he recognized not a scent or a visible track, but a memory, an *experience*: the experience of a soldier-scholar who had traveled near here. His self?

"You truly believe you are the only such soldier in all her weaving?" A hint of irony sharpened the voice now.

No. Of course not. Jhared searched for other aspects of who he was.

Brother. Son.

"Yes," the old man muttered. "And?"

Jhared glided closer to the weaving and closer again, until he could identify individual blue and red strands and sense the memories of himself as a brother and a son that left traces.

Comrade. Friend.

"That's better," the voice encouraged. "But what is it about those names that make them yours?"

Jhared thought on the reasons he named himself so, and images tumbled through his head: reading a story to Branlen; listening to a lesson from Tierzen; patrolling the border with Jase; laughing at some jest from Anzo. Blue and red strands laid themselves out before him, strands that held bits of himself. Still, there were too many to choose the moment where he belonged.

The old man made a *tsk* sound. "For such a young one, your Path has already split many times. To find your present, you must think on the names you would claim for yourself now."

Jhared thought of himself with Maya: accepting her grey feather; telling her about the Becoming; killing his own countrymen. He thought of the Path he had just witnessed. His future?

Traitor.

"Perhaps. Traitor may be a true name for you in the end, but it has hovered over you for a long while. Who are you *now*?"

Musician?

Healer?

The last names came out tentatively, but Jhared recalled his own voice low and pure as he sang Mahla's lullaby. He saw himself tending Maya's injuries and felt the deep joy of easing another's pain. His perception of the tracks on the gleaming strands of the weaving wavered for an instant before coming suddenly as clear as footprints in damp earth. When he looked at the Paths again, his own trail shone distinctly from the myriad trails around it.

"You're still missing something," the old man observed, making a clicking sound that reminded Jhared of Anzo tapping his pipe against his teeth. "It's a name you've worked hard to avoid. I suspect you'll find some grief before you claim it."

"Will you tell me what it is?" Jhared asked.

The man chuckled, not unkindly, but with a resonance that hinted at great strength kept in check. "Not even I can define your self. Go on now, and take care to hang onto my blessing. I don't give my talismans without purpose."

A puff of tobacco-scented air struck Jhared and tossed him through emptiness until he collided with his own still body. He smelled woodsmoke and felt the rocky ground beneath him. Before he completely understood where he was, a warm hand touched his cheek. His eyes flew open to find Maya crouched at his side.

Jhared sent a prayer to Riana, then added another word of thanks in case it might mean something to an odd old man on the Paths.

"It's about time you found your way back," Maya said. "I was just getting ready to come looking for you." Her tone was wry, but firelight revealed lines of strain in her face.

"Where are we? There were men." Jhared sat up, causing the world to pendulate sickeningly.

"Slow down," Maya urged, steadying him with one hand. "You were gone a long while. We're just below Parnas Pass. Far enough we needn't worry about drunken hunters."

He closed his eyes. "You should have left me. You should have run. If they had caught you . . ."

"*Should* is a word you use too freely," she said, ruffling her feathers. "And I haven't seen it bring you any peace."

He started to respond, but a shudder jolted through his body, clicking his jaws together.

Maya's hand tightened on his shoulder. "What is it?"

"The Paths have come. To claim their toll."

The cold knocked the air from his lungs and threw him back to the ground. Jhared dug his fingers into the dirt and braced his body, willing himself to calm, but he had traveled far, and the weaving wanted what he owed. His muscles contracted so hard they curled him up like a dead leaf. An iron fist clenched around his chest.

"Jhared, breathe! Take a breath!"

Somewhere above him, Maya cursed in languages he didn't know. As he fought the Paths for the remnant of his spirit's heat and breath, the vague thought came that he might lose the battle this time. He could die here. An absurd and worthless death. The world buzzed in his ears, and blue lights danced behind his eyelids. From far away, someone called his name.

Warmth descended upon him then, enveloping him like a dream of summer. An insistent weight pressed against his body, coaxing it to uncurl. The warmth and pressure loosened his muscles a little, enough that he could suck in a lungful of relief. Then another. As the scent of berries and sunlight filled him, he groped toward the life-saving heat and found flesh and feathers: Maya enfolded him in her arms and wings.

The fire of her embrace beat back the deadly cold and left in its place a new ache. Jhared begged the goddess for mercy, or perhaps it was only a woman he begged.

He knew the reasons he must maintain control and tie away his desire. Longing filled him, so much longing. But what of that? He knew how to bridle desire. A necessary skill. A discipline hard won over years. He sought the stillness within him and the absence of need. *Desire in a Shorn man is death.*

Then Maya shifted over him, holding him close to keep the Paths from stealing his life. As her body moved over his, all his discipline shredded. With a cry of defeat, he reached for her, tugging at the laces of her shirt until he could kiss smooth skin. He tasted the curve of her shoulder, the line of her collarbone, and the arch of muscle beneath. His fingers found the soft strength of her feathers and stroked the leading edge of her wings.

A low, desperate sound escaped her. She set her palm against his chest and pushed some distance between them. Her other hand swept up to cup his cheek, drawing his gaze to hers.

"I have nothing to offer you but myself," she gasped. "Do you understand, Jhared? I cannot make you whole."

The very miracle of her existence astounded him. As she held him in her gaze, he was certain she saw, not merely a cursed man or a doomed soldier, but the truth of him. In that moment, none of the rest mattered.

"You are gift enough."

Gently, he took her hand where it pressed against his heart, and leaned forward to cross the last inches that separated them. He kissed her brow, her eyelids, her lips. And then they were soaring.

Truly, he couldn't imagine anything nearer to flight. He felt weightless as she tumbled into his arms, weightless as they embraced amidst the trees, shedding clothing like fall leaves. Moonlight shone on the marvel of her body. His fingers trembled as he reached out uncertainly to learn the shape of her. No other woman had dared to offer so much to him. As his hand brushed her belly, she made a small sound that grew sharper as his palm drew upward and over the contour of one breast. Astonished, heart pounding, he realized that before him lay the mystery of an unknown trail, and all he need do was stay attentive to the signs she offered to guide him.

He leaned forward to let his lips learn the places his hands had traveled, and her wings unfurled like a black and silver fan. She pressed herself close to him in a way that made him arch against her and sent Shorn energy coursing through him.

"Wait," he begged, "I can't—"

"Shhh." She silenced him with a kiss, then slid her legs around his hips to kneel over him. Her wings beat the air in a slow, inevitable rhythm as she gathered him with a rough, warm hand and drew him inside her.

He bit back a cry and clung to her, tense and motionless, crushed between the most powerful desire he had ever known and the terror of it.

"Jhared?"

"I can't," he hissed between clenched teeth. "I'll hurt you."

She uttered a sound of surprise, then slowly stretched over him to entwine her arms around his neck. He flinched as her fingers touched his scars.

"Enough self-loathing," she murmured. "You fear your body because they taught you to fear it. Because they do. Let me teach you a reason for joy."

Her wings struck the darkness, lifting her weight so that, for an instant, she seemed to hover above him. Quickly she descended, drawing him into the very core of her. He did cry out then, and the last of his restraint snapped.

His hands clutched her waist as he reached toward the wonder of connection. He had shared her Path on the day the Arionade came to make her Shorn and the night by the lake when she sought the sky. Now, by the incomprehensible patterns of Riana's weaving, they were together, and she welcomed him. Jhared's boundaries dissolved until he didn't know whether what he sensed rose from his need or hers. Distantly, he was aware of a storm rising around them and the music in it—the tree branches creaking and leaves spinning in a wind that echoed the sounds of Maya's passion. What was not distant, what was impossibly immediate, was the fire of Shorn energy in his veins, lifting him toward the mountain heights. Maya's eyes reflected his own urgency as they approached the pinnacle. With a gasp, she pulled him close, her face burrowing into his neck and her body rippling over his, sending him exploding far beyond his own borders.

The skies roared as he spun into the center of the storm. Joy, affection, and unlooked-for completion rushed across his fevered skin—the emotions transformed into a strange song that fueled the storm, offering a power he had never known, but that felt precisely right. When darker emotions blew through him—fear, anger, loneliness—they did not overwhelm him, but only became a countermelody to balance the rest.

Gradually, gradually, he regained awareness of the night around him and his own pulse, steadying now, although he still felt himself a part of the music.

"Jhared? What are you doing?" Maya whispered in his ear.

He startled and tried to draw away, afraid he had harmed her after all. She held onto him.

"No, don't go," she said. "The Paths. You're wide open again."

She had nestled against his side, one leg slung across his thighs and one grey-black wing stretched over his chest like a blanket. The wind riffled her hair across his shoulder.

Jhared took a deep breath, and the wind gentled around him, fluttering Maya's feathers. "It's all right," he murmured sleepily. "You are the anchor that keeps me where I'm meant to be."

"You have a bard's grace," she said, her voice low and warm, "but I have no skill to hold you here. Don't fall asleep or you're bound to drift away."

He was already drifting, his limbs heavy and comfortable and his mind quiet. It was the most peaceful moment he could remember.

"No, no, that's no good. Wake up!" She shifted and pain pierced him where she brought her teeth to bear. He sat bolt upright, causing Maya to slide off him into a heap.

"I'm sorry," she said, looking not at all repentant.

The sight of her bare and smiling tethered him with a surety to his own Path. All sleepiness gone, he reached for her again, then halted suddenly as something in the crystalline night tapped his attention.

"What—?" Maya began.

He held up a hand for quiet, uncertain what had broken the pattern. No unusual sounds disturbed the darkness. The horses slept, heads drooping. Jhared let out a breath in the cool night and watched the thin stream of vapor dissipate in the breeze. At his feet, dead leaves danced in little spirals, and Maya pulled her wings around her against the blowing chill. Jhared scanned the forest, looked back at Maya, then at the forest again. There it was: the thing that should not have been. Beyond Maya and himself, all was motionless. The leaves didn't so much as tremble on the branches. Uneasiness shivered through him.

Maya's hand slipped into his. "Are you still with me?"

He nodded, turning to look around him again. "The wind. It touches only us."

Curiosity carved a line between her brows. She stared at Jhared, then at the trees beyond him, and frowned.

A terrifying possibility scraped the edge of his awareness. "Do you still feel the Paths open around me?"

Maya tightened her grip on his hand and leaned forward to kiss his cheek. Strands of her black hair whipped across his throat. "Yes," she said, pulling back. "Wide open."

"Stay here." He withdrew his hand from hers and, without bothering to clothe himself, strode away from the campfire, past the horses and into the trees. A soft whoosh of air followed him, lifting fleshbumps along the backs of his arms.

Even before he turned, he heard Maya draw a shocked breath. "Gods," she cried softly.

Jhared looked back toward the camp. Maya's hair was tousled but motionless around her face, and the leaves lay flat around her, yet at his feet the deadfall now swirled and shifted. Twigs and leaves blew off the trees and rained across his shoulders. The wind whistled, a melody so high-pitched it sent a painful prickling up his spine. He knew that sensation; always before it had preceded devastation and death.

His legs grew weak. He sucked great breaths and tried to collect his thoughts, but through an ocean of numbness only one thought penetrated over and over:

I am not the one. I am not the one. Please, Goddess, tell me I am not the one who carried the killing winds into Avelos.

He stumbled back to Maya. Inside, a part of him was screaming denials, but he heard himself speak with exaggerated calm as he pulled on his clothes. "The winds must have something to do with the Paths, then. No one ever guessed."

Maya watched the swirling leaves, fascination and horror twined in her expression. "Are they rising from the doors you opened?"

"I think so. There's old emotion at the heart of them, it seems. Someone must tell Leita."

The breeze had gained enough momentum to sting. Jhared felt a faint thrumming against his breastbone. Soon that thrum would turn into a destructive roar and the sting would become the slash of invisible knives. He drew on his boots.

"I'll go as fast and as far as I can toward the west," he said, moving to saddle Maya's gelding. "Fewer villages in that direction. You take the horses and run south. If the wind hasn't dropped in a few miles, don't wait. Take shelter."

He glanced up. Maya hadn't made any motion to depart.

"Please, Mayavana! You can't linger."

"What do you plan to do once you've fled to the edge of nowhere?" she asked. "You can't outrun yourself."

He didn't care to think so far ahead; it mattered only that he lead the threat away from the hundreds of people sleeping in villages around them, away from her. "I'm a cursed soldier. I'll do what I must to protect Avelos."

Her expression darkened and one wing swatted the air. "You find it comfortable to prove yourself cursed, don't you? What twisted need makes you so eager to sacrifice yourself for those who tore you apart?"

Her vehemence cut him, carving his fear into anger. "Nothing I give could possibly be sacrifice enough for what the killing winds have already destroyed."

Beloved of Cael. No one who stands beside you is safe.

Desire in a Shorn man is death.

The sound of the wind was the sound of his spirit keening. He tightened his sword belt and prepared to set out.

"Jhared, wait! You needn't chain yourself to the solutions they would choose for you. Think! If this wind truly is your doing, then you can stop it as well."

"Maya, I can't even close the Gate."

"If your Teachers gave you anything, it was the means to subdue your own strength." She glanced at him as she pulled on her clothes. "I have a cave above the pass. It's as far from a town as you'll get without running all the way to Avarel Forest. It will do for shelter if it must. Come!"

She threw herself awkwardly into the saddle and turned to wait for him. He stood for a moment, awed by her confidence. Despite the curse that tainted them both, despite the destruction that hovered over them, she gave him a sense of hope.

"I'm coming."

The wind faded to a breath as they set off into the Parnas Mountains. Maya tossed a smile over her shoulder at him, but her optimism was premature. As they cantered along a game trail, Jhared's mind went to Branlen as he had seen the boy on another Path, brokenhearted at the bottom of the city wall: *"You were going to save us, Brother."* Jhared's heart began to pound and the doors to the Paths around him slammed wide. The wind escalated to a whine that made the horses call out in fear.

When they reached Maya's shelter, they were forced to free the beasts. Although the cavern was large enough for ten men, the entrance was too low and narrow for a horse to pass through. Jhared refused to doom the animals by tying them. Swiftly, he and Maya stripped off their saddles and packs. Jhared offered the beasts the rest of the grain, but the black mare was already skittering in fear. With a ringing whinny, she galloped into the trees. The gelding took one wistful look at the oats then fled after her.

Jhared stood beside Maya, watching them disappear. An ancient pine tree groaned and popped as it swayed. Clouds raced before the wind in a milky predawn sky.

"Do you know I could not bear it if I brought you harm?" he said into the darkness.

Maya's wings lifted, as though he had startled her. "Better not to profess such things," she said softly. "You are a Shorn soldier. You'll do what you must to protect Avelos." She rested her hand on his arm a moment before drawing away. "Inside now. Before that grandfather pine comes down on us."

For hours, Jhared battled the wind. He struggled to shut the Gate, as Leita taught him. He tried meditation, reaching urgently for a space of stillness inside himself, as if calming his own roiling emotion might calm the storm, but it was no good. He was wrestling a monster he didn't understand. Each time he attempted to reach for stillness, some bloody memory intruded itself: the villagers he had pulled dead from the winds' wreckage; the ruined faces of comrades who had died in the attack on Velantar; Branlen, bruised and battered, lying unconscious in his family's home. Even as Jhared faced those images, faced the possibility that he had played a part in those horrors, the winds howled out a dark, wild melody formed of fury and despair, passion and freedom. It called to him, making the blood burn in his veins. He loathed that melody and loved it. For hours, he fought the winds and himself until nothing of calm remained in him. Three times he had fallen through the Gate, only to return to shudder away his strength on the hard ground.

Trembling with fatigue and frustration, he stood at the mouth of the cavern and tried not to listen to the seductive melody as the storm whipped to its killing speed. He felt like a broken thing. All the defenses that for so many years had kept his Shorn urges contained had given way. Yielding to his physical desire seemed to have been the last breach. For the sake of a moment of connection, he had lost himself entirely.

Over the roar of the winds, someone called his name. A hand touched his shoulder. When he looked at Maya, her expression was intent and concerned. He wondered how long she'd been calling him. At her insistence, he followed her back down the narrow neck of the cave to the main chamber.

"You can't continue," she said bluntly. "I'm afraid of what will happen if you fall through the Gate one more time."

He bowed his head. "I'm sorry. I've tried everything I can think of. They've only grown stronger."

"Perhaps that means they've nothing to do with you, after all."

"No. I feel them." He leaned against the stone. "I don't know how to explain it. They feel familiar. Like a song . . . about myself."

She stroked a feather thoughtfully, as if pondering how to deal with that truth. "You said emotion is at their heart. What if your struggles feed them?"

"Perhaps." He scrubbed his hands over his face and thought about the possibility. If somehow his own experiences formed the core of the storm, it made a kind of sense that his anxiety and effort would maintain them. And it wasn't only anxiety he fed them. Despite everything, there was still desire. He dug into his belt pouch to pull out the sleeping drug Leita had given him and showed the half-plug of russet leaves to Maya. "If they feed on my emotion, perhaps this would suffice to starve them."

Maya sniffed the plug and wrinkled her nose. " '*Viremur*' it's named in Sona. 'Gods' Oblivion.' Potent and dangerous. How did you come by it?"

"It was given to me to keep me from the Paths."

"No doubt it would keep you from the Paths," she said dryly. "It would keep you from waking if your boots were on fire."

"If I take it, then I'll have to trust you to watch where the sparks land." He smiled without levity. The thought of oblivion was more appealing than he cared to admit.

Maya nodded soberly, as though she heard what he didn't say. "It's all right. You need rest. If nothing else, the viremur will see to it you're untroubled by dreams."

"And if the winds grow worse when I'm gone?"

She gave him a look. Once the winds grew brutal enough to kill, "worse" didn't really matter. "We won't find better protection than this cave."

"The viremur then," he said. It was the most reasonable choice. He had no strength left to lead the threat away. If he continued to struggle with the Gate, it wouldn't be long before he lost himself in the weaving. He didn't want to imagine what might happen then. Would the winds roar endlessly while he wandered? Would they roar until he died?

Maya spread a blanket at the back of the cave, and Jhared sat, remembering how quickly the drug had flattened him the first time he tried it.

He put the viremur into his mouth and bit down. The tart juice stung his tongue and throat. The cave walls began to shimmer and ripple. Jhared looked at Maya, the magnificence of her. Had he truly known this woman's need and fire? He listened to the winds as they destroyed the land and wondered again whether he had somehow wandered onto the Path of another man, someone with true strength and terrible power.

"Will you be here when I return?"

At least, that's what he meant to ask. The words might have come out differently. Maya frowned a question and bent over him. He saw her reach out, but couldn't feel her hand on his arm. Her lips formed words, but his mind floated away before he discovered what she meant to say.

Silence gripped the world. Jhared only knew he was awake because of the warmth on his left side that was the Avelun. She slept curled against him, one arm across his chest with her palm against his heart, so close that her breath stirred his eyelashes. Even amidst the aftereffects of the viremur, Jhared's body roused at her touch and the intriguing scent of her. Gently, so as not to cause her to draw away, he kissed the tip of a primary feather.

"Filthy creature. More beast than woman." Shrill made a sound of disgust. *"For this you couldn't control your own animal need?"*

Jhared froze. *"Leave her be."*

"What?" Boar said. *"You don't still think her innocent after all this?"*

"I think you hate my kind so deeply you have nothing of value to say of her."

"The Avelun is your own kind now, is she?" Boar observed.

Jhared didn't answer. He hadn't expected to say such a thing.

"If we hated you," Shrill went on, *"would we spend such effort trying to help you survive? No Shorn soldier, not even one as intractable as you, could bring the killing winds upon his own people."*

"What are you trying to say?" Jhared demanded.

"Don't be obtuse. We know you see it: she did this. You lay with her and awoke her desire, creating something that should never have been."

"No! The winds were waiting within me. She's not to blame for my lack of discipline."

Boar made a dismissive sound. *"Don't you think we would have known if such a thing hid inside you?"*

Jhared went quiet, considering that. *"What then? You're going to tell me again that I must kill her?"*

"No!" Shrill snapped. *"We want you to learn exactly what you did to her or what she did. You must learn how to control the winds."*

"In order to return to your life," Boar added hastily.

"Go on, boy. Take the beast into your arms again and sate your desire. See what she might teach you." Shrill's voice was low and prurient. *"You can't conceal your need from us."*

Jhared could conceal nothing from his Teachers; if they wanted his thoughts, they had only to listen, but that had rarely troubled him. He had often considered the Teachers to be a gift, counselors who knew him as no one else could; he had always considered them as necessary. Now, for the first time, their presence was an invasion. He gazed at the sleeping Avelun and was heated by the memory of her body around his, her hands clutching his shoulders, her hips—

"Stop it!" he gasped. *"Those memories belong to me!"*

Shrill chuckled. Jhared felt ill.

Without another word to his Teachers, he rolled to his feet. It took a moment in the dark to find his sword. He left Maya still sleeping, with Shrill's laughter chasing him out of the cavern.

The forest seemed a great dead creature. Icy light from the waning moon revealed a tangle of broken branches and small trees that had been tossed like bones across the hillside. The killing winds had done this. *He* had done this. Whatever his Teachers said, he could feel it in his core. Jhared took off along the slope above Parnas Pass, twisting around the debris. He ran as though speed would be enough to escape his Teachers, to escape this new terrible understanding of who he was. His mind could hardly bend around the truth: the most devastating threat to Avelos came not from Sahiste or Laebek, but from within the country, from within him. Many miles burned behind him before he could gather his thoughts enough to think clearly.

I am not the only one.

He took hollow comfort from that realization. He couldn't be alone in this. The winds had attacked Avelos all across the south, in places he had never seen. Three attacks besides the one tonight had occurred in his presence: in Parnas Pass when the patrol had just set out; at Ebilan; and in Velantar. Velantar, the city of the goddess. The Heart's Hold of Alende Isan.

Jhared's breath dragged raggedly in and out of his lungs. He refused to believe he had anything to do with that devastation. He couldn't have.

He squeezed his eyes shut and kept running, letting Riana decide if he would trip over the edge of the trail to the sheer drop below. Was this the true curse of the Shorn? Was this the unholy power Tumal the Just had tried to tear out of the Avelune to protect Avelos?

His own Becoming had been distorted by the elders who had wanted him to fail. By Leita's admission, he should have died rather than survive to travel Riana's Paths. Who else had evaded the protection of the Becoming? Who else might carry the potential for destruction? The answer came to him with an image of golden hair and mad green eyes and the sound of a heartrending laugh.

Alende. The unbound.

Avelos had meant to kill the waylayer and his band of outcasts. Now it was possible they held the power to destroy the country.

"Halt!"

Two figures stepped from the brush to block the trail. Moonlight glanced off steel in their hands. Jhared scrambled to check his speed, but the slippery scree made his boots skid.

"Riana's tits!" one of the figures called out. "Stop! Or taste a Forest Guard blade!"

Still half-sliding, Jhared twisted sideways just in time to eel between the guards' swords. He stumbled to a stop behind them.

They were Shorn: one silver haired and wiry with age; the other young, near Jhared's height, but heftier. Both bore unadorned blades and red-bordered cloaks. At once they turned on Jhared, and a glimpse of their features evaporated his hope they might be soldiers he knew. As the silver-haired man leveled a sword near Jhared's throat, the younger one swung around to press a blade against his back.

"Steady there!" Jhared panted. "I'm with the Guard! Patrolman Denaban of the Fourth."

"The Fourth's at Ravia," the older man said emotionlessly. "I see a Shorn stranger in someone's Forest Guard uniform." The soldier indicated the hem of Jhared's cloak, which had been missing its red border since Ebilan. "Like to try again?"

Jhared looked into the old guard's face. The left side of Silver-hair's features dragged downward, pulling half his expression into a scowl, while the right side remained level, reflecting cool dispassion, as though two minds dwelt in one body. Jhared wondered if it was age or some other thing that so split a man from himself.

"I'm with Commander Carn's patrol. We were sent with Lieutenant Sevar to—"

"To hunt for some answer to the killing winds," Silver-hair finished. "I know about the lieutenant. If you're with them, where's the rest of your patrol? And what happened to your mission? We just watched the winds sweep the tops off the mountains."

"I know. I . . . saw them. I'm on to Velantar with a dire message for the high chieftain from the lieutenant. As a courier, I must be allowed to pass."

The guard behind Jhared made a mocking sound.

"Courier?" Silver-hair said. "Boy, you're just building yourself a taller pyre. Shorn couriers were relieved of duty weeks ago. Right before the rest of us were put on barracks time."

"My money says he's a deserter," offered the younger guard with a tone of disgust.

"How many deserters beg passage to Velantar?" Jhared snapped. "I've been on the march since the winds hit the city at the gathering. I've heard nothing of restrictions on Shorn soldiers. Why would General Nadel put aside men he needs?"

There was a pause. The right side of the old man's face matched the scowl on the left for a moment, but only a moment, before flattening again. "Legacy says Shorn soldiers are all traitors. That my years of service mean nothing."

Jhared swore under his breath. The Legacy had gathered a great deal more power in the past weeks if Toren Abrigado could force Rumar to reduce the general's forces. "If Shorn men are assigned to the barracks, why are you here?"

Silver-hair shook his head. "Enough questions from you. You say you're a courier? Then it's time we saw this message of yours."

The blade against Jhared's back kept him still as Silver-hair sheathed his own weapon, then reached forward and ripped the pouch from Jhared's belt. Ignoring Jhared's protest, he loosened the tie strings and poured the contents into his hand: a few coins, a fire-steel and striking stone, Branlen's talisman, some dried apples, and Maya's feather. The ice-colored one she had given him when he accepted her hospitality.

Jhared groaned inwardly as the soldier plucked up the oblong feather and stared at it.

"Well now, the grey feather curse is some message," Silver-hair muttered.

"It's not meant for a curse. Truly, it's not." Jhared trailed off, seeing the futility of his dissent in the emotionless right side of his captor's expression.

"Don't bother," the old man said. "It's not my job to get the truth from you. You'll be formally questioned when we take you back."

"Back to the city?" Jhared asked hopefully.

"Oh, I don't expect you'll get so far as Velantar," Silver-hair replied. "Shorn men are being executed for far less than concealing the grey feather."

Jhared thought of Leita and his comrades at the mercy of Aglar's clanguard; he thought of Maya waking alone to believe he had abandoned her. The decision before him was an easy one. He dropped into a crouch below the blade of the guard behind him and propelled himself forward. Low and fast he took the old man's legs out from under him. The guard tumbled backward, cursing and flailing.

His knee caught Jhared in the throat. Jhared rolled away, gasping as he staggered to his feet. He wanted only to run. The way before him was clear. He heard the younger guard call a warning and ignored it. Moonlight dribbled across the trail ahead. Jhared broke away, knowing he had it in him to outstrip pursuit. He thrust into a hard sprint, sending stones spraying out behind him.

He was falling before he even felt the fire at the back of his leg. With outstretched hands, he caught himself, rolled quickly, and tried to rise. His left knee buckled. Jhared discovered himself on the ground again, not far from the edge of the trail. He reached down and found sticky wetness and a blade protruding from the back of his lower thigh.

Running footsteps caught up with him. This time, the young guard aimed his sword at Jhared's heart; his gaze was layered with smug superiority and barely bridled anger. Jhared recognized those emotions; he had felt the same himself—toward Ziabela and her traitorous group, toward Alende, and toward all the Shorn who didn't acknowledge the importance of reparation.

Silver-hair came up more slowly, limping. No anger registered in either half of his face, no judgment at all as he smashed his fist into Jhared's jaw.

"You. You're the reason people fear us," the old man said.

"Yes," Jhared answered, his head ringing and blood seeping from his leg. "Yes. I am."

28.

REUNION

"Would you like a walk, my lady? I'm sure it wouldn't be too wet if you wear your heavy cloak."

From his place beside Nemiah's chair, Capalino pricked his ears and thudded his tail to show his support for the offer. Nemiah glanced up from where she had begun to drowse near the brazier, her letter to Kaliska unfinished. The icy rain had started over Parnas Pass on their first night, as the Arionade set up her tent. Three days later it was still falling, constant and inescapable. The narrow clearing overlooking the southern end of the pass was churned to mud by men and horses. The rain pattered against the tent walls until Nemiah carried the sound into her dreams. Her clothes and blankets smelled of damp and smoke.

The hollow chill inside her had started well before the rain, however. Every sacred journey recorded since the Exile had been stolen. Her legacy, that loss. Nothing else she did before or after could compare to such a tragedy. No matter how much steaming boldblood she drank or how she hovered over the smoldering brazier, she could not drive out that inner cold or fill the emptiness.

"Just a very *short* walk, my lady?"

Nemiah looked at Ziabela, who was making a valiant effort not to pace. The northern prefects were already two days overdue, and the Shorn woman did not fare well locked up for any length of time. It had not been a wise decision to bring her—surrounded as they were by the remaining members of the council—but Nemiah had been forced to leave Kaliska behind to hold the reins on the Higher Circle; Rom lay in the care of the heretics, still precariously balanced between the Paths of the living and the dead; and Nemiah could no longer deny she needed someone close, someone observant enough to keep her anchored in the present.

"No, Ziabela, we're not going for a walk. The last thing I need is for Toren Abrigado or one of the others to discover that you're here. Can you not occupy yourself with your songs?"

"It's too damp to write," the Shorn woman replied, ignoring Nemiah's half-written letter on the table. "Shall I play something for you?"

"Not now. Evorales should return soon, perhaps he'll have some news."

"Perhaps," Zia said listlessly. She stood near the tent flap, chewing on one slender finger and rolling her shoulders as she squinted out the gap in the fabric. "How long, do you think, before the killing winds return?"

When the storm struck the opposite side of the mountain two nights before, they had all hunkered down in the caverns along the pass. There had been nothing else they could do. The tents wouldn't have lasted one heartbeat, and Murita, the closest town, was built of timber and might have lasted two. It had been purest luck the storm didn't cross the mountain.

"I wish I had such clarity of sight to say," Nemiah sighed. "Come away from the door, before you distract the Arionade." She gave up on her letter and pushed it aside. Capa rose with a grunt and came to rest his heavy head on her thigh. She stroked his coarse fur. "I'd be grateful if you'd put out a meal for us. I could do with a bite of something."

A small lie, but the scribe perked up a bit at that. Zia left off her brooding to bring out plates and a tray from among their baggage, and took her time laying out cheese and cured meats, with slices of apples and hard bread. The supplies Nemiah had gathered for the trip to Sahiste had allowed her to make the two-day journey from Velantar without delay when word came of the northerners' expected arrival.

That had been five days ago. The winds had struck the mountains two nights past, and now the northerners were overdue. Evorales had gone with a detail of Rumar's soldiers to learn if the prefects had been caught in the storm.

In the waiting time, Rumar kept the council busy. He was running the country from his damp, temporary quarters, and everything moved with his particular type of hectic order. Nemiah never saw him at fewer than three tasks at a time. While the council debated whether to loan funds to the watermen's guild to speed the rebuilding of the barges destroyed in the winds, Rumar was dictating a letter for the dyers' guild about new levies and another letter to the elders of Clan Valador expressing condolences for the losses at Obled. The maps and letters spread across the field table were frequently endangered by cups of wine or tottering lamps. Nemiah had used the disruption of council routine as an opportunity to insinuate herself into the proceedings. Rumar had only given her a wry look when he saw it. She doubted he had time to chase her out, even if he wished it. In the depths of night, when Nemiah lay sleepless on her cot, she could see light still glowing through the walls of his tent. This morning before dawn, the council courier had galloped off toward the south. Letters to Sahiste and to General Nadel, Rumar had said when she asked. Even now, he worked simultaneously to prevent and prepare for war.

"The commander's back," Zia said excitedly, setting down a wedge of cheese and brushing crumbs from her dress.

Nemiah blinked and set down her cup. After a moment, she heard a familiar voice speaking a greeting outside. Leather creaked as the Arionad on watch saluted. Then Evorales announced himself and she called him in.

He hovered at the tent flap, water dripping from his white coat, his boots full of mud. Capa trotted over to give him a sniff. "Forgive me, Lady. I'm not fit for your presence. I only came to let you know I'd returned and to give what news there is."

"It's all right, Commander. We've no precious rugs or fine linens to muddy. Come in and dry off."

Evorales bobbed his head and nudged the hound aside. Zia surrendered her chair with a sweet smile, and the Arionad took it a little stiffly as she hurried to warm the tea.

"Well, the winds did a good job of it," he announced. "The forest to the south is a tangle, and the valley's not much better."

"The villages?" Nemiah asked.

"Intact. Thank the Lady. The storm kept to the wilds. We may have lost a shepherd's hut or two and a few fool sheep, but no villages."

"Good news, Evorales."

The Arionad's blue eyes lit on the plate of meat. Nemiah pushed it in his direction, with a smile. "Eat. It was a long journey. You must be famished."

"Thank you. I have to say it was a bit of a ride."

No doubt it was a good deal more than a *bit*. Most of the Arionade had no reason or care to ride. For the rare occasions when Nemiah journeyed out to visit a chapterhouse or traveled to one of the clans, Rom kept a detail of men drilled and limber, those who had the most aptitude on horseback. Evorales hadn't been among them.

"What of the prefects?" Nemiah asked.

"No sign," he reported, layering meat and cheese onto a slice of bread. "It could mean we missed them in the wreck of the valley, but I don't think so. For all that the Forest Guard can be full of themselves, those Shorn boys are good trackers. They turned up nothing. Probably just means the northerners haven't reached the pass yet."

"Well, that's something hopeful, I suppose."

"I'm not sure how hopeful, if I may say it, Lady. This waiting's a bad thing. Especially for Shorn soldiers with so few officers about. I've heard some things. You see, a few of the boys invited me to dice. As men often talk when they gamble, I thought . . . well, I thought Riana might see the order in it." He ducked his head sheepishly.

"I believe that's reading more into the Lady's judgment than a mortal man should do," Nemiah said dryly. "However, at the moment, games of chance are the least worrisome offense against order. Say an extra prayer at the evening devotion to repair the weaving and tell me what you heard."

Evorales nodded contritely and made a spiral. "They say men are beginning to desert. One soldier was caught and summarily executed in the forest yesterday. The watchmen on the north end of the pass brought back another last night. I suppose they'll do him soon." The Arionad shook his head. "It'll be a hard thing for the others to witness."

Thunder rumbled through the Paths and through Nemiah's spirit. "How horrible."

"Yes. It is horrible." Zia stood on the other side of the tent, the bread knife gripped in one hand.

Evorales set down his food and glanced at the Shorn woman. "Horrible as the end of a young man's Path will always be, but when they run, it's an oath to both Riana and Rumar they're breaking."

"And every one of those Shorn soldiers was told by the high chieftain and the Legacy just days before that he wasn't good enough to serve that oath!" Zia's eyes glittered. "When you snatch away a man's purpose and leave him nothing, you crush his spirit. If it wasn't crushed already."

"Zia, have a care!" Nemiah gasped. Thunder rumbled inside her chest: rumbled and paused, rumbled and paused, rumbled.

The Shorn woman turned her green gaze on Nemiah, and all the angry glitter went out of her. "Lady, beware! You're slipping."

"No. No, it's not me," Nemiah breathed.

"Lady, surely—"

"Someone else is traveling the Paths. Someone close. Ah, Goddess, it must be Leita. Leita's back!"

"Lieutenant Sevar's patrol!" Zia cried.

Evorales looked doubtful. "Perhaps the northerners have arrived after all."

Nemiah stood. "I have to find her. Wait here, Zia. Hold onto Capa!"

She ran out of the tent into the rain, Evorales at her heels. In the narrow clearing that served as the center of the camp, she stopped, trying to reach into herself to sense the footsteps on the Path and to reach outward to understand her surroundings at the same time. On the south side of the clearing stood the high chieftain's tent, Clan Manitar's oak and sickle moon and the mountain banner of Avelos hanging sodden and limp above it. Nearby, the councilors shared smaller quarters. The soldiers' tents formed orderly rows among the trees on the north side of the clearing. Beyond the Forest Guard tents, uphill from the camp, lay the entrance to Parnas Pass.

Amalia had called Nemiah a skilled tracker, but it had been years since she had truly practiced. After Lady Pahlina died and Leita took the Blade, Nemiah had no need or opportunity for it. The thunder rumbled along the Paths again, pulling her forward, but in the outer world there were no signs of a company coming out of the pass. The camp remained quiet. A pair of soldiers strode by.

One of them gave Nemiah a curious look. Water trickled steadily off the roof of the high chieftain's tent and splattered into the mud.

She went on more slowly, letting the footsteps guide her until she came to the place where the tents gave way to the trees. Against one sturdy pine, she glimpsed an arm and the curve of a dark head.

"There!"

She ran again, her boots slipping on the slick ground, until she came around the tree trunk and saw the figure fully. She stopped short, filled with disappointment and confusion. It was not Leita, but a man, his arms bound around the tree behind him, his head drooping over his chest.

"Who?" she asked Evorales.

"The deserter," he replied. "Looks like no one's bothered with him since they brought him in last night. Lady, will you come out of the rain?"

"Leita's here," she said softly. "She's so close. He might have seen her."

She continued to scan the boundary of the forest, but saw no one. No one but the prisoner.

He was a young soldier, long-limbed and lean. Rain plastered his sable hair to his skull and streamed over his bruised face. His clothes were torn and a bloody rag was tied around his left thigh. He'd been beaten. She supposed he had struggled against capture, knowing only death awaited him in camp.

The thunder was fading. Leita was moving off, down Paths long forbidden to her. Ignoring Evorales's protest, Nemiah dropped to her knees in the mud and reached out a hand to touch the young man's shoulder.

"Where is the Bearer of Cael's Blade?" she demanded.

At her touch, his eyes flew open. They were green and brilliant, as sun on new leaves, but they wandered past her, unfocused.

"Soldier!"

His gaze caught her, held her. He drew a long, shuddering breath and then another. Both his hands clutched the tree trunk.

"Lady Nemiah? Are you *here*?"

Even marred with uncertainty and pain, his voice was low and resonant.

"The Bearer of the Blade passed near these trees," Nemiah said. "You must have seen or heard her."

The soldier shook his head, not as if in answer but as though to clear it. He strained once against his bonds, so hard it must have cut his flesh, then slumped back against the tree, panting.

The echo of footsteps died as though a door had slammed shut on them.

"Please!" Nemiah cried. "Look at me and tell me what you know."

He looked up at her, comprehension and relief slowly replacing the confusion in his gaze. "Ah, Lady. You truly are here. At least the goddess has allowed me that."

She had the sense she should know him: the complex light and darkness of him; the well-mannered irony; and the bridled emotion of his tone, a tone that better fit an elder than a soldier.

Or perhaps an elder's son.

"You're Tierzen Trianor's fosterling!" she cried. "Denaban. Jhared Denaban. You went out with the Bearer to find the secret of the killing winds!"

"Yes," he said softly. "The Bearer is not with me, but I have word of her." The young man paused, glancing from Nemiah to Evorales, and then with a frown, to the tents beyond. "The Forest Guard is here? Then you've already heard something. Please, Lady, I beg you to tell the commanding officer I bring a message from Lieutenant Sevar."

The earth rose and dropped under Nemiah like a wave. She grasped the tree for support. "Commander Evorales, seek the high chieftain. He will come for this, I think."

The Arionad turned without question and went running toward the center of camp.

"Rumar himself?" the soldier whispered. "Why? What did they say that brought you both to this place? Away from the safety of the city?"

Nemiah was disconcerted by how quickly he understood what was happening. "The northern prefects requested to speak their grievances to Rumar."

"But how did they convince you to come to the pass? Ah wait, the symbol of it. They refused Velantar as the seat of the high chieftain's power, didn't they?"

Nemiah nodded uneasily.

"So that's where the rest of Ciam's clanguard went," he murmured, more to himself than to her. "To the city. They mean to delay Rumar."

"Why are *you* here?" she demanded. "You were sworn to guard the Bearer. To give your life for her. Why are you here if she is not?"

He looked up at her, an ocean of regret in his eyes, raindrops streaming across his cheeks. One side of his face was swollen and purple. "I am sorry, Lady."

Agitated voices came from the mist behind Nemiah; then a group of men emerged. Evorales led the high chieftain and several others: Elder Trianor, Elder Abrigado, and a Forest Guard officer whose name she didn't know.

Someone gasped as they caught sight of the injured soldier.

"Why is he bound?" Rumar asked, turning to the officer.

Nemiah could see that the officer had been tall and broad once, but now was bent with age and old injuries. "Well past his marching years," Enrian would have said. But Enrian was in the south with the heart and muscle of the Forest Guard. Rumar had only the Shorn soldiers who had been left behind in Velantar and a handful of old men to order them.

"He's a deserter, sir. Most likely. The story he told the watchmen made no sense. And his uniform—"

"Did he tell your watchmen he bore a message for me from Lieutenant Sevar?"

The old soldier shifted uncomfortably. "Yes, sir."

A muscle flexed in the high chieftain's jaw. "Untie him."

"My lord, he carried the grey feather! We wouldn't dare to bring such a one into your presence."

Abrigado brushed an icy gaze over the prisoner. "We've long known that this boy had no proper Teaching. Who among us can be surprised he's willing to use such a curse?"

"Let it be, Toren," Elder Trianor replied. "Jhared Denaban passed the Becoming months ago. By declaration of the Chosen Lady of Avelos and the council. No more can be said against his Teaching."

Nemiah flushed, remembering the boy's Becoming more clearly than she wished. He *had* passed, despite her own sacrilege. Despite how very close she had come to breaking him.

Rumar made a gesture of impatience. "If all it takes is a feather to undo us, we might as well have stayed hidden behind the city walls. I said untie him."

With help from Evorales, the Forest Guard officer cut the prisoner free. When the soldier staggered to his feet, Elder Trianor stepped forward as if to assist, then checked himself. Evorales offered a hand instead. Nemiah thought she saw sadness cloud the young man's bright eyes, but he straightened and faced the high chieftain.

Rumar appraised him and gave a tight nod. "Very well, Patrolman. Let us hear what news you bring from Lieutenant Sevar."

Abrigado cleared his throat loudly. "Are you truly going to take his report? As though we might trust him?"

The young man's gaze landed on Abrigado with sudden keenness. "Your pardon, Elder, but which part of what I have to say would you prefer them not to hear?"

Nemiah suppressed a smile. Jhared Denaban owned the same schooled wit as his foster father.

Toren laughed. "I couldn't begin to guess what you have to say, boy, but whatever it is will be tainted by your tendency for deceit. More's the shame for us that you've been taught to cloak it in cleverness and manners."

"What do you mean to imply?" Rumar asked the patrolman, his tone turning dangerous.

"Lord Rumar, if I am allowed to speak, you may judge my words and their implications for yourself." He lifted his gaze, peering past the high chieftain. "However, there may be more ears listening now than is wise."

Nemiah glanced behind her and saw that a number of soldiers lingered among the trees, curious to learn what had caused the high chieftain and his councilors to hurry out into the rain. She saw Abrigado take in all the red-bordered cloaks around him and grimace, an expression somewhere between anger and apprehension.

Rumar nodded at Denaban. "True enough. Lieutenant Mavriel, see this soldier to my tent. I'll be there shortly."

With a salute to the high chieftain, the Forest Guard officer took charge of the young man. Elder Trianor moved as though to walk with his fosterling, but Rumar caught him by the arm.

"Tierzen, I would speak with you," he said, leading the elder away.

Nemiah watched the others go, the ground rising and dropping beneath her. The shifting was constant now. It had been so since before she left the city, but she felt no more footsteps. Whoever or whatever had happened on the Path, it had passed.

"Poor Trianor," a smooth voice murmured above her. "Rumar will be telling him not to interfere in whatever is about to happen to his son."

Nemiah startled. She hadn't noticed that Abrigado had stayed behind. "Oh? What is to happen?"

"The boy will tell his story, and then we shall see. Perhaps nothing, if he stays with the truth, but these Shorn soldiers have such a distorted understanding of what that means." Abrigado shook his head in a show of dismay. "I did not mean to trouble you, Lady. It's only that we have a bit of time alone now, and I had hoped to speak with you long before this." He brushed water from the shoulder of his cloak. "And in better weather."

The Elder of Clan Amerre had exchanged his fine city clothes for more sturdy garments and a pair of well-made boots. His thick cloak of rich blue turned his eyes to lapis. His honey-colored hair slid over his brow appealingly. He smiled at Nemiah as he fell into step beside her. Someone once told her that the Verael always smiled before closing their teeth on the throats of their prey. She wondered if it were true.

"Forgive me, Elder. Temple matters have occupied me."

"Yes, I imagine. I was disturbed to learn of the attack on the high temple. A terrible thing. I hope you didn't suffer losses."

"Thank you for your concern. We are doing well enough."

"My little scribe suffered no harm, I trust?"

My little scribe. Ziabela. The warmth in Abrigado's voice made Nemiah queasy. "She was not taken by the poison."

"That's a relief," the elder said. "If she had died, I suppose everyone would have sought to blame me."

"Would they have?" Nemiah replied coolly.

"Oh, very good, Lady." Toren's gaze reflected mirth; he savored this game. "As soon as this business with the north is complete, we must settle that matter.

It's dragged on too long. The woman may be lovely and bright, but she is also dangerous."

"Dangerous to your position, do you mean?"

"Oh, score again, Lady!" Abrigado leaned closer, his breath brushing against her hair, his levity gone. "Has it occurred to you that the reason Ziabela Marcalo admitted her wrongdoing so quickly is that she knew it would cause some elders to paint her as the hapless victim and point their fingers at me? It serves her to stir disorder among us. You make a grave mistake if you take my devotion to Avelos for malevolence and believe she is an innocent."

Nemiah said nothing, only pulled away, thinking of how he must have used his power to subdue such a lively spirit as Ziabela.

"Very well," Abrigado said, straightening. "I cannot expect you to indulge me at every turn. You are Riana's Chosen, after all. What of your sworn man? What was his name? I notice he's not with you on this journey. He wasn't taken in the attack, I hope?"

Goddess, the minister was at the height of clever malice today. Nemiah struggled to keep her tone neutral. "Captain Rom is recovering."

"That's another relief, indeed. When I saw palace guards at the temple, I feared it meant you had replaced him with a new consort of somewhat higher standing."

Score for Elder Abrigado. Nemiah flushed. This, she should have expected. The high chieftain had repealed the ban on the Tests of Rona and placed his own guards at her door.It was a rational interpretation on Abrigado's part, but memory checked the protest that formed on her lips:

Do you know how the Legacy dreads what would happen if you and Rumar came to terms?

Ahead, the others were entering the tent. Nemiah paused, causing Abrigado to do the same.

"I can't imagine there's any cause for fear, Elder. With such threats before us, is it not a wise thing for the leaders of Avelos to lay aside their differences and unify their strength?"

Abrigado's expression stretched thin. "I only beg you to take care," he said softly, bowing his head close to hers once more. "In times of upheaval, leaders can change quickly. If you entwine yourself with the Firebrand, you may find yourself burned before the end."

Offering her a last handsome smile, he held the tent flap open. Nemiah thought again of the Verael. She had no choice other than to let him usher her through.

The tent was crowded and smelled of men and wet wool. Elders who had been unwilling to venture into the mud to investigate the case of a Shorn deserter were eager to learn the fate of Lieutenant Sevar's company. Or perhaps, Nemiah thought less charitably, with the Legacy leaders in attendance and Tierzen Trianor's Shorn fosterling returned, they sensed the potential for drama to enliven the dreary day.

Rumar might have held a similar thought about the elders, for he looked none too happy about the gathering. He banged the staff of warding against the table and the councilors began to sort themselves into their proper places. Evorales set himself behind Nemiah where she sat not far from Tierzen.

In the midst of it, Jhared Denaban stood at attention, waiting to be addressed. He was an exceedingly tall man, but he had a way of lowering his gaze and tucking his chin that made him seem smaller. It was a way to appear less threatening, Nemiah realized. She had seen Zia do the same when questioned. Although a glance at the soldier's impassive features would lead most to believe him undaunted by the significance of his audience, Nemiah saw him surreptitiously clenching his nails into his palms.

The staff of warding fell again. It took several moments before the discussions dropped off and quiet descended.

"Patrolman Denaban," Rumar began, "we understand you have come from the north under orders from Lieutenant Sevar. We will hear your report."

Beside Nemiah, Tierzen cleared his throat and stood. "Lord Rumar, before we begin, I would like to confirm that it is a military report we are about to hear. Is that correct?"

Whispers ran through the gathering. Rumar's expression was guarded. "Yes, Elder Trianor. That is correct."

"Then by the Code of the Council of Clans, this is a Forest Guard not a council proceeding. Elders have no right to question the soldier while he gives his report. That right belongs to the senior Forest Guard officer present," he nodded at the grizzled Lieutenant Mavriel, "and to you, Lord Rumar. Do you agree?"

Rumar sent the elder a potent look of displeasure. "Yes, Elder. That interpretation is consistent with council and military code."

"Thank you. Let it be recorded thus." Tierzen sat, his shoulders rising and falling with a deep breath.

Whispers turned to muttering. Nemiah saw Jhared Denaban throw a swift, grateful glance toward his foster father. The elder had just provided him a shield against Legacy mischief, at least a temporary one, but the resentment it stirred would cost Rumar.

"Quiet all!" The high chieftain banged the staff against the table a third time. "Your report, Patrolman Denaban."

The soldier straightened. "If I may, sir, a question first?"

Someone snickered.

"Trianor's Folly, indeed," another elder chuckled.

Rumar looked unamused. "Yes, Patrolman?"

"Sir, a courier was sent from Brenia with word of the killing winds at Obled and . . . other matters. Did it reach you?"

"Yes. The council knows about the Sahisten spies. We expect you to give your full and unedited report to this gathering."

"Of course, sir. Then you've had no word from the patrol since the first courier?"

The soldier searched through the crowd and found Nemiah. The intensity of his gaze made it seem he meant the question not just for Rumar but for her. She frowned and shook her head slightly.

"No word," the high chieftain said.

"Then my report must begin in Obled. After establishing that a Sahisten was fleeing north, Lieutenant Sevar sent me to Brenia with the Bearer of Cael's Blade to reach the courier and speak with Lady Esania. The rest of the patrol pursued the second spy."

The patrolman launched into a description of his company's success and failure in capturing the Sahisten. The loss of the spy to suicide and the discovery that Sahiste was also likely searching for the killing winds was precariously balanced by the capture of a map that depicted Lady Sabela's temple. The councilors remained silent and considering. No one could help but fear what it would mean if Sahiste gained control of the winds before Avelos did. As the soldier spoke of the Bearer's meeting with Lady Esania, his words came more slowly and sounded carefully chosen. His gaze went a second time to Nemiah. Esania had given the Bearer directions to a Sky Tower, where the Bearer had hoped to find a reference to Sabela's temple. As it happened, there had been no need to seek the tower. Then the soldier paused.

Stiffly, he shifted his weight off his injured leg. His wet clothes dripped rivulets into the dirt. He seemed to be deciding how to go on with the next part of his story. Although his features remained unrevealing, a river of emotion swept across the Path before him, rocking Nemiah with its intensity.

She thought she understood why when he continued, taking the patrol out of Brenia, north toward the Sandien Mountains, and into a night of blood and death—an attack by a Verael queen's pack in Alende's Pass. A third time his gaze met hers as he told that the Bearer had played a role in ending the Verael attack. For a heartbeat, his impassivity fled and something needful in his expression reached toward her. Before she could consider how to answer it, his gaze had passed her and he was telling the council how the guard from Clan Aglar had come upon the crippled company and forced Lieutenant Sevar to stop at Ebilan rather than go on to the garrison. In an even tone, the soldier told how Leita had put herself at risk so that he might remain free; he told of his ride to Aglar Tower, the smoke of pyres, and the injured General Orn. As details emerged of a plot by the northern prefects, the room exploded with cries of anger and disbelief.

"Silence!" Rumar bellowed. "Silence or I'll have the Forest Guard drag you all out! Patrolman, I command you to clarify. Be very certain before you answer, for you are speaking of treason and a threat to the integrity of Avelos. Are you saying that the northerners have killed soldiers at Aglar Tower and now hold the garrison for their own interests?"

The young man licked his lips. "Sir, by General Orn's report, any soldiers who resisted the overthrow were put to the sword. Those who laid down arms are hostages."

Rumar stood silent and motionless. Around him, the councilors shouted at one another. Lancion Makri declared that the story was all the lie of a Shorn man intent upon sowing destruction. Others seemed to find that idea more palatable than northern perfidy and echoed it, but Clans Nadaren and Everen berated the northern prefects as madmen with no care for order. Abrigado remained as composed as the high chieftain. Nemiah saw the two men shrewdly considering the group and one another. It couldn't be denied that they shared many qualities: strength and cleverness, and even perhaps love for Avelos, but beneath Rumar's stony expression lay a hint of something deeper, something Nemiah had never witnessed in Toren Abrigado. Compassion had caused Rumar to run into the street in the dark to rescue an injured stranger and compassion caused him to mourn the loss of the men he sent to war. It was compassion that balanced the use of power.

"Loyal men have died," Rumar began in a low tone that forced the others to quiet to hear him. "For the sake of those men, we must listen to the rest of this report, and then we must make decisions. Go on, Patrolman."

The room vibrated with fury and grief. The soldiers who had been slain would have come from all across Avelos. They would have been the kin and clansmen of the elders sitting here. It seemed apparent now why the elders of the northern five had disappeared.

Jhared Denaban coughed and continued. "From Aglar Tower, I returned to Ebilan and found the patrol. Commander Ciam had maintained the facade of hospitality, and although our men had been well treated, they were carefully guarded. Aglar had no cause to fear only so long as we didn't know about the garrison. Lieutenant Sevar and Lei . . . the Lady Bearer planned for me to return to them in two nights to aid the patrol's escape, but when Commander Ciam appeared, I had to run. Lieutenant Sevar ordered me to carry word to Velantar."

Nemiah gripped her chair as the young man ended with a brief telling of what could only have been an arduous journey back toward the city, where he was stopped and taken captive by the Forest Guard at the northern end of Parnas Pass.

"Why would the prefects come south?" Rumar asked. "When they could sit snug behind the Sandien Mountains all winter?"

"I think they had hoped to sit snug, sir, but they knew I escaped to warn you. They're trying to avoid the chance that you'll bring up the army before the snows come."

Someone snorted. "What army? We can't fight Sahistens and rebels both."

Rumar ignored the interruption. "Then you believe this meeting is nothing more than a stratagem to delay us."

The soldier grimaced. "Sir, I am a Shorn patrolman, I mustn't—"

"You have observed more of this conflict than any man here," Rumar said. "Tell us what you have deciphered."

"Yes, sir. Delay is almost certainly part of their plan. They sent clanguards after me and more men riding for Velantar at a killing pace to be certain they would reach you in case they—" The soldier winced.

"In case they didn't stop you," Rumar finished. "Patrolman, how do you know about the clanguard?"

"Half a patrol flashed past me at night on a slippery pass. Part of the same group who captured my comrades."

"The ones who brought the message to me, I suppose." Rumar's fingers made a fist around the seal of Avelos hanging from his neck. "And the other half of the patrol? Where were they?"

A ragged breath tore from the soldier. Nemiah felt the world swinging as he clenched his nails hard into his palms. "They set an ambush for me."

"And how did you escape that ambush, Patrolman."

Jhared Denaban stared straight ahead. "I killed them, Lord Rumar."

"Five men?"

The soldier glanced down, then dragged his gaze back up until he met the high chieftain's. "Yes, sir."

The council burst into chaos again. Antipathy rumbled through the men that Nemiah thought was aimed as much at the Shorn messenger as the northern prefects. Evorales stood close beside her.

"Enough!" Rumar roared. "This will *not* devolve into accusations against a Shorn soldier for killing his countrymen. We have larger matters to deal with now. Until a time when the Forest Guard can look into the incident more thoroughly, it will be recorded that Jhared Denaban defended himself against men he had reason to believe were traitors. In truth, this soldier has taken a long step toward reparation."

One of the elders laughed, an ugly, mocking sound.

A random lull quieted the room for a moment. From it, Abrigado's cold, composed voice arose: "So this is what ten years of rule by Adan Rumar have brought us to."

Then the next wave filled the calm and all was argument and speculation again. The soldier stood silently, momentarily forgotten. He was swaying, as though he felt the same swing of the world Nemiah did, as though the terrain was changing beneath him. All the color had left his face.

Nemiah came to her feet. "Lord Rumar, look to your injured man!"

Tierzen was the first to leap from his chair, but too late. The young man's knees folded and he went down. There was a soft *thump* as his body struck the dirt.

In the midst of the arguments, someone called for the Forest Guard healer. Someone else asked, prosaically, if the company had brought one.

Ziabela leaped up as eagerly as Capalino when Nemiah entered the tent. "Oh, Lady, at last! I thought I would go mad with the waiting. Have the northerners arrived? Is Lieutenant Sevar's patrol with them?"

"Ease off, girl!" Evorales snapped. "Let the Lady take a breath."

"It's all right, Commander. She's in a difficult situation: here and not here." Nemiah glanced up at Evorales as he helped her to a chair. "Think how you would feel."

Ziabela pressed her lips together, nearly quivering with the effort of restraining her questions. "I'm sorry," she said, handing Nemiah a mug of tea. "I can see it wasn't an easy time, my lady."

"It was not." Nemiah took a sip of the hot drink, chamomile for the evening, not boldblood. Zia did truly know her rhythms. "Evorales, go along now. Get yourself cleaned up and properly fed."

The commander's expression was grateful. He'd not had the chance even to take off his cloak since returning from his exploration of the northern valley. "As you say, Lady. I'll take the high moon watch tonight. If you need me before, send Avjay to fetch me." He offered a spiral and left the tent. Nemiah heard him addressing the Arionad on guard before striding away.

Outside, a night bird called and then another, beckoning the darkness. Capa lay down and settled his brindled head on Nemiah's feet.

"It wasn't Leita or the patrol," she said to Zia with a sigh. "But we know something more about what's happened to them."

She gave Zia an abbreviated version of Jhared Denaban's story. Nemiah had expected the Shorn woman to show some relief that the soldier was not in danger of execution, and perhaps some polite concern for him and for the Bearer, but by the end, Zia sat in pensive quiet.

"I'm sure he will be well," Nemiah offered. "I suspect Elder Trianor will keep an eye on his care."

"What? Oh that." Ziabela shook herself. "No, of course he'll be fine. I was just thinking that the patrol didn't find Lady Sabela's temple before they were taken, so there's no chance they learned anything about how to control the killing winds, is there?"

"I think not," Nemiah said.

"The soldier, Jhared Denaban, did he bring the map with him?"

"No. It's still with the Bearer."

"Or with the northerners." Zia sat back, her expression dismal.

"I imagine that's likely." Nemiah pressed two fingers against her forehead. "I wonder if Denaban saw the map himself."

Zia brightened a little. "Possible. Surely, it's possible. Someone must speak with him right away. Lady, couldn't we go see him?"

"No, *we* cannot," Nemiah snapped. She set down her tea and shrugged out of her cloak, finally beginning to feel the brazier's warmth. "He's a strange one. Too many Paths shifting around him. When he looked at me, I could almost feel . . ." Nemiah rubbed her eyes and shook her head. She had spent too many days drifting at the edge of the Gate; it was growing difficult to discriminate her Path from any other. "When he's recovered, I'll speak with him about the map."

"That's a sharp idea, my lady. Very sharp." Zia's eyes glittered. "You'll want a scribe, of course, to record what you hear."

"Ziabela, let it rest!" Nemiah cried. "I know you're weary of this tent, but I cannot take more risks."

Without True Balance, the weaving will tear itself apart. Every infinite Path will be flung into blackness.

Yarla's words, the words of a heretic. They still flooded Nemiah with uneasiness.

"Forgive me, my lady. I press too hard. It's long been a flaw." Ziabela dropped to Nemiah's feet. "Here now. Can I help?"

Nemiah held out one foot and then the other to let the scribe pull off her muddy boots.

"It needn't always be a flaw, Ziabela. You've taken a hand in shaping your own Path, even when you possessed little power to do so. Riana recognizes the courage of such efforts."

The Shorn woman looked up, her green eyes filled with surprise. "Lady, your kindness continues to astonish me."

"Then perhaps you will allow kindness to curb your impulsiveness and temper your anger."

Zia remained silent as she set the boots aside and picked up a brush. With a nod from Nemiah, she began to unbind Nemiah's golden braids and draw them into silky waves.

The scribe's gentle touch unknotted some of Nemiah's tension and subdued a little of the spinning that never left her now. "That's a marvel," she sighed.

"Shall I roll the braziers into the sleeping chambers?" Zia motioned to the curtained space that held Nemiah's bed and the smaller area with her own cot.

"Yes. Yes, I think I might sleep soon. For a while, anyway. Perhaps you'd play something for me?"

"Of course, my lady."

Nemiah closed her eyes. "Ziabela, you will take care, won't you?"

There was a pause. "My lady?"

"The need to shape our own Paths is part of what defines us, but if that need blinds us to the truth of our world, it becomes a danger. Do you understand?"

The Shorn woman stopped brushing. She held very still. "What if we choose not to accept the *truths* of our world? As you chose not to accept the temple's losses? You have put yourself back into the affairs of state, when men of influence told you it could not be."

"And there are costs for crossing those boundaries," Nemiah said quietly, thinking of Abrigado's warning and Yarla's fears. "It is likely I will pay them yet."

"Still, you *chose* to cross boundaries. I do not fear the cost, my lady. All I desire is to be free to choose my own direction."

Nemiah let out a sigh and bowed her head. "Ah, Ziabela, but your choices have led you to be accused of treason and to face a traitor's death. Don't you see? Avelos cannot afford to give you such freedom. And neither can I."

Smooth wood clicked on the table as Zia set down the brush. A brazier sent a tendril of smoke curling into the damp air.

"I understand, my lady. No matter which way the Paths turn, I hope you know that I do understand."

29.

BITTER TRUTHS

Bound to a tree in the rain, Jhared had promised himself he would tell everything. To speak the truth of what he had become was the only way he knew to keep any of his self intact, even if in the end it meant they must destroy him. He had promised himself he would tell them about Vesarian and Pathwalking and the killing winds, but when they stood him before the council and he had seen the faith in Tierzen's gaze and the hatred in Abrigado's, his thoughts had flown to Maya, to her strength and kindness, her acceptance of his scars, and her wings around his body. In that moment, he lost the courage to speak the truth, for the truth was that he didn't want to die. He told only what he must about the north and his patrol and allowed the elders to believe he had accomplished something worthy. A long step toward reparation, Rumar had said. Once, those words had been the dream for which he lived.

Of the whole ordeal, it was Tierzen's support that had been unbearable. His foster father had gone so far as to risk Rumar's ire to protect him from the Legacy. Jhared hadn't expected that. While Tierzen listened to his report with an expression of trust, Jhared's mind played pictures of the killing winds rising from his own desire. Guilt and grief had overwhelmed him; he had needed to escape. The faint hadn't been purely cowardice, though. The walk through camp had started his leg bleeding again. Near the end of his story, bright snowflakes had spotted his vision, and the Gate had returned, flaring against his thoughts and demanding his spirit. If he hadn't found a way out, he would have fallen onto the Paths right in front of them. Lady Nemiah had already sensed him fall once; she would have understood where he had gone, and then the deadly truths he had kept to himself would have come out.

On the way to the ground, he had an instant to wonder if they would know he was malingering, but as his thigh struck the packed dirt, an arrow of blinding pain shot up his spine. Darkness had taken him in earnest.

The warm muzziness enveloping him now wasn't unpleasant. They had stripped him of his sodden clothes and left him on a cot, his left leg propped on folded blankets. The pain was distant, like the idea of someone else's injury. Under the blankets, he made an experimental attempt to move. Hot pins pricked his toes and fingertips. They had fed him dreamsease.

Beside the bed, someone drew a hitched breath.

Jhared opened his eyes. Tent walls filtered the evening light, painting everything a dull grey-red. Slowly, he took in the figure beside him: a slender man on a stool, his shoulders stiff and his hands folded in his lap. Jhared thought it a vision from the drug. Tierzen Trianor never sat so still, not even when engrossed in a book. There was always a coin flashing over his fingers or a reed tapping against his chin.

"Sir?"

"You know, I almost never dream," the man said softly. "Perhaps more precisely, I don't remember what I dream. Yet just after you left the city with Lieutenant Sevar, I had a nightmare that you would not return. All manner of cursed creatures came to my door: a dove, a hawk, a raven, but never the boy I taught. That dream has haunted me. I didn't realize how very much until I saw you tied under the tree."

Jhared's throat closed around any greeting he might have made. Tierzen rose, crossed the tent to a small table, and poured a cup of water from a skin. He brought it to the bed.

"Thank you." Jhared wrestled with the blankets to sit up. The warm, heavy hands of dreamsease tried to pull him back down, but he fought them. The cold water helped. He looked around the sparsely appointed quarters: one cot, a small field table, and two stools. "These are your quarters?"

"Not mine," Tierzen said. "You needed a proper rest, so I made them shift the soldiers from this tent in with the others to make an infirmary. There's no actual healer with us, but one of the old commanders seems to know what he's about."

Jhared winced. Fighting men had no tolerance for favoritism. He would be made to pay for such well-intentioned intervention when he returned to the ranks.

"Thank you," he repeated. "I'm relieved to see you, sir. Is Branlen well? And Madam Trianor?"

"They have managed." The elder sank back onto the stool.

Jhared frowned at the evasion. "Sir?"

"Oh, Branlen's injuries healed without complications, but his spirit isn't the same since the killing winds tore Velantar."

"Nightmares?"

"Yes. And more than that. An anxious kind of listlessness." Tierzen lifted his hands in a gesture of helplessness.

You were supposed to save us, Brother.

Jhared swallowed. "Those injuries will heal, too. They take longer."

"I'll trust you in that. You would know better than most."

Jhared looked away. What did he know of healing? He knew better than most who was responsible for such damage.

"It would do him good to see you," Tierzen said.

"I would like that. I imagine when all is settled, I'll be sent back to Velantar with the rest of this company."

When all was settled? What could that possibly mean? The north had rebelled. And he was more dangerous to Avelos than any weapon the Sahistens could bring to bear. Reflexively, Jhared put a hand to his hip, seeking the consolation of Bran's talisman. Then he recalled that the guards had taken it, along with his belt pouch and Mayavana's feather.

"Very good." Tierzen smiled faintly. "When you're back, I'll speak to someone about assuring you have leave."

Jhared cleared his throat. "What's going to happen now? Do the elders believe me?"

"Believe that the north has committed the most hideous act of treason since the Avelune attempted to assassinate Lord Tumal? What do you imagine?"

"Ah."

"That's not to say they all doubt you. Abrigado's supporters are debating, but more on principle than fact, I think. In truth, Toren didn't seem particularly shocked, but it's to his advantage for the council to view the north's actions as the result of Rumar's rule. He wants them to invoke the Law of Integrity."

Jhared frowned. "With the chaos in the council, why hasn't Abrigado invoked it himself?"

"He can't. Not even his closest supporters would allow the Law to be pushed forward with five of the fifteen first-clans absent." Tierzen made an unhappy gesture. "He doesn't seem impatient over it. I have the sense he's waiting for something. I wish I knew what."

"When the northerners arrive, will the high chieftain have enough support to act?"

"That depends on what he plans to do."

"And what will he do?"

The elder chuckled. "It really does take unconsciousness to stop your questions, doesn't it?"

Jhared grimaced and leaned back on the pallet. It was Tierzen and General Nadel who taught him to question, to pull aside the veils that distort understanding in order to find the truth. Pain lay in that thought, although he couldn't think clearly enough to understand exactly why.

"Don't be sorry," Tierzen said. "I've missed your questions."

Silence drifted over the room. "Sir, what is it?"

"What do you mean?"

"You've always taken care not to show me favor. What you've done today will cause trouble, for you and for the high chieftain."

"Oh, that matter with the report?" Tierzen waved a dismissive hand. "That was about maintaining council order, not about showing favor. Sevar's message would have been lost under a crush of argument had I not forced Rumar to openly acknowledge the military code."

"It's not just the report, sir, and I think you know it. You pushed at least five soldiers out of their places so I could have a night's sleep. And you just offered to intervene with my commanders to gain me leave." Jhared looked into the shadows that were the elder's blue-grey eyes. "What are you afraid is going to happen?"

Tierzen didn't answer immediately. In the dim light, he looked grizzled and tired. Jhared waited, apprehension beating steadily against his ribs.

Finally, the elder sighed. "Oh, my boy. Don't you see? Rumar is in an untenable position. He's going to be forced to make compromises."

"Compromises. Like pulling Shorn soldiers from the ranks?"

"Like that. Worse. Somehow, he will either have to bring the north back into the Council of Clans or pacify Abrigado. He cannot go to war while fighting two battles at home."

"What will it take to pacify the Legacy?"

"That's what I'm afraid to find out," Tierzen said. "The case of treason against his Shorn scribe gave Toren leverage enough to deprive General Nadel of good soldiers. And he's not done with her yet."

"What?" All the other implications of Tierzen's words abruptly dropped away. Jhared's insides contorted with something that might have been relief or dread or desire. He thought of Ziabela's demand that he steal the secret of the killing winds and help her to free the Shorn from Avelos. He thought of her compelling gaze and fierce spirit. He remembered her long fingers stroking his neck and the sweet-sad sound of her flute as she played music his mother had composed. "Ziabela is alive?"

"Primarily because the council hasn't had time to deal with her. Lady Nemiah took custody of her under the Right of Advocacy." Tierzen's gaze sharpened. "Jhared? Are you listening to me?"

Jhared pulled back from a parade of confusing, seductive memories. Tierzen was staring at him with a knowing look. He flushed. "Don't fear, sir. I have no reason to try to see her."

"Good. Because you mustn't. Abrigado has not yet made any connection between you two. If he does, I would have no influence that could save you."

"I understand. You must never risk yourself that way."

The words came out with an edge Jhared hadn't intended. He grimaced and shook his head. "I only meant that I wouldn't want you to—"

Tierzen stopped him with a raised hand. "It's all right. I know what you meant. Ah, Jhared, no matter how we work at it, we all have our own veils. In the past weeks, I've found a few of my own. I think it was my nightmare that finally made me recognize them."

Jhared fidgeted with the edge of the blanket, unable to meet his foster father's gaze.

"*I* made you Trianor's Folly," Tierzen continued. "*I* made you a target for the Legacy in ways no other Shorn man has ever been."

"Sir, that's of no matter. You took me in, a cursed child. When no others would."

"It is of some matter. I gave you burdens of my creation. They had nothing to do with the curse or reparation. Now I would offer you what protection I can, while I can, and hope it will shield you somewhat when the worst comes."

"Sir, please be careful." *I am the thing you most fear. A bearer of destruction.*

Tierzen shook his head. "Don't, son. The debt has narrowed between us. When you left, after Lieutenant Sevar's accusations of insubordination and all you had revealed about the unbound, I doubted you could overcome the weakness of your tainted blood. I wondered if my Teaching had failed. I doubt you no longer. If you hadn't found your strength, you would not have returned." Tierzen smiled. "Even Rumar had cause to defend you tonight."

Jhared let out a breath. He didn't realize how wretched he sounded until he saw Tierzen's quick look of concern.

"Pain?"

Jhared only nodded.

"I've kept you too long. I'll go. It's time I returned to the council. There will be bitter debates tonight." The stool creaked as the elder rose. "The commander left more dreamsease for you. Do you need it?"

Jhared nodded again.

When Tierzen presented the bitter brew, he gulped it down.

"Sleep. Later I'll have them send food." The elder took the cup away and smoothed the blankets. "One thing more I have to say. About the clanguard ambush."

Despite the drug beginning to work in his blood, Jhared's heart drummed hard. "Yes, sir?"

"Others will question it, but I was your Teacher. I know what agony it would have caused you to put a blade to a countryman. I know you could only do such a thing for the sake of Avelos. Grieve the necessity of it, but don't let it overwhelm you."

Jhared felt his spirit tearing. "As you say, sir."

There was comfort, a small easing of burdens, before Jhared recognized the first flash of desire. She had stretched her body beside his and wrapped one arm across his chest, warm and soft in the cold night. Her breath kissed his cheek, as sweet as spring. A deep ache filled his center. It terrified him how swiftly she could unbind his need. He drew his hand out of the covers and slipped it beneath her shirt. She sucked a breath as his fingers found smooth skin and the curve of her breast. Then, with a sigh, she relaxed against him, sliding a leg upward until her knee brushed his inner thigh.

"I missed you," she whispered.

"You're a dream," he answered.

"Am I?" Her hand on his chest smoothed its way to his belly, and lower. Nails raked across his flesh.

He groaned. She laughed, softly.

"I was so afraid you would think I had abandoned you," he murmured.

She kissed him. "You could never abandon me. You know who I am."

Need thrummed like a taught bowstring inside him. His body moved instinctively, seeking hers, seeking the rhythm of flight.

"Come to me," she whispered, pressing herself against him.

The weight of her hips on his made him shudder. Urgently, he scrabbled the blankets aside, desperate to feel the heat of her, to be enfolded within her. He wrapped his arms around her shoulders. His hands sought the grace of feathers…

And found the long, gnarled knots of scars.

"Oh, Goddess! What have they done? *What have they done to you?*"

He rolled free of her, out of bed, and onto his injured leg. His knee buckled and he tripped to the ground.

"Jhared, hush! Hush or Abrigado will have us both killed! What's wrong?"

He struggled to understand. The ground was cold and hard. It was very dark. But he was not in one of Maya's grottos. The Avelun had not come to comfort him. Above him, he could make out another woman glaring down. Her exposed body shone pale in the darkness.

"Ziabela," he panted. "How did you get here? What are you doing?"

"I *thought* I was welcoming you back."

He closed his eyes, trying to catch his breath and his hurtling thoughts. "I'm sorry. I didn't mean . . . I didn't know . . . .I thought I was dreaming."

She glanced at him sidelong. "You seemed awake enough to me."

Abruptly, he realized that his body was having no trouble grasping the fact of her presence, although his mind hadn't entirely accepted it. He limped back to the bed and grabbed up a blanket to cover himself.

She chuckled low in her throat. "Did I scare you?"

She was beautiful, fierce and subtle. He thought of Alende's love for her, and his grief. He thought of Maya.

"You do scare me."

It was hard to tell in the dark, but he thought he saw her smile. She reached forward to tug the blanket away from him. "Well then. Shall I give you a true cause to fear?"

Her fingers brushed his thigh, and he let out a strangled sound. "Goddess, woman, have mercy! You just said yourself Abrigado would have us killed."

She relented a little at that, sitting back on the bed, but leaving herself uncovered. The curve of her breasts seemed almost a challenge. "I came to Parnas Pass with Lady Nemiah. No one but the Lady, her men, and now you, knows I'm here."

"Zia, stop toying with me. Why would the Lady of Avelos bring you here?"

"There are reasons for it, but they belong to the Lady. I think . . . I think I will not tell them to you."

The sudden uncertainty in Zia's voice surprised him, and made him remember she was a prisoner held by the temple, awaiting word as to whether or not she would be executed. With a sigh, he wrapped the blanket around his waist and sat on the bed a safe distance from her. "Tierzen told me the Lady claimed you. Are you all right?"

"Better than I've a right to expect." She gave a little shrug. "I've been of some use in the temple. And I've kept up with council matters. If I don't have the channels I had when I was Abrigado's scribe, I still have Kaliska to bring me news."

"I'm glad," he said truthfully. "I've thought of you."

Her smile this time was quicksilver. "I've thought of you, too. Every day I wondered if you had found the key to the killing winds. Our chance to leave Avelos is coming, Jhared. With the council so distracted, all we need—"

"Zia, don't."

"Don't what?" Her gaze glittered. "Don't speak of our right to have done with the debt? Don't speak of the way Avelos is splitting apart like a rotten log? I'm not asking you to take action for yourself. All you need to do is tell me where Sabela's temple can be found. I know others who will hunt the answers there. When we hold the secret to the killing winds, we will seek our own lands."

When we hold the secret to the killing winds. How many of the Shorn—the Kin, the unbound, the anathema like himself—already owned that secret and didn't know it? What was he going to do about it?

Outside, a breeze gusted and one side of the tent belled inward with a soft *whoosh*. The bed rustled. When he turned back, Ziabela was sitting beside him, her hand on his arm, her eyes vibrant and persuasive. From the first moment he had seen her playing her flute at the Black Mountain Inn, he had ached with longing. He had loved her for her boldness and for the connection she offered to a time before he understood the meaning of shame.

She leaned closer and ran a gentle finger along the bruise above his cheekbone. Her bare breasts brushed his chest. "Mahla would rejoice to know you played a part in freeing the Shorn. She didn't want you to spend your life in chains."

"Ah, Goddess." He swallowed and pulled back from her touch, fighting against his rising need. A part of him—the part that was all undisciplined desire—wanted to push her down on the bed and sate the hunger she had awakened. A part of him yearned to do her bidding simply in the hope that it would have been his mother's wish. He sucked a ragged breath. He was no longer willing to be compelled. He was more than Ziabela's tool or Mahla's son. He need not be bound by a woman who would use and discard him as she had discarded Alende. He had found compassion and courage in another heart. Jhared studied Zia's clever face, framed by long, tousled curls. Her green eyes delved into his. Finally, he found the strength to turn away, not because of what he saw in her, but for what he didn't see.

"My mother would be disappointed with me, then." He rose from the bed and took a step away from her. It took effort, even now. "Ziabela, the north has committed a crime as heinous as that of our own ancestors. Good soldiers have already died for no reason other than the fact that they kept their oaths. How can you come to me with words of treachery?"

"Soldiers die," she said, not ungently but with no acknowledgment that those losses had meaning. "You can't make yourself responsible for every death, or the choices of the people who caused them."

"I don't call myself responsible for the north. Of course I don't! But some answer is needed from us—we who were spawned from deceit. Do you not recognize the terrible echoes of it? The lessons of the Avelune's betrayal have not been heeded. Avelos is at the brink of dissolution."

"Which is why we must find the winds now! With Sahiste and the north occupying the council, we could truly separate ourselves. Establish a free territory for the Shorn."

"Zia, how can you think so? We are bound to Avelos!" He shook his head and raised a hand against her protest. "No, not just by blood and loss. Even I have debts of love I must repay. Is there no one you care for enough to protect in this land?"

Her head jerked upward, and the answer flashed unguarded across her face. For an instant, Jhared saw tenderness and concern in her. Then, with a defiant gesture, she dashed a hand across her eyes, crushing tenderness and replacing it with steel.

"Do you understand that I am guilty of everything of which Abrigado has accused me?"

Tierzen had told Jhared about the accusations before he left the city: that Zia had used Abrigado's name to organize Legacy speeches, incite riots, and spread word of insubordination among General Nadel's Shorn soldiers, all actions that sparked hatred and spread fear. People had died, Shorn and not.

"No. I don't understand. Tell me."

She folded her arms across her breasts. "Alende has ever been right about one thing: the Shorn have been tamed. When our people bother to think on reparation at all, they think of it as a necessary burden. Every time the council lashes a whip at us, they see it only as the way of the world. Something we must endure. The tamed ones must be shown the truth of the Legacy. They must hear the Legacy demanding our blood and see the council killing us on traitors' wall before they will stir enough to throw off our chains."

"So you took it as your task to provoke the Legacy to spill more of our blood?" Jhared's stomach churned. It was the height of irony that a Shorn woman had manipulated the most influential political faction for her own purposes. But, Goddess, the cost. "And Abrigado? Was it you who roused his hatred as well?"

"Now you credit me with more cunning than I deserve," she said, her tone at once sharp and fragile. "Abrigado has malice enough of his own. You may take my word on that."

Jhared dragged a hand over his face. "You've given the council more cause to act against us than it's had in years. Soldiers have been pulled off the line and scribes turned out of Elders' Hall. There have been executions!"

"Oh, Jhared, Avelos has stolen everything we're meant to be. What loss matters after that?"

It was a grim echo of Maya's words. He wasn't the same man who had flatly rejected such thoughts when he first heard them from Ziabela and Elian at the Black Mountain, but though he could no longer throw them away, he still didn't know what to do with them. How did he find a balance between what had been done to him and what he owed? He *was* a danger, after all, a very real danger.

"It's not so simple, Zia. We carry more than just a history of treason. Tumal the Just was right. The capacity for destruction is in our blood!"

The wind gusted again, catching the tent flap. Jhared glanced up. A dark, stocky figure pushed inside, carrying a shuttered lamp. For a disorienting instant, Jhared saw winglike shadows behind the smaller figure who followed. Then the shutter was pulled off the lamp and the shadows fled.

"Oh, Ziabela," a woman sighed. "I told you to take care."

Zia shot off the bed as though she'd been bitten, grabbing up her shirt. Jhared leaped backward, holding tightly to the blanket.

Lady Nemiah stood before them, her expression heartrending, her body swaying like a sapling in the wind. Beside her loomed the same broad-shouldered, plain-faced Arionad Jhared had seen earlier that evening. The man's angry blue eyes moved from Ziabela to Jhared.

"Lady, I didn't intend any harm," Ziabela cried. "You were asleep. I just needed a walk. I just thought—"

"Stop!" Lady Nemiah's voice rang with power. "Don't damage the weaving with your lies. Did you think I couldn't see your longing when we spoke of the map? Did you think I wouldn't guess where you had gone?"

Zia hung her head, her long hair curtaining her expression. "I did come to ask him about the map," she said, misery thick in her voice. With a start, Jhared realized that, until this moment, he had never seen genuine remorse in her.

"And was this the price for him to tell you?" The Lady of Avelos gestured at Zia's half-clad form and Jhared's blanket.

Jhared gasped. "No, Lady! I would not—"

"Quiet, soldier! The question was not for you."

Ziabela looked up. Jhared saw her wrestling with an answer. He wondered if she would blame him for her crimes.

"There was no price. He refused to tell me."

Lady Nemiah sighed. "Then why, Zia?"

"Because we share a history. Because, even though he refuses to walk the same road I do, he knows who I was meant to be."

Ah, Goddess. How many times could the spirit be torn and a man remain intact? Jhared tried to catch Zia's gaze, to show her all the confusing, complex things she meant to him. She wouldn't glance in his direction.

"Evorales, take her back to my tent before someone else sees her. I suppose you'll have to do something about Avjay, too. He must have let her go."

"It wasn't Avjay's fault!" Zia cried. "I convinced him you had sent me on an errand."

Nemiah shook her head sadly. "Oh, Ziabela, Leita and Amalia were losses enough. You were the one I expected, the Shorn woman accused of treason. So why does this hurt as it does? Go on, Commander. Leave the lamp. I have words for the soldier."

Zia shrank into herself. The Arionad glared at Jhared. "Lady, I wouldn't trust him alone with you."

"Jhared Denaban owes me for helping him to deliver his message to the high chieftain. He'll not offer any affront. Isn't that true, Patrolman?"

Jhared made a swift spiral. "Yes, Lady. Of course."

The Arionad relented, but gave Jhared a last threatening glower before turning to Ziabela. "You, come along." He retrieved her cloak from the ground and shoved it into her hands.

As Zia drew up her hood, she looked over her shoulder. Lamplight reflected from the depths of her eyes. "Mahla disagreed with me about many things, Jhared. In the end, I made choices she didn't support. The truth is that you are not so unlike her."

She stepped into the darkness, leaving Jhared staring after her, clutching that unanticipated gift.

"I am sorry to find that gentleness and trust are not enough to shift her Path after all," Lady Nemiah said.

Jhared forced himself to turn from the empty space where Zia had been. "She didn't mean to hurt you. If I've ever seen anything clearly in Ziabela, I saw that."

"That's a kind observation. I don't know what it might mean, but I thank you."

He bowed his head, unsure what he was feeling and certain that, for now at least, he had to shove the question aside. "You said you wished to speak with me, Lady. Shall I dress?"

Nemiah gave a startled little laugh, as if she had forgotten he was bare. For a moment, her tone slipped from its imperious timbre. "Please. Here's the making of a scandal neither one of us can afford."

She turned her back while he hastily pulled on the clean clothes Tierzen had left for him. As he drew on his boots, he gazed at the Forest Guard cloak folded neatly on the table, a Shorn patrolman's garment to replace the one he had shredded. The red border shone against the deep green wool, a reminder of innocent blood spilled. It seemed an age since he had slipped free of that border in Brenia, stealing Bevan's cloak to conceal his identity. He left the new one lying with his sword belt on the table. Decently dressed and as composed as he could be, he faced the Lady of Avelos.

She perched on a stool, no more levity in her expression. "You're a clear-sighted one, I've heard. I wonder if you know why I've stayed."

He was terrified that he did know, but he steadied himself and clasped his hands behind his back. If she had figured him out, she wouldn't be speaking matter-of-factly of kindness and clear-sightedness. There was something else. Of course there was. "You wish to know more about the Bearer's part in our travels."

"That's right. There are things I should know. Things that could matter."

Jhared didn't think she was playing games with him, but she seemed somewhat lost, and that made her unpredictable. Worse, she had seen him with Ziabela. He needed to be careful.

"Lady, I gave a detailed report. What is it exactly you wish to hear?"

"Why don't we start with the story of how Cael's Chosen attacked your company?"

"I said what happened. The Bearer saved my patrol from the Verael. We would have taken more losses if she hadn't intervened."

"Yes, you did say that. Now, what can you tell me about what she *did*?"

Ah, careful indeed. Jhared closed his eyes. He didn't want to lie to the priestess, but he wasn't ready to end up on traitors' wall, either. He braced himself. "She called a Pathguide, who ordered the beasts to retreat."

Lady Nemiah's gaze grew keen. "A Pathguide? How do you know? How could you?"

"The Bearer told me," he said. It was the truth, if not the full truth.

"I see. So she trusted you."

Trust? That word was too simple to describe his tie to the Bearer. "Lady, I was her bodyguard. She trusted me to keep her safe. In that, I failed."

"Now *that* is a different matter. You will yet need to make reparation for it. When Leita spoke of Pathguides, she trusted you with a mystery. Something that could have her name scarred in the Book of Circles. Why would she do that?"

Paths twirled around him. The Gate burned. He immersed his awareness in the present, afraid the Lady would sense what was happening. "Perhaps because she knew I had no reason to question her."

"No." The priestess frowned. "That's not it. At least, not the core of it. Leita doesn't spill secrets to a man just because he knows how to keep them. What is it about you?"

She studied him from across the tent, then rose and glided closer. It always startled him to realize how small she was: the top of her head didn't even reach his shoulder. She seemed worn thin since the last time he had seen her. Hollows carved her cheeks and her eyes darted over him with a preternatural shine. Jhared thought fleetingly of Alende.

"The Paths are writhing around you. It was the same at your Becoming. I remember that now. Even after all you survived, they never stopped twisting. Leita believed they would settle in time, but they haven't."

She walked around him, laying light hands over his shoulders, his heart, his back. Her touch held none of Zia's passion or possessiveness; rather it seemed more like the touch of a blind woman trying to comprehend what faced her. "There's more," she murmured. "So many open doors leading to myriad Paths. I know some of these Paths, I think. They have Leita's footsteps on them."

Jhared stood vulnerable to her inspection, wondering how long it would take before she considered the impossible. He decided he would not wait for it to happen. "Lady, what is it you truly wish to know?"

The high priestess drew her hands away and came around to face him. "What drove the Bearer to heresy?"

Jhared froze. *Careful. Be careful.* She wasn't talking about Leita's choice to teach a Shorn Pathwalker. He didn't believe she would keep that accusation silent. She knew something else about the Bearer. What? He thought of Leita, with eyes that consumed the light and secrets she doled out in perplexing bits. Abruptly, he recalled one of those secrets: Cael's messengers fluttering in a woven basket, a dove perched upon her arm.

"I'll release him at dawn, and he'll make his way home, where his mate is waiting."

"All the way to the high temple?"

"To those who have made a home for him."

Lady Nemiah tilted her head, watching his reaction. "I've frightened you."

"Yes," he said, acknowledging fear to a woman for the second time that night. "That's a dangerous question for a Shorn soldier."

"If you knew my Higher Circle, you would realize it's nearly as dangerous for the Chosen Lady. Something about you provokes candor, Jhared Denaban. But the question was unfair and probably unwise. I withdraw it. I just need to know what the Bearer was after."

He released a breath. "Lady, I can tell you she was also scared."

"Of what?"

Another choice: another point where he could offer her what he knew or hold back and evade the risk. He glanced down at the most powerful woman in Avelos and saw equal parts of hope and apprehension in her eyes, eyes as green as his own. "She spoke to me of the destruction of the Paths. The unraveling of Riana's weaving. She told me she was striving to prevent that horror."

"By achieving True Balance?" The priestess's tone was unreadable.

Jhared thought of the day after the Verael attack, when he had confronted the Bearer. "She used those words. I don't know what they mean."

"Oh, Leita, how did you stray so far?" Lady Nemiah sank back onto the stool, her head bowed into her hands.

"Lady, is it wrong for me to ask you of this True Balance?"

The priestess shook herself and blinked up at him, grief heavy in her gaze. "Why does it matter to you?"

"Because the Bearer gave me incomprehensible glimpses of a future of utter darkness." He threw out his hands. "Lady, since I met her, I've felt as though I've been hurtling blindfolded toward a cliff."

"Ah, yes, that's Leita, certain enough." She smiled sadly. "I begin to wonder if too little knowledge rather than too much has brought us to where we are now. It seems we've all been blind in one way or another." She went quiet. "You're more than a simple soldier, aren't you, Jhared Denaban?"

He refused to flinch under her penetrating gaze. "I think you know my history, Lady."

"Some of it. Enough to know you've read more about our past than most Shorn soldiers have and you've been allowed to question more than you should. Leita must have liked that about you." She studied him a long moment. "The concept of True Balance comes from an ancient heretical teaching."

She told him, then, of True Balance and True Chaos, and the heretics' belief that Riana and Cael were only two parts of something far more ancient, something they named the "Unbroken One." He reeled as she went on to tell him how the temple had been poisoned, how the maps of every sacred journey since the Exile had been stolen and her Arionade had died. When she finished, she sat in silence, looking small and tired.

He shuffled these strange new pieces in his mind. The followers of the Unbroken One, who didn't fear Cael. Were they the home to which the Bearer's doves returned? Did they know of Leita's purpose? Given a bit of time, he might solve some mysteries with these pieces.

"I thank you, Lady."

The priestess shivered and shrugged more deeply into her cloak. "You should not thank me for exposing you to such ill-formed beliefs."

If the Lady genuinely believed the story to be heresy, she would have already condemned and discarded it, but the conflict in her expression said she hadn't discarded it at all. Jhared recalled something Leita had asked him at the start of their journey, when she told his patrol the improbable tale of Alende Isan and Lady Sabela: *Might not valuable stories ever be lost? Might not a tale be shunned and forgotten if it holds a truth too painful to face?*

"What if this story is a true part of the goddess's tale?" he asked. "A part that's long been lost? Should we call that heresy, then?"

The priestess gave a choked laugh. "You are indeed Tierzen Trianor's fosterling and Enrian Nadel's pupil."

"Isn't that why you chose to tell me?"

"Perhaps," she admitted. "I also pointed out that you ask more questions than is wise."

He closed his mouth on what he might have said then.

The priestess made a face. "In all honesty, I'm not entirely certain why I told you. There's something remarkable about this point where our Paths have crossed. Possibilities may exist here." She folded her arms across her chest, her fingers digging into her flesh. "It's impossible to discuss such things now. We've something yet to settle before I go."

Her tone made him uneasy. She wasn't done wondering about him. "As you say, Lady."

"Jhared Denaban, I know you understand what would happen if the elders learn Ziabela has been here with you."

He willed himself to stillness. "A woman accused of treason found in the tent of Trianor's Folly would be a gift for Abrigado. Lady, I have earned my own demise, but Elder Trianor—"

"Wait. I did not mean it as a threat. Too many people stand to suffer if it became widely known. I only ask something from you in exchange."

He glanced at her. "I have little that's mine to give."

"You have an oath. You swore to protect the Bearer, and you left her in the hands of Clan Aglar. I would claim what you owe her."

A silence fell. "You want my oath as your guard?"

"No," she said plainly. "I want to guard you."

"Lady, you have more than enough reason to doubt me, but I did not seek out Ziabela. I would not."

"This is not about doubting you. Or not exactly." Her brows gathered above her green gaze. "I don't *understand* you. You upset the Paths like a boulder dropped into a small pond. I don't know how your decisions might shift our course, but I will feel better if I'm close enough to ward off those as reckless as Ziabela and as spiteful as Abrigado who might pressure you to make ill-advised choices. Will you accept it?"

In her presence, falling through the Gate would be a constant danger, yet Jhared couldn't deny the symmetry here. Two trained Pathwalkers existed in Avelos: a woman of Cael and a woman of Riana. By abandoning one he had found the other. Cael had led him down a road of bewilderment and loss; perhaps the Goddess of Order might grace him with the guidance he needed.

He bowed his head and formed a spiral. "I will."

The blue flames roared upward. Lady Nemiah staggered against the wall of the tent. Jhared caught her, even as he ground his teeth against the side of his mouth to anchor himself. Beyond him, beyond the tent, beyond the edges of the camp came a familiar rhythmic pounding.

"Something's happened," he panted.

"Yes, something indeed." She drew away from his support and sank onto the edge of the bed. He saw her wince as she gouged her thumbnail into her wrist.

"No, Lady. I mean here and now. A horseman's riding hard toward camp." He caught the snort of a mount reined in too hard, then the challenge from one of the watchmen.

She gasped. "Whatever it is, it's influencing our direction."

"You've claimed me to stand beside you, Lady. Shall we go find out?"

The sound of hoofbeats grew louder as the rider was passed into the perimeter. A man called out; another answered.

Lady Nemiah glanced up at him with an expression that made him pause. It wasn't a look like the Bearer's that consumed the stars and held the secrets of the spheres. It was open and ephemeral, the last, clear light of a summer evening. Jhared wondered at it. Such openness as she revealed required courage, for it made a person vulnerable. Amid the conflicts and intrigues of the council, it was a rare touch of grace. It reminded him of Mayavana.

"I've frightened you again," she said softly. "What do you see?"

"No, not frightened, Lady. Awed."

"Ah. Then it's Riana you perceive. Some few gifts the goddess has left me." Lady Nemiah glanced with a rueful expression at the bruise blossoming on the inside of her wrist.

Jhared didn't explain that it was her very mortal honesty, not the goddess's power, that touched him.

"Come," she said, rising from the bed. "Let us learn in what direction we're hurtling now."

30.

SHIFTING ALLIANCES

The ground rocked again as Jhared stepped out of the tent. Lady Nemiah's gaze swung toward the east, past the ragged tails of fog that entwined the dusky camp, toward a thread of predawn light that snaked across the horizon. Sunrise: the transition to the new day in the midst of the transition to the new season as Avelos stood at the threshold of an uncertain future. The Paths split over and again, agitating the weaving with all the endless possibilities. Jhared wondered if the high priestess would change her mind about rushing to confront whatever news was heading toward the center of camp, but she only shook herself, like someone trying to escape a bad dream, and hurried on.

The horseman thundered ahead of them across the north side of the clearing. Horses on the lines bugled in anxious response. On either side of Jhared, soldiers peered from their tents as they pulled on clothes, calling to one another for word. By the time Jhared and Lady Nemiah reached the high chieftain's tent, elders and soldiers were gathering around a mud-splashed scout and his weary mount.

The scout was a man Jhared recognized, a thickly built Shorn soldier named Jech. They belonged to the same company and had fought the winds together in the south. From their first meeting, Jhared had detested the man for his lazy attitude toward duty and the debt. Jech had scorned him for his belief in final reparation. That might have been a lifetime ago, but it had only been last spring.

"Inside," Rumar ordered the scout, nodding toward the tent. "Councilors. Lady Nemiah, if you will." He frowned at the scattered soldiers standing around; none were in proper uniform and one or two looked as though they'd found too much wine the night before. "Lieutenant Mavriel, get these men in order. I suspect we're going to need them to look like Forest Guard soon."

As the elders filed inside, Rumar's gaze skated over Jhared. He gave Lady Nemiah a bemused look.

"It's a longer story than we've time for," she said.

"I'm sure," Rumar murmured dryly.

417

Tierzen half-turned from where he was speaking with Elder Nadro of Clan Nadaren. His eyes widened when he saw Jhared, but there was nothing to be done.

"Sir, a party'a northerners are minutes behind me," Jech panted. "Prefects Aglar and Lasla with a handful'a men."

Rumar raised a brow. "Only two of the five prefects? With a single patrol?"

"That's not all," Jech said. "The bulk'a their force is traveling down the pass more slowly. Sir, they have more than a hundred armed and mounted fighting men."

Dark murmurs rose from the elders. Someone wondered aloud how the north was possibly funding such a force. Jhared's hands closed into fists.

"Good," the high chieftain said fiercely.

"Good?" Elder Makri echoed.

"It means they're nervous. Afraid to meet us without a small army of swords to back them."

"Lord Rumar, we've fewer than fifty men." Elder Nadro tapped the blessing tattooed on his cheek.

"Fifty Shorn men who'd just as soon stab us in the back as defend us," Elder Makri muttered.

"We won't need fifty," Rumar answered. "We won't need five. Whatever they've done or not, the prefects would never dare to attack the council. This is about showmanship."

If showmanship it truly was, it was neatly done, and more subtle than Jhared expected from the north. Aglar and Lasla would guess that Rumar had scouts in the pass. They would approach the council with an unimposing party and make their demands courteously, knowing that Rumar was well aware of the larger force backing them.

"What of the other three prefects?" Tierzen asked.

"What of the Bearer of Cael's Blade?" Lady Nemiah called at the same time.

Jech's gaze picked out the high priestess first. "I didn't spy the Lady Bearer, but I couldn't put a wager on whether or not she's with them. Fog's thick as stew in the pass, and I didn't have much time. When Lasla and Aglar broke away from the company, I had to scramble to get around them." He shook his head at Tierzen. "Sir, I saw no sigils but Lasla's Mavaye stallion and Aglar's lightning."

Elder Nadro made a face. "Do we intend t'welcome them?"

"Of course we welcome them," Abrigado said. "The five have requested a meeting with the council, and we agreed to it. Or do you think the word of Trianor's Folly should be given more weight than that of the leaders of the first-clans?"

Tierzen opened his mouth, but the high chieftain held up both hands in a quieting gesture. "No debate. We let the northern clans speak for themselves."

The declaration was met with a few grimaces. But Rumar needed the north under his control. He would not sever ties on the word of a Shorn soldier.

Outside, Lieutenant Mavriel bellowed commands for the men to fall into rank. Clan banners had been spotted by the watch. Jech was released to join his fellows. Jhared heard the familiar sound of soldiers hurrying to muster. He wished he were among them.

Someone tied the tent flap aside, so the council could watch the northerners trot into the center of camp and down a double column of the Forest Guard. The two prefects led the patrol on shaggy mountain horses, followed by two standard bearers partially obscured by their fluttering banners: Lasla's rampant Mavaye stallion and Aglar's triple lightning bolts. Five northmen followed.

Jhared couldn't help but stare, filled with a perverse need to see the prefects who were capable of betraying Avelos, capable of slaying the soldiers of their own army. All his life, his image of such traitors started with the scars on their backs. How did he fit the country's leaders into that image? Prefect Ondal Aglar was an intimidating figure, all iron and leather, with thick grey hair, a long grey beard, and iron-grey eyes set deeply in his weathered face. He sat his horse with ease and dressed in the same practical vest and breeches as his clanguards. The man on his right, Prefect Bilar Lasla, was much younger, not more than a handful of winters older than Jhared. He was a lean creature of bone and gristle. City men told stories of the wild, bloody-minded Lasla clansmen who lived by the Tregata Sea. Their prefect might have walked straight out of one of those stories. An axe swung from his belt; fox pelts lined his cloak; and twin scars ran down his cheeks into the silver-beaded braids of his black beard.

At Prefect Aglar's signal, the party halted and dismounted together. As the standards were planted beside the horses, Jhared caught his first clear glance of the two standard bearers. With a hiss of dismay, he took a quick step backward.

Lady Nemiah inclined her head in his direction. "Which one?" she whispered.

"With Aglar's standard. Commander Ciam."

She turned, tracking the burly, brown-eyed clanguard. "Will he recognize you?"

"Likely," Jhared muttered.

"Then pull up your hood and keep quiet. We have need of subtlety."

Jhared did as she directed, his heart pounding to see Ciam striding toward the tent. This man had held Leita at his mercy, perhaps still did.

"We *must* find her," the high priestess murmured, as though hearing his thought.

"We will," Jhared promised.

He sank another step backward as the prefects entered with the other riders. Prefect Aglar sent an appraising gaze around the tent, looking calm and self-possessed. Too calm. The prefects couldn't be certain whether or not the council had been warned of their treachery. Aglar and Lasla had the right to fear they might be taken as hostages in trade for the soldiers at Aglar Tower or executed outright for treason.

Only Ciam showed the wariness his prefect seemed to lack. Indeed, the clan-guard didn't look anything like the confident fighting man he had been in the Sandien Mountains. His skin was pale, his hair lank, and great blue circles hollowed his eyes. From behind Prefect Aglar, he studied the room anxiously. When his gaze reached Lady Nemiah, it narrowed a moment, then flinched away.

Jhared didn't have time to determine what that meant. Something was happening. Names were being muttered. Elders were nodding at the five men standing soberly beside the prefects. It seemed they were the northern five's missing elders.

"Greetings from the north to the councilors'a the first-clans," Prefect Aglar said, not waiting to be formally recognized. "I wasn't certain ya'd trade your soft beds and full tables for hard ground and soldiers' rations, but I'm glad ta see ya managed it."

The soft city men, lazy and decadent: it was an old, easy insult, the kind used to start tavern brawls. Aglar's failure to acknowledge the high chieftain was a more serious breach. The elders remained quiet, eyeing their northern counterparts with suspicion. Jhared stood vigilant behind Lady Nemiah. It was still possible men would die as a result of this gathering.

Rumar's expression revealed nothing. Dressed like a soldier in dark forest colors, with his rough features and calloused hands, he looked a match for the northerners. "Ondal Aglar, Bilar Lasla, Elders, the council welcomes you."

"Ay, we have your attention now, sure enough!" Prefect Lasla tossed his head, causing the beads in his beard to rattle like bones.

"As you say," Rumar replied. "You requested this council session and we have come. Shall we begin with the matters you have brought for resolution?"

Aglar's gaze shone hard and bright. "Time was when each leader'a the first-clans ruled as a chieftain in his own right. In that time, the staff'a warding shifted to each chieftain for a span of six years, clan by clan. No one man stood above another then, and no clan ruled over the fifteen. We've lost too much'a that time."

"How many years now has Clan Manitar held the staff for its own?" Lasla asked.

Every eye turned to the high chieftain, some shocked, some shrewd. In front of Jhared, Lady Nemiah drew a breath.

"More than one hundred sixty years," called out Lancion Makri. Since Tumal the Just had taken the staff before the Exile War.

"What is it you want?" the Elder of Clan Ontera demanded.

"We want what's right for the north!" Bilar Lasla growled, leaning over the smaller elder.

"What's right for *all* clans," Prefect Aglar added. "Return ta us the rights Alende Isan gave us as chieftains. Give over management'a the silver mines to the clans that rightfully own them. Stop stealing the best'a our men for a Forest Guard that does only Adan Rumar's will. Return us ta the time when we of the first-clans had the strength and the right ta protect ourselves."

"That time," the high chieftain said without moving, "was all of blood and feuding. People starved because the chieftains couldn't agree well enough to move grain from the fields to the cities. Because they couldn't coordinate their armies, we nearly ended as an Amurian duchy. Is that truly where you would see us return, Ondal?"

"Ya speak through the veils'a one who likes his own power too well," Aglar answered. "Ya've spent ten years sapping the strength'a the clans and drawing it ta Velantar. Of course ya see any other form'a rule as chaos."

"Return individual rule to the clans? Create fifteen independent provinces that bicker and spit at each other?" Rumar shook his head, his expression rueful. "You are asking for changes that would unravel the country. We are at the brink. If you do this, you will push us into the chasm."

"In Lasla, we know how to jump the chasms." Bilar Lasla bared his teeth in a grin.

"Just like an unblooded boy t'seek glory in conflict." Elder Nadro glowered at the young prefect. "Have ya really brought us here t'argue over these absurd demands while we face war?"

"If ya think me unblooded, take a closer look at this axe-head!" Lasla strode an angry step forward. Light gleamed off the weapon at his belt. "Alende Isan set foot on northern soil first, of all'a Avelos. The wealth'a the country lies buried in our lands. Let's see the council go without our strength a time and then tell us we have no right ta demand our due!"

"Peace, Elder Nadro! Prefect Lasla, peace!" Lady Nemiah stalked between the seething prefect and the elder. Her voice reverberated with the goddess's power. "The north bears many of Riana's gifts. Indeed, Alende Isan set foot on northern soil with Lady Sabela's guidance. But this kind of argument leads only to turmoil. What happened to the proud men of the north who understood the importance of order? More than any other clans, the northern five know order must rule the seasons and shape the discipline of survival. Bilar Lasla, your father understood it well. He offered silver to the high temple each Dawnings' Eve. Your own aunt served Riana at the sea's edge." Lady Nemiah turned her stern gaze upon the older prefect. "And you, Ondal Aglar, you spring from a line of men who ran the Tests of Rona for the gift of Riana's blessing. Where is your spiral for the Chosen Lady?"

"Some might think the Chosen Lady has abandoned order ta stand too close ta Adan Rumar," Aglar said, his gaze heated.

"And some might think that one hundred men make an army rather than a company of leaders come in good faith to resolve their differences," the Lady replied. "Will you not lay aside animosity for the memory of Alende Isan? The hero of our people stepped first on northern soil but gave his blood to Velantar. It was all of Avelos he loved. Together did the fifteen first-clans survive the fires of Altan Mar and the hard years of the migration."

The Lady's words reached them, at least Prefect Aglar. Jhared saw it in the dip of the man's grey head and the flash of reverence in his eyes. Then Aglar glanced at Toren Abrigado and ferocity returned to his gaze.

"It's easy ta speak'a love for Avelos so long as the resources'a my clan and the clans'a my brothers are flowing into your city, Lady Nemiah. I see no disorder in changing the laws that govern us. As ya say, the changing seasons are part'a her order. Even winter that kills the weakest."

In that unyielding tone, Jhared heard no chance for compromise. The northerners had committed to one Path. They would not be turned.

As if in confirmation, the blue flames leaped upward and the world swung wildly. Jhared saw Lady Nemiah start to fall, but he was already reaching for her, pulled by the force that moved them both. The Paths surged in response to the prefect's decision, shooting the consequences through the weaving like runners of ivy through the dirt. Could anyone know where and when those consequences would sprout? Did Lady Nemiah know? Is that what caused such dread to mask her features?

Jhared's fingers gouged her skin, and her green eyes met his. She gasped, and he realized that she knew. She *knew* he saw her falling toward the Gate.

Her body wilted toward the ground, drawing him downward. He sank to his knees on the packed dirt, cradling her. She was ethereal; not enough of her remained to keep her from floating away. Jhared saw the flames dancing behind her eyes. She gripped his hand and whispered something, but he only heard his name. In just that instant, someone else cried out, a voice of surprised recognition and malice. Then others were exclaiming over the Lady. Hands reached toward her: Elder Nadro's and the high chieftain's. Jhared let them free her limp figure from his arms.

"I'll get her out'a here. Into the clean air," Nadro said.

There was a quivering within Jhared's chest, like the rustle of leaves, and he knew Lady Nemiah had slipped away to some other Place or Parallel. Misery filled his heart. He caught the stench of death. "Send for the Arionade," he gasped, struggling to rise without tumbling after her. "They'll know what to do."

"It's easy ta speak'a love for Avelos so long as the resources'a my clan and the clans'a my brothers are flowing into your city, Lady Nemiah. Disorder isn't needed to change the laws that govern us. As ya say, the changing seasons are part'a her order. Even winter that kills the weakest."

Nemiah heard the finality in the prefect's voice and knew the Paths would respond. She knew the flames must come, but still she lost her balance and sagged toward the rippling earth.

Jhared Denaban reached for her as though drawn instinctively. With swift grace, he caught her under the elbow. As his fingers dug into her flesh, his green eyes met hers. She caught a breath at what she saw. He knew. Somehow he *knew* that she was near to spinning across the Gate. Dear Goddess, what had Leita taught him?

Nemiah thought of Ambri, Amalia's Arionad guide. Is that what Leita had hoped for? After such heresy as the Bearer had dared, why wouldn't she take one more forbidden step onto the Paths? They had ever called to her. If she had crossed the Gate, she would have needed her own guide. She had sent Nemiah the warning, after all.

"Too many open doors may explain uncontrolled journeys. Traveling is perilous without your guide. Don't cross the Gate alone."

What had the Bearer dared to teach a Shorn man? What could be taught to one who couldn't sense the Paths? Unless . . .

"Jhared Denaban, do you see the way? Can you find me?" She flung the words across a growing abyss, uncertain whether they made it to the young man who held her, uncertain whether he would understand them if they did.

"Oh, dove, you should never have returned."

Misery struck Nemiah like a cold hand, slapping away the remnants of her own Path. The stench of death filled her head. She stumbled in the darkness and knocked into a wall of slick, damp stone. Something metallic rattled at her feet. She jerked backward.

"Who's there?"

"Do you truly not know me, little one? Or is it only that you refuse to know?"

Infinite grief resonated in that low voice. If Riana ever mourned for her children, the goddess's voice could not hold more sadness. Nemiah strained to see through the black of the prison cell. "Lia? Is it you?"

"Yes. At least, for a short time longer."

It had found her: the Path Nemiah had been raised all her life to despise and fear; the Path she had dreaded since she learned the name of the woman who had become as a sister. Her legs gave out and she sank to the ground. "Oh, Lia."

"You sound surprised, dove. Yet you are the one who predicted my doom."

"Lady, help me understand!" Nemiah begged. "You revered Riana's order. I saw that in you. Why this? Was there truly no other way than for you to kill your high chieftain?"

The Avelun went still. Behind Nemiah, a creature gnawed and scrabbled. Sharp wet claws skittered across Nemiah's hand. She pulled her knees to her chest and hugged her arms around herself.

"I did not threaten any life," Lia said eventually. "It was Ambri."

Nemiah shivered with something much deeper than cold. "What do you mean Ambri? It was a plot by the Avelune. You are their leader. You are Lady Amalia."

"Ambri believed Tumal would come to kill me. He meant to prevent it. I never guessed he would act against my wishes. Against all order." Lia paused. When she went on, each word echoed with despair. "I don't know what happened. Perhaps Tumal guessed he would come. The palace guard caught him. Tortured him. Only then did I learn of it."

Nemiah shook her head. "I don't understand. How did you?"

"It was the pain. Ambri couldn't keep himself from falling into the weaving. He was so accustomed to finding me. He didn't intend it. It was just . . . habit."

"Goddess mercy," Nemiah breathed.

"I stayed with him. While they beat him. While they slowly cut him apart. My beautiful guide. Ah, Ambri. I begged him to surrender to them, to give them what they sought, but he refused. When Tumal finally realized my Arionad would not implicate me in any crime, he ordered him killed."

Nemiah choked on a cry. She thought of the confident young Arionad, with eyes the pale green of new apples and a fondness for kissing his beloved beneath the Ulaye tree. "They killed him. While you shared the same Path?"

"Not at the very last. Else I would not be here. He found the strength to throw himself apart from me at the end. Would that he had held me close instead, that we could have traveled to the Hidden Paths together. That I need not know what happened after."

"Tumal accused you of conspiracy," Nemiah whispered.

"But of course. You would know that part." A chain rattled as Lia shifted. "Indeed. Tumal showed himself with a bloody face before the people and flung Ambri's body into the streets with lies about a confession. The people went mad over it. The high chieftain's vipers killed the Sahisten ambassador as he tried to escape the city. I had been traveling the Paths with Ambri for six days. When they came for me and my women, I had no strength left to repel them."

"No, oh no," Nemiah cried. "Goddess, why do you play such cruel games with your servants?"

"War comes next, doesn't it, dove? Sahiste won't tolerate such an affront. And then death in the temple."

And then so much more. Nemiah couldn't tell Lia how the Avelune would be shot out of the sky and driven from the country, couldn't tell her that this day would rip through the Paths and across the years until Nemiah herself shed infants' blood over the altar.

In the darkness, she crept toward Lia's voice, stretching out her hand until her fingers touched something soft and firm, feathers, a wing unfurled and lax on the cold ground. Hesitantly, Nemiah stroked the unfamiliar contour, following it upward until she found a shoulder. Lia lay huddled against the wall, chains binding her wrists. The manacle on her ankle was bolted to the floor. Nemiah drew the Avelun as close as she could and wrapped her arms around her.

"Oh, my sister. Evil and lies have poisoned the weaving. Forgive my blindness. Oh, Amalia, forgive us all."

Elder Nadro carried Lady Nemiah out of the tent. Jhared tried to follow them, but a heavy hand landed on his shoulder and dragged him backward.

"Shorn soldier! It *is* you!" The familiar voice crackled with animosity. Jhared turned to face Commander Ciam.

"Ya attacked my men at Ebilan! Does the Council'a Clans and the Chosen Lady select mad deserters for guards now?"

Jhared stared, open-mouthed and uncertain. Ciam was the one who stood to lose here. By admitting he knew Jhared, he admitted to holding the patrol. What was the clanguard doing?

The blue flames roared hungrily. Jhared focused on the sensations of the moment—the angry lines of Ciam's face, the horrible downy lining of his vest, the pungent scent of his sweat.

"Commander, you kept my patrolmates against their wills, else I never would have used force against my countrymen."

The commander didn't flinch or hesitate. "Ya truly are mad! Lieutenant Sevar said it was so. My men fed and cared for your people. And a good thing, too! Else ya might have succeeded in your abduction'a the Lady Bearer. If we hadn't run ya off, I expect ya'd have done a great deal'a damage. You've a lot ta answer for, boy."

Jhared's insides jerked into a knot. "I tried to *free* the Bearer. Lieutenant Sevar sent me south to win aid."

"Aid?" Ciam spat. "Your lieutenant says you're a menace and a disgrace and that he should'a pushed you from the wall in Brenia!"

Ice and daggers pricked Jhared's chest.

"Enough!" Rumar demanded. "What in the name of the demon is all this?"

"We would ask the same," Prefect Aglar replied.

"Commander Ciam, you will tell us the rest of it."

Ciam offered an extravagant bow. "As ya command, Lord Rumar."

Tierzen was white faced. "Lord High Chieftain, is this not a matter for the Forest Guard? The council has no authority here."

Rumar whipped around to face the elder, frustration and anger a mask across his features. "Elder Trianor, are you suggesting I don't have the authority to demand the truth from my own soldiers?"

"No, my lord. I only ask that you stop—"

"Take care, Elder. Take great care, lest you ask one thing too many." Rumar pointed at Ciam. "You, get to the rest of your tale."

Ciam drew away from Jhared and adjusted his vest. "After this soldier attacked two'a my people in Ebilan, the lieutenant told me the boy had lost 'is mind to Shorn fever in Brenia. He attacked clanguard there as well, but only after he took it into 'is head ta free a convicted criminal. When they came ta arrest 'im for the deed, he threatened the Lady Bearer and put down two unarmed guards. Then he ran off. Later, when Lieutenant Sevar caught 'im farther north skulking around camp, the boy drew a blade on the lieutenant 'imself!"

Deadly quiet dropped over the tent. Jhared heard his own breathing, harsh and shallow.

"These allegations are indefensible!" Tierzen cried. "The boy would never have returned to us if they were true."

"But Elder, he didn't return," Abrigado observed coolly. "He was captured."

Jhared hurt as though he had been cut open. Tierzen stared at him with a terrible question in his gaze. Rumar was the one brave enough to ask it.

"Patrolman Denaban, did you free a criminal convicted by the elders of Brenia?"

Ah, Goddess. The complex elegance and cruelty of the Paths overwhelmed Jhared. How neatly his crime had twisted around. Even had he been inclined to attempt a lie, the Brenian clanguard would eagerly confirm the truth. Jhared swallowed and drew a breath. "Yes, sir."

The elders hissed in shock. Tierzen flinched. Rumar's craggy features steeled.

"Did you attack unarmed Clan Valador guards and desert your patrol?"

Another sword through the gut. Jhared straightened and bore it. He had made decisions of his own, and they had led to this.

"Denaban?" The high chieftain's voice was a hammer on the anvil.

"Yes, sir."

"And did you draw a knife on your commanding officer, Lieutenant Sevar?"

"Not with the intention of harming—"

"Answer the question!" Rumar roared.

"Yes."

Rumar braced both hands on the table and glared at the cluttered surface. Jhared didn't own the courage to look at Tierzen. His foster father's position as Minister of the Teaching was finished, and that was only the start. No bit of his own report on the northerners' treason would stand. The prefects would have a stronger position than ever from which to leverage their demands. And no one would ever know what had happened to Leita and his patrolmates.

The high chieftain growled an order to Lieutenant Mavriel, who called four soldiers out of the ranks. Two of them gripped Jhared by the arms, sending a rush of helpless anger crashing over him. He could fight now, fight until he forced them to kill him. He had known a Shorn man who had done such a thing. Micah had claimed it to be a means to reach final reparation. Jhared had not understood until now that it was an escape from shame.

He could not escape. Not that way. He relaxed in his captors' grip, earning a nod of acknowledgment from the wind-scarred soldier on his left.

"Where is the Bearer of Cael's Blade?" Jhared demanded, looking straight at Ciam.

Surprise filled the clanguard's eyes and a hint of the anxiety he had shown earlier, then something disturbing appeared, there and gone before Jhared could name it. "I couldn't say where she is."

Rumar turned on the northern guard. "You took the priestess into your care and claimed she offered the Blade to you in token of her support. How is it you don't know where she is?"

"I have no extraordinary talents ta touch others' hearts or see them as Riana's Ladies do!" Ciam's laugh was overloud. "As soon as Lieutenant Sevar and his men were fit ta travel, they left Ebilan with the lady. I imagine they're deep in the western Sandien by now."

He offered Jhared a hostile grin. "Did ya think ta stalk her there, soldier?"

The high chieftain tugged on the seal of state around his neck and gave Jhared a look of disgust. "Take him," he ordered Lieutenant Mavriel.

The guards shoved Jhared forward, past the northern prefects and through the mass of enraged elders. Tierzen leaned heavily against the table, as though he had been stabbed and left to bleed. Jhared looked away from his foster father and stumbled out of the tent into the cold morning. This moment was not his; it was too strange and terrible. He had taken some wrong step on the Path and ended in a place not meant for him.

The camp had no formal detention pen, so they flung him back into the tent that had become the infirmary. Jhared heard the lieutenant barking at someone on guard, but the words rumbled meaninglessly in his ears. With no recollection of moving, he found himself standing over the field table by the bed, a cup gripped in his hand. Dreamsease sloshed at the bottom, enough for two doses, maybe three. Without hesitation, he swallowed it all, then dropped onto the bed and waited for oblivion to take him.

31.
CHAINS AND PRISONS

In the dank prison cell with no window, no candle, not even a sliver of light beneath the door, Nemiah discovered the texture of darkness. It was thick and heavy and cold, as the murky water of a stagnant pool, pressing against her face, smothering her. When Nemiah's dread grew unbearable, she rested her cheek on Lia's feathers and inhaled their sweet herbal scent. She would not panic here; she had no right to it, not after all she had learned.

"I did not threaten any life, dove."

One sentence spoken by a woman at the edge of despair. One sentence. Enough to rip apart the veils of a nation. Nemiah could hardly comprehend it, but she could not reject it. Had some part of her begun to see the wrong long ago? Had something in the losses Avelos suffered or in the forgotten knowledge and the scarred lives warned her? Order was not only undone by this thing, but shredded, slashed. One sentence had turned a justified sacrifice for the welfare of Avelos into the worst of injustice. Into evil? Nemiah lifted her hands, but the darkness was too absolute to see them. She had cut the flesh of babes to preserve them, she believed, from weakness and deceit. She had done those things. They had been necessary. One sentence had changed that.

Lia hadn't spoken since their first exchange. Nemiah felt the other woman's exhaustion in the slackness of her limbs and the ragged pattern of her breathing. Nemiah shifted slightly, trying to ease her cramped back without disturbing the Avelun, but a wing trembled and Lia coughed.

"You believe I am the one who tried to kill Tumal, don't you, dove?"

Nemiah bowed her head. "Yes."

"You've no notion about Ambri?"

"On my Path, that's not . . . that's not the way the story is told."

Lia was quiet. "How many years have passed since?"

"One hundred fifty-two." It was a number no priestess in Nemiah's time had to pause to recall.

"A century and a half gone, and I'm the traitor. That's what Tumal hopes, I suppose. He means to paint my people with the colors of treachery." Lia's wings fluttered weakly, then settled.

"Why?" Nemiah whispered.

"Oh, little one, whatever the historians claim, too many moments shape a man to ever truly understand what drives him. I could say he craved power or he feared Sahiste or his council pushed him to bring down the temple. All of those things played a part in his decisions. Those and the one other: Marinen Tumal has never reconciled himself to being unfeathered. He has long coveted the sacred skies, and his frustrated desire has turned to cruelty."

Tumal the Just he was called on Nemiah's Path. How to confront such irony? "Oh, Lia. I am sorry."

"Do not say so. Every loss your temple suffers—of knowledge, of skills, of access to Riana's power—Ambri brought about."

"But Ambri acted out of love. I saw the intensity of his dedication to you. That should mean something in the order of things."

"Why should it? Love has nothing to do with order. Nothing else in the world can move a person so quickly toward chaos as love can." Lia's fingers tightened around Nemiah's. There was quiet; then Lia said more softly, "I understand now why you were drawn to my Path. Do you see it?"

Nemiah did. This moment was a point of influence that had slashed through one hundred fifty-two years of the weaving, right through to her own Path. "If I hadn't found you, my friend, I never would have understood what we've lost." Nemiah did not mean just the profound strength and skills that Lia and Ambri had possessed, but the deeper loss—of truth itself—that darkened the weaving from this moment to her own.

Lia bent stiffly and kissed her brow. "I wish I could give you something—a last gift of knowledge for you to take from here—but there's too much. If even your Avelune are no longer Pathwalkers, I'm not certain where to begin."

Nemiah caught a breath. The weaving could not be unwoven, although her heart might crack with grief because of it.

Lia must have sensed her hesitation. "What is it, dove?"

"Nothing. Nothing that matters now."

"Tell me."

"I cannot. Please trust me, Lia. There is a limit to the pain we should endure."

The Avelun straightened. Nemiah felt her marshalling her strength, felt the potency of her gaze, even in the darkness. "Do not speak of enduring pain until you have shared your Arionad's torture and watched your priestesses dragged away in chains. Before I die, I would know what has been wrought here. All of it."

"My lady, you should not have to know this thing." But she heard Lia's need and couldn't refuse it. Reluctantly, she spoke of the Shorn, of the Teaching and the Becoming, and of the Laws that structured them. She spoke gently and with care, but nothing could temper the image of blades against feathers and flesh. Beside her, the Avelun did not pray or curse or rant; she grew very still.

"Lia?"

There was no response. Dripping water echoed against the stone.

"Please, love, do not leave me yet."

Nemiah felt only the shallow rise and fall of Lia's chest to prove she was alive. They sat that way, in silent darkness, until Nemiah began to hum softly, and then to sing. It was one of Ziabela's songs, about the hope and sadness of Lady Elia. Nemiah owned no skill as a singer—her older sister had often teased her about that as a girl—but her voice pushed against the darkness, pushed it back just a little, enough perhaps to create a space for mourning. As the melody went on, simple and clear, Lia's breathing grew unsteady and her body shook. Finally, her grief spilled out in fierce, uncontrolled sobs. Her keening rang against the stone. In the depths of Lia's grief for the maimed children, the loss of the sacred skies, and the loss of love, there pulsed something sacred.

Nemiah continued to sing, spinning her poor melody against the black. When her voice turned hoarse and faded, she held Lia without speaking. Words were insufficient. The weaving could not be unwoven.

Time passed in the darkness with no marker. Gradually, the Avelun's shuddering subsided.

"Oh, little one, it's no wonder you say the weaving is shredding and the Paths turn toward their ends. The history of the Avelune is the history of all of Avelos."

Nemiah lifted her head. "What do you mean?"

"You don't know it? Even this? You truly don't know?"

"Lia, please help me."

"My people see the Paths from a perspective none other can. Flight allows us that perspective. We are Riana's mortal web-weavers, yet still a part of the pattern itself. We keep the balance. We open the doors to the Paths and see them closed again. Can you understand, then, what it means to tear us apart, to chain us to the ground and bar us from the Paths?"

Nemiah bit her lip. All her life, and for generations before, the Avelune had been cursed; tainted blood ran in their veins. How swiftly could a person release those veils? "I'm not sure."

Lia shifted against her chains. "Try imagining what happens to a pattern on the loom if you slash apart the warp."

In her mind, Nemiah saw a tapestry falling to pieces. As the pattern unraveled, she realized it held images from her own Path: her poisoned Arionade and a failed Becoming; Sahiste threatening war and Ziabela playing forgotten songs; the banners of the northern five and an injured Shorn soldier tied to a tree.

She did understand then. She wondered if her understanding came too late. "The fate of the Avelune is entwined with the fate of Avelos."

"Not just Avelos, dove. With the weaving itself."

"If I find a way to return to my own Path, will it matter? Can the direction be changed?"

"I don't know. I no longer own the strength to look for the answer to that question."

Nemiah swallowed against the tightness in her throat. Here was another piece of knowledge, another truth that smashed against her lifelong understanding. She must find a way to open herself to it or shatter. "Lia, I don't want to leave you."

"You told me that once before, while we watched the stars on a summer night from the top of my sky tower. You said then that you could not bear to leave behind such beauty, but no beauty remains here now."

"You cannot say so, my friend. I saw the goddess in you that night. In the heart of your courage, I sense her still."

Nemiah heard laughter, gentle and sweet, an unexpected light in this place of despair. Lia wrapped great wings around her and kissed her cheek. "This sacrifice is mine, little one. Do not seek death here. Your end has not yet been woven."

A shout went up from the heart of the camp, voices raised in something between protest and fear. Jhared rose to consciousness ready to fight. As he flung himself up from the bed, the stark realization burned before him: Leita was in danger of death, could possibly be dead already. The uneasiness he had seen in Commander Ciam's eyes had been guilt.

Jhared padded across the small space. The sleep had done him good. He felt calmer now and acutely aware. Afternoon light filtered through the tent fabric. At the entrance, he could see the profile of the man on guard. No one had come to question him, but why would they? He had already admitted his wrongdoing. When they came next, it would likely be to finish him. He might have been willing to accept that once, to call it reparation. Even now, he did not deny there might be justice in it, but with dawning comprehension, he realized he carried a burden too large to answer only to the narrow justice of the Council of Clans. He could not die and take the secret of the killing winds with him.

How was it that a man could feel such relief and fear at the same moment? He had no notion what to do with his secret, but he did know he must find the

Bearer. The steps to accomplish that task were clear. After, he would confront the other larger thing, and if, beyond that, some grace remained on this Path for him, he would be allowed the chance to bid farewell to the woman who understood who he was meant to be.

Another outcry rose from the center of camp. The guard outside muttered to himself. It was the scarred man who had dragged Jhared to his detention.

Jhared peered out the gap in the tent flap trying to catch a glimpse of the protestors. "What's happened?"

"The northerners have returned to their camp," the guard said without turning. "And the elders have just invoked the Law'a Integrity against Lord Rumar. Our boys aren't happy. We know who's likely t'come out on top'a that battle, eh?"

A rock dropped into Jhared's middle. Not the Law of Integrity now. Not while one hundred armed northerners glared across the road at Rumar's little company, not while Tierzen's political strength was demolished and Sahiste aimed its spears at the south.

Now was the worst possible moment, but of course *now* must be exactly when someone meant for it to happen.

"So that's why Aglar and Lasla brought their elders," Jhared murmured. "So the council would have enough clans in attendance to call a vote."

The guard spat into the dirt. "Probably."

There would be a hearing next. The elders who invoked the Law would make their case against the high chieftain. Rumar would be given the chance to answer, and another vote would be cast. If Rumar lost, the elders would appoint a new leader from among their own.

When the northerners had arrived, Abrigado had looked so smug. Tierzen had said the Minister of the Treasury was waiting for something. Had Abrigado somehow known what the north would do, or had he merely seen the opportunity to invoke the Law of Integrity and grabbed it?

The guard stepped closer to the entrance. "I'm Surian. Of the Forest Guard Second. That is, I was until Minister Abrigado got us ripped away from our stations."

Jhared grimaced. "I imagine you know well enough who I am."

"Well enough, Jhared Denaban. Ya were one who faced the first attack'a the killing winds at Lamirna."

Of all the ways Jhared might have been identified, he hadn't expected that one. "I was at Lamirna," he agreed. "If you're with the Second, you must have earned your scars when the winds hit Renida."

"That's right," Surian said, looking pleased Jhared knew it. "That storm came down on us while we chased raiders. I wasted time putting an arrow in one'a them instead'a running like mad, like the rest'a my patrol. Only survived cause a tree fell over me and gave some shelter." Surian grinned, twisting the scars on his cheeks into interesting patterns. "Sometimes we get unexpected gifts on this Path, eh?"

"Sometimes," Jhared said carefully, beginning to wonder why Surian was talking to him.

"Now, it would'a been a true gift if you and your boys had found the answer to those damned winds."

"We didn't."

"Right. I heard that. Unfortunate." The guard gave an easy shrug. "I suppose we've the north t'thank for that, eh? The trouble they've been causing. I heard ya had some trouble in Brenia, too. Trouble with the clanguard there."

"You hear a lot. You must have heard what the northerners said of me, then."

"Naw. Not that. I heard the truth." Surian scratched at a scar. "See, I have Kin in Brenia."

Ah. There it was. The Kin. Jhared thought of Enaro, self-righteous and gaunt, warning him to stay clear of the sky tower. "Strange coincidence. I met some Kin in Brenia. We didn't get along."

Surian grinned again. "Family's like that, eh? Can fight like wolves and hounds, but in the end they still care about what happens to ya. Might help a man out'a a tough spot."

"The last time I had family 'help,' the Clan Valador guard arrested me. I can't afford any more of that type of care, thank you."

"I see what ya mean. Perhaps then ya'd accept their aid as part'a what they owe ya? What other plan do ya have, Jhared Denaban? Ya don't intend t'let the council kill ya, surely."

"I intend to learn what happened to my patrolmates. To find them, if they're alive. The threat from the north is real. They can prove it."

"Ya need t'escape t'do that," Surian said.

"Who told you to talk to me? Was it Alende? Is he near?"

Puzzlement flashed across the guard's features before he covered it with another smile. Not Alende then. "I have a sizable family," the man said simply.

Jhared didn't trust Surian or those who ordered him, but in truth, he had no other plan. He could try to manage an escape on his own—with no weapon, a host of guards, and a long way between himself and the wilds—or accept the help of the Kin and deal with the consequences later. "Very well. What can you offer?"

"Stay alert. Not all the men assigned to ya are as vigilant as the others."

Jhared swore. "Stay alert? That's your idea of aid?"

"And keep your mouth shut. You shouldn't be so willing t'share your business with strangers." Surian grinned a last time, then stepped away from the tent flap and straightened to attention.

After that, nothing remained for Jhared to do but take Surian's advice. The waiting was maddening. He wondered if Lieutenant Mavriel would bring the execution orders, but as darkness fell, no one came at all.

Camp grew still and too quiet. It felt wrong, dangerous, like the moment of balance on the mountainside just before the avalanche falls. Outside the tent, a lamp swung gently from its pole, sending little waves of light lapping against the tent's sides. Jhared watched for an opportunity to slip his guard, but the sentry changed twice without compromise. He began to think Surian might be playing some new game for the Kin. Zia had sacrificed Shorn lives in an attempt to enrage the bound ones. Did the Kin mean to sacrifice him as well?

The moon had risen to its zenith when the guard changed a third time. Jhared wasn't certain whether he felt more relief or frustration when Surian once again took up the watch. As the old guard left and quiet returned, Surian pushed inside the tent. "Well, here we are. Time for ya t'be on your way, eh?"

Jhared rose from the bed, wary. "How did you manage to win a second watch?"

"I lost at dice." Surian's hands went to the buckle of his sword belt. "You ready?"

"Just like that you're letting me go?"

"Almost." The man tugged his belt free and offered it over. "If ya have a care, you're not likely t'get stopped. Off-duty soldiers are restricted to quarters tonight. With the Law'a Integrity invoked and the boys unsettled, the elders are scared'a trouble."

Jhared hesitated, then took the belt, which held a plain Forest Guard longsword and a dagger. "How many sentries on the perimeter?"

"Six. And three more watching the road north."

"And if I head for the pass, am I going to be stopped by someone who's been warned of my plans?"

Surian snorted. "What'd be the point'a that? If we wanted ya dead, we'd leave ya in here. I told ya, Kin take care'a their family. Now, I think ya're going t'enjoy this next part." He spread his arms wide and lifted his chin. "Go on."

Jhared stared a moment, before shaking his head. "A bloodied nose won't be enough. At best, you'll get the lash for neglect of duty."

"Felt the lash before," Surian said with a shrug.

If the council didn't believe Jhared had escaped on his own, Surian could get far worse than the lash; he could be named a traitor and shoved from the wall. Jhared pressed the thought aside with the memory of Leita's composed smile and midnight gaze. "You're certain?"

"Night's passing, boy. Get on with it."

Jhared gritted his teeth and threw a punch. His fist landed with a solid crack against the other man's face. As the guard staggered backward, Jhared caught him by the shoulder, spun him around, and tripped him to the ground. A second blow sent Surian to the brink of unconsciousness. Strips of cloth torn from the bedding served well enough to gag and bind him.

"Thank you," Jhared murmured.

He stood and grabbed his cloak. As he pulled up the hood and slipped into the night, he felt a stab of anticipation. Once more, he would break through the boundaries Avelos had constructed to contain him. He kept his focus on the necessity of it and away from the fear of its cost.

32.

FIRE AND WIND

Jhared paused in a pool of shadow, breathing lungfuls of the sweet autumn air and studying the dark to see if his way was clear. Braziers inside the soldiers' tents lit the orderly rows to a ghostly grey, but no campfires burned. The dusky quiet was an uncomfortable contrast to the multitude of lights and cheerful noises coming from the northerners' camp across the road. Ciam would be at one of those fires and so would the prefects, perhaps drinking to their successes.

Layers of stars gave depth to the crystalline sky. Although a chill breeze bit at Jhared's nose and fingers, Shorn energy warmed his blood. It lightened his steps, making him stealthy and silent. Luck or Riana's weaving had placed his little prison near the end of a row, close to the edge of camp, so he hadn't far to go to reach the perimeter: a few tents, the horse lines, a creek, then the forest and freedom.

He kept to cover as long as he could. When no cover existed, he strode with his head up and his eyes forward, a soldier carrying out an order. With his hood drawn up, he was unlikely to be distinguished from any other Shorn soldier. If someone called out a challenge, his only choice would be to bolt and hope he could outrun the men on watch. He passed one tent, then another. At the third tent, a sudden roar from inside made him hesitate, until laughter broke the tension: someone had lost at dice, it seemed. As he left the tents behind, the clearing gave way to scattered saplings and low brush

His way remained clear as he crossed the narrow creek and approached the camp perimeter. Jhared crept along the border, searching for the most likely place to cross the watch line. Merged with the shadows, he waited until the nearest watchman had turned his back to walk his patrol, then slid out of camp like a wraith.

He ran south first, away from the pass and into the hills. The soft ground gave readily under his boots; he would be easy to track come daylight, but by then he hoped it wouldn't matter. In the southern sky, Lord Arion's star shone brighter than any other. Jhared said a hasty prayer that Riana's Lord would bless her servant, a poor soldier.

437

When he had traveled far enough to be confident of crossing the pass without being observed, he made his way to the east side of the road, clambered up the short, rocky incline, and slipped north into the forest again. He approached the northerners' camp in a wide circle, appraising his surroundings as he drew closer. Northmen knew how to survive through cruel winters and wild coastal storms. They were renowned hunters and woodsmen, but they were also overproud and devastatingly independent. They did not readily come together as an army, and it showed. Nearly one hundred-twenty clanguard with their horses, supplies, and some score of camp followers sprawled throughout the forest. Their campfires dotted an area too large to defend effectively. The supply wagons were poorly guarded, and the privies had been dug too far from the perimeter. Two square tents squatted like grass hens on each side of the camp, but the body of the company made its place without any organization or shelter. Most men were drinking, dicing, or rolling with the women under carts and beside the fires.

The sentries at the perimeter seemed sober enough—one of them lifted his head as Jhared stole by—but there were only five of them. Jhared pressed against the trunk of an old walnut tree, considering the best way to enter the camp. It would be little challenge to sneak between the sentries, but what then? He needed to find Ciam or perhaps the prefects. He needed them to tell what they had done with his patrolmates, and then he needed to get out alive.

The task seemed more daunting now that it loomed before him. Perhaps he shouldn't have been so determined to set off alone. He scrubbed a hand over his face and rested his head against the walnut's trunk, looking up into the canopy. Thick, sturdy branches wove one tree to the next. Fall leaves still clung densely enough in places to blot out the starlight. It was an ancient forest, this one, part of the same forest that rippled down the foothills into the Parnas Valley, where he had run in his earliest years to escape the city walls. It was a part of Avelos he loved. And the northerners had laid themselves beneath the heart of it.

Beneath it, indeed. Jhared patted the trunk. Here was his way into camp: not so easy as sneaking between the sentries, but with more hope of moving undetected. With a little smile, he left his hiding place and glided along the edge of camp. He found the right tree for the task, one with branches that reached for the other trees beside it. He concealed his cloak under a mound of deadfall and tightened his sword belt. Then he rubbed his palms together as he gauged the distance to the first branch. Raising his arms toward the sky, he leaped and caught the rough wood with both hands. His body jerked taut as the earth pulled him downward. For an instant, he dangled in the air; then he began to swing. The breeze shivered across his skin, awakening longing. He swung harder. When his backward arc lifted him to the level of the branch, he drew his legs to his chest, released his grip, and landed with a soft thud. As his left leg threatened to buckle, he threw a hand toward the trunk and caught his balance.

Heart thudding, Jhared evaluated his position. Already, he could see deeper into camp: another horse line; more campfires; a tent that flew the sigils of the northern five. He turned to take the next step. To reach the branch that would take him to the adjacent tree, he had to shimmy a long span straight up the wide trunk. The bark tore his hands and caught at his clothes as he drove himself upward with his legs. The soles of his boots held well, though, and soon he was pulling himself onto the high branch. More slender than the first, it swayed under his weight. Leaves tickled his cheek.

He crouched there, breathing quickly, suddenly aware of where he was, so far from the ground. A pristine stretch of sparkling stars shone above him and a draft rose from below. It whispered to him, caressed him, kissed him. Desire roared through his body. His back ached and twitched. It would be so easy to fall . . . to jump. He wanted to feel the world rushing past him, to lean on the thermals beneath him. Jhared let out a half-strangled moan and sank against the trunk. The urges were dangerous, self-destructive. His Teachers had told him that all his life. They were right. They had always been right.

"You only fear your body because they taught you to fear it. Because they do."

As he lay paralyzed with need, Maya's words returned to him. For several moments, he recalled just what she had been doing when she said it, which did nothing to calm him. He wrapped an arm around the tree trunk and focused on the reassuring stability of the century-old wood. Maya suffered the same longings he did, but she had leaned over the cliff edge, her wings stretched to their full length. She did not deny her desires, but immersed herself in them. They did not drown her but were only a part of her. Jhared closed his eyes and tentatively stretched out his arms to cup the breeze. *"You fear your body because they taught you to fear it."* He did have a reason to fear, but was it possible that fear needn't be all he knew? If he permitted it, might his intimate understanding of wind and balance carry him safely over the arching branch to the next tree and into the camp itself? He rose and edged away from the trunk to the tip of the branch. It rocked him above the forest floor. He didn't look down, simply drew a breath and quieted his mind. Then he eyed the gap between his tree and the next one and leaped. This time his landing was solid.

The mingled scents of woodsmoke, animals, and grilled meat hung among the leaves as Jhared crept from tree to tree, noting everything and searching for anything that might lead him to his patrol. He could only move where the trees allowed him to go. Gradually, he worked his way inward, surveying the men at the fires intently, so intently he didn't realize that he had crept too far out on a branch until it dipped beneath him. Abruptly, his feet lost their purchase and he was falling. He twisted his body and grabbed for the branch as he dropped past it. With muscle-straining force, he caught it with one hand, held it. For agonizing seconds he hung in midair, his legs dangling. He flung his other arm over the branch. Below, footsteps were approaching. With a desperate heave, he pulled himself up and into the leaves just as someone strode past.

The lean, hard figure was Prefect Ondal Aglar. Jhared rested his brow against the branch, sucking deep breaths. The prefect strode two trees farther from Jhared, then paused just beyond one of the fires where others drank and gambled. Aglar pulled on a pipe and puffed out smoke in white wisps. His thick grey hair shone silver in the dusky light. He looked composed and watchful, a stallion guarding his herd. His partner in treachery, Bilar Lasla was at the fire, a woman under his arm and a drink in his hand.

Slowly, Jhared crossed the length of the branch toward the prefect. With exquisite care, he dared to move one tree closer, and then another. The vanilla-and-earth scent of Aglar's pipe smoke filled Jhared's nose. Watching men come and go to speak with the prefect or receive orders, Jhared began to recognize distinctions among the clanguard who were going about their duty and those who were carrying on at the fires. The more disciplined northerners wore the lightning sigil; they were Aglar's. Was it Aglar who bound the fractious northern five together? Strong steel could be made of iron and just the right measure of coal but only if a skilled smith bound them together. Ondal Aglar might very well be that smith.

At the nearby fire, men cheered. Jhared looked over in time to see Lasla kiss his woman, then untangle himself from her and stand and stretch. Despite all he had been drinking, no sign of unsteadiness showed in the young prefect's movements as he stalked over to Aglar.

"Your boys are celebrating too hard," Aglar observed, knocking his pipe against the bottom of his boot to empty the bowl. He straightened and drew a pinch of tobacco from a pouch at his belt.

Lasla grinned and scratched at the root of his braided beard. "It was . . . a long, hard ride south. . . . They're just . . . the turn'a things."

Jhared crept forward on the branch to hear the conversation better. As he moved over the northerners, the wood creaked. The branch swayed. Jhared went still.

"Nothing's turned yet," Aglar said, tamping the tobacco into his pipe with two fingers. "We're still south'a the Sandien and Rumar still has support."

"Ay, but his friends are tainted or fleeing. Tierzen Trianor's done for. Nadaren and Ontera are more pious than steadfast. And with Sahiste threatening the south, the others will look ta restore stability quickly. Only Clan Manitar and maybe Everen will stand by him. Abrigado has it now."

It was a fist in the gut to hear Tierzen spoken of so. Jhared cursed himself with silent vehemence. Aglar only inclined his head like a teacher acknowledging a student's point. He walked to the campfire, lit his pipe from a burning twig, and strode back. "Do ya trust that southerner?"

A subtle tension vibrated between the two prefects. Aglar's question seemed more a kind of test than a request for an opinion. The entire interaction reminded Jhared how very young Bilar Lasla was.

"Abrigado's no better than Rumar." Lasla shrugged. "Just as interested in consolidating power and more arrogant, but he wants Rumar gone. He could not'a invoked the Law'a Integrity without our help. He owes us."

"You're not wrong, but we won't see the truth of Abrigado till he's holding the staff'a warding. If he gets ta like his power too much, he may not keep his promises. Then we'll be fighting this spring after all."

"Sir, ya sent for me?"

Jhared's pulse accelerated. Ciam approached from behind the tree.

Aglar nodded. "You've a task to complete, Commander. It's time we rid ourselves'a the southern weight dragging at us."

"Past time," Lasla said. "Those soldiers are a liability now."

Ciam shifted and spat. "They always were."

"Wrong!" Although Aglar didn't raise his voice, his tone grew honed and sharp. "Those soldiers were our assurance'a freedom. We didn't know what the council had learned about Aglar Tower. We didn't know what a mad Shorn boy told them and whether he would be believed. Until this morning, Sevar and his men were important."

"And now?" Ciam asked.

"Now they must end their service to Avelos."

Lasla grunted agreement. "Do it tonight. I won't have our luck turn bad because one'a them slipped away."

"As ya say, sir." Ciam fidgeted and crossed his arms over his chest. "I won't kill the woman."

"Then find a man who will," Lasla said. "Shouldn't be hard. I've two swords to lift for her."

Jhared clutched the branch so tightly the bark crumbled under his fingers.

"No." Again, Aglar's voice was a knife edge. "We will *not* draw Cael's curse by shedding a Bearer's blood. Ciam could'a killed her when she turned her dark strength on him in Ebilan. It would'a been self-preservation then. Now she's helpless. We can't kill her without provoking the demon."

At the last word, Ciam shuddered, hunching his shoulders as though to conceal it.

Lasla looked amused. "I'd say the commander's already got a taste'a that curse."

Ciam's expression steeled. "Don't forget the killing winds've come north," he said. "She knows where ta find the key ta stop them. We might need her."

"Leave it be," Aglar ordered. "I've already said she's not ta die."

Ciam ignored Lasla's sneer. "How do ya want it done? They're soldiers. They shouldn't die trussed in a tent like lambs. There should be some honor in it."

Aglar looked down at the pipe in his hand, rubbing the bowl with a thumb. "Commander," he said, his voice gone cold and dispassionate, "the honor lies in saving the north from those who bleed her. Choose two men ta help ya and make it quick."

Jhared stared down through the branches at the prefect and felt a surge of anger potent enough to send him pouncing from the tree. He could do it; he could end Aglar's life before Ciam or Lasla took a breath. But Aglar's death and his own would not free Leita.

Carefully, so carefully, he retreated from the tree branch back to the trunk and peered over the disorderly camp. *They shouldn't die trussed in a tent.* There were three tents: a small one that had no guard and attracted no traffic, perhaps a dry place to store the company's tack; a larger one on the north end of camp with the banners of the northern five above it, and another small one on the east side. He had assumed the marked tent was meant for the elders and prefects, but that was inconsistent; the northmen shunned shelter, sleeping in the open near the fires. And the larger tent was the only one with a guard.

It took some time studying the scene before Jhared figured out how he would reach the tent. He had no wish to relive the attempt he had made trying to reach the Bearer near the Sandien Mountains. The plan he finally decided upon would be straightforward, although it depended upon the northerners' disorganization more heavily than he liked.

He started through the trees in a northwesterly direction. He had learned his lesson and was cautious of where he set his weight, but traveling in the dark among the leaves was still tricky. Twice he found himself at a dead end and was forced to leap back to the previous tree. Each transition exposed him to anyone who might chance to peer upward. Still, Shorn energy had pushed the pain of his injuries into a distant corner of his mind, and his muscles had warmed to the work. He reveled in it, each airborne arc like a burst of flight.

The northerners' supply wagons were four-sided, flat-bottomed affairs, with large, sturdy wheels that traveled reliably through the mountains. Two wagons had been settled unwisely outside the bustle of the center of camp, but not too distant from the horse lines. Jhared hoped they might hold fodder. Tarps kept the contents dry—and hidden—so he had to pray they didn't hold something so fire resistant as water barrels or sacks of potatoes. When he had clambered as close as he could manage in the canopy, he climbed out of the branches and set his feet back on the ground.

For once, the Path seemed to turn in his direction. Under the tarps, the carts held crisp, dry hay bales and sacks of grain. It took very little time for Jhared to begin the destruction. He pilfered the two lanterns that had been set near the wagons and splashed their oil across the hay. When he set a flame to the oil, the bales caught with a rush of air as soft as a woman's sigh. Eagerly, the fire leaped and danced from one bale to the next. Climbing up on a wagon wheel, Jhared levered two of the burning bales onto the ground, then kicked them apart to spread the flames further. He had just made it clear of the flames when an outcry began behind him. He tossed aside the lantern and sprang away.

Shouts of "Fire!" shot chaos through the camp. Men rose in confusion, trying to shake off the fog of sleep or drink or to extricate themselves from their companions. A few grabbed up weapons as they ran. Jhared serpentined his way through the shadows, but when he neared the tent with the northerners' banners, he was forced to stop. The camp's center still roiled with fighting men. From behind the bole of a tree, he watched as the clanguards gathered their wits and headed for the growling flames. No one emerged from the tent. The single guard posted at the entrance fidgeted as his companions ran off. Jhared hesitated, weighing his options. But with a shout, the guard finally gave in and joined the others who were hurrying away. Jhared moved swiftly, dagger in hand. He slipped up to the tent's entrance and inside before anyone could spot him.

The innards of the tent were black and smelled of unwashed bodies. Jhared crouched, blade at the ready, his night vision destroyed by the firelight. "Men of the Forest Guard Fourth?"

The sound of movement, slow and effortful, came from his left.

"That's right. Dare t'put a blade in my hand and I'll show ya what it means t'cross us." It was Esran, his voice dusty and tired.

"Denaban?" Lenaro called quietly from the other side of the tent.

"Yes, sir. It's me."

"Damn, but you've the prettiest voice I've ever heard," Anzo muttered. "Get over here and untie us."

Jhared followed the voices, nearly tripping over Lenaro. The soldier lay on the hard ground, tightly bound wrist to ankle. It took time to work a blade between flesh and rope to cut him free.

"What beehive did ya knock over out there?" Lenaro asked as Jhared helped him to sit up.

"Fire," Jhared said, moving to free the next man. "I doubt it will occupy them long. The ground's too damp. Where's the lieutenant?"

"Over here," Anzo called.

Jhared found Lieutenant Sevar on his side, gagged as well as bound. As Jhared tugged lightly on his bindings to slip his blade beneath them, Sevar winced. More gently, Jhared slid a hand over the lieutenant's cheek, seeking some slack in the gag. His fingers discovered swollen, heated flesh.

Lenaro came to aid the lieutenant to his feet. Jhared hurried on to free Anzo and then the rest. The last man was Grion. That made six. "Where are the others?"

"Dead." Sevar's voice rasped like rusted iron across stone.

Twitch, Bevan, and Commander Carn, gone. Murdered at the hands of their own people. Not even Bevan had deserved such a fate.

"We tried to escape at Ebilan," Anzo said, "but Ciam was better prepared for us than we expected."

"The rest'a us would've been lost as well if the lady hadn't caught him." Esran's tone was thick with fury. "We owe her. A debt we can't repay."

Jhared straightened, easing his weight off his left leg. "Where is she now?"

"This morning when they stowed us away, I saw them take her toward the east side'a camp," Esran said.

Jhared nodded. "I spied another tent there."

"That's most likely it. They wouldn't risk some man'a Rumar's accidentally laying eyes on her."

"She's being held as surety for our conduct," Anzo added. "Ciam must die, Jhared."

"Enough talk," Sevar growled. "We need to move. Where are the rest waiting for us, Denaban?"

Jhared thrust his dagger into its sheath. "I'm the only one."

"What? Couldn't Rumar spare any beside the Folly?" Bitterness edged Grion's voice. Bevan had been a close companion.

Sevar stared at Jhared, his keen eyes gleaming in the dim light. "Rumar didn't send you at all, did he?"

"No. He didn't. Ciam recognized me and had some things to say to the council about the kind of soldier I am. After that, no one was willing to believe my report." Jhared matched Sevar's taut tone, realizing how furious he was at the man. No doubt Alende would have had something ironic to say about that.

"Denaban, what did ya expect the lieutenant t'tell them?" Lenaro hissed. "They were going t'send out half an army t'hunt ya down. We needed t'convince them ya weren't worth the effort."

"The truth served well enough for that," Jhared muttered.

"It did," Lenaro replied. "Until the prefects decided t'come south t'deal with the high chieftain themselves."

Sevar's gaze hadn't wavered. "You made it all the way back to Rumar. On your own. Now you've broken out of council custody and violated Shorn Law to risk freeing us?"

Something unexpected rang in the lieutenant's voice. Jhared didn't know what to do with that. "Sir, you should know that today the council invoked the Law of Integrity against Rumar."

Someone whistled softly. Sevar's expression hardened.

Anzo pulled his head back from where he had been watching at the entrance. "Time to go, boys. It's as open as it's gonna get out there."

With stifled groans, the men straightened and stretched stiff limbs. The lot of them were battered and done in. Jhared feared what would happen if they ran into clanguard. "I'll find the Bearer," he said. "The rest of you get out. Head north out of camp and run for the road—"

He stopped, hearing the command in his tone and realizing what he had done.

Sevar's expression was sardonic. "You go for the Bearer, Denaban. Anzo, Afiro, and Esran will go with you to keep the way clear. Grion and Lenaro, you head southwest. Use the campfires to start some new spots of trouble as you go. Draw the guard farther from the Bearer."

"Sir?" Anzo asked. "Which direction will you be going?"

"The one that might end this debacle. Up now, men. Gather your strength. We're only steps from our own troops."

Determination iced the lieutenant's tone. Jhared knew Sevar recognized the complex implications of the moment. He wondered if the man had seen the same thing about the northern five that he had. "Sir, Ondal Aglar seems to be the heart of this treachery."

"It seems so," Sevar agreed emotionlessly.

"If he were gone, the rest of the northern prefects would likely fall to squabbling among themselves. Their plan might break into pieces."

Anzo looked alarmed. Understanding etched his weathered face. "Lieutenant, Aglar's committed treason. There's no need to risk hunting him now."

"Denaban?" Sevar prompted.

Jhared shifted his weight uneasily. "The high chieftain can't order the execution of a prefect. Not with the Law of Integrity over his head. He'll look as though he's trying to kill off his opposition. It has to happen now. In the chaos."

Sevar laughed thinly. "Always as subtle as an elder." He scowled at the others, whose expressions varied from stunned to resolute. "You all have orders. Complete them and get to the road. The northerners' game is up once our own soldiers have sight of us. Denaban, see the Bearer is safe. Esran spoke the truth. We owe her."

They slipped from the tent in twos and threes and scattered among the trees. Westward, the disruption continued to grow. A red-gold glow against the leaves showed the fire had spread, but here near the center of camp it was quiet.

Jhared and Anzo were the last to move out.

"Once you have her, boy, head as straight east as you can. It'll put you farther from the road, but get you out of camp the quickest. We'll be waiting."

Jhared drew his sword and offered it to the little veteran. "Take it. You're the more skilled swordsman. You'll make better use of it."

Anzo waved the blade away. "Won't need it. I have plans to take one for myself." His lips curled into an unpleasant grin. "Some of those northerners are carrying Amurian steel."

After a moment's delay, Jhared nodded and returned his blade to its scabbard.

Anzo opened his mouth as though to speak again, but closed it without saying a word. Briefly, he gripped Jhared's shoulder instead.

They stepped into the night together. Anzo slid to Jhared's left and melted into the forest. Jhared had a sense of the man's presence as they both worked their way toward the far end of camp. When the third tent came into view, he turned. The veteran saluted him from the shadows, then hurried on after Esran and Afiro.

The tent was placed out of the way of the flow of foot traffic, as though the clanguard had not wanted to deal with the sight of it. A campfire crackled merrily before it, but the fire had been abandoned and there was no sign of a guard.

Pressed flat against the tent's side, Jhared listened, then peered through the flap. It was silent and too black to see. Warily, he pushed the flap aside and crept in, pausing near the wall.

"I hear your footsteps," hissed a voice. "I hear the rustle of your clothing and the very sound of your heart beating. Be warned: the darkness is a friend to me. If you touch me, I will rip off your stones and feed them to the ravens."

Jhared swallowed. "Lady Bearer, I would never knowingly harm you. I only grieve the harm I've caused by leaving you."

"Jhared Denaban."

Just his name, then a slow breath, then stillness.

"It's me, Leita. We can leave this place now."

A soft rustling came from one corner. "The patrol?"

"Slipping away. Anzo will see to it the way is clear for us."

"Good. Very good."

His vision had adjusted again. He stepped farther into the tent. In the corner to his left lay a pile of blankets. The priestess sat stiffly in their midst, wrapped in her cloak with the hood drawn forward. Her hands were braced on either side of her.

"It's not far, Lady. We only need to make it out of camp. Our men will be waiting."

He took another step, crouched, and touched her arm. She flinched.

"Forgive me," he said, drawing back.

She didn't reply. Then, "Perhaps," she said softly.

A darkness swirled around her deeper than anything Jhared had ever sensed from her. "Lady, we must go. Prefect Aglar is no fool. He'll send men to be certain you don't flee in this chaos."

"Flight is unlikely," she murmured, then shook her head. "I'm ready. Lend me your hand."

He offered his arm for support. She reached for it. In the wrong direction.

"I'm here." His mouth went dry. His heart thudded hard. He touched her fingers.

She startled again, then checked herself, cursing.

Jhared peered down. The edge of her hood obscured her face. "Leita? What did they—?"

"Not now, Jhared. Nothing of fear or grief or pity from you or I *will* curse you by every demon I can name. Let's go."

She held out her hand. He pretended not to notice how her fingers shook or how tightly they gripped him as he set them on his left arm and helped her to rise.

Outside, the shouting had grown in ferocity. He caught a whiff of smoke and a scent like burned bread. Lenaro and Grion were apparently having some success.

"Wait. Give me your dagger," Leita ordered.

Jhared hesitated. "Lady, if it comes to a fight—"

"I won't be caught helpless. Do you think the Bearer of Cael's Blade can't wield a knife in the dark?"

In that moment, her tone returned to its familiar timbre, confident and commanding. He drew his dagger and placed it in her palm. She closed her fist around it.

"Ready?"

She nodded. He drew her closer and lifted the tent flap.

And was nearly bowled over by Ciam.

Jhared twisted to avoid the collision as the clanguard burst into the tent swinging an unshuttered lantern. Half-blinded by the sudden brightness, Jhared felt Leita step around him and saw the commander falter, his expression changing from angry to anxious. That hesitation saved them. With the side of his fist, Jhared smashed the lantern out of Ciam's hand. It spattered droplets of hot oil and yellow flame, causing the clanguard to take a backward step as it struck the ground. In that fraction of time, Jhared ripped his sword free and pressed it to the man's throat.

Ciam went still.

"Lady, I came ta see ya safe," he drawled. "We've been attacked. But it seems ya've already heard." The commander's voice was calm, lazy even, but from the flickering spots of firelight still burning on the ground, Jhared saw the deep circles of sleeplessness around his eyes and the sheen of sweat across his brow."

The Bearer was silent.

Careful not to drop the tip of his blade, Jhared stepped forward to take the clanguard's sword belt. As he did, he glimpsed the down lining of Ciam's vest, soft grey down from the small wings of creatures too young for flight. Anger shot through Jhared so fast it dizzied him. He flung the commander's sword across the tent.

The northerner gave him a look of disgust. "I see Adan Rumar cares so much about the Bearer he sent a condemned Shorn man ta find her."

Ciam must die.

Jhared had to draw a breath before he could trust his voice. "What would you have of him, Lady?"

"Nothing. Nothing more need be done. He will take his own life."

The Bearer's words were the sounds of crows cawing, of ice cracking. Jhared shivered.

Ciam gave a forced laugh. "Do ya think a northman so weak in spirit—"

"Don't speak!" Leita commanded. "I know your nightmares have started. I can hear it in your voice. Do you realize what I've done to you?"

Something thudded against Jhared's breastbone. Air rushed past his face, as though he stood beside an open window. "Lady," he said quietly, "we must finish this. Now. Others will come."

The Bearer took a step closer to Ciam. "I have rent a hole in your spirit that will never mend."

Another thud reverberated in Jhared's chest. Ciam's gaze darted over the shadow that was the Bearer. His burly figure hunched into itself.

"If you dare to peer into the darkness of that hole, it will consume you," Leita went on. "Every moment you have ever feared will drown you. What are the darkest moments you have suffered, Commander? What moments of childhood terror, of tearing pain, of approaching death? They will join as one demon to shred your courage. To shred your very self. Each time you draw your sword or ride through the mountains or love a woman, you will shiver and cry like a lost child."

Ciam hissed a breath and tucked his chin, but nothing could hide the shudder that traveled through his shoulders. Jhared stared in growing horror. Another reverberation struck deep within him and another. They set his bones to vibrating. Again, the rush of air over his body. Not like an open window, but a door, many doors slamming open. Blue flames licked the corners of his vision.

"Leita, please stop!"

She did not. Her voice gained strength. "Do not think you can forget these moments or put them aside. The more you seek to evade your fears, the more their grip will tighten. Though you turn away from the hole in your spirit, foul things will slither into your dreams. They will hunt you, chasing you through darkness and daylight, until madness eats your reason."

Jhared reached forward and clutched his blade with a bare hand. Blood welled between his knuckles and pain arrowed up his arm. His sight cleared a little, but his knees were soft wax. "Please, Lady," he gasped. "The Gate!"

Leita took one more step. "Commander Ciam, you have stolen Riana's gift from the Bearer of Cael's Blade, and to pay that debt, I promise, you will take your own life."

It was a mistake. Jhared knew it even as it happened, but that was already too late. The Bearer's last step placed her between him and the clanguard, enough to make a clear strike impossible. Ciam must have recognized it just as Jhared did. With a cry that was both wrath and terror, the clanguard lurched forward. His feet tripped like a man tearing free of tar, but he fell into the Bearer and his hands caught around her shoulders.

"Lady, one thing at least will bring me joy: knowing your darkness is as deep and endless as mine." With a wild laugh verging on panic, Ciam jerked back the Bearer's hood.

Her long, glossy braid had been cut away. Only a cap of lank black hair remained, leaving her pale neck bare and vulnerable. Above her brow, a ragged gash angled toward her scalp. A blindfold covered her eyes. From beneath the blindfold, down her left cheek, ran a dark trail, like tears. Jhared realized it was dried blood. Then Ciam tugged the blindfold free.

The hollows revealed there were so deep they devoured the light of the stars. Jhared's mind refused to understand what he saw, at first. Then the grief of it struck him full in the chest. Leita's eyes had ever been the depthless blue of a midnight sky. They could hint at secrets or threaten storms. He had both feared and craved what he had seen in them, for they had been an outlet of her power. The northerners had burned all that away.

"Oh, Leita. Oh, Goddess. What have they dared?"

Heat raced in his veins. His head buzzed and his limbs felt light. The need that had been building in him all night neared its apex: the need to release his fury, to shed his helplessness, to touch the sky. Some part of him strained against the chains that bound him—his oath to Avelos and his faith in Shorn Law—and found them already weakened.

By the time he forced himself back to the moment, Ciam was already striking. The blow took Jhared just above the wrist. He cried out as his sword fell from his numbed grasp. Ciam spat into his face and slammed him in the gut.

Jhared dropped to his knees. "Leita!" He wanted to shout at her to run. Ciam could not hold him and chase her, too. But she was trapped in darkness. Blind and injured, she could stumble into a fire or into the hands of a clanguard who didn't suffer the commander's curse and had none of his qualms about slaying the Bearer.

Ciam wrenched Jhared's right arm behind his back and launched him to his feet. The muscles of his shoulder screamed.

"How?" Jhared cried, anger and confusion roiling in him. "How do you betray your own people? Look at what betrayal has already cost us!"

"*Us?* Ya southerners are no more my people than the Amurians," Ciam hissed through clenched teeth. "Most'a ya less so. Come on. The both'a ya. Chieftain Aglar will decide what ta do with ya now."

"Jhared?" Leita called, her arms held out uncertainly.

"Take her," Ciam growled, shoving him forward.

With his free hand, Jhared touched her gently, forcing himself to look at the ruin of her face. "I'm here," he murmured.

"I know." She clutched his wrist and a cold, sharp weight slid up his sleeve. "Don't forget, soldier. Someone must walk the dark Paths."

Outside, fire was joyfully claiming the camp. Orange flames danced in the underbrush, over blankets and packs, around the bases of the trees. Loose horses blundered about madly. On the other side of camp, someone was roaring orders, rounding up men and mounts. The northerners had given up attempting to contain the conflagration, and through the smoke, Jhared saw armed men moving in orderly groups. Some had managed to catch their horses and were astride. The entire company was heading west, toward the road, toward Rumar's encampment.

Ciam laughed. "Looks like the chieftain's already decided what ta do with ya. All'a ya."

Nearly one hundred-twenty clanguard were rushing toward fewer than fifty soldiers, fifty Shorn men who would be desperately trying to shield the high chieftain, the elders, and Lady Nemiah. Most of those Shorn men would die. Jhared thought of Tierzen, his earnest smile, his ink-stained fingers. He thought of the soldiers betrayed at Aglar Tower, of his comrades needlessly slain, of Leita tortured and maimed. Deep within him, where the forbidden doors had been flung open and the blue flames burned his spirit, his need broke free. In the sky above him, a keening started as sharp as glass.

"Cael's long cold one, Denaban! It's time to be out'a here!"

Ciam's laughter faded as Esran, Afiro, and Anzo stepped from the trees, swords in hand. Leita released her hold on Jhared and took a sideways step away from him.

"To me!" Ciam cried. "To me, men'a Aglar!"

Jhared snapped his free arm downward, dropping the dagger from his sleeve into his palm. It was awkward in his left hand, but with a hitch of his shoulder, he turned the blade and thrust it backward.

Ciam bellowed and turned Jhared loose as the dagger pierced his thigh. The keening sharpened and was joined by a roar that reached from within Jhared's center up to the clouds. Jhared heard the meaning in it: it was a song shaped from a melody of high-pitched sorrow and a countermelody of inexorable rage.

Anzo reached Leita and put her behind him. Esran guarded her flank. Afiro leaped after Ciam.

From a distance, a voice took up Ciam's call for aid. Jhared heard the thrum of a bow, saw the arrow sprout from the center of Afiro's chest. The wiry Forest Guard stared down at the shaft with a look of surprise as his knees folded. Another arrow hummed past Jhared's shoulder, tearing fabric and stinging his skin.

"Anzo," he heard himself say, clear and calm, "take the Bearer and run for stone. You'll find caves in the rocks along the road. Run. Now."

Anzo caught Jhared's gaze, held it for a heartbeat with his bright, knowing eyes. Then without question, he grasped Leita under the elbow. She tried to pull free. "Anzo, no! He mustn't die here. We need him!" But the stocky veteran only gripped her close and dragged her away. Jhared didn't have time to think on them further. A third arrow parted the air. This one thunked into a tree trunk behind him. He turned to cover Leita's escape. He only need hold off the clanguard until the killing winds reached their peak, then arrows and swords wouldn't matter. Already, the accelerating breeze tore at him as though it might fling him into the sky.

Ciam snatched up Afiro's sword and came at him. Clutching the bloody dagger, Jhared danced backward, light-footed, out of the archer's line and into the tangle of trees. His injuries were a distant ache. He was treading the dark path, dancing in Cael's shadow. No chains could hold him.

"Of all your moments of terror, Ciam, which is the one that leads to your death?" he asked, grinning madly.

The clanguard's jaw tightened as he moved after Jhared, limping, but not as badly as Jhared had hoped. "You are no part of what I fear, boy."

Ciam must die.

The northerner held his sword angled before him and stepped deliberately, with no wasted motion. His eyes, locked on Jhared's, reflected nothing but the orange of the flames around him.

Jhared brandished his dagger, as though it were a threat. "Only an ignorant man does not fear me!"

Ciam lunged, steel gleaming in his hand. Jhared spun to the side and the sword sliced air. He stumbled a little, then caught himself against a tree.

Instantly, Ciam struck again, with a blow meant to cut Jhared's legs out from under him. Again, Jhared danced backward. This time, Ciam put too much into the swing, overbalanced and tripped two steps forward. Jhared darted in and slashed at his exposed right side, grazing the clanguard's forearm before Ciam brought himself around and forced Jhared to withdraw or lose his hand.

Panting now, Jhared led the clanguard another step away from Leita, and another. Without warning, Ciam's longsword sliced the night a fourth time.

A tree root fouled Jhared then. If it had caught his right leg instead of his injured left, he might have recovered fast enough to slip out of steel's reach. But as his weight came down on his left foot, his knee buckled. He saw the arc of Ciam's sword, ugly and cruel as only an earth-bound thing could be, and knew it would land in his flesh.

He fell to one knee. Above him, Ciam's face twisted with purpose, his fear quenched in hatred. In this, it didn't even matter that Jhared was Shorn; the northerner had found a way to see all who lived below the Sandien Mountains as something other than his own people. He had distanced himself from Avelos enough to betray his own countrymen. As the sword completed its arc, Jhared recognized his death.

A gust of sorrow and rage exploded through the forest. Agony blossomed across Jhared's chest as he felt himself ripped open.

An owl burst out of the trees above him and took to the sky on silent wings. Red flames turned to blue. Points of starlight stretched into long, entwined threads. The dusky forest vanished into blackness.

Jhared thought of Branlen and the place that had been his home. Then he thought of Maya and wished, just once, he had had the chance to see her fly.

33.

TRAVELING

Jhared sucked in one breath, then another, trying to dispel the dizziness that spun the world around him. Hot, dry air rushed into his lungs. He thought of the fire spreading through the underbrush and struggled to push himself free. Unexpectedly, someone pushed back. He opened his eyes and found himself blinking at a stranger's shoulders under the blaze of a midday sun. No fire. No forest. Lightheaded, he turned in a slow circle, trapped in the midst of some festival throng. All around him, people shifted and jostled one another, part of a crowd that overfilled the plaza where he stood, while somewhere else on Riana's weaving, the killing winds destroyed the people he loved.

Ah, Goddess, why this?

It was unmistakably the center of Velantar, but so different from the city he knew—taller, brighter, more *complete*. The buildings all stood where he expected them—the high chieftain's palace, the high temple, Elders' Hall—but beyond the plaza, the walls of Shorn Circle loomed smooth and whole, the granite gleaming silver and rose. No statue of Alende Isan stood before Elders' Hall. Instead, the dome of the temple dominated the sky, and the temple walls were bright with color, every carving gloriously painted. Jhared stared at the circle of the Chosen carved beside the temple's grand staircase. All his life he had looked upon the five Aye that made up the top half of the shattered circle. On the day of his Becoming, he had said a prayer before them, wondering if he would survive to see them again. Now the circle gleamed before him, complete and undamaged. The top of the circle, still so familiar, depicted the Aye, but curving up to join Riana's Chosen were a serpent, a scorpion, a spider, a condor, and a large wolfish beast. Jhared said the names of the spirits in his head as though it might change what he saw: Semule, Creaben, Aranila, Kilzaro, and Verilen. Cael's Chosen. The high temple's circle was composed of Aye and Ael together.

Uneasily, Jhared studied the crowd again. He spied the Avelune then. Only a few stood on the ground. Those few kept to themselves and wore long cloaks over the bulk of their wings. On the taller buildings surrounding the plaza, rows of small, open balconies jutted from the walls. Forbidding faces stared down from those flight-rests, and wings of every color mantled over strong shoulders. Several Avelune perched on the edge of the palace roof. One dark-winged man stood alone on the top of the temple's dome, a murder of crows at his feet.

Jhared shivered in the sun. It was no festival around him. The murmured conversations were tense and hostile. Instead of candles and flowers, soldiers lined the palace portico and the temple stairs. Instead of food vendors and performers, City Guards marched in groups through the crowd. Jhared saw a fight break out in front of Elders' Hall. Half-a-dozen guards took down the offenders with swift, ungentle efficiency. Jhared shivered again. The Paths were infinite; he might have fallen anywhere, but blood called to blood, Leita had told him. What other day in all the history of his ancestors could have so strong a pull? The pieces of the pattern came together, and he understood: this was the moment that had made him Shorn.

A bell tolled, low and grave. Jhared knew its resonance. On his Path, it marked temple devotions, completed Becomings, and executions. "They're coming!" a girl shouted, dashing up the street from the direction of the gate, from Aelend prison if Jhared were correct. The crowd quieted, a dangerous type of quiet. Up the broad street leading to the city's center, two patrols of soldiers marched in the green and grey of High Chieftain Rumar's livery. No, not Rumar's livery, Clan Manitar's. Lord Tumal had been the first son of Manitar to wrest the staff of warding from Clan Amerre after the clan wars. Through the soldiers, Jhared glimpsed a dark head and pale feathers. He knew who it was, the High Priestess of Avelos, the cause of more suffering than any other individual in the country's history. Jhared didn't remember her name, wasn't certain he had ever known it. Her name didn't matter. She was the faceless symbol of Avelune greed and deceit.

He shoved his way through the mob, trying to find an unobstructed view and leaving a stream of people cursing in his wake. Someone elbowed him in the ribs. Another man tried to trip him. It would be easy for a blade to find his back in such a throng as this, but he didn't stop until he had reached the edge of the street and could see the little parade making its slow progress.

He saw her wings first, long and elegant, nearly white but for a light wash of blue-grey, the color of a cloud's belly on a bright morning. They made his heart ache even before he took in the rest of her. She had been horribly bound, with shackles on her wrists and ankles. A chain wrapped around her throat and trailed down her body to a large iron weight. As she dragged the chain to keep from being strangled, steel thorns along the length of the metal slicked her hands with blood. Still, she moved with focused grace, a preternatural beauty about her that cruelty had not extinguished. Jhared thought of a hawk knocked from flight with an arrow in its breast. He had found beauty there where he least expected it. He thought of Tavia and her lover shot from the sky at Maren's Burn. He thought of Maya. Trembling, he pressed a hand against his heart.

As if drawn by a whisper he hadn't uttered, the woman slowly turned her head and looked at him. His breath caught. He tried to turn away, but couldn't. Her gaze was gentle and compassionate, as a mother to her child; clear and penetrating, as a raptor to its prey. With that gaze, she stripped him of all defenses, yet somehow he knew he had no need of them. She was Riana's high priestess, the center of the infinite weaving, the one who balanced the Paths with her insight and courage.

In the crowd beside him, someone gave an agonized cry. At a glance, he thought she was a girl. Then he saw her face and realized she was a woman somewhat older than himself. She was slight, near to gaunt. Her wings gleamed in the sunlight. They were delicate and as green as a hummingbird's, as green as her eyes. He imagined he recognized her, but that made no sense. This was not his Path. As she straightened, she didn't try to hide the tears streaming down her cheeks. Her sadness touched his own.

"How can they do it?" he asked, gesturing toward the high priestess.

The woman bowed her head. "They do not see in her what you and I do."

He startled, confused. He had expected to find nothing but evil. "What is it we see? What is she?"

The green-winged woman closed her eyes and went very still, as though any sudden movement might break her into pieces. "The heart of Avelos."

A thick-limbed guard shouted at the captive to move faster. A swing of his heavy blade landed with a flat smack against her right wing. Pale feathers puffed into the air and the priestess cried out in pain. As she stumbled toward the stones, Jhared pushed free of the crowd and caught her.

Weary. So weary. Mustn't fall. One foot goes before the other. And again. Ah, Lady and Lord, give me strength! *Unable to stretch wings, unable to call the breeze and take to the air.* Oh, Ambri, my love, I would you had not failed. *Anger and shame entwined with that wish. Depthless grief for the inevitability of war, for every child who will feel a blade cut feathers and bone, for all the lost brilliance that will mean the end of Avelos, perhaps the unraveling of the weaving itself.*

Jhared's legs threatened to fold. With the woman in his arms, he was drowning in emotions that didn't belong to him. As he fought to steady himself, her head snapped up and she staggered free of him. Abruptly, his thoughts were his own again.

"Lord Arionad!" she gasped. "Forgive me. I'm slipping beyond my Path."

"Oh, my lady," he whispered. "If I were truly Arionad, you would not suffer here."

A faint light brightened her eyes, almost a smile. It was a gift Jhared knew he would never forget. "You were right to come," she murmured. "Lady Nemiah would not make it back without you. Go now. Please—"

"Move away from the traitor or share her chains!"

The big guard had come around. Several of the other soldiers moved into place on either side of him. The crowd rumbled with anger. Jhared had no illusions: the mob would happily tear him apart. Yet as the guard's sword swung, Jhared put himself in front of the chained woman, twisting so that the flat of the blade smashed against his shoulder. The bone-bruising impact made him exhale sharply.

"Stop this," he begged. "The Paths should not turn this way!"

An incredulous expression warped the guard's features. "Feather-lover!" he spat. "You are risking your life for a vulture."

Jhared looked at the Avelun. Despite his years of study, he realized he didn't truly know what she had done or not done. His Teachers named her the Bane of Avelos. Zia named her an unjust sacrifice. Maya offered an uncertain guess at her innocence. One hundred-fifty years of fear and hatred had veiled her true self. Jhared longed to know from her own lips all that had led to the stories of betrayal. He was desperate to know it, but he would not be allowed. All he could know for certain was that standing in this moment, just before her death, she was more than a faceless representation of evil. He saw love and strength in her. He felt her grief for the Avelune children who would come after her. He could not bear to watch her broken.

With grim determination, he faced the guard. "I will gladly risk my life to warn you. This way leads only to bloodshed and misery. Please. The high chieftain must reconsider. Do not make these next years about war and vengeance."

Behind him, the green-winged woman gasped. Jhared cast a glance at her and saw Lady Nemiah's shocked gaze shining from someone else's features. At the same time, a hand touched his shoulder. "Lord Arionad, nothing can be done for me. Your courage must be used to spare another Lady of Avelos. Please go, and take with you my trust words. Perhaps, on some other Path, I shall be given the honor of meeting you again."

The chained priestess whispered words into his ear, the sounds of integrity and fortitude. Then the hand on his shoulder slipped away. From the corner of his eye, Jhared saw the guard nod to his men. He had time to register the movement of three soldiers as they reached for their blades and to realize that salvation was as impossible on this Path as on his own.

"You're back? So soon? No, no, no. This isn't a good place for your kind."

Jhared drifted in the cool, dewy blackness that was Nowhere. He had tumbled so far from the web that the Paths were beyond him, a glorious blue-red glow. The voice that held him was familiar, rough like an old man's, but somehow far more. It creaked with the weight of centuries. Jhared imagined that an ancient oak might own such a voice, or the slope-shouldered Parnas Mountains. "I know I don't belong here," he said wearily. "I'm sorry. I didn't intend to bring the curse."

"That's not what I meant," the voice replied querulously. There was a quick *tap-tap*, like the sound of a pipe against teeth.

Despite the irritable tone, Jhared had the sense of being gently cradled. It was an unexpectedly secure feeling for one floating beyond the edge of all existence. The voice seemed to read his thoughts.

"Don't get comfortable, boy! You need to hurry back before you forget where you've been."

Jhared sighed. "Will you tell me what you are?"

"Bah! You're wasting time. And you already hold a name or two for me."

For no reason he could explain, Jhared's thoughts went to Branlen's stone and the old man carved in it. Maya had once called him "Blessed of Lumati," but that old god's strength lay in Sahiste. He had pushed her words aside in disbelief. *"Muvanhi ri Lumati?"*

Deep, indulgent laughter echoed through the dark. "That is a blessing I know."

"But why? Why would you—?"

"You think that knowing why I've favored you will tell you who you are. It won't. You must decide for yourself whether you have value on your Path. Let it suffice to say that those like you who walk the borders intrigue me, for I know what it is to be shunned by two worlds. My Favored live in the in-between spaces."

Jhared didn't respond, startled to silence by the depth of insight he felt from the entity holding him. He gazed upon the exquisite gleaming strands that were the infinite Paths, twisting and splitting time and again, always interweaving, with every new decision born into the world. It was heartrending in its beauty and incomprehensible in its complexity. "It's more than a mind can bear to look upon."

"For your kind, yes. Though some of your people can bear it longer than others. Do you sense the music?"

Jhared tilted his head, straining to listen. He didn't think he heard it at first; then as his focus improved, he realized he had actually been hearing it for so long his mind had stopped attending to it. "I do. It's familiar."

The music was a collection of physical sensations and emotions as much as sounds—a low-pitched pluck of fear against the rhythm of his heart, a slow caress across his cheek, a needful thrumming deep within his bones. Abruptly, he realized why it was familiar: it was the same eerie combination of sound, sensation, and emotion that composed the music of the killing winds. That music had flowed through him as he held Maya, as he fought Ciam, as the winds had roused to their deadly speed.

"I am the cause of the storms, aren't I?"

"Ah, boy. Is the wolf the cause of his sharp teeth? Is the horse the cause of his strong legs? Cage a wolf and it will bite. Beat a horse and it will kick. Who is at fault then? You are a creature of the wind. It is not my place to lay blame for the way your nature has been twisted. The years have shaped you to kill."

Jhared closed his eyes. It was true: he carried devastation and death in his blood. He couldn't think on that now, *mustn't* think on it. Slowly, he gathered himself and opened his eyes. "People I care about are trapped in the midst of that violence. I must return to them."

"You will, I think. If the Nowhere does not swallow your memories. Have you already forgotten where you've been?"

Jhared struggled with it. The memory lay far away, as though it were not truly his. He approached it carefully and slipped around it, like a scout around an enemy's lines, and then—"Ah, Goddess! The high priestess. The crowd. Lady Nemiah."

Lady Nemiah will not make it back without you. . . .

"Nemiah. Yes," the Old Man agreed. "That is what they call Inhena's Lady in your moment."

"Sir, I must beg your aid in this. I've no skill to guide another home."

There was the *tap-tap* and then a long sigh. "It's not mine to take the burden from you, boy. No more than I can give you your names or tell you your worth. I am only the one who marks your success and shares your grief."

Deep empathy resonated in the ancient voice, an understanding born perhaps from ages of observing the Paths of men. "I must let you go now. The Nowhere will swallow you if you're not quick. Are you ready?"

Only once had Jhared deliberately tracked his own way back from the Paths. On another journey, Maya had carried them both. He had learned something from those experiences. It would have to be enough.

He drew a breath and opened his senses. "Yes."

Jhared hadn't realized how strong the Old Man's grip on him had been until it was released. Instantly, the tide of black Nowhere caught him and tumbled him like a pebble in a river. If he hadn't prepared himself, he would have lost his bearings entirely, but he already had the names and images in his mind: *soldier, scholar, brother, son; healer, musician, lover, friend.* He offered up every memory that defined those names for him, then hunted the Paths for any trace of them.

The joy he found in the hunt was soon eclipsed by the effort it took to hold himself intact. Tantalizing glimpses of the weaving's infinite moments split his attention in every direction. To keep his focus, he employed every exercise of discipline General Nadel and Elder Trianor had ever taught him. And then he thought of Lady Nemiah, adding what he knew of her to his search. The night she had chased Zia from his tent, she had allowed him to see something of who she was. He hoped it would serve now to track her.

He first spied the mob from high atop the temple dome. He mantled his wings and flapped twice to steady himself against the breeze. The Avelun priestess had been pressed beyond the plaza and was halfway to the wall. The growl from below spoke of violence and blood. They would force her up to the top of the battlements, the chains still about her neck, then they would push her. Jhared hopped in a small circle and chortled low in his throat, knowing there would be easy feeding later.

He froze, mortified, abruptly realizing where he'd fallen. His dismay must have slipped past his own borders, for his black-winged cousin poked curiously at his awareness. *"What? Who? Will there be play? Will there be meat?"* Jhared's pulse thudded in his ears as he tried to decide how to free himself. Terrified that he would become stuck there, he did the only thing he knew, opened his awareness to the blue flames and leaped. As he tore free, he felt a painful *snap* in his chest, and the crow cawed after him in irritation. Desperately, before he could lose the moment, he thought of Lady Nemiah and threw himself onto the Path again.

Agony jolted through him with such intensity it nearly knocked him free a second time. He gasped for breath and scrambled to find other sensations to anchor himself: the heat of the stone soaking through his shirt; the mutter of people hurrying away from his prone body; the sight of the green-winged woman kneeling at his side.

"It is you," Lady Nemiah murmured. "Jhared Denaban. I didn't believe it."

It struck him that he should have some clever reply to her astonishment, but the best he could manage was a sickly smile. "I've come to help you home, Lady." He tried to sit up, but a wave of dizziness washed black snow across his vision. An ugly gash revealed his insides just below the ribs.

"Tumal's men have made an example of you," she said, easing him back to the stone. "You must leave this Path or you will die here with this body."

He groaned in horror, realizing what she meant. "By trying to shield the priestess, I've killed a man."

"No. The web cannot be unwoven." Lady Nemiah's tone was flat with despair. "The man whose perspective you've borrowed died here long ago. Perhaps for the same reason."

"Then nothing may be done for the high priestess? This Path cannot be turned?"

Lady Nemiah shook her head. "Amalia is lost."

"Amalia." Jhared whispered the name as a sudden roar from the crowd suggested Lady Nemiah's words were about to be made true. He stretched out his hand, his heart pumping his blood onto the street. "It's time to return to our own place. Please, Lady. Come with me."

She looked down on him sadly. "I'm sorry. I have walked this Path for days. I do not own the strength to find the way back. You will have to leave on your own."

Cold sweat trickled down Jhared's neck. He swallowed and forced himself not to falter. "I am a scout, Lady. I have never yet failed to find my way home. Come with me. I will take you safely."

She stared. Jhared feared she would call him an abomination and turn away, but her gaze was reflective. "An Arionad has ended Amalia's life. Now a Shorn man seeks to see me home. There's a symmetry in this you can't understand. I will come with you. May Riana lead us where we're meant to be."

Her cool fingers wrapped around his. Jhared had no time for any preparation before the world dropped out from under him and he saw the gleam of blue flames.

When he traveled with Maya, it had been a smooth, fearless glide through darkness and blue. Trying to hold onto Lady Nemiah was like trying to cup a butterfly in his fist. He feared to clutch her too tightly, lest he crush her, but if he loosened his fingers, he knew she would slip away. As he struggled, the Paths blew past him like storm clouds. He had no time to track his way. No time to note whether the moments shooting by belonged to him. Panic beat in his chest. He would lose Lady Nemiah in a tangle of the weaving. He would float all eternity through the Nowhere—

"Easy, soldier." The quiet thought brushed against his mind. "Steady your thoughts."

"Lady?" He gasped and realized she had sensed his fears.

"I will not break in your hands. Focus on finding our Time and Place. I can hold us together."

"Are you certain?"

Her expression quirked. "Riana has left me a few gifts, still."

Releasing his unskilled hold on the priestess sent a flood of relief over him and gave him the resources to attend to the trail. It grew easier then. Going home was not as difficult as seeking a foreign moment. It came to him that traveling beyond his own place disturbed the pattern of the weaving. He was a thread that had slipped from the warp, and the wrongness of that slip was an ache in his spirit. He must return to where he belonged to heal it.

They were close, so close he began to perceive distinct images of relevant places and moments. He spotted landscapes he recognized—a mountain range, a twisting river, a lakeside town—places he had perhaps read about or traveled long ago. The signs of his passage were faint, but growing.

"Careful," the Lady murmured. "These Paths don't yet belong to you. The doors will fight you—"

A breathless squeak cut off her words as they swooped suddenly over open fields. In the distance, mountains glowed apricot with early light. With another turn, they were racing over a clifftop.

"Lady Nemiah? Are you well?"

"Yes. I . . . yes." Jhared sensed amazement and a trickle of uneasiness in her. "It seems the doors pose no trouble for you."

Jhared grinned, marveling at the delight of tracking his own steps. He was aware of Lady Nemiah, small and steady beside him, and of the weaving around him, making him a part of the pattern. It was beautiful. Glorious! He laughed aloud, intoxicated, as he soared beyond the reach of any chains. They were so close to home. He had done it; he had carried them across the weaving to the space where they belonged. For just a moment, he felt whole.

"What have you done? She sees you! She knows you! They will kill you for this!"

The shock of his Teacher's voice was a stone wall and he struck it at speed. His focus shattered, scattering images of the Paths in every direction. Lady Nemiah cried out as she flew apart from him. He grasped for her and missed.

"How could you do this? After all we've done for you!" Shrill's anger lashed him like a whip, slicing through his thoughts, his self.

"Stop! Please, stop! I must catch the Lady or she'll be lost."

"The Lady does not matter on our Path. We cannot lose you now. We are owed!"

Fury blazed in his Teacher as he had never before known it. She raged in his mind, battering his thoughts as though he were no more than the helpless child he had been when she first came to him. Stunned and disoriented, Jhared could do little more than stand against her blows as he scrambled for some way to defend himself.

"You would throw away your life now? Now! When finally you might offer us what we deserve! For this, I will see you suffer before they end you! For this, I would see them strip the feathers from your beastly love and nail her wings to the city walls!"

Shrill hurled the threat with a malice that cut like an arrow into Jhared's breast. It was too much. His anger erupted. All the strength he had gathered to travel the Paths he turned on his Teacher. He wrapped his emotion around her and shook her, like a dog shakes a rat to snap its neck.

"Enough! More than enough! I have given you every part of myself. You will not also claim my death."

He shook her again, taking grim satisfaction at his sense of her thoughts, wild and panicked. With a final surge of strength, he flung her presence as far into the darkness as he could manage. Pain burst behind his eyes as her last rage-filled curse lashed back at him. Then there was silence.

Unsteadily, Jhared began to collect his awareness. He reached for Lady Nemiah, but his grasp was ineffective. He felt her spirit fluttering in the distance before it vanished. He dropped through something stiff and unyielding. Perhaps the door Lady Nemiah had warned him of. Then he felt nothing.

34.

BELONGING

"...Nemiah!"

Jhared jerked awake to the sound of his own shout and slammed his head against something solid behind him.

Wood. A hollow. With a curse, he darted a look about. He was wedged in a small space with his knees to his chest. Light streamed in from a hole in the tree that revealed an oval of storm-torn forest. He knew that forest. It was Avelos, and the killing winds had been here. It was his Path. He had no recollection of crawling away after Ciam struck him, but somehow he had ended crammed into the hollow of a beech tree. It had saved him from the knives of the wind. No sense of Lady Nemiah remained within him.

"Ah, Lady, where are you?"

As he freed himself from the tree, he caught the unexpected scent of mint and rosemary. Then a shiver ran up his spine and through his jaw, and he had no more opportunity to notice his surroundings. The cold frosted over him and into him, as though somewhere a door had been left open and the Nowhere spilled out. He fought the life-stealing ice with memories of heat and anger. Leita had told him he must remember his journeys, and this journey he could never forget. As his body shuddered helplessly, he thought of that day of drought when a high priestess had gone to her death. He thought of the warm presence of the woman in his mind: *Amalia*, Lady Nemiah named her. A word of trust had been given to him, a gift. It would take time to figure out what that memory meant for him. Now, it served to keep his heart beating.

When he caught his breath and wrangled his limbs back under control, he sat up slowly. His chest hurt where Ciam's blade had scored him. Blood still oozed from the wound, which was long, but not as deep as it should have been. It should have killed him. He had been down and undefended, or perhaps not entirely undefended: the winds had come to him. He ground his teeth together at the thought.

He set out for his own camp at a limping trot. Sunlight dappled the wreckage of the northerners' site in incongruously cheerful pink and gold. The wind had extinguished the fire and decorated the charred underbrush with odd bits of detritus—grain sacks, broken pottery, a pair of pants. A wagon lay upside down, perfectly intact, but for the loss of one wheel, which hung above, slowly spinning, from the branch of a tall tree. Jhared saw no sign of anyone living. Only bodies remained, of men and horses. He didn't look closely at them. He knew what the storm's knives did to unprotected flesh. He paused only once, pulling up short as he encountered Ciam's body impaled on a branch like a cloak on a hook. He might have called the commander's death justice, but too many others had paid the cost for Jhared to take any satisfaction in it.

He climbed down the rocky incline to the road. The sun hadn't yet peeked into the pass, and it was colder in the shadows. Jhared wrapped his arms around his chest as he scanned the view. Nothing remained of the orderly Forest Guard camp. The neat rows of tents had been flung about and torn into piles of kindling. Not far down the road, however, he spotted the black mouths of the caverns that lined the stone and men moving about in them. He continued with caution, uncertain whether the survivors were clanguard or Forest Guard, until the flash of a dirty white coat caught his eye. Then he ran.

Commander Evorales, more grey than white now, was carrying an armload of firewood. At Jhared's swift approach, he whipped around defensively, dropping the wood.

Jhared halted and showed both his hands, palms outward. "Commander, where is the Lady? Is she *here*? Is she well?"

No welcome showed in the man's narrowed gaze. "You? She's been asking for you. We heard you ran off. I figured you were dead with the rest."

"The rest?"

"Lieutenant Mavriel, Clan Delsio's elder, and near a quarter of the Forest Guard. No one has the full count yet."

"The northerners?"

"Fled or dead." Evorales gave a humorless laugh. "The winds saved us from the traitors. Then sliced us apart."

Jhared's insides churned. He bent to pick up the fallen firewood. "I must speak with Lady Nemiah. Please."

The commander nodded toward a cavern a little further along the ridge. "Have a care, Forest Guard. The Lady honors you with more trust than I do."

The cavern bore no ancient carvings and had a thick, musky animal smell, but the roof was high enough for a Shorn man to stand without hunching. Nearly a dozen wounded soldiers sat or sprawled on the uneven floor. The high priestess walked among them, leaning heavily on the arm of a tall, cloaked acolyte, her big brindled hound pacing beside her. Her movements were slow and deliberate as she offered water and words of comfort to the men. Her golden hair was dusted to dull brown and twisted free of her braid. As Jhared watched, she murmured a blessing over an unconscious soldier. Then she lifted her head and turned.

Jhared sucked a breath. It fed his lungs as though it were the first breath he had taken since awakening in the forest. He staggered the five steps to the high priestess's side and sank to his knees. "Oh, Lady, I thought I'd lost you."

"Jhared Denaban." She didn't smile, but her eyes were clear and steady. Despite her fragile appearance, her voice had strength in it. "I'm not lost. In fact I . . ." She glanced up at the acolyte looming protectively beside her. Jhared looked up too, and with a start, met Ziabela's green gaze. "We can't discuss these things here," Lady Nemiah murmured. "I just hope you know how much—"

He held up a hand. "I know how much we can't say now, Lady. I must tell you of the Bearer."

Lady Nemiah's expression flickered, and for a heartbeat, Jhared saw the effort of will that kept her on her feet. "Is she alive?"

"She was last night. Before the winds struck."

The priestess didn't flinch, but only turned and led him back to where Evorales was stirring the fire. "Tell me everything," she demanded, sinking onto a large stone. Zia stood behind her. The hound settled at her feet and stared at Jhared with amber eyes.

Jhared looked down, then back at the high priestess. There was no easy way to speak of the horror Leita had suffered, but at least he knew Lady Nemiah would understand the significance of it. Not knowing how else to start, he began with his reconnaissance of the northerners' camp and let the story carry him forward.

By the end, Lady Nemiah had risen to her feet, her small frame trembling with anger. "She's in the caverns. She must be. Commander, I'll take Avjay and two others to find her. You remain with the wounded." She looked at Jhared. "You stay as well. Have your injuries tended. There is more than one way to be lost, Jhared Denaban."

"Lady, before anything else, I must find the high chieftain and give my report."

"No. Not now. And not alone." The high priestess's tone turned unexpectedly sharp. "Have you forgotten the charges pending against you? It will be worse since you escaped your detention. Your case is not going to be straightforward."

They will kill you for this! Jhared grimaced.

"Soldier, not long ago you agreed to let me guard you. I ask now that you place yourself in the custody of the Arionade until I return."

Reflexively, he drew back. "What do you intend, Lady?"

Her expression clouded. He could see her considering everything she had learned of him. "In truth, I cannot say, but I don't intend for you to speak to the high chieftain without an advocate."

He bowed his head, only now beginning to feel the full weight of what he had done. "As you will, Lady."

Ziabela accompanied the high priestess, moving beside her like a guardian shadow. When they'd gone, Jhared offered Evorales what aid he could to tend the wounded. The Arionad accepted without comment.

"Has the high chieftain sent a rider to Velantar?" Jhared asked, moving a dented kettle over the flames to heat water.

"And to Murita," Evorales replied.

"Murita? The village wasn't hit?"

"The Forest Guard scout says the storm stretched less than a mile beyond the camp. If we had but known, we could have escaped its borders and spared ourselves the horror."

"It might just as well have followed us," Jhared said wretchedly. "There's no guessing where the winds will blow."

"At least it means we should see aid from the village before nightfall."

With nothing more than hot water, clean rags, and a cracked jar of bitterbalm, Jhared helped Evorales distribute what poor comfort they could to the injured soldiers. The cuts, bruises, and broken bones caused by the killing winds were all too familiar, but today each wound pierced Jhared to the heart. He had done this. The Old Man had told him as much. He had caused this misery. After spending most of the morning confronting his comrades' agony, the last soldier he came upon was deeply unconscious. Falling debris had struck him a blow to the head. Jhared looked more closely and realized it was Surian. Bound and gagged, the man would have been unable to seek shelter when the winds struck. Jhared helped Evorales to bind a gash on the soldier's arm; then helplessly he strode away to collapse in front of the fire. He closed his eyes and wished for a plug of viremur or a flask of brandy to knock him senseless.

In the end, he had no need of any drug. Oblivion dragged him under without effort. His next awareness was of afternoon light slanting across his face and a hand on his shoulder. Ziabela knelt beside him.

"Murita has come," she said quietly. "We're moving out."

Jhared blinked his gritty eyelids. "Please tell me you found the Lady Bearer."

"She's with Lady Nemiah and your patrolmate Anzo. They're already in one of the wagons."

The Bearer and his patrolmates were safe from Clan Aglar. It was the thing that had driven him since he had escaped at Ebilan. With the winds untamed, however, no one had truly been saved. He stretched, feeling the imprint of the rocks on his limbs and back. The injured were being helped or carried outside, where the elders and soldiers were gathering to leave. He cast a worried glance at Zia. "What will happen if Abrigado discovers you here?"

The scribe sighed, her expression shifting. "I'm not sure that matters anymore."

Jhared frowned. "Zia?"

"I could have run," she murmured. "When the northerners attacked, everything was in confusion. The Lady was lost. The Arionade were struggling to get her to shelter. I *meant* to run."

"Up, Patrolman! Ziabela! You're to come with me."

One of the Arionade, a lanky, black-haired man, strode up to the smoldering embers and stamped them out with his boot.

"Of course, Avjay," Zia answered, bowing her head.

Jhared shook his head at the man. "I can't delay my report to the high chieftain any longer. He must know all the northerners have planned."

"He knows," the Arionad said gruffly. "He's spoken to one of your comrades. Right now he's got more difficult things to deal with than you. Come along."

Murita was a village of Clan Manitar, and the villagers had been unstinting in their response to the high chieftain's need. Two wagons drawn by great, sleek horses had been sent to carry the wounded and a small mule cart draped in green and blue to bear the dead. Food had been sent as well. The soldiers were already passing baskets hand to hand, gratefully drawing out cheeses and loaves of bread, slices of roast mutton and ham, and flasks of ale.

Avjay handed Jhared the reins of a dust-covered bay colt and warned him to stay out of trouble before leading Zia away to join Lady Nemiah and the Bearer in one of the wagons. The soldiers who could ride were already mounted. Jhared lengthened the stirrups and tightened the girth on the bay, then swung into the saddle. He spotted Anzo and Grion in a wagon and Lenaro on horseback. His heart nearly stopped when Tierzen appeared, looking bruised and frail, and was helped into a seat by Elder Nadro. Neither man looked in Jhared's direction.

It was a tedious process to organize elders, soldiers, and temple servants into some semblance of a marching line, but eventually the teamsters, a pair of cheerful, grey-eyed men, alike as brothers, took their places in the wagons and gave a sharp whistle to their teams. The big horses tossed their heads, causing the harnesses to creak. At the front of the company, High Chieftain Rumar, grimy and wind-torn, led the troops on a dappled stallion.

Jhared kept to himself on the slow ride into the hills, eavesdropping as the soldiers relived their own parts in the night's chaos. From a dozen different tales, he pieced together what had happened in the pass while he was in the northerners' camp. He knew that the prefects had organized a charge against Rumar, but he hadn't realized that the large, disorganized force of clanguard had not taken Rumar's men unaware. Long-drilled by General Nadel to recognize and respond to the signs of the killing winds, the Shorn soldiers had roused the elders at the first of the high-pitched strains, and the entire company was already running for the caves when the northmen came plunging into the pass. Instead of taking the camp by surprise, the clanguard had crashed against the Forest Guard's disciplined blades. Although Aglar's superior numbers would soon have told against Rumar, the storm struck the pass at strength, sending both forces into flight. After that, rumors varied wildly about what had happened to the prefects. Some said that, overwhelmed with shame, Prefect Aglar and his commander had taken their own lives, and Lasla had commanded the attack by himself. Some said Prefect Lasla rode a horse deaf to the winds, while Aglar's horse went mad and killed its rider. Lieutenant Sevar was likely the only one who could say for certain if the rumor of Aglar's death held any truth, but the lieutenant had been slow to make it to shelter and the winds had torn him deeply. His unconscious figure lay stretched in the wagon among the most seriously injured.

Night closed around the company, bringing with it a cold drizzle. Eventually, they crossed a bridge over a tributary of the Heartsblood River, ascended a wooded hill, and passed through the timber walls that enwrapped Murita. As Jhared rode through the darkened streets, he had a vague impression of well-kept shop fronts, neat homes, and busy drinking houses.

The tired, soggy company drew to a halt in the yard of a large, well-lit inn. Before anyone had even dismounted, a half-dozen men and women hurried out to greet them. Dazed-looking elders climbed stiffly out of the wagons. Lady Nemiah slid down and was immediately enveloped by the protective presence of two stout women. Jhared swung out of the saddle and turned to help Leita.

As he stepped toward the Bearer, her cowled head swiveled in his direction with precision. Almost he could have believed that her blindness was only a part of his nightmares. Then he saw how tensely she sat, shoulders hunched and head tilted, and realized she was straining for a clue to determine who approached her.

"It's only Jhared, Lady."

"Of course," she murmured, straightening. "Do you think I could mistake your step on the Path?"

He bobbed his head to her, then caught himself and cleared his throat. "May I help you down?" He waited for her nod before wrapping one arm around her shoulders and placing his other hand under her elbow. Her frame felt depleted and thin as he lifted her from the wagon. Such a short time ago she had been the one who offered him forbidden mysteries, the one who held all his choices. Now she leaned against him wearily as he set her on her feet.

Immediately, the Arionade closed around her. "Thank you, Patrolman," Avjay said with a tone that indicated dismissal.

It was true; this wasn't his place. Jhared would have drawn away, but Leita's fingers tightened on his arm. "Much remains for us to do, Jhared Denaban. Your skills will be needed. Do not think that has changed just because the Path has twisted."

Power vibrated through her touch, enough to make Jhared shiver, but only for a handful of heartbeats, then her grip became needful again.

"Lady, I remain a servant of Avelos," he said, because it was all he knew to say.

Lady Nemiah turned about, introducing Leita to a young, broad-shouldered woman named Dree.

Slipping free as Lady Nemiah and Dree helped Leita into the inn, Jhared followed one of the teamsters into the stable, where he rubbed down and watered his muddy colt. Then he lent a hand with the other mounts, cleaning, feeding, and turning them out into an enclosure behind the stable. When he had turned the last horse into the pen and closed the gate, he rested against the fence, watching the animals settle for the night. The drizzle had turned to a fine mist that muffled sound. It was quiet here, away from the cries of the wounded and the commotion of the company. The horses were large drowsy forms in the dark. It was more peaceful than anything Jhared had known in days. He let the fence bear his weight, his arms folded on the top rail. His head sank into his hands and he drifted.

A loud *crack* from inside the stable made him start. A hoof striking wood. He heard an angry whinny. A familiar, angry whinny. Bewildered, he strode back inside the stable in time to see a tall, silver head poke over a stall door.

"Pretty lady, that one, but proud as an elder's wife." One of the teamsters paused near Jhared with a pail of grain in his hand. "Yesterday, she gave my brother a nasty bite. Then splintered a board in her stall for good measure. As if I've nothing better to do than patch up after her."

Jhared glanced around, half expecting to spot Alende lounging against a beam with a flask in his hand. "I know that horse. Where did you find her?"

"She found us. Came striding into town a couple evenings ago all on her own. Bold as a sailor's whore. Was a bit scratched up, like she'd been running through the underbrush, but well cared for otherwise. I figure she jumped a fence on one of the estates down valley. I sent a message down. Might be there's a reward for her. If I don't hear soon, I'll let her go to the best bidder. She's already cost me good silver."

"You won't have to sell her. She belongs to the high temple."

"That so?" The man's eyes brightened with thoughts of compensation. "I suppose the Lady will want her back then, eh?"

Jhared walked over to Seravina's stall. The elegant mare peered at him consideringly, then ambled over to snuffle his hair. Jhared stroked her neck. Where was Alende? Dead? Or had he just fallen onto the Paths and forgotten about the horse? "Yes. I'm sure she'll want her."

When he had finished in the stable, Jhared searched out Anzo and found him with the rest of his patrolmates in the yard. They greeted him with weary expressions. Lenaro, who had unofficially taken up the position of commander, saw to it that Jhared was quartered with them in one of the two inns the high chieftain had commandeered. He trudged with the others into the common room and found it crowded and noisy with their own people. Anzo pointed them toward a bench in the corner, and with a smile to a serving man, earned them bowls of thick lamb stew, good brown bread, and the innkeeper's amber cider. They ate mechanically and, after a toast to their lost patrolmates, fell mostly into silence. In the undemanding company, Jhared realized how tired he was. He'd be grateful for a quiet night and some real sleep. Then he glanced up and caught sight of Elder Abrigado at a table with the elders of Clans Makri and Rehamra.

He sighed, more loudly than he intended apparently, for Anzo peered up from his meal.

"What's wrong?"

"We've been quartered in the same inn as the elders."

Lenaro looked over his shoulder to frown in Abrigado's direction. "They won't bother with ya. Not with all ya've just done."

All he'd just done was exactly why they would bother with him. He ducked his head as Abrigado scanned the room. "Maybe not tonight, but they will. They have to."

Jhared finished his meal quickly and pulled himself up the stairs to their room, eager to escape the crowd. The six of them shared a small chamber at the top of the inn. By a soldier's standards it was luxurious, with rugs, a fireplace, and even a narrow, wooden tub. Against one wall, two sets of bunks were stacked three high. It had been so long since Jhared had slept on a bed within walls that he considered going out to join Seravina instead, but the possibility of a bath changed his mind. With his patrolmates, he took turns hauling water up the stairs for the tub. After he had scrubbed the blood and wind-driven dirt from himself, he did his best to scrub his clothes, then hung them over the hearth beside the others' wet things.

A long time passed before the inn quieted. Lying awake in the top bunk of the short bed, Jhared imagined he heard the strain of a flute, and thought of Ziabela. He hadn't seen Lady Nemiah or Leita again since their arrival and hoped they had been well cared for. Sleep had just started to court him when a tentative knock brought him back to the night. Lenaro, closest to the door, was up first.

"Lord Rumar sends for Patrolman Denaban, sir."

Jhared rolled over to see one of the younger serving boys from the common room looking up at Lenaro with an awestruck expression.

"Denaban," Lenaro said through a yawn. "I'm afraid ya were right."

"You'd think they'd leave you to sleep one full night," Anzo muttered in the bed below Jhared's. "It's not as if you have something to report the high chieftain didn't already hear from Lenaro."

"It's all right. I didn't make the most courteous exit when I set out to find you. This was bound to come."

As Jhared dropped out of bed, the impact throbbed painfully through his leg and chest. His clothes were still damp, but he drew them on, tamed his hair into a tail, and tugged on his boots.

"Remember, they're the ones meant t'ask the questions," Lenaro said wryly.

"I'll try." Jhared turned to the serving boy, and saw with a pang that he was of an age with Branlen, an age when being a soldier still sounded like nothing so much as a series of heroic adventures. "Patrolman Denaban ready to report."

The boy gave him a shy smile and led him down the stairs. "Are you one of the men who fought the killing winds?"

"Fought them?" Jhared asked, curious about the boy's choice of words.

"Cook says the high chieftain and his soldiers slayed the vile beast who caused the winds. They kept it from reaching Murita. Saved us all!"

Jhared coughed on a caught breath. "I wish I could claim to be brave enough to put an end to that beast."

The boy glanced over his shoulder and looked Jhared up and down with an appraising eye. "Not every man can be as brave as another," he said with youthful conviction. "You must be quite good at something, else Lord Rumar wouldn't have sent for you."

The lamp was burning low by the time Nemiah received Rumar's message. Rom's young niece Dree had offered Nemiah and all the temple servants her family's hospitality at their home on smiths' row, but Nemiah had declined it, knowing this message would come. Instead, she had let Dree see them settled at the inn with hot baths, clean clothes, and the attention of a competent healer for Leita. Nemiah glanced to where her Bearer had been tucked into bed under thick blankets, with Capa curled beside her. She prayed that Leita slept deeply and dreamlessly. It was too soon for them to have spoken of any of the matters they must. Leita had said only two things to her when they'd first been reunited. Held close in Nemiah's arms, she had whispered, "It will be good to sleep safely again." Then drawing away, as though to allow Nemiah to inspect what had been done to her, she said firmly, "It has been a long time since the Bearer of Cael's Blade lived her life in darkness. A return to the old ways may serve us now." Perhaps those words should have frightened Nemiah, but the old ways meant something different to her since she had met Amalia, and the Bearer's strength gave her hope.

"Is it troubling news, my lady?"

Zia sat on the window seat near the fireplace, her flute in hand and her interrupted melody still lingering in the air.

"Expected news." Nemiah folded the note in half and dropped it into the fire. "I must meet with the high chieftain. Will you . . . ?"

"If the Bearer wakes, I'll send for you."

"Thank you."

"Lady? Perhaps Rumar might give you some word of the injured when you meet."

"I'm certain he could," Nemiah said softly. "Is there someone in particular you'd like me to ask after?"

The Shorn woman lowered her gaze. "It's only that I heard some of the men who were held by Aglar were badly hurt. And their lieutenant . . . I just thought Riana might hear a prayer for the soldiers of Avelos tonight."

"Of course, Zia." Nemiah was aware that Ziabela was dealing with a recent decision of her own. It was another thing that had not yet been spoken, but it would have to wait. Nemiah hurried off to find Rumar.

Elder Nadro greeted her inside the high chieftain's door with a bow. "Lady of Avelos, it lights my way t'see ya well."

"And mine to see you, Elder."

Rumar had already set his mark upon the suite of rooms—every available flat surface was covered with letters and maps, cups of boldblood and glasses of wine. Of course Adan would have started sending communications the instant he'd arrived in Murita. He would be alerting the clans to the northerners' treason and reminding them of their obligation to impede the prefects and clanguard, if they could. Likely, Rumar had also written to Enrian Nadel to discuss the possibility of drawing Forest Guard to the north. Amidst the busy room, bruised and bedraggled elders stood in distinct groups or sat at the table, grumbling over their wine. Nemiah took in the scene, stunned.

"Elder Nadro, I hadn't anticipated a full council session tonight."

"It wasn't meant t'be," he muttered, leaning closer. "Abrigado agitated some of the others for it. They're saying that with the Law'a Integrity invoked upon Rumar, he hasn't the right t'convene a closed meeting."

"Riana save us from fools and their ambitions," Nemiah said.

"Indeed," Nadro agreed sagely, tapping the tattoo along his cheek.

Nemiah excused herself and worked her way through the men. Rumar caught her eye over his cup and gestured subtly to a chair beside him, so subtly that she could choose not to see it. His hold on the staff of warding was uncertain; he was allowing her to make the decision to distance herself from him. She nodded openly at his gesture and took the seat.

"We will begin," he said, silencing the murmurs. "Elders, our country has been torn—by our own pride as much as by the killing winds. Let us make this moment about the integrity of Avelos and not waste our resources stabbing at one another." Without permitting a pause for comment, Rumar gestured to Elder Nadro. "Bring in the soldier."

Jhared Denaban entered the room, tall and composed. Nemiah saw him check sharply, registering the crowd as she had, then continue to the front of the room with his gaze lowered. There was an unsettling grace about him she hadn't noted before. He moved like a man who still remembered what it was to embrace the sacred sky, and perhaps in truth he did. It set him apart in a way that had become dangerously apparent. Nemiah wished she had found time to speak with him before now. Some things must not be revealed in this setting.

The elders shifted in their chairs. Few of them looked directly at the soldier. Even Elder Trianor did not greet his fosterling. Trianor's gaze was grave and tense; the fingers of one hand rubbed nervously at a small, glossy pebble. Nemiah was uneasy. Jhared Denaban should have been welcomed as a hero, but his actions had shown the elders they had been gullible and rash to trust the north, and no man rejoiced to see himself made a fool.

Rumar folded his arms across his chest. "Patrolman, you will give us a report of your actions from the time of your escape from detention to your return to the pass this morning. I must remind you that you have already confessed to a number of serious crimes, and it is alleged that additional crimes have been committed. Thus, the things you say here may influence the consequences for your conduct. Do you understand?"

Denaban nodded. "Yes, sir."

"Good. Go on, then."

Nemiah hadn't yet heard the details of the young man's escape from camp. Now, he painted his description of the events in their purest form, without offering any interpretation or motive. It reminded Nemiah of Enrian, and no doubt it was considered laudable for a soldier to so remove himself from his observations, but as she looked at the elders, she could see them filling in their own interpretations based on their beliefs about Shorn men, or about *this* Shorn man. As Denaban spoke of attacking a Forest Guard watchman and sneaking through camp, she knew it wasn't serving him well.

"Once I was able to move among the northerners undetected, I found Prefect Aglar and overheard a conversation he shared with Prefect Lasla and Commander Ciam."

The soldier paused, his gaze flickering warily over the assembled elders.

"Yes, Patrolman?" Rumar prompted. "What did you hear?"

Denaban still hesitated, one hand pressed to his chest. Blood stained his shirt.

"Riana's lights, Adan! Can't the boy have a chair and a cup'a cider?" Elder Nadro looked indignant. "This isn't a prisoner interrogation!"

Rumar nodded and someone dragged a stool to where the soldier stood. Nadro offered him a drink, which he accepted gratefully, but he remained standing. He set the cup on the stool and cleared his throat.

"The prefects spoke of the Law of Integrity and the odds that Elder Abrigado would be appointed high chieftain. They said . . . Elder Abrigado owed them for their aid in invoking the Law of Integrity and that he had made promises to them for it."

Nemiah darted a glance at the others. A few brows went up. Tierzen Trianor stared at the Minister of the Treasury with disgust. Abrigado yawned.

"Toren?" Rumar said, deceptively mild. "Would you like to offer a response at this time? Or should we save that investigation for when we return to the city?"

"Investigation?" Abrigado sat up and brushed at his vest, as though the word had spattered him. "My intention regarding the Law of Integrity has been an open secret for some time, has it not? Of course, the vote could not have been carried without the elders of the northern five, so I suppose I could understand why Prefect Aglar would choose to believe some debt lay between us."

"He said promises had been made," Denaban repeated. Rumar shot the boy a warning glance.

"We are statesmen," Abrigado said with an unruffled shrug. "If I belch, someone will choose to interpret it as a promise that all men will be provided free ale. People hear what they desire to hear."

"I wonder what Ondal Aglar heard that led him t'interpret it as your promise," the elder of Clan Everen mused.

"I wonder as well," Abrigado said, his composure fraying a little, "but not so much as I wonder how we'll bring the north to heel. Or what we're going to do with a Shorn soldier who has repeatedly and intentionally broken Shorn Law!"

Rumar leaned back in his chair, observing Abrigado with an astute gaze. "Your response is noted, Toren. It is well noted. Go on, Patrolman."

The young man glanced down, visibly disheartened, but he went on with an unembellished description of his discovery of his comrades and Leita, and his combat with Commander Ciam. His gaze landed briefly on Nemiah when he spoke of waking after the winds' attack, and she realized it was during the attack that he had fallen onto the Paths. It was a wonder he hadn't died at Ciam's hand or been slashed apart by the storm. Riana must truly hold her hand over him.

"When I awoke, I discovered the northerners' camp abandoned. I set out to find our people and encountered them in the pass." The soldier let out a breath. "That's the extent of it, sir."

"I see." Rumar tugged thoughtfully on the seal of state around his neck. "Patrolman, why did you risk your life to search for your comrades when you could have remained safely within Forest Guard custody?"

"It is what I have sworn to do for Avelos, sir. To hold the lives of others more dear than my own. Regardless of my oath, I could not leave my comrades in harm's way. No soldier could."

"*Regardless* of the oath?" an elder muttered. "There's a disturbing phrase from a Shorn man."

Nemiah bit her lip. Denaban was not speaking for his audience; he was speaking of his true self, and that was a dangerous thing to do amidst men of power.

"If it were only for Avelos you acted, why did you attack a Forest Guard soldier and flee alone?" Elder Makri asked. "What were the chances you would successfully find and free six men held by a force of more than one hundred?"

Denaban frowned as though the questions troubled him. "It was not the road I would have chosen had I another option."

"Are you saying that the high chieftain's company would have been incapable of accomplishing the task?" Makri pressed.

"No, sir. I'm saying that the council had decided not to act on my report."

Nemiah winced at the misstep. Toren Abrigado pounced.

"Patrolman, had you just lied to the council? Had you neglected to tell us of heinous crimes you had committed, including desertion?"

The boy grimaced. "Yes, sir."

"Given that you had proved yourself false, would it have been wise for the council to trust you?"

"Sir, I . . . no."

"So by lying, you destroyed your comrades' chance for a—"

"The point has been made," Nemiah interjected firmly. "Soldier, your patrolmates were freed and you were in the wilds alone. You could have fled and avoided facing the charges against you. Why did you return to us?"

Denaban lifted his head and eyed her guardedly. She hoped he realized she was trying to help him.

"I needed to be certain Riana's priestess had reached safety," he said, speaking the truth directly to her. "If she hadn't returned, no one would have known where to search for her."

The Elder of Rehamra scowled. "Then the only reason you returned was for the Bearer of Cael's Blade?"

Denaban looked startled. "That's not what I said."

"No?" Abrigado raised a neat brow. "Tell us again what you said."

Reporting against Abrigado had earned the young man this retaliation, and Nemiah saw that he knew it, but he sat staunchly before the elder's predatory glare. "With the veils between us, Elder Abrigado, it doesn't matter how many times I say it, you will never hear me."

A collective murmur rose from the council.

"We've all heard it well enough," Rumar said, before Abrigado could strike again. "Soldier, you are dismissed. You will remain with your patrol until we have determined your status."

"As you say, sir." The boy saluted tiredly and turned to go.

"I have one more question for the patrolman."

Denaban froze at the door and slowly turned to face his foster father.

Elder Trianor had been uncharacteristically silent during the proceeding, his eyes rarely touching his fosterling and his fingers moving restively over the pebble in his hand. Now he spoke as if each word weighed like iron on his tongue. "Jhared, what does Anarava say about the need to take care on a journey when the destination is far and difficult?"

Vigor drained from the boy's face. His green gaze was stricken. Nemiah saw him grasp the door handle as if he would flee, but instead, he stood very still. "In *Loyalty and Will*, Anarava writes that only wickedness will come at the end of a journey if it takes corruption to arrive there."

"Indeed. I'm pleased you remember that lesson." Tierzen's tone was wry and sad.

The boy glanced down, his voice hardly more than a whisper. "I remember them all, Father."

Without waiting for a second dismissal, the soldier opened the door and disappeared. Silence held like a bubble over the room. Nemiah's eyes stung. Rumar scrubbed a hand over his face.

"What are we going t'do with him?" Elder Nadro asked.

"How can there be any uncertainty?" Toren replied. "He deserted his patrol. He freed a convicted criminal."

"He uncovered treason!" Nemiah cried. "He rescued soldiers and the Bearer of Cael's Blade!"

"We might have believed him had he not lied to the council," someone at the end of the table mused. "It was his first lie that compounded the rest."

Elder Makri shrugged. "Ay, well, it's always so with the Shorn, isn't it?"

Rumar nodded across the table. "Elder Trianor, you raised this boy. Some will say that makes you the man least able to say what should be done with him. I believe it makes you the most qualified."

Trianor looked aged beyond his years. His shoulders were bowed and his slender hands shook as he pressed his closed fists against the table. "Jhared Denaban accomplished a brave thing in freeing his comrades. His bravery should not be overlooked, nor should it surprise anyone here, for he is genuinely devoted to Avelos. But . . ." The elder's ever-steady voice went hoarse. "In the matter of my son, I can only be forthright with this council, as I ever have been. I suspect, Lord Rumar, that he is no longer bound."

"There it is," Abrigado said. "He must be executed."

Tierzen flinched like a man struck. Nemiah glared at Abrigado. "Lord Rumar, surely not."

"No need t'go so far as that," Elder Ontera protested. "Discharge him and pack him off to prison at Barlona. He'll be harmless there."

The high chieftain raised his hands. "All right, all right. Be calm. I had not meant for us to make this decision tonight. We've been distracted by this small matter because it's the only one we can control." Rumar sighed deeply. "Go to your beds. I'll not seal the boy's fate when we're still stinging from northern treachery and the killing winds. Think on it carefully. We've larger troubles to address tomorrow."

A stocky Shorn soldier Jhared knew stood at his door when he returned.

"Hello, Jech," he said unenthusiastically. "You're here for me, aren't you?"

" 'Fraid so, Bright Burning. You're to have an escort from now on."

"I see."

"Rumor is you took out Surian and ran away." Jech's lip curled in a grin. "Don't worry. I didn't believe it. I said our Bright Burning wouldn't bend his oath that way."

Jhared looked down.

"You still searching for final reparation, boy? You plan to free us all from Shorn Law and be our bright hero?"

"There is no final reparation," Jhared muttered, pushing toward the door.

Something in his words or his tone caused the older man to step aside. "What's that?"

"Final reparation does not exist because it can't," Jhared said. "Shorn Law will never be enough to keep Avelos safe."

He slipped into the chamber, trying not to wake his comrades. Instead of climbing into bed, when he knew he wouldn't sleep, he took the chair near the fire. His thoughts twisted like the curls of smoke drawing up the chimney as he attempted to understand the disaster he had just fled. The council had feared him from the start. He surprised himself with that insight, but he didn't doubt it. When they looked at him, they had seen a Shorn man who had slipped his guard and evaded one hundred twenty northerners. It didn't matter what he had done for Avelos; the elders dreaded what would happen if he turned on them. He supposed it was what they had always dreaded. It was the reason they worked so hard to keep him within the Law, within safe borders.

None had worked harder to keep him within the borders than his foster father. Ah, Goddess, Tierzen. Earnest, honest Tierzen. Jhared's throat constricted. *What does Anarava say . . . ?* Tierzen had done all he could: he had given Jhared love to strengthen him and insights from the historians and philosophers to guide him. It hadn't been enough.

Jhared drew a ragged breath. His love for Tierzen, for Branlen, was the bond that kept him on the right path when doubt or the urges weakened him, but so many things had changed in the few short weeks of his journey. Old veils had frayed. He had found goodness and courage where Tierzen himself said he would find only avarice and deceit. When Jhared had stepped before the council, even his foster father had looked away. Tierzen, who had taken him in and nurtured him when none other would.

Tierzen, who had grabbed the opportunity to test his new methods of Teaching on an orphaned Shorn child.

There's nothing good about what Avelos has done, Jhared.

Hesitantly, fearfully, knowing he was standing at the edge of a precipice and could find himself falling, Jhared wondered whether his love for his father and for his family was only a pathetic, warped thing formed from the desperate need of a lonely child. A bond that had been deliberately forged by his Teachers to keep him dutiful. Had they ever truly cared for him at all?

Nausea slipped around his innards like a cold hand. He groaned faintly and sank backward in the chair. The Paths writhed around him. It was too much. He flung the thought aside and turned away from it.

Goddess, help him. He had accomplished what he meant to—he had left Maya so he could find the Bearer and reveal the north's treachery, but there would be no peace in it. How could there be? He *was* something to be feared: a creature of the wind.

Jhared leaped up from the chair and clutched his hands into fists as he stood before the flames. He had done what he must for Leita and his comrades. He had given his blood and spirit for Avelos. But breaking through borders he had never been meant to cross left him outside the laws meant to keep him secure, outside all the limits meant to hold him. He no longer fit the bonds Avelos required. He could no longer pretend that he belonged.

With the last lit candle in one hand, Nemiah bent over Ziabela's sleeping figure, smoothed the blanket, and rested a hand briefly upon the Shorn woman's shoulder where the scar of binding lay. The wood-plank floor creaked softly as she crossed the room to Leita's bed. For a long moment, she let the candlelight flicker over the signs of hatred that had been carved upon the Bearer's flesh. With great care, Nemiah touched Leita's brow and murmured a prayer for her and Zia, and for all those who had been cut by fear and hatred.

Jhared Denaban was one of those, but a prayer would not be sufficient to help him now. He had done something remarkable for her and for the Bearer—he was himself something remarkable—but he was not allowed to take pride in any of it. The council might very well kill him. With the shadow of the northerners' treason heavy over them, Nemiah suspected that some of the elders *needed* to execute the boy as a way of proving to themselves that order still remained in the world. Men felt easier when their friends and foes could be readily distinguished. The red ribbon that marked the Shorn was comforting for the way it put a boundary around evil. How some men would stagger if they realized that evil could not be identified by a color or a scar.

Nemiah sat at the edge of Leita's bed, listening to the soft breathing of the two sleeping women. It stunned her to realize she no longer feared for herself. No, that wasn't quite it: she no longer *feared herself.* Although the unraveling weaving was an ache in her spirit, she felt stronger on her Path than she ever had. The sense of wrongness in the world that she had so long attributed to her own flaws, she knew now had come from the strain of being bound to laws and rituals that had been warped from their true purposes. Tumal had torn the temple's rites away from the goddess. Some part of her had known it long before she met Amalia. Over the years, she had spent so much energy trying to silence the part of her that sensed the truth. She had punished herself and let others punish her.

The moon had set and she had heard no movement in the hall for some time, yet she still had things to accomplish. There were debts she owed now, to Jhared Denaban, to Amalia, and perhaps to herself. Rumar would be awake. He would be mourning the men who had died and evaluating the cost of betrayal. He would be struggling to decide which direction to turn next. She splashed the sleep from her eyes with cold water from the basin, then brushed her hair and plaited it simply, letting the braid hang long down her back. Before she left, she told the Arionad on watch where she would be if the Bearer needed her. Come morning, there would be matters about which she and Leita must speak.

Then she went to take her first step on a very different Path.

Tierzen rapped his fist against the table, demanding attention. "Jhared, what does Anarava say about the creatures of the winds? Think, now! They will kill you for this!"

The rapping came again. Jhared jerked out of the dream and found himself sprawled diagonally across his bunk. Milky light slid through the shutters to puddle across the room.

It took a third knock to realize someone was at the door. Muttered curses rose from his comrades still in their beds around him. Anzo was the one who finally shuffled across the room to open it.

"Ah, Lady Nemiah. This is unexpected."

Anzo glanced over his shoulder. There was the sound of movement and a few groans as men rolled over in bed, pulling up blankets or grabbing for their clothes.

"Forgive me for waking you and your comrades, soldier. I wish to speak with Jhared Denaban."

Jhared sat up, but didn't slide out of bed. His clothes lay in a pile on the floor. "Lady?"

She peered up at him. "I have errands in Murita, Patrolman, but my Arionade are occupied. I hoped you would ride with me."

"Now, Lady?"

Her expression didn't flicker. "Jhared Denaban, do you question your commanders the same way that you question the Lady of Avelos?"

Anzo snorted, not softly.

"Of course not, Lady. That is . . . forgive me. If you need me, of course I will join you."

"Good." She smiled faintly. "I will wait here."

Anzo closed the door, sucking his teeth. "Just what is it between you and the women of the high temple, boy?"

"I don't know. She was there last night, with the council. Perhaps she has questions about my report." He gathered his clothes and began to dress. No doubt the Lady's interest had more to do with the things he had not said last night.

"They stood ya before the full council?" Lenaro pushed himself up on one elbow to peer down blearily.

Jhared forced a shrug. "I suppose every elder wanted to hear for himself what the north had done." He yanked his shirt over his head and buckled his belt. Better his comrades had no idea how badly things had gone. That way they wouldn't guess at what was to come. "Save some breakfast for me. I don't know how long I'll be."

"The least we owe you is breakfast," Anzo said.

Jhared pulled on his boots and gave the old soldier a smile. He had missed Anzo, would miss him.

When he was dressed, he stepped into the hall and shut the door on his comrades' last well wishes. Lady Nemiah was speaking to the guard on the morning watch.

"Will you be coming with us?" Jhared asked the man.

"No need. You go under the Lady's supervision."

Lady Nemiah looked pleased. "Shall we then?"

She was dressed to ride, in soft boots, fitted brown breeches, and a heavy wool tunic and cloak the color of frost. She didn't speak as they descended the stairs, but in the common room she paused to win him two thick slices of honeyed bread. The big room was nearly empty, and Jhared realized it was far later in the morning then he had thought. Exhaustion and the dark day seemed to have disrupted his sense of time. Licking honey from his fingers, he followed Lady Nemiah outside into a world of pewter and steel. The temperature had dropped during the night, and every wet surface was now sheathed in ice that reflected the gravid, grey clouds. For an unreal moment, Jhared felt as if he had stepped onto a Path where neither color nor joy existed. Then he heard an eager whinny and the illusion splintered. Two horses were saddled and waiting in the yard. Beside the Lady's long-legged mare, a haughty silver shape pranced like a ghost in the gloom.

"Seravina."

The silver mare pricked her ears at her name and stretched her neck to blow steamy breath in Jhared's face. He rubbed her cheek, taking comfort in the animal warmth.

"The Bearer said you and Sera have come to appreciate one another." Lady Nemiah patted the mare's neck. "I think she must have found her way back to you for a purpose."

Jhared ducked his head toward the priestess and lowered his voice. "Lady, she is sensitive to the Gate. She warned me more than once when the Paths were shifting. It just took me some time to understand her."

Lady Nemiah's expression didn't change. "Leita mentioned that as well. Her Chosen grandsire left his mark on her. Come along."

They rode out of the yard into the streets at an easy trot. Seravina danced and shivered at the restrained pace. The priestess was silent and contemplative. Jhared followed her lead, and soon realized that she was heading toward the village gate. Damp fingers crept down the neck of his shirt and cold clung to his skin, but he was glad to be free of the inn. Whatever he learned of Murita now would make his way easier later. When he and the Lady reached the gate, she trotted through without pausing and turned her horse onto the road leading south.

"Lady, you said you had errands?"

"That is so. I wanted to be certain we were well away from town before I set to them. I have the sense that you should be clear of walls and gates when you hear this story."

Jhared shifted in the saddle. Seravina tossed her head. "Whose story?"

"The temple's. Our country's. Your own, Jhared Denaban. The name of the woman at the beginning of the story is Amalia. She was Riana's Chosen Lady and she possessed a grace and strength greater than any I have known on my own Path. I will speak of her with you because you have already seen some of the truth. You are sensitive to the Paths and you see behind veils. I suspect that beside the lies you are forced to live, the small bit of truth you possess would drive you mad. You must hear the rest."

They walked the horses along a lonely road, with only the ice-sheathed trees to hear it as she told him a story of the Avelun priestess whose final moments he had shared. He had been only five winters the first time he heard the tale, and Sarena Trianor had told it to him. Since then, he had heard it from Tierzen, from Ziabela, and from Maya. He had read it in the histories and seen it acted by players on the streets: the story of the Avelune and Lord Tumal, of betrayal and war and the creation of Shorn Law. All of those stories had come to him through more than a century of veils. Only Lady Nemiah told him the tale as she had lived it.

By the time she had finished and gone quiet, the walls of Murita hung above them, a tarnished crown at the crest of a ragged hill. Seravina had drifted to a halt before a fork in the road. Jhared stared into the distance.

"Are you all right?" Lady Nemiah asked softly.

"I don't know." His voice sounded small in the grey, empty world.

"I imagine that's the best you can hope for just now."

The Avelune had not conspired against Tumal. One man had acted alone. It had been a desperate act driven by love. The war, the Exile, and the Shorn were created by the country's fears.

Inside, Jhared was reeling, unable to hold it all. The Gate could steal him now. He would welcome it. The world was beyond control. Ah, Goddess, it was unbearable to consider. Everything he had lost, everything that had been taken from him—

A firm hand smacked down on his wrist and grasped him tightly. "No, Jhared. We've trouble enough keeping our feet beneath us, you and I. Don't seek the Gate as a means to escape."

He nodded dazedly.

"You should be taught to journey safely. On another Path, you would have been. You might even have served as an Arionad in the high temple. But we do not live on that Path. For now, the best I can do is to keep you alive and out of chains."

"What are you telling me?"

"You must go. Let your name be lost for a time." Lady Nemiah unbuckled one of the bags from her horse's saddle and tossed it to him. "Take this. There is food enough to get you beyond the city, some coin, and a few other things I thought you might find of use. Leita has included the names of folk you may seek out safely to send word to her. What you send to her will reach me. Goddess, only forgive me for consorting with heretics."

Jhared stared at her, understanding crashing over him. "You came to my room to be sure there would be witnesses. You want the council to know that you set me free."

"I don't want anyone to think you plotted and escaped of your own accord. Some few will approve of my intervention. I hope it might stir enough debate to keep them from pursuing you, but I can't promise it."

"But this will put you in danger," he protested. "I cannot abandon you in such a circumstance. Not as I abandoned the Bearer in Ebilan."

"No. You didn't abandon her. The Bearer *told you* to leave her. If you had not complied, you would likely have been the first Forest Guard to die at Ciam's hands, and Leita would still be his prisoner. Do not worry for me. Lord Rumar is not Tumal."

The high priestess spoke with calm certainty. Jhared saw the color rising in her pale cheeks and wondered: did Rumar know? Had she told him about Lady Amalia?

"What does this mean for Avelos?" he asked.

She sighed and looked back at Murita's walls. "Something is coming for us on this Path, Jhared. Something that's tearing the weaving itself. I suspect you will be needed, at least to bear witness to my journey with Amalia. Perhaps for much more. You must keep yourself safe. Will you do that?"

"I will try, Lady."

The High Priestess of Avelos leaned across the space between their horses and rested her hand on his brow. Her skin was dry and soft, like the brush of a feather. He felt a moment of warmth, sun on his shoulders, before she withdrew.

"Lady, I must ask . . . Elder Trianor, have you told him?"

"Oh, wait. I almost forgot." From a pocket in her cloak, she drew out Branlen's talisman stone. "After you left last night, the elder asked that I give this to you."

Jhared took the grey stone with the old man's face and squeezed it in his fist. "Then he knows about this?"

"He knows nothing. I couldn't be sure of him."

"Tierzen would not have let me die," Jhared said, strongly enough that he sounded certain. "But it's good you didn't tell him. It would only do him more harm."

"I'm afraid I've not made your Path easier, Jhared Denaban."

"My lady, I no longer have a Path." His life's goal had been shattered, his bonds destroyed. The ties of love that had given him strength and purpose now looked ugly and perverted. For all the direction he had, he might as well be drifting in the Nowhere beyond the weaving. The realization terrified him, and at the same time, somewhere very deep, it stirred a small flame.

Lady Nemiah searched him with eyes as green as his own. The clarity of her expression made him think she understood something of what he felt. "You have the skill of a guide, Jhared. I have cause to know and be grateful for it. The Paths have twisted beneath you, and you may wander for a time, but you need not lose yourself."

"If you say it, Lady." He bowed his head; then met her eyes again. "How can I leave you to travel back to the village unguarded?"

"Ah, an Arionad indeed." She smiled. "However, after all we've shared, I believe I need time by myself to consider my own place on this Path."

He answered her smile with a sober nod, aware that her world also had changed.

"Farewell, Jhared Denaban. May you be safe on whatever Paths you travel."

"And you, Lady Nemiah."

He stared at the two roads splitting before him: one turned east, back toward the pass and then to Velantar. The other ran west, into thickening forest and rolling foothills. He nudged Seravina toward the west. From the stillness behind him, he knew that Lady Nemiah remained at the fork. He held Sera to a walk, wanting to hear the moment when the priestess finally turned away, taking with her his last connection to Avelos.

Nearly a mile passed before hoofbeats rang out behind him, then gradually faded. She had gone. The absence opened a chasm in Jhared's chest. He faced only forward, afraid he might still go plunging back—even just to wish Anzo well or to see Zia's sly smile—knowing no place would remain for him if he did.

Seravina was fresh and eager to run. Jhared let her go, putting miles between himself and the elders. By late afternoon, the foothills gave way to the broad bowl of the Parnas Valley. As he traversed the high western rim of the bowl, the city lay nearly directly to the east. With effort, he picked out the rose-grey smudge of the walls and the glint of the high temple's dome, and felt another pang.

In early evening, sunlight finally tore through the clouds. Rays streamed in brilliant blades over the forest, and the world blazed as every ice-caught branch and leaf turned to silver and crystal. It came to Jhared that somewhere between here and Sona, one reason might exist for him to care whether he found a new Path.

Mayavana was the truth behind all the veils that Avelos had woven for him. She had revealed herself without fear. She had looked upon him—his weakness and his terrible strength—and had not turned away. He had tumbled into her on the infinite Paths before ever finding her on his own. Surely, with time, he could find her again.

High above the forest floor, beyond the shadow of the mountains, a bird gave a long, joyful shriek. Jhared glanced up to spy a golden hawk soaring in elegant ellipses. It was a young bird, bold with newfound freedom. Jhared stretched one arm toward the sky, and the breeze welcomed him, kissing his cupped fingers and ruffling his hair. The old desire raced through his body, but he didn't try to curb it or pull his gaze from the raptor's flight. Instead, he immersed himself in the heat of longing.

He didn't know how to name this moment if he no longer need call it cursed. Only as he left the Parnas Valley behind and the city finally disappeared from view did he realize that a possibility might exist to create another name, for his Path and for himself.

ᴅᴇᴀʀ Reader

Ihope you enjoyed *Cael's Shadow*, book two of The Sky Seekers. It would mean a lot to me if you would take just a minute to leave your review on Amazon and Goodreads to let others know what you thought about the book.

To stay updated about the release of *Avelune*, book three of The Sky Seekers, get a sneak peek at a chapter, and find an author interview about the series, please go to the publisher's website, www.StoneRavenPress.com.

WITH WARM REGARDS,

LARISSA N. N. DAVILA

Book Club
Discussion Questions
for Cael's Shadow

1. Why is Jhared so disturbed by the similarities he sees between himself and the unbound waylayer, Alende?

2. How does Leita continue to remind Jhared of his oppression by Avelos, even as his experiences with her help him feel more confident in his own abilities?

3. How does Lady Nemiah's shame about the curse in her own lineage prevent her from taking a stand against Elder Abrigado and other leaders of the Council of Clans? Does her growing friendship with Ziabela change that? What experiences in our own reality might be similar to Lady Nemiah's situation?

4. Anzo Nevia, Jhared's patrolmate, is kind to Jhared and seems unfazed by the fact that Jhared is Shorn. Why do you think Anzo is different from those who treat Jhared with contempt or fear?

5. Alende insists he is free of the controls that Avelos inflicts upon the Shorn—is he truly?

6. What do Lady Nemiah's interactions with Lady Lia teach her about her own situation? What do her interactions with Ziabela Marcalo reveal to her?

7. What astonishes Jhared about Mayavana, and what makes her seem so familiar to him? Why does Mayavana get angry when Jhared tells her that he owes her for her help?

8. Jhared's relationships with his fellow soldiers are a complex mix of trust and distrust. How does that instability affect him emotionally? How does this make his patrol, in many ways, like a family?

9. Near the end of the novel, Elder Trianor tells the council that he believes his son "may no longer be bound." What does that mean? Is it a good or a bad thing?

10. Jhared was raised to believe that his purpose in life is to make reparation for the crimes of his ancestors. If Jhared escapes Avelos, what purpose and identity will remain to him?

Photo by Gail Spiro

ABOUT THE AUTHOR

Daughter of first-generation Latine and Polish parents, Larissa N. N. Davila is a child psychologist and professor. She lives in Michigan, where in addition to writing fiction, she directs a mental health clinic for children and conducts research to improve psychological treatments for underserved families. Her work has been highlighted in outlets such as NBC *Today* and *Insight Daily Radio*. When not writing, Dr. Niec can be found riding horses through Michigan forests. Find out more at www.LarissaNNDavila.com.